SASHENKA

Also by Simon Sebag Montefiore

FICTION

The Moscow Trilogy:

Sashenka

One Night in Winter

Red Sky at Noon

NONFICTION

Catherine the Great and Potemkin

Stalin: the Court of the Red Tsar

Young Stalin

Jerusalem: the Biography

The Romanovs: 1613–1918

Written in History: Letters that Changed the World

CHILDREN'S FICTION
(WITH SANTA MONTEFIORE)

The Royal Rabbits of London series

SIMON SEBAG MONTEFIORE

SASHENKA

A Novel

THE MOSCOW TRILOGY

PEGASUS BOOKS
NEW YORK LONDON

Sashenka

Pegasus Books, Ltd.
148 West 37th Street, 13th Floor
New York, NY 10018

First Pegasus Books hardcover edition December 2018

ISBN: 978-1-68177-909-6

10 9 8 7 6 5 4 3 2 1

Printed in the United States of America
Distributed by W. W. Norton & Company, Inc.

To Santa

MOSCOW UNIVERSITY

SCHOOL OF HUMANITIES DEPARTMENT GAZETTE

12 MARCH 1994

PERSONAL ADVERTISEMENTS

SEARCHING!

WE SEEK YOUNG HISTORIAN, EXPERIENCED IN RESEARCH IN RUSSIAN STATE ARCHIVES.
THE PROJECT—A FAMILY HISTORY,
THE TRACING OF LOST PERSONS, etc.
SIX MONTHS. ABSOLUTE DISCRETION REQUIRED.

*

SALARY: US$ PLUS EXPENSES.
VALID PASSPORT/ID PAPERS TO TRAVEL.
ONLY GRADUATES WITH TOP SCORES MAY APPLY.
APPLICANT TO START AT ONCE.
CONTACT: ACADEMICIAN BORIS BELIAKOV,
DIRECTOR, DPT OF MODERN STUDIES AND LATER MODERN STUDIES, SCHOOL OF HUMANITIES.

There where the waves spray
The feet of solitary reefs . . .
A loving enchantress
Gave me her talisman.
She told me with tenderness:
You must not lose it,
Its power is infallible,
Love gave it to you.

Alexander Pushkin, "The Talisman"

Now and again in these parts, you come across people so remarkable that, no matter how much time has passed since you met them, it is impossible to recall them without your heart trembling.

Nikolai Leskov, *Lady Macbeth of Mtsensk*

Here I am abandoned, an orphan, with no one to look after me,
And I will die before long and there'll be no one to pray at my grave,
Only the nightingale will sing sometimes on the nearest tree . . .

Song of Petrograd street children, 1917

CONTENTS

PART ONE

ST. PETERSBURG, 1916

1

The shy northern sun had already set by teatime when three of the Tsar's gendarmes took up positions at the gates of the Smolny Institute for Noble Girls. The end of term at the finest girls' boarding school in St. Petersburg was no place for policemen but there they were, unmistakable in their smart navy-blue tunics with white trimming, shiny sabers, and lambskin helmets with sultan-spikes. One clicked his fingers impatiently, another opened and closed the leather holster of his Mauser revolver and the third stood stolidly, legs wide, with his thumbs stuck into his belt. Behind them waited a traffic jam of horse-drawn sleighs, emblazoned gold and crimson with family crests, and a couple of gleaming limousines. The slow, slanting snowfall was visible only in the flickering halo of streetlights and the amber lamps of touring cars.

It was the third winter of the Great War and it seemed the darkest and the longest so far. Through the black gates, down the paved avenue, the white splendor of the pillared Institute rose out of the early twilight like an ocean liner adrift in the mist. Even this boarding school, of which the Empress herself was patron and which was filled with the daughters of aristocrats and war profiteers, could no longer feed its girls or heat its dormitories. Term was ending prematurely. The shortages had reached even the rich. Few could now afford the fuel to run a car, and horsepower was fashionable again.

The winter darkness in wartime St. Petersburg had a sticky arctic gloom all of its own. The feathery snow muffled the sounds of horses and engines but the burning cold made the smells sharper: gasoline, horse dung, the alcohol on the breath of the snoring postilions, the acrid cologne and cigarettes of chauffeurs in yellow- and red-trimmed uniforms, and the flowery perfumes on the throats of the waiting women.

Inside the burgundy leather compartment of a Delaunay-Belleville landaulet, a serious young woman with a heart-shaped face sat with an English novel on her lap, lit by a naphtha lamp. Audrey Lewis—Mrs. Lewis to her employers and Lala to her beloved charge—was cold. She pulled the bushy lambskin up over her lap; her hands were gloved, and she wore a wolf-fur hat and a thick coat. But still she shivered. She ignored the driver, Pantameilion, when he climbed into his seat, flicking his cigarette into the snow. Her brown eyes never left the door of the school.

"Hurry up, Sashenka!" Lala muttered to herself in English. She checked the brass clock set into the glass division that kept the chauffeur at bay. "Not long now!"

A maternal glow of anticipation spread across her chest: she imagined Sashenka's long-limbed figure running toward her across the snow. Few mothers picked up their children from the Smolny Institute, and almost no fathers. But Lala, the governess, always collected Sashenka.

Just a few minutes, my child, she thought; my adorable, clever, solemn child.

The lanterns shining through the delicate tracery of ice on the dim car windows bore her away to her childhood home in Pegsdon, a village in Hertfordshire. She had not seen England for six years and she wondered if she would ever see her family again. But if she had stayed there, she would never have known her darling Sashenka. Six years ago, she had accepted a position in the household of Baron and Baroness Zeitlin and a new life in the Russian capital, St. Petersburg. Six years ago, a young girl in a sailor suit had greeted her coolly, examined her searchingly and then offered the Englishwoman her hand, as if presenting a bouquet. The new governess spoke scarcely a word of Russian but she knelt on one knee and enclosed that small hot hand in her own palms. The girl, at first hesitantly then with growing pressure, leaned against her, finally laying her head on Lala's shoulder.

"Mne zavout Mrs. Lewis," said the Englishwoman in bad Russian.

"Greetings to a bespoke guest, Lala! I am be-named Sashenka," replied the child in appalling English. And that had been that: Mrs. Lewis was henceforth "be-named" Lala. The need met the moment. They loved each other on sight.

"It's two minutes to five," said the chauffeur tinnily through the speaking tube.

The governess sat forward, unhooked her own speaking tube and spoke into the brass cup in excellent Russian (though with an English intonation). "Thank you, Pantameilion."

"What are the pharaohs doing here?" said the driver. Everyone used the slang term for the political police, the Gendarmerie. He chuckled. "Maybe the schoolgirls are hiding German codes in their petticoats?"

Lala was not going to discuss such matters with a chauffeur. "Pantameilion, I'll need you to come in and get her trunk," she said sternly. But why were the gendarmes there? she wondered.

The girls always came out on time. Madame Buxhoeven, the headmistress, known to the girls as Grand-maman, ran the Institute like a Prussian barracks—but in French. Lala knew that Grand-maman was a favorite of the Dowager Empress Maria Fyodorovna and the reigning Empress Alexandra.

A cavalry officer and a gaggle of schoolboys and students in gold-buttoned uniforms and caps walked through the gates to meet their sweethearts. In Russia, even schoolboys had uniforms. When they saw the three gendarmes, they started, then walked on, glancing back: what were the political police doing at a boarding school for noble girls?

Waiting to convey their masters' daughters home, the coachmen, in ankle-length padded robes lined with thick white lamb's fur, red sashes and bowler hats, stamped their feet and attended to their horses. They too observed the gendarmes.

Five o'clock. The double doors of the Smolny swung open, casting a ribbon of canary light down the steps toward the gates.

"Ah, here they come!" Lala tossed her book aside.

At the top of the steps, Madame Buxhoeven, severe in her black cape, serge dress and high white collar, appeared in the tent of light—

as if on wheels like a sentry on a Swiss clock, thought Lala. Grand-maman's mottled bosom, as broad as an escarpment, was visible even at this distance—and her ringing soprano could crack ice at a hundred paces. Even though it was freezing, Lala pulled down her window and peered out, excitement rising. She thought of Sashenka's favorite tea awaiting her in the little salon, and the cookies she had bought specially from the English Shop on the Embankment. The tin of Huntley & Palmers was perched beside her on the burgundy leather seat.

The coachmen clambered up onto their creaking conveyances and settled themselves, whips in hand. Pantameilion pulled on a beribboned cap and jacket trimmed in scarlet and gold and, stroking a well-waxed mustache, winked at Lala. Why do men expect us to fall in love with them just because they can start a motorcar? Lala wondered, as the engine chugged, spluttered and burst into life.

Pantameilion smiled, revealing a mouthful of rotten fangs. His voice came breathily through the speaking tube. "So where's our little fox then! Soon I'll have two beauties in the car."

Lala shook her head. "Hurry now, Pantameilion. A trunk and a valise, both marked Aspreys of London. *Bistro!* Quick!"

2

It was the last class: sewing for the Tsar and Motherland. Sashenka pretended to stitch the khaki breeches but she could not concentrate and kept pricking her thumb. The bell was about to ring, releasing her and the other girls from their eighteenth-century prison with its draughty dormitories, echoing refectories and alabaster ballrooms.

Sashenka decided that she would be the first to curtsy to the teacher—and therefore first out of the classroom. She always wanted to be different: either the first or the last but never in the middle. So she sat at the very front, nearest the door.

She felt she had grown out of the Smolny. Sashenka had more serious matters on her mind than the follies and frivolities of the other schoolgirls in what she called the Institute for Noble Imbeciles. They talked of nothing but the steps of obscure dances, the cotillion, the *pas d'espagne*, the *pas de patineur*, the trignonne and the chiconne, their latest love letters from Misha or Nikolasha in the Guards, the modern style for ball dresses and, most particularly, how to present their décolletage. They discussed this endlessly with Sashenka after lights-out because she had the fullest breasts in her class. They said they envied her so much! Their shallowness not only appalled but embarrassed her because, unlike the others, she had no wish to flaunt her breasts.

Sashenka was sixteen and, she reminded herself, no longer a girl. She loathed her school uniform: her plain white dress made of cotton and muslin with its precious pinafore and a starched shoulder cape, which made her look young and innocent. Now she was a woman, and a woman with a mission. Yet despite her secrets, she could not help but crave her darling Lala waiting outside in her father's landaulet with the English cookies on the backseat.

The staccato clap of "Maman" Sokolov (all the teachers had to be addressed as Maman) broke into Sashenka's daydreams. Short and lumpy with fuzzy hair, Maman boomed in her resounding bass: "Ladies, time to collect up your sewing! I hope you have worked well for our brave soldiers, who are sacrificing their lives for our Motherland and his Imperial Majesty the Emperor!"

That day, sewing for Tsar and Motherland had meant attaching a newfangled luxury—zippers—to breeches for Russia's long-suffering peasant conscripts, who were being slaughtered in their thousands under Nicholas II's command. This task inspired much breathless giggling among the schoolgirls.

"Take special care," Maman Sokolov had warned, "with this sensitive work. A badly sewn zipper could in itself be an added peril for the Russian warrior already beset by danger."

"Is it where he keeps his rifle?" Sashenka had whispered to the girl next to her. The other girls had heard her and laughed. None of them was sewing very carefully.

The day seemed interminable: leaden hours had passed since breakfast in the main hall—and the obligatory curtsy to the huge canvas of the Emperor's mother, the Dowager Empress Maria Fyodorovna with her gimlet eyes and shrewish mouth.

Once the ill-zippered trousers were collected, Maman Sokolov again clapped her hands. "A minute until the bell. Before you go, *mes enfants*, I want the best curtsy of the term! And a good curtsy is a . . ."

"LOW curtsy!" cried the girls, laughing.

"Oh yes, my noble ladies. For the curtsy, *mes enfants*, LOW is for NOBLE GIRLS. You'll notice that the higher a lady stands on the Table of Ranks granted to us by the first emperor, Peter the Great, the LOWER she curtsies when she is presented to Their Imperial Majesties. Hit the floor!" When she said "low," Maman Sokolov's voice plunged to ever more profound depths. "Shopgirls make a little curtsy *comme ça*—" and she did a little dip, at which Sashenka caught the eyes of the others and tried to conceal a smile—"but LADIES GO LOWWWWWW! Touch the ground with your knees, girls, *comme ça*—" and Maman Sokolov curtsied with surprising energy, so low that her crossed knees almost touched the wooden floor. "Who's first?"

"Me!" Sashenka was already up, holding her engraved calf-leather case and her canvas bag of books. She was so keen to leave that she gave the lowest and most aristocratic curtsy she had ever managed, lower even than the one she had given to the Dowager Empress on St. Catherine's Day. "*Merci, Maman!*" she said. Behind her she heard the girls whisper in surprise, for she was usually the rebel of the class. But she did not care anymore. Not since the summer. The secrets of those hazy summer nights had shattered and recast everything.

The bell was ringing and Sashenka was already in the corridor. She looked around at its high molded ceilings, shining parquet and the electric glare of the chandeliers. She was quite alone.

Her satchel—engraved in gold with her full name, Baroness Alexandra Zeitlin—was over her shoulder but her most treasured possession was in her hands: an ugly canvas book bag that she hugged to her breast. In it were precious volumes of Zola's realist novels, Nekrasov's bleak poetry and the passionate defiance of Mayakovsky.

She started to run down the corridor toward Grand-maman, who was silhouetted against the lamps of limousines and the press of governesses and coachmen, all waiting to collect the Noble Young Ladies of the Smolny. But it was too late. The doors along the corridor burst open and suddenly it was flooded with laughing girls in white dresses with white lacy pinafores, white stockings and soft white shoes. Like an avalanche of powdery snow, they flowed down the corridor toward the cloakrooms. Coming the other way, the herd of heavy-hoofed coachmen, their long beards white with hoarfrost and bearing the freezing northern night in their cloaks, trudged forward to collect the girls' trunks. Resplendent in his flashy uniform with its peaked cap, Pantameilion stood among them, staring at Sashenka as if in a trance.

"Pantameilion!"

"Oh, Mademoiselle Zeitlin!" He shook himself and reddened.

What could have embarrassed the ladykiller of the servants' quarters? she wondered, smiling at him. "Yes, it's me. My trunk and valise are in dormitory twelve, by the window. Wait a minute—is that a new uniform?"

"Yes, mademoiselle."

"Who designed it?"

"Your mother, Baroness Zeitlin," he called after her as he lumbered up the stairs to the dormitories.

What had he been staring at, Sashenka asked herself: was it her horrible bosom or her overwide mouth? She turned uneasily toward the cloakroom. After all, what was appearance? The shallow realm of schoolgirls! Appearance was nothing compared to history, art, progress and fate. She smiled to herself, mocking her mother's scarlet and gold taste: Pantameilion's garish uniform made it obvious that the Zeitlins were nouveaux riches.

Sashenka was first into the cloakroom. Filled with the silky furs of animals, brown, golden and white, coats, *shapkas* and stoles with the faces of snow foxes and mink, the room seemed to be breathing like the forests of Siberia. She pulled on her fur coat, wrapped her white fox stole around her neck and the white Orenburg shawl around her head and was already heading for the door when the other girls poured in, homebound, their faces flushed and smiling. They threw down shoes, slipped on little boots and galoshes, unclipped leather satchels and bundled themselves into fur coats, all the time chattering, chattering.

"Captain de Pahlen's back from the front. He's paying a visit to Mama and Papa but I know he's coming to see me," said little Countess Elena to her wide-eyed companions. "He's written me a letter."

Sashenka was almost out of the room when she heard several girls calling to her. Where was she going, why was she in such a hurry, couldn't she wait for them, what was she doing later? If you're reading, can we read poetry with you? Please, Sashenka!

The end-of-term crowd was already pushing, shoving through the door. A schoolgirl cursed a sweating old coachman who, carrying a trunk, had trodden on her foot. Freezing outside, it was feverishly hot in the hall. Yet even here Sashenka felt herself quite separate, surrounded by an invisible barrier that no one could cross, as she heaved her canvas bag, coarse against the lushness of her furs, over her shoulder. She thought she could feel the different books inside—the anthologies of Blok and Balmont, the novels of Anatole France and Victor Hugo.

"Mademoiselle Zeitlin! Enjoy your holidays!" Grand-maman, half blocking the doorway, declared fruitily. Sashenka managed a *merci* and a curtsy (not low enough to impress Maman Sokolov). Finally, she was outside.

The stinging air refreshed and cleansed her, burning her lungs deliciously as the oblique snow nipped her cheeks. The lamps of the cars and carriages created a theater of light twenty feet high but no more. Above her, the savage, boundless sky was Petrograd black, tempered with specks of white.

"The landaulet is over there!" Pantameilion, bearing an Asprey traveling trunk over his shoulder and a crocodile-skin valise in his hand, gestured across the drive. Sashenka pushed through the crowd toward the car. She knew that, whatever happened—war, revolution or apocalypse—her Lala would be waiting with her Huntley & Palmers cookies, and maybe even an English ginger cake. And soon she would see her papa too.

When a valet dropped his bags, she leaped over them. When the way was blocked by a hulking Rolls with a grand-ducal crest on its glossy flank, Sashenka simply opened the door, jumped in and climbed out the other side.

Engines chortled and groaned, horns hooted, horses whinnied and stamped their hooves, servants tottered under pyramids of trunks and cases, and cursing coachmen and chauffeurs tried to find a route through the traffic, pedestrians and grimy ice. It was as though an army were breaking camp, but it was an army commanded by generals in white pinafores, chinchilla stoles and mink coats.

"Sashenka! Over here!" Lala was standing on the car's running-board, waving frantically.

"Lala! I'm coming home! I'm free!" For a moment, Sashenka forgot that she was a serious woman with a mission in life and no time for fripperies or sentimentality. She threw herself into Lala's arms and then into the car, inhaling its reassuring aroma of treated leather and the Englishwoman's floral perfume. "Where are the cookies?"

"On the seat, darling! You've survived the term!" said Lala, hugging her tightly. "You've grown so much! I can't wait to get you home. Everything's ready in the little salon: scones, ginger cake and tea. Now you can have the Huntley & Palmers."

But just as she opened her arms to release Sashenka, a shadow fell across her face.

"Alexandra Samuilovna Zeitlin?" A gendarme stood on either side of the car door.

"Yes," said Sashenka. She felt a little dizzy suddenly.

"Come with us," said one of the gendarmes. He was standing so close that she could see the pores of his pockmarked skin and the hairs of his ginger mustache. "Now!"

3

"Are you arresting me?" asked Sashenka slowly, looking round.

"We ask the questions, miss," snapped the other gendarme, who had sour milky breath and a forked Poincaré beard.

"Wait!" pleaded Lala. "She's a schoolgirl. What can you want with her? You must be mistaken, surely?" But they were already leading Sashenka toward a plain sleigh parked to one side.

"Ask *her* if you want to know," the gendarme called over his shoulder, gripping Sashenka tightly. "Go on, you tell her, you silly little bitch. You know why."

"I don't know, Lala! I'm so sorry! Tell Papa!" Sashenka cried before they pushed her into the back of the sleigh.

The coachman, also in uniform, cracked his whip. The gendarmes climbed in after her.

Out of sight of her governess, she turned to the officer with the beard. "What took you so long?" she asked. "I've been expecting you for some time." She had been preparing these lines for the inevitable moment of her arrest, but annoyingly the policeman did not seem to have heard her as the horses lurched forward.

Sashenka's heart was pounding in her ears as the sleigh flew across the snow, right past the Taurida Palace and toward the center of the city. The winter streets were quiet, swaddled by the snow. Squeezed between the padded shoulders of the two gendarmes, she sat back, enveloped in the warmth of these servants of the Autocrat. Before her, Nevsky Prospect was jammed with sleighs and horses, a few cars, and streetcars that clattered and sparked down the middle of the street. The gas streetlamps, lit day and night in winter, glowed like pink halos in the falling snow. She looked past the officers: she wanted to be seen by someone she knew! Surely some of her mother's friends would spot her as they came out of the shops in the arcades of Gostiny Dvor, the Merchant's Row bazaar with its folksy Russian clutter—icons, stuffed bears and samovars.

Flickering lanterns and electric bulbs in the vast facades of the ministries, ocher palaces and glittering shops of Tsar Peter's city rushed past her. There was the Passazh with her mother's favorite shops: the English Shop with its Pears soap and tweed jackets, Druce's with its English furniture, Brocard's with its French colognes. Playful snowflakes twisted in a little whirlwind, and she hugged herself. She was nervous, she decided, not frightened. She had been put on earth to live this adventure: it was her vocation.

Where are they taking me? she wondered. The Department of Police on Fontanka? But then the sleigh turned fast on Garden Street, past the forbidding Mikhailovsky Castle where the nobles had murdered the mad Tsar Paul. Now the towers of the Peter and Paul Fortress rose through the gloom. Was she to be buried alive in the Trubetskoy Bastion? But then they were heading over the Liteiny Bridge.

The river was dark except for the lights hung across the bridges and the lamps of the Embankment. As they crossed, she leaned to her left so she could look at her beloved St. Petersburg just as Peter the Great had built it: the Winter Palace, the Admiralty, Prince Menshikov's Palace and, somewhere in the gloom, the Bronze Horseman.

I love you, Piter, she thought. The Tsar had just changed the city's name to Petrograd because St. Petersburg was too German—but to the natives it was always St. Petersburg, or just Piter. Piter, I may never, ever see you again! Adieu, native city, adieu Papa, adieu Lala!

She quoted one of Ibsen's heroes: *All or nothing!* This was her motto—and always would be.

And then there it was: the drear dark-red brick of the Kresty Prison, looming up until its shadows swallowed her. For a moment the great walls towered over the little sleigh as the gates swung open and then clanged shut behind her.

Not so much a building, more of a tomb.

4

The Delaunay-Belleville careered down Suvorovsky and Nevsky prospects with Pantameilion at the wheel and pulled up outside the Zeitlin family house, a Gothic façade of Finnish granite and ocher, on Bolshaya Morskaya, or Greater Maritime Street. Weeping, Lala opened the front door into a hall with a checkered floor, almost falling onto three girls who, with cloths tied to their hands and knees, were polishing the stone on all fours.

"Hey, your boots are filthy!" howled Luda the parlormaid.

Lala's shoes left melted slush on the gleaming floors but she did not care. "Is the baron at home?" she asked. One of the girls nodded sulkily. "And the baroness?"

The girl glanced upstairs and rolled her eyes—and Lala, trying not to slip on the damp stone, ran to the study door. It was open.

A mechanical sound like the shunt of a locomotive came from inside.

Delphine, the surly and ancient French cook, was getting her menu approved. A wife would normally take care of such matters—but not in this uneasy house, as Lala was well aware. The color of a wax candle, as thin as a broomstick, Delphine always had a drip on the end of her long nose, which hung perilously over the dishes. Lala remembered Sashenka's fascination with it. What happens if it falls into the borscht? she'd ask, her grey eyes sparkling.

"*They* don't help you, *mon baron*," the cook was saying, haggard in her creased brown uniform. "I'll talk to them if you like, sort them out."

"Thank you, Delphine," said Baron Zeitlin. "Come in, Mrs. Lewis!" The cook stood up straight like a birch tree, stiffened proudly and passed the nanny without a glance.

Inside the baron's study, Lala could savor the leather and cigars even through her tears. Dark and lined with walnut, the room was crammed with expensive clutter and lit by electric lights in flounced green shades. Palms seemed to sprout up every wall. Portraits suspended on chains from the ceiling looked down on sculpted heads, small figurines in frock coats and top hats, and signed sepia photographs of the Emperor and various Grand Dukes. Ivory fans, camels and elephants mingled with oval cameos lined up on a baize card table.

Baron Samuil Zeitlin was sitting in a strange contraption that shook rhythmically like a trotting horse as he manipulated its polished steel arms, his hands on the wooden handles, his cheeks slightly red, a cigar stub between his teeth. The Trotting Chair was designed to move the baronial bowels after meals.

"What is it, Mrs. Lewis? What's happened?"

Trying not to sob, she told him, and he jumped straight off the Trotting Chair. Lala noticed that his hands were shaking slightly as he relit the cigar that never left his mouth. He questioned her closely, all business. Zeitlin alone decided when their conversations would be warm and when they would be cold. Not for the first time, Lala pitied the children of people of quality who could not love like more middling people.

Then, taking a deep breath, she looked at her employer, at the intense gaze of this slim, handsome man with the fair mustache and Edward VII beard, and realized that if anyone could be trusted to bring her Sashenka home, the baron could.

"Please stop crying, Mrs. Lewis," said Baron Zeitlin, proprietor of the Anglo-Russian Naphtha-Oil Bank of Baku and St. Petersburg, handing her a silk handkerchief from his frock coat. Calmness in moments of crisis was not just a requirement of life and a mark of civilization but an art, almost a religion. "Crying won't get her out. Now sit down. Gather yourself."

Zeitlin saw Lala take a breath, touch her hair and smooth down her dress. She sat, hands together, bracing herself, trying to be calm.

"Have you mentioned this to anyone else in the house?"

"No," replied Lala, whose heart-shaped face seemed to Zeitlin unbearably appealing when decorated with her crystal tears. Only her high voice failed to fit the picture. "But Pantameilion knows."

Zeitlin walked back round his desk and pulled a velvet bellrope. The parlormaid appeared, a light-footed peasant girl with the snub nose that marked her as a child of the family estates in Ukraine.

"Luda, ask Pantameilion to decarbonize the Pierce-Arrow in the garage," said Zeitlin.

"Yes, master," she said, bowing slightly from the waist: peasants from the real countryside still bowed to their masters, Zeitlin reflected, but nowadays those from the cities just sneered.

As Luda closed the study door, Zeitlin sank down in his high-backed chair, pulled out his green leather cigar box with the gold monogram and absentmindedly drew out a cigar. Stroking the rolled leaves, he eased off the band and smelled it, drawing the length of it under his nose and against his mustache so that it touched his lips. Then with a flash of his chunky cufflinks, he took the silver cutter and snipped off the tip. Moving slowly and sensuously, he flipped the cigar between finger and thumb, spinning it round his hand like the baton of the leader of a marching band. Then he placed it in his mouth and raised the jeweled silver lighter in the shape of a rifle (a gift of the War Minister, for whom he manufactured the wooden stocks of rifles for Russian infantrymen). The smell of kerosene rose.

"*Calme-toi*, Mrs. Lewis," he told Lala. "Everything's possible. Just a few phone calls and she'll be home."

But beneath this show of confidence, Zeitlin's heart was palpitating: his only child, his Sashenka, was in a cell somewhere. The thought of a policeman or, worse, a criminal, even a murderer, touching her gave him a burning pain in his chest, compounded by shame, a whiff of embarrassment, and a sliver of guilt—but he soon dismissed that. The arrest was either a mistake or the fruit of intrigue by some jealous war contractor—but calm good sense, peerless connections and the generous application of gelt would correct it. He had fixed greater challenges than releasing an innocent teenager: his rise from the provinces to his current status in St. Petersburg, his place on the Table of Ranks, his blossoming fortune, even Sashenka's presence at the Smolny Institute, all these were testament to his steely calculation of the odds and meticulous preparation, easy luck, and uninhibited embrace of his rightful prizes.

"Mrs. Lewis, do you know anything about the arrest?" he asked a little sheepishly. Powerful in so many ways, he was vulnerable in his own household. "If you know something, anything that could help Sashenka . . ."

Lala's eyes met and held his through the grey smoke. "Perhaps you should ask her uncle?"

"Mendel? But he's in exile, isn't he?"

"Quite possibly."

He caught the edge in a voice that always sounded as if it were singing a lullaby to a child, his child, and recognized the glance that told him he hardly knew his own daughter.

"But before his last arrest," she continued, "he told me this house wasn't safe for him anymore."

"Not safe anymore . . . ," murmured Zeitlin. She meant that the secret police were watching his house. "So Mendel has escaped from Siberia? And Sashenka's in contact with him? That bastard Mendel! Why doesn't anyone tell me anything?"

Mendel, his wife's brother, Sashenka's uncle, had recently been arrested and sentenced to five years of administrative exile for revolutionary conspiracy. But now he had escaped, and maybe somehow he had entangled Sashenka in his grubby machinations.

Lala stood up, shaking her head.

"Well, Baron, I know it's not my place . . ." She smoothed her floral dress, which served only to accentuate her curves. Zeitlin watched her, fiddling with a string of jade worry beads, the only un-Russian hint in the entire stalwartly Russian study.

There was a sudden movement behind them.

"*Shalom aleichem!*" boomed a broad-shouldered, bearded man in a sable greatcoat, astrakhan hat and high boots like a hussar. "Don't ask me about last night! I lost every kopek in my pocket—but who's counting?"

The door to the baron's sanctuary had been shoved open and Gideon Zeitlin's aura of cologne, vodka and animal sweat swept into the study. The baron winced, knowing that his brother tended to call on the house only when he needed his funds replenished.

"Last night's girl cost me a pretty fortune," said Gideon. "First the cards. Then dinner at the Donan. Cognac at the Europa. Gypsies at the Bear. But it was worth it. That's paradise on earth, eh? Apologies to you, Mrs. Lewis!" He made a theatrical bow, big black eyes glinting beneath bushy black brows. "But what else is there in life except fresh lips and skin? Tomorrow be damned! I feel marvelous!"

Gideon Zeitlin touched Mrs. Lewis's neck, making her jump, as he sniffed her carefully pinned hair. "Lovely!" he murmured as he strode round the desk to kiss his elder brother wetly, twice on the cheeks and once on the lips.

He tossed his wet fur coat into the corner, where it settled like a living animal, and arranged himself on the sofa.

"Gideon, Sashenka's in trouble . . . ," Zeitlin started wearily.

"I heard, Samoilo. Those ideeeots!" bellowed Gideon, who blamed all the mistakes of mankind on a conspiracy of imbeciles that included everyone except himself. "I was at the newspaper and I got a call from a source. I haven't slept from last night yet. But I'm glad Mama's not alive to see this one. Are you feeling OK, Samoilo? Your ticker? How's your indigestion? Lungs? Show me your tongue?"

"I'm bearing up," replied Zeitlin. "Let me see yours."

Although the brothers were opposites in appearance and character, the younger impecunious journalist and the older fastidious nabob shared the very Jewish conviction that they were on the verge of death at all times from angina pectoris, weak lungs (with a tendency toward consumption), unstable digestion and stomach ulcers, exacerbated by neuralgia, constipation and hemorrhoids. St. Petersburg's finest doctors competed with the specialists of Berlin, London and the resorts of Biarritz, Bad Ems and Carlsbad for the right to treat these invalids, whose bodies were living mines of gold for the medical profession.

"I'll die at any moment, probably making love to the general's girl again—but what the devil! Gehenna—Hell—the Book of Life and all that Jewish claptrap be damned! Everything in life is here and now. There's nothing after! The commander-in-chief and the general staff"—Gideon's long-suffering wife Vera and their two daughters—"are cursing me. Me? Of all people! Well, I just can't resist it. I won't ask again for a long time, for years even! My gambling debts are . . ." He whispered into his brother's ear. "Now hand over my bar mitzvah present, Samoilo: gimme the *mazuma* and I'm off on my quest!"

"Where to?" Zeitlin unlocked a wooden box on his desk, using a key that hung on his gold watch chain. He handed over two hundred rubles, quite a sum.

Zeitlin spoke Russian like a court chamberlain, without a Jewish accent, and he thought that Gideon scattered his speech with Yiddish and Hebrew phrases just to tease him about his rise, to remind him of whence they came. In his view, his younger brother still carried the smell of their father's courtyard in the Pale of Settlement, where the Jews of the Tsarist Empire had to live.

He watched as Gideon seized the cash and spread it into a fan. "That's for me. Now I need the same again to grease the palms of some ideeeots."

Zeitlin, who rarely refused Gideon's requests because he felt guilty about his brother's fecklessness, opened his little box again.

"I'll pick up some London fruitcake from the English Shop; find where Sashenka is; toss some of your vile *mazuma* to policemen and ink-shitters and get her out if I can. Call the newspaper if you want me. Mrs. Lewis!" Another insolent bow—and Gideon was gone, slamming the door behind him.

A second later, it opened again. "You know Mendel's skulking around? He's out of the clink! If I see that *schmendrik*, I'll punch him so hard his fortified boot will land in Lenin's lap. Those Bolsheviks are ideeeots!" The door slammed a second time.

Zeitlin raised his hands to his face for a few seconds, forgetting Lala was still there. Then, sighing deeply, he reached for the recently installed telephone, a leather box with a listening device hooked on to the side. He tapped it three times on the top and spoke into the mouthpiece: "Hello, exchange? Put me through to the Interior Minister, Protopopov! Petrograd two three four. Yes, now please!"

Zeitlin relit his cigar as he waited for the exchange to connect him to the latest Interior Minister.

"The baroness is in the house?" he asked. Lala nodded. "And the old people, the traveling circus?" This was his nickname for his parents-in-law, who lived over the garage. Lala nodded again. "Leave the baroness to me. Thanks, Mrs. Lewis."

As Lala shut the door, he asked no one in particular: "What on earth has Sashenka done?" and then his voice changed:

"Ah, hello, Minister, it's Zeitlin. Recovered from your poker losses, eh? I'm calling about a sensitive family matter. Remember my daughter? Yes, her. Well . . ."

5

At the Gendarmerie's Temporary House of Detention within the red walls of the Kresty Prison, Sashenka was waiting, still in her sable coat and Arctic snow fox stole. Her Smolny dress and pinafore were already smeared with greasy fingermarks and black dust. She had been left in a holding area with concrete floors and chipped wooden walls.

A pathway had been worn smooth from the door to benches and thence to the counter, which had slight hollows where the prisoners had leaned their elbows as they were booked. Everything had been marked by the thousands who had passed through. Hookers, safecrackers, murderers, revolutionaries waited with Sashenka. She was fascinated by the women: the nearest, a bloated walrus of a woman with rough bronze-pink skin and an army coat covering what appeared to be a ballerina's tutu, stank of spirits.

"What do you want, you motherfucker?" she snarled. "What are you staring at?" Sashenka, mortified, was suddenly afraid this monster would strike her. Instead the woman leaned over, horribly close. "I'm an educated woman, not some streetwalker like I seem. It was that bastard that did this to me, he beat me and . . ." Her name was called but she kept talking until the gendarme opened the counter and dragged her away. As the metal door slammed behind her, she was still shouting, "You motherfuckers, I'm an educated woman, it was that bastard who broke me . . ."

Sashenka was relieved when the woman was gone, and then ashamed until she reminded herself that the old hooker was not a proletarian, merely a degenerate bourgeoise.

The corridors of the House of Detention were busy: men and women were being delivered to their cells, taken to interrogations, dispatched on the long road to Siberian exile. Some sobbed, some slept; all of life was there. The gendarme behind the counter kept looking at her as if she were a peacock in a pigsty.

Sashenka took her poetry books out of her book bag. Pretending to read, she flicked through the pages. When she came across a piece of cigarette paper with tiny writing on it, she glanced around, smiled broadly at any policeman who happened to be looking at her, and then popped it in her mouth. Uncle Mendel had taught her what to do. The papers did not taste too bad and they were not too hard to swallow. By the time it was her turn to be booked at the counter, she had consumed all of the incriminating evidence. She asked for a glass of water.

"You've got to be joking," replied the policeman, who had taken her name, age and nationality but refused to tell her anything about the charges she faced. "This isn't the Europa Hotel, girl."

She raised her grey eyes to him. "Please," she said.

He banged a chipped mug of water onto the counter, with a croaking laugh.

As she drank, a gendarme called her name. Another with a bunch of keys opened a reinforced steel door and she entered the next layer of the Kresty. Sashenka was ordered into a small room and made to strip, then she was searched by an elephantine female matron in a dirty white apron. No one except dear Lala had ever seen her naked (her governess still drew her a bath every evening) but she told herself it did not matter. Nothing mattered except her cause, her holy grail, and that she was here at last, where every decent person should be.

The woman returned her clothes but took her coat, stole and book bag. Sashenka signed for them and received a chit in return.

Then they photographed her. She waited in a line of women, who scratched themselves constantly. The stench was of sweat, urine, menstrual blood. The photographer, an old man in a brown suit and string tie, with no teeth and eyes like holes in a hollow pumpkin, manhandled her in front of a tripod bearing an enormous camera that looked like a concertina. He disappeared under a cloth, his muffled voice calling out:

"OK, full face. Stand up. Look left, look right. A Smolny girl, eh, with a rich daddy? You won't be in here long. I was one of the first photographers in Piter. I do family portraits too if you want to mention me to your papa . . . There we are!"

Sashenka realized her arrest was now recorded forever—and she gave a wide smile that encouraged the photographer's sales patter.

"A smile! What a surprise! Most of the animals that come through here don't care what they look like—but you're going to look wonderful. That, I promise."

Then a yellow-skinned guard not much older than Sashenka led her toward a holding cell. Just as she was about to enter, an official in a belted grey uniform emerged from nowhere. "That'll do, boy. I'll take over."

This popinjay with some stripes on his shoulder boards appeared to be in charge. Sashenka was disappointed: she wanted to be treated like the real thing, like a peasant or worker. Yet the Smolny girl in her was relieved as he took her arm gently. Around her, the cold stone echoed with shouts, grunts, the clink of keys, slamming of doors and turning of locks.

Someone was shouting, "Fuck you, fuck the Tsar, you're all German spies!"

But the chief guard, in his tunic and boots, paid no attention. His hand was still on Sashenka's arm and he was chatting very fast. "We've had a few students and schoolboys in—but you're the first from Smolny. Well, I love 'politicals.' Not criminals, they're scum. But 'politicals,' people of education, they make my job a pleasure. I might surprise you: I'm not your typical guard here. I read and I've even read a bit of your Marx and your Plekhanov. Truly. Two other things: I have a fondness for Swiss chocolates and Brocard's eau de cologne. My sense of smell is highly sophisticated: see my nose?" Sashenka looked dutifully as he flared narrow nostrils. "I have the sensory buds of an aesthete yet here I am, stuck in this dive. You're something to do with Baron Zeitlin? Here we are! Make sure he knows my name is Volkov, Sergeant S.P. Volkov."

"I will, Sergeant Volkov," Sashenka replied, trying not to gag on the suffocating aroma of lavender cologne.

"I'm not your typical guard, am I? Do I surprise you?"

"Oh yes, Sergeant, you do."

"That's what everyone says. Now, Mademoiselle Zeitlin, here is your berth. Don't forget, Sergeant Volkov is your special friend. Not your typical guard!"

"Not at all typical."

"You'll miss my cologne in a minute," he warned.

A guard opened a cell door and manhandled her inside. She turned to reach for the chief guard, even raising a hand, but he was gone. The smell of women crowded into a confined space blasted her nostrils. This is the real Russia! she told herself, feeling the rottenness creeping into her clothes.

The cell door slammed behind her. The locks turned. Sashenka stood, shoulders hunched, aware of the dark cramped space behind her seething with shadowy, vigilant life. Farting, grunting, sneezing, singing and coughing vied with whispers and the flick of cards being dealt.

Sashenka slowly turned, feeling the rancid breath of twenty or thirty women, hot then cool, hot then cool, on her face. A single kerosene lamp lightened the gloom. The prisoners lined the walls and lay on mattresses on the cold dirty floor, sleeping, playing cards, some even cuddling. Two half-naked crones were picking lice out of each other's pubic hair like monkeys. A low partition marked off the latrine, from whence came groans and liquid explosions.

"Hurry up!" shouted the next in line.

A plump woman with slanting oriental eyes lay reading Tolstoy's *Confessions*, while a cadaverous woman in a man's army greatcoat over a peasant smock declaimed from a pornographic pamphlet about the Empress, Rasputin and their mutual friend, Madame Vyrubova. "'Three is better than one,' said the monk. 'Anya Vyrubova, your tits are juicy as a Siberian seal—but nothing beats a wanton imperial cunt like yours, my Empress!'" There was laughter. The reader stopped.

"Who's this? Countess Vyrubova slumming it from court?" The creature in the greatcoat was on her feet. Stepping on a sleeping figure who howled in complaint, she rushed at Sashenka and seized her hair. "You rich little bitch, don't look at me like that!"

Sashenka was afraid for the first time since her arrest, properly afraid, with fear that lurched in her guts and burned in her throat. Before she had time to think, she was punched in the mouth and fell, only to be crushed as the creature threw herself on top of her. She struggled to breathe. Fearing she was going to die, she thought of Lala, Grand-maman at school, her pony in the country . . . But suddenly the attacker was lifted right off her and tossed sideways.

"Careful, bitch. Don't touch her! I think this one's ours." The plump woman holding an open copy of Tolstoy stood over her. "Sashenka? The cell elders welcome you. You'll meet the committee in the morning. Let's get some sleep. You can share my mattress. I'm Comrade Natasha. You don't know me, but I know exactly who you are."

6

Captain Sagan of the Gendarmerie dropped into his favorite chair at the Imperial Yacht Club on Greater Maritime Street and was just rubbing a toke of cocaine into his gums when his adjutant appeared in the doorway.

"Your Excellency, may I report?"

Sagan saw the blotchy-skinned adjutant glance quickly around the enormous, empty room with its leather chairs and newspapers in English, French and Russian. Beyond the billiard table hung portraits of bemedaled club chairmen, and at the far end of the room, above a blazing fire of apple-scented wood, the watery blue eyes of the Emperor Nicholas II. "Go ahead, Ivanov."

"Your Excellency, we've arrested the terrorist revolutionaries. Found dynamite, chargers, Mauser pistols, leaflets. There's a schoolgirl among them. The general says he wants you to start on her right away before her bigshot papa gets her out. I've a phaeton waiting outside."

Captain Sagan got to his feet and sighed. "Fancy a drink, Ivanov, or a pinch of this?" He held out the silver box. "Dr. Gemp's new tonic for fatigue and headaches."

"The general said you should hurry."

"I'm tired," Sagan said, although his heart was racing. It was the third winter of the war, and he was overworked to the point of exhaustion. Not only was he a gendarme, he was also a senior officer in the Okhrana, the Tsar's secret police. "German spies, Bolsheviks, Socialist Revolutionaries, every sort of traitor. We can't hang them fast enough. And then there's Rasputin. At least sit for a moment."

"All right. Cognac," Ivanov said, a shade too reluctantly for Sagan's liking.

"Cognac? Your tastes are becoming rather expensive, Ivanov." Sagan tinkled a silver bell. A waiter, as long and thin as a flute, glided drunkenly through the door, as if on skis. "Two cognacs and make it quick," Sagan ordered, savoring the aroma of cigars, cologne and shoe polish, the essence of officers' messes and gentlemen's clubs across the Empire. When the glasses arrived, the two men stood up, toasted the Tsar, downed their brandies and hurried into the lobby.

They pulled on their uniform greatcoats and *shapkas* and stepped out into a numbing cold. Disorderly, shapeless snowflakes danced around them. It was already midnight but a full moon made the fresh snow glow an eerie blue. Cocaine, Sagan decided, was the secret policeman's ideal tonic in that it intensified his scrutiny, sharpening his vision. There stood his phaeton, a taxi-carriage with one horse snorting geysers of breath, its driver a snoring bundle of clothing. Ivanov gave him a shove and the driver's bald head appeared out of his sheepskin, pink, shiny and bleary-eyed, like a grotesque baby born blind drunk.

Sagan, heart still palpitating, scanned the street. To the left, the golden dome of St. Isaac's Cathedral loomed ominously over the houses as if about to crush them. Down to the right, he could see the doorway of the Zeitlin residence. He checked his surveillance team. Yes, a mustachioed figure in a green coat and bowler hat lurked near the corner: that was Batko, ex–NCO Cossack, smoking a cigarette in the doorway of the apartments opposite. (Cossacks and ex–NCOs made the best "external agents," those who worked on surveillance.) And there was a sleeping droshky driver a little farther down the street: Sagan hoped he was not really asleep.

A Rolls-Royce, with chains on its wheels and a Romanov crest on its doors, skidded past. Sagan knew that it belonged to Grand Duke Sergei, who would be going home with the ballerina mistress he shared with his cousin Grand Duke Andrei.

From the Blue Bridge over the Moika came the echo of shouts, the thud of punches and the crunch of boots and bodies on compacted snow. Some sailors from the Kronstadt base were fighting soldiers—dark blue versus khaki.

Then, just as Sagan had one foot on the phaeton's step, a Benz limousine rumbled up. Its uniformed driver leaped out and opened the leather-lined door. Out of it stepped an overripe, ruddy-cheeked figure in a fur coat. Manuilov-Manesevich, spy, war profiteer, friend of Rasputin, born a Jew, converted to Orthodoxy, pushed past Sagan and hurried into the Imperial Yacht Club. Inside the limousine, Sagan glimpsed crushed scarlet satin and mink on a pale throat. A waft of sweat and cigar smoke disgusted him. He got into the carriage.

"This is what the Empire has come to," he told Ivanov. "Yid spies and influence peddlers. A scandal every day!"

"Yaaaa!" the driver yelled, cracking his whip a little too close to Sagan's nose. The phaeton lurched forward.

Sagan leaned back and let the lights of Peter the Great's city flow past him. The brandy was a bullet of molten gold scouring his belly. Here was his life, in the capital of the world's greatest empire, ruled by its stupidest people in the midst of the most terrible war the world had ever known. Sagan told himself that the Emperor was lucky that he and his colleagues still believed in him and his right to rule; lucky they were so vigilant; lucky that they would stop at nothing to save this fool Tsar and his hysterical wife, whoever her friends were . . .

"Y'wanna know what I think, *barin*?" said the driver, sitting sideways to his passengers, his warthog nose illuminated by the phaeton's swinging lantern. "Oats is going up again! One more price hike and we won't be able to feed our horses. There was a time, I remember it well, when oats was only . . ."

Oats, oats, oats, that was all Sagan heard from the damn drivers of carriages and sleighs. He breathed deeply as the cocaine-charged blood gushed through his temples like a mountain stream.

7

"Where are you going tonight?" Zeitlin asked his wife.

"I don't know," sighed Ariadna Zeitlin dreamily. She was reclining on the divan in her flesh-colored boudoir, dressed only in stockings and a slip. She closed her eyes as her lady's maid primped her hair with curling tongs. Her voice was low and husky, the words running together as if she were already a little high. "Want to come along for the ride?"

"It's important, my dear." He took a chair close to the divan.

"Well, maybe Baroness Rozen's for cocktails, then a dinner at the Donan, some dancing at the Aquarium—I love that place, have you seen the beautiful fish all around the walls?—and then, well, I'm not sure . . . Ah Nyana, let's see, I fancy something with brocade for tonight."

Two maids came out of her dressing room, Nyana holding a jewelry box, the other girl with a heap of dresses over her arm.

"Come on, Ariadna. I need to know where you're going," snapped Zeitlin.

Ariadna sat up sharply. "What is it? You look quite upset. Has the Bourse crashed or . . ." and here she gave him a tender smile, flashing her white teeth, "or are you learning how to be jealous? It's never too late, you know. A girl likes to be cherished."

Zeitlin inhaled his cigar. Their marriage had diminished to these brief exchanges before each plunged, separately, into the St. Petersburg night, though they still attended balls and formal dinners together. He glanced at the unmade bed, where his wife spent so much time sleeping during the day. He looked at the dresses in batiste, chiffon and silk, at the bottles of potions and perfumes, at the half-smoked cigarettes, at the healing crystals, and all those other fads and luxuries, but he looked longest at Ariadna with her snow-white skin, her wide shoulders and her violet eyes. She was still beautiful, even if her eyes were bloodshot and the veins stood out in her temples.

She opened her hands and reached out to him, her tuberose perfume mixing deliciously with that of her skin, but he was too anxious to play their usual games.

"Sashenka's been arrested by the gendarmes," he told her. "Right at the school gates. She's in the Kresty for the night. Can you imagine the cells there?"

Ariadna blinked. A tiny frown appeared on her pale face. "It must be a misunderstanding. She's so bookish, it's hard to imagine she'd do anything silly." She looked at him. "Surely you can get her out tonight, Samuil? Call the Interior Minister. Doesn't he owe you money?"

"I've just called Protopopov and he says it's serious."

"Nyana?" Ariadna beckoned to her lady's maid. "I think I'll wear the mauve brocade with the gold leaf and flounces from Madame Chanceau, and I'll have the pearl choker and the sapphire brooch . . ."

Zeitlin was losing his patience. "That's enough, Ariadna." He switched to Yiddish so the servants could not understand. "Stop lolling there like a chorus girl, dammit! We're talking about Sashenka." He switched back to Russian, casting a black glance around the disorderly room: "Girls! Leave us alone!" Zeitlin knew that his tempers were as rare as they were fearsome and the three maids abandoned the dresses and jewels and curling tongs and scurried out.

"Was that really necessary?" asked Ariadna, her voice quivering, tears welling in her kohl-smeared eyes.

But Zeitlin was all business. "Are you seeing Rasputin?"

"Yes, I'm visiting the Elder Grigory tonight. After midnight. Don't speak of him in that mocking tone, Samuil. When Dr. Badaev's Mongolian lama hypnotized me at the House of Spirits, he said I needed a special teacher. He was right. The Elder Grigory helps me, nourishes me spiritually. He says I'm a gentle lamb in a metal world, and that you crush me. You think I'm happy in this house?"

"We're here to talk about Sashenka," he protested, but Ariadna's voice was rising.

"Remember, Samuil, when we used to go to the ballet, every set of binoculars was aimed at *me*, not the stage? 'What is Baroness Zeitlin wearing? Look at her eyes, her jewels, her lovely shoulders . . .' When the officers looked at me, they thought, There's a fine racehorse, a Thoroughbred—it might be worth having a guilty conscience for that one! Weren't you proud of me then, Samuil? And now—just look at me!"

Zeitlin stood up angrily. "This is not about you, Ariadna. Try to remember we're talking about our child!"

"I'm sorry. I'm listening . . ."

"Mendel's back from exile." He saw her shrug. "Oh, so you knew that? Well, he's probably played some part in our daughter's incarceration."

He knelt down beside the divan and took her hands. "Look, Protopopov doesn't control things. Even Premier Sturmer has no influence—he's about to be replaced. Everything's in the hands of the Empress and Rasputin. So this time I *want* you to go to Rasputin's—I need you to go there! I'm delighted you have access, and I don't care how long you spend being pawed by the sacred peasant. Tell him he's in luck tonight. Only *you* can do this, Ariadna. Just get in there and petition all of them—Rasputin, the Empress's friends, whoever, to get Sashenka out!"

"You're sending me on a mission?" Ariadna shook herself like a cat flicking off rain.

"Yes."

"Me on a political mission? I like the sound of that." She paused and Zeitlin could almost hear the wheels turning as she came to a decision. "I'll show you what a good mama I am." She rose from the divan and pulled the braid cord by her side. "Girls—get back in here! I've got to look my best." The maids returned, looking gingerly at Zeitlin. "And what will you be doing, Samuil?"

"I'm going to hold my nose and go to Prince Andronnikov's. They'll all be there."

Ariadna seized Zeitlin's face between her hands. Her spicy breath and tuberose scent made his eyes water.

"You and me on a mission, Samuil!"

Despite the coarseness of her skin—the mark of drink and opium—her face, he thought, was still magnificent; the bruised lips, the overbite and long upper lip utterly, selfishly greedy; her shoulders and legs still superb despite the protuberant belly. Whatever her flaws, Ariadna had the look of a woman to whom rough pleasure came almost too easily, as easily as bruises to a ripe peach. Now, with the kohl on her eyes smeared with tears, she looked like a drugged Cleopatra. "Samuil, can I take the Russo-Balt?"

"Done," said Zeitlin, happy for her to use the limousine. He stood up and kissed her.

Ariadna gave a little shiver of pleasure, opened the top of her diamond and gold clock, took an Egyptian cigarette out of the hidden compartment, and looked up at him with eyes that held the echo of empty rooms.

Thinking how she had become like a lost child and blaming himself, he lit her cigarette and then the cold cigar he was holding.

"I'll be off then," he said, watching her inhale and then open her lips to let the blue smoke dance its way out.

"Good luck, Samuil," she called after him.

He did not want to be late for Prince Andronnikov—Sashenka's welfare depended on him—yet he stopped and glanced back before he closed the door.

"How does this look? And this? Look, it moves as I walk. See, Galya?" Ariadna was laughing as the maids bustled around her. "Don't you agree, Nyuna, Worth's dresses put the rest to shame! I can't wait for them to see this at the Aquarium . . ."

With a sinking heart, Zeitlin realized that the moment his wife left the house she would forget all about him and Sashenka.

8

Throughout the night, Sashenka clung to Natasha's whale-like bulk.

The older woman snored and when she turned over she pushed Sashenka, who was almost too afraid to move, off the mattress. Sashenka lay there, her hips ground into the freezing stone floor, but grateful just to be next to Natasha, safe. Her mouth felt as if it were ballooning where she had been hit, and her hands were shaking. She was still afraid the monster would hit her again—or maybe she would come and stab her in a frenzy during the night? They would all have knives. Sashenka peered through the semidarkness at the tangle of female bodies—one half naked with bare shriveled breasts and long nipples like bottle stoppers—sensing the heat and rot rising around her. She prayed someone would come soon to rescue her.

Lanterns flickered outside the cell, as a guard double-locked the doors. A cleaner mopped the corridors. The smell of naphtha and disinfectant temporarily defeated that of piss and shit, but not for long. Sashenka hoped every grunt and creak and slam signaled her deliverance, but no one came. The interminable night stretched out before her, cold, frightening, hostile.

"We got a message on the cell telegraph that you were coming," Natasha had whispered to Sashenka. "We're almost family, you and I. I'm your uncle Mendel's wife. We met in exile. I bet you didn't know he married a Yakut? Yes, a real Siberian. Oh, I see—you didn't know he was married at all. Well, that's Mendel for you, the born conspirator. I didn't even know he had a niece until today. Anyway, he trusts you. Keep your wits about you: there are always opportunities . . ."

Now Natasha grunted and heaved in her sleep, saying something in her native language. Sashenka remembered that Yakuts believed in shamans and spirits. A woman shouted, "I'll cut your throat!"

Another whimpered, "Lost . . . lost . . . lost." There was a brawl in the men's cell next door; someone was wounded, and guards dragged him away groaning and brought a mop to clean up. Doors opened and slammed. Sashenka listened to consumptive coughing and squelching bowels, the footsteps of the guards, and the bubbling of Natasha's stomach. She could not quite believe this was happening to her. Even though Sashenka was proud to be there, the fear, the stink and the endless night were making her desperate. Yet hadn't Uncle Mendel told her prison was a rite of passage? And what had Natasha the Yakut whispered before she fell asleep? Yes: "Mendel trusts you!"

It was because of Mendel that she was here, because of their meeting the previous summer. The family's summers were spent at Zemblishino, an estate south of the city near the Warsaw Highway. Jews were not allowed to live in the capital or own property unless they were merchant princes like Baron Zeitlin. Sashenka's father owned not only the mansion in town but also the manor house with white pillars, the woodlands and the park. Sashenka knew that her father was not the only Jewish magnate in St. Petersburg. Another Jewish baron, Poliakoff, the railway king, lived in Prince Menshikov's old red-brick palace, the first house built in Peter the Great's new city, on the new quay almost opposite the Winter Palace.

Each summer Sashenka and Lala were left to their own devices in the country, though sometimes Zeitlin persuaded them to play tennis or go bicycling. Her mother, usually in the frenzy of a neuralgic crisis, mystical fad or broken heart, rarely left her room—and would soon rush back to the city. Lala spent her days collecting mushrooms and blueberries or riding Almaz the chestnut pony. Sashenka read on her own; she was always happy on her own.

That summer, Uncle Mendel had been staying too. A tiny twisted man with thick pince-nez on a big bent nose and a clubfoot, he worked all night in the library, smoking self-rolled *makhorka* cigarettes and brewing Turkish coffee that filled the house with its scalded, nutty aroma. He slept above the stables, lying in all morning, rising only after lunch. He seemed incapable of adapting to the summer, always wearing the same filthy dark suit and a crumpled shirt with a grimy collar. His shoes always had holes in them. Alongside her dapper father and fashionable mother, he really was a stranger from another planet. If he caught Sashenka's eye, he scowled and glanced away. He looked terribly ill, she thought, with his pale blotchy skin and asthmatic wheeze, the fruit of years in prison and exile in Siberia.

The family despised Mendel. Even Sashenka's mother, Mendel's own sister, disliked him—but she let him stay. "He's all on his own, poor sad creature," she would say disdainfully.

And then one night Sashenka could not sleep. It was 3:00 a.m. The summer was hot and the heat gathered in her room under the roof. She wanted some lemon juice so she came downstairs, past the portrait of Count Orlov-Chesmensky, a former owner of the manor, the fifteen crystal peacocks on the shelf, and the English grandfather clock, and into the deliciously cool hall with its black and white flagstone floor. She saw the library lights were still on and smelled the coffee and smoke blending in the warm, rosy night.

Mendel opened the library door and Sashenka stepped aside into the cloakroom, from where she watched her uncle limp out with a gleam in his bloodshot eyes, a sheaf of valuable papers gripped in his claw-like hands.

The trapped miasma of an entire night's chain-smoking poured out like a ghostly tidal wave. Sashenka waited until he had gone and then darted into the library to look at the books that so gripped him that he was happy to go to prison for them. The table was empty.

"Curious, Sashenka?" It was Mendel at the door, his voice incongruously deep and rich, his clothes defiantly moth-eaten.

She jumped. "I was just interested," she said.

"In my books?"

"Yes."

"I hide them when I've finished. I don't like people knowing my business or even my thoughts." He hesitated. "But you're a serious person. The only intellectual in this family."

"How do you know that, Uncle, since you've never bothered to speak to me?" Sashenka was delighted and surprised.

"The others are just capitalist decadents and our family rabbi belongs in the Middle Ages. I judge you by what you read. Mayakovsky. Nekrasov. Blok. Jack London."

"So you've been watching me?"

Mendel's pince-nez were so greasy the lenses were barely transparent. He limped over to the English collection, the full set of Dickens bound in kid with the gold Zeitlin crest, and pulling out one, he reached behind and handed her a well-thumbed old book: *What Is to Be Done?* by Chernyshevsky.

"Read it now. When you finish, you'll find the next book here behind *David Copperfield.* Understood? We'll take it from there."

"Take what? From where?"

But Mendel was gone and she was alone in the library.

That was how it started. The next night, she could hardly wait until everyone was asleep before she crept down, savoring the smells of coffee and acrid *makhorka* tobacco as she drew closer to the set of Dickens.

"Ready for the next? Your analysis of the book?" Mendel had said without looking up.

"Rakhmetov is the most compelling hero I have ever known," she told him, returning his book. "He is selfless, dedicated. Nothing stands in the way of his cause. The 'special man' touched by history. I want to be like him."

"We all do," he replied. "I know many Rakhmetovs. It was the first book I read too. And not just me but Lenin as well."

"Tell me about Lenin. And what is a Bolshevik? Are you Bolshevik, Menshevik, Socialist Revolutionary, Anarchist?"

Mendel observed her as if she were a zoological specimen, narrowing his eyes, inhaling the badly rolled *makhorka* that caught in his throat. He coughed productively.

"What's it to you? What do you think of Russia today, the workers, the peasants, the war?"

"I don't know. It seems as if . . ." She stopped, aware of his scathing stare.

"Go on. Speak up."

"It's all wrong. It's so unjust. The workers are like slaves. We're losing the war. Everything's rotten. Am I a revolutionary? A Bolshevik?"

Mendel rolled a new cigarette, not hurriedly and with surprising delicacy, licked the paper and lit it. An orange flame flared up and died down.

"You don't know enough to be anything yet," he told her. "We must take our time. You are now the sole student on my summer course. Here's the next book." He gave her Victor Hugo's novel of the French Revolution, *1793*.

The next night she was even more excited.

"Ready for more? Your analysis?"

"Cimourdain had never been seen to weep," she quoted Hugo's description of his hero. *"He had an inaccessible and frigid virtue. A just but awful man. There are no half measures for a revolutionary priest who must be infamous and sublime. Cimourdain was sublime, rugged, inhospitably repellent, gloomy but above all pure."*

"Good. If Cimourdain were alive today, he'd be a Bolshevik. You have the sentiment; now you need the science. Marxism is a science. Now read this." He held up a novel called *Lady Cynthia de Fortescue and the Love of the Cruel Colonel.* On its cover stood a lady with vermilion lipstick and cheeks like a puff adder, while a devilishly handsome officer with waxed mustaches and narrowed eyes lurked behind.

"What's this?" she asked.

"Just read what I give you." Mendel was back at his desk, scratching with his pen.

In her bedroom, when she opened the book, she found Marx's *Communist Manifesto* hidden inside. This was soon followed by Plekhanov, Engels, Lassalle, more Marx, Lenin.

No one had ever spoken to Sashenka like Mendel. Her mother wanted her to be a foolish child preparing for a life of overheated balls, unhappy marriages and seedy adulteries. She adored her father but he barely noticed his "little fox," regarding her as no more than a fluffy mascot. And darling Lala had long since submitted to her place in life, reading only novels like *Lady Cynthia de Fortescue and the Love of the*

Cruel Colonel. As for Uncle Gideon, he was a degenerate sensualist who had tried to flirt with her, and once even patted her behind.

At meals and parties she barely spoke, so rapt was she by her short course in Marxism, so keen was she to ask Mendel more questions. Her mind was with him in his smoky library, far from her mother and father. Lala, who sometimes found her asleep with the lamp shining and some vulgar novel beside her, worried that she was reading too late. It was Mendel who exposed Sashenka to the grotesque injustice of capitalist society, to the oppression of workers and peasants, and showed her how Zeitlin—yes, her own father—was an exploiter of the working man.

But there was a solution, she learned: a class struggle that would progress through set stages to a workers' paradise of equality and decency. The Marxist theory was universal and utopian and all human existence fitted into its beautiful symmetry of history and justice. She could not understand why the workers of the industrial world, especially in St. Petersburg and Moscow, the peasants in the villages of Russia and Ukraine, the footmen and maids in her father's houses, did not rise up and slay their masters at once. She had fallen in love with the ideas of dialectical materialism and the dictatorship of the proletariat.

Mendel treated Sashenka as an adult; more than a woman, as an adult *man*, a co-conspirator in the worthiest, most exclusive secret movement in the world. Before long they were meeting almost like lovers, in the twilight, at dawn and in the glowing night, in the stables, in the birch woods and blackberry thickets, on expeditions to collect mushrooms, even whispering by night in the dining hall, sealed within its yellow silk walls that were fragrant with carnations and lilac.

Yes, Sashenka thought now, the road to this stinking prison in the black St. Petersburg winter had started on her father's fairy-tale estate on those summer nights when nightingales sang and the dusk was a hazy pink. But was she really such a threat to the throne of the Emperor that she should be arrested at the gates of the Smolny and tossed into this hell?

A woman behind Sashenka got up and staggered toward the slop bucket. Somehow she tripped over Sashenka and fell, cursing her. This time Sashenka grabbed the woman's soft throat, ready to fight, but the woman apologized and Sashenka found she suddenly didn't mind. Now she was tasting the real misery of Russia. Now she could tell them she did not just know big houses and limousines. Now she was a woman, a responsible adult, independent of her family. She tried to sleep but she could not.

In the sewers of the Empire, she felt alive for the first time.

9

For his foray into the St. Petersburg night, Zeitlin dressed in a new stiff collar and frock coat to which he attached his star of the Order of St. Vladimir, second class, an honor enjoyed by only a very few Jewish industrialists.

At the bottom of the stairs, pausing for a moment with a hand against the exquisite turquoise tiles of the Dutch stove in the hall, he decided he had better tell his parents-in-law about Sashenka. He knew his wife would not bother. He passed through the empty drawing room and dining room, walled in canary and damask silk, then opened the baize door that led to the so-called Black Way, the dark underbelly of the house. The smell was quite different here, where the air was thick with butter, fat, boiling cabbage and sweat. It gave, thought Zeitlin, a hint of the other, older Russia.

Downstairs lived the cook and the chauffeur, but that was not where he was headed. Instead, Zeitlin started to climb the Black Way. Halfway up he leaned on a doorpost, exhausted and dizzy. Was it his heart, his indigestion, a touch of neurasthenia? Am I about to drop dead? he asked himself. Gideon was right, he had better call Dr. Gemp again.

A hand touched his shoulder and he jumped. It was his old nanny, Shifra, a bone-white specter in an orange housecoat and fluffy slippers who had cared for Sashenka before Lala's arrival.

"Would you approve the menu today?" she croaked. The household kept up the pretense that old Shifra was still in charge though Delphine now ran the kitchens. Shifra had been retired in tactful stages, without anyone telling her. "I've consulted the powers, dear boy," she added softly. "I've glanced into the Book of Life. She'll be all right. Would you like a hot cocoa, Samoilo? Like the old days?"

Zeitlin nodded at the menu that Delphine had already shown him but refused the cocoa. The old woman floated away like a cobweb on the wind, as silently as she had emerged.

Alone again, he found to his surprise that there were tears in his eyes: it was that sensuous pull of childhood starting in the belly. His house felt suddenly alien to him, too big, too full of strangers. Where was his darling Sashenka? In a blinding flash of panic, he knew that his child was all that mattered.

But then the thousand threads of worldliness and wealth weaved around him again. How could he, Zeitlin, fail to fix anything? No one would dare to treat the girl roughly: surely everyone knew his connection to Their Imperial Majesties? His lawyer Flek was on his way; the Interior Minister was calling the Director of Police, who was calling the Commander of the Separate Corps of Gendarmes, who in turn would be calling the chief of the Okhrana Security Section. He could not bear to think of Sashenka spending the night in a police station, let alone a prison cell. But what had she done? She seemed so demure, so correct, almost too serious for her age.

Parlormaids and footmen lived farther up the Black Way but he stopped on the second floor and opened the metal-lined door that led to the apartment over the garage. Here the smells became more foreign, and yet familiar to Samuil: chicken fat, gefilte fish, frying *babke* potatoes and the bite of *vishniak*. Noticing the *mezuzah* newly nailed to the doorpost, Zeitlin opened the door into what he called "the traveling circus."

In a large room, filled with precarious piles of books, candelabra, canvas cases and half-opened boxes, a tall old man with a white beard and ringlets, wearing a black caftan and yarmulke, stood erect at a stand facing toward Jerusalem, reciting the Eighteen Benedictions. A silver pointer with an outstretched finger showed his place in the open Talmud. The book was draped with silk, for the holy word could not be left uncovered. This man, Rabbi Abram Barmakid, was not Zeitlin's father but he was another link to the world of his childhood: this, Zeitlin thought wistfully, is where I came from.

Rabbi Barmakid, once the famous sage of Turbin with his own court and disciples, was now surrounded by sad vestiges of the silver paraphernalia that had previously beautified his prayerhouse and studyhouses. There stood the Ark with its scrolls in velvet covers and silver chains: golden lions with red-beaded eyes and blue-stoned manes kept watch. It was said the rabbi could work miracles. His lips moved quickly, his face seizing the joy and beauty of holy words in a time of disorder and downfall. He had just celebrated Yom Kippur and the Days of Awe camping in this godless house, and the only happy man in it was the one who had lost everything but kept his faith.

In 1915, the Grand Duke Nikolai Nikolaievich, the Commander-in-Chief, had declared all Jews potential German spies and driven them out of their villages. They were given a few hours to load centuries of life onto carts. Zeitlin had rescued the rabbi and his wife, putting them up in St. Petersburg illegally because they had no permits. But while they denounced their godless daughter Ariadna, they were still proud, in spite of themselves, that she had married Zeitlin, a man with oilfields in Baku, ships in Odessa, forests in Ukraine . . .

"Is that you, Samuil?" a hoarse voice called out to him. In the cupboard-sized kitchen next door he found the rabbi's wife, Miriam, bewigged and wearing a silk housecoat, stirring a cauldron of soup at an old gas stove with two sideboards, the separation of milk from meat roughly enforced on a sprawl of half-washed kitchenware.

"Sashenka's been arrested," said Samuil.

"Woe is me!" cried Miriam in her deep voice. "Before the light, a deeper darkness! This is our punishment, our own Gehenna on earth, for children who all turned away from God, apostates each one. We died long ago and thanks to God, you can only die once. My son Mendel's a godless anarchist; Ariadna's lost to God: a daughter who, God protect her, goes out half naked every night! My youngest boy, Avigdor, whose very name is dead to me, abandoned us altogether, long ago—where is he, still in London? And now our darling Silberkind's in trouble too." In her childhood Sashenka had been blond, and her grandparents still called her the Silberkind—the silver child. "Well, we mustn't waste time." The old woman started to pour honey onto an empty plate.

"What are you cooking?"

"Honeycakes and chicken soup for Sashenka. In prison."

They already knew, via the household grapevine. Zeitlin almost wept—while he called ministers, the old rabbi's wife was cooking honeycakes for her grandchild. He could hardly believe that these were the parents of Ariadna. How had they produced that hothouse flower in their Yiddish courtyard?

He stood watching Miriam as he had once watched his own mother in their family kitchen in a wooden-hutted village in the Pale of Settlement.

"I don't even know what she's been arrested for," Zeitlin whispered.

Zeitlin was proud that he had never actually converted to Orthodoxy. He had not needed to do so. As a Merchant of the First Guild, he had the right to stay in St. Petersburg even as a Jew—and just before the war he had been elevated to the rank of the Emperor's Secret Councillor, the equivalent of a lieutenant-general on the Table of Ranks. But despite all this, he was still a Jew, a discreet Jew but a Jew nonetheless. He still remembered the tune of Kol Nidre—and the excitement of asking the Four Questions at Passover.

"You're as white as a sheet, Samuil," Miriam told him. "Sit! Here, drink this!" She handed him a glass of *vishniak* and he downed it in one. Shaking his head slightly, he raised the empty glass to his mother-in-law and then, wordlessly kissing her blue-veined hand, he hurried downstairs, taking his beaver-skin coat and hat from Pantameilion at the front door. He was ready to begin.

10

The surface of the frozen canal shone grittily in the moonlight as Captain Sagan's sleigh drew up outside the headquarters of the Department of Police, 16 Fontanka.

Taking the elevator to the top floor, Sagan passed the two checkpoints, each with two gendarmes on duty, to enter the heart of the Empire's secret war against terrorists and traitors: the Tsar's Security Department, the Okhrana. Even late at night, the cream of the security service was at work up here—young clerks in pince-nez and blue uniforms sorting the card indexes (blue for Bolsheviks, red for Socialist Revolutionaries) and adding names to labyrinthine charts of revolutionary sects and cells.

Sagan was one of the organization's rising stars. He could have drawn the Bolshevik chart, with Lenin at its center, in his sleep, even with its latest names and arrows. He hesitated before the chart for a moment just to relish his success. Here it was: all the Central Committee arrested, except Lenin and Zinoviev, plus six Duma members—the whole lot in Siberian exile, too broken ever to launch a revolution. Similarly, the Mensheviks: castrated as a group. The SR Battle Organization: broken. There were only a few more Bolshevik cells left to smash.

In the offices farther along the corridor, the code breakers with their greasy hair and flaky skin were poring over columns of hieroglyphics, and old-fashioned provincial officers in boots and whiskers leaned over maps of the Vyborg Side, planning raids. The security service needed all sorts, Sagan told himself, spotting a colleague who had been a revolutionary but had recently changed sides. Across the room he noticed the ex-burglar who was now the Okhrana's specialist housebreaker, and he greeted the homosexual Italian aristocrat, really a Jewish milkman's son from Mariupol, who specialized in sensitive interrogations . . . As for me, Sagan thought, I have my speciality too: turning revolutionaries into double agents. I could turn the Pope against God.

He ordered a clerk to bring the files on that night's raids and the reports of his *fileri* agents on the movements of the Jew Mendel Barmakid, and his niece, the Zeitlin girl.

11

The scent of rosewater and perfumed candles at Prince Andronnikov's salon was so powerful that Zeitlin's head spun and his chest ached. He took a glass of champagne and downed it in one: he needed courage. He started to search the crowd, but knew that he mustn't seem too desperate. Does everyone know why I am here? Has the news about Sashenka spread? he asked himself. He hoped not.

The room was crowded with petitioners in winged collars, frock coats and medals, florid men of business puffing on cigars, but they were outnumbered by the bare shoulders of women, and shiny-cheeked, rose-lipped youths wearing velvet and rouge, smoking scented Egyptians through golden holders.

He was pulled aside by the obese ex-minister Khvostov, who began: "It's only a matter of time now until the Emperor appoints a representative ministry—this can't go on, can it, Samuil?"

"Why not? It's gone on for three hundred years. It may not be perfect but the system is stronger than we think." In Zeitlin's lifetime, however much the cards were shuffled, they had always ended in a configuration not entirely disadvantageous to his interests. It was his future, his luck sealed in the Book of Life. Things would go well—for him and for Sashenka, he reassured himself.

"Have you heard anything?" persisted Khvostov, gripping Zeitlin's arm. "Who's he going to summon? We can't go on like this, can we, Samuil? I know you agree."

Zeitlin tugged his arm free. "Where is Andronnikov?"

"Right at the back . . . you'll never get there! It's too crowded. And another thing . . ." Zeitlin fled into the crowd. The heat and the perfumes were unbearable. Wet with sweat, the men's hands slipped and skidded on the soft, pale backs of the ladies. The cigar smoke was so dense that an acrid mist had formed, half feral, half exquisite. The Governor-General, old Prince Obolensky, real high nobility, and a couple of Golitsyns were there: knee-deep in the shit, thought Zeitlin. A pretty girl, who was kept in profitable three-way concubinage by the Deputy Interior Minister, the new War Minister and Grand Duke Sergei, was kissing Simnavich, Rasputin's secretary, with an open mouth, in front of everyone. Zeitlin took no satisfaction in this: he just thought of the rabbi and Miriam, back at home. They would not have believed that the court of the Russian Empire had somehow come to this.

In a clear tunnel through the tangled limbs and necks of the crowd, Zeitlin saw a tiny bulging eye with such dense eyelashes that they were almost glued together. He was sure that the other eye and the rest of the body belonged to Manuilov-Manesevich, the dangerous huckster, police snitch, and now, disgracefully, the chief of staff of Premier Sturmer himself.

Zeitlin elbowed his way through but little Manuilov-Manesevich was always ahead of him and he never caught up. Instead he found himself at the doorway of Prince Andronnikov's holy of holies, newly redecorated like a Turkish harem—all swirling silks, with a fountain bursting out of a gold tap that formed the penis of a gilded boy Pan and, even more out of place, a large gold Buddha. A crystal chandelier with hundreds of candles dripping their wax only intensified the heat.

I probably paid for some of this tat, Zeitlin thought as he entered the tiny room packed with petitioners jostling for position. There, puffing on a hubble-bubble pipe and kissing the rosy neck of a boy in a page's uniform, was Andronnikov himself, with the Interior Minister perched next to him. Zeitlin had never abased himself before anyone: it was one of the many advantages of being rich. But there was no time for pride now.

"Hey, you spilled my drink! Where's your manners?" cried one petitioner.

"In a hurry to get somewhere, Baron Zeitlin?" sneered another. But Zeitlin, thinking only of his daughter, pushed through.

He found himself squatting next to Andronnikov and the minister.

"Ah, Zeitlin, sweetheart!" said Prince Andronnikov, who was wearing full face makeup and resembled a plump Chinese eunuch. "Kiss-kiss, my peach!"

Zeitlin closed his eyes and kissed Andronnikov on the rouged lips. Anything for Sashenka, he thought. "Lovely party, my Prince."

"Too hot, too hot," said the Prince gravely—adding "too hot for clothes, eh?" to the youth next to him, who chortled. The red silk walls were crammed with signed photographs of ministers and generals and grand dukes: was there anyone who did not owe Andronnikov something? Entrepreneur of influence, gutter journalist, friend of the powerful and poisonous gossip, Andronnikov helped set the prices in the bourse of influence, and had just brought down the War Minister.

"My Prince, it's about my daughter . . . ," Zeitlin began—but a more aggressive petitioner, a skinny ginger-haired woman with freckles and an ostrich feather rising out of a peacock brooch on a silk turban, interrupted him. Her son needed a job at the Justice Ministry but was already on a train out to the Galician front. Protopopov, the Interior Minister, could see the price for this favor dangling before him and rose, taking the lady's hand. Zeitlin saw his chance and moved into the vacated seat next to Andronnikov, who inclined his head and put his hand on his famous white briefcase, a mannerism that meant: let us deal.

"Dear Prince, my daughter Sashenka . . ."

Andronnikov waved a spongy jeweled hand. "I know . . . your daughter at Smolny . . . arrested this afternoon—and guilty by all accounts. Well, I don't know. What do you suggest?"

"She's at the Kresty Temporary House of Detention right now: can we get her out tonight?"

"Easy now, dearie! It's a bit late for tonight, sweetheart. But we wouldn't want her to get three years in Yeniseisk on the Arctic Circle, would we?"

Zeitlin had palpitations at the thought: his darling Sashenka would never survive that! Andronnikov sank into an open-mouthed kiss with the youth next to him. When he came up for air, his lips still wet, Zeitlin pointed at the ceiling.

"My Prince, I'd like to buy your . . . chandelier," he suggested. "I've always admired it . . ."

"It's very close to my heart, Baron. A present from the Empress herself."

"Really? Well, let me make you an offer for it. Shall we say at least . . ."

12

Ariadna's companion for her nocturnal voyage from Baroness Rozen's salon and on to dinner was Countess Missy Loris, a cheerful blonde born in America but married to a Russian. Missy had begged Ariadna to introduce her to Rasputin, who, it was said, was virtually ruling Russia.

Holding Missy's hand, Ariadna dismounted from the Russo-Balt limousine and passed through the shadowy archway of 64 Gorokhovaya Street, across an asphalt courtyard and up the steps of a red three-story building. The door opened as if by magic. A doorman—unmistakably ex-military, surely an agent of the Okhrana—bowed. "Second floor."

The women walked up the stairs toward an open doorway lined in scarlet silk. A red-faced man in blue serge trousers and suspenders, clearly a policeman, pointed them inside brusquely. "Ladies, this way!"

A squat peasant woman in a floral dress took their coats and showed them into a room where a tall silver samovar bubbled and steamed. Beside it, and toying with handfuls of silks, chinchilla and sable furs, diamonds and egret feathers, sat the Elder Grigory, known as Rasputin, in a lilac silk shirt tucked into a crimson sash, striped trousers, and kid leather boots. His face was weathered, moley and wrinkled, his nose pockmarked, his hair center-parted into greasy bangs that formed arches on his forehead, and his beard was reddish brown. Yellow eyes gazed up at Ariadna without blinking, the glazed pupils flickering from side to side as if they saw nothing.

"Ah, my Little Bee," he said. "Here!" He offered his hand to the women. Ariadna tipsily fell on one knee and kissed the hand, which moved on to Missy. "I know what you've come about. Go into my reception room. My little doves are all here, dear Bee. And you're new." He squeezed Missy's waist, which tickled her, and she squealed. "Show her round, Little Bee."

"Little Bee," whispered Ariadna to Missy, "is his special name for me. We all have nicknames."

"Don't forget to mention Sashenka."

"Sashenka, Sashenka. There, I'm remembering."

The pair entered the main room, where ten or so guests, mostly women, sat round a table covered in their offerings—a heap of black Beluga caviar, half a sturgeon in aspic, piles of peppermint gingersnaps, boiled eggs, a coffee cake and a bottle of Cahors.

Rasputin was right behind them. He put his arm around Ariadna's waist and swung her round, steering her to a seat at the table. He greeted them separately. "Wild Dove, meet Little Bee, Pretty Dandy, the Calm One . . ."

Among the women sat a plump moon-faced blonde in a drab, badly ironed and poorly made beige dress—and a treble string of the biggest pearls that Ariadna had ever seen. This shiny-cheeked creature was Anna Vyrubova, and the pretty, dark lady next to her, wearing a fashionable sailor-suit dress and a black and white bonnet, was Julia "Lili" von Dehn: these, Ariadna knew, were the Empress's two best friends. The spirituality of the atmosphere was intensified by the exalted status of those present. Ariadna was keenly aware that, with the Emperor away at the front, the Empress ruled the Empire through the people in this room. She knew that Missy was not yet a devotee of the Elder—in fact she was there for the party. She was bored with sweet, banal Count Loris and adored anything that was fashionable or outré—and this was both. But for Ariadna it was different. Already drunk and high, she felt cleansed in this room. Whoever she was outside, however unhappy and insecure she felt at home, however desperate her love affairs and random her search for meaning in the universe, here things had a calm simplicity that she had never found before.

Rasputin walked around the table so that each guest might kiss his hand. When he found an empty chair, he sat down and took a handful of sturgeon in his bare fist and started to eat, smearing the food in his beard. The ladies watched in silence as he gobbled handfuls of cake, fish, caviar, without the slightest self-consciousness, his chomping loud and hearty. When he was finished, he gazed at them all and then placed his hands on Ariadna's hands and squeezed them.

"You! Honeyed friend, you need me most tonight and I'm here."

A blushing glow started on Ariadna's chest and rose up her neck and throughout her body, as if she felt something between teenage bashfulness, religious awe and sensual excitement. Vyrubova's bulging eyes, crafty yet credulous, glared jealously at her. What does our Friend see in this lowborn *zhyd*, the Jew banker's sluttish wife? Ariadna knew she was thinking—even though Vyrubova herself, and the Empress too, had benefited from Zeitlin's generosity.

Ariadna did not care even though the ugly flush was covering her neck and bare shoulders. Here she was no longer a *Yiddeshe dochte* born Finkel Barmakid in the court of the famous Rabbi of Turbin, or the troubled neurasthenic who could barely control her appetites. Here she was a woman worthy to be loved and cherished—even among the friends of the Tsars themselves. Rasputin talked to empresses and whores as though they were the same. This was the Elder's genius—he made his bewildered doves into proud lionesses, his neurasthenic victims into beautiful champions. This sacred peasant would save Russia, the Tsars, the world. Ariadna's breath hissed between her teeth; her tongue darted out to lick her dry lips. The room was quiet except for the murmur of the Elder and the humming of the samovar next door.

"Little Bee," he said quietly in his simple country accent, raising her and leading her around the table to the sofa against the wall where he sat her down, pulling up his chair, squeezing her legs between his own. A tremor ran through her. "You have an emptiness inside you. You're always balanced between despair and a void within. You're a Hebrew? You're a troublesome people but much wronged too. I will keep you all out of trouble. Just follow my holy way of love. Don't listen to your priests or rabbis"—he took in her shiny eyes in a single glance—"they don't know the whole mystery. Sin is given so that we may repent and repentance brings joy to the soul and strength to the body, understand?"

"We do, we do understand," said Vyrubova in a loud, crude voice behind Rasputin.

"How is brutalized man with his beast's habits to climb out of the pit of sin and live a life pleasing to God? Oh you are my darling, my Honey Bee." His face was so close to hers that Ariadna could smell the sturgeon and the Madeira wine on his breath, the perfume on his beard and the alcohol in his sweat. "Sin should be understood. Without sin there is no life because there is no repentance and if there is no repentance there is no joy. How are you looking at me, Little Bee?"

"With holiness, Father. I have sinned," she started. "I'd die without love. I need to be loved at every moment."

"You're thirsty, Honey Bee." He kissed her lips very slowly. "For now, Honey Bee, come with me. Let us pray." Leaving the other women behind, he took her hand and led her through the curtain into the sanctum.

13

Sashenka's jailhouse dawn was a blinding light and the heady fumes of a long night's distilled urine as every woman in the cell emptied her bladder in turn. Her Smolny pinafore was wet and bloodstained and she ached in every fiber of her body. Boots on stone, the turning of keys and screeching of locks. The cell door swung open.

A man stood in the doorway. "Ugh! It's rank in here," he muttered then pointed at Sashenka. "That's the one. Bring her."

Natasha squeezed her hand as two guards waded through the sprawled bodies and fished her out of the cell. They manhandled her through the grey corridors and deposited her in an interrogation room with a plain desk, a metal chair and walls peeling with damp. She could hear a man crying next door.

A gendarme, a lieutenant with a square head, shaved close, and a long square-cut beard, opened the door, stalked up to her and banged his fist on the table.

"You're going to tell us every single name," he said, "and you're never going to fuck around like this again." Sashenka flinched as he hoisted himself onto the table's edge and pushed his livid face up close to hers. "You've every advantage in life," he shouted. "True, you're not a real Russian. You're a *zhyd*, you're not nobility. Your Jew father probably salutes the Kaiser every night . . ."

"My father's a Russian patriot! The Tsar gave him a medal!"

"Don't answer me like that. That title of his ain't a Russian title. Jews can't have titles here. Everyone knows that. He bought it with stolen rubles from some German princeling . . ."

"The King of Saxony made him a baron." Whatever Sashenka's views on her father's class and the capitalist war, she was still his daughter. "He works hard for his country."

"Shut up unless you want a slap. Once a *zhyd* always a *zhyd*. Profiteers, revolutionaries, tinkers. You *Evrei*—Hebrews—are all at it, aren't you? But you're such a looker. Yes, you're real fresh strawberries!"

"How dare you!" she said quietly, always uneasy about her appearance. "Do not speak to me like that!"

Sashenka had not eaten or drunk since the night before. After her brave moments of defiance, her courage and energy were draining away. She needed food like the furnace of an engine needs coal, and she longed for a hot bath. Yet as she listened to the bully shouting at her, he began to lose his power. She did not fear his small pink eyes and the blue uniform of a degenerate system. The spray of his spittle was grotesque but easily wiped away.

She closed her eyes for a second, removing herself from this police bully, this Derzhimorda. Not for the first time, she imagined the effect of her arrest at home. My dear distant father, where are you at this moment? she wondered. Am I just another problem for you to solve? What about Fanny Loris and the girls at school? How I'd love to hear their trivial chatter today. And my darling Lala, kind, thoughtful Mrs. Lewis with the lullaby voice. She does not know that the girl she loves no longer exists . . .

The shouting came closer again. Sashenka felt faint with hunger and fatigue as the interrogator filled in his forms in brutish semiliterate squiggles. Name? Age? Nationality? Schooling? Parents? Height? Distinguishing features? He wanted her fingerprints: she gave him her right hand. He pressed each finger down on an inkpad and then onto his form.

"You'll be charged under paragraph one, article one hundred twenty-six, for being a member of the illegal Russian Socialist Democratic Workers' Party, and paragraph one, article one hundred two, for being a member of a military organization. Yes, little girl, your friends are terrorists, murderers, fanatics!"

Sashenka knew this was all about the pamphlets she had been distributing for her uncle Mendel. Who wrote them? Where was the printing press? the man asked, again and again.

"Did you handle the 'noodles' and the 'bulldogs'?"

"Noodles? I don't know what you mean."

"Don't play the innocent with me! You know perfectly well that noodles are belts of ammunition for machine guns, and bulldogs are pistols, Mauser pistols."

Another shower of saliva.

"I'm feeling faint. I think I need to eat . . . ," she whispered.

He stood up. "All right, princess, we're having a funny turn, are we? A swoon like that countess in *Onegin*?" He scraped back his chair and took her elbow roughly. "Captain Sagan will see you now."

14

"Greetings, Mademoiselle Baroness," said the officer just down the corridor, in a tidy office that smelled of sawdust and cigars. "I am Captain Sagan. Peter Mikhailovich de Sagan. I do apologize for the bad manners—and breath—of some of my officers. Here, sit down."

He stood up and looked at his new prisoner: a slim girl with luxuriant brown hair stood before him in a crumpled and stained Smolny uniform. He noticed that her lips, in contrast to her pale, bruised face, were crimson and slightly swollen. She stood awkwardly, her arms crossed tightly over her chest, looking down at the floor.

Sagan bowed, neat in his white-trimmed blue tunic, boot heels together, as if they were at a soirée, and then offered his hand. He liked to shake his prisoners' hands. It was one way of "taking their temperature" and showing what the general called "Sagan's steel under the charm." He noticed this girl's hands were shaking and that she carried the noxious smell of the cells. Was that blood on her Smolny pinafore? Some crazy hag had probably attacked her. Well, this was not the Yacht Club. Posh schoolgirls should think of such things before conspiring against their Emperor.

He pulled a chair over and helped her to sit. His first impression was that she was absurdly young. But Sagan liked to say he was "a professional secret policeman, not a nurse." There were opportunities for him among those who were absurdly young and spoiled and out of their depth. Insignificant as she was, she must know something. She was Mendel's niece after all.

She flopped into the chair. Sagan noted her exhaustion with satisfaction—and calibrated pity. She was really no more than a confused child. Still, it opened up interesting possibilities.

"You look hungry, mademoiselle. Fancy ordering some breakfast? Ivanov?" A gendarme NCO appeared in the doorway.

She nodded, avoiding his eyes.

"What can I get you, maga-mozelle?" Ivanov flourished an imaginary pen and paper, playing the French waiter.

"Let's see!" Captain Sagan answered for her, remembering the reports in the surveillance files. "I'll bet you have hot cocoa, white bread lightly toasted, saltless butter and caviar for breakfast?" Sashenka nodded mutely. "Well, we can't do the caviar but we have cocoa, bread and I did find a little Cooper's Fine Cut Marmalade from Yeliseyev's on Nevsky Prospect. Any good to you?"

"Yes, please."

"You've been bleeding."

"Yes."

"Someone attacked you?"

"Last night, it was nothing."

"Do you know why you're here?"

"I was read the charges. I'm innocent."

He smiled at her but she still did not look at him. Her arms remained crossed and she was shivering.

"You're guilty of course, the question is how guilty."

She shook her head. Sagan decided this was going to be a very dull interrogation. Ivanov, wearing an apron stretched lumpily over his blue uniform, wheeled in the breakfast and offered bread, marmalade and some cocoa in a mug.

"Just as you ordered, maga-mozelle," he said.

"Very good, Ivanov. Your French is exquisite." Sagan turned to his prisoner. "Does Ivanov remind you of the waiters at the Donan, your papa's favorite, or the Grand Hotel Pupp at Carlsbad?"

"I've never stayed there," Sashenka whispered, running her fingertips over her wide lips, a gesture she made, he noticed, when she was thoughtful. "My mother stays there: she puts me and my governess in a dingy boardinghouse. But you knew that." She was silent again.

They're always the same. Unhappy at home, they get mixed up in bad company, he thought. She must be starving, but he would wait for her to ask him whether she could eat.

Instead she suddenly looked straight up at him as if the sight of the food had already restored her. Grey eyes, cool as slate, examined him. The speckled lightness of the irises—grains of gold amid the grey—under the hooded eyebrows, projecting a mocking curiosity, took him aback.

"Are you going to sit there and watch me eat?" she asked, taking a piece of bread.

First point to her, thought Sagan. The gentleman in him, the descendant of generations of Baltic barons and Russian generals, wanted to applaud her. Instead he just grinned.

She picked up a knife, spread the bread with butter and marmalade and ate every piece, quickly and neatly. He noticed there were delicate freckles on either side of her nose, and now her arms were no longer crossed he could see that she had a most abundant bosom. The more she tried to hide her breasts, the more conspicuous they became. We interrogators, concluded Sagan, must understand such things.

Ivanov removed the plates. Sagan held out a packet of cigarettes emblazoned with a crocodile.

"Egyptian gold-tipped Crocodiles?" she said.

"Aren't they your only luxury?" he replied. "I know that Smolny girls don't smoke, but in prison, who's watching?" She took one and he lit it for her. Then he took one himself and threw it spinning into the air, catching it in his mouth.

"A performing monkey as well as a torturer," she said in her soft voice with its bumble-bee huskiness, and blew out smoke in blue rings. "Thanks for breakfast. Am I going home now?"

Ah, decided Sagan, she does have some spirit after all. The light caught a rich tinge of auburn in her dark hair.

Sagan reached for a pile of handwritten reports.

"Are you reading someone's diary?" she asked, cheekily.

He looked up at her witheringly. "Mademoiselle, your life as you knew it is over. You will probably be sentenced by the Commission to the maximum five years of exile in Yeniseisk, close to the Arctic Circle. Yes, *five* years. You may never come back. The harsh sentence reflects your treason during wartime and, as you are a Jew, next time it will be harsher still."

"Five years!" Her breaths grew quick and shallow. "It's *your* war, Captain Sagan, a slaughter of working men on the orders of emperors and kings, not *our* war."

"OK, here's the game. These are the surveillance reports of my agents. Let me read what my files say about a certain person I will call Madame X. You have to guess her real name." He took a breath, his eyes twinkling, then lowered his voice theatrically. "*After following the erotic religion of Arzabyshev's novel* Sanin *and taking part in sexual debauchery, she embraced the 'Eastern' teachings of the so-called healer Madame Aspasia del Balzo, who revealed through a process called spiritual retrogression that in a former life Mrs. X had been the handmaiden of Mary Magdalene and then the bodice-designer of Joan of Arc.*"

"That's too easy! Madame X is my mother," said Sashenka. Her nostrils flared and Sagan noticed her lips never quite seemed to close. He turned back to his file.

"*In a table-turning session, Madame Aspasia introduced Baroness Zeitlin to Julius Caesar, who told her not to allow her daughter Sashenka to mock their psychic sessions.*"

"You're making it up, Captain," said Sashenka drily.

"In the lunatic asylum of Piter, we don't need to make anything up. You appear quite often in this file, mademoiselle, or should I say Comrade Zeitlin. Here we are again. *Baroness Zeitlin continues to pursue any road to happiness offered to her. Our investigations reveal that Madame del Balzo was formerly Beryl Crump, illegitimate daughter of Fineas O'Hara Crump, an Irish undertaker from Baltimore, whereabouts unknown. After embracing the teachings of the French hierophant doctor Monsieur Philippe and then the Tibetan healer Dr. Badmaev, Baroness Zeitlin is now a follower of the peasant known to his adepts as 'Elder,' whom she asked to exorcize the evil spirits of her daughter Sashenka who she says despises her and has destroyed her spiritual well-being.*"

"You've made me laugh under interrogation," Sashenka said, looking solemn. "But don't think that you've got me that easily."

Sagan spun the file onto his desk, sat back and held up his hands. "Apologies. I wouldn't for a second underestimate you. I admired your article in the illegal *Rabochnii Put—Workers' Path*—newspaper." He drew out a grubby tabloid journal headed with a red star. "Title: 'The Science of Dialectical Materialism, the Cannibalistic Imperialist Civil War, and Menshevik Betrayal of the Proletarian Vanguard.'"

"I never wrote that," she protested.

"Of course not. But it's very thorough and I understand from one of our agents in Zurich that your Lenin was quite impressed. I don't imagine any other girls at the Smolny Institute could write such an essay, quoting from Plekhanov, Engels, Bebel, Jack London and Lenin—and that's just the first page. I don't mean to patronize."

"I said I didn't write it."

"It's signed 'Tovarish Pesets.' Comrade Snowfox. Your shadows tell me you always wear an Arctic fox fur, a gift from an indulgent father perhaps?"

"A frivolous *nom de révolution*. Not mine."

"Come on, Sashenka—if I may call you that. No man would choose that name: we've got Comrade Stone, Kamenev, and Comrade Steel, Stalin, both of whom I have personally dispatched to Siberia. And Comrade Molotov, the Hammer. Do you know their real names?"

"No, I—"

"Our Special Section knows everything about your Party. It's riddled with our informers. So back to 'Comrade Snowfox.' Not many women in the Party could carry it off. Alexandra Kollontai perhaps, but we know her revolutionary code name. Anyway she's in exile and you're here. By the way, have you read her *Love of the Worker Bees*?"

"Of course I have," Sashenka replied, sitting up straight. "Who hasn't?"

"But I imagine all that free love is more your mother's style?"

"What my mother does is her own business, and as to my private life, I don't have one. I don't want one. All *that* disgusts me. I despise such trivia."

The ash-grey eyes looked through him again. There is no one as sanctimonious as a teenage idealist (especially one who is a rich banker's precious daughter), reflected Sagan. He was impressed with her game, yet was not quite sure what to do: should he release her or keep working on her? She might just be the minnow to hook some bigger fish.

"You know your parents and uncle Gideon Zeitlin all tried to get you released last night."

"Mama? I'm surprised she'd bother . . ."

"Sergeant Ivanov! Have you got last night's report from Rasputin's place?" Ivanov clomped into thc room with the file. Sagan leafed quickly through handwritten papers. "Here we are. *Report of Agent Petrovsky: Dark One*—that's our code name for Rasputin in case you hadn't guessed—*talked to Ariadna Zeitlin, Jewess, wife of the industrialist, and acknowledged she had a special subject to discuss. But after a private session with the Dark One on the subject of sin and an unruly scene on the arrival of Madame Lupkina, Zeitlin, accompanied by the American Countess Loris, left the Dark One's apartment at 3:33 a.m. and was driven to the Aquarium nightclub and then the Astoria Hotel, Mariinsky Square, in the same Russo-Balt landaulet motorcar. Both appeared intoxicated. They visited the suite of Guards Captain Dvinsky, cardsharp and speculator, where . . . champagne ordered . . .* blah, blah . . . *they left at 5:30 a.m. The Jewess Zeitlin's stockings were torn and her clothes were in a disordered state. She was driven back to the Zeitlin residence in Greater Maritime Street and the car then conveyed the American to her husband's apartment on Millionaya, Millionaires' Row . . .*"

"But . . . she never mentioned me?"

Sagan shook his head. "No—although her American friend did. Your father was more effective. But," he raised a finger as her face lit up in expectation, "you're staying right here. Only as a favor to you, of course. It would ruin your credibility with your comrade revolutionaries if I released you too soon."

"Don't be ridiculous."

"If I do release you now, they may think you've become one of my double agents—and then they'd have to rub you out. Don't think they'd be kinder because you're a schoolgirl. They're ice cold. Or they'd assume your rich parents scurried to Rasputin or Andronnikov and bought you out. They'd think—quite rightly in my view—that you're just a frivolous dilettante. So I'll be doing you a favor when I make sure you get those five years in the Arctic."

He watched the flush creep up her neck, flood her cheeks and burn her temples. She's frightened, he thought, pleased with himself.

"That would be an honor. *I'm brave and fear neither knife nor fire*," she said, quoting Zemfira in Pushkin's "Gypsies." "Besides, I'll escape. Everyone does."

"Not from there you won't . . . Zemfira. It's more likely you'll die up there. You'll be buried by strangers in a shallow unmarked grave on the taiga. You'll never lead any revolutions, never marry, never have children—your very presence on this earth a waste of the time, money and care your family have expended on it."

He saw a shudder pass right through her from shoulder to shoulder. He allowed the silence to develop.

"What do you want from me?" she asked, her voice shrill with nerves.

"To talk. That's all," he said. "I'm interested in your views, Comrade Snowfox. In what someone like you thinks of this regime. What you read. How you see the future. The world's changing. You and I—whatever our beliefs—are the future."

"But you and I couldn't be more different," she exclaimed. "You believe in the Tsars and landowners and exploiters. You're the secret fist of this disgusting empire, while I believe it's doomed and soon it'll come crashing down. Then the people will rule!"

"Actually we'd probably agree on many things, Sashenka. I too know things must change."

"History will change the world as surely as the sun rises," she said. "The classes will vanish. Justice will rule. The Tsars, the princes, my parents and their depraved world, and nobility like you . . ." She stopped abruptly as if she had said too much.

"Isn't life strange? I shouldn't be saying this at all but we probably want the same things, Sashenka. We probably even read the same books. I adore Gorky and Leonid Andreyev. And Mayakovsky."

"But I love Mayakovsky!"

"I was in the Stray Dog cellar bar the night he declaimed his poems—and do you know, I wept. I wasn't in uniform of course! But yes, I wept at the sheer courage and beauty of it. You've been to the Stray Dog of course?"

"No, I haven't."

"Oh!" Sagan feigned surprise with a fleck of disappointment. "I don't suppose Mendel is too interested in poetry."

"He and I don't have time to visit smoky cabarets," she said, sulkily.

"I wish I could take you," he told her. "But you said you loved Mayakovsky? My real favorite is

Whorehouse after whorehouse
With six-story-high fauns daring dances . . .

—and she took up the poem, enthusiastically:

Stage Manager! The hearse is ready
Put more widows in the crowds!
There aren't enough there!
No one ever asked
That victory be

—and Sagan picked up the verse again:

Inscribed for our homeland
To an armless stump left from the bloody banquet.
What the hell good is it?

Sashenka marked the rhythm with both hands, flushed with the passion of the words. A vision, thought Sagan, of rebellious, defiant youth.

"Well, well, and I thought you were just a silly schoolgirl," he said, slowly.

There was a knock on the door. Ivanov strode in and gave Sagan a note. He rose briskly and tossed his files onto his desk, sending the particles of dust, suspended in the sunlight, into little whirlwinds.

"Well," said Sagan, "that's that. Good-bye."

Sashenka seemed indignant. "You're sending me back? But you haven't even asked me anything."

"When did your uncle Mendel Barmakid recruit you to the Russian Socialist Democratic Workers' Party? May 1916. How did he escape from exile? By reindeer sleigh, steamship, train (second-class ticket, no less). Don't worry your pretty eyes, Comrade Snowfox, we know it all. I'm not going to waste any more time trying to interrogate you." Sagan pretended to be slightly exasperated while actually he was well satisfied. He had got exactly what he wanted from their meeting. "But I've enjoyed our conversation greatly. I think we should talk about poetry again very soon."

15

Sashenka swathed herself in her snow fox stole and Orenburg shawl as the chief guard held open her sable coat. Stepping into its sleek silk-lined warmth was like sinking into a bath of warm milk. She shivered at the pleasure of it, scarcely aware of the warblings of Sergeant Volkov about "politicals" and "criminals," Swiss chocolates and Brocard's cologne (which he had applied liberally for just this moment).

Sashenka's arrival at the Kresty seemed decades ago, not just the previous night. And when the sergeant said, "You see, I'm not your typical prison guard," she suddenly wanted to hug him. He handed her the canvas book bag.

As she left the prison, she felt she was floating on air. Guards bowed. Door after door opened, bringing the light closer. Gendarmes wielded giant keys on swinging key rings, locks ground open. The gendarme at the counter actually touched the brim of his cap. Everyone seemed to wish her well, as if she were a scholar leaving a school for the last time.

Who would meet her? she wondered. Papa? Flek, the family lawyer? Lala? But before she could even formulate a prediction, Uncle Gideon was opening his strapping arms at full span and dancing toward her, almost falling sideways as if the world were tilting. He wrapped her in his fur, his beard scratching her neck, almost lifting her off the ground.

"Oh my heart!" he bellowed, regardless of the gendarmes. "There she is! Come on! Everyone's waiting!" At that moment, she loved his cognac-and-cigars scent and inhaled it hungrily.

And then she was outside in the freezing light of northern winter. Her father's Russo-Balt landaulet, with chains on its wheels against the ice, lurched forward. Pantameilion, a flash of scarlet and gold braid, ran round to open the door and Sashenka almost collapsed into that leather-lined, sweet-smelling compartment with its fresh carnations in the silver vase. Lala's arms enveloped her and Uncle Gideon climbed into the front seat, swigged some brandy from his flask and took up the speaking tube.

"Home, Pantameilion, you young ladykiller! Fuck Mendel! Fuck the Revolution and all the ideeeots!" Lala rolled her eyes and the two women laughed.

As they crossed the bridge, Lala handed Sashenka the tin of Huntley & Palmers and her babushka Miriam's Yiddish honeycakes. She ate every delicacy, thinking that she had never so loved the spire of the Admiralty, the rococo glory of the Winter Palace—and the golden dome of St. Isaac's. She was going home. She was free!

Uncle Gideon threw open the door at Greater Maritime Street as Sashenka, running up the steps, rushed past Leonid, the old butler who, with tears in his eyes, bowed low from the waist like a village *muzhik* before his young mistress. Gideon tossed his shaggy furs at the butler, who almost crumpled under the weight, and demanded one of the footmen help him pull off his boots.

Sashenka, feeling like the little girl who was occasionally presented to her busy father, ran to his study. The door was open. She prayed he was there. She did not know what she would do if he wasn't. But he was. Zeitlin, in winged collar and spats, was listening to Flek.

"Well, Samuil, the prison governor demanded four hundred," said the toad-like family lawyer.

"Small change compared with Andronnikov . . ." But then Zeitlin saw her. "Thank God, you're here, my darling Lisichka-sestrichka—Little Fox Sister!" he said, reverting to one of her childhood nicknames. He opened his arms and she leaned into him, feeling his tidy mustache on her cheek, bathing in his familiar cologne, pressing her lips against his slightly rough skin. "Let's get your coat off before we talk," he said, releasing himself from her arms and leading her into the hall. Leonid, following dutifully in her wake, removed her coat, stole and shawl, and then she noticed her father was looking her up and down distastefully, his nostrils twitching. Sashenka had quite forgotten that she was still wearing her soiled Smolny pinafore. Suddenly she could smell the filth of prison that clung about her.

"Oh Sashenka, is that blood?" her father exclaimed.

"Oh dearest, we must get you bathed and changed," cried Lala in her high breathy voice. "Luda, draw a bath at once."

"Sashenka," murmured Zeitlin. "Thank God we got you out."

She yearned to wash yet she stood still, reveling in the shock of her father and the servants. "Yes!" she proclaimed, her voice breaking. "I've been to prison, I've seen the tombs that are the Tsar's jails. I'm no longer the Smolny girl you thought I was!"

In the silence that followed, Lala took Sashenka's hands and led her upstairs to the third floor, which was their own country. Up here, every worn piece of carpet, every crack on the landing walls, the damp stain on the pink wallpaper of her bedroom with its playful pictures of ponies and rabbits, the yellowed enamel of the basin in her English washstand, reminded Sashenka of her childhood with Lala, who had decorated her room to create a loving sanctuary for an only child.

The landing was familiar—a mist of Pears pine bath essence and Epsom salts. Lala brought her straight into the bathroom, which was lined with the most indulgent British toiletry products, beautiful blue and amber and green bottles of lotions and oils and essences. The chunky bar of Pears soap, black, cracked, beloved, waited on the wooden bath rack.

"What are we having today?" asked Sashenka.

"Same as always," replied Lala. Sashenka, even though she now regarded herself as an adult, did not resist as Lala undressed her and handed her stinking clothes to Luda.

"Burn them, will you, girl," Lala said.

Sashenka loved the feel of the soft carpet under her feet and the misty essences curling around her. She glanced at her nakedness in the foggy mirror and winced at a body she preferred not to see as Lala helped her into the bath. The water was so hot, the bath (English again, imported from Bond Street) so deep that immediately she closed her eyes and lay back.

"Darling Sashenka, I know you're tired," said Lala, "but just tell me, what happened? Are you all right? I was so worried . . ." And she burst into tears, large teardrops trickling down her wide cheeks.

Sashenka sat up and kissed the tears away. "Don't worry, Lala. I was fine . . ." But as she settled into her bath, her mind traveled back to her final conversation with Mendel last summer holidays . . .

It had been *soomerki*, that beautiful word for summer dusk. The oriole sang in the pine forest. Otherwise, it was quiet in the lilac light.

Sashenka had been lying in the hammock behind their house at Zemblishino, rocking gently and reading Mayakovsky's poetry to herself, when the sleepy swinging stopped. Mendel had his hand on the hammock.

"You're ready," he said, sucking on a cigarette. "When we get back to the city, you'll take on some workers' circles so you can teach them what you know. Then you'll join the Party."

"Not just because I'm your niece?"

"Family and sentiment mean nothing to me," he replied. "What are such things compared to the course of history itself?"

"But what about Mama and Papa?"

"What about them? Your father is the arch exploiter and bloodsucker of the working class and your mother—yes, my own sister—

is a degenerate haute bourgeoise. They're enemies of the science of history. They're irrelevant. Understand that and you're free of them forever."

He handed her a pamphlet with the same title as the first book he had given her weeks earlier: "What Is to Be Done? Burning Questions of Our Party" by Lenin. "Read it. You'll see that to be a Bolshevik is like being a knight in a secret military-religious order, a knight of the grail."

And sure enough, in the weeks that followed, she had felt the joy of being an austere and merciless professional in Lenin's secret vanguard.

When she returned to the city, she began to lecture the workers' groups. She met ordinary workers, proletarians in the colossal Petrograd arms factories, men, women, even children who possessed a gritty decency she had never encountered before. They slaved in dangerous factories and existed in airless grimy dormitories without bedding or baths or lavatories, without light or air, living like rats in a subterranean hell. And she met the workers who manufactured the rifles and howitzers that had made her own father a rich man. Daily, she worked with the most fiery and dedicated Party members who risked their lives for the Revolution. The clandestine world of committees, codes, conspiracy and comrades intoxicated her—and how could it not? It was the drama of history!

When she should have been at dance lessons or visiting Countess Loris's house to play with her friend Fanny, she started to act as Mendel's courier, carrying first leaflets and spare parts for printing presses but then "apples" (grenades), "noodles" (ammunition), and "bulldogs" (pistols). While Fanny Loris and her schoolfriends composed scented letters in curling, girlish handwriting to young lieutenants in the Guards, Sashenka's billets-doux were notes with coded orders from "Comrade Furnace," one of Mendel's code names; and her polkas were rides on public streetcars or her father's sleigh bearing secret cargoes in her lingerie or her fur-collared *sluba* cape.

"You're the perfect courier," said Mendel, "because who would search a Smolny schoolgirl in a snow fox stole riding in a bloodsucker's crested sleigh?"

"Sashenka!" Lala was shaking her gently in her bath. "It's lunchtime. You can sleep all afternoon. They're waiting for you."

As Lala rubbed her back, Sashenka thought of her interrogation by Sagan, the whispers of Natasha, Mendel's woman, and her own ideals and plans. She realized she was stronger and older than she had been yesterday.

16

Five minutes later, Sashenka stood at the door of the drawing room.

"Come in," said her father, who was warming his back against the fire and smoking a cigar. Above him hung an Old Master painting of the founding of Rome set in a colossal gold frame.

She was surprised to see that the room was full of people. In Russian tradition, a nobleman held open house at lunchtime every day, and Zeitlin liked to play the nobleman. But she had expected her parents to cancel this mockery on the day she was released from prison. As she looked around the room, she wanted to cry—and she remembered a time when she was a little girl and her parents were giving a dinner party for the Minister of War, a Grand Duke and various grandees. That evening she had longed for her parents' attention, but when she appeared downstairs her father was in his study—"I asked not to be interrupted, could you take her out please"—and her mother, in a beaded velvet gown with gilded acanthus leaves, was arranging the placement—"Quick! Take her upstairs!" As she left, Sashenka secretly seized a crystal wine glass, and when, on the third floor, she heard the fuss as the Emperor's cousin arrived, she dropped it over the banisters and watched it shatter on the flagstones below. In the fracas that followed, her mother slapped her, even though her father had banned any punishment, and once again, Sashenka had found Lala her only source of comfort.

Sashenka recognized the inevitable Missy Loris (in an ivory-colored brocade dress fringed with sable) talking to her husband, the simian but good-natured count. Gideon held up his glass for another cognac and addressed the lawyer Flek, whose bulging belly was pressed against the round table.

There was an English banker too—a friend of Ariadna and Mendel's long-departed brother, Avigdor, who had left in 1903 to make his fortune in London. Two members of the Imperial Duma, some of Zeitlin's poker cronies, a general in braid and shoulder boards, a French colonel, and Mr. Putilov, the arms manufacturer. Sashenka gave him a satisfied smile, as she had spent many hours instructing his workers to destroy his bloodsucking enterprise.

"Would you like a glass of champagne, Sashenka?" her father offered.

"Lemon cordial," she answered.

Leonid brought it.

"What's for lunch?" she asked the butler.

"The baron's favorite, Mademoiselle Sashenka: Melba toast and terrine, blinis and caviar, Pojarsky veal cutlets cooked in sour cream with English Yorkshire pudding and *kissyel* cranberries in sugar jelly. The same as ever."

But everything had changed, Sashenka thought. Can they not see that?

"A quick chat in my study first," her father said.

I am to be tried, decided Sashenka, and then I shall have to talk to this bunch of shop dummies.

They went into the study. Sashenka remembered how, when her mother was away, her father would let her curl up in the cubbyhole under the desk while he worked. She loved being near him.

"Can I listen?" It was Gideon who threw himself onto the sofa and lay back, sipping cognac. Sashenka was delighted he was there; he might help counteract her mother, who sat down opposite her, in her father's chair.

"Leonid, close the door. Thank you," said Zeitlin, leaning on the Trotting Chair. "Do sit." Sashenka sat. "We're so glad you're home, dear girl, but you did give us a hell of a shock. It wasn't easy getting you out. You should thank Flek."

Sashenka said she would.

"You really might have been on your way to Siberia. The bad news is that you're not going back to Smolny . . ."

That's no funeral, thought Sashenka, that institute for imbeciles!

". . . but we'll arrange tutoring. Well, you've shown us your independence. You've read your Marx and Plekhanov. You've had a close shave. I was young once—"

"Were you?" asked Ariadna acidly.

"Not that I recall," joked Gideon.

"Well, you may be right, but I went to meetings of *narodniks* and socialists in Odessa—once when I was very young. But this is deadly serious, Sashenka. There must be no more fooling around with these dangerous nihilists." He came over and kissed the top of her head. "I'm so glad you're home."

"I'm so happy to be here, Papa."

She gave him her hand and he pressed it, but Sashenka knew this loving scene with her father would provoke her mother. Sure enough, Ariadna cleared her throat.

"Well, you look quite unscathed. You've bored us long enough with your views on 'workers' and 'exploiters' and now you've caused us all a lot of trouble. I even had to bring this up with the Elder Grigory."

Fury reared up inside Sashenka. She wanted to shout out that she was ashamed that a creature like Rasputin was ruling Russia, ashamed that her own mother, whose love affairs with cardsharps and fads with charlatans had long embarrassed her, was now consorting with the Mad Monk. But instead, she could not stop herself answering like the petulant schoolgirl she still was. Searching for a target, she aimed for the dress chosen by her mother.

"Mama, I hate sailor suits and this is the last time I shall ever wear one."

"Bravo!" said Gideon. "A figure like yours is wasted in—"

"That's enough, Gideon. Please leave us alone," said Ariadna.

Gideon got up to go, winking at Sashenka.

"You'll wear what I say," said her mother, in her flowing crêpe de chine dress with flounces of lace. "You'll wear the sailor suits as long as you behave like an irresponsible child."

"Enough, both of you," Zeitlin said quietly. "Your mother will indeed decide what you wear."

"Thank you, Samuil."

"But I propose a deal, darling girl. If you promise never to dabble in nihilism, anarchism and Marxism ever again, and never to talk politics with Mendel, your mother will take you shopping for your own adult gown at Chernyshev's, on my account. She'll let you have your hair done at Monsieur Troye's like her. You can get your cards and stationery printed at Treumann's and you and your mother can take Pantameilion and make 'at home' calls. And you'll never have to dress in a sailor suit again."

Zeitlin opened his hands, thought Sashenka, as if he had cut the Gordian knot or solved the mysteries of the Delphic oracle. She did not want dresses from Chernyshev's and she certainly did not need them where she was going. Her dear, silly father so longed for her to leave her cards and write love letters to pea-brained counts and guardsmen. But she already had what she needed: a plain high-necked blouse, a sensible skirt, woollen stockings and walking shoes.

"Agreed, Ariadna?"

Ariadna nodded and lit a Mogul cigarette. Then they both turned to Sashenka.

"Sashenka, look into my eyes and swear solemnly to this."

Sashenka peered into her father's blue eyes and then glanced at her mother.

"Thank you, Papa. I promise that I will never ever talk politics with Mendel and never dabble in nihilism again."

Zeitlin pulled a brocade cord.

"Yes, Baron," replied Leonid, opening the door. "Lunch is served."

17

A stunted man in pince-nez, an oversized coachman's sheepskin and a leather peaked cap with earmuffs stood on the Nevsky Prospect, watching the streetcar rumble toward him. It was dark, and a bitter blizzard whipped his face, already red and raw. The colossal General Staff building was on his left.

Mendel Barmakid looked behind him. The *shpik*—the secret-police spook—was still there, a mustachioed man with a military bearing in a green coat, trying to keep warm. Spooks tended to work in twos but he could not see the other one. Mendel was outside the illuminated windows of Chernyshev's, one of his sister's cheaper dressmakers. In a display window of mannequins in that season's velvet and tulle, he saw himself: a dwarf with a clubfoot, fat lips and a neat beard on the end of his chin. It was not an attractive sight but he had no time for sentimental indulgences. Nevsky was almost empty. The temperatures were falling—tonight it was minus twenty and the spooks had found him again when the Petrograd Committee met at the secret apartment in Vyborg. It was only ten days since his escape from exile, and now those police clods would debate whether to arrest him again or allow him to lead them to more comrades.

The streetcar stopped with a ringing of bells and a little meteor shower of sparks from the electric cables above. A woman got out. The spook beat his gloves together, his Cossack earring catching the light of the streetlamp.

The streetcar creaked forward. Suddenly Mendel ran toward it, his bad limp giving him a peculiar gait. His body twisted like a human parabola but he ran very fast for a cripple. The streetcar was moving now. It was hard to run in the snow and even though Mendel did not look back, he knew that the young, fit spook had already spotted him and was giving chase. Mendel grabbed hold of the bar. The conductor, shouting, "Well run, old man!" seized his other arm and pulled him up.

Sweating inside his sheepskin, Mendel glanced back: the spook was running behind—but he was not going to make it. Mendel saluted him, noble-style, touching his brim.

He traveled two stops, then slipped off the streetcar at the pink Stroganov Palace and again checked his tails. No one—though they always found him again. He passed the colonnades of the Kazan Cathedral, where he sometimes met comrades on the run from exile. The snow was slicing at the orange lanterns and he had to keep rubbing the lenses of his pince-nez. He saw only the shops of the bloodsucking classes—the Passazh with its English tailors and French jewelers; the Yeliseyev Emporium piled obscenely high with hams, sturgeons, cakes, oysters, clams, Indian teas and Fortnum & Mason fruitcakes; the labyrinthine Gostiny Dvor, with its bearded merchants in caftans selling antique icons and samovars.

Mendel heard the clipclop of horsemen—two gendarmes on patrol, but they were chatting to each other loudly about a whore in Kaluga and did not see him. He waited at the window of Yeliseyev's till they were gone. Then a Rolls-Royce sped by, and coming the other way a Delaunay: perhaps it was Zeitlin?

He reached the Hotel Europa, with its doormen in scarlet greatcoats and top hats. Its foyer and restaurant were the most heavily spied-upon square feet in the whole of Europe—and that was why he felt safe. No one would expect an escaped exile to linger here. But his coat was ragged and darned, while the folk around here were in sables, frock coats, guardsmen's rig. Already the doorman, who was a police agent, was staring at him.

Mendel heard the dry swish of the sleigh. He limped over to a doorway to watch it come, searching for signs of *shpiki* and *fileri*, external agents. But the sleigh looked kosher, just one old hunched coachman.

Mendel hailed it and climbed in.

"Where to, sir?"

"The Taurida Palace."

"Half a ruble."

"Twenty kopeks."

"The price of oats is up again. Can hardly feed the horse on that . . ."

Oats and more oats, thought Mendel. Prices were rising, the war was disastrous. But the worse, the better: that was his motto. The coachman, decided Mendel, was really a petit bourgeois with no role in the future. But then in Russia there were so few real proletarians on the Marxist model. Nine out of ten Russians were obstinate, backward, greedy, savage peasants. Lenin, with whom Mendel had shared sausages and beer in Cracow before the war, had mused that if the peasants did not accept the progress of history, their backs would have to be broken. "Cruel necessity," muttered Mendel.

Mendel was grey with exhaustion and malnutrition. It was hard to sleep, hard to eat on the run—yet somehow this existence suited him almost perfectly. No family—but then children bored him. Marriage—yes, but to Natasha the Yakut, another dedicated comrade whom he met only sporadically. Always on the move, he could sleep as easily on a park bench as on a floor or a sofa. Lenin was in Switzerland and virtually the entire Central Committee—Sverdlov, Stalin, Kamenev—were in Siberia, and he was almost the last senior veteran of 1905 on the loose. But Lenin had ordered: "You're needed in Piter: escape!" He had sent Mendel a hundred rubles to buy "boots"—his false identity papers.

All that mattered was the Party and the cause: I am a knight of the holy grail, Mendel thought, as the sleigh approached the domed portico and splendid Doric colonnade of the Taurida Palace, where the bourgeois saps of the talking-shop parliament—the Imperial Duma—now held their absurd debates. But before the sleigh was there, Mendel leaned forward and tapped the padded shoulder of the coachman.

"Here!" Mendel pressed some kopeks into the coachman's mitten and jumped off. Cars stood with their engines turning outside the Duma but Mendel did not approach the palace. Instead he limped into the lodge attached to the guardhouse of the Horse Guards regiment next door. An old Adler limousine with the crest of a Grand

Duke, bearing a Guards officer and a flunkey in court uniform, stopped and trumpeted its horn.

The gateman, simultaneously bowing, buttoning up his trousers and holding onto his hat, ran out and tried to open the gates. Mendel glanced around and knocked on the dusty door of the cottage.

The door opened. A ruddy-cheeked doorman in a Russian peasant smock and yellowed longjohns let him into a dreary little room with a stove, samovar and the fusty atmosphere of sleeping men and boiling vegetables.

"You?" said Igor Verezin. "Thought you were in Kamchatka."

"Yeniseisk Region. I walked." Mendel noticed the doorman had a pointed bald pate the shape and color of a red-hot bullet. "I'm starving, Verezin."

"*Shchi* soup, black Borodinsky bread and a sausage. The samovar's boiling, comrade."

"Any messages for me?"

"Yes, someone pushed the newspaper through the door earlier."

"Someone's coming tonight."

Verezin shrugged.

"Where's the paper? Let me see. Good." Mendel threw off his coat, checked the back window and the front. "Can I sleep?"

"Be my guest, comrade. The sofa's yours though I might bed down myself there in a minute." There was no bed in the dim little room and the doormen took turns sleeping on the sofa. "So how did you escape?"

But Mendel, still wearing his hat, boots and pince-nez, was already stretched out on the sofa.

There was a rap on the door, and the doorman found a teenage girl in a gleaming fur coat, undoubtedly sable, and a white fox-fur stole, who stepped hesitantly into the room. She was slim with a wide mouth and exceedingly light grey eyes.

"I'm in luck today!" joked Verezin. "Excuse my pants!"

She gave him a withering look. "*Baramian?*" she asked.

"Get inside, milady," joked Verezin, bowing like a court flunkey. "With that coat you should be going in the main gates with the field marshals and princes."

Mendel stood up, yawning. "Oh it's you," he said, aware that his voice was his most impressive feature—deep and sonorous like a Jericho trumpet. He turned to Verezin. "Could you take a walk? Round the block."

"What? In this weather? You've got to be joking . . ." But Mendel never joked—except about the gallows. Instead the little man looked pointedly toward the stove behind which his "bulldog"—a Mauser revolver—waited, wrapped in a cloth, and Verezin hurriedly changed his mind. "I'll go and buy some salted fish." Pulling on a greatcoat, he stomped outside.

When the doorman was gone, Sashenka sat down at the wicker table beside the stove.

"Don't you trust him?" She offered Mendel one of her perfumed Crocodile cigarettes with the gold tips.

"He's a concierge." Mendel lit up. "Most doormen are Okhrana informers—but when they sympathize with us they guard the safest safe houses. So as long as he doesn't turn, no one would look for a Bolshevik at the Horse Guards headquarters. He's a sympathizer and may join the Party." He blew out a lungful of smoke. "Your father's house is under surveillance. They're waiting for me. How did you get away?"

"I waited until everyone was asleep. Mama's out every night anyway. Then I used the Black Way into the courtyard and out through the garage. Streetcars, back doors, shops with two entrances, houses with courtyards. They never expect a girl in sable and kid boots to outwit them. You trained me well. I've learned the codes. I'm getting good at the craft. Like a ghost. And I'm fast as a mountain goat."

Mendel felt an odd sensation, and realized he was happy to see her. She was sparkling with life. Yet he did not give her the hug he wanted to give her. The child was spoiled enough already.

"Don't get overconfident," he said gruffly. "Comrade Snowfox, did you deliver the message to the safe house?"

"Yes."

"Did you collect the pamphlets from the printing press?"

"Yes."

"Where are they now?"

"In the apartment on the Petrograd Side. Shirokaya Street."

"Tomorrow they need to reach the comrades at the Putilov Works."

"I'll do it. Usual arrangements?"

Mendel nodded. "You're doing well, comrade."

She looked so young when she smiled, and by the dim lantern of the mean little room Mendel noticed the little shower of freckles on either side of her nose. He knew from her quick replies that she wanted to tell him something. He decided to make her wait.

Her intensity made him feel like an old man suddenly, conscious of his skin like porridge speckled with broken veins, of the strands of grey in his greasy hair, of the aches of his arthritis. That was what exile and prison did for you.

"Dear comrade," she said, "I can't thank you enough for your teaching. Now everything fits. I never thought the words 'comrade' and 'committee' would excite me so much, but they do. They really do!"

"Don't chatter too much," he told her sternly. "And watch yourself with comrades. They know your background and they look for signs of bourgeois philistinism. Change the sable. Get a karakul."

"Right. I feel that I'm a cog in a secret world, in the universal movement of history."

"We all are, but in Piter at the moment you're more important than you realize. We've so few comrades," said Mendel, inhaling his cigarette, his red-rimmed eyes half closed. "Keep reading, girl. You can't read enough. Self-improvement is the Bolshevik way."

"The food shortages are getting worse. You've seen the lines? Everyone is grumbling—from the capitalists who come for lunch with Papa to comrades in the factories. Surely something will happen now?"

Mendel shook his head. "One day, yes, but not now. Russia still lacks a real proletarian class and without one, revolution isn't possible. I'm not sure it'll happen in our lifetimes. How can one jump the stages of Marxist development? It can't happen, Sashenka. It's impossible."

"Of course. But surely—"

"Even Lenin isn't sure we'll live to see it."

"You get his letters?"

Mendel nodded. "We've told him about the Smolny girl called Snowfox. How's the family?"

She took a breath. Here it comes, he thought.

"Comrade Mendel," she said, "I was arrested yesterday and spent the night at the Kresty."

Mendel limped to the stove and, taking a greasy spoon, he leaned over the *shchi* soup and slurped a mouthful. The cigarette somehow remained hanging in the corner of his mouth.

"My first arrest, Uncle Mendel!"

He remembered his own first arrest twenty years ago, the appalled reaction of his father, the great Turbin rabbi, and his own pride on earning this badge of honor.

"Congratulations," he told Sashenka. "You're becoming a real revolutionary. Did the comrades of the cell committee take care of you?"

"Comrade Natasha looked after me. I didn't know you were married."

Sometimes Sashenka was a real Smolny schoolgirl. "I'm married to the Party. Comrades are arrested every day and very few are released the next morning."

"There's something else."

"Go on," he said, leaning on the stove, an old exile's trick to ease the ache of Arctic winter. He chomped on a hunk of cold sausage, cigarette miraculously still in position.

"I was interrogated for several hours by Gendarme Captain Peter Sagan."

"Sagan, eh?" Mendel knew that Sagan was the Okhrana case officer assigned to finish off the Party. He moved back to the little table, dragging his heavy boot. As he sat down, the table creaked. Now he was concentrating, watching her face. "I think I've heard the name. What of him?"

"He was trying to lead me on, but Uncle Mendel," she said, joining him at the table and gripping his arm, the Smolny schoolgirl again, "he prides himself on his humanity. He's something of a bourgeois liberal. I know I'm a neophyte but I just wanted to inform you—and the Petrograd Committee—that he seemed keen to be my friend. Naturally I gave him no encouragement. But at the end, he said he would like to meet me again and continue our conversation—"

"About what?"

"Poetry. Why are you smiling, Uncle Mendel?"

"You've done well, comrade," Mendel said, thinking this new development through.

Sagan, a penniless nobleman, was a slick and ambitious policeman who specialized in turning female revolutionaries. But he might well be sympathetic to the Left, because the secret police knew how rotten the regime was better than anyone. It could be a signal, a trick, a seduction, a betrayal—or just an intellectually pretentious policeman. There were a hundred ways it could play out and Sashenka understood none of them, he thought.

"What if he *does* approach me?" she asked.

"What do you think?" answered Mendel.

"If he comes up to me in the street, I'll tell him never to talk to me again and curse him for good measure. Is that what you want me to do?"

Silence except for the flutter of the kerosene lamp. Mendel peered at her as intensely as a priest at an exorcism. The child he had known since her birth was an unfinished but very striking creature, he reflected, guessing that Sagan wanted to turn her into a double agent to get to Mendel himself. But there were two ways of playing this, and he could not miss a chance to destroy Sagan, whatever the cost.

"You're wrong," he said slowly.

"If the committee wished it," she said, "I would kill him with Papa's Browning—it's in his desk—or there's the Mauser behind the bookcase at the safe house on Shirokaya. Let me do it!"

"In the end, we'll put them *all* up against the wall," said Mendel. "Now, listen to me. You might never hear from Sagan again. But if he turns up, talk to him, draw him out. He could be helpful to the Party and to me."

"What if he tries to recruit me?"

"He will. Let him think that's possible."

"What if a comrade sees me with him?" she said anxiously.

"The Inner Bureau of the Committee will be informed of this operation. Three of us—a troika—just me and two others. Are you afraid?"

Sashenka shook her head. Her eyes were almost glowing in the dark. He could see she was scared and excited to have such a mission. "But I could be killed by my own comrades as a traitor?"

"We're both in danger every minute," he replied. "The very second you become a Bolshevik, your normal life is over. You walk forever on burning coals. It's like leaping onto a sleigh galloping so fast you can never get off. Chop wood and chips fly. We're in a secret war, the Superlative Game, you and I. The Party against the Okhrana. You do as I tell you, nothing more, and you report every word to me. You know the codes and the drops? Be vigilant. Vigilance is a Bolshevik virtue. You've become an asset to the Party quicker than I could have predicted. Understand?"

Mendel took care to moderate his voice and hoped he sounded convincing. He offered his hand and they shook. Her hand felt as silky, delicate and nervy as a little bird whose bones could be crushed with ease. "Good night, comrade."

Sashenka stood up and pulled on her coat, stole, boots and *shapka* and wrapped her head in the scarf. At the door she turned back, pale and serious.

"I'd hate you to protect me because I was family."

"I never would, comrade."

18

"See the filly over there?" said the old coachman in the sheepskin, his cheeks as red as rare beef.

"Her again. Is she nursing a broken heart?"

"Is she a working girl or planning a bank robbery?"

"Perhaps she's booked a room at the hotel?"

"Is she slumming it for a lover who knows how to clean a horse's arse? Me, for example!"

"Hey, girl, have a vodka on us!"

In the middle of St. Isaac's Square, not far from Greater Maritime Street, somewhere between the Mariinsky Palace and the cathedral, stood a flimsy wooden hut, painted black, with a tarpaulin roof so it looked like a giant one-horse cab with the hood up. Here in the bleary realm of overboiled cabbage and winter sweat, the coachmen of the one-horse cabs—the *izvoshtikis*—came to drink and eat in the early hours in a world beyond exhaustion.

Sashenka, a rough karakul coat and leather cap beside her, sat on her own and put some kopeks into the noisy automatic barrel organ. It started to play "Yankee Doodle" and then some Strauss waltzes and presently "Yankee Doodle" again. Lighting a cigarette, she stared through the window at the Rolls-Royces outside the Astoria Hotel, the falling snow, and the horses tapping their hooves on the ice outside, waiting patiently, their breaths and whinnies all visible in the cold.

Two days had passed since her meeting with Mendel. At eleven that night, Lala had looked in on her in her bedroom.

"Turn your lights out now, darling," she said. "You look tired." Lala sat on her bed and kissed her forehead as always. "You'll hurt your eyes with all that reading. What are you reading about?"

"Oh Lala . . . one day I'll tell you," Sashenka said, curling up to sleep, anxious that her governess should not discover that under the bedclothes she was dressed ready to go out.

Once she knew Lala was asleep, she crept outside, taking a streetcar and then an *izvoshtik* over to the factories on the Petrograd Side. She spent an hour at the workers' circle at the Putilov and, together with another young intellectual, a boy from the Gymnasium, and a couple of lathe turners, they delivered the spare parts for a printing press to a new hideout in Vyborg.

Afterward she had an hour to kill so she walked along the Embankment and then along the Moika over her favorite little bridge, the

Bridge of Kisses, past the ocher Yusupov Palace that more than any other building represented the iniquitous wealth of the few. She came here to the coachmen's hut because it was close to home—and yet in another dimension.

She ordered spicy *ukha* fish soup, goat's cheese, black Borodinsky bread and some tea—and sat listening to the men's gossip. When they talked about her as a dish, a looker, she did not quite understand what they meant. She could see her reflection in the little window and felt dissatisfied as always. She preferred to picture herself out in the freeze, buried in her high-necked coat, stole and *shapka.*

Cut out the vanity, Sashenka told herself. Her looks did not interest her. Like her uncle Mendel, she lived for the Revolution. Wherever she looked in the streets, she saw only those who would benefit from the beautiful march of the dialectic.

She dipped the bread and cheese into some mustard, and spluttered as the burn raced up her nose into her sinuses. Afterward, she nibbled at a shapeless sugar lump and reflected that she was happier now than she had ever been in her entire life.

As a child, her parents had taken her to Turbin to visit the rabbinical court of her grandfather, Abram Barmakid, the saintly rabbi, with his beadles, disciples, students and hangers-on. She was very young and her father was not yet such a swell, and they lived in Warsaw, which was full of Hasidic Jews. But nothing had prepared Sashenka for the medieval realm of Abram Barmakid. The honest fanaticism, the rigid joy, even the guttural Yiddish language, the men with ringlets, fringed shawls and gabardine coats, the bewigged women—all of it scared her. Even then, she had feared their medieval spells and superstitions.

Yet she now reflected that her grandparents' world of golems and evil eyes was no worse than the secular money worship of her father's marketplace. Since childhood, she had been shocked by the injustices she had seen at Zemblishino and the manor house on his vast estates on the Dnieper. The luxury and debauchery of her parents' wretched marriage seemed to her to epitomize the rottenness of Russia and the capitalist world.

Mendel had rescued her from all this wickedness, and had changed her life. *If you love then love with verve; if you threaten mean it well*, the poet Alexei Tolstoy had written. That was her: "*All or nothing!*" She reveled in the delicious, almost amorous feeling of being part of a secret, a giant conspiracy. There was something seductive about sacrificing the old morality of the middle classes for the new morality of the Revolution. It was like sitting in this café: the very unromance of it was what made it so romantic.

She glanced at her watch: 4:45 a.m. Time to go. She pulled on the coat and hat again, tossed down some coins. The coachmen watched, nodding at her. On the street, the draymen were delivering the milk crates, the patisserie van loading up with freshly baked bread. Carters dragged in sacks of coal. Janitors cleaned the steps. Piter was awakening.

The freezing air was so refreshing after the musk of the little hut that she inhaled it until it burned her lungs. How she loved Piter with its peculiar climate, almost arctic in its gummy winter blackness, but in summer, when it never grew dark, as bright as Paradise before the Fall. Its gorgeous facades in eggshell blue and ocher were magnificently imperial. But behind them were the factories, the electric streetcars, the yellow smoke and the crowded workers' dormitories. The beauty that surrounded her was a lie. The truth might seem ugly but it had its beauty too. Here was the future!

She crossed St. Isaac's Square. Even in winter, you could spot the approach of dawn because the golden dome began to shine darkly long before there was as much as a glow on the horizon. The Astoria was still feasting—she could hear the band, glimpse in the gloom the diamonds of women, the orange tips of men's cigars. The Yacht Club was still open, troikas and limousines waiting outside for the courtiers and financiers.

She headed down Greater Maritime. She heard the rumble of a car and sank back into a doorway, like the ghost she had described to Mendel.

The Delaunay stopped outside her home. Pantameilion, in his long shining boots, opened the door of the car. Her mother climbed out.

First one gorgeously clad foot in the softest kid boot appeared. Then a glimpse of silk stockings, then the satin dress, the sequins glittering.

A white hand studded with rings held the car's doorframe. Sashenka was disgusted. Here she was, coming from serving the working class; here, with perfect symmetry, came her mother, fresh from servicing the desires of some corrupt man who was not her father.

Sashenka did not know what exactly it was that lovers did, though she knew it was like the dogs on her father's estate—and she was repulsed, yet rapt. She watched her mother pull herself out of the car and stand swaying. Pantameilion rushed to catch her hand.

Sashenka wanted to scratch her mother's face and throw her to the ground where she belonged, but she stepped out of the shadows to find Pantameilion crouched on the snow, pulling at a writhing sequined form on the pavement. It was her mother struggling to get back on her feet.

Sashenka ran up to them. Ariadna was on all fours, her stockings torn and naked knees bleeding. She fell forward again, one gloved hand clawing at the snow, the other trying to fight off Pantameilion's proffered arm.

"Thanks, Pantameilion," said Sashenka. "Just check to see that the doors are open. And send the watchman back to bed."

"But miss, the baroness . . ."

"Please, Pantameilion, I'll look after her."

Pantameilion's face bore the double anguish of servants faced with the collapse of their employers—they hated the topsy-turviness of a humiliated mistress just as they feared the insecurity of a fallen master. He bowed, shuffled into the house and emerged a moment later, climbing back into the growling Delaunay and jerking it into gear.

Mother and daughter were alone in the street under the mansion's lantern.

Sashenka knelt beside her mother, who was weeping. Her tears ran in black streams from black eyes on dirty white skin, like muddy footprints on old snow.

Sashenka pulled her to her feet, threw her arm over her shoulder and dragged her up the two steps into the lobby of the house. Inside, the great hall was almost dark, just an electric light burning on the first-floor landing. The giant white squares shone bright, while the black ones were like holes dropping to the middle of the earth. Somehow, she got her mother up to her room. The electric light would be too bright so she lit the oil lamps instead.

By now, Ariadna was sobbing quietly to herself. Sashenka raised her mother's hands to her lips and kissed them, her anger of a few moments earlier forgotten.

"Mama, Mama, you're home now. It's me, Sashenka! I'm going to undress you and put you to bed." Ariadna calmed down a little, though she continued to speak slivers of nonsense as Sashenka undressed her.

"Sing it again . . . loneliness . . . your lips are like stars, houses . . . the wine is only mediocre, a bad year . . . hold me again . . . feel so sick . . . pay it, I'll pay, I can afford it . . . Love is God . . . am I home . . . you sound like my daughter . . . my vicious daughter . . . another glass please . . . kiss me properly."

Sashenka pulled off her mother's boots, threw off the sable and the hat with ostrich feathers, unhooked the satin dress embroidered with sequins and misty with faded tuberose, untied the bodice, unrolled the shredded stockings, unclipped the brooches, the three ropes of pearls and the diamond earrings. As she pulled off the underdress and the lingerie that was inside out, she was enveloped in the animal smells and sweated alcohol of a woman of the town, aromas that repelled her. She vowed she would never let herself descend into such a state. Finally she heated water and washed her mother's face.

Amazed at herself, she realized that she had become the mother, and the mother the child. She folded and hung her mother's clothes, laid her jewels in the velvet box, threw her lingerie into the laundry basket. Then she helped her mother onto the bed, under the covers and kissed her cheek. She stroked her forehead and sat with her.

"You and me . . . ," said Ariadna, as she fell asleep, rolling and tossing in her sad dreams.

"Sleep, Mama. There, there. It's over."

"Darling Sashenka, you and me . . ."

When Ariadna finally slept, Sashenka wept. I don't want children, she told herself. Never!

19

Sashenka was still asleep in the chair in Ariadna's boudoir when she heard her mother calling her: "Sashenka! I'll take you shopping today, just as your father wanted. Chernyshev's for your day dresses! You might even be lucky enough to have a gown from Madame Brissac like the little Grand Duchesses!"

"But I've got to study," said Sashenka, stretching, and going into her mother's bedroom.

"Don't be foolish, my dear," said her mother cheerfully, as if nothing shocking had happened. "Look at how you dress. Like a schoolteacher!"

Ariadna was having breakfast off a tray on her bed, and the room smelled of coffee, toast, caviar and poached eggs. "We've become firm friends, haven't we, *sladkaya*—my sweetie?"

As Leonid finished serving and left the room, Ariadna winked at Sashenka, who asked herself how her mother could possibly have recovered so absolutely, so shamelessly, from the night's indulgences. The dissipated require constitutions of steel, she thought.

"I'm not sure I can come."

"We leave at eleven. Lala's drawing you a bath." Sashenka decided to acquiesce. Her days were interminably boring anyway. She lived for the dark hours.

An hour later, the two-tone coffee-hued Benz, the third family car, piloted by Pantameilion sporting what Sashenka privately called his "bandmaster's garb," delivered them before the famous windows of mannequins in hats, toques and ball dresses: the Chernyshev couture atelier on the corner of Greater Maritime and Nevsky.

The doors of the fashion emporium were opened by flunkeys in green frock coats. Inside, women wearing white gloves, hats like fruit bowls and tight-waisted dresses, pleated and whaleboned, tried on racks of dresses. The air was dense with perfume and the scent of warm bodies.

Ariadna commandeered the entire right side of the shop, much to Sashenka's embarrassment. A smiling fever of submissive enthusiasm attended Ariadna's every whim. At first Sashenka thought the staff were cringing like her at her mother's brashness but then she realized that the atmosphere reflected the jubilation felt in all luxury shops at the arrival of a very rich client with little taste and less restraint.

A stick insect in a red gown speaking poor French presided over this jamboree, barking orders. The assistants were almost too assiduous: weren't they smirking a little? Models (who, Sashenka thought, wore far too much foundation) walked up and down in dresses that did not interest her. Her mother pointed at this one or that one, in brocade or lace, with flounces or sequins, and even made her try on a couple. Lala, who accompanied mother and daughter, helped Sashenka into the dresses.

Sashenka had decided to enjoy the trip in order to avoid a quarrel with her mother. But the dressing and undressing, the pulling and pushing, the staring and poking by the skinny non-Frenchwoman, who whipped pins in and out of the fabric with invisible speed, began to rile her. She hated the way she looked in every dress and found herself becoming angry and upset.

"I'm so ugly, Lala, in this. I refuse to wear it! I'd burn it!" Her mother, in her velvet skirt and fur-collar bolero jacket, was a gorgeous swan while Sashenka felt lumpier and fatter than a warthog. She could not bear to look in the mirrors again.

"But Mademoiselle Zeitlin has such a perfect figure for the latest fashions," said the couturier.

"I want to go home!"

"Poor Sashenka's tired, aren't you, darling?" Another wink. "You don't have to have everything but there were some you liked, weren't there, sweetie?"

Feeling somewhat sheepish at this, Sashenka nodded.

A wave of relief now passed over the staff. Glasses of Tokai were brought for Baroness Zeitlin, who threw her head back and laughed too loudly, paying in big green notes, and then the satisfied assistants helped the ladies rearrange their furs. Pantameilion followed them out of Chernyshev's, carrying their purchases in bulging bags, which he quickly stowed in the trunk.

"There!" said Ariadna, settling herself in the car. "Now you have some grown-up dresses at last."

"But Mama," replied Sashenka, sickened by the expense and surprised such shops were still open in wartime, "I don't lead that life. I just wanted something simple. I don't need ball dresses and tea dresses and day dresses."

"Oh yes you do," answered Lala.

"I sometimes change six times in a day," declared Ariadna. "I wear a day dress in the morning. Then a tea dress and then today I'm going to call on the Lorises in my new chiffon dress with brocade, and then tonight . . ."

Sashenka could hardly bear to think of her mother at night.

"We women have got to make an effort to find husbands," explained Ariadna.

"Where to, Baroness?" asked Pantameilion through the speaking tube.

"To the English Shop, Sashenka's favorite," answered Ariadna.

Inside the shop, behind the windows that displayed Penhaligon's bath oils and perfumes, Pears soaps and Fortnum's Gentleman's Relish and Cooper's jams, the women bought a ginger cake and cookies while still lecturing Sashenka about the need for dresses.

"Hello, Sashenka! Is it you? Yes, it is!" Some young students in uniformed greatcoats and caps were lingering outside Chernyshev's, smirking and pushing against one another. "Naughty Sashenka! We heard about your scrape with the gendarmes!" they called.

Sashenka noticed that the "aesthetes" wore berets, the "dandies" peaked caps. One of the aesthetes, who was heir to some magnate or other, had written her love poems. Sashenka smiled thinly and walked on ahead of her mother and Lala.

"Mademoiselle, what a pleasure to meet again!"

For a moment Sashenka froze, but then her senses returned as Captain Sagan walked briskly through the lurking students. He wore a tweed coat, a tartan tie and a derby hat, all probably bought at the English Shop. He bowed, with a slight smile, raised the derby and kissed her hand.

"I was buying some cufflinks," he said. "Why is everyone so keen on English style? Why not Scottish or Welsh or even Indian? They're our allies too."

Sashenka shook her head and tried to remember what Mendel had ordered her to do. Her heart was thumping in the rhythm of a speeding train. This is it, Comrade Mendel! she told herself.

"I'm sure you never want to see me again, but there's Mayakovsky to discuss, and remember we never got to Akhmatova? I must rush. I hope I haven't . . . embarrassed you."

"You've a hell of a nerve!" she exclaimed.

He raised his derby, and she could not help but notice that he wore his hair long, more like an actor than a policeman.

Sagan waved at a waiting sleigh that slid forward with its bells ringing and carried him off down Nevsky.

Ariadna and Lala caught up with her.

"Sashenka!" said her mother. "Who was that? You could have been a little more friendly."

But Sashenka now felt invincible, however many silly dresses they had made her try on. She adored the secret nocturnal work of a Bolshevik activist. Now, she thought, I'll be a real asset to the Party. The house was watched. Sagan must have guessed that they would visit the English Shop, where he would stand out less than at Chernyshev's. He had spoken to her out of earshot of her mother and governess because he wanted her to know that he had his eye on her. She could not wait to tell Mendel.

On the way home, Ariadna squeezed her daughter's cheek.

"Sashenka and I are going to be firm friends, firm friends, aren't we, darling?" her mother kept saying.

Sitting on the tan leather between Ariadna and Lala, Sashenka remembered that in the past, whenever she had run to her mother for a cuddle, Ariadna had withdrawn from her, saying, "Mrs. Lewis, Mrs. Lewis, this is a new dress from Madame Brissac and the child's got a dirty mouth . . ."

Last night she had finally got her hug but now she no longer wanted it.

When they reached home, Ariadna took Sashenka's hand and coaxed her upstairs into her boudoir.

"Come out with me tonight in a new dress that shows off your figure!" she whispered huskily, sniffing the tuberose on her wrist. "After last night, when I saw you coming home late, I know about your secret lover! I won't tell Papa but we can go out together. I thought you were such a prig, dear Sashenka, never smiling—no wonder you had no suitors—but I was wrong, wasn't I? Creeping home in the early hours like a pussycat! Who was the tomcat? That tweed suit and derby we saw just now? We'll wear our gorgeous new gowns and people will think we're sisters. You and me, we're just the same . . ."

But Sashenka had to deliver a Party rubber stamp and the receipt book for contributions. At the safe house, she would meet the comrades and boil the gelatin used to print the leaflets on the hectograph.

Before all those duties, she had to contact Mendel and tell him about her meeting with Sagan.

She longed for the mysteries of the night like the embrace of a lover.

20

Sashenka left the house at 1:00 a.m. Noting the two spooks on the street, she walked up to Nevsky Prospect and into the Europa Hotel. From the lobby she took the service elevator down to the basement, walked through the kitchens, where bloody-aproned porters with shaggy beards were delivering eggs, cabbages and the pink carcasses of pigs and lambs, and out into the street again, where she hailed a troika and left a coded note for Mendel at the Georgian pharmacy on Alexandrovsky Prospect.

At the coachmen's café outside the Finland Station, she was eating a lukewarm pirozhki and listening to "Yankee Doodle" on the barrel organ for the third time when a young man slipped into the seat opposite her. He was older, but they shared the grey fatigue of the night dweller and the radiant conviction of the revolutionary.

"C-c-collect the b-b-bulldog from the comrade at the Horse Guards," stuttered the student, who had little hazel eyes, thick steel-rimmed spectacles and a leather worker's cap on a peculiarly square head. This was Comrade Molotov, Sashenka realized, and he was twenty-six years old. He, Comrade Mendel and Comrade Shlyapnikov were the last Bolshevik leaders at liberty in the whole Empire. When he took off his leather coat, he wore a short jacket and stiff collar like a clerk. Without his cap, his forehead bulged unnaturally. "Ask for C-c-comrade Palitsyn. Anything to report?"

She shook her head.

"G-g-good luck, comrade." Comrade Molotov was gone. Sashenka felt a thrill run down her spine.

At the Horse Guards, the concierge Verezin let her in again.

"What happened to the sable? And the Arctic fox?" he asked.

"Attracted too much attention," she said. "Is someone here for me?"

Comrade Ivan Palitsyn sat waiting beside some bottles at the round table by the stove. He stood up when she entered.

"I'm Comrade Vanya," he said. "I know you. I saw you talk to the workers' circle at the Putilov Works." He offered a big red hand.

"I remember you," she said. "You were the only one who asked a question. I was very nervous."

"No wonder," said Vanya, "a girl and an intellectual among us lot. You spoke passionately and we appreciated a girl like you coming to help us."

Sashenka knew what he meant by "a girl like you" and it touched a nerve. He must have noticed because he added gently, "We come from such different worlds, but you tell me what you know, and I'll share what I know."

She was grateful. Shaggy haired and six feet tall with the cheekbones and slanting eyes of his Tatar forefathers, Vanya Palitsyn personified the pure Russian brawn of peasant stock and the plainspoken, practical fervor of the worker. She knew that, unlike Mendel or Molotov, he was the real thing, one who had toiled in the Putilov Works since he was eight, and he talked in the argot of a proletarian. This, thought Sashenka, is the hero for whom Marx had created his vision and for whom she had joined the movement.

"Comrade Snowfox, I've got something for you, several things in fact. You know what to do with them?"

"I do."

"Sit. Do you want a drink of cognac or vodka? Comrade Verezin and I are having a bit of a feast aren't we, Igor?"

"I've joined the Party," said Verezin.

"Congratulations, Comrade Verezin," said Sashenka. Only Party members deserved the respectful moniker "comrade." But Mendel had told her not to socialize, not to chatter. The intellectuals were much more paranoid than the real workers, she thought.

Vanya Palitsyn, who wore a fringed peasant blouse, boots and breeches, handed her the bulldog and a small package. The oiled metal of the pistol gleamed liquidly.

"Deliver this to the printer in the cellar bar on Gogol Street—he's a Georgian, a handsome devil. Don't lose your head!" Vanya looked her in the eye and smiled. "The bulldog is for you."

She walked past the Taurida Palace just after 3:00 a.m, and caught a streetcar down Liteiny. She felt the weight in her coat. The bulldog—a Mauser pistol—was in her pocket, fully loaded and with a spare cardboard box of ammunition. She ran her fingers over the weapon; the steel was freezing. For the first time, the Party had armed her. She had never fired a gun in earnest. Perhaps it was just one of Mendel's little tests? But what was revolution without dynamite? Did the Party need her to liquidate an agent provocateur? That set her thinking about Sagan. She knew he would find her again.

She hailed a one-horse sleigh to the Caravanserai bar on Gogol, a subterranean cavern with Turkish alcoves, used by poorer students, soldiers, some workers. The entrance was unremarkable but once inside she found that a passageway led under the street. She could smell cigarettes, sausages, stale wine, and felt a table of ragged students go quiet as she passed.

In a dark alcove on his own sat a man in a dashing Caucasian hood, white but lined with fur, and an army greatcoat. He raised a glass of red wine.

"I was waiting for you, Comrade Snowfox. I'm Hercules Satinov," said the Georgian comrade, who had Russianized his real name of Satinadze. "Follow me, comrade."

He led her deeper into the bar, opening the door into a beer cellar. The air there was moist and fetid. Crouching, he lifted a manhole cover. Curling metal steps led down to the printing press. She could hear the deep rhythm of it turning over, like a mechanical bumblebee. Men in peasant smocks were bringing out piles of rough newspapers, which they bound up with red rope. The space reeked of oil and burnt paper.

Satinov pulled back his dashing white hood. "I'm just back in Piter. From Baku." His stiff, thick hair shone blue-black, growing low on his forehead. He was tall, wiry and muscular, and he radiated clean virile power. "You have the newsprint for me?"

She handed over the package.

"Pleased to meet you, Comrade Snowfox," he said without a hint of mockery, taking her hand and kissing it.

"Quite the Georgian knight!" she said a little defensively. "Do you dance the *lezginka* too? Can you sing 'Suliko'?"

"No one dances better than me. Perhaps we can sing some songs and drink some wine tonight?"

"No, comrade," replied Sashenka. "I've no time for such frivolities. Nor should you."

Satinov did not seem to take offense. Instead he laughed loudly, raising his hands in surrender. "Forgive me, comrade, but we Georgians aren't as cold-hearted as Russians! Good luck!" He led her to a different exit that emerged in a deserted courtyard behind Gogol Street.

At the end of the narrow alley, she checked her tail according to Mendel's training. No one. She waited. No one on the street at all. Suddenly she experienced a sort of dizzy jubilation: she wanted to laugh and dance gaily at the bleak glamor of these conspirators—Palitsyn at the Horse Guards, Satinov at the printer's, young men from different worlds but united in their determination. She knew in her heart that these characters were the future, her future. Her conviction made the dark roughness of this existence shine so bright. Small wonder that men like Mendel were addicted. Normality? Responsibility? Family, marriage, money? She thought of her father's delight at receiving his latest contract to supply 200,000 rifles, and her deluded, unhappy mother. That was death, she told herself, dreary, drab, living death.

She walked through an archway into another courtyard. This was one of Mendel's rules: try to avoid entering any building through the front door and always check there are two exits. In Russia, janitors and doormen lingered on the street and tended not to watch the courtyards.

Inside, she hurried to the rear door, opened it and sprang up the cold dark steps, using the half light of the streetlamps to guide her to the top floor. She had been here earlier but her comrade had missed the rendezvous. Perhaps he would be here by now.

She unlocked the door, closing it behind her. The apartment was in darkness but it was somber even in daytime, a cavern of Asiatic rugs, old kerosene lamps, comforters and mattresses. She inhaled the friendly aroma of mothballs, salted fish and yellowing books: an intellectual lived here. She went into the kitchen and tested the samovar as Mendel had taught her: it was cold. In the bedroom, the walls were covered in bookcases, *Apollo* and other intellectual journals in piles on the floor.

Yet something was not right. Her breath caught in her throat. Bristling with Bolshevik vigilance, she moved silently, nerves like forked lightning that jazzed down her spinal column. She turned into the sitting room. There was the rasp of a rough strike and a kerosene lamp sprang to life.

"Greetings! I thought you'd never come." A familiar voice—so why did it give her such a shock?

"Don't mess with me," she said, swallowing hard. She had the Mauser. "Lift up the light."

He illuminated his face. "Did you buy some sweet dresses, Zemfira?"

Captain Sagan sat in the chair, wearing an ill-fitting black suit with a string tie. A fur coat lay on the floor.

"What are you doing here?" She was conscious that her voice sounded high and a little squeaky.

"Your comrade's not coming. We picked him up. Tomorrow, the Special Commission'll sentence him to two years of Siberian exile. Nothing too serious. So rather than leave you to waste your evening, I came instead."

She shrugged, struggling to remain calm. "So? This safe house will no longer be safe. If you're not arresting me, I'll go home and get some sleep. Good night." As she turned, she remembered Mendel's order. She needed to get to know Sagan better. Besides, she was curious as to why he was here. "Or perhaps it's too late for sleep?"

"I think so," he said, pushing back his hair and looking younger suddenly. "Are you a night owl?"

"I feel lazy in the mornings but I come to life at night. All this conspiracy suits me. What about you, Captain? If I'm a night owl, you're a bat."

"I live on a knife-edge. Like you and your uncle Mendel. I sleep so little that when I go home to bed, I find I can hardly settle. I get up and read poems. This is what happens to us. We enjoy it so much that it changes us and we can't do anything else. We conspirators, Sashenka, are like the undead. The vampires. We feed on the blood of the workers, and you feed on the blood of the bloodsuckers themselves who suck the blood of the workers. Quite Darwinian."

She laughed aloud and sat on the edge of a metal bed, where the mattress was dyed sepia yellow by the hissing lamp.

"We conspirators? There's no parallel between us, you police pharaoh. We have a scientific program; you're simply reacting to us. We'll win in the end. You'll be finished. You're digging the grave of the exploiters for us."

Captain Sagan chuckled. "Yet I see no sign of this. At the moment, your vaunted Party is just a few freaks: the intellectual Mendel Barmakid, a worker named Shlyapnikov, a middle-class boy named Scriabin (Party alias Molotov), a few workers' circles, some troublemakers at the front. Lenin's abroad, and the rest are in Siberia. That leaves you, Sashenka. There can't be more than a thousand experienced Bolsheviks in the whole of Russia. But you're having a lot of fun, aren't you? Playing the revolutionary."

"You're deluding yourself, Sagan," she said hotly. "The lines are growing longer, the people getting angrier, hungrier. They want peace and you're asking them to die for Nicholas the Last, Nicholas the Bloody, the German traitor Alexandra and the pervert Rasputin . . ."

"Whom you know all about from your mother. Let me try some thoughts on you. Your parents are the very definition of the corruption of the Russian system."

"Agreed."

"The aspirations and rights of the workers and peasants are totally ignored by the present system."

"True."

"And we know that the peasants need food but they also need rights and representation, and protection from the capitalists. They must have land, and they are desperate for peace. Your father's dream of a progressive group taking power is too little, too late. We need a real change."

"Since we agree on everything, why aren't you a Bolshevik?"

"Because I believe a revolution could come soon."

"So do I," said Sashenka.

"No, you don't. As a Marxist, you know a socialist revolution isn't yet possible. The Russian proletariat isn't yet developed. That's where we differ. According to you, there'll be no Bolshevik revolution."

Sashenka sighed. "Our beliefs are so close. It's a shame we don't agree on that."

They were silent for a moment then Sagan changed the subject. "You've heard the new Mayakovsky?"

"Can you recite it?"

"Let me try:

To you who lived from orgy to orgy
To you who love only wine and food . . .

Sashenka took it up:

Why should I give my life for your convenience?
I'd be better off serving pineapple water
To the whore at the bar.

"Beautifully declaimed, Mademoiselle Zeitlin. I salute you!"

"In our country, poetry's more powerful than howitzers."

"You're right. We should use poetry more and the gallows less."

She watched him closely, keenly aware that both of them were risking their lives in what Mendel called the Superlative Game.

Her hand was on the frozen butt of the Mauser. A few weeks previously, Mendel had arranged for her to be taken out of the city to the birch forests and taught how to shoot: soon she could hit the target more than she missed it. When the Party ordered her to kill Sagan, she would do so.

"What are you carrying?"

The gun at her fingertips made her heart thump. She heard her voice and it did not sound like hers anymore. It was stranger, deeper, surprisingly calm. "Arrest me if you wish. Then you can have some Medusa of a policewoman search me."

"There's only one big difference between us, Sashenka. I believe human life is sacred. You believe in terror. Why do your comrades have to kill? I wonder if there is something in their mentality that suits them to this creed? Are they criminals or madmen?"

She stood up again. "Do you have a home to go to, Captain? Are you married?"

"Yes."

"Children?"

"Not yet."

"Happy?" Sashenka rubbed her eyes, now weary.

"Are any marriages happy?" he answered.

"I pity you," she said. "I'll never marry. Good night."

"One thing, Zemfira: do you think there's anywhere I'd rather be than here?"

Sashenka frowned. "That's no compliment. I suspect most men don't want to go home. Particularly when they're vampires like you and me." We are both armed, she thought almost deliriously. We could both die tonight.

Outside again, Sashenka walked through the streets with a light sleet caressing her face and eyelashes. Sagan was certainly an odd sort of gendarme, she reflected. She was playing along with him, drawing him out. He was older than her, much older, and he had recruited many double agents but his smug confidence in the his gamesmanship was his Achilles heel. Somehow, she'd break him down and deliver him to the Party, like John the Baptist's head on a platter.

Far away, a train rushed whistling through the night. The black smoke of the factories encircled a silver moon. It was almost dawn: the sky was tinged with pink; the snow a deep purple. The muffled trot of a sleigh approached, and she hailed it.

The bulldog was so cold in her pocket, it burned her fingers.

"The price of oats is up again," said the coachman, pulling on his tangled beard as they trotted toward the Zeitlin house on Greater Maritime Street.

21

Zeitlin knocked on the door of Ariadna's boudoir and entered without waiting for an answer. It was midday but she was still in bed, wearing a silk nightgown with blue bows that revealed the bruised white skin of her shoulders. The room smelled of coffee and tuberose. Leonid had brought her breakfast earlier, and the painted wooden tray with its dirty plates and empty glasses now stood on a stand beside the bed. Luda the maid was laying out the dresses for that day—one for a luncheon, one for calling on friends, one for drinks, then one for a dinner. Four outfits, Zeitlin noted. Were so many dresses really necessary?

"Will this do for tea, Baroness?" Luda appeared from the boudoir holding up a crêpe-de-chine dress. "Oh Baron! Good morning." She bowed.

"Leave us alone, Luda."

"Yes, Baron."

"Sit down, Samuil," said Ariadna, stretching. She was enjoying letting him see her flesh, he could tell. "What is it? Has the Bourse crashed? That's all you care about, isn't it?"

"I'll stand." He was conscious that he was clenching his cigar between his teeth.

She stiffened. "What's happened? You always sit down. Shall I send for coffee?" She reached for the bell but was distracted by the smoothness of her upper arm, which she nuzzled against her lips.

"No, thank you."

"Please yourself. I had such fun last night. I saw the Elder again. He told me such fascinating things, Samuil. Everyone was talking about the new Premier. Samuil?"

"I want a divorce, Ariadna." There—he'd said it.

There was a long silence, then Zeitlin saw the words register. She shook her head and raised a hand as if trying to speak.

"You? But why? We've lived like this for years. You're not a jealous man. You're too . . . too confident for that. You're joking surely, Samuil. We've been married for eighteen years. Why now?"

Zeitlin took a puff of his cigar, trying to appear calm and rational. "It's just . . . weariness."

"Weariness? You're divorcing me out of weariness?"

"You'll have a generous allowance. Nothing will change. You'll just be living in a different house. Is it such a shock?"

"You can't!" He had turned to leave but she jumped out of bed and threw herself to the floor at his feet, knocking the cigar out of his hand. He bent to catch it and she gripped him so hard that he lost his balance and fell beside her. She'd begun to weep, her eyes wild, the whites rolling. He tried to release himself but, in the process, tore her nightgown, exposing her breasts. Yet still she held on to him so hard that the diamond studs on his stiff shirtfront popped out onto the floor.

They lay side by side, breathing heavily. He looked down and noticed her long dark-brown nipples peering through her thick tresses. She looked like a gypsy dancer. This is how her lovers must see her, he thought, marveling at her uninhibited wantonness. How strange are we humans, he reflected. The light is dark, the night is bright.

Over the years, while they were strangers by day, they had still shared a passion by night. In daylight she either worried or disgusted him, but then she would come to him in the early hours, her breath stale with old champagne, fresh brandy and yesterday's perfume, other men's cigars, and whisper to him of adventures of startling depravity. She hissed an argot of peasant Polish and gutter Yiddish, the language they had spoken when they first met at the court of her father, the Turbin rabbi, in that Jewish village near Lublin.

What things she told him, what delicious visions! Desires and exploits almost incredible for a respectable lady! One night a lover had taken her to the Summer Gardens, a place of dogs and prostitutes . . . she spared him no detail. Roused to a fever, he performed erotic feats worthy of an athlete, he the most moderate of men who regarded passion as a dangerous thing. But in the morning he awoke feeling filthy and remorseful, as if he had met a whore in a seedy room and made a fool of himself. And this was his own wife!

"Aren't I still beautiful?" she asked him, smelling of tuberose and almonds. "How can you leave *this*? You can make love to me. Go on, push me down. You know you want to. But you're so cold. No wonder I've been so unhappy. You're joking about the divorce, aren't you? Samuil?" She began to laugh, almost to herself, but then she threw back her head, laughing huskily from her belly. He could feel the warmth radiating from her skin like heat from a burning coal, could smell the taint of her excitement. She took his hand and plunged it between her thighs, then pointed at the mirror. "Look at us! Look at us, Samoilo! What a good-looking pair! Like when we met. Remember? You said you'd never met a girl like me. What did you say? 'You're like wild horses.' "

Samuil had meant it differently—he had wondered even then if she was too unpredictable to marry.

He stood up, not without difficulty, adjusting his clothes. "Ariadna, we've become ridiculous."

The servants had talked: Pantameilion had told Leonid, who had agonized how to tell the master that Sashenka had rescued her mother, drunk in the street. The butler had dispatched Shifra, Zeitlin's own ancient governess, to tell him this unpalatable news. Zeitlin had not reacted, simply thanking Shifra politely, kissing her blue-veined hand and showing her to the door again. Historians, thought Zeitlin, try to find a single explanation for events but really things happen for many reasons, not one. Lighting up his Montecristo cigar, he reflected on Sashenka's arrest, on Mrs. Lewis's belief that he barely knew his own daughter—and on the unwelcome arrival of Rasputin in his life (which was somehow worse than Ariadna's lovers). While his irrepressible brother Gideon sought his pleasures recklessly because "I might croak at any minute and go straight to hell," Zeitlin had believed that calm discipline would ensure a long life.

Then last night he had been visited by dreams of sudden death, train crashes, gunshots, smashed automobiles, the house on fire, overturned sleighs, revolution, blood on the snow, himself on a deathbed dying of consumption of the intestines and angina pectoris, with Sashenka weeping beside him—and at the very gates of heaven, he had realized he was carrying nothing. He'd invested in treasure, not love. He was naked and he had wasted his life.

At dawn, he had gone to Shifra in the pantry—but the old witch, crouched in the chair like a translucent spider, already knew his dreams. "You need love in your life too," she'd told him. "Don't always live for the future. There might not be a future. Who knows what's written for you in the Book of Life?"

Zeitlin hated change and feared shaking the foundations of his world. But something in the Chain of Being was shifting and he could not help himself. Against his better judgement, in a trance that he believed might be the presence of Fate, he'd gone to Ariadna's room.

Now he looked down at his wife, still lying in a tangle of easy limbs on the floor.

"Is there someone else?" she asked. "Are you in love with some ballerina from the Mariinsky? A gypsy bitch from the Bear? If there is, I don't care. You see, you selfish, cold fool, I just don't care! I'm going to be as good as a nun. The Elder is showing me the rosy path to redemption. We have another appointment next week, on December sixteenth. Just Rasputin and me. 'I will teach you, Honey Bee,' he says. 'You've sinned so much, you ooze Satan's darkness. Now I'll teach you love and redemption.' That was what he told his Honey Bee. He's kind to me. He listens to me for hours on end even when his antechamber is filled with petitioners, generals, countesses . . ."

Zeitlin clicked his studs onto his shirt and retied his cravat.

"I just want to live a normal life," he said quietly. "I'm not so young and I might drop dead at any minute. Is that so strange? Flek will arrange everything." And feeling a quiet sorrow and fear of the future, he left, closing the door behind him.

22

On the broad glowing screen of the Piccadilly Cinema on Nevsky, the matinee that afternoon was entitled *Her Heart Is a Toy in His Hands.* Sashenka was late and missed the beginning but as she raised her face to the screen and lit up a cigarette, she soon gathered that the gentleman in question was a supposedly handsome dandy (who actually looked like a stuffed dummy) wearing tails and white tie on a beach while the lady in a red-tinted ball dress stared out at a sea of blue-tinted waves.

Onstage a quartet of students from the Conservatoire were playing music chosen to represent the sea breeze. The lady's heart had been toyed with enough, and she'd begun to wade into the ocean. A fat man in a tailcoat ran onto the stage and started to turn a wheel on a brass machine. The quartet ceased playing and the machine produced a sound that resembled the crunch and swish of the surf.

In the darkness of the half-full Piccadilly, the air was dry with electricity, and silvery cigarette smoke curled through the beam of light that projected the images. A peasant soldier sitting with his sweetheart commented loudly: "She's in the water! She's stepping into the sea." A couple in the back were kissing passionately, both probably married and too poor to afford a hotel. A drunk snored. But most stared at the images in rapt amazement. Sashenka had just delivered a message from Mendel to Satinov, the Georgian comrade who wore the hood, and she had an hour to kill before meeting Comrade Vanya over in Vyborg. Then it was home for supper as usual. *The End* declared the ornate letters on a black background before a new picture show was announced: *The Skin of Her Throat Was Alabaster.*

Sashenka sighed loudly.

"You think it's nonsense?" said a voice beside her. "Where's your sense of romance?"

"Romance? You're the smiling cynic," she said. It was Sagan. "You realize that we'll conquer Russia with the silver screen? We will paint the world red. I thought you slept during the day?"

Since Sashenka's arrest, they had been meeting every two or three days, sometimes in the middle of the night. She reported to Mendel on every detail. "Be patient," he said. "Keep playing. One day, he'll offer something."

"He thinks he can flatter me as a fellow intellectual."

"Let him. Even the Okhrana are human and will make human mistakes. Make him like you."

She never knew when she would see the secret policeman. In between discussions about poetry, novels and ideology, he had asked questions about the Party—was Mendel still in the city? Who was the new Caucasian comrade? Where did Molotov live? And she responded by asking, as specified by Mendel, what raids were planned, what arrests, was there a double agent in the committee?

On the screen the new moving picture had started. The quartet played a sweeping melody on their strings.

"I'm not here for the film," said Captain Sagan, suddenly serious. "I've got a troika waiting outside. You need to come with me."

"Why should I? Are you arresting me again?"

"No, your mother's in trouble. I'm doing you and your family a favor. I'll explain on the way."

They climbed into the troika, pulled the bear rug over their laps and sat swathed in furs as the sleigh skated over the ice with that effervescent swish that felt like flight. The streets were already dark but the electric lights were shining. Low Finnish sledges decorated with ribbons and jingling bells and screaming students rushed through the streets, their silhouettes forming cutouts against the snow. The food shortages were spreading, prices rising, and Sashenka spotted a massive line of working women jostling outside a bakery. The worse, the better, she thought gleefully. The sirens of the

Vyborg factories whistled. The snow, so rarely white, glowed a gritty orange.

"Are you taking me home?"

Sagan shook his head. "To Rasputin's place. He's disappeared. Dead, I think."

"So? That's a shame for us: he's won us more recruits than the *Communist Manifesto*."

"On that, Zemfira, we differ. For us, it's a blessing from heaven. The body's under the ice somewhere—we'll find him. The Empress is distraught. He never came home from a party at the Yusupov Palace. Young Felix, the transvestite Prince Yusupov, is up to his neck in it but he's married to a Grand Duchess."

"And my mother?"

"Your mother was waiting for Rasputin at his apartment. I thought, after the other night, you'd be the one to help . . ."

Police in grey uniforms with lambskin collars guarded the doorway of 64 Gorokhovaya Street. Shabby young men in student overcoats with notebooks and unwieldy cameras tried to talk their way past the barriers but Sashenka and Captain Sagan were let straight through.

In the courtyard, gendarmes in their handsome dark blue uniforms with silver buttons sheltered from the cold. Sashenka noticed that even though Sagan was in plain clothes, they saluted him.

At the top of the stairs, the stiff shirts, well-cut suits and smart two-tone shoes marked out the urbane Okhrana officers from the grizzled beards, red noses and grubby shoes of the police detectives handling the murder investigation. The Okhrana officers greeted Sagan and updated him in coded jargon that reminded Sashenka of the Bolsheviks. Perhaps all secret organizations are the same, she thought.

"Come to collect her mother," Sagan told his colleagues, taking her wrist. She decided not to withdraw it.

"Go on up—but hurry," his Okhrana colleague told him. "The Director's on his way over. The Minister's been reporting to Her Imperial Majesty at Tsarskoe Selo but he'll be here soon."

As they neared the apartment, Sashenka could hear the sound of howling. It was raucously uninhibited in the way that peasants grieved. She thought of the air-raid sirens and then a dog she once saw, its legs sliced off by a car. She entered a lobby; to the left, the steamy kitchen with the samovar; a table spread with silks and furs; and then right, into the main sitting room, in the middle of which was a table with a half-drunk glass of the Elder's Madeira. The place reminded Sashenka of the huts of the peasants on the Zeitlin estates in Ukraine but, among the soupy cabbagey smells, there was a hint of Parisian perfume. Nothing in the place quite fit, she thought: it was a peasant *izba* crossed with a government office and a bourgeois family home. It was like the hideout of a gypsy gang of robbers.

There was a sudden flurry of activity behind them and a general of the gendarmes, surrounded by an entourage, entered the main room.

Sagan hurried out, saluted, conferred and returned. "They've found the body. In the Neva. It's him." He crossed himself, then raised his voice. "All right. We've got to get her home now. She's been here since last night."

The howling grew louder and more shrill. Sagan opened the double doors into a small dark room with scarlet rugs and pillows and a large divan.

The shrieking was so animalistic, the shapes within the room so hard to identify that Sashenka stepped back, but Sagan caught her around the waist and again took her hand. She was grateful but most of all shocked. Bloody spots danced before her as her eyes adjusted to the gloom and she was able to see.

"She's in there. I have a car waiting for you downstairs but she should go before the press get in here. Go on. Don't be afraid," Sagan said gently. "It's just noise."

She stepped inside.

It was hard at first to see how the bodies and limbs fit together. Some women, arms around one another, crouched on the floor, rocking together, sobbing hysterically and ululating like Asiatics. Among them Sashenka saw her mother, her head shaking convulsively, her features hollow, her mouth a gash of scarlet screaming.

"Where am I?" cried her mother, her voice high and rough from wailing. "Who are you?"

The air inside was a broth of raw sweat and expensive soaps. Sashenka knelt down and tried to reach Ariadna but her mother rolled away.

"No! No! Where's Grigory? He's coming, I know it."

Sashenka, now on both knees, tried to get hold of her mother but this time Ariadna slipped through her fingers, with a manic laugh. A fat woman on all fours began to bellow. Sashenka had a sudden urge to get up and run away, yet this was her own mother and she now realized, if she had never grasped it before, that Ariadna was not just a bad mother, she was sick, almost demented. A tall, black-haired ox of a young peasant, with black hair on her upper lip and eyebrows that grew together, seized Sashenka, shouting curses. Sashenka fought back but her attacker, whose mouth was edged with a white paste, sank her teeth into her arm. Sashenka shouted in pain, tossing aside this peasant woman, who Sagan later told her was Rasputin's daughter, and reached for her mother in earnest. She took her arm and then her leg and dragged her out of the fray. The other women tried to stop her but Sagan and an ordinary policeman pushed them back.

The creature who had been her mother lay at her feet, shivering and sobbing, under the cool eyes of Sagan and the policemen, who were discussing the postmortem on Rasputin's body and who might have murdered him. There was a pain in her forearm: Sashenka could see the individual toothmarks of her assailant. She noticed that Ariadna wore a simple floral dress quite unlike anything she had seen her wear before, and understood that she had intended to come before the Elder Grigory as a poor supplicant.

Sashenka fell to her knees, her hands clasped. She wanted to cry too. Sagan's hand came to rest on her shoulder.

"Pull yourself together, Mademoiselle Zeitlin. You've got to get her out of here *now*," said Sagan, donning his derby hat. "I'll help you."

Sashenka and Sagan took Ariadna by the arms and dragged her to the door.

On the landing, Ariadna started screaming again. "Grigory, Grigory, where are you? We need you to soothe our souls and forgive our sins! Grigory! I've got to wait for him! He'll come back for me . . ." She struggled out of their hands, scratching and kicking, and tried to bolt back into the apartment but, moving fast, Sagan caught her.

"Gentlemen, we could do with a hand!" he called to the two city policemen guarding the door. One of them took Sashenka's place on Ariadna's left arm; Sagan took the right. The other policeman pulled down his hat, and in a fluid motion swept up Ariadna's two feet in his arms. The three of them carried Ariadna down the stairs, her dress riding up to reveal the shreds of her stockings and her bare legs.

Sashenka averted her gaze and walked ahead of them, horrified and helpless yet grateful for their assistance. She crossed the courtyard, feeling the eyes of the policemen on her, hoping they would not know that this mess was her mother. Pity and shame engulfed her.

A car with a gendarme sergeant at the wheel was backing through the archway into the courtyard.

"Get her inside," said Sagan breathlessly. Another gendarme opened the back door and helped guide Ariadna into the compartment. "Take her home, Sashenka." Sagan slammed the door. "Good luck." He leaned in toward the driver. "Thank you, Sergeant. Greater Maritime Street and fast!" Sagan banged the roof of the car.

Sashenka was alone in the compartment with her mother—and it took her back in time to the years after the revolution of 1905. She could just remember the Cossack horsemen and the furious shabby crowds and how Zeitlin had sent them out of Russia, to the west. They had traveled through Europe in a private railway carriage. Ariadna, always soused even then, wore scarlet brocade and held court at the Grand Hotel Pupp in Carlsbad, the Carlton in Nice, Claridge's in London, always accompanied by some new "uncle." There was the pink-cheeked Englishman, a Guards officer with a gold breastplate and a bearskin hat; a nimble Spanish diplomat in a frock coat; and Baron Mandro (known to Sashenka as "the Lizard"), an aging Galician Jew with an eye patch, rouged cheeks and hairy hands like cockroaches, who had once patted her bottom. When she bit him—she could still taste his coppery blood on her tongue—Ariadna had slapped her. "Get her out of here, vicious child!" and Sashenka was carried out of the room, struggling and screaming. And now, a decade later, Ariadna was being carried out, kicking and howling.

Sashenka peered out of the window. She longed to be in the streets, factories and safe houses with her comrades, away from this domestic farrago. The restaurants and nightclubs were filled with people. Whores trooped past St. Isaac's toward the Astoria dressed in so much scarlet, gold and shining leather that through the snow and darkness Sashenka thought they resembled a regiment of Chevalier Guards. St. Petersburg was in a fever. Never had the stakes in the poker games been so high, never had there been so many revelers, so many limousines outside the Astoria . . . Was it the last mazurka?

As Ariadna's head fell onto her daughter's shoulder, Sashenka told herself she was a Marxist and a Bolshevik, and she had nothing to do with her parents anymore.

23

"Your guest is already here, *mon baron*."

Zeitlin had asked a woman to meet him at the Donan at 24 Moika. At night the restaurant was crowded with ministers, nabobs, courtesans, profiteers and probably spies but during the day they held court in the foyer and café of the Europa Hotel. In the afternoon the Donan was deserted, which was why Zeitlin often used its private rooms to hold discreet meetings: it was here in his usual private dining room, known as the baron's *kabinet*, that he had met the War Minister in August 1914 to clinch the deal to supply the army with rifle butts.

That morning he had called Jean-Antoine, the maître d'. Born in Marseilles, Jean-Antoine was celebrated for his discretion, his ability to recall everyone he had ever met, and his tact in resolving the most outrageous scenes.

"*Mais d'accord, mon baron*," Jean-Antoine replied. "Your *kabinet*'s ready. Champagne on ice? Your favorite crayfish? Or just English tea, English cakes and Scotch whiskey?"

"Just the tea."

"I'll send over to the English Shop right away."

Zeitlin usually took the automobile but that afternoon he had donned his *shapka* hat with earmuffs, his black coat with the beaver collar and his *valenki* galoshes over his patent-leather grey shoes (from Lobb's of London) and picked up his cane with the silver wolf's head—and he had let himself out of his house without ringing the bell.

Zeitlin relished the anonymity of moving through the dark streets without chauffeur or footman. It was not snowing but the ice was grinding into an adamantine freeze all over again. He could almost hear the grey glaze of the Neva River fusing together its fractures and fissures. In the streets, the gas lamps were being lit, the streetcars clattering over their rails. Behind him, bells and laughter pealed. A sleigh bearing students crammed together and holding on for dear life slid past him and was gone. These days, youngsters did what the hell they liked, Zeitlin thought. They had no values, no discipline.

Was he happier now that he was rich? Look at his crazy wife! And there was his darling Sashenka, a riddle to her own father. He loved her and longed to protect her. Yet she no longer seemed interested in her own family. She was almost a stranger, and sometimes he thought she despised him.

He wished he could weep as freely as a child. Like an old man singing his school song, he found himself humming the Kol Nidre tune from his childhood, which told of a vanishing world. He had hated it then but now he wondered: what if it was the right way?

He popped into Yegorov's, the bathhouse with its Gothic mahogany walls and stained-glass windows, and a page in white tunic and black breeches showed him to a cubicle. Stripping naked, he entered the icy bath and slipped under the iron bridge, draped in lush foliage, that arched over the water. Then he steamed for a while on a granite table. Several naked men, their bald heads and buttocks oddly alike in their pinkness and shininess, were being beaten with birch twigs. Zeitlin lay there ignoring everyone and thinking.

I'd pray to God if I were sure there was one, he told himself, but if he exists, we are just worms in the dust to him. Success is my religion. I make my own history.

Yet in his heart Zeitlin believed there was something out there greater than mankind. Behind his cigar smoke, studded shirt, frock coat, striped English trousers and spats, he was still a Jew, a believer in God in spite of himself. He had studied at the cheder, learning the Shulhan Aruk, the rules of living, the Pentateuch, the five books of the Bible that formed the Torah, the Jewish law, and the pedantic, wise, archaic poetry of the Talmud and the Mishnah.

After about an hour he dressed, splashing on his cologne, and walked back to Nevsky. The tall, glassy effulgence of the Fabergé shop glinted out of the darkness.

"Good evening, *barin*! Jump in, I'll give you a ride!" called out a Finnish sledge driver, flicking his whip and slowing his stumpy-legged ponies, their jingling bells ringing festively.

Zeitlin waved the sledge driver away and walked on with a spring in his step. I have been safe but captive for decades, he thought. I'm returning to life after a long hibernation. I am going to reclaim my daughter, show her how I love her, interest myself in her tutoring and her further studies. It is never too late, never too late, is it?

At the Donan, Jean-Antoine greeted him. Zeitlin threw off his coat and hat and kicked off his galoshes. He was looking forward to greeting his guest.

Inside the scarlet womb of his private *kabinet*, Lala awaited him in a prim shantung tea dress decorated with mauve flowers. She stood up when he came in, her gentle heart-shaped face quizzical.

"Baron! What's so urgent?"

"Don't say anything," he said, taking her hands in his. "Let's sit down."

"Why here?"

"I'll explain."

There was a knock on the door, and waiters brought in the tea: fruitcake, muffins with strawberry jam, fresh cream and two thimble glasses of amber. Lala stood up to serve, but he stopped her and waited until the waiters had poured the tea and closed the door.

"A brandy," he said. "For both of us."

"What is it?" she asked. "You're worrying me. You don't seem yourself. And why the cognac?"

"It's the best. Courvoisier. Try it."

They eyed each other anxiously. Zeitlin knew he looked old, that his face was lined, that there were new fingers of grey at his temples. He was exhausted by relentless meetings and his own bonhomie, desiccated by columns of figures. Everyone expected so much of him, his obligations seemed unending. Even the profits of his own companies ground him down.

Lala seemed older too, he thought suddenly. Her cheeks were plumper, the skin weathered by the winters. Fear of the future and of solitude, secret disappointments, had made her a little older than her years.

Ashamed of these thoughts, he hesitated as the little wood fire surged up, dyeing their faces orange. She sipped the cognac. Slowly the fire warmed them.

She stood up. "I don't like the cognac. It burns my throat. I think I should go. I don't like the feel of this place. It's not respectable . . ."

"This is the Donan!"

"Quite," she said. "I've read about it in the newspapers . . ."

It was no good. He could restrain himself no longer. He threw himself at her feet and buried his face in her lap, his tears wetting her shantung dress.

"What's wrong? For heaven's sake, what is it?"

He took her hands. She tried to push him away but somehow the kindness that was so much a part of her overcame her habit of prudence. Gently, she stroked his hair, and he could feel her hands soft and warm like a girl's.

He stood up and took her in his arms.

What am I doing? he thought. Have I gone mad? My God, the lips have their own rules. Just as magnesium burns on contact with oxygen, so skin on skin unleashes some sort of chemical reaction. He kissed her.

She sighed quietly under her breath. He knew she was an inveterate giver of affection—but didn't she want some for herself too?

Then something magical happened. He kissed her again and suddenly she kissed him back, eyes closed. His hands ran over her body. The very plainness of her dress, the cheapness of her stockings, the ordinariness of her rosewater cologne delighted him. When he touched higher, he could barely conceive of the silkiness of her thigh. The smell of soap on skin, the smoke from the fire, the steaming tang of the India tea entranced them both.

I am doing something utterly reckless, out of character and foolish, Zeitlin told himself. I who have control over everything I do. Stop right now, you fool. Don't be like your absurd brother! I'll be a laughingstock! I'll shatter my perfect world.

But it was already shattered, and Zeitlin found he did not care.

24

At fourteen, Audrey Lewis had left the village school in Pegsdon, Hertfordshire, to take a job as junior nanny with the family of Lord Stisted in Eaton Square, London.

Her story, as she herself said later, was as sadly predictable as one of the cheap novels she enjoyed reading. Seduction and impregnation by the feckless son of the house (who specialized in servant girls), and her subsequent arranged marriage to Mr. Lewis, the fifty-year-old chauffeur, "so as not to frighten the horses." Her abortion was humiliating, painful and she almost died from a hemorrhage; the marriage did not prosper, and she left her position with the bribe of a glowing reference. Her adoring parents begged her to come home to their pub—the Live and Let Live in Pegsdon, which they had named to reflect their philosophy of life. But then she saw the advertisement in the *Lady*. One word was enough for her: Russia!

It was high summer in St. Petersburg when the Zeitlin carriage met the young English girl as she disembarked from the German liner. Samuil wore a white suit, spats, a boater, an opal ring, a snake-shaped silver tiepin and an air of generous optimism that immediately included Audrey in his family's happiness. He was slim and young with his auburn hair and boulevardier's mustache. The Zeitlins did not yet live in the mansion on Greater Maritime but in a spacious apartment on Gorokhovaya. They were rich but still provincial: Ariadna, with her violet eyes, her blue-black hair and her queenly bust, remained the girl who had dazzled the private boxes at the theaters in the southern cities where her husband conducted his business. Ariadna was still busy keeping up with those snobbish provincials, the wives of the Russian viceroys and officers, and the Armenian and Muslim oil barons in Baku and Tiflis.

The Zeitlins, Lala discovered, were Jews. She had never met Jews before. There were no Jews in her village in Hertfordshire and Lord Stisted knew no Jews, although Lady Stisted talked disdainfully of the unscrupulous Jewish diamond millionaires from South Africa and the thousands of filthy Jewish cutthroats from Russia who had turned the East End into a "rookery of crime." Audrey had been warned that Jews were not good people to work for—but she knew her own position would not stand too much scrutiny. The Zeitlins for their part were delighted to find a girl who had worked in a noble London household. They suited each other—especially as the Zeitlins seemed very civilized Israelites.

The moment Mrs. Lewis arrived, indeed before her cases had been taken to her room, Ariadna, who looked dazzling in a dress of turquoise crépe de chine, led her into a nursery to meet her charge.

"Here she is! *Voilà ma fille,*" said Ariadna in her pretentious Franco-English. "She almost killed me when she was born. Never again. I've told Samuil—from now on, I deserve some fun! She's an unbiddable child, ungrateful and unruly. See if you can tame her a little, Mrs. Linton—"

"Lewis, Audrey Lewis, madame."

"Yes, yes . . . from now on, she's yours."

It was at that meeting that Mrs. Lewis had become Lala, and had fallen in love with Sashenka. She herself was in her teens; this child not that much younger. Her doctor in London had told her after the abortion that she would never have a child of her own and suddenly, passionately, she wanted to nurture this young girl.

The child and her governess needed each other and so Lala became Sashenka's mother, her *real* mother. What fun they had: skating and sleigh rides in winter, carriage rides, mushroom collecting and blackberry picking at Zemblishino in the summer, always laughing and always together.

The Zeitlins traveled constantly, to Odessa and Baku and Tiflis, by train but in a private compartment. Lala studied Russian on the long trips.

In Baku they stayed in a palace that Zeitlin's father had had copied from a French château: they promenaded on the seafront surrounded by a phalanx of *kochis*, armed bodyguards sporting fezzes, wielding Berdana rifles. In Odessa they stayed at the Londonskaya Hotel right on Seaside Street, just above the famous Richelieu Steps; Lala spent her free time sitting in cafés, eating sturgeon kebabs on Deribaskaya. But her English heart remained in Tiflis.

Spring was a glory in Tiflis, magical Tiflis in Georgia, Tiflis the capital of the Caucasus, midway between the Zeitlin oil wells in Baku, on the Caspian Sea, and the Zeitlin oil tankers in Batum, on the Black Sea.

There the Zeitlins rented the mansion of a penniless Georgian prince, on a cobbled lane nestled into the steep slopes of Holy Mountain. Russian colonels and Armenian millionaires called at the house. Ariadna greeted them, laughing under her breath, from among the vines on the balcony, her hungry white teeth and violet eyes glistening. She never visited the nursery.

"Lewis and child are coming with the baggage" was her line. But even though he was so busy, Zeitlin would drop in on the nursery. He seemed to prefer it to Ariadna's "at homes" full of officers and bureaucrats in frock coats and top hats, sashes and shoulder boards. In the highest circles, children were to be admired briefly and then removed from sight, but Zeitlin adored his Sashenka and kissed her forehead again and again.

"I must go back to work," he'd say. "But you're so sweet, darling Sashenka. Your skin is like rich satin! You're good enough to eat!"

One day, during a rare evening off work, Lala dressed in her Sunday best and a parasol and promenaded down the main avenue, past the white Viceroy's Palace (where, she'd heard, Ariadna had shocked the officers' wives with her bare shoulders and her frenzied dancing). The Tiflis streets smelled of lilac and lily of the valley. She passed theaters, opera houses and mansions on her way to Yerevan Square.

She'd been warned to be careful of the square and she soon realized why. The noisy, filthy side streets seethed with Turks, Persians, Georgians and mountain tribesmen in the brightest and wildest costumes, wielding daggers and blunderbusses. Urchins or *kintos* scampered through the crowds. Water sellers and porters pushed wheelbarrows. Officers walked their ladies but there were no women on their own. Barely had Lala stepped into the square when she was surrounded by a mob of urchins and salesmen, shouting in their own languages, all offering their wares—carpets, watermelons, pumpkin seeds and lobio beans. A fight broke out between a Persian water seller and a Georgian urchin; a Chechen drew a dagger. It was early evening and still boiling hot. Jostled and harassed, with sweat pouring down her face, Lala was afraid. Then, just as she began to panic, the crowd parted and she found herself being pulled into a phaeton.

"Mrs. Lewis," said Samuil Zeitlin, in an English blazer and white trousers, "you're brave but silly venturing out here on your own. Would you like to see the Armenian bazaar? It's not safe for a lady on her own but it's most exotic: would you join me?" She noticed he carried a cane with a wolf's head.

"Thank you, but I should be getting back to Sashenka."

"It's a joy to me, Mrs. Lewis, that you so treasure my only child but she'll be fine with Shifra for an hour," said her master. "Are you all right? Then let's stroll. You'll be safe with me."

Zeitlin helped her down from the phaeton and they plunged into the wild crowd. Urchins offered Georgian snacks, Persians in fezzes poured water from wineskins; Russian officers in jodhpurs and gold-buttoned tunics strode past; Circassian tribesmen with sabers and coats with pouches for bullets dismounted from their tough ponies. The sounds of hawkers shouting, "Cool water, over here!" and the smells of fresh bread, cooking vegetables and heaps of spices were intoxicating.

Zeitlin showed her the steep alleyways and dark corners of the bazaar where bakers baked flat Georgian *lavashi*, Armenians displayed *kindjal* daggers and silver-chased saddles, Tatars sold sherbet prepared by their veiled women in back rooms, stopping sometimes to kneel on Persian carpets to pray to Allah, and a Mountain Jew played a hurdy-gurdy. As they walked, she put her hand through Zeitlin's arm: it seemed only natural. In a little café behind a stall selling spices, he bought her an iced sherbet and a glass of Georgian white wine that was stone cold, fruity, slightly sparkling.

It was dusk. The warm streets, steaming with the smells of hot Georgian cheesecake—*khachapuri*—and Armenian shashlik lamb, and reverberating with the laughter of women from balconies and the clip of horses on the cobbles, were still crowded and mysterious. Men brushed against her in the shadows. The wine made her head spin a little.

She dabbed her forehead with her handkerchief. "Perhaps we should go home now."

"But I haven't shown you old Tiflis yet," he said, leading her down the hill, through tiny winding streets of crumbling houses with leaning balconies embraced by ancient vines. No one else was out in these streets and it was as if Zeitlin and she had stepped out of real life.

He opened an old gate, using a chunky key. A watchman with a spade-shaped white beard appeared and gave him a lantern. They were in a lost garden, draped in rich vines and honeysuckle that breathed out a heady perfume.

"I'm going to buy this house," said Zeitlin. "Doesn't it remind you of a Gothic novel?"

"Yes, yes," she said, laughing. "It makes me think of ghostly women in white gowns . . . What was that book by Wilkie Collins?"

"Come and see the library. Do you like books, Audrey?"

"Oh yes, Monsieur Zeitlin . . ."

"Call me Samuil."

They entered a cobbled courtyard, thick with creepers that reached up to the balconies. Zeitlin opened some bolted wooden doors into a cold stone hall decorated with bronze engravings. Inside, they found themselves in a high-ceilinged room paneled in dark wood and hung with dark lace curtains. He paced around lighting bronze lanterns with green shades until she could see this was a library. The Karelian pine bookshelves were full and more books were piled so high that in the midst of the room they formed a table and one could sit on them like chairs. The walls were covered with the strangest curiosities—the heads of wolves and bears, ancient maps of the world, portraits of kings and generals, Chechen sabers, medieval blunderbusses, pornographic postcards, socialist pamphlets, Orthodox icons, the cheap mixed with the priceless. A lost world. But it was the books in so many languages—Russian, English, French—that delighted her most.

"Take any books you want," Zeitlin told her. "While we're here, you must read whatever you like." She followed him outside.

Their eyes met and glanced away and then met again in the darkening light of this perfume-heavy garden, the air so thick with the breath of vines and that special Georgian apple-and-almond scent of *tkemali* blossom that she could hardly breathe. She could smell his lemon cologne, his acrid cigar, and the sweet wine on his breath.

She would have done anything at that moment in the garden of the old house in Tiflis, anything he asked of her—yet just when she thought he was going to kiss her, he'd stepped back abruptly and left the garden. They hailed a phaeton on Golovinsky Prospect.

Next morning, when she brought Sashenka in to see Zeitlin at breakfast—madame of course was still sleeping—Lala was grateful that he had not touched her. Giving her a distant smile and a "Morning,

Mrs. Lewis," he kissed his daughter and returned to reading the shipping prices in his *Black Sea Gazette.* Neither of them had ever mentioned that evening again.

Since then, Lala's days had been full of Sashenka and she had no time or inclination for gentlemen friends. But recently, Sashenka had grown up much too fast. The Silberkind had darkened and slimmed down, becoming quiet and thoughtful. "You and I will never marry, will we, Lala?" she had once said.

"Of course not."

"Promise?"

"Promise."

Lala did not understand politics but lately she realized that Karl Marx had taken her place in Sashenka's heart and she knew this was a bad, dangerous thing and it filled her with sorrow. She blamed that cripple with the trumpeting voice, Mendel.

Often, when she had turned out the oil lamp in her little room at the top of the house on Greater Maritime Street, her sleep was interrupted by dreams, wonderful dreams, of that moment with the master in that Georgian garden. As she turned over in bed, her skin flushed, and she imagined her breath against his chest, his lips touching her breasts, his hand between her thighs. Sometimes she awoke trembling all over.

And then, out of the blue, Zeitlin had invited her to the Donan.

"I really want my daughter back and you know her better than anyone," he had said. "Let's meet outside the house and plan her future. It's too late to enrol her in the Gymnasium on Gagarin Street. I was thinking of Professor Raev's Academy on Gorokhovaya . . ."

How differently things had turned out. At the restaurant he had never mentioned Sashenka. It had been like one of her disturbing dreams—yet Lala knew it was wrong and it alarmed her. She needed stability. If the master became reckless, what would happen to the household, to her, to Sashenka?

Lala feared change. The start of the war had been thrilling: she had stood among hundreds of thousands of peasants, workers, maids and countesses on Palace Square. She had seen the Tsar, Tsarina, the pretty Grand Duchesses and the little Heir on the balcony of the Winter Palace, blessing the crowd. Lala, now almost a Russian, had sung the Russian anthem and rejoiced as the recruits marched down Nevsky singing, "*Nightingale, nightingale, you little bird!*"

Now she sensed something terrible was about to happen to her adopted country, yet it was too late for her to return home; she was too worldly, with her fluent Russian and visits to Biarritz and Baku; too set in her ways to start again in another household, and too attached to Sashenka to mother another child. She had saved a lot but not enough to live on.

She saw the bread lines in the streets, and the fast women outside the casinos and nightclubs of St. Petersburg. She read in the newspapers how the armies were retreating, how the Germans had conquered Poland and many of Zeitlin's forests. She had to be civil to Ariadna's parents, who were camping in the house, talking in guttural Yiddish and chanting in Hebrew. The Tsar was at the front. Her hero Lord Kitchener, victor over the Mahdi and the Boers, had set out to visit Russia but his ship had hit a mine and he had drowned. But she still believed that, even though there might be trouble, her Samuil, her baron, would get them all through it.

In all these years, Lala had kept herself to herself, knowing her responsibilities, living modestly, already a spinster destined for a solitary old age, the ghost in the attic of a grand family. Like Shifra, in fact. And yet, well concealed beneath her dutiful blandness, like a frothy brook rushing down a mountainside under a carapace of thick ice, her blood was foaming. That night, as she prepared for bed, she replayed her teatime encounter with the baron. Curiously unembarrassed, they had lain together naked in the *kabinet* at the Donan.

"I'm divorcing Ariadna," he said afterward. "Marry me, will you?"

For so long her body had been untouched, ignored, that every slightest caress, inside and out, had left marks as if tiny bee-stings had grazed her skin.

Now, as she looked at herself in the little mirror in her well-ordered bedroom, she could feel, deliciously, where he had been. Her skin scintillated. Unused, unknown muscles in tender places fluttered like captive butterflies. Her legs kept turning to rubber. As she waited for Sashenka to return, she tried to read a new book from England but she had to put it down.

She trembled inside and out with the wildest joy.

The bell suddenly rang in her room. This was unusual. As Lala came out, she heard a woman shouting and ran downstairs. Sashenka, pale and drained, stood in the lobby with the front door open, and a bedraggled, murmuring Ariadna reclined on a chair with her head in her hands.

"Oh Lala, thank God you're here. Help us to the bedroom. Then—let me think—call the maids and Dr. Gemp." Sashenka paused, then looked at Lala. "Where's my father?"

25

Captain Sagan stood wearily at the window of the safe house on Gogol Street, lighting a thin cigar. It was a new year but the Russian defeats were worsening. He took a pinch of cocaine from his snuffbox and rubbed it into his gums. Instantly the blood fountained through his veins and his fatigue was transformed into a roaring optimism that galloped through his temples.

In the early hours of a January night, lanterns blinked across the Neva from the ramparts of the Peter and Paul Fortress. To his right, along the Embankment, the lights burned in the Winter Palace too, although the Tsars had not lived there since 1905. The Empress lived outside the city at Tsarskoe Selo and the Emperor at headquarters near the front. But the fortress represented the power of the autocracy: in its church lay buried Peter the Great, Catherine and their successors all the way down to the present Emperor's father. But it was a prison too: the freezing cells of the Trubetskoy Bastion held the anarchists, nihilists and socialists he himself had trapped.

He heard the door click. Footsteps behind him. Perhaps it was her? Or was it one of their assassins? One day, that click and this view might be the last thing his senses recorded before the shot that blew off the back of his head. It might even be her foolish finger on the trigger. But this was the Superlative Game, the risk of the life he led, the crusading work he did, his service to the Motherland. He believed in God, believed that he would go to Heaven: remove God and his son Jesus Christ and there was nothing, just chaos and sin. If he died now, he would never see his wife again. Yet it was meetings like this in the fathomless night that made his life worth living.

He did not turn round. Thrilling to the sight of the red Menshikov Palace, the fortress, the frozen river, Peter's city, he waited. He knew it was her coming into the room behind him, sitting on the sofa. He could almost taste her.

Plainly dressed in a grey skirt and white blouse, like a virginal teacher, Sashenka was looking at a book. Sagan marveled at how she had changed since her arrest. Although her hair was pulled back into a severe bun and her drawn face bereft of any makeup, this only made those dove-grey eyes more intense, those little islands of freckles all the more exquisite. The less flirtatious she was, the more she concealed her figure, the more he looked at her when she was looking away. She seemed to him even more compelling . . . yes, even beautiful.

"So, Comrade Petro"—that was what she now called him—"have you got something for us or not? Is the samovar boiling? Can I have some tea?"

Sagan made the *chai*. They had met often and become quite informal. He could not know whether she was meeting him because she was beginning to like him or because the Party had ordered her to do so. We men are absurd, he thought, even as he hoped it was the former. It was fine to be attracted to her, even if she was barely a woman. But he did not need to remind himself that to become attached in any way, even fond, let alone in love, could risk not just his career but his sacred mission in life. He knew the rules. If Mendel was pulling the strings, the Bolshevik cripple would want Sagan to lust after her. This must never happen. It never would. Sagan was always in control.

"Happy New Year, Zemfira," he said and he kissed her cheeks three times. "How was the coming of 1917 in your house?"

"Joyful. Our house was more like a sanatorium this year."

"How's your mother?"

"Ask your spies if you really want to know." Accustomed to conspiracy, she seemed more confident than ever. Yet he was sure that, since Rasputin's death, she had started to trust him, in spite of her Bolshevik vigilance. When they met the night after Rasputin's death, she had thanked him. For a moment he even thought she might hug him in her prim comradely way, but she did not. Yet they kept meeting.

"Is the baroness's opium working? Is she trying hypnosis? I understand it works."

"I don't care," she replied. "She's better, I think. She's getting another dress made and grumbling about Uncle Gideon's outrages."

"And the divorce?"

"Papa should divorce her but I don't think he'll dare. She's a lost soul. She believes in nothing but pleasure. I'm hardly at home now." There was a pause. "The Party's growing. Have you noticed? Have you seen the bread lines? There are fights every day for the last loaves."

He sighed, suddenly craving more cocaine, fighting an urge to tell her more about himself, more of what he knew. He was surprised by a wave of hopelessness that seemed to blow in from the streets of the city and sweep over him. Were Tsar, Empire and Orthodoxy already lost?

"You know the truth from your reports," she said, leaning forward, "and I know you sympathize with us. Come on, Petro. Show me a little of yourself—or I might get bored and never meet you again. Tell me something I don't know. Tell me what your reports say."

The perceptive grey eyes studied him unforgivingly, he thought.

He said nothing.

She raised her eyebrows and gestured with her hands. Then, jumping up, she gathered her karakul coat and *shapka* and headed for the door. She opened it.

"Wait," he said, his head tightening like a vise. He did not want her to go. "I've got a headache. Let me have a toke of my tonic."

"Go right ahead." She watched him open his crested silver box, an heirloom set with diamonds, and, wetting his finger, take a thick layer of white power and rub it into his gums. His arteries distended, the blood gushed once more to his temples, and he wondered if she could see the seething swell of his lips.

"Our reports," he started to tell her, "warn the Tsar of revolution. I've just written one that reads: *If food supplies are not improved, it will be hard to enforce law and order on the streets of Petrograd. The garrison remains loyal but . . .* Why do we bother? The new government's a joke. Sturmer, Trepov, now this antique Prince Golitsyn, are pygmies and crooks. Rasputin's murder hasn't solved anything. We need a new start. I don't agree with everything you believe in, but some of it makes sense . . ."

"Interesting." She stood right in front of him so that he thought he could smell her—was it Pears lavender soap? Her finger stroked her lips. He understood that she had grown up faster than he had realized. "We've been back and forth, haven't we, Comrade Petro? But now we're getting impatient! If you think I like meeting you, you might just be right. We might almost be friends . . . but are we? Some of my comrades don't think I should see you anymore. If you really sympathize with us, there are things we need to know. 'It's a waste of time,' my comrades say. 'Sagan wouldn't give us ice in winter.' In any case, you know your work's all for nothing. Your world's about to end. You need to give us something to persuade us to spare you."

"You're too optimistic, Sashenka, deluded. I don't think much of the standard of your newspapers but, between ourselves, they tell the truth about the situation in the factories and at the front. I've agonized about this. But I might have something for you."

"You do?" Sashenka's smile as she said this made it worthwhile. She tossed off her coat and sat again, still in her *shapka*.

Not for the first time, Sagan wrestled with the infinite possibilities of who was playing whom. Sashenka's new confidence informed him that she was still telling Mendel about their meetings. Sagan was disappointed that she was not coming just out of affection—maybe he was losing his touch—but she was surely a little fond of him? "Almost friends," she had said. In spite of himself, the secret policeman felt a tinge of hurt. But they talked about their families, poetry, even health.

So how much did she tell Mendel? He hoped she was keeping back their closeness, because this was how it worked: the holding back of small things led to small lies and then the holding back of larger things led to big lies—this was how he recruited his double agents. He wanted to destroy Mendel, and Sashenka was the tool to do it. Duplicity, not honesty, was his métier—but if he was honest for once, she was not only a tool. She was his delight.

"Listen carefully," he said. "They're planning a raid tomorrow night on your printing press down the road. You need to move it. I don't need to know where."

She tried to conceal her excitement from him, but the way she knitted her eyebrows to assume a military briskness made him want to laugh.

"Are you leading this raid?" she asked.

"No, it's a Gendarmerie operation. To find out the details, I had to promise to trade some information in return."

"That's presumptuous, Comrade Petro."

He flicked his wrist impatiently. "All intelligence work is a marketplace, Sashenka. This has kept me up night after night. I can't sleep. I live on Dr. Gemp's powder. I want to help your Party, the people, Russia, but everything inside me rebels against giving you anything. You know I'm risking all by telling you this?"

Sashenka turned to leave. "If it's a lie, this is over and they'll want your head. If your spooks follow me from here, we'll never meet again. Do we understand each other?"

"And if it's true?" he called after her.

"Then we'll meet again very soon."

26

A gentle sepia light shone through the clouds, reflected off the snow, and burst brighter through the curtains: the opium sailed through Ariadna's veins. Dr. Gemp had called to give her the injection. Her head dropped onto the pillow and she drifted in and out of dreams: Rasputin and she were together in Heaven, he was kissing her forehead; the Empress was inspecting them, dressed in her grey nursing outfit. Rasputin held her hand and, for the first time in her life, she was truly happy and secure.

In her bedroom, she could hear soft voices speaking in Yiddish. Her parents were sitting with her. "Poor child," murmured her mother. "Is she possessed by a dybbuk?"

"Everything is God's will, even this," replied her father. "That's the point of free will. We can only ask for his mercy . . ." Ariadna could hear the creak of the leather strap as the rabbi tied his phylactery onto his arm and he switched to Hebrew. He was reciting the Eighteen Benedictions and this familiar, reassuring chant bore her like a magic carpet back in time . . .

A young and handsome Samuil Zeitlin was standing in the muddy lane outside the Talmudic studyhouse, near the workshop of Lazar the cobbler in the little Jewish-Polish town of Turbin, not far from Lublin. He was asking for her hand in marriage. She shrugged at first: he was not a Prince Dolgoruky or even a Baron Rothschild, not good enough for her—but then who would be? Her father shouted, "The Zeitlin boy's a heathen! He doesn't eat or dress like one of us: does he keep kosher? Does he know the Eighteen Benedictions? That father of his with his bow ties and holidays in Bad Ems: they're apostates!"

Then she was circling the Jewish wedding canopy—the chuppah—seven times; Samuil was smashing a wineglass with a decisive stamp of his boot. Her new husband was borne aloft by the singing Hasids, with an expression on his face that said: I just pray I never have to see these primitive fanatics ever again—but I've got her! I've got her! Tonight I make love to the most beautiful girl in the Pale! Tomorrow, Warsaw! The day after, Odessa. And she would escape Turbin, at last, forever.

Then it was years later and she was caressing Captain Dvinsky in a suite at the Bristol in Paris, where she amazed even that connoisseur of flesh with her depravities. In a torn camisole, she was on all fours, pressing her loins down onto his face, smearing his face, revolving like a stripper, delighted by the wantonness of it, hissing swear words in Polish, obscenities in Yiddish. Even now, waves of lust, the stroking of naked men, the kisses of women, washed over her.

She sat up in bed, cold, sober. She thought she saw the Elder: yes, there was his beard and his glittering eyes at the end of the bed. "Is it you, Grigory?" she asked aloud. But then she realized that it was a combination of the curtain pelmet and a dress on a stand that somehow suggested a tall, thin man with a beard. She was alone and clear-headed suddenly.

Rasputin, who offered me a new road to happiness, is dead, she thought. Samuil, whose love and wealth were the pillars of my rickety palace, is divorcing me. Sashenka hates me—and who can blame her? My Hasidic parents shame me and I am ashamed of my shame. My whole life, every step of the way, has been a fiasco. My happiness has been tottering on a tightrope, only to tumble through the air. Even my pleasures are like the moment that high-wire artiste starts to tremble and loses her footing . . .

I mocked my father's world of holiness and superstition. Perhaps my mother was right: was I cursed since birth? I mocked Fate because I had everything. Does the Evil Eye possess me?

Ariadna lay back on the pillow, alone and adrift on the oceans like a ship without a crew.

27

Sashenka left an emergency message for Mendel at Lordkipadze, the Georgian pharmacy on Alexandrovsky Prospect, and then walked home down Nevsky. The clouds billowed into creamy cauliflowers that hung low over the city. The ice that curled from the drainpipes and the roofs was stiffening. The thermometer was sinking to minus twenty. In the workers' districts, the sirens and whistles blared. Strikes had started to spread from factory to factory.

On Nevsky, right in the center, clerks, workers, even bourgeois housewives lined up outside the bakeries for bread. Two women rolled around in the sludge fighting for the last loaves: a working woman repeatedly hit the other in the face, and Sashenka heard the crack as her nose broke.

At Yeliseyev's Grocery Store, where the Zeitlins ordered their food, Sashenka watched as workers burst in and grabbed cakes and fruit. The shop assistant was bludgeoned.

That night, she could not even pretend to sleep. Her head was buzzing. The anger of the streets replayed in her mind. Outside, the sirens of the Vyborg echoed across the Neva, like the calling of whales.

She rose from her bed, and in the early hours Comrade Molotov met her at the coachmen's café outside the Finland Station.

"Comrade Mendel is busy now. He sent me." Molotov was humorless and stern but also meticulous and he listened carefully to Sashenka's tip-off.

"Your s-s-source is r-reliable?" Molotov stammered, his forehead bulging.

"I think so."

"Thank you, c-c-comrade. I'll get to work."

At dawn, Comrades Vanya and Satinov were already dismantling the printing press. Sashenka and other comrades removed the parts in beer barrels, milk churns, coal sacks. The bulky press itself was placed in a coffin, collected by a stolen undertaker's hearse and accompanied by a carriage of weeping (Bolshevik) relatives in black to the new site in Vyborg.

At dusk the following afternoon, Mendel and Sashenka climbed the stairs of an office building down the street from the printing press. For Mendel, every step was an effort as he dragged his reinforced boot behind him.

They came out on the roof and Sashenka gave Mendel one of her Crocodile cigarettes, its gold tip incongruous beside his worker's cap and rough leather coat. Together, they watched as three carriages of grey-clad police and two carloads of gendarmes pulled up outside the cellar and broke down the door.

"Good work, Comrade Snowfox," said Mendel. "You were right."

She flushed with pride. She really was an asset to the Party, not the spoiled child of the degenerate classes.

"Do I continue to meet Sagan?"

Mendel's eyes, magnified by his bottle-glass lenses, pivoted toward her. "I suppose he's in love with you."

She laughed and shook her head simultaneously. "With me? You must be joking. No one looks at *me* like that. Sagan talks mostly about poetry. He really knows his stuff. He was helpful about Mama but he's very proper. And I'm a Bolshevik, comrade, I don't flirt."

"Fucking poetry! Don't be naïve, girl. So he *lusts* after you!"

"No! Certainly not!" She blushed with confusion. "But he sympathizes with us. That's why he tipped us off."

"They always say that. Sometimes it's even true. But don't trust any of his *shtik*." Mendel often used the Yiddish of his childhood. While Ariadna had completely lost the accent, Sashenka noticed that Mendel still spoke Russian with a strong Polish-Jewish intonation.

"If you're right about his immorality, comrade, I don't think I should meet Sagan again. He sent me a note this morning, inviting me to take a sleigh ride with him in the countryside. I said no of course and now I certainly shan't meet him."

"Don't be such a *schlamazel*, Sashenka," he replied. "You don't know what's best here, girl. Beware bourgeois morality. We'll decide what's immoral and what isn't. If the Party asks you to cover yourself in shit, you do it! If he desires you, so much the better."

Sashenka felt even more flustered. "You mean . . ."

"Go on the sleigh ride," he boomed, exasperated. "Meet the scum as often as it takes."

"But he needs something to show for it too."

"We'll give him a morsel or two. But in return, we want a gold nugget. Get me the name of the traitor who betrayed the press in the first place. Without that name, this operation is a failure. The Party will be disappointed. Be vigilant. *Tak!* That's it." Mendel's face was livid with the cold. "Let's go down before we freeze. How's your mother coping with the divorce?"

"I never see her. Dr. Gemp says she's hysterical *and* melancholic. She's on chloral, bromine, opium. Father wants her to try hypnotism."

"Is he going to marry Mrs. Lewis?"

"What?" Sashenka felt this like a punch in the belly. Her father and Lala? What was he talking about? But Mendel was already on his way downstairs.

The factory whistles started up again across the city, yet the black slate of the rooftops revealed none of the seething furies beneath. The world really was going mad, she thought.

28

The next day was warmer. The sun and the moon watched each other suspiciously across a milky sky. The sparse clouds resembled two sheep and a ram, horns and all, on a snowy field. The factories were on strike.

As she took the streetcar to the Finland Station, Sashenka saw crowds crossing the bridges from the factories, demonstrating for bread for the third day running. The demonstration had started on Thursday, International Women's Day, and grown since then.

"Arise, you starvelings, from your slumbers!" the crowds chanted, waving their red banners. "Down with autocracy! Give us bread and peace!"

The Cossacks tried to turn them back at the Alexander Bridge but tens of thousands marched anyway. Sashenka saw women in peasant shawls smash the windows of the English Shop and help themselves to food: "Our men are dying at the front! Give us bread! Our children are starving!" There were urchins on the streets now, creatures with the bodies of children but with swollen bellies and the faces of old monkeys. One sat on the street corner singing and playing his concertina:

Here I am abandoned, an orphan, with no one to look after me,
And I will die before long and there'll be no one to pray at my grave,
Only the nightingale will sing sometimes on the nearest tree.

Sashenka gave the boy some money and a Red pamphlet: "After the Revolution," she told him, "you'll have bread; you'll be the masters; read Marx and you'll understand. Start with *Das Kapital* and then—" But the boy had scampered off.

Sashenka had no special orders from the Party. At first light, she'd checked with Shlyapnikov at the Shirokaya safe house. "The demonstrations are a waste of time, comrade," he insisted. "Don't squander any of our leaflets. This'll lead to naught like all the other riots." On Friday, a police officer had been killed by the workers on the bridge—and a mob had broken into Filippov's, the patisserie where Delphine the cook bought Baron Zeitlin's millefeuille.

Now the authorities were striking back. The city was filled with Cossacks and soldiers, and it seemed to Sashenka like an armed camp. Every side street, every bridge was guarded by machine-gun nests and armored cars; squadrons of horsemen massed on the squares; horse manure steamed on the snow.

The theaters were still playing and Ariadna was so improved that she and Zeitlin were off to the Alexandrinsky to see Lermontov's *Masquerade*, a most avant-garde production. The Donan and the Contant were still crowded, and the orchestras played waltzes and tangos at the Europa and Astoria hotels.

Sashenka was meeting Sagan. She hurried first to the safe house at 153 Nevsky but Mendel, who was with Shlyapnikov and Molotov, ordered her to calm down. "Give these workers a few shots over their heads and a loaf of bread and the movement will be gone." The others agreed. Perhaps they were right, Sashenka thought uncertainly.

At the Finland Station, Sashenka checked her police tails out of habit. There was one spook who fitted the bill but she lost him easily before she caught the train, traveling third class. In the cold, the steam seemed to wheeze out of the train, whirling around it like a wizard's spell.

She had arranged to meet Sagan at Beloostrov, the small town nearest the Finnish border. When she arrived—the only passenger to leave the carriage—Sagan was waiting in a troika, a sleigh with three horses, smoking a cigar, shrouded in furs. She climbed in and he covered their laps with the fur blanket. The coachman spat out a spinning green gobbet of phlegm, cracked his whip and they were off. Sashenka remembered such trips with Lala in the family sleigh with its ivory fittings, the family crest on the doors, the sable rug. Now this flimsy sleigh, creaking and clattering, flew over the fields, the coachman in his sheepskin and fur hood leaning to one side, drunkenly flicking his whip over the mangy rumps of the skinny piebalds. Every now and then he talked to the horses or his passengers but it was hard to hear him over the swish of the sleigh and the thud of the hooves.

"Giddy-up . . . Oats . . . prices rising . . . Oats . . ."

"Shouldn't you be in Piter fighting the wicked pharaohs?" Sagan asked her.

"The workers are just hungry, not rebels at all. Aren't you worried though?"

He shook his head. "There'll be riots but nothing more."

"The Party agrees with you." She peered up into Sagan's face. He looked exhausted and anxious—the strain of his double life and miserable marriage, the headaches and insomnia, the rising turbulence in the city, all seemed to be catching up with him. She shook her head at Mendel's accusations. How could he know what Sagan felt when he had never met him and certainly never seen them together? No, Sagan had become a sort of friend—he alone understood the pain of having a mother like Ariadna. She felt that he liked her too, for her own sake, but *not* like *that!* Not at all! Sagan was not even suited to police work. He was much more like a vague poet than a frightening policeman with his feathery blond hair that he wore much too long—and yet it suited him. They were enemies in many ways, she knew that, but their understanding was based on mutual respect and shared ideas and tastes. She had a serious mission and when it was over they might never see each other again. But she was glad Mendel had ordered her to see Sagan again. Very glad. She had family news to tell him and who else could she confide in?

"Something has happened at home," she began. There was no harm in recounting harmless gossip. "Mrs. Lewis! My Lala! Mendel has a spy in the Donan. That's how I discovered. When I confronted Papa, he blushed and denied it and looked away and then finally admitted that he had considered marrying her for *me*, to make me a happier home. As if that would make the slightest difference to my life! But now he says he's not going to divorce Mama. She's too fragile. I asked Lala and she hugged me and told me she refused him on the spot. They're all such children, Comrade Petro. Their world's about to end, the inevitable dialectic's about to crush them and they're still playing like that orchestra on the *Titanic*."

"Are you hurt?" he asked, leaning toward her. She noticed his blond mustache was cut just like her father's.

"Of course not," she answered huskily, "but I never thought of Lala like that!"

"Governesses are prone to it. I had my first love affair with my sister's governess," said Sagan.

"Did you?" She was suddenly disappointed in him. "And how's your wife?"

He shook his head. "I'm spiritually absent from my home. I come and go like a ghost. I find myself doubting everything I once believed in."

"Lala was my confidante. Who do you talk to?"

"No one. Not my wife. Sometimes I think, well, maybe *you're* the only person I can be myself with because we're half strangers, half friends, don't you see?"

Sashenka smiled. "What a pair we are!" She closed her eyes and let the wind with its refreshing droplets of snow sprinkle her face.

"There!" shouted Sagan. He pointed at an inn just ahead.

"Right, master," cried the sleigh driver and whipped the horses.

"We're almost there," Sagan said, touching her arm.

A tiny wooden cottage, with colorful wooden carvings hanging from its roof, stood all alone in the middle of the snowfields with only a few birches on either side like bodyguards. Sashenka thought the place belonged in a Snow Queen fairy tale.

The sleigh swished to a stop, the horses' nostrils flared and steaming in the cold. The wooden door opened, and a fat peasant with a jet-black beard came out in a bearskin caftan and soft boots to hand her down from the sleigh.

Inside, the "inn" was more like a peasant *izba*. The "restaurant" was a single room with a traditional Russian stove, on top of which a very old man with a shaggy white beard lay full length, snoring noisily in his socks. Inside the half-open stove, Sashenka saw game sizzling on a spit. The black-bearded peasant showed them to a rough wooden table and thrust a generous shot of *cha-cha* into their hands.

"To a strange pair!" said Sagan and they drank. She had never been out for a meal with a man before. The *cha-cha* burned in Sashenka's belly like a red-hot bullet, and this unlikely idyll—the open fire, the sleeping old man and the aromatic game in the stove—softened her concentration. She imagined that they were the only people alive in the whole of the frozen north. Then she mentally shook herself, to keep her wits about her. Joking with Sagan, whom he seemed to know, the peasant served them roast goose in a piping-hot casserole, so well done that the fat and flesh almost dripped off the bones to flavor a mouthwatering beet, garlic and potato broth. They so enjoyed the food that they almost forgot the Revolution, and just made small talk. There was no dessert, and the old man never awoke. Eventually they left, very satisfied, after another *cha-cha.*

"Your tip checked out, Petro," said Sashenka as the sleigh sped over the featureless snowfields.

"It was hard to give you that."

"But it wasn't enough. We want the name of the man who betrayed us."

"I might get it for you. But if we're going to keep meeting, I need to show my superiors something . . ."

She let the silence develop as she prepared herself, excited by the danger of their game. "All right," she said. "There is something. Gurstein escaped from exile."

"We know that."

"He's in Piter."

"That we guessed."

"Well, do you want to find him?"

He nodded.

"Try the Kiev boardinghouse, room twelve." This was the response she'd rehearsed with Mendel, who had warned her that she would have to trade some information of her own. Gurstein was apparently expendable.

Sagan did not seem impressed. "He's a Menshevik, Sashenka. I want a Bolshevik."

"Gurstein escaped with Senka Shashian from Baku."

"The insane brigand who robbed banks for Stalin?"

"He's in room thirteen. You owe *me,* Comrade Petro. If this was known, the Party'd kill me by morning. Now give me the name of the traitor who betrayed the printing press."

There was just the crispness of blades slicing frozen snow, and Sashenka could almost feel Sagan weighing up the price of a man's life versus the value of an agent.

"Verezin," he said at last.

"The concierge of the Horse Guards barracks?"

"Surprised?"

"Nothing surprises me," Sashenka said, exultantly.

The sky was furrowed with scarlet, as if ploughed with blood. Rabbits jumped out ahead of the horses and crisscrossed one another, making jubilant leaps. What joy! Sagan gave orders to the coachman, who whipped the horses.

Sashenka sat back and closed her eyes. She had the name. Her mission was successful. The Party would be pleased. She had got what Mendel wanted—not bad, she decided, for a Smolny girl! Somehow, together, she and Sagan had delivered. They had shared the adrenaline that all operatives feel after a successful mission. She had tricked him and, for whatever reason, he had given her his nugget of gold.

A cottage appeared in the distance, probably on the edge of some estate. The temperature was falling, and the ice was stiffening again. A clump of pines looked as if they were made of tarnished silver.

"See, there!" said Sagan, taking her gloved hand in his own. "Isn't it beautiful? Far away from the struggle in the city. I wanted to show you an exquisite little place that I love."

"There you are, *barin*," said the coachman, raising his eyebrows and spitting. "Just as you ordered."

"I could live here forever," said Sagan passionately, pulling off his *shapka*, his flaxen locks flopping over his eyes. "I might escape out here. I could be happy here, don't you think?"

A little curl of smoke puffed out of the distant tin chimney. Sagan took her hand and slipped her glove off. Their hands, dry and warm, cleaved together, breathing each other's skin. Then he took her left hand and slipped it inside his own glove, where her fingers rested closely against his, buried in kid leather and the softest rabbit fur. It seemed impertinent, yes, and horribly intimate, but she found it delicious too. She gasped. The tender skin of her palm seemed to become unbearably sensitive, glowing and prickling against his rough skin. She felt a flush rising up her neck and withdrew her hand from his glove abruptly.

She could feel his eyes on her, but she looked away. That, she decided, had been a step too far.

"Faster! *Bistro!*" Sagan barked at the driver. The three horses jumped forward and suddenly the driver lost control. The sleigh bounced left and right, the driver shouting, but the snow was uneven, tipping them one way, then the other and finally flipping the sleigh in a powdery tornado of whirling snow until Sashenka found herself flying through the air.

She landed in a soft drift, facedown, and was still for a moment. Sagan was close to her but not moving. Was he alive? What if he was dead? She sat up. The horses were still galloping away, the driver chasing after them and the sleigh upside down. Sagan was still, his face covered in snow.

"Petro!" she called out, crawling over to him. She touched the dimple in his chin.

Sagan sat up laughing, wiping the snow off his long narrow face.

"You gave me a shock," she said.

"I thought we were *both* dead," he replied, and she laughed too.

"Look at us!" she said, "we're soaked . . ."

". . . and cold," he said, looking for the sleigh. "And I fear quite alone!"

She saw that his dark pupils were dilated with the excitement of the crash. She put his hat back on his head and they could not stop laughing, like children. Sitting there in the midst of the snowfields, the cottage still far away, the sleigh invisible, he moved his head to rest on her shoulder just as she did the same and they bumped heads, then looked at each other.

Without missing a beat, he kissed her on the lips. No one had ever kissed her before. Thinking of the Party, relishing her success, and remembering that perhaps Mendel was right after all, perhaps Sagan did like her, she allowed him to press his lips on hers. His tongue opened her mouth and licked her lips, teeth, tongue. Her lips tingled and she became drowsy and dreamy. For a moment, just a moment, she closed her eyes and let her head rest against his, and her hand did what it had always wanted to do: stroke the pale hair that reminded her of cotton candy. They had shared personal confidences—the poetry, his marriage and headaches, her family—but nothing so all-embracing as the Superlative Game of conspiracy. The deadly exchange of information formed the climax of a slow, voluptuous polka on the thinnest ice. Sashenka was dizzy and shaky, yet sparks of nervous excitement and a flick of sensuous heat flashed through her.

"Here we are, *barin*!" cried the sleigh driver, whose entire beard was frosted like a fungus. He had righted his sledge and driven his troika of lathered horses in a big circle to pick them up again. "Apologies for the bump but, well, no broken bones, I see. A picture of health!" and he cackled coarsely. Sagan's skin was warm, prickly, rough on her cheeks and chin. It burned her—and she broke away. "Whoa!" cried the driver. The sleigh came to a halt beside them with a slushy crunching that sprinkled a shower of frozen stars onto their faces.

Sagan helped her up and brushed the snow off her and then handed her back onto the sleigh. Her hands and knees were quivering. She wiped her lips with her sleeve. She was unsure of herself, unsettled.

Moments later, they arrived at the cottage. Spears of ice with fine points hung down from the eaves, and intricate blossoms of frost made opulent patterns on the windows. The nailed wooden door opened and a smiling pink-cheeked peasant girl in a sheepskin caftan came out, bearing a tray with two glasses of *gogol-mogol*. The glowering sky spread its soft blanket over the snow, turning it a deep purplish blue.

Afterward, Sagan and Sashenka parted at the station.

She had a rash on her chin. She touched it with her fingertips and, remembering his lips against hers, she shivered.

29

Captain Sagan watched Sashenka's little train pull away and gather speed, its steam billowing like the sultan-spike of a gendarme's helmet.

He showed his pass to the stationmaster, who was almost overcome with excitement as Sagan commandeered the fool's cozy office.

Warming himself by the Dutch stove and helping himself to a shot of cognac, he wrote a report to his boss, General Globachev.

Sagan's temples were tightening, always the start of a reverberating headache. He quickly rubbed some of the medicinal powder onto his gums then sniffed two tokes. Things were not going well. He and the general were more worried about St. Petersburg than he had let onto Sashenka. But both men agreed that a crackdown and a dismissal of the Duma were necessary: it was time, he considered, for the Cossack to wield his *nagaika* whip. The coca tonic replaced his anxiety with a feeling of all-conquering satisfaction that drummed in his temples.

Ever since his days in the Corps de Pages, Sagan had been one of the top students, winner of the highest prize during the two years of courses at the School for Detectives. He had learned the anthropometric tables of the Bertillon system for describing the features of those under surveillance, won the bull's-eye prize in Captain Glasfedt's practical course on firearms and mastered the "Instructions on Organizational Conduct of Internal Agents," which he had applied punctiliously to Sashenka. He had memorized the urbane orders of Colonel Zubatov, the genius of the Okhrana, who had written: *You should look on your informer as a mistress with whom you are involved in an adulterous affair.* It was indeed impossible to turn female revolutionaries into double agents without exploiting chivalry in some form, even if that meant what he called "antichivalry"—allowing silly teenagers to believe they were serious intellectuals who would never contemplate the slightest flirtation, yet alone sexual approaches. Sagan had followed Zubatov's recommendations with one of his female double agents in the SRs and another in the Bolsheviks. Neither was a beauty but, in bed, the drama of espionage more than compensated for the often dull athletics.

Sagan always prepared himself meticulously for his meetings with Sashenka, listening to the latest tango, learning reams of that doggerel by Mayakovsky that had turned her head. Her devotion to Bolshevism made it child's play: the humorless ones were always the easiest to crack, he told himself. Like so many of the revolutionaries, she was a *zhyd*, a kike, one of that race of turncoats who supported either godless Marxism or the German Kaiser. He smiled at his own liberal posturing, he who believed so passionately in Tsar, Orthodoxy and Motherland, the old order.

Now, using the stationmaster's pen and ink, he started to write his report to the General:

Your Excellency, I am most satisfied with the case of Agent 23X ('Snowfox') who has finally started to prove useful. As Your Excellency knows, I have now met clandestinely with this member of the RSWP (Russian Socialist Workers' Party: Bolshevik faction) eleven times, counting the first interrogation. The hours of work have paid off and will yield considerable gains later. Using our surveillance teams of external agents, Snowfox's movements have enabled us to arrest three nihilists of middling rank and to track the new printing press.

The price for the recruitment of this agent has been 1. philosophical—her conviction of my sympathy for her cause and her person (the rescuing of her mother from the Dark One's apartment was particularly successful in gaining trust); and 2. tactical—the handover of the name of the doorman (new Party member code named Horseguards), which has cost our service nothing since we earlier failed to recruit him as an internal agent, despite the offer of the usual financial inducements (100 rubles/month) as per P. Stolypin's "Instructions on Organizational Conduct of Internal Agents."

At today's meeting, the agent surrendered the name of two revolutionists, a Menshevik factionist and a Bolshevik terrorist, who had long been sought by the Security Sections of Baku, Moscow and Petrograd. I will organize surveillance according to General Trusevich's "Instructions for External Surveillance" and arrest forthwith. I request your permission to continue to handle Agent "Snowfox" in the future as I believe that her usefulness for the service depends on my management. It is possible that her Bolshevik handlers have ordered her to hand over these names but I believe that the threat of exposure to her own comrades will now make her submission easy to accomplish.

Our primary mission remains the arrest of Mendel Barmakid, her uncle (codename Clubfoot; alias Comrade Baramian, Comrade

Furnace, etc.) and the Bolshevik faction's Petrograd Committee, but I have absolute confidence that this organization is now hopelessly broken and incapable of any threat in the short to medium term . . .

Poor little Sashenka, he thought smugly—yet in his heart he knew she was the brightest star in his firmament.

He did not look forward to seeing his wife or General Globachev. If he had had his way, he would have met Sashenka at the safe house every night.

Her diffidence, those teenage doubts, her awkward stance, the prim way she dressed in grey serge, dreary wool stockings and buttoned blouses with her thick hair in a virginal Bolshevik bun, the absence of any makeup or even perfume—all this had wearied him initially. But in recent weeks she had began to grow on him and now he looked forward to the smell of her fresh skin and her sumptuous hair when she was near him, the way her columbine eyes bored into him so intensely, her fingers touching her short upper lip when she talked about her mother, the way her slim body was shaping into a woman's curves that she was determined to conceal and scorn. And nothing was so adorable as the way she suppressed her humor and joie de vivre, knitting her brows to play the dour revolutionary. He laughed at the tricks of the Almighty, for, however matronly she wanted to be, God had given her features—those lips that never closed, those scathing grey eyes, that lush bosom—that undermined her wishes at every turn and made her even more delicious.

And when he had tasted her lips, his hands had actually started to shake. Her reluctance to return his kiss made her obvious enjoyment of it even more poignant and delightful. Or did I imagine that? he asked himself. Any man of almost forty would lose judgment when faced with that skin, those lips, and the husky bumble-bee voice he had come to know so well. He raised his hands and thought he could divine the scent of her skin, her neck . . .

Yet she was his agent. The cause, Tsar and Motherland, always came first. It was a desperate struggle for survival between good and evil and she was on the wrong side. If he had to . . . Well, he hoped it would never come to that. The Okhrana was special. The battle to defend the Empire was a war that had to be fought with merciless conspiracy—as his colleague General Batiushin had told him: "All honor to him who dishonors his name and ends the case with silence as his only reward." He wet his finger and dipped it into Dr. Gemp's powder and applied cocaine to nose and gums. He chuckled to himself.

The door opened. A livid snout and ginger whiskers appeared, followed by a uniformed paunch and the rest of the stationmaster.

"Did you say something, Your Excellency?" he said. "Anything I can do? A note to my superiors would be a help. I'd be so grateful . . ."

"Why not?"

"We hope you're destroying our enemies, German agents and *zhyd* nihilists!" The stationmaster rubbed his hands.

"Absolutely! When's the next train to the Finland Station? I have a report to file."

"Five minutes, Your Excellency. God Save the Tsar!"

30

The Grand Duke's crested Benz was already parked among the carriages outside the Radziwill Palace on Fontanka when Pantameilion's Delaunay swung into the forecourt, the chains wrapped around the wheels just gripping the ice. Samuil and Ariadna Zeitlin waited their turn while the French Embassy Renault dropped Ambassador Paleologue and his wife.

The Izmailovsky Guards in green tunics, the gendarmes with their sultan-spikes and the Cossacks in leather trousers and high furs, flicking their thick whips, bivouacked around bonfires in the squares and guarded the street corners. The air steamed with horse sweat and manure and sweet woodsmoke; the cobbles clattered with the clipclop of a thousand hooves, the rumble of howitzer carriages, the metallic rattle of rifles, horse tackle and scabbards.

The melody of waltzes and laughter wafted down the marble stairs of the palace. The Zeitlins greeted the French ambassador and his wife at the top of the steps. The foursome were just agreeing how quiet the city was when a gunshot echoed over the rooftops. Dogs howled, sirens wailed and somewhere out toward the Vyborg Side the city herself seemed to growl.

"How are you, dear Baron? Are you better, Baroness?" The French ambassador bowed, speaking fluent Russian.

"Much better, thank you. Did you hear that?" asked Ariadna, her eyes iridescent as whirlpools. "A firework!"

"That was gunfire, Baroness, I fear," replied the ambassador, immaculate in black coat, top hat and white tie. "There it is again. The metal factory workers are marching in their hundreds of thousands from Petrograd, Vyborg and Narva."

"I'm freezing," shivered Ariadna.

"Let's go in," said the Frenchwoman, taking her hand.

The ambassador's wife and Ariadna, both in floor-length furs, one in ermine, the other in seal, walked inside, handing their coats to the staff. Ariadna, like an angel stepping out of a fountain, emerged glistening and pale in a mauve brocade gown embroidered in diamonds with a high bosom and low-cut back. She embraced the richest couple in Lithuanian Poland, Prince and Princess Radziwill.

"You're so good to come, Ariadna, and you, Madame Paleologue, on such a night. We wondered whether to cancel but dearest Grand Duke Basil absolutely banned it. He said it was our duty, yes, our duty. We've spoken to General Kabalov and he's most reassuring . . ."

More gunshots. Zeitlin and the ambassador remained outside on the steps, peering into the night. Puttering limousines and whispering sleighs dropped off the guests. Diamonds and emeralds hung like dewdrops on the ears of the women who moved like animals in their sleek furs. Perfume vied with the biting cold for possession of the air. Zeitlin lit a cigar and offered one to the ambassador.

They were both silent. The ambassador, knowing how prices were rocketing and the secret police warning of imminent unrest, was amazed to find ministers and Grand Dukes at play on a night like this.

Zeitlin was lost in his private thoughts. He had lived through riots, demonstrations, pogroms, two wars and the 1905 revolution, emerging richer and stronger each time. Things at home were calm again; his uncharacteristic flash of madness and doubt was over.

Dr. Gemp's injections of opium had restored Ariadna; the divorce was off; Sashenka was enrolled in Professor Raev's classes; and Lala seemed calm and acquiescent. The only worry was Gideon. What was that scallywag, that *momzer*, up to?

31

Gideon Zeitlin was on his way home, driven by Leonid the butler in the big touring car, the Russo-Balt, with two hundred rubles in his pocket. Cossacks and guardsmen had erected checkpoints around the official Liteiny cordon that guarded the General Staff, War Ministry and Winter Palace. But as Gideon crossed Nevsky, some workers threw stones at the car.

"Filthy speculator!" they shouted. "We'll teach you to fleece the people."

The stones drummed on the roof but Gideon, always slightly screwed even when sober, was not scared. "Me? Of all people? It's my brother you want, you fools!" he muttered, slapping his thigh. "Drive on, Leonid! It's not our car they're smashing up! Ha ha!" The butler, a nervous driver at the best of times, was less amused.

They pulled up on Tenth Rozhdestvenskaya, a narrow street of tall new apartment buildings. Gideon leaped out of the car, tugging his coat with its beaver collar around his shoulders.

"I'll be off then," said Leonid.

"Hmm," said Gideon, who had promised his wife, children and brother Samuil to spend some time at home. But he could not quite commit himself. "I'd like you to wait."

"Sorry, Gospodin Zeitlin, I don't like to leave the car out for too long," replied the servant. "The baron said, 'Drop him off and come home,' and I work for the baron. Besides, the motorcar could get stoned by the workers and this is a beautiful machine, Gospodin Zeitlin, many times more beautiful than the Delaunay or—"

"Good night, Leonid, godspeed!"

Nodding cheerily at the doorman (while thinking, You informing Okhrana scum!), Gideon strolled through the marble lobby and caught the elevator, an Art Nouveau beauty of polished amber brass and black carving, to the fifth floor. The cognac and champagne he had drunk with Samuil rollicked through his body, making his heart burn, his bowels churn and his head spin. His wife Vera, mother of his two daughters, was pregnant again and he had spent all his meager earnings on dinner at Contant's and games of chance. Oh, the tragedy, he chuckled to himself, of being born rich and growing up poor!

Once again his brother had bailed him out, opening his handsome teak strongbox to hand over the *mazuma* in two fresh green Imperial notes. But this time the baron had insisted he would not be opening it again for a long time.

"Oh, there he is!" said Vera, who was at the stove, in a shabby housecoat and slippers.

"That's a fine welcome for a returning prodigal," said Gideon, kissing her sallow cheek. "Me? Of all people!" Despite his bad behavior, Gideon was always amazed at how people treated him. He placed a colossal, hairy hand on her belly. "How are you feeling, Commander-in-Chief?"

How firm and tight and tidy and full of life her belly feels, he thought. It's mine, the fruit of my seed—but who am I to bring another child into this pantomime of a life? The earth is spinning out of control . . .

Vera's strained voice softened. "Good to see you, dear."

"And you, and you!"

Then her weary face hardened again. "Are you eating with us? How long are we to be honored with your company, Gideon?"

"I'm here for you and the children," answered Gideon so sunnily that anyone who did not know him would be convinced he was the best husband in Piter. Here, no one helped with his fur or galoshes. The apartment was messy and steamy with fat and cabbage, like a peasant's place. Like many disorderly men who never tidy up anything, Gideon hated mess and he inspected the unwashed dishes, the unmade beds with their yellowed sheets, the piles of shoes and boots, the footmarks on the carpets and the crumbs on the kitchen table with accusatory fury. It was a handsome apartment, painted plain white with ordinary Finnish birch furniture, but the pictures were still not hung. "This place is a sewer, Vera. A sewer!"

"Gideon! We don't have a kopek. We must pay the butcher twenty rubles or we lose our credit. We owe the doorman eight, we owe—"

"Feh, feh, dearest. What's for dinner?"

"Kasha and cheese. We couldn't get anything else. There's nothing in the city to eat. Viktoria! Sophia! Your papa's here!"

There was the thud of reluctant feet in heavy lace-up shoes. A girl stood in the doorway, peering at her father with sullen, muddy eyes as if he were a Martian.

"Hello, Papa," said Viktoria, known as Vika.

"Darling Vika! How are you! How's school? And that admirer of yours? Still writing you poems?"

He held open his arms but his darling fifteen-year-old daughter neither approached nor altered her expression.

"Mama's very tired. She cries. You haven't visited for a long time. We need money."

Tall, olive skinned with lanky hair, wearing horn-rimmed spectacles and a dressing gown, Vika reminded Gideon of a censorious librarian. He could not get close to her.

"Where have you been?" the girl went on. "Drinking? Chasing women of easy virtue?"

"What a thing to accuse me of! Me? Of all people!" Gideon's eyes fell. Even though his big mouth, dancing black eyes, wild hair and beard were made for grand gestures and belly laughs, he felt hollow and ashamed. Where did she get such a phrase as "women of easy virtue"? From that mother of hers of course.

"I've got homework to do," said Vika, slouching away.

Gideon shrugged to himself: Vera was poisoning the children against him. Then he heard a cascade of light steps. Sophia, a dark girl with frizzy jet-black hair and eyes, threw herself into his arms. He stood up and whirled her round and round in her shabby nightshirt.

"Mouche!" he bellowed. "My darling Mouche!" That was Sophia's nickname because when she was a baby she had resembled a mischievous fly. Now she was older, with black curls, black eyes and a strong jaw, she radiated energy just like her father.

"Where've you been? Is there a revolution? We saw a fight at the bakery! I want to be out there, Papa. Take me with you! How are your revolutionary friends? Did you see anything? I support the workers! How are you, Papa? Are you writing something? I've missed you. You haven't been bad, have you? We hope not! We are very prissy here!" She wrapped herself around him like a monkey. "What are you writing, you old papa *momzer*?"

He loved the way she called him "papa scallywag" in Yiddish and tickled his beard. "Shall we write something now, Mouche? I owe them a quick article."

"Oh yes!" Mouche took his hand and dragged him into the study, where it was difficult to step without knocking over piles of papers and journals—yet the fleet Mouche dodged them all and pulled out his green leather chair, adeptly placed the paper on the typewriter and wound it into position.

"*Pravilno!* Right!" he said.

"Now, who are we writing for today? The Kadets? The Mensheviks?"

"The Mensheviks!" he replied.

"So you're a Social Democrat this week?" she teased her father.

"This week!" He laughed at himself.

"How many words?"

"Five hundred, no more. Do we have something to drink?"

Mouche scurried off to get a thimble of vodka.

He swigged it and sat down in the chair.

Mouche settled into his lap, rested her hands on his arms and cried out: "Type, Papa, begin! How about this? 'The regime's reactionary follies are almost played out.' Or 'In the streets, I saw a hungry wraith of a woman, a worker's widow, shake her baby at a rich war profiteer.' Or . . ."

"You're so like me," he said, kissing her forehead.

Gideon was one of those journalists who, in a few minutes, could dash off an article decorated with ringing phrases and sharp reportage, without any real effort. Since he could never quite make up his mind whether he was a Constitutional Liberal (a Kadet) or a moderate Social Democrat (a Menshevik), he wrote for both their newspapers and several other journals, using different names. He had traveled widely and his pieces contained references to foreign cities and forgotten wars that impressed the reader. His phrases, so carelessly constructed, often hit home. People repeated them. Editors asked for more. He never regretted that he had let Samuil buy him out of the family business, though if he had kept his share he would now be a very rich man. He regretted nothing. Besides, money never stuck to his fingers.

He had promised the Menshevik editor a rousing article that evening on the atmosphere in the streets. Now, with Mouche excitedly feeling the tendons in his brawny arms as he typed, he worked fast, fingers banging into the keys and crying out, "Return!" at the end of each line. Then Mouche returned the typewriter to begin another line, humming to herself with enjoyment, jiggling her knees with nervous energy.

"There," he said. "Done. Your papa's just earned himself a few rubles for that."

"Which we never see!" said Vera from the doorway.

"I might just surprise you this time!" Gideon was feeling virtuous. He had enough cash to pay off the debts, satisfy Vera, buy the girls new books and dresses, and some fine meals. He looked forward to handing over the *mazuma*: Vera would smile at him; Mouche would dance; even Vika would love him again.

When Vera served the kasha, a buckwheat porridge, sprinkled with goat's cheese, she again asked about the money, not mentioning there was a revolution afoot. Outside, the factory sirens started to blare and whine; a shot, more shots and then a barrage rang out; stolen cars raced down the streets, skidding, grinding their gears as peasants enjoyed their first driving lessons.

"Is Sashenka really a Bolshevik, Papa? How's Aunt Ariadna? Is it true the doctor prescribed her opium?" Mouche asked questions and hummed to herself as he tried to answer them. Vika glared at her father each time her mother pressed her lips together, sighed or sniffed sanctimoniously.

No one could ruin a meal for Gideon. Whether it was kasha in his dreary apartment or a sturgeon steak at the Contant, he was a vigorous trencherman, recounting the family news, smacking his lips, sniffing the nosh like a happy dog and soiling his beard without the slightest embarrassment.

"You don't eat as you taught us to eat," said Vika. "Your manners are terrible, aren't they, Mama?"

"Don't do as I do," replied Gideon. "Do as I say!"

"How can you tell the children that?" asked his wife.

"It's hypocrisy," said Vika.

"You two are a regular trade union of sulking women! Cheer up," said Gideon, putting his feet up on a filthy chair, already marked by his boots on other occasions.

"No more jokes, Gideon," said Vera, sending Vika and Mouche to do their homework.

The moment he was alone with Vera, everything changed. Her drawn sallow face, made for martyrdom, irritated him. She was always wiping her nose with a green-stained rag. Her prissiness maddened him. He adored his daughters—or rather he adored Mouche—but what had happened to Vera? A child of the provincial bourgeois, the daughter of a Mariupol schoolteacher, she had been educated, an intellectual who worked on the literary journal *Apollo*, full of vim and enthusiasm, with a high bosom, blue eyes and golden hair. Now the bosom hung around her waist like udders, the eyes were watered down to a tepid pallor, and the hair was greying. How he had been so foolish as to get her pregnant again, he could barely believe! But on Mouche's birthday he had been overcome with a sort of erotic nostalgia for how she had been, forgetting how she was now. The fact that he himself had done this to her and that he felt guilty about it made him resent her all the more.

Only Mouche delighted him, and he decided that when she was a little older he would invite her to live with him. As for now, he could hardly stand it here another moment. Great events were taking shape on the streets; parties were throbbing in the hotels; a writer must see history being made; and he was stuck here with this straitlaced harridan.

Vera droned on with her complaints: the morning sickness was gone but her back ached and she could not sleep. The doorman made comments about Gideon's carryings-on. Vika had told her friends that her father was a revolutionary and a drunkard; Mouche was insubordinate and rude, the teachers complained about her and she was growing out of all her boots and dresses. But there was no money; it was hard to get meat in the shops and impossible to find bread; the neighbors had heard from someone else in the building that Gideon had been seen drunk in the early hours in the Europa Hotel; and how did he think *that* made her feel?

A full belly never made Gideon sleepy; it went straight to his loins. It fortified his libido. For some reason, he cast his mind back to the lunch last week at his brother's house. The Lorises were famous for their happy marriage but the boring count was not at the lunch so Gideon had given Missy what he called the Gideon Manifesto: let us pleasure ourselves now for life is short and tomorrow we die. (Obvious as it was, the manifesto was surprisingly successful!) Now Gideon recalled how, as he was saying good-bye to Missy, she had looked into his face with her crinkly, twinkling eyes—her laughter making creases around them—and squeezed his hand unmistakably, saying, "It would be wonderful to talk more about Meyerhold and the new theater. I suppose you won't be at Baroness Rozen's at the Astoria on . . . ," and she named a date. It happened that it was tonight. Gideon had neglected to follow up—but now his refreshed and well-fed phallus, a brilliant interpreter of female intentions, stirred. He had to get to that party right away.

Missy had never paid him the slightest attention. She was worldly enough—she had to be open-minded to be friends with Ariadna. But she had never really flirted with anyone and certainly not with him. Gideon reflected that the war, the loss of respect, the ever-changing ministers and the disturbances on the streets must be shaking free some ripe fruit that would never otherwise have fallen to the ground. He thought about Missy Loris's body—that bobbed blonde was skinny and had no bosom—yet he suddenly hungered for the sheer unadulterated joy of tasting new skin, lips, the satin of her inner thighs. He smiled to himself: this ursine giant was capable of Herculean erotic feats that no one—except the women themselves—would have believed possible. He proposed the most deliciously outré acts of lovemaking in delicate French phrases that liberated the restraint of chorus girls and countesses alike. Yet he had never become complacent about this erotic success. Why did these lovely *bubelehs,* these babes, choose me? he thought. Me? Of all people! I'm an ugly brute—like a Jewish innkeeper! But what the hell, I'm not complaining!

He just could not help himself: he had to find Missy right away that night. But if he handed over the two hundred rubles to Vera now, he would have nothing to buy the ladies drinks and snacks. What to do? He groaned. He'd do what he always did.

Moments later, as Vera washed up morosely, Gideon fled, leaving a hundred rubles on the hall table and keeping the rest for himself. Mouche helped him pull on his felt boots and handed him "our Menshevik article!" while Vika shook her head, pursing her lips.

"You're leaving already, Papa? I knew it. I knew it. I knew it!"

"We'll change the locks, you deadbeat!" shouted Vera, but he was gone.

Outside in the streets, Gideon could not find a sleigh. As for Vera, the whiner would manage, he thought. Vera and Vika: what a pair of sourpusses! I'm a coward, an incorrigible shameful hedonist—but I'm so happy! Dizzy with anticipation! What's wrong with happiness? We make our own lives! What are humans? We're just animals. I'll die young. I won't make old bones so I'm just doing what my species does. Besides, I had to go! I have an article to deliver to the newspaper.

He smelled the icy air. Strange sounds echoed in the distance. Gunshots crackled, factory whistles sang, engines revved and screeched, voices chanted—but here all seemed oddly quiet. But as he strode toward the Astoria Hotel, his mind racing with the anticipation of Missy's bare shoulders, her soft belly, her smells of female sweat and perfume, he stepped out into the wider streets. It started as a murmur, became a throbbing and grew into a roar. The broad boulevards were filling with masses of people, their covered heads and heavy coats making padded bundles of them as if they were automata all marching in the same direction.

Gideon weaved in and out, sometimes letting the current carry him, sometimes standing aside and watching it rush past. He was excited. As a writer, he was witnessing something. But where was the army, the Cossacks?

He stepped into the hotel, home again among its gleaming parquet floors, the shiny gold and black elevators, the dark oak bar.

"The usual, Monsieur Zeitlin?" asked Roustam the barman. Inside the Astoria, the polished formality had given way to a wild and carefree holiday. Tossing his coat and hat at the hat-check girl and forgetting to remove his boots, Gideon padded toward the private room where Baroness Rozen was holding a soirée. A girl in a backless orange dress, a feather boa and yellow shoes—what Vera called a woman of easy virtue, but what Gideon affectionately called a *bubeleh*—hailed him like an old friend, and he beamed at her. She was holding a drink and offering him a sip. The receptionists laughed at her: were they drunk too? A couple, an officer and what appeared to be a respectable lady wearing a double rope of pearls, sat kissing on the sofa in the foyer as if they were in a *kabinet*, not a public place. A doorman opened the double doors to the party and Gideon noticed that the red-faced servant did not bow, just smirked as if he knew what was inside Gideon's head.

Gideon almost fell into the room, pushing through uniforms and shoulder boards, frock coats and gowns, hearing them discussing the situation in the streets—until he saw a helmet of blond hair, some pale shoulders and a long gloved arm with a gold-tipped cigarette and the smoke curling round above it like a snake from a basket.

"So you came," Missy Loris said in her American accent.

"Was I meant to?"

Her smile raised those comely laughter dimples in her cheeks. "Gideon, what's happening out there?"

He put his lips to her little high-set ear. "We could all die tonight, *bubeleh*! What shall we do in our last moments?" It was one of his favorite lines from the Gideon Manifesto, and any moment now it was going to work.

32

There were no cabs at the Finland Station when Sashenka arrived back in the city. There was hardly anyone on the train except for two old ladies, probably retired teachers, who were earnestly discussing whether the *Thirty Abominations*, a lesbian novel from before the war, by Lidia Zinovieva-Annibal, was a classic exposition of female sensuality or a disgusting unchristian potboiler.

The argument started politely enough but as the train pulled into the Finland Station the two ladies were shouting at each other, even cursing. "You philistine, Olesya Mikhailovna, it's pornography plain and simple!"

"You hidebound reptile, Marfa Constantinovna, you've never lived, never loved, felt nothing."

"At least I feared God!"

"You've so upset me, I'm having a turn. I need my pills."

"I won't give them to you until you admit you're being utterly unreasonable . . ."

Sashenka could only smile as she heard the ricochet of gunshots over the city.

The station was eerily empty of its tramps and urchins. Outside, it was dusk but the streets were filled with running people, some with guns. It was snowing again, big dry flakes like barley seeds; the half moon cast a lurid yellow light. Sashenka thought the people looked oddly swollen but realized that many were wearing two coats or padding to fend off the knouts of the Cossacks. A worker from one of the vast metal factories told her there was a standoff at the Alexander Bridge, but before she could ask any more there was shooting and everyone began to run, unsure what they were running from. A female worker from the Putilov Works told her there had been battles on Alexander Bridge and Znamenskaya Square; that some of the Cossacks, the Volynsky Guards, had changed sides and charged the police. An old drunk claimed he was a socialist but then tried to put his hand into Sashenka's coat. He squeezed her breast and she slapped him and then ran. On the Alexander Bridge, she thought she saw the bodies of policemen. There were no streetcars.

She walked slowly toward home down the famous avenues, now seething with dark figures. Bonfires were lit in the streets. Urchins danced around the flames like demonic gnomes. An arsenal had been stormed: workers now carried rifles. She tramped onward, exhausted yet vibrating with fear and excitement. Whatever Uncle Mendel claimed about the Revolution, the people had not melted away at the first sign of resistance. There was the crackle of more shooting. Two boys, young workers, kissed her on both cheeks and ran on.

She came upon a crowd of soldiers on Nevsky. "Brothers, sisters, daughters, mothers, I propose that we don't fire on our brethren," shouted some NCO to cries of "Hurrah! Down with the autocracy!" She tried to find her comrades but they were at none of the coachmen's cafés or the safe houses on Nevsky.

Hurrying on, Sashenka felt wildly joyful. Was this it? A revolution without leaders? Where were the machine-gun nests and Cossacks and pharaohs? She heard a roaring engine. The people in the streets froze and watched, raising white faces like moons: what could it be? Like a dinosaur, a grey Austin armored car mounted with a howitzer drove haphazardly, gears screaming, in random accelerations and jerking turns, down Nevsky. The crowd scattered as it mounted the pavement and drove straight over a bonfire outside Yeliseyev's grocery store, and then stopped beside a group of soldiers.

"Can anyone drive this thing?" shouted the driver.

"I can!" A young man with shaggy black hair and bright brown eyes jumped up. "I learned in the army." It was her comrade Vanya Palitsyn, the Bolshevik metalworker. Sashenka hurried toward him to ask for instructions but he was already inside the armored car, which revved, shook and then accelerated off down the prospect.

"Are you for the Revolution?" asked a stranger, a boy with a Ukrainian accent, a blue nose and a military jacket. It was the first time anyone had used that word.

"I'm a Bolshevik!" Sashenka said proudly. They hugged spontaneously. Soon she was asking the question herself. Strangers embraced around her: a grizzled sergeant-major, a Polish student, a fat woman wearing an apron under her sheepskin, a leather-clad metalworker in a tool belt, even a fashionable woman in a seal coat. Closer to home, cars filled with soldiers waving banners and rifles skidded down Nevsky and Greater Maritime.

Dizzy with the momentum of this chaotic night, Sashenka kept thinking of Sagan. She was keen to make her report to Mendel. She had got the name of the traitor, established Sagan as a Bolshevik source inside the Okhrana, and was now a fully fledged practitioner of the art of conspiracy. She could hand over the direction of their double agent to another comrade. The mission was over, and away from Sagan and the effect he had on her, she was relieved. The Party would be satisfied.

She racked her brain for other Party safe houses. She tried 106 Nevsky. No answer. Then 134. The door was open. She flung herself upstairs, her senses bristling. The door was just opening and she could hear the Jericho trumpet of Mendel's voice. "What are we doing?" he was shouting.

"I just don't know," replied Shlyapnikov, wearing a padded greatcoat. "I'm not sure . . ."

"Let's go to G-g-gorky's apartment," suggested Molotov, rubbing his bulging forehead. "He'll know something . . ."

Shlyapnikov nodded and headed for the door.

"This is it," she said. Her voice squeaked, not her own. "The Revolution."

"Don't lecture the committee, comrade," answered Shlyapnikov as he and Molotov clumped down the stairs. "You're a puppy."

Mendel lingered for a moment.

"Who's in charge?" asked Sashenka. "Where's Comrade Lenin? Who's in charge?"

"We are!" Mendel smiled suddenly. "Lenin's in Geneva. We are the Party leadership."

"I met Sagan," she whispered. "Verezin the Horse Guards concierge is the traitor. But I don't suppose it matters anymore . . ."

"C-c-comrade!" called Molotov from the lobby, stammer reverberating up the stairs.

"I've got to go," said Mendel. "Check the other apartments for comrades. There's a meeting at the Taurida Palace. Tell them to report there later."

Mendel limped down the stairs, leaving Sashenka alone.

She returned to Nevsky, heading home. She ate some *solianka* soup and a chunk of black Borodinsky bread at the carriage-drivers' café, which was full of workers and coachmen, each telling stories of mayhem, orgies, slaughter, hunger and treason in loud, tipsy voices without listening to anyone else. Coal and oat prices had quadrupled. Even a bowl of soup in the café had gone up seven times. There were German agents, Jewish traitors and crooks everywhere.

As Sashenka put some coins into the barrel organ, which incongruously played "God Save the Tsar," raising guffaws from the coachmen, the streets grew darker. There were distant sounds like lions coughing in the night, the groan grew into a deafening roar and the hut shook. At first she could not understand why—then she realized that as she had been eating, the coachmen's café had been surrounded, overrun by a sea of people in dark coats. They were blocking the streets. There was shooting in the distance and smoke rising, pink against the pale darkness: the Kresty Prison was on fire.

As she walked down Greater Maritime, Sashenka saw a soldier and a girl kissing against a wall. She could not see their faces but the man groped up the girl's skirt past her stocking tops while the girl tore open his fly buttons. A leg rose up his side like one of the Neva's bridges opening. The girl mewed and writhed. Sashenka thought of Sagan and the sleigh ride in the snowfields and hurried on.

Outside the Astoria, some soldiers were stealing a Rolls-Royce, punching a uniformed chauffeur. The doorman, an officer and a gendarme ran outside, shouting. The soldiers calmly shot the officer and the gendarme, and the car drove off with its horn blowing.

Presently, a bearded man staggered heartily past her singing, "*Nightingale, nightingale,*" with a blond woman in a fur coat and Sashenka recognized Gideon and Countess Loris. She was relieved to find friends and was about to hail them when Gideon cupped Missy's buttocks and pulled her out of the crowd and into a doorway where they started kissing frenziedly.

A volley of shots distracted Sashenka. Figures were climbing up the facade of the Mariinsky Palace and tearing down the double-headed eagle of the Romanovs.

The gendarme's body lay in the street, splayed so that his white belly bulged out of his trousers, like a dead fish. Exhausted beyond belief, Sashenka stepped over it and hurried down Nevsky—toward the Taurida Palace.

33

"What are you all standing around for?" Ariadna called from the top of the stairs, her hair up, elegant in a flounced dress of shantung silk. The faces of Leonid the butler, the two chauffeurs and the parlormaids were raised toward her as she started to descend.

"Haven't you heard, Baroness?" It was Pantameilion, always the cheekiest, his neat mustache, oiled hair and sharp chin thrusting impertinently.

"Heard what? Speak up!"

"They've formed a Workers' Soviet at the Taurida Palace," he said excitedly, "and we've heard that—"

"That's yesterday's news," snapped Ariadna. "Please get on with your work."

"And the crowds say . . . the Tsar's abdicated!" said Pantameilion.

"Rubbish! Stop spreading rumors, Pantameilion. Go and decarbonize the car," replied Ariadna. "The baron would know if anyone did—he's at the Taurida!"

At that moment, the front door opened and Zeitlin swept in, a commanding figure in his floor-length black coat with a beaver collar and *shapka.* Ariadna and the servants stared open-mouthed as if he alone could settle the great question of the epoch.

Zeitlin cheerfully tossed his hat at the stand. He appeared years younger, radiating confidence. So there! thought Ariadna, the Tsar is back in control. What nonsense the servants talk! Fools! Peasants!

Zeitlin leaned on his cane and looked up at Ariadna like a tenor about to sing an Italian aria.

"I have news," he said in a voice quivering with excitement.

There! The Cossacks are guarding the streets, the Germans are retreating, everything will settle down again as it always does, decided Ariadna. Long live the Emperor!

On cue, Lala came down the stairs, Shifra emerged from the Black Way and Delphine the cook from the kitchen, her customary drip dangling from the end of her nose.

"The Emperor has abdicated," announced Zeitlin. "First in favor of the Tsarevich then in favor of his brother Grand Duke Michael. Prince Lvov has formed a government. All political parties are now legal. That's it! We're entering a new era!"

"The Tsar gone!" Leonid crossed himself then started to sob. "Our little father—abdicated!"

Pantameilion grinned insolently, twisting his mustache and whistling through his teeth. The two parlormaids paled.

"Woe is me!" Shifra whispered. "Thrones tumble like in the Book of Revelation!"

"What next? George the Fifth?" said Lala. "What'll become of me here?"

Delphine started to weep and her perpetual drip separated itself from the cozy berth of her nostrils and fell to the floor. The household had waited twenty years for this historic event but now that it had happened, no one noticed.

"Come on, Leonid," said Zeitlin, offering the butler his silk handkerchief, a gesture that, Ariadna noted, he would never have made a week earlier. "Pull yourselves together. Nothing changes in my house. Take my coat. What time is lunch, Cook? I'm ravenous."

Ariadna gripped the marble banisters, watching the servants pull off Zeitlin's boots. The Emperor was gone. She had grown up with Nicholas II and suddenly felt quite rootless.

Zeitlin leaped up the stairs, taking two at a time, like a young man. Following her into her bedroom, he kissed her on the lips so energetically that it made her head spin and then talked about the new Russia. The crowds were still out of control. The police headquarters was burning; policemen and informers were being killed; soldiers and bandits were driving automobiles and armoured cars around the streets, shooting their rifles in the air. The former Emperor wanted to return to Tsarskoe Selo but was now under arrest, soon to be reunited with his wife and children—they would not be harmed. Grand Duke Michael would turn down the throne.

Zeitlin was elated, he told his wife, because many of his friends from the Kadets and Octobrists were serving in Prince Lvov's government. The war would go on; he had already been commissioned by the new War Minister to deliver more rifles and howitzers; and it turned out that Sashenka was still a Bolshevik. He had seen her at the Taurida Palace with her comrades—a motley bunch of fanatics—but youth will be youth.

"There, you see, Ariadna? We're a republic. Russia's a sort of democracy!"

"What will happen to the Tsar?" asked Ariadna, feeling dazed. "What will happen to us?"

"What do you mean?" replied Zeitlin affably. "There'll be changes of course. The Poles and Finns want independence, but we'll be fine. There are opportunities in all this. In fact, when I was in the Taurida, I had a word with . . ."

Ariadna barely noticed when Zeitlin, still babbling about new ministers and juicy contracts, checked his gold fob watch and went downstairs to his office to make telephone calls. Almost in a trance, she followed him out of her room and watched him descend. She heard the Trotting Chair rumble into action.

Leonid rushed to the front door. Sashenka came into the hall, pale and elated, dressed in that plain blouse and grey skirt, her hair in an ugly bun, and no rouge at all. Ariadna was disappointed in her daughter: why did she dress like a provincial schoolteacher? What a sight the child was! She stank too, of smoke, soup kitchens and the people, the rushing gadding people. Even a Bolshevik needed to use powder and lipstick, and why did she refuse to wear her new dresses from Chernyshev's? A decent dress would improve her no end.

But somehow Sashenka was utterly triumphant, glowing even. "Hello, Mama!" she called up but then, throwing off her fur *shuba* and boots, she swept on to answer the questions of Lala and the servants.

Excitedly, Sashenka told them that the Soviet of Workers' and Soldiers' was sitting; that Uncle Mendel was on the Executive Committee. And that Uncle Gideon was there too—he was writing about it—and his friends, the Mensheviks, dominated the Soviet.

Ariadna did not care about this politicking but she could see that Sashenka needed to sleep. Her eyes were red, her hands shook from coffee and exhilaration. Yet as she watched her daughter's animated face, she saw Sashenka anew. It was as if she had grown strong and beautiful, like a grub eating her mother's flesh from the inside. Now she was shining with life while Ariadna was lifeless and empty.

Stifling a longing to weep, Ariadna retreated to her bedroom.

Feeling not so much calm as becalmed, Ariadna measured out Dr. Gemp's opium tonic and swallowed it. But this time it did not work. Her limbs were heavy, as if moving through molasses. The earth seemed to slow down, almost stopping on its axis. Time became excruciating.

She lay down on her divan. She could not rejoice in the news that made her husband feel younger and her daughter seem beautiful; it merely aged her. The ground was splintering beneath her feet. No Tsar; Rasputin dead; Zeitlin had talked divorce; and somehow what most upset her was Sashenka's joyous luminosity. She was playing grown-up politics, laughing at her parents. She had a mission in life—but what did Ariadna have? Why was Sashenka happy? Why so smug? The clock ticked more and more slowly. She waited for each tick but it took ages to come and when it did, it was like the tolling of a distant bell.

When Ariadna was growing up in Turbin, she knew the Tsars were no friend of the Jews, but the Jews were convinced that without the Tsars it would be much worse. The Tsar was far away and he did much harm to the Jews and to the Russians too, even if his intentions were not too bad. But the Tsar had protected the Jews against the Cossacks, landowners, anti-Semites and pogromists. Now he was gone, who would protect them? Who would look after her? Suddenly she craved her mother's embrace, her mother whom she had ignored. Miriam was in the same house, so was her father—but they might have been in another universe. To reach them would take an eternity.

The sounds of the household were muffled. She had nothing to do and the nothingness took forever to pass. The world was soaked in blood, just as Rasputin had warned her it would be; the streets of Piter were in anarchy. Outside, she heard tramping feet, hooting cars, cheering and gunfire. The sounds meant nothing; everything had lost its taste; her perfume had turned to dust. Everything, even her scarlet dresses, her sapphires, looked grey.

She rose with a sigh and wandered toward Sashenka's room. She realized that she had not visited it for years.

34

Baron Zeitlin was in his study, clanking energetically on his Trotting Chair, a cigar between his teeth. He was sure he could adapt to the new world, indeed he almost sympathized with the socialists. He was vibrating with new plans. Then he heard Sashenka's voice in the foyer and remembered how he had failed to understand her. Now he must try harder—otherwise he would lose her.

"Darling Sashenka!" She burst in breathlessly but did not sit down. "I can't believe the last few days. But life must go on. When are you starting your studies?"

"Studies? We're much too busy for studies. I lied to you about my politics, Papa, because I had to. We Bolsheviks live by special rules. I was doing what was right." Her face was firm, almost aggressive.

"It's all right, Sashenka, I understand," said Zeitlin, but he did not. He blamed himself for making his daughter into this godless avenger. She had lied to him and rejected the family. But he had taught her to disrespect faith and this was the result. And now was not the time for another quarrel. "Your mother thought you had a boyfriend."

"How absurd! She hardly knows me. I have a job now at the *Pravda* newspaper as liaison with the Petrograd Committee and the Soviet."

"But you must go back to school. The Revolution's almost over, Sashenka. The government . . ."

"Papa, the Revolution's just started. There are exploiters and exploited. No middle ground. This government's just a temporary bourgeois stage in the march to Socialism. The peasants must have their land, the workers their equality. The soldiers now take their orders from the Soviet of Workers' and Soldiers' Deputies." She was almost shouting at him now, flushed with defiance, her hands gripping his arms. "There'll be one last stage of capitalist corruption and then all this rottenness, all the bloodsuckers—yes, even you, Papa—will be swept away. There'll be blood on the streets. I love you, Papa, but we Bolsheviks don't have families and my love counts for nothing in the face of history."

Zeitlin had stopped trotting on his contraption. He looked at his daughter, at her exquisite freckles and dappled eyes, and was stunned.

Silence. From somewhere else in the house, there was a small pop.

"Did you hear that?" said Zeitlin, taking his cigar out of his mouth. "What was it?"

"It might have come from upstairs."

Father and daughter went out into the hall and then, for some reason, they were running. Leonid was at the top of the stairs, Lala on the landing. All were looking at the door of Ariadna's room. A cold hand clutched his heart, and Zeitlin rushed up the stairs.

"Ariadna!" he shouted, knocking on the door. The staff peered past him, goggle-eyed.

Ariadna was snowily naked on the divan. The smoking Mauser, dark and chunky, rested on her stomach. On her white skin, blood dripped crimson down her breast and pooled on the floor.

35

Sashenka stood at the window of the Gogol Street safe house, not far from the War Ministry, smoking a cigarette and peering out over the frozen Neva at the Peter and Paul Fortress. It was dark, yet the sky glowed an unnatural purple like a theatrical screen with a light behind it. The lantern atop the spire of the fortress's church swung a little in the wind.

The workers controlled the fortress. Mendel and Trotsky had once been prisoners in the Trubetskoy Bastion but yesterday the prisoners had all been freed. It was early evening and the streets were still teeming as excited but good-natured crowds tore down any remaining Romanov eagles. The Okhrana headquarters was on fire.

Sashenka's dreams were coming true but now she was numb. She walked the streets without seeing or hearing the remarkable sights. Her mother had pulled off the impossible: she had upstaged the Russian Revolution. People bumped into Sashenka. Someone embraced her. Vanya Palitsyn called her name from a careering car filled with Red Guards, a Romanov crest on its doors.

The apartment was too hot; she was sweating because she had not taken off her coat or hat. Why on earth had she walked straight here again? A place she had promised never to revisit. She had tried to block Sagan out of her mind; his time was past and probably he was already in Stockholm or the south. Yet here she was, in the familiar apartment, waiting for the person she was accustomed to confiding in about her mother.

She heard a sound and turned slowly. Captain Sagan, still in full gendarme uniform but haggard and bleary, stood there pointing a Walther pistol at her. Suddenly he looked his age, older even.

They said nothing for a moment. Then he put the pistol back in its holster and without a word came to her. They hugged. She was grateful he was there.

"I've got some brandy," he said, "and the samovar's just boiled."

"How long have you been here?"

"I came last night. I didn't know where else to come. Some workers went to my home and my wife has gone. The trains aren't running. I didn't know where to go so I just came here. Sashenka, I want to tell you something that will surprise you. My world—everything I cherished—has vanished in a night."

"That's not what you told me would happen."

"I'm in your hands. You can turn me in. I was a believer in the Empire. And yet I told you the truth about myself."

He took a bottle of Armenian brandy, cheap *cha-cha*, and poured out two shots, handing one to Sashenka. He downed his. She took off her coat and hat.

"Why are you here?" he asked. "I'd have thought you'd be celebrating."

"I was. And then something terrible happened. I was going to the Taurida Palace but when I passed the guardhouse at the barracks I knocked on the door. It was open. The doorman—remember the doorman, Verezin?—was lying dead on the floor, shot in the head. And then I went into the Soviet and met my comrades."

"You'd told them he was a traitor?"

She nodded.

"And you were surprised that he was dead?"

"No, I wasn't surprised. A bit shocked, I suppose. But that's revolution for you. When you chop wood, chips fly."

"But you said something terrible had happened?"

"My mother shot herself."

Sagan was aghast. "I'm so sorry, Sashenka. Is she dead?"

"No, she is just about alive. She shot herself in the chest. Apparently, beautiful women tend to avoid their faces. She found my Mauser, the Party's Mauser, under my mattress. How did she know it was there? How could she have found it? The doctors are there now." Sashenka paused, struggling to control her breathing. "I should have gone to the newspaper but instead I found myself here. Because it was here . . . with you . . . that we talked so much about her. I hated her. I never told her how much . . ."

She started to cry and Sagan put his arms around her. His hair smelled of smoke, his neck almost tasted of cognac, yet she found that just telling Sagan about her mother had calmed her. His hug restored her and, ironically, gave her the strength to pull away.

"Sashenka," he said, his hands squeezing her shoulders, "I have something to tell you. I was doing my job but I never told you how much I came to . . . be fond of you. I have no one else. I . . ."

She went cold suddenly.

"You're so much younger than me but I think I love you."

Sashenka stepped backward. She knew she had needed him, but not as the man who had kissed her in the snowfields, more as a confidant. Now his need for her, his stench of desperation, repelled her, and this specter of the fallen regime was frightening her. She wanted to be away from him.

"You can't just leave me like that," he cried, "after what I just told you."

"I never asked for this, never."

"You can't leave . . ."

"I've got to go," she said and, sensing a change in him, rushed for the door. He was right behind her.

He grabbed her around the waist and pulled her back to the sofa, where she had sat so many nights talking of poetry and parents.

She punched his jaw. "Let me go!" she screamed. "What are you doing?"

But he seized her hands and pushed her down, his long thin face terrifyingly close, pouring sweat and dribbling saliva as he struggled with her. He thrust his other hand up her skirt, tearing her stockings, driving up between her thighs. Then he turned to her chest, ripping the buttons off her blouse, rending her undergarments and clawing at her breasts.

She twisted sharply, freed her hands and smacked him in the nose. His blood burst all over her face but his weight held her down. Then she pulled the Walther out of his holster and slammed it sideways into his face. She felt the steel connect with teeth, bone and flesh, and more blood oozed over her fingers.

He rolled off her, and she was on her feet and racing for the door. As she wrenched it open, she glimpsed him curled like a child on the sofa, sobbing.

Sashenka did not stop until she was downstairs and out of the building. She hurtled into a cellar bar full of drunken soldiers but they were shocked by the sight of her and, seizing their bayoneted rifles, offered their help in killing anyone who had laid a finger on her. In the bathroom she washed the blood off her face and buttoned her blouse. The metallic taste of Sagan's blood was in her mouth, nose, everywhere, and she tried to wash it away but the smell made her gag, and she vomited. When she came out, she took a vodka from one of the soldiers and drank it down. It cleansed her a little, and gradually she felt calmer.

Outside, the streets were still heaving. She heard a burst of shooting on Nevsky. They were lynching pickpockets, and there were drunken gangs of deserters and bandits on the loose. She sensed that Sagan would want to get away from the apartment, so she hid in a doorway and watched the exit from the building. Her head was throbbing, and the lingering taste of his blood made her retch again. Her body was shaking. This had all been for the Party, and now it was over. She told herself that she should feel a sense of triumph—for she had won the Superlative Game, Sagan and his masters were finished, and his attack on her reflected his humiliation. Yet all she could feel was a corrosive shame and a savage fury. She imagined returning with her Party pistol and shooting him as a police spy, but instead, fumbling, she lit up a Crocodile.

About half an hour later, Sagan came out into the street and, in the queer purple light of night, she saw his swollen, bleeding face, his broken gait, how diminished he was. He was just a crooked, lanky figure hunched beneath a high astrakhan hat, his uniform covered by a khaki greatcoat. The streets were seething with huddled men, armed with Berdanas and Mausers, staggering in padded coats. The night was balanced on that thin spine between chanting jubilation and growing ugliness. Sagan headed down Gogol, through the small streets, and across Nevsky. She followed and saw the workers surround him outside the Kazan Cathedral. Perhaps they'd give him a good beating and punish him for hurting her, she thought, but they let him through. Then he tripped on a paving stone and they saw his uniform.

"A gendarme! A pharaoh! Let's arrest him! Scum! Bastard! We'll take him to the Soviet! We'll throw him in the bastion! Here, take this on the smiler, you weasel!" They surrounded him, but he must have drawn his pistol. He got off a shot—there it was, that popping sound again. Then they were kicking at a bundle on the ground, jeering, shouting and raising their rifle butts and bayonets. Breathing raggedly, Sashenka watched it all happen too fast for her really to understand.

Somewhere inside the cacophony of blows and cries, she heard his voice and then the squealing of an animal in pain. The moist thudding of the rifle butts told the rest. Through the workers' boots and the skirts of their greatcoats, she could see blood glistening on the dark uniform.

She did not see the metamorphosis of a man into a smeared heap on the street—and when it was over, there was a hush after the frenzy, as the crowd cleared their throats, straightened their clothes and then shuffled away. She did not wait any longer. She had seen the power of the people in action—the judgment of history.

Yet she no longer felt as if she had won. A wave of sadness and guilt overwhelmed her, as if her curse had visited this horror upon him. The dead body of Verezin, and now this. Yet *this* was what she had craved and she must welcome it: the Revolution was a noble master. Many would die in the struggle, she thought—and yet the destruction of a man was a terrible thing.

She found herself leaning on a statue outside the Kazan as tears ran down her face. It was an end but not the one she had wanted. She wished she had never known Sagan and she wished too that he had walked on down that street to a safe exile, far away.

36

A husky drawl broke the sepulchral hush of the sickroom.

"What's in the newspaper?" Ariadna asked.

The familiar voice shocked Sashenka. Her mother had not spoken for days. She had just slept, her breathing labored, the infection flourishing in her chest so that it seemed she would never wake again. Sashenka had been reading *Pravda*, the Party newspaper, when Ariadna stirred. She spoke so clearly that Sashenka dropped the paper, scattering its pages onto the carpet.

"Mama, you gave me a shock!"

"I'm not dead yet, darling . . . or am I? It stinks in here. I can hardly breathe. What does that newspaper say?"

Sashenka picked up the pages. "Uncle Mendel's on the Party's Central Committee. Lenin's returning any day." Sashenka looked up to find her mother's velvety eyes resting on her with an astonishing warmth. It surprised and then embarrassed her.

"When I finally went to your room . . . ," Ariadna began, and Sashenka strained to understand.

"Mama, you look better." It was a lie but who tells the truth to the dying? Sashenka wanted to soothe her mother. "You're getting better. Mama, how do you feel?"

"I feel . . ." She squeezed her daughter's hand. Sashenka squeezed back. The eyes dimmed again.

"I long to ask you one question, Mama. Why did you . . . ? Mama?"

At that moment Dr. Gemp, a plump, worldly man with a shiny pink pate and the theatrical air often associated with society doctors, entered the room.

"Did your mother wake up then? What did she say?" he asked. "Ariadna, are you in pain?"

Sashenka watched him lean over her mother, bathing her forehead and neck with a cold compress. He unraveled the dressing on her chest and inspected, cleaned and dabbed the wound, which looked like a congealed fist of blood.

Her father appeared beside her, also leaning over the sickbed. He looked terrible, his collar filthy and the beginnings of a prickly grey beard on his cheeks. He reminded Sashenka of an old Jew from the Pale.

"Is she coming round? Ariadna? Speak to me! I love you, Ariadna!" said Zeitlin. Ariadna opened her eyes. "Ariadna! Why did you harm yourself? Why?"

Behind him stood Ariadna's parents, Miriam, her small, dry face pointed like that of a field mouse, and the Rabbi of Turbin, with gabardine coat and skullcap, his face framed by his prophetic beard and whimsical ringlets.

"Darling Silberkind," said Miriam in her strong Polish-Yiddish accent, taking Sashenka's hands and kissing her shoulder tenderly. But Sashenka sensed how out of place the old couple felt in Ariadna's room. They had been in there before, yet they peered, like paupers, at the pearls, gowns, tarot cards and potions. For them this was the Temple of the Golden Calf and the very ruin of their dreams as parents.

Dr. Gemp, who specialized in the secret tragedies—abortions, suicides and addictions—of Grand Dukes and counts, stared at the old Jews as if they were lepers, but managed to finish dressing Ariadna's wound.

Ariadna pointed at her parents. "Are you from Turbin?" she asked them. "I was born in Turbin. Samuil, you must shave . . ."

Hours, nights, days passed. Sashenka lost track of time as she sat by the bed. Ariadna's breathing was hoarse and labored, like an old pair of bellows. Her face was grey and sallow and sunken. She had become old, tiny and collapsed. Her jaw hung open, and her chest creaked up and down, catching on clots of phlegm in her lungs so that her breath rattled and crackled. There was no beauty or vivacity left, just this shivering, quivering animal that had once been a vibrant woman, a mother, Sashenka's mother.

Sometimes Ariadna struggled to breathe and began to panic. Sweat poured off her, soaking the sheets, and she clawed the bed. Then Sashenka would stand up and take her hand. All of a sudden, there was so much she wanted to say to her mother: she wanted to love her, wanted to be loved by her. Was it too late?

"Mama, I'm here with you, it's me, Sashenka! I love you, Mama!" Did she love her? She was not sure, but her voice was saying these things.

Dr. Gemp came again. He pulled Zeitlin and Sashenka aside.

"Don't raise your hopes, Samuil," said the doctor.

"But she wakes up sometimes! She talks . . . ," said Zeitlin.

"The wound's infected and the infection has spread."

"She could recover, she could . . . ," insisted Sashenka.

"Perhaps, mademoiselle," replied Dr. Gemp smoothly, as a maid handed him his black cape and fedora. "Perhaps in the land of miracles."

37

"Would you like me to read something to you?" Ariadna heard her daughter ask the next morning.

"No need," she replied, "because I can come and read it myself." Another Ariadna rose up from the Ariadna on the bed and hovered over Sashenka's shoulder. She looked down and barely recognized the waxy creature with a dressing on her chest, breathing fast like a sick dog. Her hair was lank and greasy but she did not demand that Luda bring the curling tongs—so she *must* be dying. Ariadna wondered if she had always been cursed by the Evil Eye or infested by a dybbuk, or whether she had brought all her troubles upon herself.

She spun away from reality into wondrous dreams. She flew gracefully around the room. What visions she had! She and Samuil were together in a garden with tinkling fountains and luscious peaches.

Were they in the Garden of Eden? No, the forests were slim silver birches: these were Zeitlin's forests, soon to be the butts of rifles in the dead hands of Russian solders. The trees became ballerinas in tutus, then stark naked.

She opened her eyes. She was in her room again. Sashenka was sleeping on the divan. It was night. The room was softly lit by a lamp, not electric light. Samuil and two old Jews, a man and a woman, were talking quietly.

"I've lost myself, Rabbi," said Samuil in Yiddish. "I no longer know who I am. I'm not a Jew, not a Russian. I have long ago ceased to be a good husband or a good father. What should I do? Should I wear phylacteries and pray as a religious Jew, or should I become a socialist? I thought I had my life in order and now . . ."

"You're just a man, Samuil," answered the bearded sage.

Ariadna knew that voice: it was her father. What a fine voice, so deep and kind. Would he curse Samuil and call him a heathen? she wondered.

"You've done bad things and good things. Like all of us," her father said.

"So what should I do?"

"Do good. Do nothing bad."

"It sounds simple."

"It's very hard but it is a great thing. Don't harm yourself or others. Love your family. Ask for God's mercy."

"But I'm not even sure I believe in him."

"You do. Or you would not be asking these questions. All of us sin. The body is for sinning in this world. Without the choice, goodness would be meaningless. The soul is the bridge between this world and the next. But everything is God's world. Even for you, even for poor, darling Finkel, God's mercy is there, waiting. That is all you need to understand."

Who on earth was Finkel? Ariadna asked herself. Of course, it was her real name. Her father and her bewigged mother seemed to her at one moment like laughable cartoons; at another, they were as sacred as priests in the Temple of Solomon.

"And Ariadna?" Samuil asked.

"A suicide." Her father shook his head. Her mother started to weep.

"I blame myself," said Samuil.

"You did more for her than us, more than anyone," said her father. "We failed her; she failed us. But we love her. God loves her."

Ariadna was moved; she felt fondness for her parents, but not love. She no longer loved anyone. These were characters from her life, familiar faces and voices, but she loved none of them.

She was light as a goose feather, a draft from a window blew her this way and that. Her body lay there, croaking and wheezing. She was interested in this, but not involved in its mechanical functions. Dr. Gemp came into the room and threw off his cape like a Spanish bullfighter. She felt her forehead being dabbed; her dressing changed; morphine injected; her lips wetted with warm, sugary tea. Her belly ached; bowels groaned; the congested fist in her chest throbbed around a single bullet that she herself had placed there. This thing on the bed—the body she recognized as hers—was no more important than a laddered pair of stockings, a good pair, but an object that could be thrown away without a thought.

Her father was praying aloud, reading from the Psalms, singing in a deep chant that filled her with disinterested joy. It was the voice of a nightingale outside in the garden. But when she looked at his face, he was young, his beard a reddish brown, eyes strong and bright. Her mother was there too, full of life, even younger. She did not wear a wig but her own long blond hair in braids, and a girl's dress. And her grandparents too, all much younger than she. There was her husband as a teenager. Sashenka as a little girl. They could now be her sisters and brothers.

The rabbi's chanting carried her to Turbin three decades earlier. Her father and the beadle were walking out of the studyhouse; her mother was cooking dumplings and noodles laced with saffron, cinnamon and cloves. Ariadna was in trouble even then: she had refused to marry the son of the Mogilevsky rabbi, had been seen talking to one of the Litvak lads who did not even wear ringlets—and she had met a Russian officer in the woods near the barracks. She adored that uniform, the gold buttons, the boots, the shoulder boards. No one knew she had kissed not only the Litvak boy but also the young Russian, sipping cognac that made her glow, their hands all over her, her skin fluttering under their caresses. How that officer must have boasted and laughed to his friends in the officers' mess: "You'll never guess what I found in the woods today. A lovely Jewess fresh as the dew . . ."

I was too beautiful for the rabbi's court in Turbin, she told herself. I was a peacock in a stable. And now she was happily going back to Turbin. Or at least passing through there, on the way to somewhere else. What was written for her in the Book of Life?

But when Ariadna flew back to that familiar bedroom filled with family and re-entered her body, she realized that it was no longer her bedroom, Sashenka was no longer her daughter, Miriam no longer her mother—and she herself was no longer Ariadna Finkel Barmakid, Baroness Zeitlin. She became something else, and she was filled with joy.

Sashenka was the first to notice. "Papa," she said, "look! Mama's smiling."

38

"She's gone," said Miriam, taking her daughter's hand.

"Woe is to outlive your own child," said the rabbi quietly and then he started to pray for his daughter. Sashenka felt that she had made some peace with her mother, but her father, who had been napping on the divan, awoke and threw himself onto the body, weeping.

Uncle Gideon, now writing for Gorky's *New Life* newspaper, flirting with both the Mensheviks and the Bolsheviks, was also there, waiting in the corridor, and he rushed into the room and lifted Zeitlin off Ariadna's body. He was immensely strong and he carried the baron away and sat him in a chair outside.

The doctor sent them all out. He closed Ariadna's mouth and her eyes and then called them back. "Come and see her now," he instructed.

"She's become . . . beautiful again," Sashenka whispered. "Yet there's no one there." Sure enough, Ariadna was no longer the quivering ruin but as beautiful as she had been as a girl. She was serene, her skin white, her pretty nose upturned, and those lush lips slightly opened as if expecting to be kissed by some dashing young officer.

This is how I'll remember her, thought Sashenka. What a beauty. Yet she felt a gnawing dissatisfaction and uneasiness: she had never known her. Her mother had been a stranger.

And who was she herself in this play? She no longer belonged there. While her mother was dying, she had become her daughter again. Her father, who had been unfazed by revolutions, wars, strikes and abdications, by his daughter's arrest, his brother's mischief, his wife's affairs, who had defied Petrograd workers, Baku assassins and aristocratic anti-Semites, had crumpled under this, a domestic suicide. He had abandoned his business, left his contracts unsigned, his contacts neglected and, in a few weeks, he had lost almost all interest in money. The businesses in Baku, Odessa and Tiflis were already unraveling because the Azeri Turks, Ukrainians and Georgians were liberating themselves from the Russian Empire. But the details were in his mind, and it seemed that this unshaven, grief-stricken man was beset by doubts about everything. She could hear him jabbering and crying.

It seemed to Sashenka that she might be losing both parents in one day.

She did not cry anymore—she had cried often enough in recent nights—but still she longed to know why her mother had used her daughter's gun. Was Ariadna punishing Sashenka? Or was it simply the first weapon that had come to hand?

Sashenka stood beside the bed for a long time as people came and went to pay their respects. Gideon staggered into the room and kissed Ariadna's forehead. He ordered the doctor to sedate her father. The old Jews prayed. She watched as Turbin reclaimed the wicked she-devil of St. Petersburg.

Ariadna's smile remained, but gradually her face started to subside. Her cheeks sank, and her gentile nose, the perfect little button that had allowed her to romance Guards officers and English noblemen, became Semitic and hooked. Sashenka's grandfather covered the body with a white shroud and lit two candles in silver candlesticks at the head of the bed. Miriam covered the mirrors with cloths and opened the windows. Since Zeitlin himself seemed paralyzed, the rabbi took control. Orthodox Jews, liberated by the Revolution and allowed to visit the capital, appeared in this most secular of houses, as if by magic. Low stools were provided for the women to sit shiva.

There was a debate among the rabbis about what to do with the body. A suicide was beyond God's law and should have consigned her to an unholy burial, another tragedy for Ariadna's father. But two other rabbis had arrived and they asked what had actually killed Ariadna. An infection, Dr. Gemp replied, not a bullet. By this pragmatic and merciful device, the Rabbi of Turbin was allowed to bury his daughter Finkel, known as Ariadna, in the Jewish cemetery.

Finally, the servants, shocked and confused by the presence of these gabardine-coated Jews with ringlets and black hats, filed past the bed.

Sashenka knew she had to get back to her job at the Bolshevik newspaper. As if on cue, the door opened and Mendel, who had appeared only once for ten minutes a few days after the shooting, limped into the room between two young comrades, the powerful, thickset Vanya Palitsyn, now clad in a leather coat and boots with a pistol in his holster, and the slim, virile Georgian, Satinov, who wore a sailor's jacket and boots. They brought the welcome breath of a new age into the chamber of decay.

Mendel was wearing a long lambskin coat and a worker's cap. He approached the bed, looked coldly at his sister's face for a moment, shook his head and then nodded at his sobbing parents.

"Mama, Papa!" he said, in his deep voice. "I'm sorry."

"Is that all you have to say to us?" asked Miriam through a curtain of tears. "Mendel?"

"You've wasted enough time here, Comrade Zeitlin," Mendel said brusquely to Sashenka. "Comrade Lenin arrived last night at the Finland Station. I've got a job for you. Get your things. Let's go."

"Wait, Comrade Mendel," said Vanya Palitsyn quietly. "She's lost a mother. Let her take her time."

Mendel stopped. "We've work to do and Bolsheviks can't and shouldn't have families. But if you say so . . ." He hesitated, looking back at his parents and the deathbed. "I lost a sister too."

"I'll bring Comrade Snowfox," said Vanya Palitsyn. "You two go ahead."

Satinov kissed Sashenka thrice and hugged her—he was a Georgian after all, she remembered. "You mourn all you need," said Satinov, following Mendel as he limped out.

Vanya Palitsyn, brawny in his leathers and holster, looked out of place in the exquisite boudoir, yet Sashenka appreciated his support. She saw his brown eyes scan the room and imagined what the peasant-worker would make of the decadent trappings of capitalism: of all those dresses and jewels, Zeitlin the prostrate, sobbing industrialist, the society doctor in his cape, the half-soused bon viveur Gideon, the tearful servants and the rabbi. Vanya could not take his eyes off those wailing Jews from Poland!

Sashenka was pleased to be able to smile at something.

"I've read about deathbeds in Chekhov stories," she said quietly to him, "but I never realized they're so theatrical. Everyone has a role to play."

Vanya just nodded, then he patted Sashenka on the shoulder. "Don't rush, comrade," he whispered. "We'll wait. Cry all you need. Then go and get cleaned up, little fox," said Vanya, his tenderness all the more touching in one so big. "You'll come back for the funeral but for now I've got a motorcar outside. I'm taking you to the mansion. I'll wait for you downstairs."

Sashenka took in the room and the family in a last sweeping glance of farewell. She approached the bed and kissed her mother's forehead. She was crying again and she noticed tears in Vanya's eyes too.

"Vanya, wait. I'm coming right now," said Sashenka, her voice breaking as she backed out of the room.

39

At midday the next day, in the silk-walled splendor of the Modernist Kschessinskaya Mansion, where once the ballerina Mathilde had entertained both her Romanov lovers, Sashenka sat at an Underwood typewriter at a neat wooden desk on the first floor. She wore a white blouse, buttoned to the neck, a long brown woollen skirt and sensible laced-up ankle boots. She was not alone in the anteroom. Three other girls, two of them wearing round spectacles, also sat at desks, pivoting round to watch the door.

The mansion was manned by armed Red Guards, actually workers who wore parts of different uniforms, commanded by Vanya himself. Vanya had taken her out for a quick meal the night before and driven her home afterward. In the morning she had visited, for the first and last time, the Moorish-style synagogue on Lermontovskaya (which her father had paid for) and then seen her mother buried in the Jewish cemetery, where she, her father and Uncle Gideon seemed drowned in the sea of mourning Jews in their wide hats and coats, attired entirely in black, except for the white fringes of their prayer shawls.

Vanya had begged her to take another day off but she replied that her mother had already consumed too many days of her life, and she'd hurried back to her new office—to meet her new boss. How could a young person wish to be anywhere else in the world but here in the ballerina's mansion, the furnace of revolution, the cynosure of history?

At her desk, Sashenka heard the buzz of excitement from downstairs. The meeting in the ballroom, attended by all the Central Committee, was about to break up. Just then its doors opened, the sounds of laughter and voices and the tread of boots on the stairs coming closer.

Sashenka and the other three girls settled their bottoms on their chairs and straightened their blouses, and arranged their inkwells and blotters once again.

The smoked-glass doors flew open.

"Well, Illich, here's your new office. Your assistants are all waiting for you, ready to get to work." Mendel stepped into the room with Comrade Zinoviev, a scruffy Jewish man in a tweed jacket with a frizzy shock of black hair, and Stalin, a small, wiry, mustachioed Georgian wearing a naval jacket and baggy trousers tucked into soft boots.

They stopped at her desk: Zinoviev's nervous eyes scanned Sashenka's bosom and skirts while Comrade Stalin, smiling slightly, looked searchingly into her face with eyes the color of speckled honey. Georgians had a charming way of looking at women, she thought.

The men seemed to be borne on a wave of energy and enthusiasm. Zinoviev smelled of cognac; Stalin reeked of tobacco. He was carrying an unlit pipe in his left hand, a burning cigarette in the corner of his mouth. They turned as a short, squat man with a bald bulging forehead, neat reddish beard and a very bourgeois three-piece suit with tie and watch chain burst into the room. In one hand he held a bowler hat and in the other a wad of newspapers and he was talking relentlessly and hoarsely in a well-educated voice.

"Good work, Comrade Mendel," said Lenin, looking at Sashenka and the others with his twinkling, slanted eyes. "This all looks fine. Where's my office? Ah yes, through there." The desk was ready, paper, inkwell and a telephone. "Mendel, which is your niece, the one who studied at the Smolny?"

"That's me, comrade!" said Sashenka, standing up and almost curtsying. "Comrade Zeitlin."

"A Bolshevik from the Smolny, eh? Did you really have to bow to the Empress every morning? Well, well, we represent the workers of the world—but we're not prejudiced against a decent education, are we, comrades?"

Lenin laughed merrily as he headed toward the glass double doors of his office, then turned briskly, smiling no more. "Right, ladies, henceforth you're working for me. We're not waiting for power to fall into our laps. We're going to take power ourselves and smash our enemies into the dust. You're to be available for work at all times. Often you'll need to sleep in the office. Make arrangements accordingly. No smoking in this office!"

He pointed at Sashenka. "All right, come on in, Comrade Zeitlin, I shall start with you. I've got an article to dictate. Let's go!"

PART TWO

MOSCOW, 1939

1

Dust rose around the limousine as Sashenka watched her husband jump out like a showman from a puff of smoke. The sunlight caught the flash of polished boots, the gleam of an ivory-handled pistol and the scarlet tabs that trimmed the well-pressed blue tunic.

"I'm home," Vanya Palitsyn called up to her on the veranda, waving at the driver to open the trunk. "Sashenka, bring out the children. Tell them their daddy's here! I've got something for them. And you, darling!"

Sashenka had been lying on a divan on the wooden veranda of their country house, trying to read the proofs of her magazine. The one-story villa with white pillars had been built near Moscow by a Baku oil nabob at the turn of the century. A wave of feathery blossom sailed over her head on the hot wind. The apple and peach trees in the orchard were thick with creamy petals and the veranda smelled of jasmine, hyacinth and honeysuckle. A crackly gramophone recording of Kozlovsky the tenor sang Lensky's aria from *Eugene Onegin* over the fence from the neighboring dacha—and a male voice joined in heartily.

She had been out there for a while and found herself humming the aria too. Her son, Carlo, aged three and a half, was on her lap and he did not allow her to read anything because he was so demanding and playful. He was actually named Karlmarx but as he was a toddler during the Spanish Civil War, when Sashenka wore a Spanish beret every day, his name was given a Latin turn. "Carlo, I've got to read this. Go and find Snowy and play with her or ask Carolina to cook you something!"

"No," answered Carlo in his high voice. He was a sturdy, brown-haired boy with a broad dimpled face, already handsome, and was kissing her cheeks. He was built like a bear cub but insisted he was a rabbit. "I want to be with my mama. Look, Mamochka, I'm stroking you!" Sashenka looked down at her son, at his beautiful brown eyes, and kissed him back.

"You're going to break hearts, Carlo my little bear!" she said.

"I'm not a bear cub, Mama, I'm a bunny rabbit!"

"All right, Tovarish Zayka," she said. "You're my favorite Comrade Bunny-Rabbit in the—"

"—whole wide world!" he finished for her. "And you're my best friend!"

Then she'd heard the car bouncing up the drive.

"Papa's home!" Sashenka said, sitting up.

"Open the gates!" yelled the driver.

"All right, coming," she heard a man answer. She recognized his voice. It was one of the service staff, the old Cossack in charge of the horses.

The gates swung open. Through them, she could see the little guardhouse at the end of the communal drive with its figures in blue uniforms. They were not really guarding her house—Vanya was quite important now but some big names, Molotov and Zhdanov, both Politburo members, and Marshal Budyonny and Uncle Mendel, lived down the same lane.

The car, a green ZiS, based on the American Lincoln with a long hood and a sleek body, swung through the gates, its creaky suspension gasping. It threw up clouds of dust as it came, weaving between the chickens, ducks and barking dogs. The children's pony, tied at the gate, watched impassively.

"Look, Comrade Bunny-Rabbit, it's Daddy!"

"I only want to kiss Mummy!" insisted Carlo, but he jumped down anyway and rushed to hug his father.

Sashenka followed him down the wooden steps. "Vanya, what a nice surprise! You must be boiling in those boots!" But the wearing of boots at one's desk, even in high summer—and the Moscow plain was hot that May—was more about the military machismo of the Bolsheviks than comfort or utility. Comrade Stalin wore boots at all times.

Carlo flung himself into Vanya's arms. His father gathered him up and whirled him round and round. Carlo squeaked with glee.

"How was the parade?" asked Sashenka, watching son and father, who were so alike.

"We missed you on the VIP stand," replied her husband. "The new planes were beautiful. I saw Mendel—and my new boss with his Georgians. Satinov said he would come by later . . ."

"Next year I'll try to organize things better," she promised. She had given Carolina the morning off to see the parade but the nanny was already back. At first, Sashenka had regretted missing the show in Red Square that demonstrated Soviet power, with its ranks of shock workers, soldiers and athletes in gorgeous uniforms, and its display of planes and tanks. The might of the army filled her with pride at what they had achieved since 1917, and she enjoyed greeting the leaders beside her in the VIP seats. But this year she'd wanted to be home with her children at the dacha.

"Is Uncle Hercules coming for the party?" asked Carlo. "I want to play with him!"

"Papochka says he's coming but you'll probably be asleep, Bunny."

Vanya squeezed Sashenka's narrow waist and took her face between his huge hands and kissed her.

"You're so lovely, darling," he said. "How are you?"

She slipped out of his grasp. "I'm exhausted, Vanya, after the women's group and the plans for the school and orphanage. There was a problem at the printer's, some idiotic typographical error—"

"Nothing serious?" Sashenka saw his eyes narrow and hastened to reassure him. The Terror was over but even a proofing mistake could be dangerous. Vanya and Sashenka had not forgotten the fate of the typesetter who had put "Solin" (Man of Salt) instead of "Stalin" (Man of Steel).

"No, no, nothing like that, and then Carolina burned the pirozhki and Carlo sobbed . . . What's all that?" she asked, pointing at the boxes in the car.

"Is it a present for me?" asked Carlo.

"Wait and see," answered Vanya, laughing. He unhooked the leather strap across his barrel chest that was linked to his belt and gun holster, tossing everything to his driver, Razum. Throwing off his blue tunic, he whirled it round his head to reveal a white shirt and suspenders holding up blue trousers with red stripes tucked into boots. Returning to the car, he helped Razum, who wore the same uniform, to pull out three large parcels wrapped up in blue paper.

Razum was an old boxer with a broken nose. He was a real veteran with a scar on his right cheek that he claimed to have received from General Skuro himself in the Civil War (though Vanya joked that he actually got it by falling drunkenly through a pane of glass).

Placing the two smaller parcels by the car, Vanya and Razum slowly carried the third toward the house.

"Papochka!" Their five-year-old daughter, Snowy, holding a pink cushion, ran out of the house, in nothing but shorts, to hug her father. Vanya lifted her up in his arms and kissed her forehead.

"Look at me! Watch this, Daddy!" she said, waving her favorite cushion "friend" in the air.

"We're always watching you," replied Sashenka. "Show Daddy your cushion dance."

Snowy was tall for her age, slim and very pale, hence her nickname, with blue eyes and rosy lips. Sashenka could not quite believe that such a beautiful creature had come from her and Vanya, although she looked a little like Sashenka's father, the "former person" Samuil Zeitlin, ex-baron, ex-bloodsucker. Sashenka felt a sudden pang of sadness and could not help wondering where he was now. No one knew if he was among the living—and a Bolshevik did not ask.

Snowy kicked her legs high, waving the cushion and skipping like a colt. "Look, Papochka, do you like my new cushion dance?" She performed her crazy jig that always ended with "Giddy-gush, giddy-gush, giddy, giddy-up, giddy-gush!" Sashenka clapped. Vanya laughed. She could do no wrong in his eyes.

"Look!" Snowy pointed to a scarlet butterfly and pretended to fly after it, waving her hands as wings.

"You'll be in the Bolshoi yet!" said Vanya. "An Artist of the People!"

Snowy ran back to her father, jumping up and down with much-treasured exuberance, and he picked her up again. He was so tall that her feet were far from the ground. "What have you been doing today, Snowy?"

"I'm not Snowy. Show us the presents, Papochka!"

"Volya then."

Volya was her real name—it meant "Freedom" but also "Will," a tribute to the People's Will, an early revolutionary group—another good revolutionary name, reflected Sashenka, watching them indulgently.

She knew she was fortunate that Vanya was such a gentle father in this steely time of struggle when tenderness was not fashionable among the leaders, though Satinov had whispered to her that even Comrade Stalin did homework every night with his daughter Svetlana. Sashenka and Vanya were a real Soviet team, sharing the load when possible because both worked very hard, and they were both unusually affectionate parents. But then, as Comrade Kaganovich, Stalin's trusted ally, had told her delegation of the Committee of Wives of Commanders, "Bringing up Soviet children is as important as liquidating spies or fighting Fascists, and a Soviet wife should care for her husband and children!"

An angular, beaky woman in sensible shoes and with her grey hair in a bun bustled after the little girl.

"You must put a hat on, Snowy," scolded Carolina, the nanny, a Volga German who also cooked for the family, "or you'll get sunburned like Carlo!"

Vanya put Snowy back on the ground. "Right, time to open the presents," he said. "But first, this big one is for your lovely mother." He and Razum heaved the bulky package onto the veranda. "There! Open it!"

"Can I open it?" said Snowy, jumping up and down.

"Can I open it?" cried Carlo, struggling out of his mother's arms.

"Ask Mama!" said Vanya, smiling at Sashenka. "It's her May Day present!"

"Of course you can," said Sashenka.

"Come on then, Comrades Cushion and Bunny-Rabbit!" said their father. They tore at the paper until there in the blazing sun stood a voluptuous, cream-colored refrigerator with stainless steel trimmings and the words *General Electric* in chrome across its front. "Pleased, darling?"

Sashenka was delighted. An American fridge would make such a difference to their lives at the dacha, especially in this heat. She hugged Vanya, who tried to kiss her on the lips but she swerved slightly and he got her cheek instead. "Thank you, Vanya. But where on earth did you get it?"

"Well, it's from the Narkom—the People's Commissar—for our good work but he said that Comrade Stalin himself had approved the list." Behind them the service staff—Razum the driver, Golavaty the Cossack groom with bow legs and a waxed mustache, Carolina the nanny and Artyom the old gardener—admired the American fridge.

But Snowy and Carlo were already tearing at the other parcels, to reveal a metal frame, wheels, handlebars . . .

"A bicycle!" cried Snowy.

"Oh, Snowy, just what you were hoping for on May Day!" said Sashenka, catching Vanya's eye. "You really are a lovely daddy, thank you for all of this!" She took Snowy's hand. "Snowy, say thank you to your wonderful papochka!"

"Not Snowy. My name is CUSHION! Thank you, Papochka!" Snowy scampered up to her father and leaned into his arms.

"You've got to thank the Party too and Comrade Stalin!" said Sashenka. But the children were already trying to balance on the bikes.

"Thank you, Comrade St . . ." Snowy lost interest and chased another butterfly while Carlo tried to cycle and fell off, which led to tears, cuddles and consoling ice cream indoors.

By midafternoon it was too hot to be outside and an oriole was singing. The silver pine forest that surrounded them buzzed with spring, voices murmured nearby, glasses tinkled, horses neighed.

Sashenka swung in the hammock, watching as Vanya, still in his boots and breeches but now bare chested, broad shouldered and muscular, worked with his tools to add training wheels to Carlo's bike, cannibalizing parts from an old stroller. Sashenka marveled at his ingenuity—but of course he was a former lathe turner, a real worker since his childhood, and she remembered meeting him that first time at the safe house in Leningrad, when she was sixteen and he a little older. There had been no sentimental courtship or soppy proposal, Sashenka thought proudly, no bourgeois philistinism or rotten liberalism; they were too busy making a revolution. They had just agreed to get married, and had not even registered at the marriage office until the government had moved to Moscow. Then there'd been the civil war. She'd worked for the Party and taken evening classes at the Industrial College. She and Vanya had set off together into the countryside to squeeze the grain out of the obstinate peasants and collectivize their smallholdings. They shared digs at the House of the Soviets with other couples and owned nothing. I can't believe, she thought now, that I'm almost forty already. The Smolny Institute for Noble Imbeciles seemed as distant as the Middle Ages.

Over the fence, the neighbor changed his gramophone record and started to sing along to one of Dunaevsky's catchy songs from his jazz movie, *The Jolly Fellows.*

"Dunaevsky might come by for some *zakuski* later, Vanya," she said. "Along with Utesov and some new writers too. Uncle Gideon's bringing them. He might even persuade Benya Golden to come."

"Who?" he said, his forehead crumpled as he tightened the bolts attaching a wheel to the bicycle.

"The writer whose stories on the Spanish Civil War I read recently," she replied.

Vanya shrugged his bunched shoulders. Sashenka wished he was more interested in singers, writers and film stars. She was—and why shouldn't she be? Vanya had once called them "a rackety bunch of unreliable elements—and your uncle Gideon is the worst." She knew that Vanya preferred Party and military people but they could be so rigid and dry, and they were worse since the Terror. Besides, she was an editor, and her magazine was read by the wives of all the "responsible workers"—as the leaders were called. It was her job to know glamorous stars.

"Well, Satinov's coming and so is Uncle Mendel if you want to talk politics," she answered.

"How many have you asked?" he said, trying out the balance of the bike.

"I don't know," she answered dreamily. "It's a big house . . ."

The dacha was a recent acquisition—and sometimes, in spite of herself, the sounds and smells reminded Sashenka of Zemblishino, the Zeitlin family estate where Mendel had converted her to Marxism.

Sashenka and Vanya had been assigned the dacha a year previously, in the summer of 1938, when they had also been granted the apartment on Granovsky and their driver. The cleansing of the Party had been a brutal and bloody process. Many had failed the test and fallen by the wayside, sentenced to death, the Highest Measure of Punishment in the official terminology. Some of Sashenka's oldest friends and acquaintances had turned out to be traitors, spies and Trotskyites. She had never realized so many of them wore masks, pretending to be good Communists while actually being Fascists, saboteurs and traitors. With so many comrades vanishing into the "meat grinder," as it was known, Sashenka had, like all her friends, culled their photos from the family photograph albums, scratching out their faces. Even she and Vanya had been worried, although they were completely committed to the rapture of the Revolution. Their marriage was a Communist marriage too. Sashenka and Vanya shared faith in the Party; for them, the faith was everything. They shared so much even if, she suddenly thought, the differences in their interests had become more marked as they grew older.

But the Terror was over now; they could breathe easy again. The country was ready and united for the coming war against the Hitlerite Fascists.

Vanya stood up and called Snowy, who came scampering around the corner with little Carlo trying to keep up.

"The bikes are ready." He lifted her onto the seat. "Now take it slowly, Comrade Cushion, easy now, not too fast, feet on the pedals, now start to pedal . . ."

"Me too," piped Carlo.

"Hang on, Carlo, oh Carlo . . . Don't worry, bear cub, I've got you!"

"I'm a bunny, Papochka!" shouted the little boy furiously. His parents laughed. "Don't laugh, silly Mummy!"

Sashenka smiled, her heart full of love for her small son. It didn't matter if he was rude to her providing he was not rude to his father, who had a furious temper.

"Careful, Bunny," she called. But it was too late. Desperate to catch up with his sister, he went too fast, swerved to avoid a chicken and fell off his bicycle.

"I want my mummy!" he sobbed.

Sashenka scooped him up again, at which he instantly stopped crying and demanded to go back on the bike.

"Look at me, look at me, Papochka and Mamochka!" He was off again.

"When aren't we looking at you?" retorted Sashenka, tenderly. Turning round she could see that Snowy had mastered the bicycle. Triumphant, the little girl jumped off and danced away, waving her cushion.

"Right, it's too hot and I'm hungry," announced Vanya. "Brightness burns. I want you all out of the sun right now."

2

An hour later, Sashenka, sitting cross-legged on the floor, was playing with the children in the nursery next to the Red Corner, with its posters of Lenin and Stalin, and the family radio mounted in a varnished oak casing. She could hear Razum and Vanya in the kitchen arguing about the soccer match between Dynamo Moscow and Spartak. Dynamo Moscow had played appallingly. Spartak had fouled the Moscow striker, who had been borne off the field, but the referee had not sent off the Spartak player.

"Perhaps he's a saboteur!" Razum joked.

"Or maybe he needs new spectacles!"

No one would have laughed about a saboteur six months earlier, Sashenka reflected, even a soccer saboteur. People had been arrested and shot for lesser things. She recalled how the director of the Moscow Zoo had been detained for poisoning a Soviet giraffe, and how a schoolboy at School 118 near their Moscow apartment had been arrested for throwing a dart that accidentally hit a poster of Stalin. Whenever one of their friends was arrested, Vanya would close the kitchen door (so the children could not hear) and whisper the name. If it was someone famous like Bukharin, he would just shrug: "Enemies are everywhere." If it was a good friend with whom they had holidayed in Sochi, for example, she would be mystified and concerned. "The Organs must know something but . . ."

"There's always a reason," he'd say. "It means it's necessary."

"The masks that people wear! The evil of our enemies beggars belief. Snowy was going to play with their children—"

"Cancel Snowy's visit," Vanya would say sharply, "and don't call Elena! Careful!" He would kiss her forehead and no more would be said.

"You can't make a revolution with silk gloves," said Comrade Stalin, and Sashenka had repeated it to herself every day. But now Comrade Stalin had told the Eighteenth Congress that the Enemies of the People had been destroyed. Yezhov, the crazy secret-police boss, had been fired and arrested for his excesses, while the new Narkom of the NKVD, Lavrenti Beria, had brought back justice and moderation.

The men, their voices increasingly sticky from the succession of beers and the heat, were guffawing about a goal Vanya had scored in their amateur soccer team. Sashenka could not imagine why anyone would want to discuss soccer. She sighed. She and Vanya were opposites—he a worker of peasant origins, she an intellectual of bourgeois upbringing. But everyone knew that opposites make good marriages, and she had a kind, successful husband, two beautiful children, the drivers, the cars, this idyllic dacha—and now an American fridge.

Carolina started to set the big table on the veranda for an early May Day supper. Sashenka, who always held a party on May Day, thought about the evening ahead—and their guests. Uncle Gideon would bring his raffish friends and proposition somebody inappropriate, she supposed. There was a squeal. Carlo had grabbed Snowy's beloved cushion and she was chasing him into the sitting room and out again, careering round the Red Corner, both laughing their heads off.

Sashenka walked onto the veranda, humming a tune, one of Liubov Orlova's songs.

She stopped, jolted by a terrifying attack of happiness. She was on the right side of history; Soviet power, with its colossal steel plants and thousands of tanks and planes, was strong; Comrade Stalin was loved and admired. How much the Party had achieved! What joyous times she lived in! What would her grandfather, the Turbin rabbi, probably still alive in New York, have said about her dizzy happiness? "Don't tempt the Fates." That would have been his warning—all that nonsense about the Evil Eye and those dybbuks and golems. But this was just medieval superstition! There was much to celebrate.

"Have we got vodka?" she called out to Vanya.

"Yes, and a crate of Georgian wine in the trunk of the car."

"Well, pour me a glass! Put Utesov's jazz-tango on the gramophone."

The children and her husband joined her on the veranda. Vanya lifted up Snowy and pretended to slow-dance with her as if she were a grown-up. Sashenka held Carlo and danced with him, singing along to the music. She and Vanya turned the children upside down at the same moment and then swooped them up again. The children squealed with joy. How many comrades dance with their children like we do? thought Sashenka. Most of them are much too dull.

3

The sun was going down, suffusing the garden with the lilac light that always made Muscovites think of bygone summers in their dachas. At seven the party began and, as Sashenka had predicted, Uncle Gideon arrived first, bringing some friends—the famous jazz singers Utesov and Tseferman, as well as Masha, a pouty young actress from the Maly Theater who was his latest conquest.

Gideon, no longer young but still strong and irrepressible, was as shameless as he had been twenty years earlier. He wore a peasant blouse and blue beret from Paris, a gift, he said, from his friend Picasso, or was it Hemingway? Gideon claimed to know everyone—ballerinas, pilots, actors and writers. Sashenka depended on her uncle to bring these glamorous artists to her house on May Day night.

Uncle Mendel, roasting in a winter suit and tie, and his wife Natasha, the plump Yakut lady whom Sashenka remembered from the days before the Revolution, arrived right on the invited hour with their pretty daughter Lena, a student, who had inherited her mother's slanting eyes and amber skin.

Mendel immediately started in on foreign policy with Vanya. "The Japanese are spoiling for a fight," he said.

"Please don't talk politics," said Lena, stamping her foot.

"I don't know what else to talk about, sweet one," protested her father in his resonant baritone.

"Exactly!" cried his daughter.

Soon the driveway was jammed with drivers in ZiSes, Buicks and Lincolns trying to park along the grass shoulder, and Sashenka begged Razum to impose some order. Razum, who was blind drunk, shouted, pointed and banged the roofs of cars but ended up handing out vodka to the other drivers and having a party at the gates. The traffic jam got worse and the chauffeurs sang saucy ditties, to Sashenka's amusement. A soused Razum was a feature of her parties.

Inside, Sashenka invited guests to eat at the buffet. They piled their plates with the *zakuski* snacks laid out on the table: pirozhki, blinis, smoked herring and sturgeon, veal cutlets. They drank vodka, cognac, wine and Crimean champagne. It was hard work but she enjoyed it, especially meeting Gideon's new arty friends.

"So this is your niece, Gideon?" said Len Utesov, the jazz singer from Odessa, who would not let go of her hand. "What a beauty! I'm spellbound. Will you run away from your husband and come on tour with me to the Far East? No? She says no, Gideon. What must I do?"

"We love your songs," said Sashenka, basking in the attention and pleased she had worn such a pretty summer dress. "Vanya, let's play Len's record on the gramophone."

"Why play his records," cried Gideon, "when you can play him?"

"Behave yourself, Uncle, or you'll be doing the dishes," teased Sashenka, sweeping her thick brown bob with its streaks of auburn behind her ears.

"With Carolina?" he roared. "Why not? I love all shapes and sizes!"

Vanya called for quiet and toasted May Day—"and our dear Comrade Stalin."

As the light faded, Utesov started to tinkle on the piano, then Tseferman joined him. Soon they were singing the Odessa prison songs together. Uncle Gideon accompanied them on the bayan, a sort of accordion. The pianist from the Art Theater played on the upright piano while the writer Isaac Babel, sturdy but with laughing eyes behind round spectacles and mischief curling his full, playful mouth, leaned on the piano and watched. There was always a party, said Gideon, when Babel was around.

Sashenka had loved his *Red Cavalry* stories, and admired the way he saw things. "Babel is our Maupassant," she told Vanya when he came to watch but he shrugged his shoulders and returned to the study. She stood with the musicians, holding Carlo, who was staying up late, and sang along while the men pretended to sing to her, and Snowy danced around the room in a pink party dress, all long limbs like a new foal, waving her inevitable companion.

As the thieves' songs of the Black Sea wafted over the dacha, Sashenka's guests—writers in baggy cream suits, mustachioed Party men in matching white tunics, peaked caps and wide trousers, a pilot in uniform (one of "Stalin's Eagles"), actresses in Coty perfume and low-cut silk dresses à la Schiaparelli—talked and sang, smoked and flirted. May Days started with the parade in Red Square and ended with a Soviet bacchanalia, from the top down. Somewhere, even Comrade Stalin and his comrades were toasting the Revolution. Vanya had told Sashenka there was a little room for drinks and *zakuski* behind the Mausoleum on Red Square, after which the leaders lunched all afternoon at Marshal Voroshilov's place and then caroused at some dacha in the suburbs until the early hours.

Slightly drunk on the champagne and still strung up with an uneasy elation, Sashenka strolled into the garden and lay down in the hammock between two gnarled apple trees. She could hear herself singing those songs, watching her children, and swinging back and forth as the tipsy world spun a little.

"Sashenka." It was Carolina, the nanny. Carolina appeared dry, serious and formal—but underneath she was very affectionate and loving to the children. Sashenka had chosen her carefully. "Shouldn't we put the children to bed? Carlo's exhausted. He's still so young."

Sashenka could see Carlo, in blue pajamas embroidered with Soviet airplanes, sitting in a chair watching the musicians in a dreamy way. Uncle Gideon was playing his bayan for Snowy, shouting, "Bravo, little Cushion! Hurrah!"

"My cushion, cushion, cushion is dancing with Uncle Gideon," sang the little girl, in her own world. "Giddy-gush, giddy-gush, giddy, giddy-up!"

"Thank you, Carolina," said Sashenka. "Let's put Carlo to bed in a minute. They're having such fun." It was way past their bedtime but when they were older they would be able to boast, "We saw Utesov and Tseferman play thieves' songs together! Yes, in 1939 during the

Second Five Year Plan in the joyous period after the Great Turn, after collectivization and after the times of struggle, at our dacha!"

She congratulated herself on the success of her soirée. Why did they all come to her house? Was it because she was an editor? She was a "Soviet woman of culture" well known for her *partiinost*, her strict Party-mindedness. Was it because men found her attractive? I've never had so much fuss made of me, she thought, and was glad she had worn her white linen summer dress that showed off her tanned shoulders. And then of course there was the attraction of her husband's power. All writers were fascinated by that!

Just then the hammock lurched so violently that she almost fell off.

"So here's the comrade editor of *Soviet Wife and Proletarian Housekeeping* magazine," a mocking voice crooned from behind her.

"You gave me a shock creeping up on me like that," she said, laughing as she swiveled in the hammock to see who had ambushed her. "You should treat the comrade editor with some Soviet respect! Who are you anyway?" she asked, sitting up, pleasurably dizzy from the champagne.

"You didn't invite me," said the man, "but I came anyway. I've heard about your parties. Everyone comes. Or almost everyone."

"You mean I've always forgotten to invite you."

"Precisely, but then I'm very hard to get."

"You don't seem too shy to me. Or too hard to get." She was glad she had worn the Coty perfume. "Then why did you come?"

"I'll give you three guesses who I am."

"You're a mining engineer from Yuzovka?"

"No."

"You're a hero-pilot, one of Stalin's Eagles?"

"No. Last chance."

"You're an important apparatchik from Tomsk?"

"You're tormenting me," he whispered.

"All right then," Sashenka said. "You're Benya Golden, writer. My naughty uncle Gideon said he'd asked you. And I love your Spanish stories."

"Gee, thanks," he said in English with an American accent. "I've always really wanted to write for *Soviet Wife and Proletarian Housekeeping*. It's one of my life's ambitions."

"Now you're mocking me." She sighed, aware of how much she was enjoying talking to this strange man. "But we do need a piece for the autumn on 'How to prepare Happy Childhood chocolate cakes and Soviet Union candies—tasty and nutritious food for the Soviet family.' Or if that doesn't take your fancy, how about a thousand words on the new Red Square perfume produced by Comrade Polina Molotov's Cosmetics Trust? Don't laugh—I'm being serious."

"I wouldn't dare. No one laughs these days without thinking first, especially not at Comrade Polina's perfume, which, as every Soviet woman knows, is a revolution in the struggle of perfumery."

"But you usually handle wars," Sashenka pointed out. "Do you think Benya Golden could handle a *really* serious subject for a change?"

"Yours are truly challenging subjects, Comrade Editor," replied Benya Golden, "and I know you wouldn't tease a poor scribbler."

"Poor scribbler indeed. Your stories sell really well."

There was a silence.

"Must I stand here in holy audience," Benya asked, changing the subject, "or may I sit beside you?"

"Of course." She made space in the hammock. Benya was wearing a white suit with very wide sailor trousers and was looking at her intensely from beneath eyebrows set low over blue eyes with yellow speckles. His fair hair was balding. In the dimming pink light, she could see he had long eyelashes like a girl. She knew he was originally a Jew from Habsburg Galicia, and she remembered her mother saying that Galitzianers were jackanapes and rogues, worse than Litvaks—and Ariadna had probably had personal experience of both. I'm not sure I like him, she decided suddenly; there is something brash about him.

She found herself aware of her movements as she rearranged herself in the hammock, and felt irritated by the way he had crept up on her. He was invading her privacy, and his proximity made her feel shivery inside.

"I have an idea for our article," said Benya. "What about 'The disturbing effect of Red Square ladies' perfume and Moscow Tailoring Factory stockings on those promiscuous shock workers and Stakhanovites in the Magnitogorsk steelworks'? That will really get their furnaces stoked."

He started to laugh and Sashenka thought he must be drunk to say something so clumsy and dangerous.

"I don't much like that idea," she said soberly. She stood up, sending the hammock rocking.

"Now you're behaving like a solemn Bolshevik matron." He lit a cigarette.

"I'll be who I like in my own house. That was an un-Soviet philistine joke. I think you should leave."

She stormed toward the dacha, so furious that she was shaking. She had relaxed for a moment, her head turned by his fame, his presence in her house, but her Party-mindedness now righted her tipsy mind. Was this sneering vulgarian here by coincidence or had he been sent to provoke her into a philistine joke that could ruin her and her family? Why was she so infuriated by his boozy arrogance and pushy flirtatiousness? Wasn't he wary of her husband's position? Her anxiety about her fragile happiness made it all the more unsettling.

Then, stepping from the fuzzy darkness into the light of the house, she saw Carlo asleep in the big chair by the piano. He looked adorable, his upturned nose and closed eyes so innocent. Snowy was sitting on Uncle Gideon's knee, trying to poke the corners of her pink cushion into his mouth while he talked to Utesov about Eisenstein's new movie, *Alexander Nevsky*. Gideon's actress girlfriend, almost a child herself, sat next to them on the sofa, wide-eyed as she listened to Gideon's loud reflections on famous writers, beautiful women and faraway cities.

"Uncle Gideon?" said Sashenka.

"Am I in trouble?" he replied with mock fear.

"I don't much like your friend Golden. I want him to leave." Sashenka scooped up Carlo, kissing him, careful not to wake him.

"Come on, Snowy. Bedtime." Carolina appeared magically at the door and was beckoning to her.

"I don't want to go to bed! I won't go to bed," shouted Snowy. "I'm playing with Uncle Gideon."

Gideon slapped his thigh. "Even I had to go to bed when I was little!"

Sashenka felt suddenly weary of her party and her guests.

"Don't act spoiled, Snowy," she said. "You've had a lovely present today. We've let you stay up and now you're tired."

"I'm NOT tired, you silly—and I want a cuddle with Uncle Hercules!" Snowy stamped her foot and pretended to be very angry indeed—which made Sashenka want to laugh.

The sitting room was at right angles to Vanya's study. As she headed toward the door, Sashenka could make out her husband's curly greying head and barrel chest. He was still in his blue trousers although now sporting his favorite embroidered shirt.

Vanya sat at a desk on which were placed three Bakelite phones, one of them his new orange *vertushka*, the hotline to the Kremlin. He was arguing with Uncle Mendel, one of the few Old Bolsheviks elected to the Central Committee at the 1934 Congress of Victors and re-elected at the Eighteenth Congress. The others had overwhelmingly vanished into the meat grinder and Sashenka knew that most of them had been shot. But Mendel had survived. They were discussing jazz: Soviet versus American. Mendel liked Utesov and Tseferman's Soviet version while Vanya preferred Glenn Miller.

"Vanya," boomed Mendel's trumpet of a voice out of his tiny twisted body, "Soviet jazz reflects the struggle of the Russian worker."

"And American jazz," replied Vanya, "is the music of the Negro struggle against the white capitalists of—"

"I *won't* go to bed," cried Snowy, throwing herself onto the ground.

Vanya leaped up, effortlessly gathered Snowy into his arms and kissed her. "*Bed* before I box your ears!" Vanya put Snowy down and gave her a little push. "*Now!*"

"Yes, Comrade Papa," said Snowy, chastened. "Night, Papochka, night, Uncle Mendel." She skipped out.

"Thank you, Vanya," said Sashenka as she followed with Carlo in her arms.

A car door slammed outside, a light step sounded on the veranda, and the family favorite, Hercules Satinov, smart in a white summer Stalinka tunic, soft cream boots and a white peaked cap, peeped round the corner.

"Where's my Snowy?" he called. "Don't tell Cushion I'm here!"

"Uncle Hercules!" cried Snowy, scampering back into the room, opening her arms to him and kissing him.

Sashenka kissed their friend thrice, bumping into her daughter in the process. "Hercules, welcome. Snowy was longing to see you! But now you've seen him, Snowy, you're going to bed! Say good night to Comrade Satinov!"

"But Mama, Cushion and I want to play with Hercules," Snowy wailed.

"*Bed! Now!*" Vanya shouted and Snowy darted back down the corridor toward her room.

If anything, Sashenka reflected, Hercules Satinov had become better looking with time. His black hair still gleamed with barely a strand of grey. She remembered how he and Vanya had come to collect her when her mother died, how kind they'd been to her. Now she watched as Satinov embraced his best friend, before noticing Mendel and shaking his hand formally.

"Happy May Day, comrades!" he said in his strong Georgian accent. "Sorry I'm late, I had papers to get through at Old Square." Satinov, who had helped run the Caucasus, now worked in the Party Secretariat at the grey granite headquarters on Old Square, up the hill from the Kremlin.

"What a party, Sashenka! The jazz men singing together? Even at receptions for the leaders in St. George's Hall, I've never seen that before. I hope you don't mind, Vanya, some Georgian friends have invited themselves, and they'll be here shortly."

4

"Aren't you leaving?" Uncle Gideon loomed up over Benya Golden, smoking a cigarette on the veranda. "You ideeeot!"

"Gideon, shush. Did you hear what Satinov said? Some Georgians are coming! Which ones? Someone big?" Benya whispered.

"How would I know, you *schmendrik*! They're probably some Georgian singers or cooks or dancers!"

Gideon gripped Benya's hand and pulled him outside into the dark orchard. Benya peered around nervously.

"No one can hear us here," said Gideon, checking that Razum and the drivers were still singing dirty songs at the gates.

"If they're just cooks or singers, why have you dragged me down here and why are you speaking, Gideon, in that bellow of a whisper?"

The sky glowed rosily and warmly, an owl hooted, and the sweet scent of flowers seeped out of the orchard. Gideon liked Benya Golden enormously and admired him as a writer. They both loved women, though as Gideon liked to put it, "I'm an animal while Benya's a romantic." He put his arm around his friend.

"If these Georgians are big bosses," he said, "the less people like *them* know about people like *us*, the better." He remembered his brother Samuil, Sashenka's father, who he assumed was long dead now, and suddenly his chest hurt and he wanted to cry. "Ugh, time to go! Cure your curiosity, Benya! But I'm whispering, you big *schmendrik*, because you've offended my niece. Well?"

"I put my foot in it with the comrade editor. She's no Dushenka," Benya said, "no featherbrain. I had no idea she was so extraordinary. Is she happily married?"

"You ideeeot! Firstly she's Vanya Palitsyn's wife, my dear Benya, and secondly she's never even looked at another man! First love and they've been together ever since. What did you do, pinch her ass, or suggest that Marshal Voroshilov is a blockhead?"

Benya was silent for a minute. "Both," he admitted.

"You Galitzianer *schlemiel*, you tinker!"

"Gideon, what's the difference between a *schlemiel* and a *schlimazel*?"

"The *schlemiel* always spills his drink onto the *schlimazel*."

"So which am I?"

"Both!" Gideon told him and they roared with laughter.

"But the trouble is—I'm short of work," Benya said. "I haven't written for ages. They've noticed of course. I really do need a commission from her magazine."

"What? About how to organize a masked jazz ball for workers celebrating production targets? Have you no shame?" asked Gideon.

"Why did I tease her?" groaned Golden. "Why can I never resist saying things? Now you've got me worried, Gideon. She won't denounce me, will she?"

"I have no idea, Benya. The Organs and the Party are all around us here. You have to behave differently in such houses. Here the softness is only skin-deep."

"That's why I had to come. I want to understand what makes them tick—the men of power and violence. And that Venus with her mysterious, scornful grey eyes is at the center of everything."

"Ahhh, I see. You want to understand the essence of our times and write a *Comédie Humaine* or a *War and Peace* on our Revolution, starring our princess Sashenka from the mansion on Greater Maritime Street? We writers are all the same. My niece's life's a spectator sport, eh?"

"Well, it's quite a story, you must admit. I've met them all—marshals, Politburo members, secret policemen. Some of the killers were as delicate as mimosa; some of those who were crushed by them were as coarse as tar. At Gorky's house, I met the sinister Yagoda, you know, and I once played the guitar with that insane killer Yezhov, at the seaside." Benya was no longer smiling. He looked anxiously at Gideon. "But the meat grinder is over, isn't it?"

"Comrade Stalin says the Terror's over and who am I to disbelieve him?" answered Gideon, who really was whispering now. "Do you think I've survived this long by asking stupid questions? *Me?* Of all people? With *my* family background? I do what I have to—I'm the licensed maverick—and I console myself in holy communion with drink and flesh. I've spent the last three years waiting for the knock on the door—but so far they've let me be."

"*They?* Surely Comrade Stalin didn't know what was happening, did he? Surely it was Yezhov and the Chekists out of control? Now Yezhov's gone; that good fellow Beria has stopped the meat grinder; and, thank God, Comrade Stalin is back in control."

Gideon felt a lurch of fear. Although he regarded himself as a mere journalist, he had, like all the famous writers—Benya himself, Sholokhov, Pasternak, Babel, even Mandelstam before he disappeared—praised Stalin and voted for the Highest Measure of Punishment for Enemies of the People. At meetings of the Writers' Union, he'd raised his hand and voted for the death of Zinoviev, Bukharin, Marshal Tukhachevsky: "Shoot them like mad dogs!" he had said, just like everyone else, just like Benya Golden. Even now he was aware of his rashness in discussing such sensitive questions with the overexcitable Benya. He pulled Benya close, so close his beard tickled his ear.

"It was never only Yezhov!" he murmured. "The orders came from *higher* . . ."

"Higher? What are you saying . . . ?"

"Don't write that book on the Organs and don't tease my niece about Komsomol cakes and the 'furnaces' of female steelworkers! And Benya, you need to write something, something that pleases. We're off to Peredelkino—Fadeyev's having a party and he hands out the writing jobs so you'd better be polite to him this time, and don't hang around here anymore if you ever want to work again!"

"You're right. Shall I say good-bye to Sashenka?"

"Do you want a kick in the balls? I'll get the car and you go and get my girl and tell the frisky little minx we're leaving."

As they left, two black Buick town cars purred into the drive.

"Was that the Georgians?" hissed Benya from the back of Gideon's car. Masha sat silently in the front, lighting a cigarette.

"Don't look back," bellowed Gideon, "or we'll turn into pillars of salt!" He put his foot down and sped away with a screech of tires.

5

The party was over. The half moon poured a milky light into the well of warm darkness outside. Mendel, chain-smoking and coughing up phlegm in guttural thunderclaps, and Satinov, who both worked at Old Square, were talking about rebuilding cadres at the Machine Tractor Stations. Sashenka and Vanya started to tidy up.

Apart from the uneasiness with Benya Golden, it had been a successful evening, Sashenka reflected. In the half darkness a figurine of alabaster nakedness appeared. "Mamochka, I can't sleep," said Snowy, waving her cushion so winningly that Satinov cheered.

Sashenka felt a surge of love. She could not help but indulge her daughter, perhaps remembering her own mother's coldness, but the truth was that she was always happy to see her. "Come and have a quick cuddle! Then back to bed. Don't overexcite her—especially you, Hercules!"

Snowy vaulted into Sashenka's arms.

"Doesn't that cherub ever go to bed?" growled Vanya.

"Mama, I've got to tell you something."

"What, my darling?"

"Cushion woke me up to give Hercules a message!"

"Whisper it to me quickly and then back to bed—or Papochka will get cross."

"Very cross!" said Vanya, who caught them both in a hug and kissed Sashenka's face while Sashenka nuzzled Snowy's silky cheek.

"Mamochka, what are those ghosts doing in the garden?" Snowy asked, pointing over her mother's shoulder.

Sashenka turned and peered through the window.

The "ghosts," four crop-haired young men in white suits, were stepping up onto the veranda.

"Communist greetings, Comrade Palitsyn," said one, as the phone rang in Vanya's office—the one connected to the Kremlin, its tone high-pitched and distinctive.

A few minutes later Vanya returned, his rumpled forehead a little puzzled. He called over to Satinov. "Hercules, that was your friend Comrade Egnatashvili." Sashenka knew that Egnatashvili was a senior secret policeman in charge of Politburo dachas and food. "He says he's coming with some people. We might need some Georgian food . . ."

Satinov looked up from the sofa. "Well, he said he might come. Who's he bringing?"

"He just said Georgian friends."

"Some Georgian food?" asked Sashenka, thinking fast. "It's only midnight. Razum!" The driver appeared, swaying a little, his uniform crooked. "Can you drive?"

Razum had entered that stage of embalmed drunkenness known only to the Russian species of alcoholic: he was so soused he was almost sober again.

"Absolutely, Comrade Sashenka"—and he burped loudly.

"I'll call the Aragvi Restaurant," said Satinov, heading for the phone in the study. The restaurant was in town off Gorky Street.

"Comrade Razum, speed into Moscow to the Aragvi and bring back some Georgian food. Scram!"

Razum leaped off the veranda, lost his footing, nearly fell over, righted himself and made it to the car.

"Wait!" Satinov shouted. "Egnatashvili will bring something. He's got all the best food in Moscow." There was a pause as he and Vanya looked again at the young men in white suits guarding the gates, the suits glowing as if the moon had painted them silver.

"Who's coming, Mamochka?" asked Snowy in the silence.

"Silence, Volya! Bed now!" said Snowy's father, his eyes flashing. He did not use her real name unless he was deadly earnest. "Sashenka, we've got to give that child some discipline . . ."

"Who's coming, do you think?" Sashenka asked Vanya, with a twinge of concern.

"Maybe Lavrenti Pavlovich . . ."

"I think I'll be going. It's been a nice evening," said Mendel, whose wife and daughter had left hours ago. Sashenka noticed he was one of the few leaders who still sported an ill-fitting bourgeois suit and tie, never having embraced the Stalin Party tunic. Mendel pulled out his pillbox and placed a nitroglycerin tablet under his tongue. "Let me call my driver," he muttered to himself. "Can't take those flashy Georgians and all those toasts! Ugh. Too late!"

A convoy of cars drew up at the gate, their powerful beams illuminating the greens and reds of the lush garden. A pall of dust darkened the starry sky, reaching for the moon. The ghosts in the white suits opened the gates to reveal several black Lincolns and a new ZiS.

The piano tinkled from inside, there was laughter from a nearby dacha, and Sashenka saw a blond athletic figure in the familiar blue and red-striped uniform jump out of the front car.

Satinov called out in Georgian: "*Gagimajos!*" And in Russian: "'It's Egnatashvili and he's brought some food!" Sashenka could see that Egnatashvili was carrying a crate of wine. Guards in blue uniforms materialized, as if from nowhere, at the gates.

"Come on in, comrades," said Sashenka. "Satinov said you might join us."

Comrade Egnatashvili's eyes gleamed up at her in the dark, eyes narrowed in warning, as she moved forward to welcome the new guests, hand outstretched—and then froze.

6

Lavrenti Beria, round faced and olive skinned, in baggy white trousers and an embroidered Georgian blouse, was carrying a box full of plates. He was, as Sashenka knew well, the new People's Commissar for Internal Affairs, boss of the secret police, the NKVD.

"Lavrenti Pavlovich! Welcome!" Vanya stepped down from the veranda. "Let me help you with that . . ."

"I'll take it in, don't you worry," Beria said, with a glance behind him.

Sashenka saw Vanya stiffen to attention—and then the night went quiet and next door the singing and the clink of glasses hushed.

A statue seemed to be standing right there in her garden.

Comrade Stalin, his feline, almost oriental face smiling and flushed and still singing a Georgian song, appeared at the foot of the steps in a white summer tunic, wide trousers and light brown boots embroidered in red thread. The moon seemed to throw him his own spotlight.

"We heard Comrade Satinov was going to a party given by Comrade Palitsyn," said Stalin in a soft Georgian accent, chuckling like a mischievous satyr. "Then we heard he had invited Comrade Egnatashvili. Comrade Beria said he was invited too. This meant only Comrade Stalin was left out and Comrade Stalin wanted to chat to Comrade Satinov. So I appealed to my comrades, admitting I didn't know Comrade Palitsyn well enough to crash his party. 'Let's put it to a vote,' I said. The vote went my way, and my comrades decided they would invite me. But I come at my own risk. I won't hold it against you, comrade hosts, if you send me home again. But we do bring some wine and Georgian delicacies. Comrades, where's the table?"

Satinov stepped forward.

"Comrade Stalin, you already know Comrade Palitsyn a little," said Satinov, "and this is his wife, Sashenka, whom you may remember . . ."

"Please come in, Comrade Stalin, what an honor," said Sashenka, finally finding her voice. She had a terrifying and un-Bolshevik urge to curtsy as she used to at the Smolny before the portrait of the Dowager Empress. She was not quite sure how she managed the steps down to the garden, yet somehow she approached Stalin—smaller, older, sallower and much wearier than she remembered, his left arm held in stiffly. He had, she noticed, a slight potbelly, and his tunic's pockets were roughly darned. But then she supposed giants did not care about such things.

Stalin seemed amazed at the effect he had—and yet he reveled in it. He took her hand and kissed it in the old Georgian way, looking up at her with eyes of honey and gold.

"Comrade Snowfox, you're beautifully dressed."

He remembers my old Party alias from St. Petersburg! What a memory! How embarrassing! How flattering! she thought in confusion.

"It is lucky that you and your magazine are teaching Soviet women the art of dressing. Your dress is very pretty," he continued, climbing the steps.

"Thank you, Comrade Stalin." She reminded herself not to mention that her dress had been made abroad.

"For once, comrades, the Party has appointed the right person to the right job . . ." Stalin laughed and the others laughed too, even Mendel. "Come and join us, Comrades Satinov and Palitsyn. And you, Comrade Mendel." Sashenka noticed that Stalin did not show much enthusiasm for the austere Mendel.

Beria affably poked Palitsyn in the stomach as he passed. "Good to see you, Vanya." He clicked his tongue. "All quiet? Everything running smoothly?"

"Absolutely. Welcome to my home, Lavrenti Pavlovich!"

"What did you think of the soccer? Spartak need to be taught a lesson, and if our strikers don't play better next time I'll bust their guts!" Beria clapped his hands cheerfully. "Will you come and play basketball on my team tomorrow? We're playing Voroshilov's guards."

"I'll be there, Lavrenti Pavlovlich."

Sashenka knew that her husband admired Beria, who worked like a horse. He was young, his round face smooth and unlined.

"May I sit down here?" asked Stalin modestly, pointing at the table.

"Of course, Comrade Stalin, wherever you wish," she said.

Comrade Egnatashvili laid out the food on the table and Sashenka leaned across for the wine bottle.

"Let me open it," said Stalin. He poured glasses of the earthy red wine for everyone. Then he put some lobio beans, with their rich Georgian broth, into a bowl, tossed in some bread and added a plate on top to let the bread soak. He helped himself to shashlik lamb and Georgian spicy chicken, *satsivi*, and carried this assortment back to his place. Egnatashvili, blond and handsome in his well-cut uniform, with bulging wrestler's shoulders, stood towering over Stalin, helping himself to the same dishes. Both of them sat down and started to eat, Egnatashvili tasting his lobio a moment earlier than Stalin. He really was Stalin's food taster, Sashenka thought.

"Comrade Satinov," Stalin said quietly, gesturing for Satinov to sit beside him, with Beria on the other side. Egnatashvili, Vanya and Mendel were farther down the table.

"Lavrenti Pavlovich, who shall be *tamada*?" Stalin asked Beria.

"Comrade Satinov should be toastmaster!" suggested Beria.

Satinov rose, holding up a Georgian wineglass in the curved shape of an ox's horn, and made his first toast. "To Comrade Stalin, who has led us through such difficult times to shining triumphs!"

"Surely you can think of something more interesting than that!" joked Stalin, but everyone in the house stood up and drank to him.

"To Comrade Stalin!"

"Not *him* again," protested Stalin. His voice was surprisingly soft and high. "Let me make a toast: to Lenin!"

Other toasts followed: to the Red Army, to their hosts, to Sashenka and Soviet women. Sashenka observed everything, topping up the glasses then rejoining the table. She wanted to remember every moment of this scene. Stalin bantered with Satinov in Georgian but Sashenka sensed the Leader was watching him, evaluating him. She knew that Stalin liked simple, decent young people who were ruthless and vigorous but easygoing and cheerful. Satinov was hardworking and competent but he was always singing opera to himself.

Mendel started coughing.

"How's your lungs, Mendel?" Stalin asked, listening patiently as Mendel answered with an excess of medical detail. "Mendel and I shared a cell at the Bailovka Prison in Baku in 1908," Stalin informed the table.

"Right," said Mendel, stroking his modest goatee.

"And Mendel had a food hamper from his indulgent family and he shared it with me."

"Right, I shared with all the comrades in the cell," said Mendel in his starchy, pettifogging way, making clear there was no favoritism in his comradeship. But only one cellmate mattered, thought Sashenka.

"That's Mendel! Incorruptible author of that best-selling tome *Bolshevik Morality*! You haven't changed in the slightest, Mendel," said Stalin teasingly but with a straight face. "You were old then and you're old now!" He chuckled and the others joined in. "But we've all aged . . ."

"Not at all, Comrade Stalin," insisted Egnatashvili, Vanya and Beria simultaneously. "You look great, Comrade Stalin."

"That's enough of that," said Stalin. "Mendel once told me off for drinking too much at a meeting when we exiles shared that old stable in Siberia, and he's still giving everyone a hard time!"

Sashenka remembered how Mendel had backed Stalin in the Control Commission ever since Lenin's death, never wavering during the famine of '32, nor hesitating to smash the "bastards" to smithereens at the Plenums of '37.

"In fact," Stalin teased Mendel, "I often have to hold him back or he'll froth at the mouth and have a seizure!" Everyone laughed at Mendel because his pedantic fanaticism was notorious. But it was also the reason that Mendel was still alive.

Stalin sipped his wine, his half-slit eyes flicking from person to person.

"Would you like some music, Comrade Stalin?" suggested Satinov.

Stalin smiled like a cat. When he started to sing "Suliko," all the Georgians joined in. Then Satinov called out, "Black Swallow." Stalin grinned and, without missing a beat, took the lead in a beautiful, high tenor, backed by Egnatashvili in a baritone, and Beria and Satinov in polyphonic harmonies. Sashenka listened entranced.

Fly away, black swallow,
Fly along the Alazani River,
Bring us back the news
Of the brothers gone to war . . .

They sang more songs: hymns, and the Odessan thieves' songs "Murka" and "From Odessa Jail." They crooned Stalin's favorite gangster tunes: "*They've buried the gold, the gold, the gold . . .*" Sashenka wondered if Stalin was choosing the songs to put everyone at their ease: the Orthodox hymns for the Russians, the harmonies for the Georgians, Odessan numbers for the Jews—yes, that was Mendel's deep voice enriching "From Odessa Jail."

"We need some hot women here!" said Beria. "But I've drunk too much. I don't think I could even . . ."

"Comrade Beria, observe the proprieties! There are ladies present," said Stalin, with mock gravity and a slight smirk. "Shall we play the gramophone? Do you have records? Some dances?"

Sashenka brought out their collection. Thank God, Satinov always gave them a Georgian gramophone record for May Day and November 8, so Stalin found exactly what he wanted. He stood at the gramophone and played the records; sometimes he raised his hands and made Caucasian dance steps but mostly he directed the festivities.

The Georgians pushed back the sofa. Sashenka rolled up the carpet and when she got up she found Satinov and Egnatashvili dancing the *lezginka* to her. She preferred the tango, the foxtrot and the rumba but she knew the Caucasian moves too, so she made the dainty steps while first Satinov, then Beria and Egnatashvili set to her.

"Comrade Hercules, you can really dance," said Stalin approvingly. "I haven't seen anyone dance so well since I was a boy . . . Where's your family from?"

"Borzhomi," answered Hercules Satinov.

"Not far from my hometown," said Stalin, restarting the record. This was Georgian talk but Sashenka agreed with Stalin: Satinov danced gracefully. His dark eyes shone, his steps were lithe and agile, and his hands were elegant and expressive. He held her firmly, while Beria's hand squeezed her and he put his face too close. His lips were so fat it seemed as if there was too much blood in them. Presently, she felt tired and stood back to watch. She found herself next to the gramophone where Stalin was laying out the records.

Sashenka felt happy suddenly, and at ease, almost too relaxed. She'd been terrified when first she saw Stalin, right there in her garden. But he had relaxed them all and now she was fighting against her instinct to flirt and chatter. She was overexcited and probably drunk on that heavy Georgian red. Several times, crazy things were on the tip of her tongue. Be careful, Sashenka, she ordered herself, this is Stalin! Remember the last few years—the meat grinder! Beware!

Waves of devotion rolled over her for this tough yet modest man, so decent yet so pitiless toward his enemies. But she sensed her cloying devotion would irritate him, make him uneasy. She wanted to ask him to dance. What if he was longing to dance with her? But what if such an offer was insolent or made him uncomfortable? Yet she wanted to dance with him and he must have seen it on her lips.

"I don't dance, Sashenka, because I can't hold a woman with my arm." His left arm was a little shorter than his right—it was why he held it stiffly. They stood beside the piano and she was aware of the tense silence, of the danger that surrounded this extraordinary man.

"I adore this music, Comrade Stalin."

"Music relaxes the beast in a man," said Stalin. He looked about him. "Are you and Comrade Palitsyn happy with this dacha?"

"Oh yes, Comrade Stalin," she answered. "So happy."

"I hope so. May I look around?"

Beria and the others watched but did not follow them, and Sashenka was immensely proud and stirred that Stalin was talking only to her.

"We're so grateful for it—and today we received the refrigerator. Thank you for the Party's trust!"

"We have to reward the Party's responsible workers." Stalin looked into Vanya's study. "Is it warm enough in winter? I like the study, very airy. Are there enough bedrooms? Do you like the kitchen?"

Oh yes, Sashenka loved everything about it. She fought her giddiness, her feelings of joy and freedom as an unspeakable but powerful thought crossed her mind. She was thinking of her father, Samuil Zeitlin. Couldn't she ask Comrade Stalin now? She was so intimate with him at that moment: how could he refuse her anything? She could tell he admired her as a new Soviet woman.

"Comrade Stalin . . . ," she began.

Her father had lost his mind after Ariadna's suicide and his fortune after the October Revolution. He had stayed behind in St. Petersburg, put his financial knowledge at the service of the Bolsheviks, and during the twenties he had served as a "non-Party specialist" in the People's Commissariats of Finance and Foreign Trade, then the State Bank, before he was purged in 1930 as a "wrecker with Trotskyite tendencies." Yet they let him retire to Georgia. Beria had arrested him there in 1937—and he had vanished. Of course, they were right to "check" this class enemy, thought Sashenka. On paper, Zeitlin was among the worst of the bloodsucking oppressors. But he had "disarmed" and had served Soviet power sincerely, without a mask. Surely Stalin would see he was no longer a threat?

Stalin smiled indulgently at Sashenka. He looked, she thought, like a friendly old tiger, creases forming on either side of his mouth—and she hesitated for a second. The honey in his eyes sharpened to yellow and a shadow of embarrassment crossed his face. She suddenly grasped that Stalin must recognize her expression. He, who could divine everything, could tell she was about to ask about the arrest or execution of a relative and there was nothing he hated so much as that request.

"Comrade Stalin, may I ask a . . ." The words were forming again on Sashenka's lips and she could not stop them. She had excised her father from her memory in 1937 but now, at this most unsuitable, most fatal and yet opportune moment, she longed to say his name. What was happening to her? A Bolshevik didn't need a family, just the Party, but she loved her papa! She wanted to know—was he felling logs somewhere? Were his bones in some shallow grave out in the Siberian taiga? Had he long since faced the Highest Measure? Please, Comrade Stalin, she prayed, say he's alive! Free him! "Comrade Stalin . . ."

"Cushions!" Stalin and Sashenka turned to the doorway, and Vanya's mouth fell open. "Mamochka, I can't sleep!" cried Snowy. "There's so much noise. You woke me up. I want a cuddle!"

Snowy was wearing a nightie printed with butterflies, her long golden hair curling around her rosy cheeks, her smile revealing evenly spaced milk teeth and pink gums. She fell into her mother's arms.

7

"Snowy!" Vanya, who had been cheerfully drunk a minute earlier, stood up, his face darkening. Sashenka too sensed real peril. She had tried to teach her children to say nothing, repeat nothing, hear nothing, but Snowy was capable of anything! With Stalin in the house? One foolish word, a single stupid game could at best make a fool of her and Vanya in front of Stalin, at worst dispatch them all to the firing squad. What would Stalin say? What would Snowy say to Stalin?

"Who's this?" asked Stalin quietly, apparently enjoying Vanya's expression of panic.

"Comrade Stalin," said Sashenka, "may I introduce you to my daughter, Volya."

Stalin beamed at her daughter. Didn't all Georgians love children? thought Sashenka, as he bent down and tickled her nose. "Hello, Volya," he said. "That's a good Communist name."

"That noise woke me up," Snowy grumbled.

Stalin pinched her cheek.

"Stop!" she cried. "You're pinching me!"

"Yes, so you'll remember me," said Stalin. "I confess my guilt before you, Comrade Volya. It was me playing the music, not your mama, so be angry with me."

"She's not angry at all. I apologize, Comrade Stalin," Sashenka said quickly. "Now, Snowy, off to bed!"

"I hate sleeping."

"Me too . . . Snowy," said Stalin playfully.

"Here's my cushion!" Snowy pushed her cushion toward Stalin's face but Sashenka caught it just in time.

"Well, what's that?" asked Stalin, bemused, half smiling.

"It's my best friend, Miss Cushion," said Snowy. "She's in charge of production of cushions for the Second Five Year Plan and she wants to join the Young cushiony Pioneers so she can wear the red scarf!"

"That's enough, child," Sashenka said. "Comrade Stalin doesn't want to hear such nonsense! Off to bed!" She was aware that, on the other side of the room, her husband had raised a hand to his face.

"Yes, bed!" he said too loudly.

"Easy, Comrade Palitsyn," said Stalin, ruffling Snowy's hair. "Couldn't she stay up a little? As a treat?"

"Well . . . of course, Comrade Stalin."

Snowy performed a quick cushion dance and blew a kiss to her father.

"So you're a Cushionist?" said Stalin solemnly.

"I'm in the Cushion Politburo," said Snowy with that gummy smile. Sashenka saw she was thrilled to find herself the focus of all eyes. "Long Live Cushionism!"

Sashenka felt as though she were drowning, as she waited miserably for Stalin's reaction. There was a long silence. Beria sneered. Mendel scowled. Stalin frowned, glancing gravely round the room with his yellow eyes.

"I think, since I woke her up," said Stalin slowly, "we should let this little beauty stay up and join our singing, but if your parents think you should go to bed . . ." Sashenka shook her glossy head, and Stalin raised a finger: "I resolve: one, the Party recognizes that Cushionism is not a deviation. Two, if you stay up, you should sit on my knee and tell me about Cushionism! Three: you will go to bed when your mother says so. How is that, young Comrade Snowy Cushion?"

Snowy nodded then peered at Stalin with her very blue discerning gaze. She raised her arm.

"I know you," she said, pointing. Sashenka flinched again.

Stalin said nothing, watching.

"You're the poster in the Red Corner," said Snowy. "The poster's come for dinner." Everyone laughed, Sashenka and Vanya with relief.

Stalin sat back at the table and opened his arms. Terrified that her daughter would reject Stalin, Sashenka put Snowy onto the Leader's knee, but she was much more interested in waving the cushion to the music. They sang another round of songs. After the first song, Stalin put Snowy down, kissed her forehead and she sped round to her mother.

"Say good night and thanks to Comrade Stalin," said Sashenka, holding Snowy tightly.

"Night, night, Comrade Cushion," said Snowy, waving her pink cushion.

"I'm sorry, Comrade Stalin . . ."

"No, no. That's a first!" Stalin laughed. "Good-bye, Comrade Cushion."

Sashenka carried Snowy from the room. "Comrade Stalin, you are so good with children. She'll remember this all her life. I can't thank you enough for your kindness and tolerance to Snowy." Sighing with relief, she tucked Snowy into bed and the child was asleep a moment later.

When she returned to the sitting room, she was holding something. Stalin's eyes flicked toward her hands. "Comrade Stalin, as a small thank you for the honor of having you as our guest, but really to thank you for your patience with our daughter, may I give you a gift of a sweater for your daughter Svetlana?" She held up a cashmere sweater that would fit the thirteen-year-old Svetlana Stalin and handed it to him.

"Where's it from?" Stalin asked coldly.

Sashenka swallowed. It was from Paris. What should she say?

"It's from abroad, Comrade Stalin. I am very proud of our Soviet products, which are better than any foreign luxuries, but this is just a simple sweater."

"I wouldn't accept it for myself," said Stalin, puffing on a cigarette, "but since Svetlana is really the one who runs the country, I shall accept it for her." Everyone laughed and Stalin stood up. "Right! Who's up for a movie? I want to see *Volga, Volga* again."

Almost everyone except Sashenka, who had to listen for the children, and Comrade Mendel, who said he was too tired and ill, was up for a movie. They piled into the cars to drive back to the movie theater in the Great Kremlin Palace. Stalin kissed Sashenka's hand and complimented her dress again. Outside, he inspected the buds on the bushes.

"You grow roses here. And jasmine. I love roses." Then, surrounded by the swaggering Georgians and the young men in white suits, he lumbered away in that heavy, slightly crooked gait, toward the waiting cars. Egnatashvili opened the door for him.

As he climbed into one of the cars, Vanya waved at Sashenka, exhilarated to be in the entourage for the first time. "Back soon, darling!" he called.

Beria kissed her on the mouth with his sausagey, blood-swollen lips. "*He* likes you," he said in his thick Mingrelian accent. "Well done. He's got good taste, the Master. You're my type too!"

Satinov was last to leave, peering round to make sure the bosses were in their cars. Doors slamming, wheels screeching, the clouds of exhaust and dust rising over the moon-kissed orchards, the Buicks and ZiSes revved up and skidded out of the drive.

"Phew, Sashenka!" he said. "Long live Cushionism! Kiss my goddaughter for me, the little charmer!" Feeling weak, Sashenka kissed Satinov good-bye. Then he jumped into the last car, which sped away.

The young men in white suits had disappeared.

Alone on the veranda, Sashenka looked up at the sky. Dawn had begun to break. Wondering if she had been dreaming, she went inside and looked into the children's rooms.

Carlo had slept through it all but he had thrown off his pajamas and now lay naked with his head at the wrong end of the bed. His body was still wrapped in the pink fleshy curves of a baby and he held on to a soft rabbit. Sashenka shook her head with pleasure and kissed his satiny forehead.

Snowy slept like an angel in her pink room, her hands resting open on her pillow, on either side of her head. That damn cushion lay on her bare chest. Sashenka smiled. Even Comrade Stalin loved Cushion. What a strange night it had been.

8

Stalin sat in the middle pullout seat between the front and back seats of his new ZiS limousine, Beria in the back with Egnatashvili, and his chief bodyguard, Vlasik, in the front beside the driver. The rest were in other cars.

"To the Kremlin please, Comrade Salkov," he told the driver gently. He knew the names and circumstances of all his bodyguards and drivers, was always kind to them and they were devoted to him. "Take the Arbat."

"Right, Comrade Stalin," said the driver. Stalin lit his pipe.

They sped down avenues of birch and spruce, the blossoms bright in the moonbeams. They came out on the Mozhaisk Highway, and took Dorogomilov Street.

"She's a good Soviet woman, Sashenka," said Stalin after a while to Beria, "don't you think so, Lavrenti? And Vanya Palitsyn's a good worker."

"Agreed," said Beria.

The convoy was on the Borodino Bridge with its stone bulls, its colonnades and obelisks, and about to cross Smolensk Square.

"That Sashenka can dance all right," mused Egnatashvili, who was no politician but lived for sports, food, horses and girls.

"And she can edit too," joked Stalin, "though that magazine's hardly an academic journal. But that sort of housekeeping shit is important.

Soviet women need to know these things." They sped down the Arbat. "But what a family! She still has hints of her alien bourgeois origins—did you know she was at the Smolny? But she doesn't bore us with stupid lectures like Molotov's wife. Keeps home, makes cakes, raises children, works for the Party. She's 'reforged' herself into a decent Soviet woman."

"Agreed, Comrade Stalin," said Beria.

"This'll be about the tenth time I've seen *Volga, Volga*," said Stalin. "It's always like a holiday every time I see it! I think I know it by heart!"

"Me too," said Beria.

They were approaching the Kremlin along wide empty roads, the security cars in front, alongside and behind. The blood-red towers of the medieval fortress appeared up ahead of them, gates opening slowly, preparing to swallow them up. Guards saluted. The wheels gave rubber gulps over the cobbles. "Ivan the Terrible walked here," said Stalin quietly. It had been his home for more than twenty years, longer than he had spent in his mother's house, longer than the Seminary.

Stalin looked round at Beria, whose eyes were closed.

"Tell me, Lavrenti," he said loudly, pointing his pipe, and Beria awoke with a start. "Where's Sashenka's father, Zeitlin the capitalist? I remember we checked him out. Is he still with you at one of your places or was he shot? Can we find out?"

9

"I like the article 'How to Do the Foxtrot,'" said Sashenka, inspecting the proofs at her T-shaped desk. "Are you happy with it, comrades?"

Two days had passed, and she was in the offices of *Soviet Wife and Proletarian Housekeeping* on Petrovka. There were portraits of Stalin, Pushkin and Maxim Gorky on the walls; photographs of Vanya Palitsyn in uniform last May Day parade with Snowy and Carlo stood on her desk; and one grey Bakelite telephone and a very small grey safe sat on a table in the corner. The size of the safe, the number of phones and the quality of the Stalin portraits were signs of power. This was not a powerful office.

"We must entertain our readers, of course, Comrade Editor," said Klavdia Klimov, the pointy-faced, bug-eyed deputy editor who dressed in the hideous shrouds of the Moscow Tailoring Factory. "But shouldn't we also look at the class implications of foxtrot?"

Sashenka was a master at playing this game: she was herself a believer and took the journal's mission seriously. She might still be a little dizzy from the excitements of the May Day holiday, but she knew the rules: never talk about the bosses and especially not the Master. Nonetheless, she hoped somehow the story would leak out. She wanted Klavdia and the three other editors in her office to know who had come to visit the Palitsyns on May Day night! After all, Comrade Stalin had endorsed the journal and her work, so shouldn't she share this with her comrades? Several times it was on the tip of her tongue but even she balked at the scale of this name-dropping and she swallowed it . . . Back to the foxtrot and jazz dancing.

"Do we agree with Comrade Deputy Editor? A vote?" All five of them raised their hands. "Can we resolve to commission a further piece on jazz dancing as an expression of the American capitalist's oppression of the Negroes? Klavdia, would you write it yourself or do you have a writer in mind? And photographs? Should we pose a shot with professional dancers or send someone down to the Metropole one night?"

The editors agreed to pose a shot: there were sometimes alien elements at the Metropole. Finally they dispersed. The meeting was over. Sashenka took out a Herzegovina Flor cigarette and lit it with her lighter. She offered them round. The other four lit up too.

"You know, Utesov and Tseferman played at our house on the holiday," Sashenka said, unable to prevent herself from a little harmless boasting.

There was an awkward silence and immediately Sashenka regretted it. "Would they give an interview to the magazine?" asked Klavdia.

"Well, I couldn't ask them then and there," said Sashenka, blowing out blue smoke. "But I'll give it some thought."

Just then there was a knock on the door. Sashenka's secretary, Galya, stood in the doorway.

"There's a writer waiting to see you."

"Does he have an appointment?"

"No, but he's very arrogant. He says you'll know who he is and he wants to apologize."

There was a leap in Sashenka's belly as if she had driven over a hill too fast. "That must be Benya Golden," she said dismissively. "What impudence! A very rude man. Tell him I haven't got time, Galya."

"Benya Golden?" said their one male editor, Misha Kalman. He had gotten up to leave but now he put his briefcase down again. "Will he write for the journal?"

"How do you know *him*?" asked Klavdia almost accusingly, eyes bulging. She remained in her seat, and when she inhaled she made a wet sucking sound.

"I don't know him. But he came to the dacha on the weekend."

"It must have been quite a party," said the deputy editor in her shapeless brown shift dress. "Utesov, Tseferman—and now Golden too." Sashenka wished she had not boasted about the guest list. She turned to Galya.

"I don't wish to see him. He should make an appointment. Besides, I hear he's washed up. He hasn't written a thing for two years. Tell him to go, Galya."

"Right, comrade," said Galya.

"No, wait," said Misha Kalman, whose voice was high and quizzical.

Galya turned as if to leave the room.

"Tell him, Galya," Sashenka insisted, and Galya moved toward the door.

"Hang on!" said Kalman. "I'm a fan of his work. We so rarely get writers of his quality in the journal. *Carpe diem!*"

Klavdia's protuberant eyes, like those of a big red crab, swiveled at Sashenka. "Are you allowing individualism to penalize the collective?" she asked.

Sashenka sensed danger in overplaying her dislike. Bathing in the majesty of Stalin himself, she felt suddenly generous. Besides, maybe she had overreacted at her party? Had Benya been that bad?

"Wait a minute, Galya," she said at last, and Galya, giggling this time, stopped.

"Comrades, we need to decide if we really want him to write for *Soviet Wife and Proletarian Housekeeping.*"

Klavdia pointed out that Golden had been a member of the delegation to the Writers' Congress in Paris in 1936 with Ehrenburg, Babel and others, and that he had been involved in the Pushkin Centenary of 1937.

"His stories are unforgettable," said Kalman, ruffling his grey corkscrew curls as he praised Benya's writing on the Spanish Civil War. Sashenka recalled that some of the generals Benya knew had been unmasked as Enemies of the People and executed in 1937/8. His patron, Gorky, was dead and many other writers had been liquidated.

"But why hasn't Golden written anything lately?" she inquired. "Is this a protest against the Party or is it on 'guidance' from the Culture Section at Old Square?"

"I'll call Fadeyev at the union," said Klavdia, "and Zhdanov's cultural apparat at the Central Committee. I'll take soundings."

"Proposal accepted. What would you like him to write, Klavdia?"

"Could he write about how the Bolshevik Cake Factory has made the largest chocolate cake in the world in the shape of a tank for Comrade Voroshilov's birthday? Golden could interview the workers and reveal how they used Bolshevik ingenuity to create the tank's gun barrel out of cookies and wafers . . ."

The Bolshevik Cake Factory loomed large in the magazine's features but Sashenka frowned as she imagined Benya's reaction to a cake story, however grand and military in design.

"Or how about the dancing piece?" suggested Klavdia. "Under my close supervision."

"Comrade, you yourself had a better idea," said Sashenka. "Remember the work of our Women's Committee. You suggested a piece on the orphanage for children of Enemies of the People!"

"It's a heartwarming story of class redemption and the reforging of identity," said Klavdia.

"Surely that's the piece for a serious writer in our pages? We'll run it big, a cover story, five thousand words. I heard the place is delightful and many children are adopted into warm Soviet homes. So, comrades, shall I ask him to do the piece on the Felix Dzerzhinsky Communal Orphanage for Children of Traitors to the Motherland?"

Sashenka felt tired. It was already 7:00 p.m. and Carlo had woken at six that morning and climbed into her bed. Outside, Moscow basked in the vermilion light of a May evening. Despite the Five Year Plan and the signs of building work everywhere, there was still something primitive about Moscow. The streets were half empty and there were not many cars. A horse and carriage clipped along Petrovka, delivering vegetables.

"Thank you, comrades!" said Sashenka. "Resolution carried." Her comrades filed out of the room. "Galya?"

"Final decision, comrades?" Galya joked, popping her head round the corner.

"Send him in, and you can go home."

A moment later, Benya Golden stood in her office.

"I can't talk in this ink-shitting bureaucratic morgue," he exclaimed in his gravelly voice. "The breeze outside is so balmy, it'll make you want to sing. Follow me!"

Afterward, long afterward, when she had too much time to replay these moments, Sashenka knew this was where it had all started. Her blood pounding in her ears, she walked with him to the elevators, then stopped.

"I've left something on my desk, Benya. I must grab it. Excuse me!"

She left him in the foyer and ran back to her office. Her fingers touching her lips, she looked at her desk, her photographs of Vanya and the children, her phone, her proofs, at everyone and everything that was important to her. She told herself this preening man was bad news. He was rude, arrogant, insincere and lacking Party-mindedness (he was not even a Party member)—and not as afraid of life as he should be. She should not go walking with him.

Then, aware of what she was doing yet curiously unable to stop herself, she turned around and walked back to where Benya Golden was waiting for her.

10

"This is one of those rare moments when no one knows where we are," said Benya Golden as they walked in the Alexander Gardens beside the red crenellated fortress towers of the Kremlin, which reached up to pierce the pink sky.

"You know, sometimes you strike me as very naïve for a writer," replied Sashenka briskly, remembering his foolish comments at the dacha. "We're both well known and we're walking in the most famous park in the city."

"That's true but no one's watching us."

"How do you know?"

"Well, I told no one I was coming to your office, and you told no one we were going for a walk around Moscow. I was on my way home to my wife, and you were on your way to your husband at the Granovsky. So there was no reason to follow either of us. Your comrades imagine we're earnestly discussing commissions in your office. If they cared, the Organs would assume that we were going home as we always do."

"Except we didn't."

"Precisely, Sashenka, if I may call you that. Anyway no one would recognize me in my hat." Benya doffed his white peaked cap and bowed low.

"Well, they'd certainly recognize you now," she said, looking at the fair spiky strands of his receding hair.

"Look around you. The whole of Moscow is promenading tonight. Don't you ever want to be rid of your responsibilities? Just for an hour."

Sashenka sighed. "Just for an hour." The soothing balmy air caressed her skin and reached into her white dress, inflating and rippling the cool cotton so she felt as light and gay as a sail on the wind. Golden was walking faster, talking as quickly, and she struggled to keep up, almost running in her high heels.

She thought about her responsibilities. There was her husband, conventional, industrious and successful, and their two mercurial, spirited cherubs in the bloom of health and happiness. They had two residences, the new dacha and the huge new apartment in the pink Granovsky building known as the Fifth House of Soviets in that little street near the Kremlin. There were the service workers: Carolina the nanny and cook, Razum the driver, the gardeners, the groom. Then there were Vanya's parents, who lived with them at the apartment—they were a full-time job in themselves, especially Vanya's mother, who sat in the yard all day gossiping in a dangerously loud voice. She considered Vanya's stressful, prestigious position, and her own duties on the Women's Committee and the Party Committee. They both had hectic lives; war was coming; they had to build their socialist world; they were emerging from deep sorrow and tragedy; many had vanished beneath the waves of revolution. That night, like most nights, Vanya would work until dawn—everyone did, following the Master's nocturnal hours. Vanya told her how the leaders sat at their desks waiting until the words came down the *vertushka*: "The Master's just left the Little Corner for the Nearby Dacha."

Now, there was something big going on. After Munich, Stalin was changing his foreign policies—and his ministers. This was significant for the future of Europe—but it also meant that Vanya was busy working on the changes at the People's Commissariat for Foreign Affairs.

As usual when he had secrets to share, he had pulled Sashenka into the garden at the dacha. "Litvinov's out; Molotov's in. I'll be busy for a few days," he had told her.

Sashenka knew that meant she would not see Vanya at night either and she must not mention this to anyone. Meanwhile Vanya's parents were babysitting Snowy and Carlo at the Granovsky apartment.

Feeling lighthearted suddenly in Benya's company, Sashenka stopped and twirled around like a girl. "Just for an hour. I can be lost for an hour. What a delicious idea!"

Her words sounded indulgently extravagant somehow—not like her at all, and she wanted to take them back.

"You were a Party member before the Revolution, weren't you, Comrade Snowfox?" said Benya. "You must have been adept at dodging the Okhrana spooks. So are we being followed?"

She shook her head. "No. Our Organs have never been as good at surveillance as the Okhrana was."

"Careful, Comrade Editor! Rash talk!"

She could see that he was teasing her. "And yet I feel I can trust you."

"You can, I promise you that," said Benya. "Isn't it wonderful sometimes to be able to escape one's duties and be completely selfish for a while?"

"We Communists can never do that," she objected. "We mothers can never do it either . . ."

"Oh, for heaven's sake, just shut up and try it for a bit. Time is so short."

Sashenka said nothing, but she was shocked and her head spun with a sort of vertigo.

They walked around the Kremlin. The Great Palace shimmered glass and gold beneath the evening sky. They passed the brooding dark modernist labyrinth of Government House on the Embankment, where Satinov, Mendel and many other bosses lived, where so many had been arrested in the dark times, where the elevators had groaned all night, as the NKVD drove people away in their Black Crows. There was no traffic on the streets now, just a couple of horses and carts—and an old lady selling greasy pirozhki from a kiosk.

Moscow, thought Sashenka, once called the city of a thousand cupolas because there were so many churches, is a grim place. Comrade Stalin will beautify it and make it a worthier capital for the workers of the world, but now it's still partly palatial, partly a collection of villages—and the rest is just a building site. She had one of her periodic pangs of nostalgia for her home city: St. Petersburg—or Leningrad, as it was now called, the cradle of revolution.

I love you, Peter's creation, she thought, quoting Pushkin.

"You're missing Piter, aren't you?" said Benya, out of the blue.

"How did you know?"

"I can read you, can't you tell?"

She could, and it made her very uneasy.

They stood on the Stone Bridge, looking down on the Great Palace and the Moskva River, the whole of the city reflected and amplified in tiny detail as if it were resting on a mirror.

"Will you dance with me?" he asked, taking her hand.

"Here?" Goosebumps covered her arms and legs.

"Just here."

"You really are the most foolish man." She felt dizzy again, and recklessly young, and her skin scintillated where he touched her as he took her in his arms, confidently, and turned her left and left, back and forth in the foxtrot, all the time singing a Glenn Miller song in an American accent, in perfect tune.

When they parted, his body seemed to leave a burning imprint on her belly where he had pressed her against him. She saw there was another couple on the bridge. They did not react as Sashenka and Golden approached. They were youngsters, he in a Red Army uniform and she in a white coat over a dress with a slit up the side. She was probably one of the girls from the food shops on Gorky Street. They were openly kissing each other with an intense hunger, their mouths wide open, their tongues licking like cats at a dish of milk, faces shining, eyes closed, her curtain of thick flaxen hair getting caught in his teeth, his hands up her skirt, her fingertips on his zipper.

Sashenka felt disgusted: she remembered the couple necking on her street during the Revolution, and Gideon and Countess Loris outside the Astoria—yet she could not take her eyes off the couple and suddenly felt a starburst of the wildest wantonness in her body, and such urgency that she did not recognize herself, so foreign was it to her, so alien. This gulping spasm was so insistently physical that she feared it was her period arriving early to cramp her insides.

Benya towed her along the Embankment with insouciant arrogance, not talking anymore, just singing old romances and gypsy songs:

Ach, those black eyes have captivated me,
They are impossible to forget,
They burn before my eyes
Black eyes, passionate eyes, lovely burning eyes,
how I love you, how I fear you.
I first laid eyes on you in an unkind hour . . .

When he finished singing, her hand remained in his, first by accident, then tensely, and when she became aware of it she did not try to remove it.

He was flirting with her in an audacious and dangerous way, Sashenka told herself. Didn't he know who she was? Didn't he understand what her husband did? I'm a Communist, a believer, she thought, and I'm a married woman with two children. Yet now, in that hot Muscovite night, after twenty years of survival and discipline, and three years of terror and tragedy while thousands upon thousands of Enemies were unmasked and liquidated, she suddenly experienced a flutter of madness in the company of this slight, balding Galician Jew who had ambushed her with his frivolous dance steps, blue eyes and raffish songs.

Benya handed her down a small set of stone steps that led directly to the river's brim, a secret quay. "No one can see us!" he told her again, and they sat on the steps, their feet just over the water. It should have been muddy and scummy but tonight the Moskva was coated with diamonds that reflected light onto their faces, etching them in purple and bronze, making them both feel younger. A flush spread throughout her body, the sensation of wings beating. She had been powerfully bedded by her husband and had children by him—yet she had never experienced anything like this.

"Did you ever do this as a teenager?" he asked her. He kept reading her mind uncannily.

"Never. I was a solemn child and a very serious Bolshevik . . ."

"Didn't you ever wonder what the popular songs were about?"

"I thought they were nonsense."

"Well then," he said, "you deserve just an hour in the world of popular song."

"What do you mean?" she said, noticing his lips, his sunburnt neck, his eyes burning into her. He offered her his last Egyptian cigarette, a Star of Egypt with a gold tip—and it took her back twenty years. He lit it for her with a silver kerosene lighter, then offered her a swig from a flask. She expected vodka; instead, sweetness flooded her senses.

"What on earth is it?"

"It's a new American cocktail," he said. "A Manhattan."

It went straight to her head—and yet she was more sober than she had ever been.

A hulking barge, piled high with coal or ore like a floating mountain, rumbled past them, lying low and rusty in the water. The sailors sat around, drinking and smoking. One was playing a guitar, another an accordion. But when they saw Sashenka, in her white wide-brimmed hat and her beaded dress tight across the hips, her gleaming white stockings reflected on the dappled waters, they started to call out and point at her.

"Hey, look over there! A real vision!"

Sashenka waved back.

"Fuck her, man! Kiss her for us! Bend her over, comrade! You lucky bastard!" one of the sailors called.

Benya jumped to his feet, raising his hat like a dancer. "Who! Me?" he called.

"Kiss her, man!"

He shrugged apologetically. "I can't disappoint my audience," and, before she could protest, he kissed her on the lips. She fought it for a second but then, to her own astonishment, she surrendered.

"Hurrah! Kiss her for us!" The sailors cheered. She laughed into his mouth. He pushed his tongue between her lips, delving as deep as he could reach, and she groaned. Her eyes closed. Surely no one in the world had ever kissed like *this.*

She had never understood before. In the Civil War she'd been young, but she had been with Vanya then and men like Vanya did not kiss like this. And she had never wanted him to kiss her this way: they'd been comrades first; he had cared for her after her mother's suicide; they worked closely together during the Revolution of October 1917; and then she'd traveled through Russia on the Agitprop trains and he with the Red Army as a commissar. Afterward, they had met again in Moscow. There was no time for romance in those days: they had moved into an apartment with other young couples, all of them working days and nights, living on carrot tea and crackers. Sashenka was still the straitlaced Bolshevik and that was how she liked it. She'd always recalled her oversexed mother with horror and regret. Yet this insolent Galitzianer, this Benya Golden, had no such inhibitions. He licked her lips, nuzzled her forehead, inhaled the smell of her skin as if it were myrrh—and the pleasure of these simple things amazed her!

She opened her eyes as if she had been asleep for an age. The sailors and the barge were gone but Benya kept on kissing her. The secret places of her body purred. She shifted her position, embarrassed, but every time she moved, her loins felt liquid and heavy. She was nearly forty years old—and she was lost.

"You know, I just don't do this sort of thing," she said at last, a little breathlessly.

"Why the hell not? You're very good at it."

She must have been a little mad because now she leaned over again and took his head in her hands and started to kiss him back in a way she had never done before.

"I want you to know, Benya, I love your stories. When I read them, I wept . . ."

"And I love these freckles on either side of your nose . . . And these lips, my God, they never quite close as if you're always hungry," Benya said, kissing her again.

"So why have you stopped writing?"

"My ink is frozen."

"Don't be ridiculous." She pushed his face away roughly, holding his chin in her hand. "I don't believe you're not writing. I think you're writing secretly."

He stared out at the river, where the lights of the British Embassy in its stately mansion right opposite glowed in the water.

"I'm a writer. Every writer has to write or he'll die. If I didn't I'd shrivel up and rot away. So I translate articles from socialist papers, and get commissions to work on film scripts. But they've almost dried up too. I'm nearly penniless now, even though I still have my apartment in the writers' building."

"Why didn't you stay in Paris?"

"I'm a Russian. Without the Motherland, I'd be nothing."

"So what are you working on?"

"You."

"You're writing about the secret police and the top of the Party, aren't you? You write it by hand at night, and hide it in your mattress. Or maybe at the home of some girl in the suburbs? Am I just material for your secret work? Are you using me to see into our world?"

He sighed and scratched his head. "We writers all have something secret that keeps us alive and gives us hope, although we know we can never publish it. Isaac Babel's working on something secret, Misha Bulgakov's writing a novel about the devil in Moscow. But no one will ever read them. No one will ever read me."

"I will. Can I read what you're working on?"

He shook his head.

"You don't trust me, do you?"

"I long to trust you, Sashenka. I'd love to show you the novel because no one knows of it, not even my wife, and if I showed it to you, then I would have one reader, one beautiful reader, instead of none and I'd feel an artist again instead of a washed-up scribbler in these days when we've all become cannibals."

Benya looked away from her and she sensed, even if she did not see, that there were tears in his eyes.

"Let's make a pact," she said, taking both his hands. "You can trust me with anything, even the novel. I'll be your reader. And in return, if you swear never to hurt me, never to break this confidence, you can kiss me again after sundown by the Moskva."

He nodded and they held hands, their faces luminous in the summer night like the burnished death masks of pharaohs. Behind her, she heard the call and then the haunting creak of wings as two swans landed with a clean foamy swish on the rippling surface of the river.

She was happier at that moment, in herself and for herself, than she could ever remember.

11

Benya led Sashenka by the hand up the steps from the Embankment and toward the Metropole Hotel. She hung back as the doorman in the top hat and braided tails opened the door, but Benya could tell that she wanted to dance as much as he did.

Benya loved the atmosphere at the Metropole. Even during the Terror, the jazz band went on playing there and he would dance away his troubles to the blare of the trumpets and saxophones. Before 1937, the hotel had been full of foreigners with their Russian girls in French gowns, but now the businessmen, diplomats, journalists and social delegations from abroad sat apart. Before the killing started, Gideon had sometimes brought him here for dinners with important foreign writers. He had met H. G. Wells, Gide and Feuchtwanger. He had heard his patron Gorky give a speech here to the Party writers and theater bureaucrats such as Averbakh and Kirshon. One by one, they had all vanished. Alien elements liquidated! But he had survived, and Sashenka had survived the Terror by some miracle, and it seemed to Benya all of a sudden that tonight they should celebrate being alive.

As they walked together through the doors, they were so close and so in step, momentarily, that he could see the dark wood and polished chrome of the front desk reflected in her grey eyes. But as soon as they were in the lobby, Benya noticed how Sashenka kept apart from him. He realized she was worried that she might be recognized—but she sometimes entertained her writers for the journal here and he was her new writer.

"Relax," he whispered to her.

The waiters in black coats showed them to a black art-deco table. How different the dining room seemed. The brilliant mirrors, the curling blue smoke rising to the molded ceiling like mist on a mountain, the lights on the stage, the silhouettes of men with their hair *en brosse* and their tidy mustaches, the gleam of boots, the curve of jodhpur breeches on the Red Army officers, the permanent-wave hairdos of the girls—all were infinitely more glamorous tonight.

A girl in a white blouse with a flashlight and a tray of cigarettes and chocolates appeared before them. Never taking his eyes off Sashenka, Benya bought a pack of cigarettes, offering her one. He lit hers, then his own. They said nothing, but when she looked at him, her gaze seemed like the beam of a lighthouse shining out from a friendly shore. The smoke whirled around her in broken circles as if it too wanted to be close to her. Everything in the nightclub revolved around her.

He thought she seemed cool and calm again, the "Soviet woman of culture" in her white dress, but then her lips, which stayed just open enough for him to catch the glint of her teeth, twitched a little as she dragged on the cigarette. Her eyes closed for a second so that her dark eyelashes fanned against her skin and those rare archipelagos of freckles. The lights caught the chestnut in her thick dark hair, and he saw that beneath all the composure she was a little breathless. He was breathless himself. Tonight it seemed the world was turning a little faster and tilting a little bit more.

The show was about to start. The lights spun and then shone onto the fountain in the middle of the room. The drums rolled. It was not Utesov's band tonight but another jazz group with three trumpeters, a saxophonist and two double-bassists, all in black suits with white collars. New Orleans met Odessa in the strut of a louche, smoky rhythm.

Benya ordered wine and vodka and *zakuski*—caviar, herring, *pelmeni*—and then realized he had barely a kopek in his pocket. "I order, you pay," he told her. "I'm as broke as a cockroach on Millionaya Street!"

She drank the Georgian wine, and he watched her relish its taste and then swallow it and sigh as it quenched her thirst—and even that commonplace act seemed precious. At last, he pulled her up to dance.

"Just once," she said.

Benya knew he was good at the foxtrot and the tango, and they danced for more than one song. His body was slim and slight but he spun her around, making the steps as if he were walking on air. He suddenly felt that time was short. The circumstances that had allowed this freedom might never coincide again and he must push things as far as they could go. So he held her against him, knowing just from her breath how exhilarated she was too.

She broke away quickly and sat down again.

"I've got to go now," she said as he joined her.

"This is a night that doesn't exist in our lives," he whispered. "Nothing that happens tonight ever happened. Suppose we took a room?"

"Never! You're insane!"

"But imagine what a joy it would be."

"And how would we even book it?" she answered. "Good night, Benya." She grabbed her bag.

"Wait." He held her hand under the table and then, in a crazy gamble that would either ruin the night or make it, he put her hand right on his zipper.

"What the hell do you think you're doing?" she demanded, snatching it away.

"No," he answered. "Look what you're doing to me. I'm suffering."

"I must go at once." But she didn't and he could see the effects of his brashness in her wide grey eyes. She was drunk, but not on the wine.

"Don't you have a room here already, Sashenka? For your magazine?"

She blushed. "Room four hundred and three belongs to Litfond but, yes, the editors of *Soviet Wife* can use it for out-of-town writers, but that would be completely out of . . ."

"Anyone using it now?"

Cold anger flashed in her eyes and she stood up. "You must think I'm some sort of . . . *bummekeh*!" She stopped and he realized she was surprised by her use of the Yiddish for a disreputable woman, a relic from her childhood.

"Not a *bummekeh*," he answered quick as a flash, "just the most gorgeous *bubeleh* in Moscow!"

She started to laugh—no one had ever called her a babe, a little doll, before and Benya understood that they shared an oddly reassuring past in the old Jewish world of the Pale of Settlement.

"Room four hundred and three," he said, almost to himself.

"*Bonsoir*, Benya. You've made me surprise even myself but enough is enough. File your article by next Monday," and she turned and walked out of the dining room, the chrome and glass double doors swinging behind her.

12

Sashenka laughed at her own stupidity. She had pushed through the wrong doors, but after such an exit she could not go back into the dining room. Now, she sat on the scarlet stairs leading to the rear elevators of the hotel and lit up one of her own Herzegovina Flors. Her presence in this hidden space right in the heart of the hotel seemed quite appropriate. No one knew she was there.

Without really thinking, she walked into the service elevator and rode it up to the fourth floor. Like a somnambulist, she crept along the musty, humid corridors, smelling the stale whiff of chlorine, cabbage and rotting carpet even in Moscow's smartest hotel. She was lost. She must go home. She feared there might be the usual old lady (and NKVD informant) at the desk on the fourth floor, but then she realized that by entering the back way she had missed the crone altogether.

As she reached Room 403, she heard a step behind her. It was Benya. She opened the door with the key that she held as editor of the magazine, and they almost fell into the little room that, if she analyzed it (and she would never forget these smells as long as she lived), was like a sealed capsule of mothballs and disinfectant. Inside, the room was dark, lit only by the lurid scarlet of the electric stars atop each of the eight spires of the Kremlin outside the window. They backed onto a bed that sagged in the middle, the sheets rancid with what she later identified as old sperm and alcohol in a cocktail specially mixed for Soviet hotels. She wanted to struggle, to reprimand, to complain, but he grabbed her face and kissed her so forcefully that a lick of flame burned her to the core.

His hands pulled her dress off her shoulders and he buried his face in her neck, then her hair, scooping up between her legs. He pulled down her brassiere, cupping her breasts, sighing in bliss. "The blue veins are divine," he whispered. And in that moment, a lifetime of unease about this ugly feature of her body was replaced with satisfaction. He licked them, circling her nipples hungrily. Then he disappeared up her skirt.

She pushed him away from there, once, then twice. But he kept returning. She slapped his mouth, quite hard, but he didn't care.

"No, no, not there, come on, no thank you, no . . ." She cringed, closing her eyes bashfully.

"You're beautiful," he said.

Could that be true? Yes, he insisted and he swiped her with his tongue. No one had ever done this to her before. She shivered, barely able to control herself.

"Lovely!" he said.

She was so ashamed she actually hid her face in her hands. "Just don't!"

"See if you can pretend it isn't happening!" was his suggestion as he buried his face in her. When she finally looked down, he peered back at her, laughing. I've got a lover, she thought, incredulous. His irrepressible carnality enthralled her. It was like the first time with her husband, her only other lover—but then it was not like that at all. In fact, she reflected, *this* is me losing my real virginity at the hands of this infernal, lovable Jewish clown who is so unlike any of the macho Bolsheviks in my life.

He's a madman, she thought as he made love to her again. Oh my God, after twenty years of being the most rational Bolshevik woman in Moscow, this goblin has driven me crazy!

He eased out of her again, showing himself.

"Look!" he whispered and she did. Was this really her? There he was between her legs again, doing the most absurd, lovely things to places behind her knees, the muscle at the very top of her thighs, her ears, the middle of her back. But the kissing, just the kissing, was heavenly.

She lost all sense of time and place and decorum. He made her forget she was a Communist, he made her forget herself for the first time in twenty years—and at last she began to live in the luscious, invincible present.

13

All was silent. Lying on creased sheets, she opened her eyes like one who has been in a deep sleep, awakening after a flood or an earthquake. Were those Kremlin stars still outside the window or had they been swept away by their lovemaking? Reality returned to her slowly.

"Oh my God," she said. "What have I done?"

"You loved that, didn't you?" he said.

She shook her head, eyes closing again.

"Look at me," he said. "Tell me how much you love it. Or I'll never kiss you again."

"I can't say it."

"Just nod."

She nodded and felt her bruised face. She could hardly believe the intoxication of her pulsating body in that dark little room at the top of the Metropole on a night in May 1939 after the Terror was over.

Her dress and her underwear were on the floor but her bra was still on her stomach; one stocking was still in place but the other draped the lamp, casting a brassy sepia light on their limbs. Their mouths were salty and the taint of pleasure and sweat made her giddy with sheer delight.

Benya was kissing her again on the lips, then between her legs—it was so sensitive there now that she winced. He gave her a kiss on the mouth and then delicately there again. She shivered, blisters of perspiration on her rounded belly. Then she pulled Benya up and turned him over so she was on top and he was inside her again. Somehow they just slotted together. Why did she feel so at home in his arms? Why did it seem so natural?

The enormity of what had happened struck her like a blow. She had betrayed kind hearty Vanya, her husband and friend of all these years, the father of her children. She loved him still but this earth-tilting fever was another love, utterly foreign, and contradictory to that cozy habitual love of home and children. Women aren't supposed to be able to love two men at once but now I see that's absurd, Sashenka thought. Yet a tremor of guilt slipped down her throat to her uneasy heart.

"I've never done anything like this before," she whispered. "I bet everyone says that to you . . ."

"Well, funny you should ask but according to 'The Soviet Proletarian Guide to the Etiquette of Adultery,' it is the traditional female comment at this very moment of the first encounter."

"And according to this . . . 'Soviet Proletarian Guide to the Etiquette of Adultery,' what is the correct male answer?"

"I'm meant to say, 'Oh, I know!' as if I believe you."

"Which you don't."

"Actually, I do believe you."

"And who is the author of this famous book of wisdom?"

"A certain B. Z. Golden," answered Benya Golden.

"Does it say what happens next?"

He was silent, and she saw a shadow pass over his face.

"Are you afraid, Sashenka?"

She shivered. "Slightly."

"We need never meet again," he said.

"You don't mean that, do you?" she asked, suddenly terrified that he might indeed mean it.

He shook his head, his eyes very close to hers. "Sashenka, I think this is the most joyful thing that has ever happened to me. I've had lots of girls, I sleep with lots of women . . ."

"Don't boast, you filthy Galitzianer!" she scolded.

"Perhaps it's the times. Perhaps we live everything so intensely now. But we deserve a little selfishness, don't we?" He took her face in his hands and she was surprised how serious he became. "Do you feel anything for me?"

Sashenka pushed him away and stumbled to the window, sweat drying on her back, a pulse still beating between her legs. They were in the eaves of the old building. In the moon-blanched night, she looked down at the Moskva River, the bridges, the gaudy onion domes of St. Basil's, and into the Kremlin, sixty-nine acres of ocher palaces, emerald rooftops, blood-red battlements, golden cupolas and cobbled courtyards, and saw where Comrade Stalin worked, in the triangular Sovnarkom Building with the domed green roof. She could even see the light on in his office. Was he there now? The people thought so but she knew he was probably at Kuntsevo. He was her friend, Josef Vissarionovich . . . well, not quite. Comrade Stalin was beyond friendship, but the Father of Peoples—yes, her new acquaintance and sometime guest who had promoted her husband and admired her magazine—was the greatest statesman in the history of the working class. She did not doubt it, and she remained a Bolshevik to her fingertips. What had happened in this room had not changed that.

But something *had* changed. Benya was lighting a cigarette, lying stretched out on the bed. He was watching her silently, barely breathing. The band might still have been playing downstairs, but in the room it was quiet and calm. She had everything but this in her life. She was a Communist woman and a mother, while Benya was a blocked writer out of tune with the boldest ideals of his time, alienated from the great dialectic of history, a piece of faithless flotsam who regarded Comrade Stalin and the workers' state with sneering zoological interest. Yet this vain, impertinent and flashy Galitzianer with his dimpled chin, his low-set brows over dancing blue eyes, his forlorn last tuft of blond hair on his balding forehead, and yes, his sex, had made her savagely happy.

He got up and stood behind her. "What is it?" he asked, wrapping his arms around her.

"I've done something worse than be unfaithful—something I thought I would never do. I've become my mother."

But he wasn't listening. "You don't even know how erotic you are," he said, running his hands up her thighs from behind. And they started again, another shuddering tournament. When it was over, they had become creatures of the sea, their bodies as sleek and wet and lithe as leaping dolphins.

Later, she rested her elbows on the windowsill so she was looking at the Kremlin again and he touched her, from behind, with such delicate tracery, such gleeful tenderness, that she barely recognized the geography of her own body. "What a glutton you turn out to be!" he teased her. He seemed to live with joyfulness, a gaiety that dyed her monochrome world all the wild colors of the rainbow.

So *this*, she mused to herself, *this* is what all the fuss is about.

14

Her body still tingling and burning, Sashenka walked home past the Kremlin, higher and brighter than ever in the searchlights that sent strange white columns boring into the sky, across the Manege and alongside the National Hotel. When she looked back at the Kremlin, its eight red stars made her think of Benya. They were, she'd read in the newspaper, made of crystal, alexandrite, amethyst, aquamarine, topaz—and seven thousand rubies! Yes, seven thousand rubies to celebrate her and Benya Golden. What had happened to her? she wondered. She could not believe Benya's uninhibited carnality or the fog of sweat that had blurred that little room. Passing the old university on her right, she turned down little Granovsky Street. Her pink turn-of-the-century wedding-cake home, the Fifth House of Soviets, was on the left with guards outside. The guards nodded at her. The janitor was hosing down the yard.

She let herself into the apartment on the first floor. She did not turn on the lights but she relished the shining parquet floors that smelled of polish and caught the meager light; she enjoyed the high ceilings, molded so beautifully; and the woody aroma of the Karelian pine furniture, issued by the government. Her parents-in-law were asleep round the corner of the L-shaped corridor but she turned on the lamp by her bedside, its base a muscular golden bicep holding a bulb surrounded by a green shade. She sat on her bed for a second and caught her breath. Was she betraying everyone she loved? Could she lose it all? Yet she could not regret what she had done.

She opened the door to the children's rooms and looked in on them. Would they smell the reek of sin on her? But they slept on angelically. She had not betrayed them, she told herself firmly. She had just found a part of herself.

Sashenka stood looking down on them, then kissed Snowy's forehead and Carlo's nose. Carlo held one of his many bunnies in his arms. She suddenly longed to wake them up and cuddle them. I am still their mother, I am still Sashenka, she told herself.

Just then Snowy, holding her cushion, sat up. "Mama, is it you?"

"Yes, darling, I'm back. Did Babushka put you to bed?"

"Did you go dancing?"

"How did you know?"

"You're still singing a song, Mama. What song are you singing? A silly song?"

Sashenka closed her eyes and sang softly just for her and Snowy:

Black eyes, passionate eyes, lovely burning eyes,
how I love you, how I fear you.
I first laid eyes on you in an unkind hour . . .

What a song she had sung with Benya Golden, she thought. Was he still singing it?

Snowy grabbed her mother's hand, folded it into her floppy cushion, put them both under her golden head and went back to sleep.

Sitting on the bed, her hand trapped under Snowy's alabaster cheek, Sashenka's uneasiness evaporated. She was not Ariadna; she could not remember Ariadna ever kissing her good night. Her mother had become a wanton creature, a lunatic animal. But sitting there on Snowy's bed, she remembered her mother's death. She wished they had talked. Why had Ariadna killed herself with her Mauser? Sashenka would never forget sitting beside her wheezing mother, waiting for her to die.

Listening now to the soft breathing of the children, she thought of her father again. How proud she had been that he had not fled abroad but had renounced capitalism and joined the new regime. But she had not seen him since 1930, when he fell from being a "non-Party specialist" to a "former person" and "saboteur" and was sent into a lenient exile in Tiflis, where he'd lived in a single room. During the Terror, Sashenka might have been vulnerable as a "capitalist's daughter" but she was an Old Bolshevik, an enthusiast even for the Terror, and she had "reforged" herself as one of Stalin's New Soviet Women. Vanya's working-class credentials and success protected her, but she'd accepted that she could not appeal for her father, help him or even send him packages.

"Let him go," Vanya had told her. "It'll be best for him and us." She had almost appealed to Comrade Stalin, but Snowy had stopped her just in time.

She had last heard Samuil Zeitlin's gentle, urbane voice—its tone and mannerisms so redolent of their old mansion and life before the Revolution—on the telephone just before his arrest in 1937. Her children had never met him: they believed that her parents had died long before. Sashenka never criticized the Party for the way it treated her father, not even in her own mind, but that did not stop her wondering now: are you out there, Papa? Are you chopping logs in Vorkuta, in the wastes of Kolyma? Or did they give you the seven grams of lead—the Highest Measure of Punishment—years ago?

Slowly she went back to her room, showered, then, collecting Carlo in her arms, she got into bed with him. Carlo awoke and kissed her on the nose. "You've found a baby bunny in the woods," he whispered, and with his mouth still close to her ear, they slept.

The next morning, she had just sat down at her T-shaped desk in the office when the phone rang.

A low humorous voice with that Jewish Galician intonation that immediately, embarrassingly, resonated between her legs, said: "It's your new writer, Comrade Editor. I wasn't sure—did you commission that article or not?"

15

Ten days later, Benya Golden lunched as usual at the Writers' Club with Uncle Gideon. Later they visited the Sandunovsky Baths and Benya continued on to Stas, the Armenian barber, in his little shop right next door. There was a portrait of Stalin on the wall, an array of metal clippers and naked razors stuck on a magnetic strip, and a plastic plant in the window. The radiogram, always playing at Stas's place, reported clashes with the Japanese in Mongolia. War was coming. Benya sat in the soft leather chair as Stas bathed his face in foam and warm water.

"You seem happy enough," said Stas, an old Caucasian with thick oily hair dyed an unnatural jet black and a small raffish mustache. "You've got a commission? Or you're in love?"

"Both, Stas, both, simultaneously! Everything in my life has changed since I last saw you."

As he luxuriated in the warm towels wrapped around his face and neck, Benya's spirits soared. He didn't give a fig for his commission. All he could think about was Sashenka. Her meltingly husky voice, how she would stroke her short upper lip when concentrating; how they danced, made love, sang, talked, and understood each other "as if we were born under the same star," he said aloud, shaking his head slowly.

Not a day, not an hour, not a minute passed when he wasn't consumed by his need to see her, talk to her, touch her. He wanted to feast his eyes on her and fill up his stores of memories, so that even if she was not with him he could almost reach out and feel her. Now he viewed even the most familiar places with reverence, if they were associated with her. That day he had wandered down Gorky Street. The stars and towers celebrated not the Tsars or Stalin, but her, Sashenka. When he ambled past Granovsky, where she lived, a diaphanous halo illuminated that very street. The NKVD guards were not guarding marshals or commissars, they were guarding his heart, which dwelled there.

Yet with love, there was always suffering: she was married. So was he. And they had met in cruel times. He had once loved his wife, but the struggle of everyday life had ground their passion into routine; they had become brother and sister—or, worse, lodgers in the same apartment that they shared with their little daughter. And Sashenka was—highfalutin romantic phrases failed him—simply the loveliest woman he had ever met. He felt he was sitting atop a dizzying peak, peering down on the glowing earth, crowned with stars. Could it last? We mustn't waste a second, he thought.

"What time is it? I'm late. Hurry up, Stas!" He felt impatient suddenly as if he had to tell someone about his ardent secret. "I'm in love, Stas. No, more than love, I'm crazy about her!"

Across town in the Kitaigorod, Moscow's Chinatown, Sashenka, in the smart scarlet suit she wore sometimes for work, was climbing up a small staircase to the atelier of Monsieur Abram Lerner, the last old-fashioned tailor in Moscow. He worked for the special services section of the NKVD, and it was he who had designed the new marshals' uniforms when Stalin had restored the old ranks of the army. It was said that he made Stalin's own tunics but the Master hated new clothes and it was probably just a rumor.

Lerner had taken on Cleopatra Fishman to serve the leaders' wives. Sashenka knew that Polina Molotov and the other wives all came to her (and that some insisted on paying, while some did not pay at all). Now, at the end of a busy day, she had arrived to collect another new outfit. She waited impatiently in the reception area, where there were piles of *Bazaar* and *Vogue* magazines from America. If a client liked a certain design, she pointed to it in *Vogue* and Cleo and her team of seamstresses would work it up for her. Lerner and Cleopatra, who were not related but had worked together for decades, existed in an island of old-world courtesy: their atelier was probably the only institution in the entire Soviet Union where no one had been denounced or shot over the last decade.

Cleopatra Fishman, a stocky little woman with grey, curly hair who smelled of chicory, escorted Sashenka into the dressing room, where she unveiled the blue silk dress with the pleated flounces on the skirt.

"Do you want to try it now or just take it?"

Sashenka looked at her watch.

"I'll put it on." She quickly threw off her clothes—in a way, she reflected, that she would never have thrown them off before—and folded them away into a bag and pulled on her new outfit. She shivered as the silk settled onto her new-cast body.

"You've had a new hairdo too, Sashenka."

"The permanent wave. Do you approve?"

The older woman looked her up and down. "You're glowing, Comrade Sashenka. Are you pregnant? Anything you want to tell old Cleopatra?"

Fifteen minutes later, at 7:00 p.m., in that eyrie at the top of the Metropole, Sashenka, in her new dress and hairdo, her new brassiere, her new perfume and silk stockings, was kissing Benya Golden, who, while his white suit got dirtier and shabbier, was also primped, barbered and bathed.

They made love, they talked, they laughed—and then she brought a package out of her bag and tossed it on the bed.

He jumped up and opened it, weighing it in his hands.

"A little present."

"Paper!" He sighed. The Literary Fund Shop had refused him any more paper so she had ordered it for him. "Paper's the way to a writer's heart."

They had met at the Metropole every day for ten days, and their relationship had moved beyond mere sexual infatuation. Sashenka had told him the story of her family; he had told her of his upbringing in Lemberg, of his adventures in the civil war, and the many outrageous erotic shenanigans in which he had become embroiled. After twenty years in the grip of Bolshevik officialdom, Sashenka was bowled over by the exuberance of Golden's life: every disaster became a ridiculous comedy in which he starred as chief clown. His clashes with officialdom—dreary and heartbreaking in anyone else—became hilarious sketches peopled by grotesques. His views on the Socialist Realists, writers and filmmakers, were riotously scabrous, yet he spoke of poetry with tears in his eyes. He lent her books and took her to movies in the middle of the day; they relished Moscow in bloom—the lilacs and the magnolias—and he even bought her garlands of mimosa and bunches of violets, which came, the shopkeeper assured them, all the way from the Crimea.

"You've brought me back to life," Benya told her.

"What am I doing with you?" she answered. "I feel as if I'm in delicious freefall. When a woman lives a disciplined life for twenty years and then the discipline snaps, she may lose her mind."

"So you do like me a bit?" he persisted.

"You're always fishing for more praise, my darling." She smiled at him, taking in his blue eyes with the yellow speckles that bored into her so intensely, the dimpled chin, the mouth that was always on the verge of laughter. Sashenka realized that though she laughed so much with the children, she had not laughed enough in her life since those early days with Lala. There was precious little laughter with Mendel and Vanya, and now she discovered how many joyless people there were in the world (and especially in the Bolshevik Party). When she was not making love with Benya, they were laughing, their mouths wide open, their eyes shining.

"You need more and more praise, don't you? I can tell your mother loved you as a boy."

"She did. Is it that obvious? I was so spoiled."

"Well, I'm not going to tell you what I think of you, you silly Galitzianer. Your head's quite swollen enough. Anyway, isn't the proof of the pudding in the eating?"

"This pudding always wants to be nibbled," he said.

She sighed. "I want you all the time."

She was at the window, letting the breeze cool her sweat, wearing just her stockings. He was lying naked and spread-eagled on the bed, smoking a Belomor and wearing nothing but his white peaked cap. She went to him and lay on his limbs, resting her head on her hand, taking his cigarette for a puff and then blowing blue circles into his mouth. But for once, he did not start making love to her.

"I've written your article," he said, not looking at her.

"The Felix Dzerzhinsky Communal Orphanage . . ."

". . . for the Re-education of Children of Traitors to the Motherland."

"Well, it must be quite an uplifting institution," she mused. "The front line in the creation of the new Soviet child."

"I can't write it like that, Sashenka. Even if I turned myself into the most cold-hearted, cowardly, murderous scum, I couldn't write it . . ."

"What do you mean? It's a story of redemption." She was shocked by his sudden vehemence.

"Redemption? More like perdition, Dante's inner circle of hell!" He was shouting suddenly, and she ran a finger over her lips, surprised by his anger. "I don't know where to start. At a distance it looked very sweet—an old noble house in the woods, probably somewhat like the Zemblishino of your upbringing. Children parading at morning assembly in their white uniforms to discuss the new *History of the Bolshevik Party—Short Course.* But when I wanted to come inside and observe, the director, a brutish Ukrainian named Khanchuk, made a fuss, although he surrendered when he learned the name of the editor's husband. Inside, away from public scrutiny, the children are starving, dirty and ill educated. One six-year-old died yesterday—there were cuts and burns all over his little body. The doctors said he had also been beaten every day by Khanchuk. The teachers are savage degenerates who sexually abuse the children and treat them as slaves. The little ones are terrorized by gangs of damaged older children. It is one of the most horrifying places I've ever seen."

"But it's run by the NKVD . . . for the Party, and they care about reforging the children. Comrade Stalin said—"

"No! You don't understand!" He was shouting again and she was a little afraid. She had never seen him angry before. He shook her off him, jumped up to get a piece of paper from his jacket and began to read:

> *The Felix Dzerzhinsky Communal Orphanage for the Re-education of Children of Traitors to the Motherland is one of the most delightful examples of redemption in our Soviet paradise. Here, in a charming rustic glade, these innocent children, tainted only by the cruelties of chance in their relationships to their wicked parents, the bloodsucking terrorists, wrecking spies, snakes, rats and Trotskyite murderers, are given a wonderful new introduction to the generosity of Soviet education. No wonder at 6:00 a.m. at morning assembly, they happily sing the "Internationale," chant "Thank you, Comrade Stalin, for our happy childhood" and then start to study the* Short Course. *Meanwhile, in the Little Red Corner, a gang of hungry, dirty and brutalized teenagers have started to torture a little girl of four with a switchblade and a cigarette lighter under the negligent gaze of the corrupt and depraved Director Khanchuk. Before the end of the day, she will probably be raped again by these feral children stripped of all the kindness and innocence of childhood. No wonder, because this very morning two children celebrating their twelfth birthdays were arrested as Trotskyite and Japanese spies and marched off to be sentenced to execution or hard labor in the camps . . .*

Sashenka gasped. "We can't publish that! If I handed that to Klavdia, my deputy, she would immediately take you to the Party Committee and they would denounce you to the Organs."

Benya was silent.

"You don't want me to hand it in, do you?" she said.

"I don't want to die, if that's what you mean—but I don't want to be a Russian toady either. I didn't sleep last night. I saw my own child in that Dantean hell and I woke up sobbing. I want you to mention that place to your husband." Her husband. Following Benya's imaginary book, "The Soviet Proletarian Guide to the Etiquette of Adultery," they had agreed never to mention Vanya or Benya's wife, Katya.

"I'm not sure I should mention you to my husband at all."

"I don't suppose he'd be all that interested, especially if he's still working boisterously on those diplomats . . ." There was an edge to his voice that she did not like.

"Boisterously? He works too hard."

"Well, we've all heard about his hard work."

Sashenka looked at him a long time, her belly churning at the sting in his words, which she did not quite understand. Their lovemaking had been so frenzied and it was hot under the eaves of the Metropole. She was horrified by Benya's article, which brought back that song from her Petersburg youth:

Here I am abandoned, an orphan, with no one to look after me . . .
Only the nightingale . . .

Benya lay down beside her again and stroked her gleaming white back, his fingers exploring between her thighs, but she flicked his hand away and lit the article with her lighter, holding it as it flamed and fell.

"Do you despise me?" Her bumble-bee voice was breaking up.

He sighed, again. "'The Soviet Proletarian Guide to the Etiquette of Adultery' reveals that this is the adulteress's most commonly asked question. No, actually I think all the better of you . . ."

Craving him, she rolled him on top of her, dreaming of spending a night with him, of singing with him at the piano, and of waking up together.

16

Lavrenti Beria knew he did not suit the full blue and red uniform of Commissar-General, first degree, of State Security. His legs were too short for the pleated trousers and boots, his shoulders too broad, his neck too thick, but he had to wear the ridiculous rig sometimes.

His black Buick with the darkened windows drove him through the Spassky Gates into the Kremlin, turned into Trinity Square, and halted with a skid at the Sovnarkom Building. Security in the Little Corner, as Stalin's office was known, was very tight. The Guards Section answered only to Stalin himself, so that even the People's Commissar for Internal Affairs needed to show his pass and surrender his sidearm.

Beria had been in Moscow for only ten months, so he was still new enough to enjoy his position—but keenly aware that he had to fight to keep it. He was confident that he could handle any degree of responsibility—he was indefatigable, he could work without sleep.

Holding his leather satchel, Beria passed through the first security barrier into the office of Alexander Poskrebyshev, Stalin's chief of staff. Here he surrendered his Mauser. A bald dwarf with the face of a baboon and livid, almost burned skin, Poskrebyshev recorded his arrival in the Master's appointment book. He greeted Beria respectfully, a sign of Stalin's favor.

"Go right in! The Master's ready—and in a thoughtful mood." Poskrebyshev offered this service to important visitors: a forecast of Stalin's state of mind.

The first door opened and a group of military commanders and intellectual types came out, holding drawing boards. Beria thought he saw tanks and guns on these. The soldiers and designers glanced at him and Beria saw them blanch: yes, he was the pitiless sword of the Revolution. They had to fear him. If they didn't, he was not doing his job.

When they were gone, Beria passed through the last security checkpoint. The young men in blue saluted.

The room was empty. Beria knew that the Master was now thinking about the European situation. Madrid, the capital of the Spanish Republic, had just fallen—and that removed any obstacle to dialogue with the Hitlerite Germans. Britain and France had caved in to Hitler at Munich, and momentous changes were now on the Master's mind. That was the reason for the case against the former diplomats at the Foreign Commissariat—it was a signal to Berlin that Soviet policy was changing.

Poskrebyshev shut the door behind him.

Beria waited by the door of a large, high rectangular office with many windows. A huge table covered in green baize stood in the center. Portraits of Lenin and Marx hung on one side, and (an addition that anticipated the coming war) those of Field Marshals Kutuzov and Suvorov on the other. Lenin's death mask was illuminated by a green-shaded lamp to remind visitors that this was the holy of holies.

At the far end, behind a large empty desk, a small door, almost invisible in the wood paneling, opened and Stalin came in, carrying a steaming glass in a silver holder. Beria was always impressed with the Master's mixture of animal grace, peasant swagger and thoughtful intellect. A great statesman required all three.

"Lavrenti, *gamajoba*!" said Stalin in Georgian. Alone, they could talk Georgian. When Russians were present, Stalin did not like to talk in his native tongue because he was a Russian leader and Georgia was a minor province of the Russian Empire; "a parochial marsh," he had once called it. But when they were alone together, it was fine.

Stalin gave Beria his tigerish smile. "Ah, the new uniform. Not bad, not bad at all. Sit down. How's Nina?"

"Very well, thank you, Comrade Stalin. She sends her regards." Beria knew that Stalin liked his blond wife, Nina.

"And your son, little Sergo?"

"Settling into school. He still remembers when you tucked him up in bed when he was very small."

"I read him his bedtime story too. Svetlana's very happy he's now in Moscow. Does Nina like that nobleman's house I chose for you? Did she get the Georgian jams I sent over? You're a specially trusted responsible worker, you need some space. You need special conditions."

"Thank you and the Central Committee for your trust, the house and the dacha. Nina's delighted!"

"But she can thank me for the jam herself!" They laughed.

"Believe me, Josef Vissarionovich," Beria respectfully used Stalin's name and patronymic, "she's writing you a letter."

"No need. Sit down."

Beria sat at the green baize table and unzipped his case, pulling out papers. Stalin sat at the head of the table, stirring his tea. He squeezed a slice of lemon into it.

"Right, what have you got for me?"

"We've a lot to get through, Comrade Stalin. The case at the Foreign Commissariat is progressing well and there are German, Polish, French and Japanese spies among the old diplomats."

"Who's working it?"

"Kobylov and Palitsyn."

"We know Kobylov. He's a bull in a china shop but a good operative. He takes his silk gloves off. Palitsyn's a good worker?"

"Very," replied Beria, though he had inherited Palitsyn, not chosen him. "Here are some of the confessions already signed by the prisoners. Comrade Stalin, you asked about the former person Baron Zeitlin, father of Palitsyn's wife and brother of the journalist Gideon Zeitlin."

"Sashenka Zeitlin-Palitsyn is a decent Soviet woman," said Stalin.

Beria noted the Master was not in the mood for jokes about sex, a subject never absent from his own mind for long. Today he could see that Stalin's mind was in the fraught borderlands of Mitteleuropa. He watched the Master sip his tea and pull a new pack of Herzegovina Flor cigarettes from his shabby yellow tunic. Opening it, he lit one and started to fiddle with the pencils on his desk.

"Did she and Palitsyn ever contact him?" Stalin asked.

"No."

"They put the Party first," said Stalin, sharp eyes on Beria. "You see? A decent Soviet girl who has 'reforged' herself—despite her class and connections. I remember seeing her typing in Lenin's office. Don't forget Lenin himself was a nobleman and grew up on a country estate, eating strawberries and rolling in the hay with peasant girls."

Beria knew this trick of the Master: only Stalin could criticize Lenin in the way that one god may mock another. Beria delivered the required look of shock and the old tiger's eyes gleamed. Stalin was the Lenin of today.

Beria laid out some papers. “You asked about Zeitlin’s whereabouts. It took a bit of time to find out his fate. On March twenty-fifth, 1937, he was arrested on my orders in Tiflis, where, since his dismissal in 1930, he had been living quietly in exile with his English wife. He was interrogated . . .”

“Silk gloves, or gloves off?” Beria saw that Stalin was sketching a wolf’s head with a green crayon on the pad of writing paper headed *J. V. Stalin.* He scrawled the words *Zeitlin* and then *glove.*

“Roughly enough. We weren’t running a hotel! But he confessed nothing.”

“What? That broken reed survived Kobylov’s workout?”

“If I hadn’t supervised, Kobylov would have ground him into dust. The Bull can go too far.”

“The Revolution requires we all do some dirty work.”

“My boys and I don’t wear silk gloves. Zeitlin was sentenced under Article Fifty-eight to the Vishka”—this was the nickname among the leaders for execution, the Highest Measure of Punishment—“as a Trotskyite terrorist who had conspired to assassinate Comrades Stalin, Voroshilov, Molotov and myself.”

“Even you? You are modest!” said Stalin with a slight smirk but then he sighed a little sadly. “We make mistakes sometimes. We have too many yes-men in this country.”

Beria was used to these inquiries. Stalin’s memory was extraordinarily detailed but even he could not remember all the names on the death lists. After all, he had personally signed death lists accompanied by “albums”—brief biographies and photographs of those listed—for 38,000 Enemies. Around a million had been executed since 1937 and more had died en route to, or in, the Gulag camps. Beria was curious why the Master was interested in a forgotten antique like Zeitlin—unless Stalin was attracted to Sashenka, and in that he couldn’t fault his taste. The Master was deeply secretive about his private life but Beria had learned that he had had many affairs in the past. Another possibility occurred to Beria. Zeitlin had once had interests in Baku and Tiflis. Did Stalin know Zeitlin personally?

No matter; sometimes Stalin expressed regret for such executions. "So Zeitlin's gone?" he asked, shading in his wolf's head.

"No, he was in the album of seven hundred and forty-three names prepared for you and the Politburo by the Narkom NKVD on April fifteenth, 1937. You confirmed all the Vishka sentences but placed a dash next to the name of Zeitlin."

"One of my dashes?" murmured Stalin.

Beria knew that a tiny signal from the Master—a mere stroke of punctuation on a piece of paper, or a tone of voice, or a raised eyebrow—could change a fate.

"Yes. Zeitlin was not executed but was sent to Vorkuta, where he's now in the camp hospital with pneumonia, angina and dysentery. He got a job as an accountant in the camp store."

"Those bourgeois are still pulling their tricks, I see," said Stalin.

"He's been constantly ill."

"A creaky gate's often strongest."

"He may not survive."

Stalin shrugged and exhaled smoke.

"Lavrenti Pavlovich, do we really think former person Zeitlin poses much of a threat anymore? Come to Kuntsevo for dinner tonight. Chareuli the film director and some disreputable Georgian actors are coming. I know you're busy—only if you have time."

Stalin pushed the file across the desk and Beria knew it was a sign that he should take his leave. The meeting was over.

17

When Sashenka's uncle, Gideon Zeitlin, finished his usual lunch—borscht soup, salted herring and veal cutlets—at his usual table at the Writers' Club in Moscow, he donned his fedora and walked out into the balmy streets. He had eaten with his cronies: the "Red Count," the supple, worldly and fat Alexei Tolstoy, one of Stalin's favorite writers; Fadeyev, the drunken secretary of the Writers' Union; Ilya Ehrenburg, the raffish novelist; and Gideon's own comely daughter Mouche, now an actress who was starting to earn big parts in the movies. These literary lions enjoyed their privileges—the food, the wine, the dachas in Peredelkino, the holidays in Sochi—because they had survived the terrible years of '37 and '38.

Afterward, Gideon, a giant with his prickly beard, ox-like jaw and playful black eyes, walked in the streets with Mouche. It was early summer. Girls were promenading.

"Mouche, did you notice that, until recently, everyone dressed like prissy nuns?" announced Gideon. "Thank God that's over! Skirts are getting shorter, slits getting higher. I adore summertime!"

"Stop looking, Papa *momzer,*" Mouche scolded him, calling him a rogue in Yiddish, like in the old days. "You're too old."

"You're right. I am too old, but I'm slightly soused and I can still look. And I can still do!"

"You're a disgrace."

"But you love me, don't you, Mouche?" Gideon held Mouche's hand. His daughter was now in her thirties, married with children, and dramatically good-looking, with black eyes, thick black hair, strong cheekbones—and almost famous in her own right. Gideon was a grandfather but damn that! The girls were out in force in Moscow that May, and the old connoisseur relished the legs, the bare shoulders, the new look of permed hair—oh, he could taste their skin, their thighs. He decided to call on his new mistress, Masha, the girl he'd brought along to Sashenka's party. Masha, he mused, was one of those placid, easygoing girls who would be boring were it not for their almost insane appetite for sex in all its varieties. He was just playing the scene in his mind when he realized Mouche was pulling on his arm.

"Papa! Papa!"

A white Emka car had stopped right next to them. The driver was waving at Gideon, and his passenger, a young man in a baggy brown suit, round intellectual's spectacles and a pompadour hairstyle, jumped out and opened the car's back door.

"Gideon Moiseievich, any chance of a chat? It won't take long."

Mouche had gone quite pale. The pretty girls in the streets drifted out of Gideon's vision, and he put his hand on his chest.

"If you're not feeling well, we can talk another time," said the young man, who sported a thin ginger mustache.

"Papa, will you be OK?" asked Mouche.

Gideon puffed up his barrel chest and nodded.

"It's probably just a chat, darling. I'll see you later."

It was routine, he told himself. Nothing to worry about. He'd be back with Mouche in a couple of hours.

As Mouche watched her father get into the car, she had a terrible feeling that she might never see him again. Where was her uncle Samuil? Vanished. Half of her father's friends had disappeared. First their works were mocked in the newspapers, then their apartments were searched and sealed. When she saw those friends again, she could barely say hello. They carried the plague of death. Finally they too were arrested, and vanished. But Gideon had strode over their bodies, and Mouche saw that he was a master of survival. He did what he had to do, although his family background was utterly damning. He survived only because it was said that Comrade Stalin liked his work and his connections with the European intelligentsia.

Now swaying in the summer wind, Mouche watched the car drive off with an ostentatious skid of the wheels up the hill toward the Lubianka. As it left, she had seen her father turn and blow her a kiss.

Mouche hurried to the public telephone and rang her cousin.

"Sashenka? Papa's fallen ill unexpectedly." She knew this was all she needed to say.

"Which hospital is he at?"

"The one at the top of the hill."

18

At her apartment in the Granovsky, Sashenka was playing with the children in the playroom. Carolina, the nanny, had made them toast and peach jam for tea and was now frying calf's livers for supper. Vanya was meant to be home by seven but he was late, and Satinov and his heavily pregnant wife, Tamara, had already arrived for dinner.

"What is it?" Satinov had asked, as soon as he saw her anxious face.

"Hercules, may I show you our new car downstairs?"

Sashenka knew that Satinov understood this code perfectly. Leaving the doll-like Tamara with the children, they took the elevator down to the courtyard where an array of the most dazzling limousines were parked under the watchful eye of the janitor and an NKVD guard. Granovsky was now such a bosses' residence that it had its own wooden guardhouse.

A gaggle of elderly men and women sat in a half circle of canvas chairs in the evening light, warmed by the hot asphalt—the mottled men in fedoras, white vests and shorts, displaying creased old bellies and white-furred chests, the swollen women in cheap sandals and sundresses with floppy hats, broad in hip, white skin burning raw. The men were reading the newspapers or playing chess, while the women talked, pointed, laughed, whispered and talked more.

At their center was Marfa, Vanya's fishwife of a mother, a cheerful walrus in a straw hat.

"Hey, there's my daughter-in-law," Marfa cried out raucously. "Sashenka, I'm telling them about the May Day party and who turned up at the dacha. They can't believe it."

Her father-in-law, Nikolai Palitsyn, an old peasant, pointed proudly at Sashenka. "She talked to HIM!" said Nikolai. "HIM!" He raised his eyes to heaven.

"But HE mentioned how much he admired Vanya!" added Vanya's mother.

Sashenka tried to smile but Vanya's parents were a source of danger. The courtyard was in its way quite select: these were all the parents of bosses but any gossiping was reckless, and could prove fatal.

"Hello, Comrade Satinov," called out the old Palitsyns.

Satinov waved, impeccably smart in tunic and boots.

"I'm showing Hercules the new car," Sashenka said. "Can you believe them?" she whispered. "How can we shut them up?"

"Don't worry, Vanya will keep them quiet. Now tell me what's happened," he said.

"Mouche called. They've arrested Gideon. I thought it was all over except for a few special cases. I thought . . ."

"Mostly it's over but it's our system now. It'll never be over. It's the way we make our USSR safe, and we're living in such dangerous times. Probably it's nothing, Sashenka. Gideon's always been a law unto himself. He's probably got drunk, told a stupid joke or groped Molotov's sourpuss wife. Remember: do and say nothing."

A Buick drew up and the driver opened the door.

"It's Vanya."

Sashenka was not surprised to see her husband looking bleary, unshaven and exhausted—it was the hours he worked, and the stress.

"What is it?" he asked, before he even kissed Sashenka or greeted Satinov.

"I'm going upstairs to play with the children," said Satinov.

"Did you know about Gideon's arrest?" Sashenka asked her husband, while, for the benefit of the geriatrics and the guards, she pretended to look at the car.

Vanya took her smooth hands in his big ones. "Rest assured, they're very pleased with me at the moment. I don't know any details but they mentioned it to me and I just said, 'Let our comrades check him out.' Understand? I promise you this doesn't touch us in any way."

Sashenka looked into Vanya's reassuringly proletarian face, taking in his lined forehead, greying temples and crumpled uniform. She was so relieved that they were safe. Gideon was a special case, she told herself, a European writer who knew foreigners, who visited whorehouses in Paris, who gave interviews to English newspapers. Once again, she was grateful for her husband's rock-like stability. Then she remembered Benya's sarcasm about his "boisterous" hard work, which, in turn, was obscured by a delicious memory of Benya's lips on her body earlier that day. A trickle of unease ran down her spine.

Upstairs, Snowy and Carlo were chasing Satinov round the apartment. Sashenka came in as they caught Satinov and tickled him.

"Tell me, Uncle Hercules," said Snowy, sitting astride her godfather, "where do cushions live?"

"Cushonia, of course." Satinov had helped Snowy develop her fantasy world. "Are they Wood Cushions, Sky Cushions or Sea Cushions?"

"Hercules, you're such a sport," said Sashenka. "You'll be marvelous when you have your own!"

"I love these children," said Satinov as he surrendered to them, allowing Carlo to pull off his boots.

Carolina came in to announce that dinner was ready.

19

Gideon was numb with fear as the car crossed Red and Revolution squares, then climbed the hill toward Lubianka Square. His vision crumpled as five mountainous storeys of grey granite and three of yellow brick overshadowed the car, which turned through a side gate into Lubianka Prison.

His mind kept working. He thought remorsefully of his brother, whom he had not seen for almost ten years and whom he had not telephoned since 1935. Surely Samuil had understood that it was risky for them to be in contact? But where was he now?

Gideon remembered his brother at the mansion on Greater Maritime Street, in that study crammed with Edwardian bric-a-brac, clanking on his Trotting Chair. How could it be that he had ceased to exist?

Without even thinking, Gideon bowed his head and whispered the Kaddish for his brother, amazed he could even recall that old Jewish prayer for the dead . . . Facing death, one returns to childhood, to family. Gideon realized that he loved his daughter Mouche more than anyone in the world. Will Mouche understand me, remember me, after I get the seven grams in the back of the neck? he wondered. The pain in his chest was unbearable. He was almost weeping with fear.

"Here we are!" The young man smiled at Gideon. He did not treat Gideon like a prisoner. On the contrary, a uniformed Chekist—as all secret policemen were known, in honor of Lenin's "knights of the Revolution," the Cheka—opened the door and helped him out of the car. Well, I *am* a literary celebrity, Gideon thought, reviving a little. There was no tonic like fame.

He noticed the many Buicks and ZiSes parked there. This was not the courtyard where they brought new prisoners.

Gideon was guided through double wooden doors into a marble hall and then a wood-paneled corridor with a blue carpet runner along the middle. Officers in NKVD uniform, and secretaries, bustled about. It was like any other state office. Gideon was relieved they were not taking him to the Internal Prison but he kept searching his mind for the meaning of this summons. What had he written recently? What had he said? What was happening in Europe that could involve him? He was a Jew and they had just sacked Litvinov, the Foreign Commissar, and also a Jew. Were Jews going out of favor? Was the USSR moving closer to Hitler?

If I am going to die, have I fucked enough women? Gideon thought suddenly. Never enough! Heartburn pierced his chest and he gasped.

"This is my office," said the young man, his pompadoured hair rising in a perfectly formed wave over his pink forehead. "I'm Investigator Mogilchuk of the Serious Cases Section, State Security. Are you all right? Here!" He offered Gideon a pillbox. "Nitroglycerin? You see, I was expecting you."

Gideon swallowed two pills, and the pain in his chest diminished.

A busty freckled redhead with a slit up the side of her dress sat typing in the anteroom. Even here his mind wandered up her skirt for that delicious first touch of the new . . . There were flowers on her desk. She took Gideon's hat.

"Come on in, Gideon Moiseievich," said Investigator Mogilchuk, clean-cut and young. When they were sitting down, the freckled girl brought tea for both of them and shut the door.

"Thanks for coming in, Citizen Zeitlin," Mogilchuk started, pulling out a pad of paper and a pen. Gideon could smell the coconut sweetness of that damned pomade in the youth's red hair. "I shall take notes. By the way, have you seen Romm's new movie, *Lenin in 1918*? As a young fan of your writing, I just wondered what you thought of it?"

Gideon virtually spat out his tea: had these ideeeots terrified him in order to bring him here just for a chat on movies? No, of course they had not. Ever since the twenties, the Cheka had used sophisticated faux intellectuals to manage the real ones. This freckly youth was merely the latest in a long line.

"*Lenin in 1918* is a wonderful film, and Stalin is beautifully portrayed in contrast to the murderous terrorist Bukharin," he replied.

"You know Romm of course. And how about Eisenstein's *Alexander Nevsky?*"

"Eisenstein is a sublime artist and a friend. The movie shows us how Bolshevism is utterly compatible with the Russian nation and its stand against our national enemies."

"Interesting," said the interrogator sincerely, stroking his ginger mustache. "I must tell you I'm a writer myself. You may have read my collection of detective stories published under the name M. Sluzhba? One of them will soon be performed as a play at the Art Theater."

"Ah yes," said Gideon, who vaguely remembered a review of a volume of clichéd detective yarns by a certain Sluzhba in some thick journal. "I thought those tales had the tang of reality about them."

Mogilchuk smiled toothily. "You flatter me! Thank you, Gideon Moiseievich, from you that's a compliment. I would welcome any comments." He passed his hand over the papers before him but did not change his tone. "Now let me start by showing you these." He pushed a bound wad of papers toward Gideon.

"What are these?" Gideon's confidence sank again.

"Just some of the confessions of your intimate friends in the last couple of years."

Gideon surveyed the typed-up pages on special headed NKVD letterhead, each one signed in the corner.

"You're a big name and you appear frequently in these confessions," explained the youngster keenly, almost admiringly. "They all mention you. Look here in these Protocols of Interrogation, and see there!"

Could the wild-eyed hag in this photograph really be that lissom creature of pleasure Larissa, whose throaty laughter and delicious breasts he remembered from that summer at the Mukhalachka Sanatorium in the Crimea just four years ago? Had she really denounced him for planning to kill Comrade Stalin? But then he remembered that he had himself denounced Larissa at meetings of the Writers' Union as a traitor, snake and spy who should be shot along with Zinoviev, Kamenev and Bukharin. And no one had had to torture *him* to make him do it.

Where were these friends of his? Were they all dead?

Gideon's breath was shallow with fear; red specks rose before his eyes.

Outside that comfortable sunny office with this unctuous Soviet New Man with his pomaded hair were scores of corridors and offices where baby tyrants grew into big tyrants, where ambitious bullies became systematic torturers. And somewhere in this nest of misery was the Interior Prison with its cellars where his friends had died, where he might die yet. Gideon was amazed by the evil in the world.

"This is all totally false," said Gideon. "I deny this nonsense."

The quiff smiled affably. "We're not here to discuss that now. We just want a chat. About your relative Mendel Barmakid."

"*Mendel?* What about Mendel? He's an important man."

"You know him well?"

"He is the brother of my brother's late wife. I've known him since they married."

"And you admire Comrade Mendel?"

"We're not friends. We've never been friends. In my view, he's an ideeeot!" Gideon felt a guilty relief. He had always disliked Mendel, who had banned two of his plays at the Little Theater—but no, he wished this fate on no man. On the other hand, Gideon was in his fifties and never hungrier to embrace life, to gobble it up. Who loves life as much as me, he wondered, who deserves to live more? He thanked God they wanted Mendel, not him!

"Where did you last see Comrade Mendel?"

"At the Palitsyns' house on May Day night."

"Did you talk to him?"

"No."

"Who was he talking to?"

"I don't remember. I don't pay attention to him. He doesn't approve of me. Never did."

Gideon noted that the interrogator still called Mendel "comrade," which meant that this was merely a fishing expedition. These torturers always tried to rope in other big names to add to their invented conspiracies. That was why all his old friends had denounced Gideon himself: the NKVD was just letting him know that he was living on ice. OK, he surrendered. They owned him and that was fine!

"Comrade Mendel appears in many of the confessions we have here too. Does Comrade Mendel reminisce about his early revolutionary career in the underground? His role in 1905? In exile? In Baku? In Petersburg? The early days of 1917? Does he boast of his exploits?"

"All the time. Ad nauseam." Gideon, hands resting on his fat prosperous belly, laughed so heartily and unexpectedly that the young investigator laughed too, in a high and reedy squeak. "I know all his stories by heart. He doesn't so much boast as drone on interminably."

"Do you have enough tea, Citizen Zeitlin? Want some cakes? Fruit? We so value these friendly chats. So, tell me the stories."

The youngster opened his hands. Gideon felt braver.

"I'm happy to tell old stories but if you want an informant, I'm not right for such work . . ."

"I quite understand," said Mogilchuk mildly, collecting the files. A photograph half fell out of them. Gideon's chest constricted sharply. It was Mouche, his beloved daughter, walking with Rovinsky, the film director, who'd vanished in 1937. So Mouche was the reason they asked him about movies. Mogilchuk quickly gathered up the photograph again and it disappeared into his *papki.*

"That was Mouche," cried Gideon.

"With her lover, Rovinsky," said Mogilchuk. "Do you know where Rovinsky is now?"

Gideon shook his head. He had not known about Mouche's love affair—but she was so like him. He must protect his darling daughter.

Mogilchuk just opened his hands as if sand were running through them.

"You want all Mendel's stories?" said Gideon. "That might take all night!"

"Our State can place eternity at your disposal if you wish. Are you dreaming of Masha, that little honey of yours? She's much too young for you and so demanding! She'll give you a heart attack. No—much safer for you to think about your daughter as you tell us those Mendel stories."

20

Two days had passed and it was dusk on the Patriarchy Ponds. In the sweltering half light, couples walked like pink shadows around the cool ponds, holding hands under the trees. Their feet crunched on the gravel, their laughter tinkled and someone was playing the accordion. Two old men stared at a chessboard, neither moving.

Sashenka, in her white hat and hip-hugging white beaded dress, bought two ice creams and handed one to Benya Golden. They walked slightly apart but an observer would have known they were lovers, for they kept a constant symmetry between their bodies as if linked by invisible threads.

"Are you busy?" she asked him.

"No, I've virtually nothing to do and no money to do it with. But"—here he whispered—"I am writing brilliantly all day on your delicious paper! Can I have some more? I'm so happy to set eyes on you. I just long to kiss you again, to savor you."

She sighed, half closing her eyes.

"Shall I go on?"

"I can't believe I want to hear your talk—but I do."

"I want to tell you something crazy. I want to run away with you to the Black Sea. I want to walk with you along the seafront at Batum. On the boardwalk there's a barrel organ that plays all our favorite love songs and I could sing along, and then when the tropical sun goes down we could sit at Mustapha's café and kiss. No one would stop us, but at midnight some old Tatars I know would take us in their boat to Turkey—"

"What about my children? I could never leave them."

"I know, I know. That's one of your attractions."

"You're shamefully perverse, Benya. What *am* I doing with you?"

"You're a wonderful mother. I've behaved badly all my life—but not you. You're a real woman of milk and blood, a Party matron, an editor, a mother. Tell me, how's the magazine?"

"Wildly busy. The Women's Committee is planning a gala for Comrade Stalin's sixtieth in December; we're doing a special issue for the Revolution Holidays; I've managed to get Snowy into her first Pioneers' Camp at Artek—she's already dreaming of wearing her famous red scarf. But best of all, Gideon is back home."

"But he could still be doomed, you know. They could just be playing him like a fish on a hook."

"No, Vanya says he might be all right. Comrade Stalin said at the Congress—"

"No more Party claptrap, Sashenka," Benya said urgently. "We haven't time to talk about congresses. There's only now! Only us."

They turned a corner, away from the ponds, and suddenly they were on their own. Sashenka took his hand. "Do you look forward to seeing me?"

"All day. Every minute."

"Then why are you looking so mischievous and crafty? Why have you lured me here?"

They were approaching an archway that led into a courtyard. Checking to see that no one was watching them, Golden pulled her into the archway, through the courtyard and into a garden where there was a rickety garden shed, the sort favored by pensioners to store their geranium seeds. He flashed a key. "This is our new dacha."

"A shed?"

He laughed at her.

"You're displaying bourgeois morality."

"I am a Communist, Benya, but when it comes to lovemaking I couldn't be more aristocratic if I tried!"

"Imagine it's the secret pavilion of Prince Yusupov or Count Sheremetev!" He unlocked the wooden door. "See! Imagine!"

"How can you even think for a moment that I would . . ." Sashenka realized that the days of living with Vanya in the spartan bunk beds of their tiny room in the Sixth House of the Soviets were long ago. She was a Bolshevik—but she'd earned her luxuries. "It's rotten and it stinks of manure."

"No, that is Madame Chanel's new perfume."

"That looks like a garden fork to me!"

"No, Baroness Sashenka, that's a diamond-encrusted fork made for the Empress herself by the celebrated craftsmen of Dresden."

"And what's that disgusting old rag?"

"That blanket? That is a pelt of silk and chinchilla fur for the baroness's comfort."

"I'm not going in there," said Sashenka firmly.

Golden's face fell but he persisted. "What if I just told you, with no bullshit at all, that this door leads us into a secret world where no one can see us or touch us and where I will love you more than life itself? It's not a mansion, I know. It may be just a pathetic garden shed, but it is also the shed where I want to adore you and cherish you without wasting another second during my short lifetime in this menacing world. It may sound silly but you've arrived in the summer of my life. I'm not old, but I'm no longer young, and I know myself. You are the only woman of my life, the woman I will remember as I die." He looked very serious suddenly, as he handed her a book he'd drawn out of his jacket—a volume of Pushkin. "I prepared this so we would never forget this moment."

She opened it and on the page of her favorite poem, "The Talisman," was a single, rare dried orchid.

He began to recite:

You must not lose it,
Its power is infallible,
Love gave it to you.

"You never stop surprising me," she whispered. Sashenka felt so moved and desperate to kiss him that her hands shook. She stepped into the shed and kicked the door shut. Everything in there—tools and seeds and some old boots—seemed as alive and full of love as she was.

Benya took her in his arms, and somehow she could tell by the look in his eyes, and the cast of his lips, that he meant what he'd said, that he did love her, and that this moment, in their private world, was one of those sacred occasions that occur once or twice in a lifetime, and sometimes never at all. She wanted to bottle it, store it, keep it forever in a locket at the very front of her memory so she could always reach for it and live it all over again, but she was so entranced that she couldn't even hold that thought. She just reached for him and kissed him again and again until they had to go home. But even as they parted, she repeated to herself, *You must not lose it, its power is infallible, love gave it to you.* And she could scarcely believe her own joy and luck that someone had actually said those words to her.

21

"What now? I'll complain to the Housing Committee. Stop that rumpus! It's three a.m.!" shouted Mendel Barmakid, Central Committee member, Orgburo member, Deputy Chairman of the Central Control Commission, Supreme Soviet deputy. His daughter Lena was also awakened by the banging on the door and for a moment she lay there, smiling at her father's absurdly operatic fury, imagining him in his ancient corded dressing gown, moth-eaten and stained. She heard him open the door of the family apartment in the Government House on the Embankment.

"What is it, Mendel?" called out Mendel's wife, Natasha.

Now my mother's up too, thought Lena, and she could almost see the plump Yakut woman with the Eskimo features in her sweeping blue caftan. Her parents were talking to someone. Who could it be?

Lena jumped out of bed, put on a scarlet kimono and her glasses, and came round the corner from her room toward the front door.

She saw her father rubbing his red-rimmed eyes and squinting up at a bulging giant in NKVD uniform. In shining boots, immaculate in his blue and scarlet uniform, holding a riding crop in a hand covered in gaudy rings and a jewel-handled Mauser in the other, Bogdan Kobylov stared down at the three Barmakids. He was not alone.

"Who is it? What do they want, Papa?"

Before Mendel could answer, Kobylov swaggered into the hall, almost blinding Lena with his eye-watering Turkish cologne. "Evening, Mendel. On the orders of the Central Committee, you're coming with us," he said in a barely intelligible rustic Georgian accent. "We've got to search the apartment and seal your study."

"You're not taking him," said Lena, blocking the way.

"All right! Step back," said Kobylov in a surprisingly soft voice. "If you waste my time and fuck around, I'll grind you all to dust, the little mare included. If we keep things polite, it'll be better for you. As you can imagine, there are other things I'd far rather be doing at this time of night." He flexed his muscles.

Lena glared up at their tormentor's jewels and kinky hair but her father laid a gentle hand on her shoulder and pulled her out of Kobylov's way.

"Thank you, Vladlena," sneered the interloper with a flashy smile. Lena's full, revolutionary name, Vlad-Lena, was short for Vladimir Lenin.

"Good evening, comrades," said Mendel in that Polish-Yiddish Lublin accent that he had never lost. "As a Bolshevik since 1900, I obey any summons from the Central Committee."

"Good!" Kobylov beamed mockingly.

Lena, who was twenty and studying, sensed how this uneducated secret policeman from some village in Georgia hated the Old Bolsheviks, Soviet nobility, with their libraries, fancy airs and intellectual pretensions.

"May I get dressed, Comrade Kobylov?" asked Mendel.

"Your women will help you. One of my boys will keep an eye on you. Where are the weapons?"

Lena knew from her father how Comrade Stalin hated suicides.

"There's a Nagant in the bedside table, a Walther in the study," boomed Mendel, limping back to the bedroom.

"I've got to sit down," murmured Natasha. She collapsed onto the sofa in the sitting room.

"Mama," cried Lena.

"Are you all right, Natasha?" called Mendel.

"I'm fine. Lena, help Papa dress, please." Natasha lay down, breathing heavily.

Lena brought a glass of water to her mother, then watched the Chekists opening drawers and making piles of manuscripts in Mendel's study. During '37 and '38, there had been arrests and raids in their building every night—she'd hear the elevators working in the early hours and see the NKVD Black Crows parked outside. The next morning, she'd noticed how the doors on the apartments had been sealed by the NKVD. "The Cheka's defending the Revolution," her father told her. "Never speak of this." But that was all over. The arrests had stopped a year ago. This must be a mistake, she thought.

"Mendel," called Kobylov. "Any letters to or from the Central Committee? Old things?" He meant letters from Comrade Stalin. "Your memoirs?"

"In the safe, it's open," retorted Mendel from the bedroom. To Lena's surprise, there were a few postcards from Stalin in exile; some notes from the twenties; and typed memoirs on yellowing sheets of foolscap, marked by Mendel's spidery notes. Her father was so modest. He told stories of his adventures but never dropped names. "Lena!"

Lena followed her father into his bedroom. She opened his wardrobe and took out his three-piece black suit, his black fedora, his walking boots with the built-up sole, a leather tie, his Order of Lenin. Then, struggling to show no emotion and aware that she must not add to his troubles, she helped him dress, as her mother often did. He said nothing until he was ready. "Thank you, Lenochka."

"What's it about, Papa? Do you know?" she asked, then wished she hadn't bothered him.

He just shook his head. "Probably nothing."

Mendel entered the sitting room and kissed his wife's forehead. "I love you, Natasha," he said in his deep voice. "Long live the Party!" Then he turned to his daughter.

"I'll see you down," said Lena, feeling numb. In the hall, she helped her lame father step over a heap of family photographs, papers, letters and proofs of his famous book, *Bolshevik Morality*. The floor looked like a shattered collage of their entire lives.

They rode down in the ornate but creaking elevator. Outside, the night was warm. The Great Palace of the Kremlin glowed majestically. Even though it was so late, there were two lovers on Stone Bridge; tango music escaped from an open window somewhere in the huge building. There was no traffic, just a Packard touring car and a Black

Crow van that bore the words *Eggs, Bread, Vegetables,* both with engines idling.

In the humid street, the glossy, oversized Commissar of Security Kobylov somehow reminded Lena of a shiny papier-mâché statue on a May Day carnival float.

"Your carriage awaits, Mendel," he said, inclining his kinky-haired head toward the Crow.

Lena watched her father, limping in his old-fashioned suit, his metallic boots clicking on the asphalt, as he approached the open door of the black van. He paused and Lena gasped, her heart in her mouth, but Mendel just looked up at the super-modern apartment building they were so proud to inhabit and said nothing, though a nervous tic fluttered on his cheek. Her severe, laconic and very old-fashioned father was not a demonstrative man but Lena knew from a million little things that he absolutely loved her, his only child. Now Lena did something she had never done before. She took his hand and, placing it between both of hers, she squeezed it. He looked away, and she could hear him wheezing. He was sixty but he looked much older.

Then he turned to Lena and, to her surprise and deep emotion, he bowed formally and then kissed her thrice, the old way, *à la russe.* "Be a good Communist. Good-bye, Lena Mendelovna."

"Good-bye, Papa," she answered.

She wanted to inhale his smell of coffee and cigarettes and soap, his presence, his love; she fought an urge to hold on to his suit, to fall to the pavement and grip his legs so they couldn't take him—but it was over too fast.

Mendel didn't look at her again—and she understood why. The step was too high. Two Chekists took Mendel and lifted him into the van. Inside, there were metal cages so Mendel could not sit. They closed him into one such compartment and as they slammed the van door, Lena saw not only her father's liquid eyes catching the light—but others' too.

Kobylov banged the top of his limousine as he swung into the passenger seat. Lena stood in the street and watched the two vehicles speed across the bridge past the Kremlin and out of sight.

The janitor, so friendly, always doing chores for the family, stood on the steps staring, but he said nothing and averted his eyes. Then Lena went upstairs to tend to Natasha.

Her mother was sobbing so hard she could not speak. Lena sat down wearily and wondered what to do. She remembered that her mother had cared for Sashenka during her night in prison in 1916.

At dawn, Lena called Sashenka from a phone on the street. She could hear Snowy singing in the background, the clack of cutlery. Sashenka was serving the children breakfast over at Granovsky.

"It's Lenochka," she said.

"Lenochka—what is it?"

"Papa's fallen ill unexpectedly and they've . . . he's gone for treatment." Lena was overcome with foreboding. Tears flooded her eyes and she put down the phone.

"Who was that?" asked Snowy. "Lenochka? Aunt Lenochka's a fat cushion. What's wrong, Mama?"

"My God," sighed Sashenka, sinking into a chair, her hand at her forehead. What did this mean? First Gideon, then Mendel. She felt sick.

"Mamochka," said Carlo in his piping voice, climbing onto her knee like a tame bear cub. He wore blue pajamas. "Are you feeling poorly? I'm going to give you a cuddle and stroke your face and kiss you like this! I love you, Mamochka, you're my best friend!"

Carlo kissed her on the nose with such pliant gentleness that Sashenka shivered with love.

22

The following Saturday, Sashenka was waiting for Vanya to come home. The dacha was quiet, its stillness suffocating. The children were baking a cake with Carolina.

Doves cooed in the dovecote and crows cawed in the birch trees. The horses in Marshal Budyonny's stables whinnied and the children's pony answered. Bees buzzed; the jasmine was sickly sweet. The important neighbor next door was singing a song from the movie *Jolly Fellows*. But the phone did not ring. Satinov had not called for his game of tennis.

Everything had slowed down. Sashenka sat on the veranda, pretending to read the newspapers and her magazine proofs. There was no clue in the newspapers, no hint of the spy mania and show trials of a year earlier. People were being freed; cases were being reviewed. Perhaps she was being paranoid. She had rung Benya and told him about the uncles in code. "The geraniums are budding," he'd answered calmly and she remembered the garden shed and their talisman.

She thought about Benya all the time. They could meet next week. He would soothe her; he would make her laugh in that fatalistic Jewish way of his. How had she survived so long without the one and only Benya? She yearned to call him, but not from the dacha. There was a public phone down the lane. Benya kept teasing her, trying to make her say that she loved him. "Don't you feel something special for me?" he'd ask. After ten days? She, Party member, mother, editor and Old Bolshevik, fall in love with an idle writer? Was he mad? No, it was *she* who was crazy. Oh, Benya! What would he make of all this?

The signs were confusing. Gideon had not been arrested, and Mouche had called to report that "they" had just wanted to discuss movies with him, "movies and the history of the Greeks and the Romans." Was that a hint for Sashenka or a random throwaway phrase? Was Gideon warning them about Mendel's arrest? "The Greeks and the Romans." Mendel knew ancient history. He *was* ancient history. His arrest must stem from something in the distant Bolshevik past. Stalin's old Georgian friend, "Uncle" Abel Yenukidze, had written a history of the Bolshevik printing press in Baku—yet fatally downplayed the Master's role in it. Sashenka remembered Comrade Abel well, a sandy-haired playboy with blue eyes, wandering hands and a harem of ballerinas. He had been shot in 1937.

Yet Mendel was no Abel. Uncle Mendel had never joined an opposition and had fought for Stalin ferociously. He was the Conscience of the Party and no chatterer. Why Mendel and why now, when the Terror was really over? They could have arrested Mendel at any time since 1936. It did not make sense.

Or had Gideon meant ancient *family* history? But everyone knew about the Zeitlins and that she had typed for Lenin, she the millionaire's Bolshevik daughter, Comrade Snowfox! Were the Organs circling her and her family? Her antecedents might be bourgeois—but she was protected by her marriage to Vanya Palitsyn, by his loyal service and proletarian pedigree, and by their joint Party orthodoxy.

Or perhaps the problem lay with her husband? Was this some rivalry inside the Organs, Beria's new Georgians versus the old Muscovites? But Vanya had never been a vassal of the previous boss, Yezhov, and anyway Beria had sacked all Yezhov's homicidal lags months earlier. Those maniacs were gone. Dust.

Family arrests did not necessarily reflect on her, Sashenka told herself. They happened all the time. Even Stalin's in-laws, the Svanidzes, had been arrested. Even the brothers of Stalin's dear Comrade Sergo had been executed. Her own father had vanished. Stalin had said the sons were not to blame for the sins of the fathers but at a secret dinner at the Kremlin, attended by Vanya himself, he had also threatened to destroy Enemies of the People "and their entire clans! Yes, their clans!"

Stalin, history and the Party worked in mysterious ways, she knew this. We Party members are devotees of a military-religious order in a time of intensifying class struggle and coming war, thought Sashenka. The greater the successes of our Party, the more our enemies will struggle against us: that was Comrade Stalin's formula. We owe our loyalty to the Party and the holy grail of the Idea, not bourgeois sentimentality. Mendel is a politician and in our progressive but imperfect system, *this* is politics. It would be fine, she told herself. Mendel would return just like Gideon. This was a new, less carnivorous era. The bad times were over.

The doves in the dovecote flew up like a fan as a car drew up. Sashenka came down in her bare feet to help the chauffeur open the gates.

Her husband stepped out wearily but Sashenka felt reassured at the sight of him. Vanya was Assistant Deputy People's Commissar of Internal Affairs and, since the March Congress, candidate member of the Central Committee—and here he was, right as rain. Just a little washed out and with more grey in his thick coarse hair—but he always came home tired.

She had been a fool for worrying. Snowy and Carlo rushed outside. Carlo was naked and Snowy wore her pink summer dress: she was growing fast. Their father hugged them, squeezed them, greeted their bunnies and cushions, heard about their cakes and candies in the kitchen—and sent them back inside. Then he was looking at Sashenka, looking at her as he had never looked at her before, his raging eyes crow black. He was about to say something when Carolina announced lunch from the veranda.

He turned his back on her and walked inside.

23

The meal at the veranda table seemed longer than usual. The scent of the lilacs was heavenly but then Snowy threw some bread at her brother. Vanya snapped, jumping up and wrenching her chair away from the table.

"Stop that!" he shouted.

Snowy was shocked and started to sob. Carlo looked terrified, then his wide face melted into tears. "I didn't do anything!" he cried. He ran to his mother but Sashenka said nothing. All her senses were centered on her husband.

Vanya avoided her eyes and ate hardly anything. Instead of feeling guilty, as she expected to, she felt resentful. She longed for Benya and his irrepressible sense of fun, his Rabelaisian bawdiness and his sensitivity.

"Vanya, you need to sleep," she said finally.

"Do I? What good will that do?"

Sashenka rose. "I'm going to take the children to swim in the river." It was 2:30 p.m.

Vanya shut himself in his study.

In her bare feet, carrying the towels, Sashenka led the children by the hand down the dirt lane through the silver birches toward the banks of the Moskva. Vanya always returned grouchy from his nocturnal work, she told herself. Even walking, she felt how Benya had changed her life.

Her legs were bare, and the sun seemed to lick her cheekbones, shoulders and knees as if they were covered in syrup. Her thighs grazed each other, sticking a little, sweaty. Even the grit between her toes seemed sensual. The young Sashenka of the civil war and the twenties would never have noticed such things; the Party matron of the thirties was too serious, too full of the Party's campaigns and slogans. Then she had dressed with deliberate dreariness, in the plainest, brownest stockings, in shapeless shift dresses, her hair in the tightest bun and always tied with the same kerchief. Now everything played with her senses in a way that amazed her. The buttoned cotton dress seemed to caress her on the thighs and neck. She longed to tell Benya about the delicious smell of pine resin and every detail of what she was doing and feeling. A cool breeze lifted the unbuttoned hem and showed her legs.

She grinned at the thought of Benya and his hands all over her, of him dancing and that way he laughed, with his mouth wide open. They discussed books and movies, paintings and plays but oh, how they laughed. And the laughter led back to her thighs and her breasts and her lips: all belonged to him.

They reached the golden banks of the mud-brown river, lined with cherry trees laden with pink blossom. Snowy picked her a spray.

Other children were swimming, and she recognized some of the Party families. She waved and blew kisses, clapping for the children as they sprinted and dived. "Are you watching me, Mama?" called Carlo every time he jumped in and each time she answered, "When aren't we watching you two?" She dried and dressed them when they began to feel chilled.

They returned by the woods. An army of bluebells lay under the trees awaiting them. Snowy and Carlo started to build a camp for the Wood Cushions, immersed in a world of mossy sofas and tree-trunk palaces.

She sat on the bench by the lane and watched them. She knew why she had brought them this way. Her eyes flickered between the camp and the nearby public telephone. Should she, shouldn't she? No, she would not call.

"Darlings, we've got to go home now," she said.

"No!" shouted Snowy. "We want to play."

She knew she had to phone, that she was always going to use that phone. She closed her eyes. Benya had said he would be at his ramshackle dacha in Peredelkino, the writers' village. She had the number and longed to suggest that they meet somehow. At some garden shed—clinging together among the spades and geraniums! But she must wait until the Mendel business was settled. Besides, he was with his family.

She would call him anyway. If Benya's wife answered, she would introduce herself as his editor. She really was commissioning him to write a piece for the magazine: "How to celebrate at a real Soviet people's masked ball! How to prepare your dresses, your masks and your feast!"

As her children danced along the sandy path, she dialed Benya's number. The phone rang and rang. No answer. She found herself leaning on the aluminum shield of the telephone box, pressing herself against it, dreamily contemplating the electrical miracle that would carry his voice through the wires to her ear. She stopped herself, shaking her head at her own foolishness.

You'll have to wait, Benya Golden. I'll find a way to let you know, she said to herself. I was going to tell you I loved you.

24

At 4:00 p.m., Sashenka was back at the dacha. The white pillars of its façade, the wooden table, the swinging hammocks reminded her of summers at Zemblishino before the Revolution. The children were drowsy and Carolina took them to rest in their rooms.

Vanya sat in the garden in his scarlet-embroidered peasant shirt, boots and baggy trousers. Always the boots.

"Are you all right, Vanya?" she asked. "Any news of Mendel?"

He did not move. Then he stood up slowly, turned toward her and hit her right in the face, knocking her over. The punch was so powerful that she did not quite feel it, although as she lay stunned on the grass she could taste the blood on her tongue.

His impassive face twitching, Vanya stood over her, clenching and wringing, clenching and wringing those puffy hands of his. Sashenka got to her feet and dashed at her husband, her mouth open to scream at him, but he caught her by the wrist and flung her back onto the ground.

"Where have you just been, you disgusting slut?" He was bending right over her. Even in this fight, both were aware of the voices over the fence, the staff in the house, the guards: everyone was listening and reporting. After he had hit her, they were still whispering at each other, not shouting, beneath the buzz of a late spring day.

"We went to swim in the river."

"To the telephone."

"Well, I passed the telephone . . ."

"And you called, did you not?"

"Don't speak to me like I'm one of your cases. What if I did? I'm not allowed to make a phone call?"

"Who did you call?"

He knew already, she could tell, and it terrified her.

"You called that Jewish writer, didn't you? Didn't you? Do you think I haven't had my chances? Have I been faithful to you?"

"I don't know."

"Well, let me tell you, I've never touched another woman once in all these years, Sashenka. I worshipped you. I did everything for you. Didn't I provide for you?" Then he hissed at her: "You met him in our house, you whore! You took my children down the lane and you called that bastard writer!"

What did he know? Sashenka frantically shuffled the facts like a pack of cards: if he knew that she phoned him, what did that prove? If he knew she had commissioned an article, well, why not? If he knew about the hotel, then she was lost!

Vanya stood over her and she thought he would hit her again or kick her with his boots, right there in the garden of their dacha with their children sleeping in the house.

"Have you fucked him?"

"Vanya!"

"It doesn't matter, Alexandra Samuilovna. Now it doesn't matter. Now it's beyond that. You can't talk to him because he's not there."

She was still touching her bleeding lip as the meaning of what her husband said swept over her.

"What are you saying?"

His face was close to hers. He was sweating. "He's not there, Sashenka! He's gone now. *That's* his prize!"

Sashenka was furious, white-lipped with a wild anger that took her by surprise. "So this is your revenge? This is how Chekists make their wives faithful, is it? You should be ashamed of yourself! I thought you served the Party. And what will you do to him? Beat him up in some cellar with a bludgeon? Is that what *you* do every day, Vanya?"

"You don't understand." Vanya sat down suddenly. He rubbed his face in his hands, rubbed his hair, eyes closed. Then he got up and walked slowly back into the house.

Sashenka stood up shakily. Benya had been arrested! It could not be true. What would happen to him? She could hardly bear to contemplate him suffering. Where was he?

25

"Mamochka!" Carlo was crying. He always woke up in a bad mood.

"Why are you and Papochka talking like that?" said Snowy, dancing into the garden. "Mama, why is your lip bleeding?"

"Oh," said Sashenka, feeling ashamed for the first time. "I banged it on the door."

"I want to cure you, Mama. Can I put a bandage on your cut?" said Carlo, touching her lip and kissing her hands, while Snowy, refreshed and exuberant, trotted round the garden like a fresh pony. Sashenka looked down the corridor toward Vanya's study, the possibilities ricocheting around her brain. She was almost glad Vanya had hit her and that he had not taken it out on the children. She would rather he beat her black and blue if it meant Benya would not suffer. But what if Benya wasn't who he seemed to be? Suppose he'd been arrested not out of a cuckold's vengeance but because he was an "unclean element," some sort of Trotskyite spy? Or suppose Vanya had invented the arrest just to torment her? Or suppose Mendel was in real trouble and had somehow embroiled her and her friends? As each plausible scheme ripened in her imagination, she felt another lurch of fear until one of the children called her.

"Mamochka, are you watching me?" First Snowy, then Carlo. Sashenka almost sleepwalked through the exasperatingly slow afternoon, a perfect example of the delights of spring in the silver woods of the Moscow plain.

What have I done, she thought, what have I done?

•••

At last, it was 8:00 p.m. and bedtime.

"Will you stroke me to sleep?" Carlo mumbled, brown eyes on hers.

"Eleven strokes on your forehead," she said.

"Yes, Mamochka, eleven strokes."

Usually, Sashenka was completely engrossed in Carlo but today her mind was somewhere else. Where was she? With Benya in the cellars of the Lubianka? With Mendel in the dungeons of hell? And where did this leave her and her family? She prayed for a release from the suspense, and yet she feared it.

"Mamochka? Can I tell you something? Mama?"

"Yes, Carlo."

"I love you in my heart, Mama." This was a new expression and it hit Sashenka hard. She seized his sturdy cub's body and hugged him tightly.

"What a lovely thing to say, darling. Mama loves you in her heart too."

She laid her hands on his satiny forehead and they counted aloud: she stroked his face eleven times until his eyes were closed. Mercifully, Snowy was exhausted and went straight to sleep without a fuss.

It was a lush, sweltering night. The house was patrolled by fat fluttering moths, sleepy obese bluebottles and swarming greenflies. The ceiling fans whirred. Carolina was in her room.

No one had phoned.

Vanya went to sit on the rocking chair on the veranda, smoking and drinking. Jews, Sashenka thought, don't drink when they're in crisis, they get rashes and palpitations. She remembered her father. Vanya's chair creaked back and forth and she heard the clanking of her father's Trotting Chair all those years ago.

It was time. Crows cawed in the linden tree. Sashenka approached her husband nervously.

"Vanya?" she said. She needed to know how he had found out about Benya, what he knew. Until then, confess to nothing.

"Vanya, I did nothing," she lied. "I flirted. I'm so sorry . . ." She expected more severity from him but when he turned his face to her, it was clammy and swollen with tears. Vanya never cried except when he was very drunk, during sad movies, at regimental reunions or when he saw Snowy in the school play.

"Don't," he said.

"Do you hate me?"

He shook his head.

"Please just tell me what you know."

Vanya tried to speak but his generous mouth, swaggering jaw and teddy-bear eyes lost their definition, as he cried silently in that warm dusk.

"I know I've done something very wrong. Vanya, I am so sorry!"

"I know everything," he said.

"Everything? What is there to know?"

He groaned with an awesome, weary pain. "Don't bother, Sashenka. We're beyond husbands and wives now."

"You're scaring me, Vanya."

Tears flowed down his cheeks as the blood of the sunset spread across the sky.

26

Sashenka stood beside the rocking chair, breathing in the scent of the jasmine. She thought of Mendel. She thought of Benya. And the children asleep in their rooms.

Finally Vanya got up from his chair. He was drunk, his eyes hot and gritty—but drunk in the way that hard drinkers ride the alcohol—and he pulled her to him, lifting her feet off the ground. For the first time in a long while, she was grateful for his touch. She noticed the rabbits in the hutch and the pony gazing peacefully over the fence—but she and Vanya were as alone as they had ever been.

"I can separate from you," she said. "No one needs to know. Let me separate and you'll be rid of me. Divorce me!" (Just hours ago, this might have been a fantasy escape with Benya—now it seemed a measure of desperation.) "I did something terrible! I'm sorry, so sorry . . ."

"Don't say that," whispered Vanya, squeezing her tighter. "I'm angry with you, of course, you fool. But we don't have time to be hurt."

"For God's sake, tell me what you mean? Who knows?"

"*They* know everything—and it's all my fault," he said.

"Please! Just tell me what's happened?"

He hugged her suddenly, kissing her neck, her eyes, her hair. "I've been moved off the Foreign Commissariat case. I'm being sent down to check out our comrades in Stalinabad in Turkestan."

"Well, I'll go with you. We can all go and live in Stalinabad."

"Pull yourself together, Sashenka. They could arrest me at the station. They could come tonight."

"But why? It's me who's done something . . . I beg for forgiveness but how can this be political?"

"Gideon, Mendel, now Benya Golden—there's something out there, Sashenka, and I don't know what it is. Perhaps they have something on your writer? Perhaps he's a bastard connected to foreign spies. But they also have something on you and me. I don't know what it is but I do know that it could destroy us altogether." His feverish face was pale in the shrinking light. "We might not have any time. What are we going to do?"

The enormity of their predicament crushed Sashenka.

Two weeks earlier, Comrade Stalin had been in her house with Comrade Beria, Narkom of the NKVD. Stars of screen and stage had sung in their home; Vanya was newly promoted and trusted; Comrade Stalin admired her magazine, admired her and tweaked Snowy's cheeks. No, Vanya was wrong. It was lies. Her heart fluttered, red sparks rose before her eyes and her guts spasmed.

"Vanya, I'm terrified."

They sat at the table on the veranda, very close, cheek to cheek, hand in hand, closer now than on their honeymoon when they were young and in love, bound together now in more ways than any husband and wife would ever want to be.

Vanya gathered himself. "Sashenka, I'm frightened too. We've got to make a plan now."

"Do you really believe they're coming for us?"

"It's possible."

"Can't we ask someone? Have you called Lavrenti Pavlovich? He likes you. He's pleased with you. You even play on his basketball team. What about Hercules? He knows everything; Stalin loves him; he'll help us."

"I've called them both," answered Vanya. "'Comrade Beria is unavailable,' said his apparat. Hercules hasn't called back."

"But that doesn't mean anything. Beria's probably tomcatting. And Hercules'll call us."

"We need to decide what to do tonight. They may arrest me, or you, or both of us. Who knows what they're beating out of Mendel right now—or your fucking writer."

"But surely they can't make them invent things?"

"Christ save us!" Vanya exclaimed. "You're joking, aren't you? We have a saying in the Organs: 'Give me a man tonight and I'll have him confessing he's the King of England by morning!' You believed every confession at the trials? Zinoviev, Kamenev, Bukharin, the terrorists, killers, wreckers, spies?"

"They were true. You said they were true, in spirit, in essence."

"Oh yes, they were true all right. They were all bastards. They were enemies in spirit. They lost faith, and *faith* is everything. But . . ." He shook his head.

"You beat people to say these things, didn't you, Vanya?"

"For the Party, I'd do anything. I've done anything. Yes, I know what it is to break a man. Some break like a matchstick, some die rather than say a word. But better to shoot a hundred innocent men than let one spy escape, better a thousand."

"Oh my God, Vanya." Benya's words, and Benya's expression as he had said them, returned to her. He had known what Vanya did all night while she, she . . .

"What did you think I was doing? It was top secret but it suited you not to know."

"But the Party's right to destroy the spies. I knew there were mistakes but we all said the mistakes were worth it. Now, what if we become such a mistake? I believe in the Party and Stalin, it's my life's work. Vanya, do you still believe?"

"After what I've done for the Party, I have to believe. If I were shot tonight, I'd die a Communist. And you?"

"Die? I can't die. I can't vanish! I want to live. I love life. *I'll do anything to live.*"

"Keep your voice down, dear Comrade Snowfox." His new air of brisk conspiracy took her back to when he was an ardent young Bolshevik activist in Petrograd in 1916—it was one of the things that had attracted her to him. "Be calm! We're not going to die but we need to plan ahead. If they take us, don't confess a thing. That's the key. If you don't confess, they can't touch you. Whatever they do to us, confess nothing!"

"I'm not sure I could take it. The pain," Sashenka said shakily. "Vanya, you have your revolver here, don't you?"

Vanya lifted the peaked cap that lay before them on the table. Underneath lay a Nagant pistol. Sashenka put her hand on the cold steel and remembered the "bulldogs" in Petrograd that she'd carried for the Party. How passionately and proudly she had borne those pistols for the Revolution. How she had admired Vanya, the strapping worker with those hands more like paws, his bold face, his brown eyes! What had he become? What had they both become?

"We could kill ourselves tonight, Vanya. I could kill myself and you'd be free of me. You'd be clean. I'll do it if you just ask . . ."

"That's our first choice. We have the gun and we have tonight. But suppose they don't have anything on you? They'll beat you and humiliate you. But if you don't confess, they'll ask: 'Did she sign anything? No? Well, perhaps she wasn't a bastard after all.' They'll free you in the end. For us, for life, for the children."

The children! They'd almost forgotten the children. Death, the violence and finality of vanishing from the earth and ceasing to exist, was so horrifying, so immediate, that it bred the purest form of egotism. How could she have been so selfish?

Sashenka turned and ran into the house, Vanya behind her, and they burst into Snowy's room. Holding hands, they stared in anguish at Snowy, her white skin and fair hair spread out on her pillow, breathing so softly, her long arms curled beside her, her silly pink cushion resting against her cheek. And there was Carlo lying naked on his front, hair tousled, arms and legs still creased like a baby, head burrowed into his favorite velveteen rabbit.

Sashenka was barely able to breathe, her throat parched, in the warm, dark room that smelled of the peculiar freshness of young children in summertime, of hay and vanilla. It was as if they were the first and last parents in the world. But they were the only ones to know what they were up against. Sashenka's stomach churned. They were on the verge of losing their treasures forever.

"Snowy, Carlo, oh darlings!" She fell to her knees between the two beds, Vanya beside her, and suddenly they were sobbing silently in each other's arms.

"Don't wake them," said Vanya.

"We mustn't," agreed Sashenka, brokenly. But she could not help herself. With trembling hands, she reached into Carlo's bed and lifted him out, folded him against her, raining kisses on his satiny forehead until he stirred. Vanya was holding Snowy, his face buried in her hair, which cleaved like gold thread to his wet cheeks. Both children were drowsily sensual as they clung to their parents, gloriously unaware of the rising storm, roused from the deep slumber of that sweltering night. The four of them crouched together in the comforting darkness, the parents gasping with tears, the children stretching and sighing, settling back into their loving arms, only half awake.

Finally Vanya pulled Sashenka by the hand. "Put them back to bed!" he said. They tucked the children in again then crept outside to sit on the edge of the sofa by the open French windows. A car door slammed loudly in the night air.

"Vanya! Is this it? Is it them?" She threw herself into his arms.

He calmed her with his clumsy hands, their coarseness now so welcome, familiar.

"No, it's not them. Not yet," he whispered. "But we've got to think calmly. Stop crying, girl! Gather yourself. For the children . . ."

Then he too started to shudder—and she let out an involuntary moan until he put his hand over her mouth. Finally she left the room and washed her face with cold water. A dread soberness descended on both of them.

"Vanya, we can't kill ourselves because—"

"Stalin calls suicide 'spitting in the eye of the Party.' We save ourselves pain, but not the children. The Party will take it out on the children."

"I've got it. We kill ourselves *and* the children. Tonight, Vanya, now. We die together and we'll be together. Forever!" How strange—yet she did believe in a sort of afterlife. In eternity. That was what her rabbinical grandparents believed, and she the Communist had always eschewed it. Now those old words from Turbin came back to her—Zohar, the Book of Splendor and heart of the Kabala, Heaven and Gehenna, the golems and dybbuks that haunted those cursed with the Evil Eye, the spiritual world so foreign to scientific Marxism and dialectical materialism. And yet now she imagined her soul, and its love, living on beyond the shell of her body. There she would see her mother and father, all young again. They would all be together! She pulled out the Nagant from under Vanya's NKVD cap. She still knew how to use it.

"Do you believe that?" he asked. "I do. We'd all be together in Heaven. Maybe you're right. If they come for us, we kill them and then ourselves."

"So that's decided." But as Sashenka turned toward the bedroom, he caught her, taking the pistol from her and slipping it into his holster.

He hugged her tightly, whispering, "I couldn't. I just couldn't. Could you?"

She shook her head. It was now past midnight and Sashenka's mind was working more systematically.

"We don't have time for more crying, do we, darling Vanya?"

"They've something on us. I don't know what."

"Gideon mentioned 'the Greeks and the Romans' and then Mendel was arrested. Benya Golden knows nothing about us."

"But is he a provocateur? A spy? Is he filth?"

"He could be . . ." She was now so afraid that she was blaming her own lover. Was this what had happened? Had Benya destroyed her family? Then another meteor shower of possibilities bombarded her: "Could it be a Chekist intrigue at the Lubianka? There has to be some reason for this, Vanya, doesn't there?"

He opened his hands wide.

"There has to be a cause," he told her. "But there doesn't need to be any reason."

Just then they heard the back gate creak.

"It's *them,* Vanya. I love you, Vanya, Snowy, Carlo. If either of us live, oh Vanya . . . Shall we end it all? Where's the bulldog?"

They clung together. He had the gun in his hand and they pressed its cool steel between their palms as if it were their love token. There were no other sounds. The night turned with grinding slowness.

A whistle split the stillness, and a figure in a white hood stepped out of the shadows of the orchard.

Vanya raised the Nagant pistol.

"Who's there? I'll shoot. I'll take you all with me, you bastards!"

27

"I can only stay for a few minutes," said the visitor, removing the Caucasian hood that he had always worn in that Petrograd winter, in the early days.

"Oh Hercules, thank God you came!" Sashenka kissed him repeatedly, holding on to him. "We're going to be all right, aren't we? You've come to tell us how to fix it. Who do we need to talk to? Please tell us!"

They turned off the lights on the veranda, and Hercules Satinov sat at the table with Vanya and Sashenka. She poured the three of them shots of Armenian brandy.

"It's going to be fine, isn't it?" she said again. "We're imagining this, aren't we? Oh Hercules, what are we going to do?"

"Hush, Sashenka," said Vanya. "Just let him speak."

Satinov nodded, his eyes slits of quicksilver in the darkness.

"Listen carefully," he began. "I don't know everything but I know that something has changed. They're working on Mendel and they've found something on you."

"On me?" cried Sashenka. "Vanya, divorce me! I'll shoot myself."

"Just listen to him, Sashenka," said Vanya.

"It's beyond that now," said Satinov tersely. "I thought . . . about the children."

Sashenka's blood started to pound.

"Can't I go and see Beria? I'd do anything. Anything! I could persuade Lavrenti Pavlovich . . ."

Satinov shook his head and Sashenka sensed the tension running through him. He did not even have time to discuss them. Just the children.

"I could write to Comrade Stalin. He knows me, he's known me since March 1917 when I typed for Lenin . . . He knows me."

Satinov's eyes flashed, and Sashenka understood that somehow this came from the Instance, the top, the Instantzia.

"You must think only of the children now," he said simply.

"Oh my God," Sashenka whispered, red spots whirring before her eyes. "They'll be sent to one of those orphanages. They'll be tortured, murdered, abused. Trotsky's children are dead. All Kamenev's. All Zinoviev's. I know what happens in those places . . ."

"Quiet, Sashenka. What can we do, Hercules?" Vanya asked.

"Can they stay with any of your family?" asked Satinov but Sashenka knew Gideon and Mouche were on the edge of the precipice; his other daughter, Viktoria, was a Party fanatic who would never help tainted children; Mendel was already in the coils of the Lubianka; and Vanya's parents would probably be arrested soon after them.

"Then Snowy and Carlo must be sent away," said Satinov. "Immediately. Maybe even tomorrow. To the south. I have friends there who owe me favors. Remember, I was on the ZaKavCom for a long time. Outside the towns, there are ordinary people, unpolitical people. I was tough at times when I worked down there, I broke the backs of our enemies—but when I could, I helped people."

"Who are these people? What will happen to Snowy and Carlo?" Sashenka was drowning in hysteria: she fought for breath, her mouth gasping, yet she could not take in enough oxygen.

"Sashenka, you have to trust me. I'm Snowy's godfather. Do you trust me?"

She nodded. No choice: Satinov was all they had.

"Right, they must travel south in secret. I have to go to the Caucasus myself tonight but I can't travel with them. Someone absolutely trustworthy must take them 'on holiday'—nothing suspicious about that. Somewhere, that person will hand them over to another person I have in mind."

"What about Vanya's parents?"

"Yes, my mother loves the children . . . ," said Vanya eagerly.

"No," interrupted Satinov. "They're at the Granovsky. They're being watched at all times. They would not be a wise choice; forgive me, Vanya, but their Party-mindedness is both fervent and simpleminded, a dangerous combination."

"Do you know . . . someone who would look after the children in the south, someone really kind, kind enough for such beloved . . . such angels?" Sashenka asked.

Satinov took Sashenka's hands in his and squeezed them. "Don't torture yourself. Yes, oh yes, I promise you, Sashenka, I have in mind someone of whom you would approve. But even that person cannot know where they are finally settled."

"Will they be settled together? Please say they will. They love each other, need each other—and without us . . ."

Hercules shook his head. "No. If they were in an NKVD orphanage for children of traitors, they'd be split up, their names changed. Besides, there might be an all-Union search for a brother and sister together and they'd find them. They'll be safer separated. There are thousands of lost children now, millions even, the stations are full of them."

"But that would mean they'd lose a brother and a sister as well as their parents. They'd cease to be part of the same family. Vanya, I can't bear it. I can't go through with it."

"Yes," Vanya replied, "you will."

"They'll be settled in separate families," continued Satinov. "I have the families in mind. They're couples without children, not involved in politics in any way—but decent, kind people. If you come back, if all this is nothing, if you're just exiled, you won't be able to live in Moscow for a long time but the children'll be ready for you, I promise. And they'll come and join you wherever you are. But if not, and things look bad . . ."

"Tell me who they are, please, these families. *Who are they?*" beseeched Sashenka, her voice cracking.

"No one except me can know where they settle. Helping children of Enemies of the People would cost all of us our heads. But I can do it, Sashenka. The paperwork'll be lost, and they'll disappear safely. You're not alone. Many sent their children to the countryside in thirty-seven. So this is my offer. If you accept this, I swear that I'll watch over your children as long as I have breath in my body. It will be my life's mission. But you have to decide right now."

Vanya looked at Sashenka and she looked at him. Finally she turned to Satinov.

"Oh Hercules," she croaked—but she nodded.

She tried to hug Satinov but he shrank from her and she understood how he felt because she'd felt it herself. When doomed friends were put on ice in '37, waiting for arrest, she avoided them as if they were infectious, as if they carried the plague, because in those times such connections could be fatal. Now *she* was the leper and this dear friend was helping her.

"Thank you," she said softly. "You're a decent man, an honest Communist."

"Believe me, I'm not so great," Satinov said.

"All right," he said then. "First, I have telegrams to send. Get the children ready tonight. You can send them anytime from tomorrow. Or you can wait until one of you is taken and you know more. You depart tomorrow for Stalinabad, don't you, Vanya? But if they take you, will you be able to get a message out? I'm leaving tonight on a special Central Committee train so I'll be in Tiflis tomorrow. I'm heading a new mission and I'll be in the south for a month. It's a blessing because it means I can help you. I'll give you my telegram details. And this is important: if you're arrested, I need time to settle the children before the Organs come looking. Vanya, you know what I'm saying. Don't even think about harming yourselves. Give me the cover, whatever it costs you. I'll use it well, understand? Now, stage one. Would Carolina take them on the first part of the journey?"

Sashenka thought of the stick-thin Volga German woman. For a moment she hesitated. In her flux of fear, Sashenka wondered if the nanny would betray them. Truly they could trust no one. Then, "Yes," she said, "I believe she'd go to the ends of the earth for those children."

"Get her," said Vanya but Sashenka was already knocking on Carolina's door. When she saw Carolina's anxious face, she realized that the nanny knew something was wrong—she hardly needed to explain. A few words sufficed.

Sashenka fought back tears and understood from the grim determination on Carolina's face and her set jaw that she had observed their suffering of the past hours.

"Come and join us," said Sashenka. The distinctions of mistress and servant vanished in a second, their power to save (or destroy) each other making them equals.

"Right," said Satinov when Sashenka and the nanny returned. "You understand that whatever happens, I was never here. Vanya, Sashenka, the last time we ever met was at the Granovsky at dinner with my wife. We didn't talk politics. I know nothing of your fate. You must book Carolina's tickets and passes as soon as possible. Call the station, work out times, right now, tonight even." He placed two identity cards on the table. "These are the papers for two orphans from the Dzerzhinsky Orphanage. Carolina must travel on her own papers but the children's tickets will be in false names. There are constant inspections on the stations and trains these days. Sashenka, destroy the children's passports—don't leave them in the dacha!"

"Where should Carolina go?" asked Sashenka. "Could she take them home with her to her village?"

"They might find her even there," said Satinov. "There've been a lot of arrests of Volga Germans out of Rostov. Carolina, you should take the Moscow-Baku-Tiflis train from Saratovsky Station. When you leave the train at Rostov there'll be a message for you at the stationmaster's office under your own name—it's Gunther, isn't it? Carolina Gunther? Either a person or a message. Afterward you must return to your village. All clear?"

Sashenka noticed that Satinov did not look his old friends in the eye as he departed, but he kissed her hand just as he had when they first met more than twenty years before and he hugged Vanya.

Pulling on his Georgian hood, he left through the garden just as he had come, and the gate creaked as it closed. Sashenka had known him since the winter of 1916, when they were all young. He had seen her at Ariadna's deathbed, had been their best friend in the world. Now their relationship was ending—or perhaps it was metamorphosing. From being a friend, he might become the only family her children had on earth. Among this Russian nation of toadies and cowards, timeservers and snitches, he alone had shown the courage to remain a human being.

"Come on. We've got work to do," said Carolina briskly, placing her hands on Sashenka's upper arms and pressing. "But first we must eat. A clear mind needs a full stomach." She brought out a tray of goat's cheese, tomatoes and black Borodinsky bread with Narzan mineral water.

They did not turn on the veranda light but they fell on the food as if they had never eaten before. Time ground on slowly. Sashenka felt better now: she had a mission. She had to trust Hercules Satinov. He said her children would be settled with "kind people" but oh, how her heart was breaking! She remembered Snowy and Carlo's births at the Kremlevka, the Kremlin Hospital, on Granovsky. Snowy, the first, had been easy: she had emerged with a head of blond hair and slept her first night on Sashenka's chest . . . Now she talked endlessly about cushions and butterflies (she knew the names of Brazilian Blues and Red Admirals) and she hated eggs. Carlo needed his eleven strokes before he would sleep, and he woke up in the night and needed a cuddle. He hated yogurt and he had a collection of rabbits, and when his blood sugar ran low between meals he needed his favorite Pechene cookies, the ones with the Kremlin on the tin; and he always wanted to visit the new Metro stations with their marble halls and glass cupolas and ride on the trains . . .

Should she write these things down for these "kind people"? Could she tell someone? Who would know all this—except a mother? How could her children be happy without their mother? Sashenka began to shake again.

"Discipline yourself! We must be practical!" Vanya's voice cut into her terror.

Sashenka contracted into herself as if she had been touched by a block of ice.

She could not write anything down and the children could take little with them—above all, nothing that linked them to their parents. There was no time now for sentiment, tears, guilt. Sashenka was a mother now, nothing more, just a mother protecting her cubs. She had to save them from the orphanages that Benya had described. When everything had been prepared, if there was time, then she could savor the presence of those living treasures, and talk to them a little. Then she could sob all she liked.

Sashenka found her food tasted of nothing. The garden might have been made of cardboard; the jasmine and the lilac and the honeysuckle smelled of decay; the pony, the rabbits, the squirrels, the rest of existence could rot for all she cared, if only she could be spared to bring up her children, if only they could be free to return to her . . .

Here I am abandoned, an orphan, with no one to look after me . . . Never had that old song been so pertinent and so unbearable.

"Vanya, we must talk carefully. This may be our last night together. But what do we tell them?" she asked, choking over her words.

"The less, the better," said Vanya. "They must forget we ever existed. Snowy will remember more but Carlo's only three. He won't even . . ." He could not speak anymore. Sashenka took Carolina's hand.

"Carolina, let's pack their cases. We must find them warm things to wear so they are never cold."

They went back into Snowy's room and Sashenka started to hand the child's clothes to Carolina. Each time, when she raised a little skirt or sweater to her nose, she inhaled the scent of hay and vanilla.

I gave the children life, Sashenka told herself, but I never owned them. Now they must live on without me, as if I never existed.

28

Old Razum the driver, last night's booze oozing out of cratered pores, arrived at dawn to take Vanya to the Moscow station. He honked beyond the gate, and Sashenka came out in her mauve nightie. It was a cool, bright, bracing May morning. The dew on the grass sparkled like a shower of diamonds, and the roses were budding. The children were already up and Carlo was jumping on their bed.

"Mama, can I tell you something . . ."

Vanya had been drinking all night and was sweating vodka. Sashenka watched as he went into the playroom to kiss the children. She knew he had many things he wished to say to them: bits of advice, sayings, mistakes to be warned against, gems all fathers wish to impart to their children before going on a journey. But the children were overexcited and would not even sit on his knee.

"I don't want to kiss Papochka, do you, Snowy?" Carlo pointed at his father, who stood there in his full NKVD uniform, boots, cap, three tabs on his red collar, leather strap and holster.

"We only want to kiss Mama and Carolina. Daddy's a scary monster! Daddy will eat us up and spit us out!" shouted Snowy, skipping like a frisky lamb. They jumped around him, and Sashenka watched—tears in her eyes—as Vanya caught them each in turn and pressed his face, his lips, his nose against them, just for a moment.

"Ouch, Daddy, you're all prickly!" cried Carlo. "You hurt me!"

"I don't want to kiss your prickly face," said Snowy. "Kiss my lovely cushion instead. Take it with you!"

"You want me to take your favorite?" asked Vanya, almost overcome.

"Yes, so you remember me, but promise to send it back, Papochka!"

Vanya's lips trembled as he took the little pink cushion and put it in his pocket, then he grabbed Snowy and held her for a moment. "Let me go, Papochka! You smell all funny!" And she scampered off, jumping over the two neat little canvas cases that stood by the door.

Vanya marched out, tears streaming down his unshaven cheeks.

Carlo ran after him. "Papa! I love you here," he said, "in my heart. Let me stroke you because you're crying." Vanya stopped and picked up his son, and Carlo mopped up the tears with his bunny rabbit.

"Why are you sad, Papa?" asked Snowy on the veranda.

"I don't like going away from you," said Vanya, putting Carlo down gently. "I'll be back soon but when I'm away, if you ever wonder where I am, look up at the stars in the sky like I've shown you. Wherever the Big Bear is, that's where I'll be."

Sashenka came with him to the door. He took her in his arms, lifted her up and squeezed her so tight that her slippers fell off.

"Marrying you . . . ," he could barely articulate the words, ". . . best decision . . . ever. Don't worry, this'll blow over, but if not we have our plan." He turned to Carolina and bowed low.

Carolina looked down and pushed her strong jaw forward, then she offered her hand and he shook it, standing straight as if he were on parade. "Thank you, Carolina!" Then he grabbed her too and hugged her spare, scrawny body.

Razum had turned the car round. Vanya climbed in and they drove away. Sashenka watched it go and ran back inside and threw herself onto her bed. How could all *this* be coming to an end? She still could not quite believe it.

She tried to imagine where Benya Golden was, and Mendel, but she could not do so. A ruthlessness had entered her spirit: there was no one but her and Vanya and the children now. No one. She should feel pity for Benya who loved her, and Mendel too—but she didn't. Let *them* perish so that she and her children could be together.

She felt weight on the bed.

"What's wrong? Mamochka's crying. Are you sad Papochka's gone away?" asked Snowy.

"Mama, Mama, can I tell you something? I'm going to kiss you and stroke you, Mama," said Carlo. His brown eyes turned cloudy, like a seducer in a movie, and he kissed her hard right on the lips.

"Darlings?"

"Yes, Mama."

"You might be going on a journey, a great adventure."

"With you and Daddy?"

"No, I don't think so, Snowy. But you love Carolina, don't you? You might be going with her and you know never to talk about your family or anything you've heard at home."

"We know that already," said Snowy very seriously. "Papa always says: 'No chatter!'"

"What about you and Daddy?" Carlo asked, his eyes anxious.

"Well, Carlo, we might come along later. If or when we can . . . But we'll always be around you, always . . ."

"Of course you will, silly!" said Snowy. "We're going to be together for ever and ever."

29

Sashenka drove them back into the city on Sunday afternoon. And then it started.

The guards at Granovsky were as friendly as ever—but there was a new guy. What expression was that in his eyes? Did he know that

Vanya was in Stalinabad? Did he know why? Was there a why? Marfa and Nikolai, Vanya's parents, and the other geriatrics sat in their chairs downstairs: why didn't Vanya's father stop reading his newspaper and speak to her? What was that sly look from Andreyev's old father—had his son, a top Politburo member, mentioned something? Had he told him to be careful of those Palitsyns, not to let the children play with them for a while? The janitor waved but why didn't he say hello and help with the cases? He always helped. Did he know something?

A young man in the street in a gabardine coat and a fedora watched them drive in. A Chekist? The guards in the guardhouse made a note: they were watching her. They knew something. Outside the apartment, Marshal Budyonny's maid lingered, dusting the stairs. An informer. It was agony. It was absurd. The circle of confidence and despair turned rhythmically inside her like a creaking old carousel at a circus.

It was Sunday night, and she lay in bed. A hole gaped in her belly. Wormwood coated her tongue. The fear hit her again, the terror of losing the children, and of death. Yet she was not afraid of the final cut: young people who became revolutionaries were always a step away from the gallows. When she traveled on the Agitprop trains during the civil war, she had been ready at any time to face death if she was captured by the Whites. That was what it meant to be a Bolshevik. But since she had had Snowy and Carlo, she had sensed death creeping up on her, a thief in the night, the highwayman who would steal her children. She felt her breasts for cancerous lumps; she feared the influenza and TB—what was that cough? Please, please, she begged Fate, give me the time to love them and cherish them. Grant me those years to see them happy and married with children of their own.

When the Terror came, she saw other parents disappear and their children vanish after them, no longer playing in the courtyard at the house on the Embankment or here on Granovsky. But those parents had deviated from the Party line and acted rashly, insincerely, impurely. They had seemed honest Communists yet in reality they wore masks. The Party came first and they had erred. She had always promised she would never do that. Yet somehow, she *had* done exactly that.

It grew dark and Sashenka tried to sleep, only to be divebombed by phantasms of horror, of tortures, arrests, sobbing childish faces. She shook and her pulse raced: was she going to have a heart attack? Vanya had not called. She dropped into sleep fitfully, just touching it, never sinking into it, before skimming off it like a pebble on a pond. She saw her mother dead, her mother alive, her mother young, her father being shot in the back of the head in front of her children.

"Who is that man?" asked Snowy.

"Don't you know your own dedushka, your grandfather?"

"What will happen to him when he's dead?" Carlo was asking. "Will he become a ghost?"

Sashenka woke up sweating and trembling, went into the children's room and lay down with Carlo, barely able to believe that this adorable boy could exist in such a world. She put her face on his shoulder. His skin was soft and rich. She stroked his bare back and fell asleep again.

When she awoke, Carlo was stroking her, his sweet breath on her face. What joy!

"Mamochka, can I tell you something? Someone's knocking on the door."

She sat up. It all came back to her. Nausea and vertigo assailed her. The knocking was so loud, so angry.

She kissed both children and then approached the door.

"Open up!"

"Who is it?" cried Snowy.

"It's Razum!" said the driver. "Telegram."

Sashenka hesitated. Took a deep breath. Opened the door.

"Good morning, comrade," smiled Razum. "A beautiful day! And a message from the boss."

IN STALINABAD.
FEELING WELL.
GREETINGS TO CHILDREN.
HOME WEDNESDAY. VP

Sashenka felt jubilant, certain suddenly that nothing bad would happen. She had imagined it all. Why shouldn't an assistant deputy commissar like Vanya be sent on some temporary assignment to Stalinabad? It happened all the time; not everyone sent on missions into the regions was arrested. Satinov too had been dispatched to Georgia for a few weeks and no one suggested he was in any trouble.

She got ready for work at the magazine. She thought coldly of enemies and traitors, as she had so often before, when the Organs had "checked" those friends who never returned. Was she dangerously linked to Benya Golden via the magazine? Klavdia had called Andrei Zhdanov's cultural apparat at Old Square and Fadeyev at the Writers' Union. They had both passed him so her back was covered. She and he had met to discuss the commission. There was no personal connection between them. She was suddenly overtaken by self-disgust. She loved only her children, husband, herself—and no one else.

Perhaps Satinov had been wrong? Perhaps the only link between Mendel and Benya was that both were prominent, and it was this that put them in danger. Before he left, Vanya had told her that other writers and artists had recently been arrested: Babel for one, Koltsov the journalist, Meyerhold the theatrical director. Perhaps *they* were connected? Vanya had whispered that they were planning a fourth show trial, starring the fallen "Iron Commissar" Yezhov, and were considering tossing some diplomats and intellectuals into the cauldron. Perhaps that was what this nightmare was about?

She kissed the children; she hugged Carolina; she dressed in her favorite cream suit with white buttons and the blouse with the big white collar; she touched behind her ears with some Red Moskva perfume. Greeting the janitor and the guards, she walked to work. Granovsky was an elegant street, the apartment building pink and ornate, a wonderful place to live. Down the road, behind, stood the Kremlevka where the best specialists had delivered her babies.

She came out of Granovsky near Moscow University, where Snowy and Carlo would study one day.

The zestful breeze danced around her and she smiled as she passed the Kremlin, beaming waves of affection at the charming little window of the exquisite Amusements Palace, right by the wall of the Alexander Gardens where Stalin had lived until the suicide of his wife Nadya. As she crossed the Manege and passed the National Hotel, she caught sight of the domed and triangular splendor of the Sovnarkom Building where Stalin worked and where he lived, where the light was on all night. Thank you, Comrade Stalin, you always know the right thing to do, she telegraphed to him mentally through the amber air of a sunny Moscow day. You met Snowy, you understand everything. Health and long life to you, Josef Vissarionovich!

Walking with her slightly bouncing step, she turned left up Gorky Street. On the right stood the building where Uncle Gideon lived in a roomy apartment, near other famous writers like Ilya Ehrenburg. Trucks growled down the street, carrying cement for the new Moskva Hotel that was rising like a noble stone temple; Lincolns and ZiS limousines swept down the avenue toward the Kremlin; a dappled horse and cart was stationed outside the Mayor's office, a former palace. Moscow was still unformed, still that collection of villages, but she belonged here. Up the hill and over the top, Sashenka passed men and women working on the new buildings, militiamen on duty spinning their truncheons, children on their way to school, Young Pioneers with their red scarves. Before she reached the Belorussian Station, she saw the fine statue of Pushkin—and turned right down to Petrovka with its shabby stalls offering fried pirozhki.

At the office, she called the editors to sit at the T-shaped table. "Come in, comrades. Do sit! Let me hear your ideas for Comrade Stalin's birthday issue in December."

The days passed lightly and gracefully like new skates on glazed ice.

30

"Papa's back!" cried Snowy.

"What are you doing out of bed?" Sashenka was in her nightie and housecoat. "Back to bed! It's almost midnight."

"Razum's at the door with Daddy!"

"Daddy's back?" Carlo, in blue pajamas, emerged all tousled from bed and stomped down the parquet corridor of the apartment.

"He's at the door!" Snowy was jumping up and down. "Can we stay up? Please, Mama!"

"Of course!" She opened the door.

"Hello, Razum, you picked him up? He's late as usual . . ."

"Stand back, no crap," said Razum in an exaggerated voice with a blast of vodka and garlic. He stood, boots wide apart, pistol in his hand, in his usual shabby NKVD uniform. "Come on, boys, this is the place! See how they lived, see what the Party gave him, the fat boss—and see how he repaid it!"

Razum was not alone: four Chekists stood behind him, and behind them stood the janitor, sweaty and embarrassed, fiddling with his baroque bunch of a hundred keys. The Chekists filed past her into the apartment.

"Oh God, it's started." Sashenka's legs almost gave way, and she leaned against the wall.

A senior officer, a narrow-faced commissar with two tabs, who was too thin for his overlarge uniform, stood in front of her. "Orders to search this apartment, orders signed by L. P. Beria, Narkom, NKVD."

Razum elbowed this stick insect aside, so keen was he to be part of the operation. "We've arrested Palitsyn right at the Saratovsky Station at first light. He punched one of them, did Vanya Palitsyn."

"That's enough, comrade," said the stick insect in charge.

"Where is he?" asked Sashenka eagerly. So Vanya's train had been on time. Razum (probably excluded from the secret in case he warned his boss) had been at the station to meet him, and Vanya had been arrested then and there. Razum's grotesque pantomiming was his desperate attempt to prove his loyalty and save his skin. Sashenka knew enough to realize Vanya would have been taken straight to the Internal Prison at what they called "the Center": Lubianka.

"Not another word, Comrade Razum," said the stick insect. "This is our affair."

"I always had my suspicions about these *barins*." Razum was still chattering. "There wasn't much I didn't see. Now we're going to search the place, find out what papers that snake's been hiding. This way, boys!"

The stick insect and his Chekists were already in the study. Carolina watched from her bedroom door. Had they come to arrest her? Sashenka wondered. Frantic longings and selfish thoughts filled her again: perhaps she was safe? Perhaps they only wanted Vanya? Let Vanya be arrested. Let her stay with the children.

Sashenka and Carolina looked at each other silently. Were they too late? Would the children be tortured in that orphanage? How would they know what to do? Vanya had sent no signal. Should Carolina leave right now with the children? Tonight? Or would that bring further torment?

"What's happening, Mama?" asked Snowy, arms curling round her mother's waist. Carlo sensed the turmoil in the boots and the loud voices, the casual way the Chekists were opening drawers and slamming cupboards in the study, tossing papers and photographs into a heap on the floor. His pliant face collapsed in three stages: a slight downturn of the eyes and the lips; welling tears and crumpling features; the spread of a deep red blush as he started to howl.

"Stay in your bedroom," cried Sashenka, hiding them behind her body. "Go to Carolina."

Carolina opened her arms but the children froze around Sashenka, their hands clutching her hips and thighs, sheltering under her like travelers during a storm.

Vanya's mother burst out of her room in a purple nightdress, followed by her husband.

"What's going on?" she shouted. "What's happening?" She ran into the study and started pushing the Chekists away from Vanya's desk. "Vanya's a hero! There's been some mistake! What's he been arrested for?"

"Article Fifty-eight, I believe!" answered the stick insect. "Now, out of the way. They're removing the safe."

Sashenka saw the secret policemen fixing a seal onto the door of the study. Four of the boys were straining to get Vanya's safe to the elevator. Finally the janitor brought up a metal cart and they wheeled it out.

"Good night, Comrade Zeitlin-Palitsyn," said the uniformed stick insect to Sashenka. "Don't tinker with the seal on the study. We'll return for more material tomorrow."

"Wait! Does Vanya need some clothes?"

"The spy had a suitcase, thank you very much," sneered Razum, hands on hips, striking a pose. "I'll be right with you, lads!" he shouted over his shoulder to the stick insect and the others who were loading piles of papers into the elevator.

"Why do you hate us?" Sashenka asked him quietly.

"He'll sing! He'll confess, the hyena!" Razum said to her. "You bosses live like nobility! Think you're better than the likes of us? You've gotten fat and soft. Now you're getting your comeuppance."

"Silence, Comrade Razum, or you'll be in the soup yourself!" piped the stick insect, holding the elevator door open. Old Razum turned abruptly but as he did so, something fell out of his pocket. Shouting drunken insults, he trotted after his fellows. The elevator door closed.

Sashenka shut the door, leaned back against it and sank to the floor, Carlo and Snowy collapsing with her, tangled in her legs. She was thinking coldly, trying to plan with the icy dedication of a mother in crisis—though her hands were shaking, the red sparks rising in her eyes were blinding her, and her belly was squirming.

"Cushion!" Snowy reached out to pick up the little pink cushion with a bow. "Silly Razum dropped my lovely cushion"—and she showed the wrinkled pink object to Sashenka.

Sashenka grabbed it from Snowy, examining it, turning it over, smelling it.

"No, Snowy. Wait," she snapped as her daughter tried to retrieve it.

"I want my little cushion!" cried Snowy pitifully.

"Carolina!" The nanny was there already.

Vanya's parents emerged from their room again and stood staring at the scene.

"Where's Vanya?" asked Vanya's mother. She pointed savagely at Sashenka. "I always told him you were a class enemy, born and bred. This is your doing, isn't it?"

"Be quiet for once!" Sashenka retorted. "I'll explain everything later. Tomorrow you two should go to the dacha or to the village—but for now please go to your rooms. I need to think!"

The old peasants muttered at her rudeness but retreated again.

"That bastard Razum," spat Carolina.

"From now on, everyone's a bastard. We've just crossed from one species to another," said Sashenka, holding the little pink cushion. "Carolina, this was at the dacha?"

"Yes."

"We didn't bring it back, did we?"

"No, we didn't. It lives in the playroom there."

Sashenka turned to her daughter. "Where did this come from, darling?"

"Razum dropped it. That silly old man! He smells!"

"But who took it from the dacha? Did you see someone take it?"

"Yes, silly. Papa took it. I gave it to him to look after and he put it in his pocket."

"So your papochka remembered us," murmured Sashenka. "Dear Vanya." Snowy's cushion: what signal could be more appropriate? "Good old Razum," she added.

"Can I have it, Mamochka?"

"Yes, darling heart, you can have it."

Sashenka looked up at Carolina and the nanny looked back at her: it was an exchange of absolute maternal love, a look of gravity that tolled so poignantly that both women were stunned by it.

In that instant, Sashenka tried to touch, taste, see and feel all the treasured impressions and precious moments of her children's lives. But she could not hold them and they slipped through her fingers, carried away on the wind.

31

The next morning, Sashenka went to the office. Some would have stayed in bed, claiming illness, but that in itself might arouse suspicions. The arrest of a husband did not always lead to the arrest of the wife. No, she would edit her magazine as she always did and take what came.

As she departed, she kissed the children, inhaled their skin, their hair. She looked into each of their faces in turn. She kissed Carlo's brown eyes and pressed her lips onto Snowy's silky forehead.

"I love you. I will always love you. Never forget it. Ever," she said to each of them, firmly. No tears. Discipline.

"Mama, Mama, can I tell you something?" said Carlo. "You are a silly old pooh!" and he roared with laughter at his wicked joke.

Snowy laughed too but took her mama's side. "No, she's not. Mama's a darling cushion." High praise indeed.

Carolina stood behind them. Vanya's parents pulled their coats on. Sashenka hesitated then nodded at them. They nodded too. There was nothing else to say now.

Sashenka shook herself. She craved to kiss Carlo and Snowy again, so craved it that she could wear away their very skin with kisses—but she shuddered and pulled on her coat and opened the door.

"Mama, I love you in my heart," cried out Carlo. He blew a raspberry at her and then grabbed Snowy's cushion and trotted off with it.

"Give me that back, you pooh!" Snowy pursued him, away from the adults.

Sashenka seized the moment and was gone, taking a little canvas bag and her handbag. Just like that. The children did not even notice. One moment she was a mother with her children; the next she was gone. It was like jumping out of an airplane: a second that changed everything in life.

As she walked down the elegant wooden staircase, Sashenka could not see for the salty tears swimming across her vision.

But her senses sharpened as she came into the lobby. The guards went quiet as she approached them, and the janitor swept the parking lot with astonishing enthusiasm. When she passed Comrade Andreyev, Party Secretary, and his wife, Deputy People's Commissar Dora Khazan, coming down to their ZiS, they met her eyes but looked right through her. They were probably going to see Comrade Stalin and Comrade Molotov and Comrade Voroshilov that very day in the corridors of the Kremlin, in the land of the living. They might never cross paths again.

She waved gaily at the guards. One waved back but the other told him off.

She set out for work. The light, the flowers of the Alexander Gardens, the carts and horses, the dust and rumble of all those new building projects, the crocodile of red-scarfed Young Pioneers singing gaily, none of this registered with her.

The pavement did not seem hard. She floated on the air because her shoes, feet, bones were no longer solid. Adrenaline rushed through her, along with the fine coffee she had made during the night.

She suddenly felt the urge to run back and kiss the children again. It was so strong that her muscles actually bunched and started to move but she held them back. Stick to the plan! For them. Any folly, any stupid sentimentality could ruin it.

Her heart drummed, her vision sharpened. She reveled in her heightened senses. On the street, she noticed the janitors watching her as they cleaned their courtyards. The militiamen at the Granovsky corner whispered to one another.

She stopped at the corner and glanced back. Yes: her parents-in-law had come out into the street. On time. Vanya's mother swung her usual canvas handbag but this time none of the other gossiping peasants in the courtyard greeted her. Vanya's father looked toward Sashenka but gave no sign of recognition.

Helped by her husband, Vanya's mother hobbled on her swollen legs down the street in the opposite direction, smoking a cigarette.

Sashenka turned the corner and headed past the Kremlin on her right, the National Hotel on her left, and then up Gorky Street. Just about now, she knew that Carolina would be coming downstairs with the children, taking them for a walk.

She would lead them in the same direction as the grandmother and grandfather, left out of the door.

The guards in the Granovsky guardpost would watch them impassively: who cared? The NKVD was interested in the parents. Besides, they had no orders. Yet.

Sashenka lingered outside the National. She hoped Carolina and the children had caught up with their Palitsyn babushka and dedushka, who would hand over a tiny canvas suitcase. It belonged to Snowy. The plan was to get the children's suitcases out of the house without the guards noticing.

The children remained with the grandparents. Carolina took the next right and came into Gorky Street just as Sashenka was about to cross. They greeted each other.

"Time for a coffee, Comrade?"

"Of course." They entered the National Hotel and ordered a coffee in the café. Sashenka tried to remain caught up in the cloak-and-dagger moment—but she felt so sick, so desperate, that her gorge rose, and her belly lurched as it had the day that Lala first left her at boarding school and she wanted to chase after her. Frantic, she had broken away from her teacher and sprinted down the Smolny corridors, pushing aside other girls and running outside to the gates, where Lala saw her and cuddled her again. Now that frenzy returned. But Carolina, bony and expressionless, sipped the coffee, kissed Sashenka briskly, and then hurried off with barely a glance, carrying Carlo's little case, which contained winter clothes, underwear, soap, toothbrush and three bunny rabbits. Sashenka ran through the items: had they remembered everything? What about Carlo's cookies?

At the door of the café, Carolina turned back one more time. She and Sashenka exchanged a last beseeching gaze of the most terrible emotions—love, gratitude, sorrow. Then Carolina set her jaw and was gone. The plan was in motion. Vanya had sent the signal with Razum that Sashenka had to act now. Just as Satinov had suggested, so Sashenka and Carolina had arranged.

Sashenka watched the nanny's thin back with a desperate wild envy. As an amputee feels his absent leg walking, so she felt her own ghostly body running after them, while she still sat in the café. Then her body bunched and twitched and she was on her feet. She started to run after Carolina. She found herself tossing coins for the coffee onto the table. She was running, sweating, her heart thrashing in her chest as if she were having a heart attack, flying almost, tears splashing in her wake like rain on a car windshield. She was on the street. She looked left and right. Carolina was already gone. God, she *had* to see them again! The sob in her throat became a wild groan, a sound that she had never heard in her life. She sprinted frantically down the side street.

And then she saw them. A streetcar had stopped in the distance, casting sparks in its wake. Snowy was on the first step, waving her pink cushion and laughing, so that Sashenka could distinctly see her wide white forehead and fair curls. Carolina, holding both bags in her left hand, handed up Carlo, who was playing the fool, pretending to march, singing a song.

He was tugging at her sleeve. "Carolina, Carolina, can I tell you something?" Sashenka knew he was saying this but Carolina was up the steps now too. Two soldiers climbed on behind them, both smoking.

"Stop! Carolina! Carlo! Snowy!" Sashenka was actually screaming.

Carolina paid at the little window. Sashenka could see only the tops of their heads, Carlo's tousled brown hair and Snowy's butter-colored tresses, catching a speck of sunlight like spun gold. She was ruining everything by running. The NKVD would see her and know she was spiriting them away; they'd arrest her as a spy; they'd throw the children into the Dzerzhinsky Orphanage, shoot them. But Sashenka was out of control, careering forward now, colliding with an old lady whose shopping bag was torn, potatoes rolling on the pavement; still Sashenka ran, tears cascading down her face. But the streetcar, in a shower of sparks, jolted. The doors shut. It gathered speed. Sashenka was catching up and she saw them again: Carolina was helping them into a seat by the window. Just a blurred impression of blue eyes and a milky forehead, and brown eyes and hair—and they were gone.

A man pushed Sashenka out of his path, and she fell into a doorway and sat on the step. She heard herself howling as her mother had howled when Rasputin was killed. People hurried by, slightly disgusted at her. Slowly she gathered herself.

The grandparents would return to the apartment and tell the guards they were going back to the dacha for the summer. The guards understood because Vanya Palitsyn had been arrested, and they would shrug: who cared?

Sashenka stood up and straightened her clothes. Everyone was safe. Hoping no NKVD informant had noticed her hysteria, she tidied her face, got to her feet and crossed Gorky Street, glancing down to the Kremlin and up at Uncle Gideon's window. There was no point in calling him though she longed to do so. Her phones might be bugged and he would find out soon enough. She beamed him her love: would he ever know it? Now she thought about her father again: where was he? Would she join him in some forgotten grave? She could not, just could not conceive of her own vanishing from the surface of the turning world.

She chose a different route to Petrovka, not via Pushkin Square but taking the Stoleshnikov Alley. She tried to absorb everything—the little bars there, the Aragvi Georgian restaurant, the shoeshine stall, the kiosk selling newspapers, Zviad the Mingrelian's barbershop—but nothing stayed with her. Like the night. There was too much to take in.

Where would Snowy and Carlo be now? Don't even glance at your watch, she told herself. Suppose you are being observed: they might ask why you are checking the time constantly. But the train to the south was leaving at 10:00 a.m. and now it was 9:43. Her children were on their way.

32

The doorman straightened as Sashenka arrived at work; her secretary, Galya, blushed at the sight of her; Klavdia did not even look up as she passed. Everyone knew that Sashenka was no longer a real person. She was a Former Person; worse, they all knew somehow that she was the wife of an Enemy and Vanya was in the cellars of the Internal Prison of the Lubianka—and so was Benya Golden, her new writer whom she had met at her dacha on May Day night, with whom she had left the office, with whom she had been seen walking . . .

Sashenka sat at her desk. No one came in. She spent the entire day there, except for a brief visit to the cafeteria, where she ate some borscht alone. She tried to read the proofs of the magazine but could not concentrate. She had known many friends and comrades who had endured shadows and clouds over them but who had continued as if nothing had happened—and they had survived. Like Uncle Gideon. Keep your nerve and you might just keep your children, she promised herself.

She returned home in the evening.

The high ceilings, the shiny parquet floor, the ornate moldings on the walls, the dappled glossy brown of the Karelian pine furniture, the green lamps with the muscular bronze figures belonged to her life with the children. She hated the apartment now. It was echoingly quiet. She longed to look into the children's rooms. Don't do that to yourself. It will break you up, send you mad, she told herself. But just a glance?

Dropping her handbag and coat, she rushed down the corridor, throwing herself onto their beds and smelling their pillows, first Snowy's then Carlo's. There, at last, she could cry. She imitated their voices and she talked to their photographs. Then she burned their photographs, all of them, and their passports too. Snowy had left most of her cushions and Carlo had left most of his army of rabbits. Sashenka took them to bed with her, company for the sleepless night that lay ahead.

Presently she packed herself a suitcase with her toothbrush, warm clothes, underwear. She chose her best. Why not?

The next day she went to work again, taking her suitcase. And the next day. And the day after that. The stress was making her ill. She had a sore throat, her face was drawn and she could barely eat. At night she dreamed of Vanya and the children. Where were they now? Three nights on the road: were they with a family? Or in some railway station, lonely, hungry, lost? She talked to the children all the time, aloud, like a crazy woman.

Benya Golden came to her in the night. She awoke filled with regret, guilt, disgust—and, horribly, a feverish excitement. She hated him suddenly. She would like to kill him with her bare hands, gouge his eyes out: was it him, with his smug defiance, his refusal to write, his curiosity about the Organs, his famous friends in Paris and Madrid—was it his connections that would kill her and steal her children? Yes, she had loved him, yes, he had given her the wildest happiness, but now, compared to her love for her children—it was dust!

On the third day, she saw something different in the eyes of the guards. When she greeted the janitor, he looked up toward her apartment and she knew it was about to happen. She stopped on the stairs, almost relieved that this limbo was over.

When she let herself back into the apartment, the study was unsealed and she smelled cloves. She walked past the Red Corner into the sitting room and saw plates of half-eaten food on the dining-room table. A very large man in a specially tailored NKVD uniform lay with his patent leather boots on the sofa. High boots creaking, he got to his feet and gave Sashenka a gleaming white smile. His skin was brown and glossy, his hair kinky, and he had colorful rings on every fat brown finger. His clove-scented cologne was so pungent that Sashenka could taste it on her tongue. He was not alone. A couple of other Chekists tottered to their feet, perhaps a little drunk, sniggering.

Sashenka was wearing a pink cotton summer dress. She had had her hair styled recently, slightly curled at the front, arranged the new way in a permanent wave, and her face was made up. She drew herself up to her proudest.

"Comrades, sorry to have kept you. Have you been waiting long? I am Sashenka Zeitlin-Palitsyn, whom Lenin called Comrade Snowfox."

"Well, comrade, what a nice welcome," said Commissar-General of State Security (Second Degree) and Deputy People's Commissar NKVD Bogdan "the Bull" Kobylov. "You know Comrade Beria is an admirer of yours?"

Sashenka took a deep breath, nostrils flaring, grey eyes narrowed. "I've been expecting you any minute. I'm almost pleased . . ."

"Now I see why Comrade Beria speaks so highly of you," he said.

Like many oversized men, his voice was mellifluous, almost effete. Sashenka despised him. She thought of her children far away—they had been gone for three nights now. She knew that within minutes she would be stepping off the edge of the world but she remembered what she had to do. She coolly took out a cigarette and held it out like a film star. Kobylov, fluttering his rings on amber-skinned fingers, leaned over and lit it for her. She could smell his oily flesh—and those cloves.

"Thank you, comrade." She inhaled, closing her eyes and blowing out the blue smoke. Someone was playing the piano in a nearby apartment and a child was singing, a family in a normal world. "What do you want?"

"When it's a pretty woman," said Kobylov, wrinkling his nose at her, "I like to come and get her myself."

33

A thousand miles to the south in the small city of Tiflis, a grey-haired woman was packing an overnight bag. She lived alone in a single room, close to the city center, down a dark, overgrown lane just below the sulphur baths, the old town and the Orthodox church with the round Georgian tower.

Her tiny room, which contained a bed, a lamp, a wardrobe and old photographs of a rich family, all waxed mustaches, bowler hats, sailor suits and shiny limousines, was in an elegant mansion, once the property of a line of Georgian princes, the last of whom had been an eccentric antiquarian, book collector and owner of the sulphur baths. (He was now a taxi driver in Paris.) At the time of the 1905 revolution, he had sold the palace to a Jewish oil magnate based in St. Petersburg. Now the mansion was divided up into small apartments and the princely library on the ground floor was a café, a flamboyant venue of a kind that no longer existed in Moscow or anywhere in Russia proper. But here in Georgia, despite the recent killings that had decimated the intelligentsia, this curiosity shop of a café, with its damp old books, candlesticks overflowing with wax and dense, curling vines covering its steamed-up windows, still prospered, serving Turkish coffee and Georgian dishes.

The grey-haired lady worked in the café all day as a waitress. It was not well paid but it was a decent job for those times; she had the correct papers; it was all legal. She kept herself to herself, never chatted with customers or even with the other waitresses, who had given up gossiping about her. It was clear that she was a bourgeois and that she did not belong there, but provincial cities in those days were full of such flotsam and Georgia was more tolerant than anywhere else. It was said that Communism did not extend much beyond the limits of the capital. She had once lived with an older man but he had gone and she showed no interest in discussing her private life.

The waitress's Russian was excellent, her Georgian more than adequate, but she spoke both with an accent. She was polite to everyone but they noticed she reserved her real solicitude for the library itself. The kitchen and bar had been jerry-built between two bookcases at the end of the dark old room. The humidity of the kettles and cauldrons had rotted the woodwork; the books were peeling and warping; the old pictures were mildewed and yellowing—but she did what she could, dusting the books, sometimes drying them out in her own room upstairs.

On the previous day, the woman had asked for a week off, something that had never happened before. But she had years of unused vacation, so Tengiz, the manager, gave her two weeks instead.

Today, she rose very early and walked across Beria Square to the Armenian Market, where she bought provisions. Returning to her room, she filled her suitcase not only with clothes but also with a bag of flat Georgian *lavashi* loaves, cured meats and candies. Taking a photograph of an awkward schoolgirl in the uniform of a Tsarist boarding school off the wall, she removed its back and took out some notes. She hid two hundred rubles in her girdle, kissed the photograph and replaced it on the wall.

She checked herself in the mirror and tutted: those apple cheeks in that heart-shaped face were now weathered and coarsened; there were bags under her eyes; and her clothes were dignified but frayed at the edges. She looked fifty but she was younger. How on earth, she asked herself, did you end up here? She shook her head and smiled.

A few hours later she caught the streetcar to the station, where she bought a ticket to Baku and from there to Rostov-on-Don. She changed at Baku Station, a place teeming with Muslims, Turks and Tartars in Soviet uniforms, skullcaps and robes, carrying chickens and sheep and children. One family offered her some Turkish *plov*, cold lamb stew, and she was grateful. She waited for her train. When it was called, it seemed that the entire station charged at it but her Turkish friends helped her and pulled her up into their carriage. She sat close to them and was again grateful for their protection. On the train, she tried to sleep but could not stop reflecting on the strange events of the previous week.

Four days earlier, a sweaty official in a Party tunic had arrived to inspect the residence and work permits of the employees at the café. All were asked to go to the Party Headquarters, the old Viceroy's Palace, on Beria Boulevard to have their papers checked. Tengiz told her she was to go first. This was odd but one did not ask questions: checks, cleansings and purges were part of everyday life. Her husband was already gone, certainly dead; and she had been expecting them to come for her. Surely she would be arrested and vanish in her turn. Well, did it matter anymore?

The woman tramped up the hill to the splendid white Viceroy's Palace, from where the First Secretary ruled Georgia. The wait made her very anxious. There were many questions she longed to ask. But like everyone else, she was helpless before the clumsy and colossal state. Questions *from* you could lead to questions *about* you—it was better to keep your head down. She waited like the other coughing, scratching, grunting, depressed people, old and young, in the filthy anteroom with its battered wooden window.

When it was her turn, she passed her papers through the hole. She was then called through into a grubby, unpainted office. She braced herself for the rude tyranny of some minor Georgian bureaucrat. But the official who awaited her was not that type at all. A slim and handsome man, clearly a Party boss, stood up when she came in, drew out a chair for her and then took his place behind the desk. His Stalinka tunic fitted his broad shoulders and slim waist perfectly. He radiated the energy of the Stalin generation and appeared much too sophisticated to belong in this chipped office. He must be a Muscovite, a potentate, she thought. Yet his blue eyes were bright, questioning.

"Audrey Lewis?"

She nodded.

"Don't be nervous. I've always known you were here in Tiflis. Do you remember me?" he asked. "I saw you long ago in St. Petersburg. The house on Greater Maritime Street, the day Sashenka's mother died. Three comrades came to collect her that day. One was her uncle Mendel. The second was Vanya. I was the third. Now, Lala, there is something I want you to do."

34

The smell of sweat and clove cologne rose from Commissar Kobylov's expansive neck and thighs during the ride through the summer night in Moscow. Sashenka was squeezed next to him and he was enjoying their proximity, shifting his elephantine bottom and wrinkling his nose at her like an oversized tabby cat.

The car drove up the hill to the brooding granite of the Lubianka, the People's Commissariat of Internal Affairs, and then swerved into a side street, through the opening gates of a courtyard, driving Kobylov's spicy breath onto her neck. But already Sashenka did not care. She was trying to pace herself, to conserve her energy, as all prisoners try to do.

The lights over the courtyard—invisible from the exterior—illuminated a scene that resembled a railway station where people arrived but never left. Sashenka guessed that this hidden nine-story building was the dreaded Internal Prison. Black Crow vans and Stolypin trucks, back doors open to reveal barred cages, unloaded bleary-eyed men in nightshirts with bleeding lips, shrieking women in cocktail dresses and smeared eye shadow, piles of badly bound papers and battered leather suitcases. Each of the arrivals had the white face of a once-settled person falling into an abyss of fear.

An officer opened Kobylov's door. Breathing heavily, he raised his clumsy boots and leaned out until his weight landed him on the ground. The officer helped him out.

Sashenka's door was opened and a Chekist gripped her arm and guided her into a large basement with chipped arches and battered wooden walls, where yet more bewildered people stood in lines. The room stank of cabbage soup, urine and despair. Sashenka—a special case, she noted ruefully—was led to the front.

"I am a Soviet woman and a member of the Party," she told a bored Chekist. She had helped build this Soviet system; she believed this oppressive machine was necessary to create the new world according to the Marxist-Leninist-Stalinist science of dialectical materialism; she wanted the Chekists to know she still believed in it even though it was about to consume her. But the Chekist just shook his head and told her to empty her pockets, handbag, suitcase. He waved a yellow hand to hurry her and filled in a form. Full name, patronymic, year of birth. He peered at her. Color of hair? Color of eyes? Distinguishing marks? He pressed her fingers on a blue inkpad and took her prints. She received a prisoner number.

"Watch? Rings? Any money?" He noted her belongings and cash, gave her the form to sign and tore off a receipt. Behind her, other bodies pushed against her. "Women that way!" pointed the Chekist. Sashenka remembered her arrest in St. Petersburg and the identical questions—but now she was much more afraid. The Tsarist Empire was soft; she had helped create this man-eating USSR.

She entered a small room where a woman in a white coat sat on a desk smoking an acrid *makhorka* cigarette.

"Clothes off!" the woman barked.

Sashenka removed her dress and shoes. She stood in her underwear and stockings, shivering slightly in the night chill of the cold concrete. She remembered that her underwear was silk. The woman's beady eyes noticed too.

"Everything off! Don't waste my time, and don't be stuck up!" The woman rammed the cigarette into the corner of her mouth and pulled up her sleeves to reveal powerful hairy forearms.

Sashenka removed her brassiere and stood with her hands over her breasts. Not bad breasts after two children, she told herself stoically.

"And the rest!"

She took off her teddy, standing shyly, a hand over her pubis.

"No one's interested in you and your clipped little tail. Move it! Mouth open!"

The woman stuck her fingers into Sashenka's mouth. They tasted of stale cheese.

"Hands on desk now. Legs open."

She pushed Sashenka's head down. A finger scooped painfully into her vagina and then plunged into her rectum. Sashenka gasped at the invasion.

"Toughen up, princess. It wasn't torture! Get dressed." She took Sashenka's shoes. "Take out the laces. Give me that belt. No pens allowed." The woman measured her prisoner's height and wrote it down. "Sit!"

Sashenka fell back into a chair, relieved to be dressed again.

"Vlad!" called the woman.

A skinny old photographer with slicked-back hair, a tiny head and a worn blue suit appeared in the room: clearly an alcoholic, he was shaking and could hardly hold his heavy camera. A round flashlight blossomed out of it like a chrome sunflower.

"Look at me," he said.

Sashenka looked into the camera, wearily at first, but then she tried to primp herself up, touching her hair. Suppose one day her children saw that picture? She fixed her eyes on the lens trying to transmit a message: Snowy and Carlo—I love you, I love you! This is your mother! Remember me! Dream of me!

"Keep still! Done." The bulb flashed with a sizzling pop. Sashenka saw silver stars melting across a black sky.

A guard led her by the arm through a locked door that clicked behind them. Her shoes were loose without the laces and her dress no longer fitted without the belt. There were three guards now, one in front, one holding her, one behind. She passed metal cages, climbed up steel staircases and down stone ones, waited in concrete assembly areas, marched along rows of cells with steel doors and sliding eyeholes. She heard the percussion of prisons—coughing and swearing, the clank of locks, slam of doors and scrape of feet, the clack of bunches of keys swinging. Floors of worn parquet glistened with burning detergent.

The smell of prisons—urine, sweat, feces, disinfectant, cabbage soup, the oil of guns and locks—reminded her of Piter in 1916. Back again—

but this time Papa won't be getting me out! she thought sadly. She felt that Vanya and Benya and Uncle Mendel were all nearby, and somehow it comforted her. In one corridor, another prisoner approached with a guard—she glimpsed a pretty young woman, younger than her, with a black eye.

"Avert your eyes, Prisoner seven hundred seventy-eight," barked her guard, the first words he had spoken. He pushed Sashenka toward a corner where what appeared to be a metal coffin stood upright. He opened its door and pushed her inside, locking it. The coffin door pressed on her back. Was this a torture? She fought for breath in the airless space. The other guards and prisoner were passing. When they were gone, the coffin was unlocked and they continued until they reached a line of cells where a guard held a door open. There, *778* was scrawled on an oily card.

The cell was small and cool with two bunk beds, no window whatsoever, a bucket of slops in the corner, brick walls and a damp floor. The door shut; the locks scraped; she stood there alone; the peephole opened; eyes stared at her. Then the Judas port shut. She closed her eyes and listened to the life around her. Prisoners sang, spat, coughed and spluttered, and tapped to one another using prisoners' code that had not changed since the days of the Tsar. The giant building throbbed like a secret city. Pipes gurgled and shook. A metal pail was dragged along and then a wet mop swished outside. A cart clanked. There was the murmur of voices, the echo of metal cups and spoons. The eyehole opened and closed. The door rasped open again.

"Supper!" Two prisoners, one bearded, old and frail, the other grey but probably her own age, were serving soup out of a swinging pan in the cart. The old one gave her a tin cup while the other poured from a ladle, filling up the cup with steaming water from a kettle. Two guards, hands on their pistols, watched closely. There must be no contact between prisoners.

"Thank you!" she said.

"No talking!" said the guard. "Never look at other prisoners!"

The younger prisoner gave her a sugar lump and a small square of black bread and looked at her for a moment, with a spark of feeling on a sensitive, rather mischievous face. Before Benya she would not have recognized it but now she spoke that particular language. My God, she thought, it was lust! Sashenka was pleased: the people in here still feel desire! Perhaps lust lasts beyond many other things. When the door slammed, she drank her watery buckwheat porridge. She used the slop bucket and lay down.

Vanya, wherever you are, she thought, I know what to do. All was not yet lost: the children had gone but there might be no case against her. Vanya knew that. She could still return. She *would* return. What could they have on her, the loyalest Communist? Then aloud she said one word: "Cushion!"

The lights remained on. Sashenka tried to sleep. She talked aloud to the children but already they belonged to another world. Could she still smell their smells? The texture of their skin, the sound of their voices, everything was still utterly fresh and vivid for her. She started to cry, gently and with resignation.

The peephole slipped open.

"Silence, prisoner! Show your face and hands at all times!"

She slept and she was a child again, on the Zeitlin estate at Zemblishino: her father, in a white suit and yachting shoes, was holding a pony by the bridle—and Lala, darling Lala, was helping her climb up into the saddle . . .

35

Sashenka was woken by the grating of carts, swishing of mops, screeching of locks. The peephole opened and shut, the door rasped open.

"Slopping out! Bring your slop bucket!" A guard marched her to the washroom, where the chlorine stung her eyes. She poured out her slops and washed her face with water. Then it was back to her cell.

"Breakfast!" The same prisoner whose glance had been so slyly sensuous now wore a plywood tray like an usherette selling cigarettes. The other prisoner, a bearded old man covered in tattoos—a real criminal, Sashenka guessed—poured out the tea and handed over a small piece of bread, a lump of sugar, and eight cigarettes with a strip of phosphorus from a matchbox. Once again the long thin face of the server revealed nothing, but again his eyes roved over her body and neck and glinted with the rudest lust before the door slammed again. Already, the tea and bread tasted divine. She knew from Vanya that prisoners sometimes waited weeks even to be interrogated so it might be ages before she was able to make her stand, to defend herself as a Communist—and find out what had brought her here.

Then she lay again on the bed. Where are the children now? she wondered. And she said aloud the word that was becoming her talisman, her code to transmit her love across the vast steppes and powerful rivers of Russia to her distant children. "Cushion!"

"Prisoner seven hundred seventy-eight?" The door had opened.

"Yes."

"Come!" Three guards marched her along the corridors, up metallic steps, down concrete staircases with metal grilles to prevent suicides, over rickety wooden bridges suspended above granite canyons, across corridors, until they passed two security doors with manned barriers and entered a wide passageway with offices instead of cells. Sashenka hummed to herself—she found to her surprise it was that gypsy romance so beloved of Benya Golden, their love song:

Black eyes, passionate eyes, lovely burning eyes,
how I love you, how I fear you.
I first laid eyes on you in an unkind hour . . .

What an unkind hour for love it had turned out to be, but that tune fueled a sudden surge of optimism. She was certain now there would be no need for Vanya's terrible plan. She would easily disprove the Chekists' accusations. Then they would release her. She would wait a little then recall the children. Oh, the joy of that!

"In here!" The guard pushed her into a small clean office with a linoleum floor, an empty desk, a grey telephone and a light turned toward her. The brightness of the bulb blinded her for a second. Golden beads sparkled before her eyes and she smelled the sweetness of coconut pomade.

A young man in NKVD uniform with round spectacles, a ginger mustache and a preposterous pompadour opened a *papka* file, licking his finger as he turned the pages. He took his time and when he had finished he sat back, his boots creaking. He stroked, almost massaged, the piece of paper in front of him.

"Prisoner, my name is Investigator Mogilchuk. Are you ready to help us?" He did not call her "comrade" but he seemed gentle and reasonable. His voice was husky like that of a boyish student; the accent was southern, from around the Black Sea, Mariupol perhaps; and she guessed that he was a teacher's son, provincial intelligentsia, probably qualified in the law, summoned to Moscow to fill the boots of the old Chekists, now deceased.

"Yes, Investigator, I am but I would like to save you from wasting your time. I've been a Party member since 1916; I worked in Lenin's apparat and I'd like to ask—"

"Silence, prisoner! I ask the questions here. As the armed sword of the Party, we Chekists will decide your case. That's our mission. Now will you help us?"

"Absolutely. I want to clear this up."

Investigator Mogilchuk stretched his neck and raised his chin. "Clear up what?" he said.

"Well, whatever it is that I'm accused of."

"You know what it is."

"I can't imagine."

"Oh, come now, prisoner. I'm going to ask you: why are you here?"

"I don't know. I am innocent. Genuinely."

Mogilchuk carefully checked the crusty surface of his pompadour and knitted his eyebrows. "That's not being helpful. Are you sincere in your wish to serve the Party? I wonder. If you were sincere, you would know why you are here."

"I am a sincere Communist, Comrade Investigator, but I've done nothing wrong! Nothing! I joined no oppositions. Never! I supported every policy of the Lenin-Stalin Party line. I would never tolerate any anti-Soviet conversations. Not even anti-Soviet thoughts. My life's been devoted to the Party . . ."

"Shut up!" said the investigator and banged the table, an action so absurd that Sashenka struggled to conceal her disdain. She had a misplaced urge to laugh.

"Don't waste our time!" he snapped at her. "You think we bring you here for fun? I'm up to here in cases and I need you to confess now to what you have done. We know how to handle people like you."

"People like me?"

"Spoiled Party princesses who think the State owes them their fancy clothes, cars, dachas. We specialize in grinding your type down to size. So I repeat: look into your life, your Communist conscience, your past! Why are you here? A confession will make things much easier for you."

"But I can't . . . I'm innocent!"

"How do you reconcile the fact of your arrest with your claim of innocence? Begin your confession! Do not wait until we force you!"

Sashenka was rattled. What was he demanding? If she admitted something trivial would that satisfy him? She thought back over Vanya's careful instructions as they sat on the swinging hammock in the dark hot garden that desperate night: "Confess nothing. Without a confession, they can't touch you! Believe me, darling, I know what I'm talking about. I've broken legions of men and perhaps this'll be their revenge on me. But don't invent some little crime. It won't ease the pressure! If they have something specific, they'll confront you. If they want something specific, they'll sweat it out of you."

Mogilchuk leaned forward. The sickliness of his coconut pomade was overpowering. "You come from a bourgeois family, real bloodsuckers. Did you genuinely embrace the Party—or did you remain a member of your filthy class, an enemy of working people?"

"I worked for Lenin."

"Do you think I care about that now? If you deceived Comrade Lenin, you'll be doubly damned."

"He called me Comrade Snowfox. He himself knew my background and he told me he came from nobility—it didn't matter because I was a real Bolshevik believer."

"How dare you soil Comrade Lenin! Don't you realize where you are? Don't you realize *what* you are now? You're as good as dust! You are sitting before the Tribunal of the Revolution: the Cheka. Just answer my questions." He looked down at the file, massaging the paper, round and round. "How long have you known Mendel Barmakid?"

"He's my uncle. All my life."

"Do you believe he's a good Communist?"

"I have always thought so."

"You sound like you have doubts?"

"I know he's been arrested."

"So you know we don't arrest people for nothing?"

"Comrade Mogilchuk, I believe in the armed wing of the Party. I believe you Chekists are, as Dzerzhinsky said, the knights of the Revolution. My own husband—"

"Accused Palitsyn. Do you think he's such a paragon of Party-mindedness? Really? Search your memories, your conversations: was he ever really an honest Chekist?"

"Yes, he was." Suddenly she questioned even that: what if Vanya was a Fascist spy?

"And Mendel? He was never a real Communist, was he . . . Comrade Snowfox"—he added with a sneer—"if I may call you that?"

"An honest Bolshevik who served five exiles, imprisonment in the Trubetskoy Bastion, ruined his health in hard labor and never joined a single deviation or opposition . . ."

Mogilchuk removed his glasses. Without them, he was blearily myopic. He rubbed his face and ran his hands over his red hair. She sensed how eager he was to deliver her confession to his superior. Maybe he'd impress Beria. Perhaps even the Instantzia—Comrade Stalin himself—would hear of this ardent young investigator? He replaced his glasses. "Lift Mendel's mask, show us this jackal and disarm him for us!"

"I don't know anything," she said. "Mendel! I'm trying to think . . ."

"Think and tell me!" Mogilchuk raised his pen. "You speak and I'll write. Did Mendel ever mention the Japanese diplomat he met in Paris?"

"No."

"The English lord who visited the embassy in London?"

"No."

"What foreigners did he know? Did he ever ask you to meet them? Think—scour your mind!"

So it was Uncle Mendel they wanted! Sashenka knew it was not her. They'd invited Gideon to the Lubianka to talk about Mendel. Then Vanya had been pulled into this: perhaps someone had overheard Mendel and Vanya arguing about jazz? And, through Vanya: her. Benya was clearly unconnected to Mendel. Except via her—but that was much too tenuous. No, Benya was part of something else, the case against the intellectuals—and Mogilchuk hadn't mentioned him at all. What was clear, though, was that they needed her to denounce Mendel.

So it was Mendel who had brought this disaster upon her: it was he who had taken her children away. The mother in her was happy to sacrifice Mendel in a moment: she would do anything to see her children again. But if she invented the fact that Mendel was a Japanese spy, would they see that she was innocent and had loyally served the Party?

She went back to Vanya's instructions: "If they're creating a case against Mendel, they'll want your testimony, but remember he converted you and me to Marxism, introduced us both to the Party—and each other! That confession will destroy us all! Wait until we know what they have against us."

The investigator checked his hairdo again. "Well?"

"No, Mendel's a decent comrade."

"And you yourself have nothing to tell me?"

She shook her head, feeling exhausted and weak. But there was hope, she told herself. Like someone buried in a landslide, she thought there was a way through to a chink of light. Vanya would not confess either; and even if her darling Vanya was destined for the meat grinder, there was no case against her. Vanya, like any father, would die easier if he knew his wife was safe with their children! Be strong, confess nothing—and you will see Snowy and Carlo again, she told herself. After all, this had been polite enough. Perhaps they were just fishing . . .

"All right, you want to play games with us?" said Mogilchuk quite calmly. "You must realize, Comrade Snowfox, that I'm an intellectual like you are, like your uncle Gideon. You may have seen my stories published under the name M. Sluzhba? Well, I just like to talk to people. That's my way. I've given you every chance but you're going to get a nasty surprise if you don't start to talk." He picked up the Bakelite phone and dialed a number. "It's Mogilchuk . . . No, she won't . . . Right!" He replaced the phone. "Come with me."

36

Accompanied by a guard, Investigator Mogilchuk led Sashenka down a long passageway that she had never seen before, up some steps, across the covered bridge, down some steps, and they emerged onto a wide corridor with a parquet floor. It was lined with gleaming panels of Karelian pine, portraits and busts of early Chekist heroes, and silken banners. A blue carpet ran down the center, held in place with chunky gold tacks. Guards in ceremonial NKVD uniform stood beside a Soviet flag and a life-sized statue of Dzerzhinsky. The corridor ended in imposing double doors of oak. A guard opened them.

They entered an anteroom where two NKVD officers, probably from the regions, sat with their briefcases. Mogilchuk walked straight through a further set of double doors, which were opened by another guard. Inside, Sashenka recognized instantly the bustling apparat of a Soviet potentate: many secretaries in white blouses and grey skirts, eager young men in Party tunics, lines of Bakelite phones, piles of *papki* files, and green palms. A young officer jumped up and led them to a third closed door. He knocked and opened it.

"Investigator Mogilchuk?"

They entered an airy and bright office of monumental proportions, gleaming parquet and Karelian pine, smelling of polish and cool forests. To the left, some sofas and soft chairs were set on Persian carpets. Over the mantelpiece hung a huge oil painting by Gerasimov of Comrade Stalin, and in the corner sat a steel safe taller than a man. Marble busts of Lenin and Dzerzhinsky stood on each side of the room and, so far away that Sashenka could barely see it, another Gerasimov loomed, this time of Dzerzhinsky, Iron Felix, the founder of the Cheka, with his insane eyes and goatee.

In the middle of the room, a polished oak desk was attached to a conference table to form the T shape common to every office in the USSR. It was in pristine order, with a silver desk set, inkwells of turquoise ink, and only one or two pieces of paper on the blotter. The table behind the desk boasted eight telephones—and the *vertushka* Kremlin line. And presiding over it all, on a high-backed velvet burgundy chair, sat Comrade Lavrenti Pavlovich Beria, Narkom of the People's Commissariat of Internal Affairs.

Beria was eating from a plate of what appeared to be spinach or salad leaves. He beckoned her into the room with an open palm, masticating energetically.

Mogilchuk saluted and left the room.

"Oh Lavrenti Pavlovich," Sashenka said, "I'm so pleased to see you! Now we can clear this up."

Beria swallowed his mouthful then stood up courteously, walked round the desk and kissed her hand. "Welcome, Alexandra Samuilovna," he said formally in his rich Mingrelian accent, still holding her hand between his silky fingers. "You're wondering what I'm eating?"

"Yes," she said, though she did not give a damn what he was eating.

"Well, I don't eat meat, you see. I hate killing anything. Those poor calves or lambs! No, I can't bear it, and besides, Nina says I mustn't put on weight! I'm a vegetarian so I eat only this—even at Josef

Vissarionovich's place. 'Beria's grass!' says Comrade Stalin. 'Look, Lavrenti Pavlovich is having his grass again!' Now, let me look at you." He kept her hand and turned her around as if they were dancing. 'Ah, you're so pale. But so beau-ti-ful still. That figure's enough to drive a man like me to folly! To risk everything for just one caress. You're like a cream cake. What a shame to meet like this, eh?'"

His colorless eyes ran over Sashenka with such gobbling greed that she flinched. The stocky and bald People's Commissar with the pince-nez circled her noiselessly on his soft suede shoes. He was not in uniform, just baggy yellow slacks and a collarless, embroidered blouse, like a Georgian at the seaside. Sashenka had not forgotten that her husband used to play on Beria's basketball team at his Sosnovka dacha. When she watched the games, she had noticed that Beria was incredibly quick on his feet.

"I'm so glad to see you," she repeated. She meant it. Beria was ruthless but competent. Vanya had admired his diligence, industry and fairness after the drunken frenzy of Yezhov. "You can sort this out, Lavrenti Pavlovich! Bless you!"

"I could look at your hips and breasts all day, my cream cake, but you're tired, I can see. Will you eat something?" He picked up a phone and said, "Bring in some sandwiches."

At Beria's invitation, she took one of the leather-seated chairs at the conference table adjoining Beria's desk. He sat down too. The double doors opened and a woman in a white apron wheeled in a tea cart. Placing a white napkin over her arm (just like one of the waitresses at the Metropole Hotel), she served tea and set out some sandwiches and fish *zakuski*, then left.

"There!" said Beria, smacking his loose, balloon-like lips. "Now eat while we talk. You're going to need your energy."

Sashenka hesitated, afraid that eating these delicious snacks would somehow obligate her to betray her husband or Mendel. She concentrated and thought of her children. Now was her chance.

"I don't know what I'm accused of, respected Comrade Beria, but I'm innocent. I know you know that. You have no idea what joy it gives me to see you."

"Oh, and me you. Eat up, my dear cream cake. They're not poisoned, I promise." She started to eat the sandwiches. "You know, you're my type absolutely, Sashenka. The moment I saw you, I knew something about that overbite of yours suggests a capacity for pleasure. Yet you didn't look too happy when I flirted with you at your place on May Day, hmmm? I think of women all day, you know. I'm a real Georgian man, aren't I, eh?" Beria's eyes grew cloudy, the eyelids drooping. "You know what I'd like to do, Sashenka, I'd like to drive you over to my Moscow house. Nina and my son live at Sosnovka, at the dacha. We'd have a Georgian *supra,* you and me in my *banya,* we'd drink the best wines in that cozy bathhouse, and then I'd lay you on the divan and lift your skirt and run my nose up until I can smell your strawberries . . ."

Beria was letting her know that he could do anything he wished. Yet she did not want to encourage him. His obscenity might be a trick, a lure. Or was it a sign that he really did desire her and if she wanted to get out, there was a simple price?

But this was Lavrenti Beria, People's Commissar, a man she respected and liked, a Bolshevik trusted and chosen by Comrade Stalin himself. How could he talk like this to a comrade who had known Lenin and entertained Stalin in her house? She thought quickly, and decided right then and there that she would do anything, however vile and demeaning, to see her children again.

"You're embarrassing me, Lavrenti Pavlovich," she whispered huskily. "I'm not used to this sort of . . ."

"Aren't you? Come on, Sashenka. I was surprised myself. You're so respectable—such a decent Soviet woman teaching our housewives how to cook cakes and darn the skirts of Young Pioneers. But *we* know what a wanton creature you are. The things you cry out, the acts you demand when you're really revved up. Just like your mother. She was notorious too, wasn't she?"

A shard of ice froze her belly. Benya Golden must have betrayed their sexual secrets, and this was how her husband had known too.

Beria beamed a smile at her with lips too fat, too wide.

"We know everything, dearest cream cake," he said lasciviously. "If you'd have that Jewish writer, you could have had me too. But don't get your hopes up. You didn't confess to my boy, Mogilchuk. Have you read his stories? They're shit, you know. He writes detective yarns, whodunits—he aspires to create a Soviet Sherlock Holmes. But alas, my duty interferes with my pleasures. Your case is a serious one, Sashenka, and much as I'd love to taste you, the Instantzia is following this affair closely."

"Comrade Stalin knows I'm innocent."

"Careful, careful. Don't mention that name to me, Prisoner Zeitlin-Palitsyn. I want you to know that your only hope is to confess now. Disarm, reveal your treacherous anti-Soviet activities. We're working hard here. Are you going to make us force you?" He stood up and walked around the desk, enveloping her in his lime cologne. He stroked her hair, ran his hands over a breast. Sashenka cringed, tried not to cry out. He touched her lips, then forced a knuckle into her mouth. It tasted coppery.

He put on a silly voice: "I don't want to be rough. Don't do that to me! I love women! Oh, the taste of them! Don't make me." He sat down, businesslike again. "Think carefully. There's nothing I don't know about you, your past, family, work, your cunt . . . Eh?" Beria drummed his fingers on the desk. "Are you going to help us? Stand up! Now! If you don't we'll grind you into dust and shoot you like a partridge! In a minute you're going back to your cell and I'm going back to work. Hang on. Wait. Don't turn around! Close your eyes."

She heard him open a drawer in his desk. The single door at the other end of the office opened. She heard the breath of men and the creak of boots getting closer but passing behind her.

"Not on the Persian carpet, it's a good one. Roll out that one. That's it," she heard Beria say.

A dull thud followed. Her eyes watered—there it was again, the pungent cologne of cloves—she could taste it on her lips.

"Thank you, Comrade Bull!"

It was Kobylov again. What was this? Some sort of game? Fear clawed at her suddenly.

"Right! Now. Let's take Comrade Snowfox back to her cell—and . . . one-two-three and . . . *turn*!"

Something bludgeoned into Sashenka's right cheek so hard that it spun her round and tossed her off her feet onto the parquet in the sitting area. The world dissolved into a blizzard of red specks in a diamond kaleidoscope. She was on the parquet floor, looking back at the desk where Beria stood smiling with a black truncheon in his hands.

Holding the side of her face, which seemed to be twitching of its own accord, she peered through the shiny boots in front of her at a bundle of clothes spattered in dried mud. She realized it was alive, quivering, stirring. Her gaze was drawn to the mass of raw red and blue and yellow bruises on bare skin, to fingers that bled from the tips, to an unshaven face with red-lidded eyes so swollen they could barely open. Her mouth gaped in shock.

"What do you think you're doing bringing that in here?" asked Beria. "Didn't you know I had Sashenka in here? You didn't knock, Comrade Kobylov! Tut, tut, bad manners!"

"Sorry, Lavrenti Pavlovich, I didn't know you were busy," said the giant Kobylov. "We need to work a little on this old bag of shit, another stubborn case. But we don't want her to see anything that might alarm her, do we?"

"Absolutely not," said Beria. "Help her up and take her back to her cell."

"Nasty bruise!" said Kobylov, touching her cheek and wrinkling his shiny nose. "You must have walked into something." He helped her to her feet. Sashenka could not take her eyes off the body on the rough stained carpet. "Come on, we must protect you from this unsavory vision—it's so hard to restrain Comrade Rodos when he gets the bit between his teeth."

"Rodos?" she murmured.

On the other side of the room, a stocky man with a hairy mole on his cheek, a pointed face and a head like a chicken meatball was caressing a black truncheon.

Investigator Rodos, wearing dirty boots and a grey tunic girded with a wide army belt, shrugged modestly and, with a defiant glance at Sashenka, he started to land blows on the belly of the man on the carpet, raising the truncheon very slowly and deliberately over his shoulder as if he were lobbing a ball. The man on the floor groaned each time, like a cow that Sashenka had once seen giving birth at the Zeitlin estates in Ukraine.

"It's rude to stare but it *is* fascinating, isn't it?" said Beria as she left.

Kobylov took her arm and led her out into the corridor, where Investigator Mogilchuk's toothy smile awaited her. "We'll meet again, I hope," said Kobylov, returning to Beria's office in a waft of cloves.

Sashenka was shaking. Unable to control herself, she bent over and and vomited up the food she had eaten, which left a cheesy taste in her mouth. The thudding of the truncheons on the prone man was pulsating in her ears. She could not believe what she had seen. Who was it . . . ? She knew—or was she seeing things? Was this how Beria treated Old Bolsheviks? Was that what Vanya did all night before coming home to the dacha and the children? Was this what had happened to the former owners of their dacha and their apartment?

She recited to herself Vanya's instructions. "Confess nothing whatever happens until you know they have something so damning . . . I'll never get out, but you, Sashenka, you can see the children again. Never forget them! Sign nothing whatever they do to you!" She still did not believe they had anything on her and it was clear that none of her associates had so far confessed. She could still get out if she kept her head. She had to hold on to this, whatever it cost her.

But where was Vanya? Where was Benya? She remembered their times together in the hotel, in the garden shed, kissing in the street like youngsters, singing "Black Eyes" by the river, exchanging pressed flowers as the most romantic days of her life. The seven thousand rubies of the Kremlin stars were theirs still! She loved them both now, Vanya and Benya, differently, insistently. They were her family now. They were all she had in this fathomless canyon of shadows.

They marched her back up the stairs, and down more stairs, out of the world of Karelian pine, palms and clove cologne and back through the pungency of cabbage, urine and detergent, into the Internal Prison. She had to lean on the wall a couple of times to keep herself from falling over. She touched her cheek; it was bleeding near the eye, swelling up.

Snowy, Carlo, Cushion, Bunny! Snowy, Carlo, Cushion, Bunny! she recited.

Were they safe? She calculated it had been six days since they left; three nights, three days since she was arrested. The knowledge that Satinov would keep the children safe formed a warm and untouchable locket of love deep inside her.

"Here we are, home again," said Mogilchuk, shoving her into her cell. "Rest up. We'll talk in the morning." Sashenka sank heavily onto the bottom bunk in her cell. "Oh—and did you recognize your uncle Mendel? I think it was him—at least what was left of him."

37

That night they moved her to a new cell with bright lights—but they refused to dim them. The pipes in her cell shook, groaned and started to heat even though it was high summer. In the cells, the air was already stifling.

Sashenka banged on her door.

"Sit on your bed, prisoner." The locks rasped open. Two guards stood in the doorway.

"I wish to complain to Narkom Beria, to the Central Committee. The heating's come on and it's summer. And please turn my lights down. They are so bright they're keeping me awake."

The guards looked at each other. "We'll report your complaints to our superiors."

The doors slammed. The heat increased. Sashenka was sweating. She could hardly breathe, and she was tortured by thirst. She took off her dress and lay on the bunk in her underwear. The lights were so bright, so hot, she could not sleep, however tightly she closed her eyes. If she buried her face in the mattress, they shook her.

When she finally slept fitfully, the Judas port creaked open. "Wake up, prisoner!"

"I'm sleeping, it's nighttime."

She fell asleep again.

"Wake up, prisoner. Move your hands where we can see them."

When these shouts were not enough to keep her awake, they dropped her on the floor, kicking her, slapping her face.

Now she understood. This was what her Party had come to. One night without sleep was fine but by the second night she felt she was beginning to disintegrate. She was nauseous all the time; sweat poured off her and she was not sure if she was ill or just worn to the bone. She fell asleep on her feet; the guards found her asleep on the lavatory but even there they woke her. Worst of all, her fears enveloped her, growing on her like fungus: what if Vanya was an Enemy all along? The children were lost and they were crying for her, or they were dead.

Hours and days crept by. No exercise. No washing. She was fed thrice daily via a tray passed through the hatch, but she was always hungry, always thirsty. Alone in the cell, woken every few minutes, she heard Snowy and Carlo's voices. She must not break. For them. But their faces and smell overwhelmed her. They were lost already, she told herself. Satinov's plan would never work: they were in one of those orphanages, raped, tortured, beaten, abused, and when they were old enough, shot. She should confess to any lies, anything rather than this. Just to sleep in a cool cell. The children were dead already. Dead to her, dead in fact. They were no longer hers. They were lost forever.

She was no more in the land of the living.

38

Far to the south of Moscow, the Volga German woman in the floral scarf and the plain summer dress knocked again on the door of the stationmaster of Rostov-on-Don. Again she dragged in her three suitcases and her two children, a small blond girl and a brown-haired boy, who clung to her arms, their sunken eyes already sad and hollow.

The stationmaster's office was next to the furious chaos of the ticket office, where hundreds waited all day and where so many were disappointed. With its armchairs and portraits of Lenin and Stalin, the office was an oasis of calm and civilization. Even though the Volga German woman had come here every morning for four days and found no telegram, no signal, no friend, she still came in, appearing to enjoy her minute in this clean, quiet eye of the storm. The stationmaster and his assistant looked at each other and rolled their eyes. The nanny, with her three suitcases and two children, was just one of the desperate, grey multitudes who came in every morning hoping for some sign from above, some telegram from nonexistent relatives, some lost luggage that would never be found, some tickets for a train that would never leave.

"Comrade Stepanian," she greeted the stationmaster on the fourth day, "good morning. I wondered if there was any news? A telegram perhaps?"

The stationmaster reached wearily into a wooden in-tray and, clicking his tongue like the clipclop of a horse, began to work his way through the thick yellow paper of Soviet officialdom, moving his lips as he read each telegram.

On the first day, Stepanian had checked the papers of this Volga German woman and these two well-dressed children who were being transported to an orphanage near Tiflis. Each day they returned, looking hungrier, filthier, more forlorn. The angular and wan nanny herself was haggard with exhaustion.

"I'd like to help. Are the young ones OK?" Stepanian smiled at the children. "Are you all right, you two? What's that you've got there?"

"A cushion," said the little girl, forlornly.

"Do you sleep on it?"

"We can't sleep well here. We're beside the canteen but we want to go home. The cushion is my friend."

"We want our mummy," said the little boy, who already had the anxious eyes of a station child.

The words seemed to upset the Volga German woman. Stepanian glanced at her and she shook her head, immediately beginning to collect the bags in order to return to the platform where an Azeri family was keeping their place under the shelter just outside the canteen. She was trying to hide her anxiety but the stationmaster was a connoisseur of misery and uncertainty.

"Thank you, comrade," the woman said very politely. "I'll check in again tomorrow."

Stepanian got up and held open the door for them. "Sorry, I can't help," he said. "Come back tomorrow."

"Is she a fantasist? Maybe there's no telegram?" his assistant asked when they'd left.

"Who knows?" Stepanian shrugged, dismissing them, and returned to his desk with a click of his tongue. He had an important job to do.

Outside the office, the bedraggled threesome walked slowly back to the platforms. Rostov-on-Don station boomed with the thunder of shunting carriages while the air sang with the whistle and puffing of locomotives. Even though the turmoil of collectivization and the Terror was over, the regional stations were still mangy bedlams of confused humanity. Families camped around their suitcases, some well-to-do, some in rags, some in city clothes, some in peasant boots and smocks. Trains were overbooked and never left on time; tickets were hard to buy; the militia checked and rechecked passes and passport stamps, removing those who lacked the correct papers or the energy to dodge their sudden descents.

It was lucky it was a warm summer because the platforms resembled an encampment, crowded with soldiers, workers, peasants and children, hungry ragged children, well-fed lost children, children sitting on handsome leather suitcases, urchins with the faces of old men, little girls with painted lips and short skirts smoking cigarettes and looking for customers.

The canteen in the station offered snacks for those with rubles. An old Tatar ran a kiosk selling newspapers and candies, and behind the Moscow platform was a rusty spigot where the station's inhabitants lined up all day for water. The lavatories, down the steps under the station, were awash with a foamy stinking waste yet there were constant lines; children sobbed and wet themselves and adults fought to get to the front faster.

Carolina was more than worried now. She did not know what had happened to Sashenka and presumed the worst. She was a deeply practical woman but the stress of caring for two children in the station was eating at her. She prided herself on her cleanliness, but by now all three of them were dirty, the children's clothes stained with food, grease and piss. She had a plentiful supply of rubles for food, but Snowy and Carlo, delicate eaters, were used to fine cooking and hated the watery vegetable soup, black bread and dumplings in thin tomato sauce that were the only things available in the canteen. They were already losing weight. During the day they played with other children but Carolina could never relax because some of these urchins had become feral tricksters who were capable of anything. She had to watch the suitcases too. At night they slept together, hugging one another, on their rolled-up mattress under a blanket and some coats. Snowy and Carlo cried in her arms and asked about Mummy and Daddy. When would they see them again? Where were they going?

The actual departure from Moscow had been easy enough: Vanya's parents had reserved seats for Carolina and the children. The train had left on time; and although the journey had taken a day longer than scheduled, a kind Red Army soldier and his young wife, on their way to a new posting on the Turkish border, had taken pity on them and brought them ice creams and snacks from the stations where the train stopped. But the children knew something was terribly wrong. They wanted their mother. Carolina longed to comfort them but did not want to lie, or to encourage them to say dangerous things that might draw attention. It was agony. As they traveled away from their former life, from their parents, from Moscow, Snowy and Carlo clung to her.

"Will you be with us, Carolina? You're staying with us, aren't you? I miss Mama!"

After their visit to Comrade Stepanian, they went for their daily snack in the canteen. They sat at one of the greasy Formica tables. Carolina found that she was shaking. Weary and dispirited, she tried to fight off an attack of naked panic. The Palitsyns were gone. Perhaps Comrade Satinov had forgotten his plan? Perhaps he too had been destroyed? She counted her money in her mind: she had twenty-five rubles in her hand and the large sum of four hundred rubles in her brassiere, for emergencies. If there was no message soon, she would have to make a difficult decision. She had already decided there was no question of leaving Snowy and Carlo at an orphanage of any sort, especially not an NKVD one, but she had few connections in officialdom, and none that was independent of the Palitsyns. She would have to take the children home with her, to her German village not far from Rostov. This filled her with joy, for she loved Snowy and Carlo. They loved her too and she knew that in time she could heal the wounds of loss with her loving care. But she was too old to be their mother and how long would it be before the NKVD came to arrest the Palitsyns' nanny—and where else would they search than in her own village?

That night, she could not sleep. She listened to the chug of locomotives and hiss of steam, the never-quiet rumble of people and machines in the station. Carolina looked down at the pale faces of the children, at Snowy pressing her pink cushion against her lips for comfort, and, for the first time since she left Moscow, she started to cry.

39

"Prisoner seven hundred seventy-eight, sit down. Now, did you sleep well?"

Sashenka, disheveled, pale, dehydrated and barely strong enough to speak, shook her head.

"Is your cell comfortable? How is the air circulating in this hot summer?"

Sashenka said nothing.

Investigator Mogilchuk swept a hand over his thick pompadour and stroked the papers in front of him. It was the same as yesterday and the day before and the day before that. Sashenka had spent three days on the so-called conveyor. No sleep in an overheated cell had broken stronger prisoners than her. After breakfast and slopping out, they brought her back to this interrogation room.

"Your cheek has come up with quite a bruise. It's black and blue."

Sashenka touched it gingerly. It was very painful. Perhaps her cheekbone was fractured, she thought.

"Let's start again. Remember your uncle Mendel. Do not wait until we force you! Begin your confession! Then we'll let you sleep and solve that heating problem in your cell. Would you like a night's sleep?"

"I have nothing to confess. I am innocent."

"Then how do you reconcile the fact of your arrest with that declaration of innocence? Do you think I'm a clown and Comrade Beria's just passing the time of day?"

"I don't understand it myself. I can only think it's a mistake or the result of a misunderstanding caused by some coincidences."

"The Party doesn't recognize coincidences," said Mogilchuk. "You saw Comrade Investigator Rodos in Comrade Beria's office? He's quite a man, a legend in the Organs, more like a dangerous beast: we have to stop him killing prisoners all the time. In fact, he's damaged quite a few people close to you this very week. He says he gets a red mist before his eyes and forgets himself. He hates our sort, Sashenka. He hates intellectuals! You might have to meet him soon if you don't disarm. But you're in luck. I'm going to give you one more chance: I am going to introduce someone who might jog your memory."

He picked up the telephone on his desk. "Deliver the package!" he said genially.

He smiled at Sashenka, removed and replaced his spectacles, and checked his pompadour. They waited in silence. The phone rang.

"Yes, yes, comrade, we'll wait for you."

Mogilchuk left the room for a moment and then returned. "Just making sure everything is just so."

"Can I have a glass of water?" Sashenka repeated Vanya's instructions to herself and then, under her breath but still moving her lips, she chanted, "Snowy, Carlo, Cushion, Bunny."

Mogilchuk was pouring her out a glass when the door burst open and Kobylov pretended to creep in, raising his huge shiny hands with the many glistening rings.

"Pretend I'm not here, Comrade Investigator. I'll hide over here in the corner!" Just like a headmaster sitting at the back to observe a teacher's class, the fragrant giant leaned against the wall and crossed his boots.

There was a knock on the door.

"Your show!" Kobylov whispered and wrinkled his nose at Sashenka. She looked away. "Tired?" he hissed.

"Enter!" piped up Mogilchuk. "The confrontation starts now." The door opened. The torturer from Beria's office entered. "Welcome, Comrade Rodos," Mogilchuk said.

Butterflies of physical fear fluttered in Sashenka's belly. Rodos moved slowly as if made of rusty steel. He nodded at his comrades and then looked Sashenka straight in the eye. He sat down in the chair next to Mogilchuk and started to play with the long red hairs of the mole on his chin. This was the Sashenka team: Kobylov was in charge, with Mogilchuk and Rodos as the soft and hard men. Just to break her? No, they must be working on some bigger case, she thought; one that involved poor Mendel. Her natural optimism, barely still beating in her breast, told her she would survive this. No one had yet broken, that was clear.

So who were they bringing to surprise her? She had already seen Mendel—a heartbreaking, dreadful sight.

If it was Vanya, and he had told lies against her, she would understand that, under the ministerings of Rodos, he had crossed into the other world: she would still beam her love at him. She would not confess: she could still survive.

If it was Benya, darling Benya of the eight stars, of the seven thousand rubies, he was beyond blame now. She had rung him that day to say "I love you." Now she loved him once more, convinced he was as innocent as she. If she never got out of the Lubianka, she would always be grateful that she had known such a love.

But she would not confess, whatever anyone said, because she was still innocent. And if she did not confess, she would one day be freed. And she would reclaim Snowy and Carlo. It was all for them now.

The door opened.

Sashenka looked down at her fingers with terrible foreboding. This was it.

She sensed, through her peripheral vision, a wizened figure hesitating in the doorway.

"Sit down, prisoner," said Rodos, pointing at the chair facing Sashenka on the T-shaped conference table. "There!"

A skinny old man in blue prison overalls hesitated again, pointing at himself. "Yes, you! Sit there, prisoner. Hurry!"

A bolt of expectation hit her. Was it her father? She gulped. Was he alive? Had he testified against her? It did not matter: if he was alive, she would be jubilant.

Love welled up in her for her father, her mother, her grandparents, all of them.

Papa! Whatever they'd done to him, whatever he'd done to her, she just wanted to hug him. Would they let her kiss him?

"Accused Zeitlin-Palitsyn!" barked Rodos. "Face the prisoner."

40

Esteemed Josef Vissarionovich, dearest Koba,

I write to you as an old comrade of over twenty-five years, during which time I have served the Party and you as its ideal personification without once deviating from the Party line. I believe I owe my successful career as a responsible worker in our noble workers' and peasants' Party to your trust and kindness. I will obey any order of the Central Committee as I have always done, but I wish to protest at the methods of "investigation" used on me by the workers of the Organs. I suffer from ill health (a shadow on my right lung; angina and cardiac failure as well as physical weakness from childhood lameness and severe arthritis from hard labor and prolonged exile in Siberia during the Tsarist times) and I am now aged sixty-one. As a member of the Central Committee, I wish to report to you as General Secretary and Politburo member that on arrival here in the Internal Prison at the Lubianka, I was asked to confess to serving foreign powers. When I refused, I was forced down onto a carpet and beaten on the feet and legs with rubber truncheons by three men with terrible force. I could no longer walk and my legs became covered in red and blue internal hemorrhages. Each day, I was beaten again on the same places with a leather strap and rubber truncheons.

The pain was as intense as if boiling water had been poured on me or acid had burned me. I passed out many times, I wept, I screamed, I begged for them to tell you, Comrade Stalin, what I was enduring. When I mentioned your name, they punched me in the face, breaking my nose, my cheekbone and my glasses, without which I can barely function, and they started to beat my spine too. My self-respect as a Bolshevik almost prevents me from telling you more, Illustrious Comrade Stalin, and it pains me even to say this: when, lying in a shuddering heap on the floor, I refused again to tell the Party lies, the interrogators relieved themselves (and, in doing so, polluted the name of our sacred Party of Lenin and Stalin) on my face and in my eyes. Even in the katorga *hard-labor camps under the Tsar, I never endured an iota of this fear and pain. I am now in my cell shivering in every muscle, barely able to hold this pen. I feel such overpowering fear, I who as a revolutionary of thirty years have never experienced fear, and a terrifying urge to lie to you, Josef Vissarionovich, and to incriminate myself and others, including honest responsible workers, even though this itself would be a crime against the Party.*

I understand that our great state needs the weapons of terror to survive and triumph. I support our heroic Organs in their search for Enemies of the People and spies. I am not important. Only the Party and our noble cause matter. But I am sure that you do not know of these practices and I urge you, esteemed old comrade, Great Leader of the Working Class, our Lenin of today, to investigate them and alleviate the sufferings of a sincere and devoted servant of the Party and you, Comrade Stalin.

Mendel Barmakid, Party member since 1904

41

A cadaverous old man with yellow translucent skin and tufts of pale hair on a peeling, scabby scalp sat opposite her in blue prison uniform. He sucked his gums, jerkily glanced around him, and scratched himself in bursts, rolling his eyes, followed by long minutes of comatose stillness.

Sashenka had never met a Zek, but everything about this broken-down ruin shouted Zek, a veteran of the Gulags. She sensed that he had spent years in Vorkuta or Kolyma, breaking rocks, cutting down trees. He no longer even smelled of prisons or possessed the shifty, artful craving for survival that she herself now displayed. This meager husk existed without hope or spirit. Now she saw the true meaning of that expression favored by Beria and even her Vanya: "ground into camp dust." She had never understood it before.

At last she dared to peer into the face, tears welling: was it Baron Samuil Zeitlin, arrested in 1937? No, it could not be her father. This man did not look anything like her father.

Kobylov smacked his lips with a sportsman's glee, and Sashenka observed how the investigators noted his impatience.

"Do you recognize each other?" asked Mogilchuk keenly.

"Speak up, prisoner," said Rodos with surprising warmth. "You recognize her?"

Sashenka searched her memory. Who was he? He must be in his eighties or more.

He swallowed loudly and opened his mouth. He had no teeth, and his gums were pale with ulcerated streaks. She noticed a mark on his neck and realized it was blue-black bruising.

"It's her! It's her!" the creature said in a strikingly educated, level and delicate voice. "Of course I recognize her."

"What's her name?" demanded Rodos briskly.

"She looks exactly the same. But better."

"Speak up! Who is she?"

The husk smirked at Rodos. "You think I've forgotten?"

"Do you want me to remind you?" said Rodos, still playing with the coarse hairs that grew out of his mole.

"What will you do with me after this? Put me out of my misery?"

Rodos ran a hand over his bumpy scalp. "If you don't want any more French wrestling . . ." and then he stood up and shrieked in a voice of maniacal violence: "What is her name?"

The prisoner stiffened. Sashenka jumped, breaking into a sweat.

"Are you going to beat me again? You don't have to. That's Baroness Alexandra Zeitlin—Sashsh-enk-ka, whom I once loved."

Rodos walked to the door. "I have another appointment," he said to Kobylov.

"Enjoy it," said Kobylov. "Carry on, Investigator Mogilchuk."

"Accused Zeitlin-Palitsyn," said Mogilchuk, "do you recognize the prisoner?"

Sashenka shook her head, fascinated and horrified.

"Prisoner, your name?"

"Peter Ivanovich Pavlov." It was another man's voice, from another city in another vanished time.

"That's not your real name, is it?" coaxed Mogilchuk gently. "That's the false name under which you masqueraded as a teacher in Irkutsk for more than ten years when you were really a White Guardist spy. Now look at the accused and tell her your real name."

42

In another interrogation room, Benya Golden sat in a chair in front of Investigator Boris Rodos.

"You've been arrested for treacherous anti-Soviet activities," Rodos said. "Do you acknowledge your guilt?"

"No."

"Why do you think you've been arrested?"

"A chain of coincidences and my inability to write."

Rodos grunted and peered at his papers, with a sneer that further flattened his broad boxer's nose. "So you're a writer, are you? No wonder Mogilchuk wanted to interrogate you. I thought you were just a filthy traitor and a piece of shit. A writer, eh?"

Benya could not contain his surprise. "I wrote a book called *Spanish Stories* that was a success two years ago and then—"

"What the fuck do I care, you vain little prick?" spat Rodos. "I just see a smug Jew who I could break in half like a stick. I could grind you to dust."

Benya did not doubt it. Rodos, with his squashed bald head, overdeveloped shoulders and short legs, reminded him of a hyena. Benya was scared of losing the things he loved, his child and, above all, his darling, his Sashenka. They were all that mattered now.

"Again, why did we arrest you?"

"I honestly don't know. I lived in Paris, I was associated with French and American writers. I knew some of the generals arrested for being Trotskyites."

"So? Don't make me open the drawer on my desk where I keep my sticks and smash your Yid hook nose into pulp. I like French wrestling—that's what we call it here. Confess your criminal and amoral activities and I won't even have to raise a sweat. Tell me the full story of your sexual depravity in the Metropole Hotel, room four hundred and three."

"*That?*" exclaimed Benya. So had he been arrested because of his affair with Sashenka? Gideon had warned him about meddling with a secret policeman's wife. Even in such puritanical times that couldn't be so serious, could it? Perhaps this meant that he would be sent into provincial exile, far from Moscow, but at least he'd live. He had to protect Sashenka.

"Yes, that," answered Rodos, holding up a thick file. "We know every disgusting detail."

"I get it. Her husband's behind this. But she's innocent, I promise. She's done nothing wrong. She's a loyal Communist." Benya scanned Rodos's face but it was like trying to read a slab of meat.

"Who said she wasn't?"

"So she's not in any trouble then?"

"That's secret information, Accused Golden. Just confess how it all started . . ."

Benya prayed that Sashenka knew none of this. Perhaps she would return to being the good wife she had always been. She would assume that Benya had been arrested as a Trotskyite spy and she would despise him and forget about him and continue her life of Party-minded duty and luxury. He loved her so much he wanted to suffer for her, to save her pain.

When they arrived to arrest him, he had not been surprised. He had been so happy in those two weeks of loving Sashenka that he could not believe it would last—even though he knew that she was truly the love of his life. It was a love that comes just once, if ever.

As he sat inside the car on the way to prison, he watched the city streets pass by, the lights fluid through his tears. It was dawn, the time when cities renew themselves before the day breaks: trucks collected garbage, janitors sprayed steps, old ladies swept up paper, a man in overalls carried a pail of milk. But the red stars of the Kremlin that had lit up their room in the Metropole belonged to them both together. Now he would suffer on the rack: they would tear him to pieces, and his blood ran cold.

Sashenka would live on outside, that adorable woman whom he loved. No one would ever know what was in their hearts, no matter how much they beat him. Her existence outside the prison, like that of his own young child, meant that he would live on too as long as she lived. She had never told him that she loved him but he hoped that she did . . . Why couldn't she tell him when so much suffering stretched out ahead of him? She was making him wait for it, and probably he would have to wait to hear it in another world.

Now he asked himself—what was the right thing to say? How to protect Sashenka? Or was she beyond protecting? Such was his writer's curiosity that, even as he mocked death, he speculated on this latest twist in his own liquidation. What would his "Soviet Proletarian Guide to the Etiquette of Adultery" recommend? he wondered, recalling how he and Sashenka had laughed about it together.

"Disarm and make your confession!" Rodos shouted.

Suddenly he pulled open the drawer of the desk and smashed Benya once, twice and again across the face with a black rubber truncheon.

Benya fell to the floor, his cheek scouring on concrete. Rodos followed him, his boots smashing into Benya's nose, blood fountaining out, and the truncheon thudding into his face, his kidneys, his groin, his face again. He vomited in agony, bringing up bile and blood and teeth.

"Sashenka!" he moaned, realizing with each blow that she was not free, sensing that she was somewhere here, near and in pain—and that broke him utterly. "I love you! Where are you?"

43

"Peter Sagan, Captain of Gendarmes," the old Zek said in the most urbane and aristocratic of tones. "There, that's given her a shock."

Sashenka gasped. Hadn't he died in the streets of Petrograd? Her heart drummed, claws tweaked her insides.

"How do you know her?" asked Mogilchuk.

"I loved her once," said the husk in his Corps de Pages, Yacht Club accent.

"You had a sexual relationship with her?"

"Yes."

"That's a lie!" cried Sashenka, thinking back to that romantic but chaste sleigh ride and then the miserable night when Sagan had tried to rape her.

"Quiet or you'll be removed," said Mogilchuk. "You'll get your chance in a minute. She was a virgin?"

"Yes. She became my mistress and I corrupted her with unspeakable perversions. I also gave her cocaine, which I pretended to take as a medicine."

"Never!" shouted Sashenka. "This is not Peter Sagan. I don't recognize this man. He's an impostor!"

"Ignore her, prisoner. Let's carry on. You had a professional relationship?"

"I used her . . . I hated the revolutionaries as scum . . . but I came to love her."

"We don't want your romantic reminiscences, prisoner. Your *professional* relationship?"

"She was my double agent."

"When did you recruit her for the Okhrana?"

"Winter 1916. We arrested her as a Bolshevik. I recruited her at Kresty Prison. Thereafter we met in safe houses and hotel rooms where she betrayed her comrades."

"This is not true. You know it's not true! Whoever you are, you're telling lies!" Sashenka stood up. Kobylov's bejeweled hands fell heavily on her shoulders, jolting her back into her seat. A chill rose up her body, and she started to shiver.

"Did she recruit other agents for you, higher up the Bolshevik high command?"

"Yes."

"Tell us who."

"First, Mendel Barmakid."

Sashenka shook her head. She felt she was drowning, the waters closing above her head.

"Was Mendel a valuable agent, Prisoner Sagan?"

"Oh yes. The other leaders were in prison, Siberia or abroad. He was a member of the Central Committee in contact with Lenin."

"How long did he remain a double agent?"

"Mendel's still a double agent."

"Lies! You bastard!" she shouted again, energy draining from her. "You'll rot in hell for this! If you knew what you were doing! If you only knew . . ." She started to weep.

"Get a grip on yourself, accused," said Mogilchuk, "or Rodos will tear you apart." There was a moment of silence. "After the Revolution, Sagan, what happened to your Okhrana agents?"

"They went underground as I did myself."

"Under whose control?"

"Initially the White Guards but later we became the servants of . . . an unholy alliance of snakes and running dogs." At this, Sagan again smirked, and Sashenka sensed within him a mixture of shame and mockery. Behind his shifting, restless blue irises he seemed to be weeping, begging her to forgive him. Had they drugged him?

"Under whose command, Sagan?"

"Ultimately under the command of Japanese and British intelligence but taking orders from the United Opposition of Trotsky and Bukharin."

"So all these years you were still in contact with the accused?"

"I was the contact between her and the enemies of the Soviet working people."

"You met regularly?"

"Yes, we did."

"This is laughable," Sashenka shouted. "I've never heard of this man. The policeman Sagan was killed on Nevsky Prospect in 1917. This man is an actor!"

"What other agents did she recruit?"

"Her husband, Vanya Palitsyn. And more recently the writer Benya Golden—using the same degenerate sexual techniques I taught her as a girl."

"So Japanese and British intelligence, along with Trotsky and Bukharin, were running traitor Mendel in the Central Committee, traitor Palitsyn in the NKVD, and traitor Golden the writer for years on end?"

"Ycs!"

"You bastard!" Sashenka threw herself across the table but when her fingers came into contact with her accuser, it was like grabbing handfuls of sand. There was nothing to hold. The old man was so weak that he fell off his chair, grazing his head on the side of the table and lying on the floor in a heap.

Kobylov lifted her up from behind like a rag doll and dropped her hard onto her chair.

"Careful, girl, we've got to look after him, haven't we, boys?" said Mogilchuk as he helped Sagan off the floor. He was still floppy and could barely sit up, legs and hands a blur of spasms.

Sashenka experienced the despair of the damned. This scarecrow was tolling the bells on her entire life. She thought of her children. The unthinkable had happened. Nothing was as she had imagined.

She was not irrelevant to this case, she realized. She was its pivot—the center of the spider's web—and she would never get out, never see Snowy and Carlo again. "Give me time to settle the children," Satinov had demanded. She prayed he had succeeded.

Was it now time to put Vanya's plan into action? "Only confess when you realize you have no choice," he'd instructed. Had he held out this long?

"Good work, boys!" Kobylov clapped his hands together and left, kicking the door shut behind him with a gleaming boot.

Mogilchuk held up a file entitled *Protocol of Interrogation* and opened it.

"Here's your confession. You've signed every page and at the end, have you not?"

Sagan nodded, jiggling his knees and scratching.

The Chekist tossed it over to Sashenka. "There, Accused Zeitlin-Palitsyn! Read it! You couldn't remember all this? How could you have forgotten?"

44

"Comrade Stepanian, any sign of a telegram?"

Carolina staggered into the stationmaster's office. It was the next morning, a fan whirred overhead, and the hot office was crowded that day. An old peasant in blouse and clogs, two little eyes peering over a long white beard, sat in front of the desk; a young man in a Party tunic with a Kalinin beard waited with passport and tickets; an NKVD officer read a sports magazine with his feet up on the radiator.

Comrade Stepanian put his hand on the pile of telegrams and patted it.

"No, no, there's no telegram . . ."

Carolina was overcome with despair. Satinov had failed them; it had all been for nothing. "I'm leaving today," she said, on the edge of tears. "I can't wait any longer."

She dragged herself and the children to the door and was struggling to open it when suddenly Stepanian shook himself and clicked his tongue like a woodpecker.

"Wait! There's no telegram—but there's someone waiting for you by the samovar in the canteen. A woman. She's been here for some time."

"Thank you, Comrade Stepanian. Thank you! I could embrace you . . ." and she rushed out.

"Is it Mama?" asked Carlo as they hurried to the café.

"Mama's gone away," said Snowy seriously. "Carolina's told you already. We're on an adventure."

"Come on," said Carolina. "Run quickly. Oh, please God she hasn't left already."

Inside the canteen, a little apart from the line for tea and hot water beside the steaming samovar and farther from the trays of greasy dumplings, pirozhki and *pelmeni*, a dignified older woman with a heart-shaped face and grey curls around her ears sat stiffly. Wearing an old-fashioned lady's cloche hat and a suit, Lala was sipping a cup of tea, scanning the crowds eagerly. When she saw the bedraggled nanny and the two children, she stood up and beckoned them over.

"Hello, I've come to meet you." She smiled at them all and offered a hand to Carolina, who seemed beyond such courtesies. The two women eyed each other for a moment, then hugged like old friends.

"I'm sorry it's taken so long. The train was delayed and I'm not practiced at all this. Come, let's sit down at this table," she said, speaking slowly, looking hard at the children, her darling Sashenka's children. "I have a room in the Revolution Hotel in Rostov where we can go and wash and get some sleep. We can eat there too. I have papers stamped for the children and I was given some money."

Carolina tottered and then sat and buried her face in her hands—and Lala knew what this moment must be costing the nanny. Carlo ran to Carolina and kissed her hair. "You're my best friend in the whole wide world!" he said, stroking her cheek.

Lala placed her hand on Carolina's shoulder. "We're living in bad times and you've done so well to get here. Please, Carolina, stop crying! I never asked for this job. Like you, I'm risking a lot to do it. I too am out of my depth."

"But you have a plan? You know what to do?"

"Yes, I have instructions. Carolina, I'll do anything to carry them through." She looked once more at the children and they stared at her.

"Who is she?" asked Snowy.

"Be polite, Snowy!" Lala saw Carolina return to her brisk self. "This lady is going to help you."

"Where's Mama?" asked Carlo, his face collapsing again.

"You must be Carlo," said Lala. "I have something for you." She reached into a canvas bag and pulled out a cookie tin illustrated with a picture of the Kremlin.

Carlo could not take his eyes off the tin. Lala opened it and Carlo gasped at the yellow magic of the cookies with their delicious cream and jam fillings but did not move.

"I heard you liked these," she said, feeling Carolina smile at her.

"Look, Carlo," said Snowy, "she knows they're your favorite." Snowy took one and gave it to Carlo, who ate it. He took hold of his sister's hand.

"Hello, Snowy. Is that your friend Cushion?" asked Lala.

"You've heard of Cushion?"

"Of course, Cushion is famous. Hello, Miss Cushion! You're much blonder than your mummy, Snowy, and your eyes are blue but you have her mouth—and you, Carlo, look just like your father."

"You know Mama?" asked Snowy.

"You know Papa?" said Carlo.

"Oh yes," said Lala, remembering the day she'd first met Sashenka and had loved her instantly like her own. She recalled the nights she spent with Sashenka in her bed at the mansion on Greater Maritime Street, the sleigh rides sweeping through the boulevards of St. Petersburg, the hilarity of ice skating, the exhilaration of riding ponies on the family estate. She had been Sashenka's real mother and, although she had not seen her for almost ten years in the crazy, man-eating world that Sashenka had embraced, she had thought of her every day and talked to that portrait of the Smolny schoolgirl in her pinafore, as if they were still together. She knew too that she was here, in this station, not just for herself or Sashenka—but for Samuil Zeitlin as well, whether he was alive or dead.

Now Sashenka had been swallowed up by the Party she'd served so assiduously—and the only way Lala could express her deep love was by undertaking this troubling mission for the Zeitlin family. "I know your mummy better than anyone alive," she told Carlo and Snowy. "But we mustn't think about Mummy now. We must make plans for the future, for your next adventure. Oh, and you must call me Lala."

"So *you're* Lala?" said Snowy. "Mama told me you gave her a bath every day. I like you. You're very cushiony."

The two nannies smiled at each other, sharing their admiration of Snowy—then looked away, abruptly. It was too painful.

Turning their backs on the station, they walked into Rostov-on-Don, each holding the hand of one of the children.

"Swing me!" piped Carlo, kicking up his legs, happy for the first time in days.

As Carolina took one arm and Lala the other, Lala could not help thinking that one stage of Snowy and Carlo's lives was ending—and another was about to begin.

45

Sashenka crawled to her cell door. "Take me to Kobylov!"

The Judas port slid open, muddy, bored eyes blinked; it shut again. Sashenka lay back sweltering on her bunk, falling in and out of sleep. How many days since she had slept for longer than ten minutes? She had lost count. She had lost the sense of day and night. There was no window in her cell, just a brilliant light that penetrated and burned even the deepest and darkest and coolest chambers of her soul.

The confrontation with Captain Sagan had changed everything. She had thought about it all day and into the night, slipping in and out of delirium. Awake, she dreamed of the children, of Vanya, of Benya Golden, and debated absurd questions: could a woman love two men at the same time, one as a lover, one as a husband? Oh yes, it was possible. But each time, she passed into dreamless unconsciousness, she slipped under the surface of fathomless black water where she saw nothing.

Then she was shaken awake roughly. "No sleeping!"

She did not even know if Vanya was alive. She knew they would have been merciless. He was one of them, he knew where all the bodies lay buried, and now they were crushing him. She longed to see him.

She thought about asking to meet him to confirm that she should take the next step, but she feared that any suspicion that they had coordinated their plans would draw the investigators toward the children. They had had more than a week now, darling Cushion and Bunny, to go on their dread adventure.

What was their smell? Hay and vanilla. How did Snowy say, "Let's do the Cushion dance"? Sashenka struggled to get the children's intonation right, sketching their faces again and again, but sometimes the shape of a nose or the curve of a forehead (those delicious foreheads, her favorite places to kiss, just where the hair met the temple, oh, she could nuzzle them there forever!) confounded her and they sank beneath the remorseless black water. Perhaps this was Nature making it easier for her, allowing her to forget.

Her mind was barely functioning, she scarcely registered the life of the prison around her: she just existed on the conveyor. But if she went insane, she would be no use to Carlo and Snowy. She sensed it was time for the next step.

It was deep in the night when they came to get her. The whole Soviet government functioned throughout the night, from Stalin down. How naïve she had been about Vanya coming home at dawn, smelling like an old wolf, as if he had been in a barroom brawl. His secrecy had suited her too because she had never had to ask what he was doing all night. Now she knew the compromise they had both made.

When they reached the interrogation rooms that existed, in Sashenka's mind, in limbo, exactly halfway between the paneled offices at the front of the Lubianka complex and the dungeons of the Interior Prison, she was relieved, just as she had been oddly relieved when they had arrested her.

She walked into the room and was struck so hard on the back with a rubber truncheon that she fell over. She was kicked viciously, which made her curl up with a groan. The truncheons—there were two men in there—fell on her back, her breasts, her stomach, wherever she turned, but especially on her legs and feet. She screamed in pain, and blood ran down her face into her eyes. She tried to pretend that this was a very unpleasant medical procedure that was necessary and even therapeutic and would be over soon, but this did not work for long.

In the compacted odors of vodka sweat, cologne and pork sausage that oozed from her persecutors, in the agony of the blows that struck her breasts, in the virile grunts and heaves of these unfit men as they swung their truncheons, Sashenka recognized that her tormentors found berserk sport in beating her. Perhaps her request had interrupted a banquet in the NKVD Club—or even an orgy at a safe house somewhere.

The men halted briefly, breathing heavily. Wiping her eyes, shivering and gasping with agony, she squinted up at Kobylov and Rodos, in boots, white shirts and jodhpurs held up with suspenders. They stood together, such different men but with the same eyes: bloodshot, yellowed and wild, like wolves caught in the headlights.

"I want to confess," she said as loudly as she could. "Everything. I beg you. Stop it now!"

46

"Hurrah! Hurrah!" shouted Kobylov, jumping up and down like a schoolboy at a soccer match. "Christ is risen!"

He remembered his own mother, the big-breasted cheerful Georgian woman who so cherished him. The last time he was with her in her new apartment in Tiflis, she had warned him: "Careful of the unhappiness you cause, Bogdan! Remember God and Jesus Christ!"

He pulled on his tunic, wiping his forehead with a yellow silk kerchief. "Enough now! Get her cleaned up, Comrade Rodos, let her get some sleep, cool her cell down and give her some coffee when she wakes. Then give her a pen and paper and get Mogilchuk to charm her. I'm off back to the party where so many mares await me! Thank heaven we can stop before we ruin her looks altogether. This is hard work, Sashenka, for a man who loves women. It's not easy, pure torture, not easy at all." And with a fleshy wave of jeweled fingers and a gleaming boot kicking the door shut, he was gone.

Sashenka slept all the next day. The cell was deliciously cool and dark but her chest was agony—perhaps they had broken a rib? Some time in the night a doctor, a grey-bearded, white-coated specialist, fallen from his fancy city practice into this world of the living dead, came to see her. She was half awake but she dreamed that he was the vanished Professor Israel Paltrovich who had delivered Snowy in the Kremlin Hospital. Something about his hush of surprise when he saw it was her, something about his aristocratic and soft-spoken bedside manner, even though he himself looked so broken, something about his gentle reassurance in the middle of the night, reminded her of him. She wanted to talk to him about Snowy.

"Professor, is it you . . . ?"

He put his calm fingers on her hand and squeezed it.

"Just rest," he said, and more quietly, "sleep, dear." He gave her injections and rubbed some healing cream into her muscles.

When she woke up, she could not move. Her body was black and blue, and her urine was red. She ate and slept some more, then they let her wash and walk in the exercise yard, where, hobbling along, she stared at the gorgeous turquoise tent above her. The air was racy and fresh and warm. It was as if she had been born again today.

She had been lucky after a fashion, she told herself. What luck to be loved by Lala and raised by her; to marry Vanya and create those children; to have enjoyed the seven-thousand-ruby caresses of Benya Golden, one wild, reckless love affair in her life of good sense and hard work. She had known Lenin and Stalin in person, the titans of human history. Given that it was all about to end, thank God she had known such things. What riches, what times she had enjoyed!

They would draw it out of her, she knew, and she would deliver all they wanted—and more. The words she would utter, the confessions she would make, were a long form of suicide, but addictively indispensable to her one reader: the Instantzia, Comrade Stalin, who would find in her breathless reminiscences all he had ever wanted to believe about the world and the people he hated. Vanya had told her about Stalin's lurid visions and she would pander to every one of them. Vanya, if he was still alive, would do the same, less flamboyantly. She did not know, probably would never know now, why she, Mendel, Benya and Vanya had been arrested in the first place. The workings of spiders and webs were now beyond her. All that mattered was that she was the center of it all, she had destroyed them all. She and Peter Sagan.

They might just keep her on ice for months but by the time they sentenced her (and this part, this snuffing out, this unspeakable ending, this violent conclusion of the mysterious, boundless, vibrant thing called Life, she still found unimaginable), the children would be settled somewhere with new names and destinies, safe and sound and in the world of the living—not in her world of the dead. She beamed her love to them, her thanks to Satinov, her love for those precious to her. She had to let them go. She had been a Communist since she was sixteen. It had been her religion, the rapture of absolutism, the science of history. But now she saw, late in life, that *this*, her special fantastical confessional suicide, was her last mission. She had become a parent again, just as she ceased to be one. She was pregnant with purpose.

In the exercise yard, Sashenka saw wispy clouds in the dancing shapes of a train, a lion and a bearded rabbinical profile. Was that her grandfather, the Rabbi of Turbin? And could that be a rabbit and a pink cushion, lit by the rays of a sun just out of sight . . . Perhaps, after all, the mystics were right, life was just a chimera, a fire in the desert, a fevered trance, but the pain was real.

When the time comes for the Highest Measure, she promised herself, I'll welcome the seven grams of lead and I'll leave an expression of love for Snowy and Carlo out there on the gates of eternity. It was time for the final act.

47

"Here's your prize," said Kobylov, welcoming her into the interrogation room. The secret policeman watched as the beautiful prisoner caught first a whiff and then the strong aroma of the burnt, slightly sour coffee beans.

"You must confess your criminal and treacherous activities," said Mogilchuk, pouring her coffee out of a brass flask.

She sat in the chair, snow-white between the welts and bruises, and thin, but something about those lips that never quite closed, the little islands of freckles on either side of her nose, and that bosom distracted Kobylov, who sat on the windowsill, swinging a new pair of coffee-colored calf-leather boots. He liked this stage in a case. There was an end-of-semester chumminess in the air and he did not have to beat her anymore, even though a bout of French wrestling with a real bastard was bracing sport. He felt her grey eyes rest on him, bright again and bold and vigilant.

Kobylov winked at her and wrinkled his nose. He took out a packet of cigarettes emblazoned with a crocodile. "Your favorite Egyptians," he said, taking one and tossing her the packet.

"I couldn't have imagined when I became a Bolshevik that I would end here," she told him.

"When you chose the revolutionary life, even at sixteen, you entered a game of life and death and put the quest for the holy grail above everything else," said Kobylov, lighting her cigarette and then his own. "Comrade Stalin told me that himself."

"But I changed," said Sashenka, blowing out lacy ringlets of smoke.

Kobylov raised his eyes to heaven. "It's irreversible," he said.

"Like a sleigh ride that you can never get off . . ."

"Time to work," said Kobylov.

Mogilchuk lifted his pen and smoothed the pristine sheet of paper. "Begin your confession."

Sashenka brushed her hair back off her forehead. There was a cut on her cheek and one whole side of her face was still swollen, surrounded by a rainbow of deep blue, mustard yellow and poppy red.

Kobylov felt like the hunter who corners the noble stag and even as he aims his rifle at its heart he cannot help but admire it. He marveled at her self-possession and her courage.

Sashenka ran her fingers over her lips and met Kobylov's gaze. "I want to start on the day I was arrested by the Okhrana outside the Smolny Institute in St. Petersburg in the winter of 1916. That was how I came to be recruited by the Tsarist secret police and thence by British, German and Japanese intelligence and their hireling, Trotsky. May I start on the day it all began?"

48

Carolina heard the door of her hotel room close quietly. The room seethed with insects: the ceiling, even the bedspread, was covered in a blanket of glistening black bodies like living caviar. The children had been fascinated by them. In one twin bed, Carolina had slept with Carlo curled around her to form a single sculpture. After the station, it had seemed the most luxurious room on earth. But now, as she sprang awake from a sleep fathoms deep, she knew that click of the lock could mean only one thing.

She jumped up and ran to the window and, placing her hands on the glass, she stared, wild eyed, down at the street below. Among the horse-drawn carts, trucks and Pobeda cars, she saw women in floral dresses and red headscarves, and the pea-green uniforms of a provincial Soviet town. Then she spotted the children far across the square, walking toward the station.

They were holding Mrs. Lewis's hands, two tiny far-off figures. But she knew every mannerism of their gaits, the way Carlo stomped along and Snowy's long-legged, bouncing grace, so like her mother's. For a moment, Carolina longed to run after them and catch them and hug them over and over again . . . But already she knew this leave-taking was for the best.

The train would be shunting forward, the momentum shifting too. Soon Snowy and Carlo would be leaving another beloved figure behind and moving into a new existence.

She cried loudly and openly and for a long time in the room.

She cursed this gentle nanny, this Lala, who now had the children. Perhaps Lala would keep them, and even though she could never care for them as lovingly as she herself (no one alive could do that!), they would be better with her than with strangers. But Carolina knew too that Lala could not keep them forever; that she had some dangerous connections, and connections had to be avoided, Comrade Satinov had explained. So Lala was taking them somewhere else. She had mentioned an orphanage in Tiflis, but that was for the paperwork. There the children's identities would be laundered and their adoptions made official.

The night before, it had been hard to get the children to sleep even though they were exhausted and so grateful for the beds. They cried out for their mummy and daddy. The two nannies stroked them, hugged them and fed them their favorite cookies until in the end the children had hugged them back and surrendered to sleep.

Then the two nannies had sat in the bathroom and Carolina had talked with a frowning intensity, passing on everything she knew about the children: what they loved, what they hated, what foods, what hobbies, what books. At the end, in a sort of agony, she had whispered, "Tell the new parents about the Cushion, tell them about the bunnies. It's all they have left of their lives!"

And Lala had understood. "I know what sensitive children they are, Carolina. I cared for Sashenka for so long . . ."

"What was she like?" asked Carolina. "Was she like . . . ?" and she looked toward the bedroom—but then she could speak no longer. No more details. It would be more than either of them could bear.

The two women, the Englishwoman and the Volga German, embraced in tears. In the end, lying each with one of the children, they managed to fall asleep too in the warm hotel room looking out over the Don, where Peter the Great had once sailed.

As she packed her bag and caught the bus to return to her little village, Carolina remembered how the three figures had wound their way toward the station. They were pulling the tottering Lala in different directions, laughing, she thought, from the way Carlo was tossing his head back and Snowy was skipping. She realized that she was seeing Snowy and Carlo Palitsyn for the last time. Very soon, they would be different children with new names, belonging to other families.

"Good-bye, my absolute darlings!" she said aloud. "God bless you. May my love travel with you wherever you go and whomsoever you become."

To what awaited her, she gave not a thought.

There were such kind women as Carolina, in the agony of Russia, when even the most decent people became cruel or turned their eyes away. Such paragons were rare. But they existed. They alone kept the candles of love alight.

49

It was high summer, the time of year when Tiflis becomes a balmy, baking city of outdoor cafés and strolling boulevardiers. In the Café Biblioteka, Lala Lewis was pouring red wine for one of her regulars when the doors opened.

An ancient waxy-skinned man entered in a battered, dusty sepia-colored suit with a little leather suitcase. He sported a neat grey mustache, and walked painfully in pigeon steps toward the cashier's desk. Tengiz the manager was not sure if he recognized this ghostly wraith: could it be a miracle? One of the "lucky stiffs" back from the dead?

The Englishwoman watched his staggering progress silently for a moment, her eyes opening wider and wider, her mouth breaking into a scream before any sound came out.

Then she gave the most girlish yelp, as if she were sixteen years old, and almost skipped across the wooden floor to meet her husband. She had recognized the "former person" Samuil Zeitlin, who had been arrested in 1937, sentenced to death but reprieved by a centimeter of ink from the pen of Comrade Stalin and dispatched to the Kolyma Gulags in northeastern Siberia. Then, a few short months ago, against all the odds of Fate, Zeitlin, the ultimate class enemy, had been reprieved again.

"Good God!" said Lala in English. "Samuil! You're alive! You're ALIVE!" She threw herself into his weak embrace, nearly knocking him over. It had never occurred to her that he might still live. She quickly poured him a thimble of brandy and he swallowed it and sighed.

"Thank God you're still here, darling Lala," he said, falling to his knees, right there in the café, and kissing her hands and even her feet.

"Let's get you up," she said, pulling him to his feet, anxious not to make any more of a scene. "You really are a miracle. Since the Terror ended, a few have come back—lucky stiffs is what they call them."

"If you only knew, but you'd never believe it, the things I saw on the way to Kolyma, the things I saw men do to other men . . ."

Lala sat him down at a table and brought him a glass of brandy, a plate of lobio beans and a hot slice of *khachapuri.* He told how a strange thing had happened to him. An NKVD guard had come to the office, where he worked as camp accountant in the faraway hell of Kolyma, and summoned him to the commandant's apparat, where he was asked to sign for his belongings. He was given his old suit and shoes then invited to lunch by the commandant, who served veal cutlets, by coincidence almost the same dish cooked daily by Delphine at the mansion on Greater Maritime Street. He was taken to the barber's shop (the barber was a former nobleman). Then, with a small allowance, he was freed to set off on the long, slow journey back to Tiflis.

When he was a little restored, she and Tengiz helped him upstairs to her room. Tengiz brought them hot water. When the manager was gone, she undressed Zeitlin and washed his frail body with a warm sponge.

Samuil sat on the edge of the bed, looking at her, asking questions with his eyes. She knew he wanted to know about Sashenka—but he could not bring himself to ask.

He lay down with a sigh, closed his eyes and went to sleep immediately.

Lala lay beside him with her head on his shoulder. At that moment, she loved him so much that she regretted nothing. She felt that she had imagined her birth and childhood in England. It seemed her entire life had taken place in Russia with the Zeitlins. Her family in Hertfordshire had not received a letter from her for many years. They probably thought she was dead. And the English girl Audrey Lewis *was* dead.

She had loved Samuil for nearly thirty years and they had been together for more than twenty: his family was her family. She had mourned him and grieved in the stoical silence of the times.

She never blamed Samuil for keeping her in Russia—they had been happy together. And it had been such a blessing that she had not been arrested but was still working in the café, healthy and prepared, waiting for him to return. Here he was, her Samuil, alive and back from the camps, returned from the dead.

She kissed his face and his hands, smelled his male smoky biscuit smell. He was almost as she remembered.

He opened his eyes as if he couldn't quite believe where he was, smiled, and went back to sleep.

Lala stroked his skin, the parchment of the Gulags, and wondered how, and when, to tell him about the heroism of his daughter, what had happened in the railway station just a few weeks ago, and how together she and Sashenka had saved Snowy and Carlo.

PART THREE

THE CAUCASUS, LONDON, MOSCOW, 1994

1

"Three hours, twelve minutes and eighteen seconds until the train for London!" Katinka Vinsky cried out, running to her window in her pink nightgown, almost slipping on the wrinkled yellow carpet, throwing open the brown, damp-stained curtains. She caught a glimpse of herself smiling in the mirror and behind her a chaotic bedroom with clothes everywhere, and a half-filled carpetbag. It was dawn in the bungalow cottage on the main street of Beznadezhnaya, a village on the Russian borderlands of the north Caucasus, remote enough for locals to say that it was "lost in deafness."

"Mamochka! Papochka! Where are you?" she called, opening her door.

Then she saw the doctor and his wife, already dressed, in the kitchen–cum–sitting room. She knew her father would be reassuring her mother that their daughter's trip would be all right, that they would be at the station early enough, that the seat on the train was booked (facing the right way, because their darling felt sick if she had her back to the direction of the train), that the train would arrive in time for her to catch the bus to Sheremetyevo Airport in Moscow to check in for the Aeroflot flight to Heathrow. Her mother was reassuring her father that Katinka would have enough food for the journey and that she had the right clothes for London, where, it was said, the rain never stopped and the fog never cleared. They were, Katinka decided, much more nervous than she was.

Katinka knew her parents were of two minds about her accepting the mysterious job in London. They had been so proud when she received the top grades in history at Moscow University, but when her professor, Academician Beliakov, showed her the advertisement in the *Humanities Department Gazette*, her father had begged her not to go.

What sort of people lived in London and were rich enough to hire a historian? he asked. But Katinka could not resist it. Researching a family history, tracing the vanished past . . . She imagined a cultured young Count Vorontsov or Prince Golitsyn living in a dilapidated London town house full of ancient samovars, icons and family portraits, keen to find out what had become of his family, their palaces and works of art dating from the eighteenth century, her period, her speciality. She wished she'd been born in those more elegant times . . .

She had never been abroad before, although she had spent three years at the university in faraway Moscow. No, the offer was too good to miss: young historians specializing in eighteenth-century history do not often get the chance to earn much-needed U.S. dollars and travel to London.

Katinka's father, Dr. Valentin Vinsky, was smoking a cigarette and pacing the floor while her mother Tatiana, a soft, feathery creature with bright red-dyed hair, busied herself in the kitchen with her mother-in-law, Babushka—or Baba for short. Through the fog of cooking, Baba, a low-slung, broad-shouldered peasant in a floral dress, scarlet kerchief and some old surgical socks held up with elastic, moved slowly like a dinosaur in the mist.

Steam rose so densely, so aromatically, from the bubbling pots of vegetable broth that it was hard to see the two women. It was as if the nourishing humidity had warped the entire house. Like a million Soviet homes, everything inside, carpets, curtains and clothes, was yellowed with steam and damp and grease.

"There you are!" said Katinka, bounding into the room. "How long have you been up?"

"I didn't sleep a wink!" her father replied. He was tall and dark-skinned with brown eyes. Though his grey hair was thinning and he was always exhausted, Katinka thought he looked like one of those handsome forties film stars. "Everything packed?"

"Not so fast, Papochka!"

"Well, you must hurry . . ."

"Oh Papochka!" Father and daughter hugged, both with tears in their eyes. The family were always quick to cry and Katinka, the youngest of three children and a beloved afterthought, was its soft-hearted and much-indulged core. Her father was a thoughtful man. He did not laugh much; in fact, he did not say much at all and when he did he was tortuously inarticulate—yet he was worshipped virtually as a god in the neighborhood, where he had delivered the babies of babies he had delivered and even *their* babies. "I can't imagine how I've brought up such a confident, loquacious child as you, Katinka," he once told her. "But you're the light of my life. Unlike me, you can do anything!" He was right—she knew she possessed all the assurance of a child utterly cherished in the happiest of families.

"Your food'll be ready, don't you worry, girl," said Baba, her gums almost bare of teeth. "Go and wake up Bedbug or he'll miss your departure!" "Klop," or Bedbug, was Sergei Vinsky, Katinka's grandfather.

Katinka trotted down the corridor toward the bathroom, passing her little bedroom with its single unit of bed, light and bedside table (standard Soviet issue) and its curling posters of Michael Jackson.

She heard the faucet running in the bathroom as she called out to her grandfather. The bathroom door opened and she met the rich, sweet distillation of Bedbug's bowels and the familiar stale damp of old towels that was another ingredient of the provincial fug of home. Bedbug, a small weathered countryman in an undershirt and pouchy grey briefs, emerged from a bathroom that was so overshadowed by hanging laundry that it resembled a gypsy tent. Resting his hands on his hips and chewing his gums, he let rip an ungodly fart of orchestral proportions.

"Hear that? Good morning and good luck, dear girl!" and he cackled hoarsely. It was the same every morning at home. Katinka was used to it—but since her return from the university she had observed its customs with more detachment.

"Disgusting! Worse than a farmyard!" she said cheerfully. "At least in a farmyard the animals aren't rude too. Come on, Bedbug, hurry up! Breakfast's ready. I'm leaving soon!"

"So? Why should I hurry? I have my rituals!" He nodded at the Soviet lavatory with its unique basin-like design (guaranteed to preserve its fetid cargo as long as possible), and grinned.

"Yes, Bedbug, and no one enjoys their rituals like you. But you are coming to see me off?"

"Why bother? Good riddance!" More cackling. "Wait, Katinka! I've heard about a new murder on the radio! There's a serial killer in Kiev who eats his victims, brains, livers and all, can you believe it?"

Katinka returned to the main room, shaking her head. Bedbug, an old collective farmer, lived in a world of his own. Now that the old order had gone and the Soviet Union had been abolished, he mourned the Communist Party and fulminated with his gambling cronies in the Vegaz-Kalifornia Klub against the New Russian rich—"crooked *zhydy i chernyi i chinovniki*"—Jews and Chechens and bureaucrats! There was nothing to equal the burning bitterness of old men in small villages, Katinka thought.

For Bedbug, though, the recent disintegration of the Workers' Paradise had had one advantage. In these queer, unsettled times, Russia was enjoying a lurid harvest of serial killers, a banquet of cannibals. Apart from his bowels, Bedbug had found a new hobby for his old age—the lives of the murderers.

Katinka sighed and went back to the kitchen to eat her last breakfast before London.

2

When Katinka's grandparents and parents emerged from the house to accompany her to the station, they were dressed up in their Revolution Day best.

It was a bracing day of sharp-edged brightness in this village of mixed Russian and Caucasian folk, a day that suited a new beginning. A ragged crust of grimy ice still covered the fields and pastures and the ditches on either side of the village's one paved thoroughfare, Suvorov Street (known as Lenin Street until last year), with its dreary, squat cottages enlivened only by their blue or red shutters. There is no more thrilling time of year in Russia, for beneath this tainted whiteness Katinka could already hear the rushing of water. The ice was melting and, hidden from view, frothy streams seethed, merged and parted, unleashing the snowdrops that were already pushing through the black-edged snow. The trees oozed sap, and skylarks and finches trilled with joy, celebrating spring.

Katinka wore a rabbit-fur coat and white vinyl boots, a denim miniskirt (Turkish made) and a purple sweater, of which she was very proud, inlaid with rhinestones in rhomboid patterns. Her father, in a felt greatcoat that covered his medical smock, carried her single bag down to their white Volga. The car was old and rusty but its broad confident solidity summed up the best of the old USSR. In the village, the doctor's car signified change: when it was parked outside a house, it meant that the family was expecting either the stork—or the reaper. Bedbug, wearing a shiny, greasy brown suit, red shirt buttoned up to the top without a tie, and his war medals (Stalingrad, Kursk, Berlin), joined Baba and Tatiana in the car. Katinka, the family mascot, the village heroine, sat in the front.

The villagers came out to wave good-bye as they drove down old Lenin Street, past the prefabricated concrete apartment building, with its 1970s orange and black panels. Katinka waved at the white-coated, peachy-cheeked women of the Milk and Meat shops; at the be-suited and permed typists of the Mayor's office; at the Mayor himself, who looked like a Latin crooner with his bouffant hairdo and white suit. Beso and the Ingushetians of the Vegetable Shop tossed a brown bag of Georgian tomatoes in through the car window, and Stenka the Cossack, the tattooed bouncer/bodybuilder from the nightclub-café Vegaz-Kalifornia, in his leather vest and bleached jeans, proffered a can of Mexican beer and a little Greek-made bottle of Why Not? perfume. Gaidar, father of the dark Azeris in their sheepskins who ran the kiosk, tossed a Twix into the car—and Katinka gave it to her father, who often suffered low blood sugar during the day and would wolf down chocolate bars . . . But where was Andrei?

There he was, smiling in his soft, devoted way, with those winsome eyes that seemed meant for departing trains and long good-byes. Wearing his dark blue jeans, he was waiting for her on the steps of the little stationhouse. Like her father, Andrei hadn't wanted her to go to London, and the night before he'd begged her to wait for the late spring when they could go on vacation and sun themselves in the Crimea. His alternating kisses and reasoning had almost persuaded her—until she stopped the charade with a playful "Not so fast, Andryushka. We'll see." He sulked; she consoled him, thinking how much she liked his green eyes—but where did he rank compared to London, Moscow, the doctorate she was starting to write, her vocation as a historian? She wanted to be a writer, a historian of Catherinian Russia; she imagined herself living in Moscow, publishing respected books and perhaps, one day, gaining a seat in the Academy . . .

Andrei wanted to carry her little bag to the train, and so did her father. In the end, after a slight tug of war, they compromised and each held one strap of the carpetbag. They all boarded the train and settled her into her compartment. Dr. Vinsky hugged Katinka and kissed her forehead, leaving with tears in his eyes. Andrei whispered, "I love you."

Katinka stood at the open window, blowing kisses to family and boyfriend. Then the oil-stained steel engine clanked, jolted and, with a shrill whistle, rumbled into the distance, heading north into the heart of Russia.

Trains leaving empty provincial stations can seem sad even at the happiest of times—and partings are never that. The family said nothing for a moment then Tatiana dabbed her eyes with a handkerchief, worrying about Katinka's job: what sort of research would she be doing? How would she survive? Why did she have to go? She put her arms around Andrei.

Baba, a living study of the compatibility of Communist dogma and peasant superstitions, crossed herself. Bedbug had left Beznadezhnaya only once—in June 1941, to join the Red Army—and returned only once, in May 1945, but he had left on a locomotive with a tail of white steam that bore him all the way from Moscow to Berlin . . . The best and most dread times of his life, he'd told his wife: friends lost, friends made, "For Stalin and the Motherland!" Stalin: now there was a man!

Dr. Vinsky remained standing alone on the platform as the others left. It was just 10:00 a.m. but already his office at the medical center on Suvorov Street, between the local Party secretary's office and the Milk Products Shop, would be full of pensioners with spring colds and shrinking savings.

He lit a cigarette and looked after the train. He was very proud of Katinka's courage: would he have done the same? He had grown up with his parents, Bedbug and Baba, right here in Beznadezhnaya—and at eighteen he had left on this train too, to study medicine in faraway Leningrad. Baba had bought him a new jacket, new boots and a red chintz suitcase: they were poor but so proud he had been accepted by Leningrad Medical School. The first of the Vinsky family, and surely the first in the village, to attend a university.

Dr. Vinsky asked himself (not for the first time) why he had returned to this godforsaken place in the borderlands of the Empire as a young doctor. He could have studied more; he had dreamed of becoming a gynecologist, a specialist, a professor, in Moscow. But he came home—home to the blue-shuttered cottage where he'd been born, and still lived—to be with his old peasant parents and run the local clinic. Perhaps he would not have succeeded in Leningrad, or perhaps he was a coward, he thought now. But this was home and he craved it.

Dr. Vinsky hated partings: he hated anyone to go away; his sons were married and lived far off, and now his only daughter had gone. He himself was nearly sixty, with a weak heart, and he knew he would never leave.

He flicked his cigarette onto the tracks. What was this "family research" of Katinka's? he asked himself yet again. In Russia, it was always better to leave the past alone. Here it had a way of poisoning the present. Without Academician Beliakov's insistence that Katinka would be safe, he would never have let her go to London.

Katinka, he decided, was a bright bird of paradise stuck in a dingy cage: he had to let her fly. Unlike his old father, Dr. Vinsky was no Communist, yet, in these times of turbulence—in which chaos, corruption and democracy reigned—he yearned for stability.

Perhaps this was why he felt uneasy about Katinka's journey. She was traveling into a world where he could not protect her.

3

The trip—the train ride to Moscow, the flight from Sheremetyevo Airport—was so dizzyingly exciting that Katinka recorded every moment in a diary she had bought especially. She described the people she met on the train, the check-in at the airport, the passengers who sat on either side of her on the flight (she had never flown before); her trip into London on the grimy Metro (or the Tube, as the English gracelessly called it), which was so dark and sordid compared with the vaulted marble cathedrals that were Moscow's underground stations; and then the walk, staggering with her bag, from Sloane Square Station. And there she was, staring with wide-eyed amazement at the discreetly luxurious hotel booked for her in Cadogan Gardens, Chelsea.

The receptionist, a waxy paper pusher with a weave-over hairstyle, did not seem too pleased to see her. When he realized she was Russian, he appeared suspicious, examining her passport as if it might contain some trace of KGB biological weaponry. When he looked up her reservation and found it was prepaid in cash, she could see him re-evaluate her, reducing her status from KGB agent to gangster's moll.

"What are you doing in London? Sightseeing or . . . ," he asked, without looking up from behind the desk.

"I'm a historian," she replied, in hesitant English, trying not to giggle at his confusion. She thought she saw him shake his head a little: prostitute, spy or . . . or historian, he couldn't work it out.

Upstairs in her room, she could only wonder at the canopied double bed and the marble bathroom containing two, yes two, basins, two, yes two, fluffy bathrobes and an Aladdin's cave of free shampoos, soaps and bubble baths (all of which she immediately hid in her bag to take home), and cable television. It was so different from her home in the north Caucasus or her room in the dormitory in Moscow where she had lived for three years.

The desk was equipped with embossed envelopes and writing paper (straight into the bag with them too!). There were goosefeather pillows, bedspreads, curtains, pelmets like a palace, and downstairs a sitting room, silent except for a ticking grandfather clock, with deep well-stuffed sofas and piles of glossy new magazines such as *Vogue* and something called the *Illustrated London News.* Oh, the very Englishness of it! What a mercy, she thought, that her English had been so good at school and that she remembered some of it. When she had looked around, the receptionist gave her a note in a typed envelope:

Pick-up tomorrow 9:00 a.m. Your driver is Artyom.

This struck her as so iconic that she stuck it in her diary for posterity. Before taking a stroll around Sloane Square and down the King's Road, she called her parents from the room to tell them she was safe. She got her father, who was always agonizingly shy on the phone.

"Katinka, trust no one out there," he warned her, between gaping silences.

"They're terrified of us here, Papa. In the hotel, they think I'm a gangster or a spy!"

"Promise me you'll take no risks, darling," he said.

"Oh, Papa. OK, I promise: no risks. I kiss you, Papa. Love to Mama and Baba and Bedbug!"

She laughed to herself—how could he understand? She adored her father but she could imagine him on the phone by the bookcase, smoking a cigarette late at night, in that faraway cottage in a village "lost in deafness"—while *she* was in London now. But when she got into her sumptuously soft bed with its incredible wealth of pillows, she closed her eyes and wondered what on earth she was doing there. A spiked barb of anxiety lodged deep inside her drumming heart.

4

Next morning, after an English breakfast of toast, marmalade and fried bacon and tomatoes (she ordered much of the menu), Katinka found a shaven-headed Russian man of military bearing standing in the lobby and staring at her with ill-concealed contempt. So this was Artyom, she thought, as he nodded toward the door and directed her to a large black Mercedes that smelled deliciously of new leather.

Artyom climbed stiffly into the seat right in front of her and she heard the locks click shut on all four doors. As he swung the car aggressively into traffic, pressing her against the passenger door, Katinka examined his hulking shoulders and muscle-knotted neck with foreboding. She felt small and helpless and wondered if her father, whom she'd so recently mocked for his caution, had been right after all.

What if her entire trip was a wicked trick arranged by some Russian master criminal? Was she about to be sold into white slavery? But why would a Thief-in-Power, as Russian gangster godfathers were known, bother to ask Academician Beliakov, author of the classic work *Law-making and State-building under Catherine II: The Legislative Commission*, to place an advertisement for him in the *Humanities Department Gazette*? Beliakov had been invited to put forward his top history graduate. And why would a gangster want a historian when surely the provincial villages and Muscovite streets were seething with booted, miniskirted girls eager to be sold into white slavery in London or New York?

"Where are we going?" she asked Artyom anxiously.

"The house," muttered Artyom, as if this answer was already causing him considerable weariness.

"Who am I meeting?"

"The boss." These two words fatigued him even more.

"Mr. Getman?" she asked.

Artyom did not answer.

"Is he very rich, Artyom?"

Artyom snorted with heavy-breathed superiority, and altered the air-conditioning on his gleaming dashboard as if he were piloting a supersonic MiG fighter.

"How did you come to work for Mr. Getman?"

"I served in the Spetsnats in Afghanistan," he replied.

Katinka was amused that every thug and nightclub bouncer in Russia claimed to have fought with the Special Forces in Afghanistan. If all of them had been telling the truth, Russia might have won the war.

"Is Mr. Getman one of the oligarchs?"

There was another long, sneering pause as the Mercedes swung from the inner circle of Regent's Park into a discreet driveway. High gates shivered, then opened slowly. Katinka heard the crunch of the Mercedes's wheels on thick gravel and gasped at the beauty and scale of the house, a perfectly proportioned Queen Anne mansion hidden in the woods of Regent's Park, right in the middle of London, one of those secret places that had been owned, she was told later, by several of the legendary millionaires of the past.

Artyom marched round to open Katinka's door. "This way, girl," he said, without looking at her. He turned and loped up the steps.

Katinka followed him nervously into a black-and-white-floored hall breathing fresh paint and polish, and where portraits of ruddy-cheeked English earls in bulging pantaloons and velvet frock coats glared down at her. A charging red-coated cavalryman, saber outstretched, caught her eye roguishly from a broad gold-framed canvas hanging on the sweeping staircase with the shiny oak banisters. But where was Artyom? Katinka looked round frantically, but the house seemed silent and forbidding. Then a door concealed in the opulent chinoiserie wallpaper swung on its hinges. She opened it and saw Artyom's broad back turn a corner. Relieved, she ran after him into a gloomy corridor lined with framed English cartoons. He opened a black door. Bright sunlight pouring through a line of windows blinded her momentarily. Raising a hand to her eyes, she blinked and tried to gather herself.

She was in the biggest kitchen she had ever seen. Black marble covered every surface. A chrome fridge extended from floor to high ceiling. The gadgets—the oven, the washing machine, the dishwasher—seemed as wide as cars with control panels that belonged in a Sputnik, not a kitchen.

Was this where she was supposed to be? Perhaps she should have waited in the hall? Katinka was about to turn back and retrace her steps when a slim grey-haired woman rose from a pine table with a generous, uninhibited smile. Katinka stopped as Artyom marched past her toward a high-backed scarlet chair—almost a papal throne, she thought—which was occupied by a large, crumpled man with curly dark hair who was watching a wall of television screens that showed different rooms and approaches to the house.

"Boss," said Artyom, halting before the papal throne. "Here's the girl. Where do you want her?"

This was all a horrible mistake, Katinka decided, longing to escape, to go home, worrying about how to get a lift to the airport. But the scruffy man, who wore a checked seersucker jacket, jumped to his feet and greeted her exuberantly, hands outstretched.

"You must be Ekaterina Vinsky? Welcome, come in! We've been longing to see you!" He spoke Russian in a thick Jewish, Odessan accent that she'd heard only in old movies. "Thank you for coming to see us." Us? Who was us?

The man glanced at the driver. "All right, Artyom, see you at eleven." Artyom looked disappointed and lumbered away, leaving the kitchen door swinging behind him, but his dismissal lifted Katinka's spirits.

"Now," said the scruffy man, "come and sit down. I'm Pasha Getman."

So this, thought Katinka, was what a real oligarch looked like, a billionaire who breezed through the corridors of the Kremlin itself—but he was already showing her to a chair.

"Come on, Mama," he called to the slim lady. "Bring the honey-cakes. Are they ready?" Then to Katinka, "What sort of tea do you like? What sort of milk? Let's get started!"

Pasha seemed incapable of sitting down or even keeping still. He was bursting with sparky energy. But before he could continue, a telephone gadget, which appeared unlinked to any wires, started to ring and he answered it in Russian, then switched to English. He seemed to be discussing oil prices. Then, covering the phone with his large soft paw, he said, "Katinka, meet my mother, Roza Getman," before giving orders into the phone again.

So these people were her new employers, Katinka thought. She looked more carefully at the woman approaching her with a silver tray. Steam curled out of a blue china teapot; cakes and apple strudel were arranged on plates; and teacups stood graciously on matching saucers. Placing the tray before her, Roza Getman started to pour the tea.

"Pasha's always in a hurry," she told Katinka, smiling at her son.

"No time to spare. Life's short and my enemies would like to make it shorter. Understand that, understand everything," explained Pasha, who seemed to be able to conduct several conversations simultaneously. Katinka didn't know what to make of these Odessans, who seemed so haughty, so sophisticated, so un-Russian (she knew from her grandfather's rantings that most oligarchs were Jews) that they made her feel gawky and provincial. But just as her spirits were sinking again, Roza handed her a plate.

"Try one of my honeycakes. You're so slim, we need to feed you up. Now tell me, dear, how was your flight and did you like the hotel?"

"Oh my God, it's beautiful," answered Katinka. "I've never flown before and the hotel's palatial. I couldn't believe the breakfast and the fluffy towels . . ." She stopped and blushed, feeling provincial again, but Roza leaned toward her and touched her hand.

"I'm so pleased," she said in the same Odessan accent as Pasha. She was dressed with understated elegance, thought Katinka, admiring the silk scarf around her neck. Her hair was greying but it must once have been blond and it was curled like that of a film star from the fifties. Her blouse was cream silk, her skirt pleated and tweedy, and she wore no jewelry except a wedding ring and a butterfly brooch on her cashmere cardigan. But none of this impressed Katinka as much as her once beautiful—no, still beautiful—face, her pale skin, and her warm eyes that were the most extraordinary shade of blue she'd ever seen.

Pasha finished his call but almost instantly the big phone on the table started to ring. He pressed a button on a flashing control panel and started talking in Russian about an art auction—"Mama, you start, don't wait for me," he said, covering the mouthpiece again—so that Katinka was able to concentrate all her curiosity on this somehow alluring older woman who seemed to have everything, she suddenly realized, except happiness. What am I doing here? she asked herself again, biting into a honeycake so sweet it made her shiver.

"I'm so glad you could come," Roza said. "We wanted a historical researcher so I consulted Academician Beliakov."

"Are you a specialist in the eighteenth century?" Katinka asked earnestly, pulling a notebook out of her rucksack.

"Of course not!" Pasha interrupted, banging down the telephone. "I started selling concert tickets in Odessa and things expanded from there, first metals, then cars, now oil and nickel, so no, I know nothing about the eighteenth century and nor does Mama."

Katinka felt crushed.

"Pasha, don't be so bombastic," said Roza. "Katinka, we need the best historian, and the professor recommended you. You've done research, haven't you? In the archives?"

"Yes, in the State Archive, on Catherine the Second's Legislative Commission and recently for my doctorate on the impact on local government of Catherine the Second's 1775 *prikaz* on . . ."

"That's perfect," said Roza, "because we want you to do genealogical research."

"We want you to discover the history of our family," added Pasha, hovering over them impatiently and lighting a monstrous cigar.

"In the eighteenth century? Your family origins?"

"No, dear," said Roza, "only in the twentieth century." A trickle of unease ran down Katinka's spine. "You'll be paid well. Does a thousand dollars a month plus expenses sound about right to you?"

Katinka sat up very straight. "No, no," she said. "It's not necessary." The money worried her, it was much too much, and this meant something was wrong. What would her father say? As for Bedbug, he regarded these oligarchs as the Antichrist. "I don't think I can do this job. I only know the eighteenth century."

Pasha looked at his mother, exhaling a noxious cloud of smoke. "Are you saying you don't want the job?"

"Pasha," said Roza, "take it easy on her. She's right to ask questions." She turned to Katinka. "This is your first job, isn't it?"

First job, first trip abroad, first oligarch, first palace, first everything, thought Katinka, nodding.

"Look," said Pasha, "you've worked on one set of archives so why not another? What's the difference? Catherine's archives, Stalin's archives."

Katinka stiffened. The Stalin era! Another alarm bell! It was not done to look into that period. "Never ask people what their grandfathers did," her father once told her. "Why? Because one grandfather was denouncing the other!" Yet now her esteemed patron, Academician Beliakov, had tossed her into this snakepit. She had come all this way and now she had to escape—but how? She took a deep breath.

"I can't do it. I don't know that period and I don't want to be involved in matters that concern the Party and the Security Organs," she said, her face hot. "I don't know Moscow well enough, and I can't accept this excessive salary. You've got the wrong person. I feel guilty because you've flown me all this way and I'll never forget the hotel and I promise I'll repay the cost of the—"

"That's it!" Pasha slammed down his cup and saucer, spilling tea across the table, muttered something about "Soviet-minded girls from the provinces" and clamped the cigar between his teeth.

Katinka was shocked by his outburst and was about to stand up to say good-bye when two lines and the mobile started to ring simultaneously in a screeching cacophony.

"Pasha, take these calls in your study," said Roza briskly, "or I'll throw all those phones out of the window. And that repulsive cigar!"

When he was gone, she took Katinka's hands in her own. "I'm so sorry. Now we can talk properly." She paused and looked searchingly at Katinka. "Please understand, this isn't about vanity or even curiosity. It's not about Pasha's money. It's about me."

"But Mr. Getman is right," said Katinka. "I can't do this. I don't know anything about the twentieth century."

"Listen to me a little and if you still don't want to help us, then I understand. I want you anyway to have a lovely time seeing London before we fly you home. But if you could help us . . ." A shadow clouded her deep blue eyes for a moment. "Katinka, I grew up with a hole in my heart, an empty place right here, like a frozen chamber, and all my life I've never been able to talk about it and I've never even let myself think about it. But I do know that I'm not alone. All over Russia there are people like me, men and women of my age who've never known who their parents were. We look like everyone else, we married, we had children, we grew old, but I could never be carefree. All the time I've been carrying this sense of loss inside me, and I still carry it. Perhaps that is why I brought up Pasha to be so confident and extroverted, because I didn't want him to go through life like me." She frowned and laughed softly at herself; it was, thought Katinka, the gentlest of sounds. "I never talked about this with my late husband or even Pasha, but recently Pasha wanted to buy me a present. I told him that all I wanted was my family and he said, 'Mama, the Communists have gone, the KGB's gone and I'll pay anything to help you.' That's why you're here."

"Are you . . . an orphan?" asked Katinka. She couldn't imagine how this might feel.

"I don't even know," answered Roza. "Where are my parents? Who were they? I don't know who I am. I've never known. Look on this task any way you like—as a challenge, a historical project, a vacation job to earn some money, or just an act of real kindness. But this is my last chance. Please, please say you'll help me find out what happened to my family?"

5

It was spring in a newly schizophrenic Moscow, a city in the midst of the craziest personality crisis of its history. Grim and neon lit, it had become an Asiatic and Americanized metropolis of BMWs and Ladas, Communists and oligarchs, apparatchiks and whores.

Creaking chandeliers of gutter-soiled ice still hung off the ornate pink eaves of the Granovsky Building as Katinka found the bell for staircase one, apartment 4. On this small private street, the cascades of ice dangled so treacherously over the pavement that the janitors had fenced off sections to protect the pedestrians. Meanwhile the cherry blossom was bursting into flower; rap music blared in the street; there were Mercedeses and Range Rovers parked outside the building.

Katinka walked slowly along its wall, reading the orange plaques recording the famous Communists who had once lived here: marshals and commissars, Stalin's henchmen, names from a vanished black time. Again she wanted to escape. She couldn't do this; she shouldn't be doing this—yet here she was.

Three days had passed, three days in which Katinka and Roza Getman had drunk tea, and walked round the rose gardens of Regent's Park, and talked about Roza's childhood, her adoptive parents and her hazy memories of another life. And Katinka had agreed. Against all her instincts and her father's advice, she was here in Moscow—for Roza.

Katinka approached the wooden door with the glass windows and rang the old-fashioned brass bell hard. She waited a long time and was about to give up when there came the sound of an aged throat being cleared.

"I'm listening!" said a hoarse voice.

Katinka smiled at the superior way that old *chinovniki*—bureaucrats—answered their phones, as in "Make your submission, slave!"

"This is Katinka Vinsky. The history student? I called and you told me to come."

A long pause. Rasping breaths, then the door clicked. Katinka pushed through the battered wooden doors into a foyer and up a dingy but once glorious staircase to another door with reinforced locks. She was about to knock when it swung open into a gleaming hall lined with boots and shoes.

"Hello?" she called out.

"Who are you?" asked a swarthy middle-aged woman with a long nose and shabby black clothes. She spoke well, Katinka noted, as if she had been to the best schools.

"I'm the historian who's come to see the marshal."

"He's waiting for you," said the woman, pointing down a shining parquet corridor and retreating into the kitchen.

"Leave your shoes!" said the voice of an old man. "Come and join me! Where are you?"

Katinka took off her shoes, slipped on some yellowed foam slippers and followed the voice through an archway. So this was how the bosses lived? She had never seen an apartment like it. The ceilings were high; a chandelier glistened; the wainscoting was bright Karelian pine, as was the art-deco thirties furniture. The L-shaped corridor led off to many rooms but she turned right into the living room. The brash spring glare beamed through the four windows, but then her vision cleared and she saw, across a piano thick with family photographs, the ten-foot-high painting of Lenin at the Finland Station on one wall and on the other an original Gerasimov portrait, of a handsome, sharp-faced marshal in full uniform, gold shoulder boards and a chestful of medals like a Christmas tree.

To her right, a table was heaped with Soviet and foreign magazines; a new-fangled mobile phone was charging on the windowsill, and a Sony CD player played Mozart's Sinfonia Concertante through small black speakers on little platforms high in the four corners of the room. Katinka was amazed. It was true what they said—the Soviet leaders really did live like princes.

In a deep leather chair with its back to the light sat a dignified specimen of ancient *Homo sovieticus.*

"Hello, girl, come in!" Katinka had expected the oily Soviet comb-over hairdo, the waxy pallor (the "Kremlin tan") and the paunch of a much older man, but *this* antique, sitting erect in a blue Soviet suit with only the star of the Order of the Red Banner, for courage in the Great Patriotic War, on his lapel, was lean and chiseled. His hair was steel hewn, spiky and thick, and his aquiline nose that of a Persian shah. She recognized a shrunken version of the marshal in the portrait.

The original stood up, bowed, showing her to an upright Karelian pine chair opposite his own, then sat again. "Sit, please. That's it. Now, girl . . ."

"Ekaterina," she said, taking the seat indicated.

"Katinka—if I may—what can I do for you?"

Katinka took out her notebook and a pencil, her hands shaking a little. "Hercules Alexandrovich . . ." She turned too many pages at once, dropped the pencil, picked it up, lost her place, all while intensely aware of his eyes—an astonishing cornflower blue—scanning her.

She had never met such an important man. The marshal had known every Soviet leader from Lenin to Andropov. The provincial modesty of the doctor's daughter from Beznadezhnaya, the life-preserving urge bred into every Soviet citizen to avoid officials, Muscovites and especially secret policemen, and the dangers of power itself—all of these dueled within her. She remembered the story that Roza Getman had told her in London and was just about to ask the marshal about it when he asked her a question.

"How old do you think I am?"

"I know how old you are," she replied, deciding to pretend to be more confident that she felt. "The same age as the century."

"*Pravilno!* Right!" The marshal laughed. "Not bad then for ninety-four, eh?" Katinka noticed that his Georgian accent was still strong despite many decades in Moscow. "Do you know I can still dance? Mariko!" The middle-aged woman appeared in the doorway with a tray of tea. "This is my daughter, Mariko; she looks after me." Katinka thought that the old marshal had much more life in him than his daughter. "Put on the *lezginka*, dear!"

Mariko put the tray on the table by the window and then changed the CD in the corner.

"Don't overdo it, Father," she said. "Your breathing is already bad. No smoking! And don't scald yourself, the tea is hot." She glanced at Katinka, then stomped out of the room.

As the wild strings and pipes of the *lezginka* rang out, Marshal Satinov stood up, bowed and then adopted the lithe pose, hands on hips, one foot sideways, the other on the tips of the toes, of the Caucasian dancer. Katinka acknowledged, as he presumably hoped she would, that he was still trim and elegant. He danced a few steps, then sat down again, smiling at her. "Now . . . Katinka . . . Vinsky . . . have I got your name right? You're a historian?"

"I'm writing a doctorate on Catherine the Second's legal program for Academician Beliakov."

"You're a beautiful scholar, eh? A flower of the provinces!" Katinka blushed, pleased that she had dressed up in her good skirt, an example of fine Soviet fashion with pyramidal spangles and a high slit. "Well, I'm a piece of Soviet history myself. I should be in a museum. Ask whatever you want while I catch my breath."

"I'm working on a specific project," she began. "Does the name Getman mean anything to you?"

The blue eyes focused on her again suddenly, expression neutral.

"The rich banker . . . how do they say nowadays? An oligarch."

"Yes, Pasha Getman. He's employed me to research his family."

"Family genealogy for the new rich? I'm sure the Princes Dolgoruky or Yusupov did the same thing in Tsarist times. Getman isn't an unusual name; Jewish naturally. From Odessa, I'd guess, but originally Austrian Galicia, Lvov probably, intelligentsia . . ."

"You're right. They're from Odessa, but do you know the Getman family personally?"

There was a sharp, wintery silence. "My memory's no longer what it was . . . but no, I don't think so," Satinov said at last.

Katinka made a note in her book. "Pasha Getman's mother inspired this project of family history."

"Using his money."

"Yes, of course."

"Well, with money, you might find out something. But the name means nothing to me. Who is she trying to find?"

"Herself," said Katinka, watching him carefully. "Her maiden name was Liberhart. Does that name ring any bells, Marshal?"

A shadow crossed Satinov's face. "I just can't place it . . . I've met so many people in my life, you understand, but the names . . ." He sighed and shifted in his chair. "Tell me some more."

Katinka took a deep breath. "Pasha Getman's mother is called Roza. All she knows about her origins is this: a professor of musicology at the Odessa Conservatoire and his wife, also a teacher, adopted her in the late thirties. Their name was Liberhart, Enoch and Perla Liberhart. They had been unable to have children of their own so they adopted this five-year-old child. She was fair-haired so they called her the Silberkind—the silver child."

"What about before?" asked Satinov.

"Roza remembers fragments of a life before the adoption," Katinka said, thinking of their recent conversations in the bracing air of a London spring. "The laughter of a beautiful woman in a cream suit and a blouse with a pretty white collar, handsome men in Stalinka tunics, games with other children, journeys and train stations, and then the adoption . . ."

"A common story in those days," interrupted Satinov. "Children were often lost and resettled. In the building of a new world, there were many mistakes and tragedies. But is it possible she's imagined this story? That happens a lot too, especially now that the newspapers are digging up all this misery again and printing such lies." The blue eyes teased her obliquely, cynically.

"Well, it's my job to believe her but, yes . . . I do believe her. The Liberharts discouraged her from probing into her past because they came to love her as their own. They didn't want to lose Roza—and they were afraid to attract attention. The adoption was arranged under the aegis of a very high official and everything in those days was secret."

"But after Stalin's death, surely . . ."

"Yes," said Katinka, "after Stalin's death, Roza insisted that the Liberharts make an official inquiry. They told Roza that both her parents died during the Great Patriotic War, which fits because her adoption was around that time."

Satinov opened his hands. "And she accepts this?"

"She accepted it for decades. She loved her adoptive parents. Enoch died in 1979 but Perla lived until recently. Before she died, Communism fell. Only then did Perla admit to Roza that she had lied to her. The Liberharts had not made an official inquiry because they never knew the name of her real parents."

"Tell me, Katinka, were these Liberharts . . . good people, kind parents?" Satinov asked, leaning toward her.

Katinka sensed the sudden swirl of deeper, more treacherous waters. She thought nostalgically of her studies: of Catherine the Great at the State Archive, of nobler, more golden times. But she was a historian and what historian wouldn't be fascinated to meet a relic like Satinov, a real breath of the recent past, a past that was itself shrouded in mystery?

"Roza says they were unworldly intellectuals unsuited to having children. Professor Liberhart couldn't boil an egg or drive a car, and Roza said he once went to work with his shoes on the wrong feet. Perla was an overweight bluestocking who couldn't cook, darn or make a bed and never even used makeup or had a hairdo (though she could have done with both!). She devoted her life to translating Shakespeare's sonnets into Russian. So Roza grew up like a mini-adult caring for eccentric parents. She remembers the terrible things that happened in that war. There was the siege of Odessa; the slaughter of the Odessan Jews by the Nazis and Romanians; the Holocaust. But through everything, Enoch and Perla loved her with the love of parents who have been blessed with a child they never expected."

Satinov stirred some plum jam into his tea and licked the spoon. Then, checking no one was at the door, he pulled out a pack of Lux cigarettes and lit one with a silver lighter, holding it over the top like a young man. "I'm not allowed to smoke, but the Devil, get thee behind . . ." He inhaled deeply, eyes closed. "So why have you come to see me?"

"When Roza needed an operation in her teens and her parents were worried about her health, they called someone in Moscow who arranged everything."

"Perhaps it was an uncle?"

"Once there was a big Party conference in Odessa. Roza thinks it was in the fifties. Many bosses came to town. One afternoon, she saw a black ZiL limousine outside her school with a man in uniform inside, a big boss. She had the feeling, no, more than a feeling, she was certain that he was waiting for her. All week, he was there watching her every morning. I don't know who that man was, Marshal Satinov." Katinka looked directly at Satinov, who shifted slightly in his chair. "Roza forgave the Liberharts for their lie but she begged her mother for a name. Before she died, Perla told Roza that the Muscovite they called was you. You helped her get this treatment. Maybe you were the man in the limousine?"

Satinov took another toke of his cigarette. Katinka could tell he was listening carefully. "Stories, just stories," he said.

Katinka felt a sharp surge of impatience. She leaned forward on her uncomfortable chair. "Roza and I want to know why you helped her, Marshal. She is convinced that you know who her parents were."

Satinov frowned and shook his head. "Do you realize, girl, how many so-called historians ring me up to ask impertinent questions? Because I'm old, they expect me to undermine the greatest achievements of the twentieth century—the creation of Socialism, the victory in the Great Patriotic War, my life's work." He stood up. "Thank you for visiting me, Katinka. Before you go, I want to present you with my autobiography."

He handed her a book with his picture on the cover in full uniform. It was entitled *In the Service of the Glorious October Revolution, the Great Patriotic War and Building a Socialist Motherland: Recollections, Notes and Speeches* by Marshal Hercules Satinov.

Sexy title, thought Katinka, I'll bet the speeches are a laugh a minute. She realized she was being dismissed and was certain that he was concealing something. "Will you sign it?" she asked a little breathlessly, determined to stand her ground.

"With pleasure."

She moved toward his chair. She could tell that he liked looking at her, so she leaned closer to him, shaking her hair back as she did so.

Patting her hand playfully, he signed: *To a beautiful scientist of truth. Hercules.* "It was published in many languages—Polish and Czech," he said proudly, handing her the book. "Even Mongolian."

"Thank you, Marshal. You're the first famous war hero I've met and I know you would help me if you could. Is it possible Roza's family did die during the war? Were they repressed in the Great Terror? If so, their records would be in the KGB archives. Now, families can apply for their case records, but without a name how can we apply for anything? Could you help us apply?"

He smiled at her, looking at her quite boldly. "I've always loved women," he said quietly, "even though I'm an old ruin."

"You must have danced quite a lot of them into your arms," Katinka said.

There was a silence.

"Well, I still have a few contacts left," Satinov said at last, "although most of my friends have gone to Lenin."

"Where?"

"To the Politburo in the sky. You're not a Communist, I suppose?"

"No, but my grandparents are true believers."

"I became a Marxist at sixteen and I've never wavered."

He wasn't going to tell her anything, Katinka realized, feeling depressed suddenly. In her meeting with the only link to the Getmans' past, she had already let Roza down. Her face must have dropped because Satinov took her right hand between his own and pressed it. "Katinka, the past in our country is a dark cell. You may never find the old people but concentrate on the young. Trace the young! They deserve your attention. You understand Catherine's court but you know nothing about me or my work. You must immerse yourself in the age of building Socialism if you wish to find anything. Speak to those researchers who are digging in the archives. Search more deeply, trace the links of the chain. It was an underwater world, but not everything was submerged. There were friendships even then, in the hardest times, and if you find a name, the thread to the past, then come back and talk to me."

Katinka sensed that he did not really want her to give up, so she plucked up her courage for one final push. "Marshal, may I ask you one embarrassing question that might save me a lot of work—and then I could go back to Catherine the Second."

"You'll have to work harder to make progress in your project," Satinov said briskly, showing her toward the door, "or you'll find nothing at all. What was the question?"

Katinka's heart was thudding so loudly in her ears that she realized she was almost shouting.

"Are you Roza's real father?"

6

Katinka enjoyed the hushed mysteries that reign in all libraries. Some of her friends thought they were boring, with their musty smell and their rigid silence broken only by the occasional cough, the illicit whispers, and the turning of pages. But to her, libraries were like hotels: secret villages inhabited by passing strangers from a thousand different worlds brought together just for a few hours.

As she did not know where to start with her research, she began where everyone begins—in the reading room of the Lenin Library on Vozdvizhenka. She had worked there before and she already had a library card, but this time she noticed that the building's Stalinist

Gothic facade was covered in the bronze silhouettes of Soviet heroes—writers and scientists. As she walked through the stacks of bookshelves, steering around the messy tables with their crews of stretching, yawning students and obsessional, grey-skinned old men, eyes flicked up to watch her surreptitiously. She felt the excitement of discovery again and remembered Roza's extraordinary eyes, how she had begged Katinka for help. Katinka was on a quest, though she had no idea where she was headed.

She sat at an empty table beneath the high windows and tried to think. Where to start? Usually she only noticed the students in the library but now she stared at the old people, in their brown suits and ties, burrowing, scratching out notes in spidery handwriting on yellowed pads: why were they so hungry for information when their lives were so nearly over? Did any of them have a clue for her? If she had access to all their soon-to-vanish memories of Bolshevik secrets, one of them, surely, would be able to solve her quest. What did they know? What had they seen? As she watched an old man licking his finger as he wrinkled up his eyes and turned the pages, a sentence of Satinov's came back to her: "It was an underwater world but not everything was submerged." Everything was secret at that time—except what? Except the newspapers, of course.

She walked, then almost ran to the front desk, where the librarian directed her to the large green books of bound newspapers from the thirties. She knew Satinov had started his rise in 1939 when he joined the Central Committee. Somewhere in those old newspapers, somewhere, she told herself, there might be a clue that linked him to Roza's family. Those yellowed newspapers were another world, written in an unnatural Bolshevik language that made her smile at its absurdities, at its news of Five Year Plans, of the achievements of collective farms and motor tractor stations and iron smelters in Magnitogorsk; of heroic pilots, proletarian comrades and Stakhanovite miners. As the light outside changed from bright blue to powdery dusk, she sat there, reading *Izvestia* and *Pravda*, beginning to understand that Satinov and Roza came from a different planet, recent in time but as foreign to her life as Mars or Jupiter. Twice she found mentions of "Comrade Satinov" giving a speech on Abkhazian tea production, brought back to Moscow by Comrade Stalin, promoted in the Party apparat—but there was not a hint of personal life, of friendships or connections.

Several times she walked around the colossal library just to stay awake and get her blood running; several times she was tempted to stop and read the Western magazines or the satirical *Ogonyuk*, yet each time she returned to her newspapers and their stories of the past.

She was about to give up when she turned to page five of *Pravda* in March 1939 and found a photograph of the young Satinov, in Stalinka tunic and boots, hair brushed back *en brosse*, beside a burly barrel-chested man in NKVD uniform. An article about the first Central Committee Plenum after the Eighteenth Congress had been placed beneath the photograph.

> *Comrade Stalin praised the new generation of cadres promoted to candidate members of the Central Committee, reflecting how "some comrades had come of age in the school of the Party itself, fresh steel tempered by the Revolution . . ." Afterward, in informal comments to delegates, Comrade Stalin reminisced with paternal fondness that he had first encountered Comrades H. A. Satinov and I. N. Palitsyn together as young Party workers, in Petrograd in 1917. "They were young, they were comrades-in-arms, they were devoted Bolsheviks. The Party has given them many hard tasks," said Comrade Stalin, "but now again these brothers-in-arms are reunited at the top of the great worker state . . ."*

She read it carefully twice, noted down its details and the new name: I. N. Palitsyn. She looked round the reading room: it was emptier than it had been. Half the table lights were off. The youngsters were all gone, only the old still there, those old men with so little time, like Roza with her terrifying sense of loss. Was this the name she was looking for? "There were friendships even then . . ."

Katinka slammed the book shut with a muffled boom that made one of the older readers jump and twitch as if he were waking from a long sleep. It was time to go. She had an appointment.

7

The motorcyclist in the leather trousers, pale brown bomber jacket and horned, Viking-style helmet skidded to a halt outside the Black Dog nightclub. It was on the Moskva Embankment a few hundred yards from the British Embassy and just across from the Kremlin. An occasional chunk of ice still floated down the Moskva River and the dark earth was edged with snow like a frill of lace, but the air held the spring tang of moist earth. It was already dusk, but the night was warm and grainy.

Katinka could hear a heavy-metal band playing the Scorpions' song "Winds of Change" inside the nightclub. She wondered if she had come to the wrong place: she was no Muscovite and she barely knew the city center. It seemed a strange spot for a meeting of historians.

Then the biker dismounted and walked toward her, pulling off his horned helmet and extending a leather paw. "Katinka? Is it you? I'm Maxy Shubin."

"Oh, hi . . ." Katinka felt the flush rise up her face—much to her embarrassment—because he was so much younger than she had expected. Maxy's dark hair was a long, tousled mane, his caramel eyes were wide, and his light beard looked as if it had been grown over a weekend, by accident rather than design. When she saw he wore tight leather trousers punctuated with silver zippers, she tried not to smile. "You don't look like a researcher," she told him.

Maxy smiled. "And you don't look like an academic. Would you like a drink?"

The doorman, a punk rocker with too many piercings in his lips and nose, waved them into the club. Upstairs there was a sitting area with smoke hanging in the air, used glasses, plastic cups and decaying sandwiches on every surface. The band playing downstairs made the floor shake but at least they could talk.

Maxy found a seat on a sofa, hailed a waif-like waitress in vinyl boots, stockings and leather shorts, and ordered them two cold Ochakov beers. "You're new in Moscow, aren't you?"

"I studied here and I do research here but—"

"Let me guess from your accent: you're from the north Caucasus somewhere? Mineralnye Vody or Vladikavkaz?"

"Not bad," said Katinka, her confidence returning as she sipped the icy beer, unaware that she had left the foam on her nose and that her clothes made it obvious she was from somewhere far away. "You're a Muscovite?"

"Originally from Piter."

"The window on Europe. How romantic!"

"Do you really think so?" said Maxy. "I'm someone who still believes that. Actually it's a backwater, an elegant poetical backwater, a city of empty palaces. But it has a tradition of freedom so perhaps it played some part in my working at the Redemption Foundation." He pulled off his leather jacket. "How did you find me? And what's this project of yours?"

"I read your article on the NKVD during the Terror in *Voprosy Istorii* and of course I'd heard of Redemption's research into the victims of the Terror—so I just rang you. It was good of you to meet me so quickly."

Maxy looked somewhat sheepish—and it occurred to Katinka that he had agreed to meet her only because she was a girl—but she dismissed such base motives in this genial crusader for truth. "I'm studying Catherine the Great for my doctorate . . ."

Maxy leaned toward her, brown eyes on hers. "So why are you leaving the graceful, noble, romantic court of the Empress for the sordid psychopathic killers of Stalin?" he asked.

"I don't know," she admitted. "I didn't want this job. And I refused it at first."

"But you took it anyway?"

"Have you ever met someone who's so beautiful and intriguing that you can't resist her?"

Maxy put his head on one side and looked at her suggestively. "Only very occasionally," he said.

"I mean in your research," she said coldly, sitting back.

Maxy's face fell. "Yes, in my work I often meet people who've been so damaged by the crimes of the past that I want to do all I can to put them back together again—that's my vocation." He looked young and earnest now, and she liked him better.

"Well, I met someone just like that. Her name's Roza Getman and she's so wounded by the past that I had to help her . . ." Maxy listened carefully as Katinka recounted her trip to London, the oligarch and his palace, the walks in Regent's Park—and how she had phoned Roza's one link to the past, a powerful old Communist, and had been to see him on a quest that she had made her own . . .

"It sounds like a million stories, a thousand cases I'm working on right now," said Maxy at last. "I can't help you in detail—I'm so overstretched—but I can give you some rough guidelines. Look, call me again next week and I'll put you in touch with a coworker who might be more use." He took a sip of beer and Katinka realized he was ending the conversation. She had slapped down his flirtation and, because her case was like so many others, there was no real reason for him to help her. The sooner she got back to the eighteenth century, the better. "By the way, who was the old Communist?" he asked as he got up.

"Oh, he was called Satinov," Katinka said, wondering how she was going to tell Roza that no one would help them.

Maxy sat down again abruptly. "Hercules Satinov?"

"Yes."

"He saw you?"

She nodded.

Maxy lit a cigarette, offered her one and lit it for her. "He never sees anyone, Katinka," he said, talking fast, his face animated. "I've tried to meet Satinov for fifteen years and not one of my colleagues at the foundation, no liberal historian, has ever gotten to see him. All the other old dinosaurs are dead and Satinov's the very last of them, the keeper of the secrets, the great survivor of the twentieth century. He knows where the elephants lie buried. If he's seen you, it's because he's interested in you. It means he can help you."

Katinka looked at him witheringly.

Maxy spread his hands. "If you share the results of your research with me, I'll help you all I can. Don't look at me like that, Katinka—believe me, you're really going to need me to find your way through this vanished world. You'd find it easier charting the hieroglyphics of ancient Egypt than the labyrinth of Stalin's Kremlin. What do you say? Do we have a deal?"

Katinka thought of Roza again, and sighed. "Yes," she said, "but remember, I'm a serious historian—not some girl to be chatted up."

He laughed and called for two more bottles of Ochakov beer. They raised them.

"To our unlikely partnership." They drank and clinked their bottles. "Now," Maxy said, "tell me about your meeting with Comrade Satinov. I want everything. No detail is too small. Everything matters, even what socks he was wearing."

Maxy questioned her carefully, listened earnestly and raised further queries. Even though they were in a smoky, somewhat squalid bar, such was the intensity of their conversation that they might have been sitting in the hushed sanctuary of the archives themselves.

"Without a doubt, he knows something about the family you're looking for. And it's something important," said Maxy.

"I can't understand why he doesn't just tell me," she said. "Then I could go back to my studies."

"No, that's not the style of these people," explained Maxy. "You shouldn't think of these Bolsheviks as modern politicians. They were religious fanatics. Their Marxism was fanatical; their fervor was semi-Islamic; and they saw themselves as members of a secret military-religious order like the medieval Crusaders or the Knights Templar. They were ruthless, amoral and paranoid. They believed that millions would have to die to create their perfect world. Family, love and friendship were nothing compared to the holy grail. People died of gossip at Stalin's court. For a man like Satinov, secrecy was everything."

"But Stalin died forty years ago and Communism's been gone for three years," Katinka objected. "What's stopping Satinov telling us his secrets now?"

"You have to understand that silence and secrecy were deeply ingrained in people like Satinov. When Stalin was alive, his apparatchiks were silent partly because they believed in what they were doing, partly because they were born conspirators—conspiracy was their natural habitat—and partly out of fear. And it was the sort of fear that doesn't pass: it lives in the bones forever. After Stalin died, they were silent because they wished to protect the Idea, the Soviet Union, the holy grail. For someone like Satinov, secrecy wasn't just a habit, it was the essence of the revolutionary code."

They were both silent as they thought about this.

"So did you find anything to take back to him?" Maxy asked at last.

Katinka shrugged and blew out the smoke of her cigarette. "I hoped you might have some idea. I waded through years of newspapers and I found no personal link—except this." She handed him a photocopy of the article and picture she had found in the Lenin Library. "I don't think it'll help us much . . ."

Maxy took it and studied it carefully, and whistled. "Vanya Palitsyn. I know exactly who he was. A veteran secret policeman of the old school who vanished soon after this photograph was taken. He was important in the thirties but he appears in no memoirs, no histories. His arrest was never announced and we don't know what happened to him."

"But how does this help us?"

"Well, I never knew that Satinov and Palitsyn were friends—and they had to be very close friends, well known for their friendship, for Stalin to refer to such a thing in his 'informal comments.' It may be a dead end, but you've found a possible link to Satinov's past. Isn't this what he told you to do?"

The thrill of historical revelation, of past humanity refound and resuscitated, inflamed Katinka. The reverberating music, the chattering of the other denizens of the club, everything else seemed distant and irrelevant. All she could think about was Roza, and Roza's elusive family. "But will this be enough to make him talk to me?" she asked.

"I think you should do some more research first, just to make sure," said Maxy slowly. "You have the name Palitsyn. Apply for his file in the KGB archives—I'll file the applications for you—and find out what happened to him, if he had a family, children. That's the easy bit. Then you can go back to Satinov. You've worked in archives?"

"I love archives," she said, hugging herself.

"Why?"

"You can smell the life in the paper. I've sat in the State Archives and held the love letters of Catherine and Potemkin, the most passionate notes, fragrant with her scent and soaked in his tears as he lay dying on the steppes."

Maxy nodded. "Well, these are different archives. Where there is such suffering, there's a kind of holiness. The Nazis knew they were doing wrong, so they hid everything; the Bolsheviks were convinced they were doing right, so they kept everything. Like it or not, you're a Russian historian, a searcher for lost souls, and in Russia the truth is always written not in ink, like in other places, but in innocent blood. These archives are as sacred as Golgotha. In the dry rustle of the files you can hear the crying of children, the shunting of trains, the echo of footsteps down to the cellars, the single shot of the Nagant pistol delivering the seven grams. The very paper smells of blood."

8

Two days later, Katinka came out of the decaying Stalinist hulk of the Moskva Hotel, where she was staying, and climbed the hill past the Kremlin, the Bolshoi and the Metropole Hotel, up to Lubianka Square. The crowds of office workers poured out of the Metro past the kiosks with their collage of lurid magazines; traffic raced around the middle of the square where the empty plinth of Dzerzhinsky's statue marked the fall of Communism. There before her was the KGB headquarters, an invincible stronghold of red and grey granite, containing offices, archives, tunnels and dungeons. Once the offices of the Russia Insurance Company, this had been the home of the fearless, merciless and incorruptible knights of the Communist Party since 1917. They'd operated under many names—the Cheka, OGPU, NKVD, KGB—and now there were other dread letters, but their power was gone: Katinka was sure the KGB would never dominate Russia again.

She had not wanted to come here. No Russian ever wanted to visit the Lubianka—it was the national charnel house. But she had only to recall her phone call to Roza to walk faster toward this brutal slab that still radiated power, the power to crush human happiness. Over the telephone line from London, Roza hadn't commented on what Katinka had found but she'd urged her on . . . Yet if Katinka's father had known that her research would bring her here to the Lubianka, he would never have let her take the job.

"Leave well enough alone! Don't snoop around cemeteries. It's too dangerous," he would have said. "You know how much I love you? More than anyone else in the entire existence of mankind since the beginning of time! That's how much!" It was wonderful to have a father—and mother—who so loved you. Katinka thought, again, of Roza, and what it must be like not to know who your parents were.

She elbowed open the double wooden doors of the Lubianka and entered a vaulted marble foyer. Two corporals in blue examined her passport, called upstairs and sent her up a flight of marble steps so wide that a tank could have driven up it. A bust of Andropov, the bespectacled KGB boss and Soviet leader, stood halfway up.

She found herself in a long corridor with a red carpet, old banners and portraits of past Chekists. Maxy had told her that within this fortress stood the yellow Internal Prison where the parents of her employer might have perished, although they might also have received the seven grams at the Butyrki or the Lefortovo prisons or Beria's special torture center, the Sukhanovka, a beautiful former monastery on the outskirts of Moscow. Maxy had explained that now was a good time to apply to see files. He had called her the previous evening. "The Lubianka phoned me. Your file's ready."

"But are you sure I should be looking at Palitsyn? Marshal Satinov advised me to forget about the adults and start with the children."

Maxy laughed. "Remember what I told you about Satinov and these veteran Bolsheviks? Lies were their duty to the Revolution. That just confirms you must start with the adults and then we'll think about the children."

"I'm beginning to get the hang of this," she said.

"Wait until you see the archives. Remember, Katinka, no one ever found a jewel in full view."

She followed her instructions, turned right and then left, and saw the door that read *Colonel Lentin, Director, Department of Registration and Archives.* She knocked, a voice replied and she entered a boxy office with the flounced white blinds pulled down. The air was densely fuggy, the glass fogged up, the sofa rumpled, so she knew that the colonel had been sleeping in his office. But where was he?

"Good morning," said the voice and she turned round. A fleshy silky-haired man in civilian clothes was just buttoning up his shirt and tightening his tie in a mirror behind the door. "Excuse me! I'm just beautifying myself for visitors. Have a seat!"

She sat at the T-shaped conference table and placed her notebook in front of her. Her instinct in this place was to obey every command but at that moment her curiosity was more powerful than her fear. What had happened to Satinov's friend Palitsyn all those years ago, maybe in this very building? She realized that she was beginning to catch Maxy's enthusiasm, the thrill of the chase.

"Now." Colonel Lentin sat behind his desk and, wetting a finger with an orange tongue, opened a file on the desk. He spoke beautiful, educated Russian. "You're a historian studying eighteenth-century law under Academician Beliakov and then, fa-la-la, you suddenly apply to see files from the time of the Cult of Personality." Fa-la-la? Colonel Lentin must be a fan of those crass Mexican soap operas that now pollute Russian television, thought Katinka. His skin looked as if it had never known a razor; he had oily eyelashes that were encrusted with flakes of sleep. But the small face, prominent jaw and flat nose reminded her of an animal. Yes, Lentin was a preeningly officious marmoset. "I didn't know Catherine the Great reformed the laws of the nineteen thirties—or have I missed something?"

"I have never been interested in the Cult of Personality. I'm just doing this as a little project of family research," Katinka said casually. "To make a bit of money to pay for my Catherine studies."

"I see," said the Marmoset. "Well, your friend Max Shubin and his sort are doing some research too, but it seems to me that you should keep your little project separate from theirs. We have no problem with yours but those liberals are American flunkies who rejoice in Russia's humiliation today. They are hammering away at the foundations of the State, hoping, fa-la-la, that *we* will just disappear. But without us, Miss Katinka, Russia would be lost to corrupt speculators and American hegemony—lost, quite lost. And we Chekists take our vows seriously. We'll always be here."

Katinka sighed. This KGB claptrap was out of date in the new Russia she and Maxy lived in. "I understand what you're saying, Colonel," she said. Just then, the door opened and an old man in a white coat entered with a metal cart piled high with speckled brown paper files, corners hooked with rubber bands, each with different file numbers and stickers on the front.

"Here we are, Colonel." The old man spat thickly into a brass spittoon that rested on his cart. Beside the spittoon a fat ginger cat was sleeping deeply. "More gold in dust!"

"Good morning to you, Comrade . . . Mr. Archivist," said Katinka, standing up and bowing slightly. She recognized a real archive rat, a Quasimodo of the secret stacks. Every archive had such a man, a true descendant of the troglodytic species that thrived in the twilight tunnels and storerooms deep under the pavements of Moscow. But they had power too, and Katinka knew that historians had to give them respect and win their favor.

"Two files from the archives, Comrade Col-o-nel! Good day!" He handed them to the Marmoset, then wheeled his cart toward the door. A very skinny kitten peeped out from under the cat.

"May I ask your name, Comrade Archivist?" Katinka asked quickly.

"Kuzma," said the specter. He spat again, and Katinka saw that the spittoon was engraved with the KGB crest. Was it a gift for long service?

"I so appreciate your help, Comrade Kuzma," said Katinka. "You must know so much that you could write the histories yourself. What's her name?" She gestured toward the cat.

"Utesov," Kuzma told her.

"You're a fan of Odessan jazz?"

Kuzma nodded.

"So what's the name of the kitten? Tseferman?"

Kuzma did not look her in the eye or smile but just stood there for a moment stroking the cats, humming in a satisfied manner like a father whose children have been complimented. Katinka had guessed right.

"Little Tseferman, eh? My father loves that music so I was brought up with it. Maybe I'll bring Utesov and Tseferman some milk when I next visit?"

Kuzma responded with a specially dense gobbet of spit that did two somersaults before landing in the brimming spittoon. Katinka managed to look as though she appreciated this graceful demonstration.

"Thank you, Comrade Kuzma—and good-bye, Utesov and Tseferman."

The archivist shut the door.

"Here are your files. Some dust for you to breathe," said the Marmoset. "Let's see," and he read out:

> *Investigation File May/June 1939*
> *Case 16373 Main Administration of State Security*
> *Ivan Nikolaievich Palitsyn . . .*

He lifted up the file and dropped it on the table in front of her, making her jump: dust flew out of it, tiny particles and silvery satellites vibrating and shimmering in the light.

Katinka hesitated, letting her eyes run over its brown, speckled cover, its KGB-crested stamp, its array of printed and handwritten scrawls listing the number of its *fond*, *opis* and *papka*—the location code of the archives.

"Can I take notes?"

"Yes, but we reserve the right to check them. In 1991, we let too many files be copied by alien influences. Procedures got sloppy. What do you hope to find out?"

"Whether this Palitsyn is connected to my clients . . ."

"You might find out some answers but it's not your right to know everything, even now."

"Did he have a wife and children, do you know?"

The Marmoset nodded and placed another slim *papka* file on top of the other. "Palitsyn's wife has her own file, right here. Do you want to see it?"

Katinka picked it up and read:

> *Investigation File May/June 1939*
> *Case 16374*
> *Alexandra Samuilovna Zeitlin-Palitsyn, Prisoner 778*

"Samuilovna Zeitlin. Not a Russian name. There were a lot of *them* in the Party in those days and many turned out to be traitors," said the Marmoset, leaning over her shoulder. He opened the file. There was a photograph clipped to the few papers inside.

"There, that's the photograph they take on the day of arrest."

Katinka looked at it, her heart beating. It showed a woman with a full mouth slightly open and ash-grey eyes that burned into the lens.

"She's beautiful, whoever she was." Katinka was fascinated suddenly, and a little touched.

"Yes, she was quite well known once, that Delilah. Then, fa-la-la, she vanished!"

"May I examine the file now?" Katinka could not wait to free herself of the Marmoset's gaze.

"You have thirty minutes." He pushed the file over to her then returned to his seat and sat watching.

"For this one file?"

"For both. These are the rules."

"Do feel free to do your other work, Colonel," Katinka said self-consciously.

"Watching you," he replied, "is my work."

9

Katinka placed the photograph above the file, which she pulled closer, and looked into the woman's face: the eyes reflected the flashbulb of an old-fashioned camera but, far from a vacant self-pity, the gaze radiated warmth and a mocking jauntiness, even as Katinka traced in the set of the muscles a straining to show, at the brink of the abyss, the best face she could.

"Hello," whispered Katinka, imagining that the photograph might answer, that those beseeching eyes might blink. "Who are you?" Stapled to the inside cover of the file was a scuffed, stained scrap of paper to be signed by everyone who had looked at the file—but it was blank. No one outside the KGB had ever examined it. She grabbed at the first sheet of paper, a short biography:

Born 1900 in St. Petersburg, Alexandra Samuilovna Zeitlin-Palitsyn, known as Sashenka, Comrade Snowfox. Nationality: Jewish. Party member since 1916. Last place of work: editor, Soviet Wife and Proletarian Housekeeping *magazine, State Publishing House. Educated at Smolny Institute . . .*

"Sash-en-ka . . . ," Katinka said to herself. "Will you help Roza and me?"

Family: father, Baron Samuil Zeitlin, capitalist banker, later non-Party specialist at People's Commissariats of Finance, then Foreign Trade, then State Bank, dismissed 1928, exiled 1929, arrested 1937, sentenced to ten years Kolyma. Mother: Ariadna Zeitlin, nee Barmakid, dead 1917.
Mother's brother: Mendel Barmakid, Jewish, Party member since 1904, member Central Committee 1911–1939, arrested 1939.
Father's brother: Gideon Zeitlin, writer. Not a Party member. Jewish.
Husband: Ivan Palitsyn, born St. Petersburg 1895. Russian, Party member since 1911, married 1922, arrested 1939, last place of work: Assistant Deputy People's Commissar, NKVD.
Children: Volya and Karlmarx.

"Pleased to meet you all," said Katinka under her breath. Sashenka and her husband would be very old now but they could still be alive—there was nothing in the file to say they weren't. And their children wouldn't even be old. She didn't know if this woman was relevant to her search, yet her pulse quickened. "I wonder what happened to you."

"You're talking to yourself," said the Marmoset. "Silence, please."

"Sorry." Katinka turned over the page to find a form, filled in on May 16, 1939, giving Sashenka's description. *Color of eyes: grey. Hair:*

dark brown with chestnut streaks. And there were her smudged fingerprints. Then a creased and stained piece of paper, headed *Main Administration of State Security, Very Important Cases Department.* In the middle, typed in a large, curvaceous, open typeface that looked bold and honest as if it had nothing to hide, was the following command: *Zeitlin-Palitsyn, along with her husband Palitsyn, has been unmasked as a long-serving Okhrana and White Guardist spy, Trotskyite saboteur, and agent of Japan. It is essential to arrest her and carry out a search.*

This was surrounded by stamps, squiggles and signatures. The first name was *Captain Melsky, Head of Ninth Section of Fourth Department, Main Administration of State Security.* But a thick felt pen had been put through his name and underneath, in what appeared to be a child's handwriting and spelling, someone had written: *I will carry out this oberation myself. B. Kobylov, Commissar-General, State Security, second degree.* Then later: *Oberation compleded. Prisoner Alexandra Zeitlin-Palitsyn delivered to Internal Prison. B. Kobylov, Commissar-General, State Security, second degree.*

The Marmoset was still sitting there leering, but Katinka did not care. She was gripped. So Sashenka and her husband had fallen in 1939. Why? When she turned the page, she found the testimony of a man named Peter Sagan, ex-Captain of the Gendarmes, Okhrana officer and later (under a false name) a schoolteacher in Irkutsk. Sagan revealed that Sashenka and Vanya had been in Petersburg in 1917—just like Satinov. But soon the outpouring of crazed accusations against the Palitsyns became too much to absorb. It seemed a ghost had emerged out of the mists of time bearing a plague of lies and accusations. But then she looked at the date of the Sagan confession: it was July 5—*after* Sashenka's arrest. Sagan had not arrived in Lubianka until July 1. So Sashenka had been arrested for something else. But what?

Katinka leafed hungrily through the badly typed fifteen-page confession signed at each corner with Sagan's frail, anemic markings—how strange, she thought, that these characters' lives were reduced to strokes of the pen. She tried to imagine the personality behind the fading lines of ink, and trembled.

Next she found a single piece of paper with a paragraph headed *Extract from confession of Beniamin Lazarovich "Benya" Golden: attach to file of Alexandra Zeitlin-Palitsyn.* The writer Benya Golden. She'd heard of him and his one masterpiece, those stories of the Spanish Civil War. She read on:

> *B. Golden: Using the depraved seductive techniques of the Mata Hari type of spy, Sashenka—accused Alexandra Zeitlin-Palitsyn—first seduced me sexually under guise of inviting me to write for her magazine and persuaded me to meet her for corrupt sexual practices in room 403 at the Metropole Hotel, set aside by the Writers' Union/Litfond for the use of non-Moscow writers for* Soviet Wife and Proletarian Housekeeping *magazine, which she edited. While wearing the mask of a new Soviet woman, Zeitlin-Palitsyn admitted to me she was an Okhrana agent and Trotskyite and asked me to introduce her to the French secret service, who had recruited me in Paris in 1935 when I was traveling to the International Writers' Congress with the Soviet delegation. She had already recruited her uncle Mendel Barmakid, a member of the Central Committee, and I recruited her other relative, my friend the famous writer Gideon Zeitlin, to help plan the assassination of Comrades Stalin, Molotov, Kaganovich and Marshal Voroshilov at a party at Sashenka's house by spraying the gramophone that Comrade Stalin would use with poison. The first attempt at her house—when Comrade Stalin visited on May Day 1939—failed because I failed to spray the gramophone . . .*
>
> *Witnessed: Investigator Rodos, Very Important Cases Department, Main Administration of State Security*

Katinka recoiled. So Benya Golden, that talented, elegiac writer, had rolled over and incriminated Sashenka. It must have been Golden's denunciation that got her arrested. How could he have done so? The accusations against Sashenka seemed preposterous.

Yet this was dated August 6, even later than the Peter Sagan confession. Katinka hurriedly turned more pages. She had been reading for more than fifteen minutes. After a rather picturesque collage of stamps, triangular, square and round, she read a note dated six months later:

Office of Military Procurator, 19 January 1940
The case against the Zeitlin-Palitsyn-Barmakid terrorist spy group is now complete and must be handed over to the court . . .
Send the case to the Military Tribunal, 21 January 1940.

Katinka felt a nervous twinge as if she, or someone close to her, was going to be tried on January 21, 1940. Sashenka's eyes looked out anxiously from the photograph. Maxy was right: there was an intimacy in these mysterious old papers, and an unbearable sense of tragedy. What happened to these people at the trial? Did Sashenka live or die? Katinka eagerly turned the page. There was nothing more.

"Five minutes!" said the Marmoset, drumming his fingers on the desk. Katinka noticed he was reading a magazine on soccer, *Manchester United Fanzine.* She noted down the basic facts in her notebook and the new names: Benya Golden—famed writer. Mendel Barmakid—forgotten apparatchik. Gideon Zeitlin—literary figure.

Katinka quickly reached for the Palitsyn file. First the photograph: Ivan Palitsyn, Sashenka's husband and Satinov's friend, side and front views, a burly, athletic man, with thick greying hair, a Tatar slant to the cheekbones. A handsome specimen of that shaggy Russian proletarian type, he had been a real worker at the Putilov Works. But in the picture, he had a black eye and bleeding lip. He must have put up a fight, decided Katinka. He wore a torn NKVD tunic. She looked into his eyes and saw . . . weariness, disdain, anger, not the fear and the appealing sarcasm in his wife's eyes.

"Four minutes," said the Marmoset.

She read his biography. Vanya was a top Chekist who had guarded Lenin himself in the early years in Petrograd and Moscow, 1917–19. Rising over the bodies of his bosses during the Terror, he must have been responsible for his share of crimes until . . . She found an arrest order, shortly before that of his wife. That must be why he looked more weary and angry than afraid: yes, he understood what was to come but he was bored by the procedures that he knew so well. What happened to him? She read and reread the file, noting the dates, trying to understand the sequence. Everything was there but nothing was what it said it was: it was in Soviet gibberish, the code of Bolshevism. She leafed ahead: Palitsyn had started to confess on June 7 and continued into July, August, and September. He too had been sent for trial.

"Time's up," said the Marmoset.

"Please—one second!" She skipped some pages and jumped to the end of the file. She had to find out what had happened to Palitsyn. She found a signed confession.

Accused Palitsyn: I plead guilty to spying for the Japanese and British intelligence services, to serving Trotsky, and planning a terrorist plot against the leadership of the Soviet Union. But there was no end to his story—and no mention of Satinov, no link to a common past.

She noted down the dates in her notebook and sighed, wanting to cry. Why? For these two people whom she had never known?

"There's no record of a sentence," she said aloud. "Could they have survived? Could they be alive?"

"Does it say in the file that they died?" asked the colonel.

She shook her head.

"Well then . . ." He stood up and stretched.

"But there's a lot missing from these files, Colonel. No details of sentencing. Perhaps the Palitsyns were sent to the Gulags and pardoned after Stalin's death. I wish to apply for more files. I want to find out what happened to these people."

"Is this a game, girl? Fa-la-la! Maybe you'll be lucky. Maybe not. I'll refer your request to my superior, General Fursenko. I'm just a cog in the machine."

Katinka felt downcast suddenly. She had still not found out why Sashenka and her husband had been arrested. Captain Sagan's confession was dated after their arrest. She did not believe Benya Golden's story of his affair with Sashenka, let alone the conspiracy to assassinate the Party leaders, so perhaps this too was invented? And she still didn't know if all this was in any way connected to Satinov.

As she slid the Sashenka file across the desk to the colonel, she accidentally bent back the blank list of those who had examined the file. On the other side were some scrawled names from 1956: her heart leaped. There it was: *Hercules Satinov.*

The Marmoset started to check if each document was present, wetting his fingertips with his tongue as he turned the pages.

Katinka saw she had another minute or two. She quickly reopened Ivan Palitsyn's file—and something caught her eye.

There it was, on the State Security letterhead, a handwritten order dated May 4, 1939:

> *Top Secret.*
> *Captain Zubenko, Special Technical Group, State Security*
> *Set up immediate surveillance in Moscow city limits only on Comrade Sashenka Zeitlin-Palitsyn, editor,* Soviet Wife and Proletarian Housekeeping, *23 Petrovka, and set up listening equipment in room 403, Metropole Hotel, with immediate effect.*
> *Reports only to me, no copies.*

Katinka stared at the signature. *Vanya Palitsyn, Commissar-General of State Security, third degree.*

Sashenka's husband.

Afterward, Katinka walked through the Moscow streets, down the hill past the Bolshoi toward the Kremlin. She gripped her notebook and glanced at the stalls of the street vendors offering pirated CDs, sensationalist history pamphlets, American pornography, Italian showbiz magazines, even Peter the Great's *Book of Manners.* But she was not really looking at them. Once she bumped into a man, who shouted at her, and another time she walked right into a Lada parked on the pavement. She was trying to make sense of what she had found in the file. Finally, she walked up the cobbled hill from the river, past the Kremlin's ramparts and then round and round Red Square.

Perhaps Benya Golden's confession had been true after all. Could Sashenka really have had an affair with a famous writer in room 403 at the Metropole Hotel? But it would have been such a dangerous thing to seduce the wife of a Chekist, who had all the weapons of the secret police—surveillance, bugging, arrest—at his disposal. Somehow Vanya seemed to have found out about the affair and he himself had set the ball rolling, unleashing the thunderbolt: a personal investigation without official sanction. *Reports only to me, no copies. Palitsyn.*

Jealousy, Katinka thought. Were they all ruined because of one man's fear of being cuckolded? Did they all die because of his jealousy?

10

"So Vanya Palitsyn recorded his wife in bed with a writer?" said Maxy that evening, sitting on his motorbike in leathers, outside the nightclub near the British Embassy. "He gets the report: all the oohs and aahs of fucking . . ."

". . . Vanya was outraged," Katinka continued, "and ordered Benya Golden's arrest."

"No, no," said Maxy. "Benya Golden's a famous writer and Sashenka was well known, the niece of Mendel Barmakid, 'Conscience of the Party.' And if this just concerned adultery, why was Vanya himself arrested?"

"Benya was arrested and then denounced his mistress Sashenka who denounced her husband?"

"No, Katinka, you're missing the point. They couldn't have been arrested without Stalin's approval." Maxy lit a cigarette. "Besides, the dates don't tally. You must realize the archives are full of lies and distortions. We have to read them like hieroglyphics."

Katinka sighed. It was getting cold, and her miniskirt did not keep out the wind. "What shall I do now?"

"Don't get upset about all this. You've done really well—better than I thought possible." Maxy looked at his Red Army watch. "Wait—it's only nine p.m.: why don't you ring his eminence the marshal? You need his help to get the rest of the KGB files, the stuff they didn't show you. And now you know more, you can ask more. We need him to confirm that the Palitsyn family are the ones to follow."

Business concluded, he offered her a cigarette and struck a match. They both sheltered the flame with cupped hands. As their skin touched, his eyes narrowed, and she was conscious of him looking at her carefully.

"Tell me—are you spending all that oligarch's money? On clothes? Or makeup? No, you're too sensible, too serious. You're not spending any of it. You should enjoy life more!" He laughed. "You're too cute, Katinka, for a historian." He leaned over and brushed the hair off her face.

"Not so fast," she said coolly, allowing him to kiss her on the cheek. His stubble burned her skin.

Flicking his cigarette into the air so that it landed on the embankment by the Moskva, he pulled on his helmet, kick-started the bike and sped away toward the Stone Bridge.

Katinka watched him go then touched her cheek where he had kissed her and repeated his line mockingly to herself: *You're too cute for a historian.* What a ridiculous gambit, she thought. You may be my teacher, but you're a bit of a poser. I decide who kisses me and who doesn't.

Then slowly, thoughtfully, with the eight red stars of the Kremlin sparkling above her, she walked over to the public telephone and dialed a number.

"I'm listening," answered an old man with a Georgian accent.

"I won't be dancing this time," said Hercules Satinov with a wintry smile. He was sitting in his chair at Granovsky, surrounded as usual by the photographs of his family, beneath the portrait of himself as the bemedaled marshal. "I'm getting sicker."

"No smoking, Father! He was showing off to a pretty girl," said Mariko, bringing in the tea. "He had to go to bed afterward, you know." She sounded angry, as if this were Katinka's fault. "You shouldn't have come now. It's much too late. You should go." Mariko banged the tray on the table and left the room, tossing a sour glare at the visitor.

"It's all right, Mariko . . ." Mariko shut the door, though a creaking suggested she was never far away. "Well," said Satinov, "I am rather ancient." When Katinka sat in the same chair as last time and crossed her legs, the old man glanced at her approvingly. "You look as if you've been out dancing in nightclubs. Well, why not? Why should a flower as young and fresh as you waste her youth on dusty archives and ancient miseries?" He pulled out his cigarettes again, lighting up and closing his eyes.

"It's what I do best, Marshal."

"You might not have as long as you think for your research," he said, "or are you getting fond of me?" He looked right at her. "Well, girl, what did you find?"

Katinka took a deep breath. "In 1956 you visited the Lubianka and examined the files of Sashenka and Vanya Palitsyn. They were old friends of yours from before the Revolution. They were the link with the past you wanted me to find."

"You seem keener on the subject than you were before," he observed.

"I am. These people—they seem so real somehow."

"Ah. So the historian of Catherine the Great is getting involved in our own times. You smell the happy flowers and the bitter ashes? That shows you're a real historian."

"Thank you, Marshal."

"Tell me again," he said, leaning forward suddenly. "Your name's Vinsky. Why did *you* get this job?"

"I was recommended by Academician Beliakov. I was his top student."

"Of course," Satinov said, sucking on his cigarette, eyelids sliding down. "I can see you're a clever girl, a special person. Academician Beliakov was right to choose you out of all his hundreds of students over his many decades of teaching . . . Think of that."

"I think he wanted to help me." Katinka felt annoyed. She could see that he was toying with her, as he had with so many other inferior beings in his lifetime. This was another Satinov, sly and reptilian. The chilliness shocked her, poisoning her liking for him.

"Marshal, please could you answer my question. Sashenka and Vanya Palitsyn are the people I was meant to find, aren't they? What became of them?"

Satinov shook his head, and Katinka noticed a muscle twitching in his cheek.

"There's no record of their trial or sentencing. Could they have survived?"

"Unlikely but possible. Last year a woman found her husband, who had been arrested in 1938—he was living in Norilsk." He gave her a brief, bitter smile. "You're on a quest for the philosopher's stone, which so many have sought and none has found."

Katinka gritted her teeth and started again. "I really need your help. I need to see their files—the ones the KGB are still holding."

He inhaled, taking his time, as always. "All right," he said, "I'll call some old friends in the Organs—they're all geriatrics like me, waiting to die at their dachas, fishing, playing chess, cursing the new rich. But I'll do my best."

"Thank you." She sat forward in her chair. "The files mentioned that the Palitsyns had two children, Volya and Karlmarx. What happened to them?"

"I have no idea. Like so many children of those times, they too perhaps just disappeared."

"But how?"

"That's your job to find out," he said coldly, shifting in his chair. "Where did you say you came from? The northern Caucasus, wasn't it?"

Katinka took a quick breath of excitement. He'd changed the subject, a petty diversion. She scented her prey. "May I just ask—you knew the Palitsyns. What were they like?"

He sighed. "They were dedicated Bolsheviks."

"I saw her photograph in the file. She was so beautiful and unusual . . ."

"Once you saw her, you never forgot her," he said quietly.

"But such sad eyes," said Katinka.

Satinov's face hardened, the angles of his Persian nose and cheekbones sharpened, became more triangular. His eyes slid closed. "She was hardly alone. There are millions of such photographs. Millions of repressed people just like her."

Katinka could feel Satinov closing down, so she pressed him again.

"Marshal, I know you're tired, and I'm going now . . . but was Roza Getman one of their children?"

"That's enough, girl!" Mariko, draped in a black shawl like a Spanish mantilla, had come into the room. She placed herself between Katinka and Satinov. "You shouldn't have come here in the first place. What kind of questions are you asking? My father's tired now. You must go."

Satinov sat back in the chair, wheezing a little.

"We'll talk again," he said heavily. "God willing."

"Sorry, I've asked too much. I stayed too long . . ."

He did not smile at her again but he offered his hand, looking away.

"I'm tired now." There was a piece of paper in his hand. "Someone you must meet. Don't wait. You may already be too late. Say hello from me."

11

Two days later, Katinka was awakened by the green plastic phone in her tiny, fusty room deep inside the square colossus of the Moskva Hotel. Her bed, bedside table, light and desk were all one piece of wooden furniture. The bedspread, carpet and the curtains the color of brimstone. She was dreaming about Sashenka: the woman in the photograph was talking to her.

"Don't give up! Persevere with Satinov . . ." But why was Satinov so obstructive? Would he refuse to meet her again? She was still half asleep when she grabbed the phone.

"Hello," she said. She expected it to be her parents—or maybe Roza Getman, who was phoning regularly for updates on her progress. "Hello, Katinka, any jewels in the dust?" was how Roza always started her calls.

"This is Colonel Lentin." Katinka was amazed: it was the Marmoset of the KGB archives. "You wish to see more documents?"

"Yes," she said, heart surging. "That would be wonderful."

"Wonderful? Wonderful indeed. You're such an enthusiast. Meet us at the Café-Bar Piano at the Patriarchy Ponds at two."

Katinka pulled on her boots and the denim miniskirt with the spangles. She was earning money for the first time in her life but still it did not feel like her own. She was using it to pay for her room, food and transportation but nothing else. She was only doing this for Roza, she told herself, so that she, like Katinka, would have a family.

She took the elevator down to the grey marble lobby, damp as wet rat fur, and walked through to another hall, where she climbed the steps, followed a corridor left then right and finally opened a red curtain to reveal a little cubbyhole with three tables and an old woman in a minuscule kitchen. The tempting tang of cooking fat and the music of sizzling eggs welcomed her. A young English journalist and an ancient Armenian man were at their usual tables, sipping espresso coffees.

"Morning, senorita," said the old woman in a blue apron, speaking bad Russian. Her brown face, with its large jaw, was deeply wrinkled. "Spanish omelette?"

"The usual," said Katinka. The cook was an old Spaniard who claimed to have been cooking in this cubbyhole since the Spanish Civil War.

"The best cook in Moscow!" murmured the Armenian, kissing his hand and blowing it toward the old woman.

An hour later, Katinka walked slowly up Tverskaya—the new name for Gorky Street—and then took a left through an archway that led down to the Patriarchy Ponds, a square with a park in the middle containing two lakes surrounded by trees. Bulgakov, she knew, had lived around here, when he was writing *The Master and Margarita.* She bought an ice cream at the open-air café and sat watching the couples, the children promenading, the old folk watching her watching them. Why did the Marmoset want to meet her here and not at the Lubianka? Could he be bringing the documents? No, that was impossible. So why? She did not trust these people.

At 2:00 p.m. she walked out of the square and looked around the far end of the street. There it was—a black and white sign, *BAR-CAFÉ PIANO.* She went in. Rod Stewart was singing "Do Ya Think I'm Sexy" on the stereo. The small café was empty except for a specter-thin grey-haired man behind the bar, smoking a cigarette as he poured out three thimbles of vodka, and two men at a chrome table. One of them was the Marmoset, Colonel Lentin, wearing a green sports coat and a Wimbledon tennis tie. He stood up and offered his hand.

"Come and sit down, girl." He guided her to a chair. "Let me introduce you to my comrade here, Oleg Sergeievich Trofimsky."

"Delighted, Katinka, delighted. Yes, sit!" Trofimsky's head was wide and misshapen and looked as if it had been fired out of a medieval cannon, and his pitchfork beard gave him the air of an aging magician. The barman brought the vodkas and slammed them down on the table.

"No, no," the Magician remonstrated coarsely. "Dima, bring us your oldest Scotch whiskey. This young lady's much too cultured for mere Russian vodka."

The barman shrugged and returned to the bar.

"Dima's a retired comrade," explained the Magician to Katinka, "so we—shall we say—patronize his establishment. He's used to my tastes, aren't you, Dima?"

The barman rolled his eyes and brought the amber liquid.

The Magician turned back to Katinka. "Now, drink carefully. This is fifty years old, aged in oaken barrels in the Scottish isles. Its name? Laphroaig. Taste it: you see? You can taste the peat; that is the soil there. When I was in the London Embassy—my work was, shall we say, clandestine—I toured the Caledonian isles. The British royal family drink only this when they are hunting in the Scottish region. Go on, drink!"

Katinka drank, but only a sip.

"You're a historian, are you not?" asked the Magician, stroking his pitchfork beard.

"Yes, I specialize in the eighteenth century."

"I've studied history myself and I know the Velvet Book intimately, the Romanovs, Saxe-Coburgs, even the collateral lines," he said. "It's a hobby, shall we say. But now I've taught you something about civilized living, let me get straight to the point. You are researching something very different? The period of the Cult of Personality?"

"Yes, one family," answered Katinka, cautiously.

"I know, I know, Colonel Lentin has told me. And you weren't satisfied with the documents you were shown?"

"I would like to see others," she said.

"Well, you may, that is totally possible. You will see them."

"Thank you," said Katinka, surprised. "When?"

The Magician waved a finger at her. "We're adapting to the new era, aren't we, Colonel Lentin? We're embracing it! But we're still patriots. We don't wish to be American. Make no mistake, girl, we in the Competent Organs are the conscience of this country. We'll make it strong again!"

"But what about the documents? When can I see them?"

"You're young, in a hurry. As soon as tomorrow?"

"Yes, please," she said, as eager as she was uneasy.

"Can we do it tomorrow, Colonel?" asked the Magician.

"Three days perhaps," said the Marmoset, clearly the junior partner here. "Maybe a week."

"Then that is that," said the Magician. "And it won't be too expensive."

"Expensive?" cried Katinka. "But . . ."

"Ahhh, look at her!" cried the Magician theatrically. "Look at that worried pretty face! Ha ha. You're new in Moscow, just a kitten in the big city, I can tell. Yes, everything has its price. The Colonel and I are embracing the new mentality! More whiskey, Dima. Let's drink to it!"

12

Just after midday next day, Katinka walked through the high halls, past window displays and along vestibules of the new shops in the GUM arcade on Red Square. She had an appointment at the Bosko Restaurant, where slim, tanned girls with long legs in boots and skirts and gleaming Versace chains sat with squat men in Italian suits. The aromas of ground coffee and scented skin filled the air. The place was so chic that Katinka felt she might be in Venice or New York, even though she had never been anywhere but London.

What a place! she thought, not noticing the maître d', an Italianate Tatar with the profile of a pigeon, scowling at her spangled skirt and white boots. "Oh look!" she burst out. "What a view!"

She sighed with the sensual pleasure of a provincial girl at Bosko's wall-sized panorama of Red Square and its expanse of shiny cobbles. From here, the gaudy ice-cream cones of St. Basil's seemed more Tatar than Russian. Just under the Kremlin walls stood that strangely unslavic Egyptian mausoleum in freckled red granite wherein lay the mummified Lenin. There, farther away, almost hidden against the Kremlin Wall, was the little green marble bust of Stalin himself, rudely removed from its resting place in the Mausoleum. The Russianness of the Kremlin, with its Orthodox churches, its green and ocher Tsarist palaces, even those red stars, filled Katinka with Slavic pride.

She could see the domed roof of the Council of Ministers Building, where Lenin and Stalin had worked. Now President Yeltsin held office there. Sashenka had known Lenin and Stalin in the early years of Soviet power, Katinka remembered—and her obsession jolted her: she was relating to a woman whom she knew only from a photograph and a file.

"Can I help you, mademoiselle?" said the Tatar maître d'. "A table with a view?"

"She's with me," said a voice behind her. Pasha Getman towered awkwardly over her. He moved clumsily and none of his clothes quite seemed to fit even though they looked expensive. The trousers were too baggy; the shirt, open necked, was wrongly buttoned, yet he exuded cosmopolitan confidence, and Odessan haughtiness with the pungent smoke of his oversized cigar.

Katinka had spoken to Roza after her meeting with the Magician and the Marmoset, and Roza had asked her to talk to Pasha, who had agreed to meet her straight away.

She was now not sure if he would embrace her. Both leaned toward each other but at the last minute he withdrew and offered his hand. Katinka blushed but was rescued by the maître d'.

"Welcome, Gospodin Getman! Your usual table in the alcove? Sir and mademoiselle, please follow me!"

Getman's three bulky, shaven-headed bodyguards, tattoos peeping over their shirt collars, sat at the neighboring table. Katinka followed Pasha, noticing that he walked like a juggling bear with his paw-like hands ready to catch the balls.

"I haven't got long," said Pasha when they were seated.

"I didn't know you were here. I thought you were in London."

"Water?" Pasha reached for the water and spilled it. Waiters rushed to clear up but he did not seem to care. "I came home again. There's going to be an election soon. The President needs our help—we must keep out the Communists. Mama's on her way back from London. You understand that this is her last chance to find out who she really is. Imagine not knowing, Katinka! I knew my parents so well, so intimately, but she has always this burning sense of loss inside her. Do you know your parents?"

"Of course."

"Happy childhood?"

She nodded, unable to conceal her pleasure in the thought. "My father's a doctor. They really love me and we live with my grandparents in their old house."

"We're so lucky, you and I. Now I know you've been talking to Mama"—Katinka was amused that this bear of a billionaire in his mid-thirties still called his mother "Mama"—"but I'd like to know myself what you've found so far."

As Katinka explained, Pasha's mobile phone continued to ring. Once the bodyguards took a call and gave him a message; a red-haired girl in a leather miniskirt and Chanel boots and belt greeted him; and several businessmen came to shake hands—but navigating these interruptions, she managed to reveal her story. While she talked, Pasha leaned forward and listened to her, chewing on his cigar, his sharp, dark eyes looking straight into hers.

"So Satinov does know something but he's very old and mysterious. Typical of that generation for whom secrecy is a fetish. You're doing well."

Katinka flushed with pleasure. "But the documents were incomplete and I met with the KGB to discuss the ones that were missing and I'm so embarrassed—and of course, I told them it wasn't possible—but they asked . . ."

"Asked what?"

"For money! It's disgusting!"

"How much?" asked Pasha.

"I told them it was ridiculous."

"Look," said Pasha, "I don't mean to sound . . . I'm older than you so . . . I'm sorry I lost my temper in London. Mama told me off. But you're so unworldly. I meet a lot of greedy girls. I understand you're not like that. Mama says too that you're not doing this for the money—that you genuinely want to help us. So I hope you'll keep working on this day and night. How much do they want?"

"But we shouldn't pay them," Katinka objected. "Not the Organs! These are not decent people."

"Just tell me how much they've asked for."

"They mentioned . . . it's so much, it's a crime and they're Mafiosi . . . ," she sighed. "Fifteen thousand dollars. A sin! What has happened to Russians these days?"

Pasha shrugged, the juggling paws opening and closing. "Well, this is my gift to Mama. Truth is expensive, but I think family is priceless. Understand that, understand everything. I'll pay it."

"No."

"Stop telling me what to do!" he growled and crumpled up the tablecloth, almost sending all the cups to the floor. "It's my money, and we need their information."

"Well, OK . . . ," Katinka said at last. "And there's one other thing. Satinov gave me this and said I must meet this person and not leave it too long." She handed over a scrap of paper.

"But this is a Tbilisi number. In Georgia."

"Yes."

"Well, what are you waiting for? You must go immediately, Katinka."

"Now?"

"Sure, pick up your passport and suitcase from the hotel. When you get back, I'll give you the cash and you can meet your KGB crooks." He dialed on his cell phone. "It's me. Book a flight to Tbilisi for this afternoon. Four o'clock? Fine. Ekaterina Vinsky. Put her in the Metechi Palace Hotel. Bye." He called to the next table. "Hey, Tiger!" One of the bodyguards lumbered over. "Take Katinka back to the hotel and then on to Sheremetyevo. Right now."

13

It was already dark in Tbilisi—once known as Tiflis—when Katinka arrived at the airport, a bazaar of shouting taxi drivers, gunmen, traders, soldiers and footpads. But there was a driver waiting for her with a sign that read *Vinsky*—and a Volga that apparently could only be started with two wires and a hummed song. As they drove into town, the gunshots of a small wild land in the midst of a civil war ricocheted over the half-lit city. The Metechi Palace Hotel, an ugly modern construction with glass elevators and a big open foyer with ranks of green metal balconies reaching up toward a giant skylight, was patrolled by Georgian gunmen in glittery gun holsters toting battered Kalashnikovs.

Leaving her bags at the hotel, Katinka caught a taxi into the city, passing through checkpoints manned by militiamen of motley uniform belonging to any of several private armies. The police themselves looked shabby and lost in their own city. The buildings were grandly decayed, and the streets had the flavor of a Levantine dream of a Paris that never was.

Katinka had never been to Georgia—her family spent their holidays in Sochi on the Black Sea—but she had heard a lot about it, of course: the fruit basket, the wine barrel, the playboy capital, the jewel in the crown, the pleasure dome of the Soviet Imperium with its luscious harvests of grapes and vegetables, its sulphurous Borzhomi water in those famous green bottles, its earthy red wines, its privileged, corrupt Communist bosses who lived like sultans, its argumentative intellectuals and its flashy Casanovan lovers. But Georgia had its dark side too. It had produced Stalin and Beria—and other famous Communists with unpronounceable, slightly ridiculous Georgian names: Sergo Ordzhonikidze, Abel Yenukidze—and Marshal Hercules Satinov.

The taxi took her right to the city center through Freedom Square (once Yerevan Square under the Tsar, then Beria Square, then Lenin Square) and into the broad and handsome Rustaveli Avenue (Golovinsky during Tsarist times) with its theaters and palaces. The driver did not know the way to the house she wanted: he shouted at people to ask. He turned the car round, oblivious to the hooting traffic, and showed her the burnt-out wreck of the Tbilisi Hotel, once the grandest south of Moscow. Finally they stopped on a steep cobbled hill, beneath a church with a round tower in the Georgian Orthodox style, and the driver pointed into the dark.

"There!"

Katinka paid him in dollars then walked carefully down the darkened street. Behind high walls the mansions were embraced by long-fingered vines, their courtyards overhung by flower-draped balconies where laughter and lanterns flickered. A bearded man with the thick white hair that Georgians never seem to lose held up a lantern.

"Where are you going? Are you lost?"

She saw he had a shotgun but did not feel afraid. "Café Biblioteka?" she asked.

"Come on!" His Russian was abysmal but he took her arm and led her down the cobbled street until they reached a house almost completely concealed in the vines. He opened the wooden double doors into a crumbling marble hall, lit with a candle, that reeked of Georgian feasts. To the right was a large shabby door and he pushed it open, jabbering in Georgian, the shotgun angled alarmingly over his shoulder. "Come on! Here is Café Biblioteka!"

With a gasp of wonder, Katinka entered the café, in the flickering light of candles decorated with wings of wax. She thought it smelled delicious: of *tkemali*, ginger, apple and almond. It was an old library, the bookshelves still standing in between the tables and behind the bar. Maps, banners of Tsarist Guards regiments, Georgian brigades and Bolshevik workers, drawings, noble and obscene, paintings, icons, pieces of old Georgian uniforms, swords and daggers, busts of Mozart, Queen Tamara, Stalin and Roman senators covered the walls. Some of the bookshelves had rotted and collapsed, tossing their priceless antique volumes onto the floors, where they lay, their yellow parchment pages open like fans.

At small tables, a single old man in a black fedora read in the half light; a group of American backpackers in yellow Timberlands and big shorts with their wallets on belts round their waists (advertising their Western riches to any brigands present) toasted one another in Georgian wine; and two grey-haired Georgians argued loudly about their politicians.

"Shevardnadze's a traitor, a spy, KGB!" shouted one.

"Zviad's a lunatic, a spy, KGB!" retorted the other.

"Do you want a table? Wine? Dinner?" asked a tall slim Georgian man with a blue beret on his head and a *chokha* coat, wasp-waisted with pouches for bullets, and a jeweled dagger in his belt. He bowed. "I'm Nugzar. Who are you? You look lost."

"Do you know Audrey Zeitlin? I want to see her."

"The old English lady? She's our icon, our lucky charm! We feed her every day. She worked here for a long time, she taught us English and our children! Upstairs, come on!"

Katinka followed Nugzar to the first floor, along a corridor where the vine had punched its way through the wall and joined up with another of its limbs through a window that could no longer be closed. He knocked on the door at the end.

"Anuko!" he called.

Those Georgians, Katinka thought,with their funny diminutives!

"A visitor, Anuko!"

No reply.

Peering tentatively into the gloom, Nugzar opened the door.

14

"I always hoped you would come," said Lala in the squeezed pitch of the ancient.

She wore a housecoat over a nightgown, and had long white hair. There was little left of her, just a bag of bones held together by white skin so delicate one could almost see through it. But it was her eyes, which seemed enormous in their glowing opalescence, that drew in Katinka, for they had a bold, exuberant will that held the spotlight and challenged the energy of the young. "I've waited for fifty years. What took you so long?"

"Hello," Katinka said hesitantly, afraid she had come to the wrong place, yet surprised that this antique woman seemed to know who she was. "Marshal Satinov sent me to see you."

"Ah—Satinov. He was our hero, our guardian angel. He's old now, of course. Not as old as me, though. Sit down, sit down."

Katinka sat in the soft chair in the corner of the small room musty with tissues and hand cream. There was a single candle beside the bed; sepia photographs of grandees in stiff white collars and bowler hats; a haughty schoolgirl in a white pinafore; a silver model of an oil derrick; and many old books.

"Here, girl, puff up my pillow behind me, and bring me a glass of wine. Ask Nugzar downstairs. Then we must talk. All night. You don't sleep much when you're as old as me. Who wants to be alive at my age? It's miserable. All my friends are dead and that's no fun! My husband's been dead for forty years. But I think I've been waiting. I've been waiting for you, darling child. And now you're here, sent by Marshal Satinov. He wants you to find my lost children, doesn't he? Are you taking notes, dear?"

Feeling as though she had stepped into a dream, Katinka dug into her bag for her notebook and pen.

"I'm going to tell you about Sashenka, Snowy and Carlo."

"Wait, I know Sashenka but who's Snowy and . . ."

"Don't you know anything, girl? Snowy and Carlo were Sashenka's children. Their real names were Volya and Karlmarx. I'm going to tell you their story but first, open the window, will you?" Katinka was only too glad to let in the fragrant air. The dreamy garden seethed outside. The scent of violets, roses and that almondish, appleish *tkemali* blossom slowly penetrated the stuffy room in waves through the slats of the old-fashioned shutters. From the rooms below, the kitchen cauldrons in which *chakapuli* was boiling released powerful aromas of ginger and nutmeg.

And so it was that, as she drank her wine and ate slices of *khachapuri* brought up by the Georgian warrior from the café, Katinka traveled back in time to an unimaginable epoch in a house on Greater Maritime

Street in St. Petersburg, where a rich Jewish banker and his flighty wife brought up a daughter named Sashenka with the help of a young English nanny whose parents had run the Live and Let Live public house in a village named Pegsdon, not far from the market town of Hitchin, Hertfordshire. "Lala" Lewis, as Sashenka had once called her, "and you must call me that too, Katinka," seemed to know everything about the Zeitlin family. She described the solemn gawky child, bullied and disdained by her mother, loved distantly by her father, nourished by the devotion of her nanny.

What a picture Lala Lewis painted of those times: of cars with split windshields, chrome lights, leather and teak upholstery, carriages and sledges with postilions in top hats and sheepskins; millionaires, counts and revolutionaries, uncles and chauffeurs, breakdowns and suicides.

"I fell in love with Baron Zeitlin right here in this Tbilisi house—it had belonged to him, long, long ago," Lala told Katinka, and that later he'd asked her to marry him in a *kabinet* at a smart restaurant, the Donan in St. Petersburg.

"Samuil lost everything in 1917, but he rebuilt his career in the Soviet service then lost it all again in 1929, and we returned here. We thought it would be safer. We felt that we didn't have long so we didn't waste a moment," she said. "We so loved each other. Every day was a honeymoon, every kiss was a bonus, a gift. In Moscow, Sashenka and Vanya—as everyone called her husband—were bosses. They knew everyone, even Stalin—Sashenka was a magazine editor and Vanya a secret policeman, probably a terrible butcher, although he seemed a jovial fellow. We longed to see them—I loved Sashenka as much as Samuil did. It was our love of Sashenka that first brought us together, you know. When the NKVD took Samuil away, I knew he was doomed, and I waited for them to take me too. I kept working here in the café; I taught English; I looked after children; I became the best English teacher in the town. I taught the bosses' children and I still do a little teaching today! But I'm getting ahead of myself. When they took Samuil, I grieved for him. The mail and money I sent him was returned: that meant he was dead. Then they took Sashenka and Vanya too. I despaired then. So imagine my amazement when Samuil came back. Oh, the randomness of death in those times!"

"How did Samuil take Sashenka's disappearance?"

"When Samuil was sinking in and out of coma on his deathbed, he said, 'Sashenka darling, my *lisichka*, my little fox, will you kiss me, Sashenka, before I die?' He was sure Sashenka would come back. So I promised that I'd wait for her instead."

"Are you tired, Lala?" asked Katinka, anxious about Lala's strength yet greedy for her stories. "Do you want to sleep for a bit?" She noticed tears seeping down the old lady's cheeks.

"I'm tired but I've waited so long to tell this. You see, when Samuil was in the camps, Comrade Satinov called me to the Viceroy's Palace with a proposal that I could not refuse. Listen to me, Katinka. I only have the strength to tell this once."

"I'm listening, I promise!"

"Hercules Satinov was a hero. He had a young wife and new baby and all the privileges of his rank. He could have been shot for helping Sashenka's children but he fixed everything. When everyone else was a lackey, a coward and a killer, he alone dared to be decent. If you write this story, write that!"

"I will," said Katinka, remembering the sly old marshal and his expression of pain when she asked him about Sashenka and her children.

"At the Viceroy's Palace—it was then the Communist headquarters—Satinov told me that something terrible had happened to Sashenka and Vanya, and I needed to care for their children. He told me to go to Rostov Station, where I found the children and their nanny, Carolina, in the canteen. They were exhausted, hungry and filthy, but I loved them instantly. It was as if I'd raised them myself because Sashenka had cared for them just like I'd cared for her. Snowy so reminded me of Sashenka that I kissed her the moment I saw her and she melted into my arms! Carlo was adorable, bold and playful—like his father but with Samuil's eyes and smile, even his dimple. They immediately trusted me, who knows why—perhaps they sensed a connection to their mama. Oh, it was heartbreaking! First they were parted from father, then mother, then Carolina: she was like a mother to them herself. I left the hotel in Rostov when she was still asleep—I still feel guilty about that—but I hope she understood because she too had risked her life for those children."

"What happened to her?" asked Katinka but the old lady did not stop, as if afraid to waste an ounce of energy on anything not strictly necessary. Katinka understood suddenly that Lala Lewis was telling her the story that perhaps Satinov could not bear to tell her himself.

Lala sipped her red wine, spilling some on her nightie. A shaky hand tried to wipe it but she missed the stain and soon gave up.

"I begged him to let *me* keep the children but he told me I would be arrested myself and then what? I knew then that I would only have them for the briefest of times, and I needed to make the most of it. Our five days and nights together were too short for me. I'd lost Samuil but gained them. Satinov had given me enough money to feed the children well and we had papers so we could move about openly. I was with *family*. 'Where's Mama? When's Mama coming back?' the children asked, but Satinov had told me that I had to tell them their parents had died in an accident. That was a terrible moment. More than ever, they clung to me and to that cushion, that absurd cushion, that became mother and father to darling Snowy, and to that pink rabbit that Carlo kissed at night. I wanted to kiss and hug those children, spoil them, soothe them, heal them. I wanted to cover them in love. But I couldn't let them get too close because I knew that I would soon have to disappear too. They slept in my bed, yes, this very bed, and I relished those nights with them, every second. As I lay there between them, with their soft limbs and sweet breath on me, I sobbed for them and Sashenka, but I couldn't move or make a sound so the tears flowed silently. Like an underground stream. In the morning the pillow was soaked.

"One morning, Snowy kissed me. 'Can we go home, Lala? Where is Mummy now?' she asked.

'I think she's watching you.'

'Like the stars in the sky?'

'Just like that. She'll always watch you, darling!'

'Why did she go away and leave us?'

'She didn't want to, darling. I know she loved you and Carlo more than anything in the world. At night, wherever you are, I think she'll kiss your forehead just like this and you won't awaken. But in the morning, you'll just feel a light breeze over you and you'll know she's been there.'

'What about Daddy?'

'Daddy will kiss you too, on the other side of your forehead.'

'Will you be like our mummy for us?'

"Oh, Katinka, dear child, can you imagine such a conversation? I had to take them to the Lavrenti Beria Orphanage outside town. A hellish place. Even visiting was a bad experience. But there they got the stamps on their papers assigning them to the families who would adopt them. Satinov had arranged it meticulously so they weren't registered as children of Enemies of the People, just ordinary orphans. How he did it all I don't know. I dreaded parting with them. I loved them both, Snowy and Carlo. Dear child, I can still smell their skin now, still look into their eyes, still hear their voices—I had to leave them and, worst of all, I had to part brother and sister. They would never see each other again. It was one blow after another!"

Tears ran down her lined cheeks. Katinka was so moved that she too burst into tears and, without a word, she sat on the bed and they held each other. Finally Lala drank a little wine, ate some *khachapuri*, and cleared her throat.

"Are you strong enough to go on?" Katinka asked.

"I am. Are you?" said the old lady, wiping her eyes. "I'm not bad for my age, am I?"

"Who were the families who took them? Can you remember?"

"I never knew the names of the families. Satinov made sure of that. Only he knew. But I remember the day I met them both as if it were yesterday. Oh, it was agony! Carlo was playing with trains in one room at the orphanage. Snowy was creating a dinner party of pillows and cushions. And then the families came. I suppose they were good people but they weren't like Sashenka or me—not cozy. The Jewish couple—they didn't say but they were from Odessa or Nikolaev, somewhere on the Black Sea—were kind enough, I think, but quite unsuited to looking after children—he was already middle-aged with wild fuzzy hair, some kind of intellectual, and she was a bluestocking. I wanted to tell them that Snowy's mother was Jewish too so they were her sort in a way. I did explain about Snowy's favorite toys and games, and in their stiff way they started to play along with her. That comforted me later. I left Snowy with them, hoping they would get to know one another. But they didn't. Snowy kept running back to me. 'Where's Lala?' she'd scream. 'Lala, you won't leave us, will you, Lala? Where's Carlo, I want to stay with Carlo! Carlo!' "

"When they took her away, Snowy howled. 'Lala, you promised, Lala, help me, Lala!' She wanted me, she wanted her brother. Finally, the nurses and guards had to force her into their car. She was kicking and crying, 'Lala, you promised!' At last, her new parents got into the car and drove off into the distance. And I sank onto the floor and howled too, like an animal, in front of everyone in that orphanage . . ."

Katinka felt exhausted, and yet, in spite of the tragedy, excited too. "That couple from Odessa must have been the Liberharts," she said. "Roza *is* Snowy." But Lala kept talking as if she hadn't heard. "It was the same with Carlo and the peasants."

"The peasants?" asked Katinka, taking notes.

"The couple who took Carlo. The moment Snowy was gone, he started crying: 'Where's Snowy? I want to cuddle Snowy! Lala, you won't leave me, will you, Lala?' I barely survived that day. He struggled too as they took him. I can still hear his voice right now . . . In some ways it was easier for him as he was only three. I prayed he wouldn't even remember Sashenka and Vanya, and perhaps he didn't. They were going to rename him. They say three is the borderline between what you remember and what you forget."

Katinka took Lala's hands in hers again. "Lala, I've got wonderful news for you."

"What? Is it Sashenka?" She peered at the shadows by the door. "Is Sashenka here? I knew she'd come."

"No, Lala. We don't know where Sashenka is."

"I dream of her so often, you know. I'm sure she's alive because we all thought Samuil was dead and *he* came back from the dead. Find her, Katinka. Bring her to me."

"I'm going to do my best, but I have something else to tell you. I think I've found your Snowy. The family who adopted her were called Liberhart and they renamed Snowy Roza. I'm going to phone her tonight and bring her to you. Then you can tell her these things yourself."

Lala looked at Katinka and turned her face away, a hand over her eyes. "I knew I hadn't waited in vain. That Satinov's an angel, an angel," she whispered. Then, sitting up straight, she faced Katinka. "I want to meet Snowy. But don't leave it too long. I'm not immortal."

When Katinka stood up, she was dizzy. It seemed as if she had experienced the tragic partings herself. "I must go back to my hotel and phone Roza."

But the old lady reached up to her. "No, no . . . stay with me. I've waited so long, I'm afraid you won't return and that this is just a vision. There's a dream I've had so often. Samuil, holding a glass of Georgian wine, leads me into the library, full of old books and strange curiosities, in a ruined mansion wrapped in vines and lilacs. And Sashenka, on a sleigh with bells galloping through the streets of Petersburg, is laughing and saying, 'Faster, Lala, faster . . .' And then I wake up, here in this little room, alone."

"Of course I'll stay," said Katinka, settling down again in the comfortable chair in the corner. She was glad not to have to go back to her unfriendly hotel on the outskirts of town.

During the warm night, she was woken by Lala, who was sitting up in bed. "She was arrested at the school gates, Baron. Yes, the gendarmes arrested her . . . What shall we do today, Sashenka? Shall we go skating, darling? No, if you're a good girl, we'll buy a tin of Huntley & Palmers biscuits at the English Shop on Nevsky. Pantameilion, bring round the sleigh . . ."

Katinka approached the bed. Lala's eyes were open and she was holding a photograph to her breast: it was Sashenka in the white pinafore of the Smolny Institute, with the same amused eyes.

"Go back to sleep, Lala. Go back to sleep," Katinka hushed her, stroking her forehead.

"Is that you, Sashenka? Oh, my darling, I knew you'd come back. I'm so happy to see you . . ." Lala's head sank back onto her pillow. Katinka thought her sleeping face was ageless, the tender heart-shaped face of the girl who had come from England all those years ago.

Then she returned to her chair and sobbed—she wasn't quite sure why—until she fell asleep again.

15

It was a balmy morning in the Georgian spring. When Katinka woke, the curtains were open. Lala, wearing a frayed pink dressing gown, was holding a small cup of Turkish coffee and a flat loaf of *lavashi* bread, delivered by Nugzar the warrior from downstairs.

Outside the window, Georgian men were singing "Suliko" on their way to work. There was so much music in Tbilisi. That very Georgian *tkemali* smell of almonds and apple blossom rose from the garden, the zest of fresh coffee, and the clatter of kitchens, came from the café beneath them.

"Good morning, dear child," said Lala. "Run downstairs and get some coffee."

Katinka sat right up. She rubbed her eyes. She had to get back to the hotel and call Roza. Her job was almost done, yet there was still so much to find out. Was Carlo still alive? And she was burning to know what had happened to Sashenka and Vanya. As if reading her mind, Lala said, "I know in my heart that Sashenka's alive—and I know someone who might help us find her."

•••

By 10:00 a.m. next day, Katinka was back in Moscow and walking up Tverskaya Street. As a student, she had browsed at the World of Books shop on Tverskaya. Now she rang the bell on the third door of the building. The door clicked open into a naked stone hall with the usual stench of cabbage and she rode up to the penthouse in a tiny, dyspeptic elevator that reminded her of a sardine tin hanging on a cable. But when the doors groaned open, she gasped in surprise. Instead of a landing with three or four doors, the elevator opened into a high-ceilinged apartment decorated in gracious, airy pine, filled with the sort of dark, noble furniture she usually saw in museums. The walls were stacked high with books and thick magazines of the Soviet era, and hung with paintings in gold frames and old movie posters. It was not overpoweringly grand like Marshal Satinov's place but cozy and aristocratic, the apartment of a well-off aesthete of Tsarist times.

"Welcome, Katinka," said a striking elderly woman standing in the middle of the room. Well dressed, with a busty figure neatly shown off in one of those tweed suits worn by Marlene Dietrich in the forties and a hairstyle to match, she suited the room so well she might have been posed there by a fashion photographer. Katinka guessed she was well over eighty, yet with her strong eyebrows and thick hair dyed black she held herself like an actress on her very last tour.

"I'm Mouche Zeitlin," the woman said, holding out her hand. "Come on in and I'll show you round. This was my father's study . . ." She led Katinka into a small room still heaped with papers and books, pointing out a wall of volumes. "These are all his works. You probably remember some of them—or maybe you're too young . . ."

"No, I knew his name," answered Katinka. "In my father's bookcase we have all the Gideon Zeitlin books along with Gorky, Ehrenburg and Sholokhov . . ."

"A giant of the Soviet era," said Mouche, who spoke the noble Russian of a trained actress. "Here!" She pointed at the large black and white photographs on the wall that showed a beaming black-eyed man with a grey-black beard and the same eyes and smile as his daughter. "That's my father with Picasso and Ehrenburg in Paris, and that's him with Marshal Zhukov at Hitler's Chancellery in 1945. Oh, and that's him with one of his many girlfriends. I used to call him *Papa momzer*—that's Yiddish for 'Daddy the rogue.' As for us, my sister and mother died in the Siege of Leningrad but my father and I, with our sense of humor, survived wars, revolutions and terror. In fact, we flourished—I'm a little ashamed to say. See those posters? That's me in my films. You've probably seen a few. Let's have tea." They crossed the impressive hall and Katinka found herself sitting at a big kitchen table. "Are you writing about my father or me?"

"No, actually, that's not why I came see you . . ." Katinka blushed but Mouche Zeitlin waved it away.

"Of course not, why should you, dear? You're the new generation. But you said you were a historian." She lit up a Gauloise, which she smoked in a silver holder, offering a cigarette to Katinka.

"No, thanks," said Katinka. Then she told Mouche about meeting Roza and Pasha, and the story up to the previous day with Lala. "Lala sent me to you. She had your address; I think she must have kept it when Samuil died. And now we know that my client Roza Getman is Snowy, Sashenka's daughter."

"God! Snowy!" Mouche lost her brashness and suddenly she dissolved in tears. "I can't believe it! How we longed to find that child. And what about Carlo?"

"I hope we can find him somehow."

"But Snowy's alive and well? I can't believe it!" Mouche held out her arms to Katinka as if the visitor herself were long-lost family. "You're a messenger bringing us blessings! Can I phone her? When can I meet her?"

"I hope very soon," replied Katinka. "But there's still so much to discover. I came to tell you this good news but also to ask you—did you ever look for Sashenka and Vanya?"

"Right up until his death, my father tried to find out what had happened to them and the children. There were many times during Stalin's reign when my father was close to destruction himself, even though he was one of the dictator's pet writers. At the end of the war, my father traveled down to Tbilisi to meet up again with his elder brother Samuil—and Lala Lewis, of course. They were very happy together. It was such a joyous reunion, the two brothers hadn't seen each other for so many years. Anyway, Samuil made my father promise that as soon as he could, he would find out about Sashenka and her family."

"Did you find anything?" asked Katinka, taking out her notebook.

"Oh yes. Even during Stalin's lifetime, Papa inquired of the Cheka and was told that Sashenka and Vanya had received ten years in the camps in 1939. We applied again in 1949, when Sashenka was due to be released, but were told that she had received another ten years without rights of correspondence. During the Thaw after Stalin's death, we were told that they had both died of heart attacks in the camps during the war."

"So there's really no hope for her."

"We thought not," said Mouche. "But in 1956 a female ex-prisoner, a newly released Zek, called on us here and told us that she'd been with Sashenka in the Kolyma camps, that she'd last seen Sashenka very recently, and she was alive when Stalin died in March 1953."

Katinka's heart leaped.

Later that day, a black armored Mercedes collected Katinka from the Moskva Hotel and drove her to Pasha Getman's headquarters, a former prince's mansion off Ostazhenka Street. Katinka was curious to see "The Palace," as it was known in the press. It was said to be a hive of political and financial intrigue so she was almost disappointed when they drove through the security gates and stopped in front of a graceful but small two-story residence in white marble with curling oriental-style pilasters. Inside, the hall was decorated, decided Katinka, like a Turkish sultan's harem, with many divans and fountains. She was met by a beautiful black-haired secretary, a Russian girl not much older than she, in a little black suit with a tiny skirt and colossal high heels, all set off by a clinking gold belt. Katinka knew at once, just from the girl's proprietorial slink, that this "Versace girl" was not exclusively Pasha's typist.

With her heels clicking on the marble floors, the assistant led Katinka, feeling dowdy in her denim skirt, past a room filled with electronic equipment and television screens, watched by guards in blue uniforms; then a dining room where a young man was checking place settings, flowers and cutlery; and then an airy modern office, all glass and chrome, where Pasha Getman waved at her.

He was on the phone but Roza was sitting on the sofa beneath some pieces of expensive (and hideous, in Katinka's view) modern art.

"Dear girl, you've done so well already," said Roza, kissing Katinka thrice and holding on to her warmly. "I just can't believe that you've found all this. I'm going to call Mouche right away . . . As soon as you mentioned the name Palitysn, Sashenka and Vanya, it was as if I already knew them."

"You didn't mention you also had a brother."

"I wanted to start with my parents, and even now I find it hard to say his name, to talk about him . . ." Roza stopped and closed her eyes for a second. "Anyway, I wasn't sure what you'd find. But oh, Katinka, I just can't thank you enough. You've given me back a slice of myself, my identity." Now that those violet eyes were open again, Katinka saw how hard Roza was fighting not to break down.

"Do you want me to go on?" Katinka realized she very badly wanted to find out what had happened to the rest of Roza's family, especially Carlo, but she felt guilty too. Was she becoming addicted to the drama of someone else's tragedy?

"Yes—and here's the cash for the KGB," said Pasha Getman, coming around the desk to embrace her. He handed her an envelope. "I knew I'd hired the right person." Katinka caught Roza's eye as he said this, and they exchanged a conspiratorial smile. "But now, go and find the other Palitsyns. If any of them are alive . . ."

Katinka felt very nervous about carrying the money in her handbag. She had never held so much and was sure it would be stolen, or she would drop it. She was relieved when she entered the Café-Bar Piano near the Patriarchy Ponds to meet the two KGBsti, the Marmoset and the Magician.

She played with the thick envelope for a minute, then opened it in front of them to show the U.S. greenbacks.

"For this much cash, we'd like the files fast. You said tomorrow, didn't you?"

"It's all there?" asked the shiny-cheeked Marmoset, eyeing the envelope.

"Yes, against my advice," said Katinka, "Mr. Getman insisted on paying."

"All in Abraham Lincolns?" asked the Magician.

"I have no idea," she said, disdainful of this gangster jargon.

"An angel of the north Caucasus! You'll learn the way things work!" The Magician laughed and stroked his coarse gingery hair. As she pushed the envelope across the table, he slapped his hand onto hers. "Beautiful, girl. Beautiful, like you."

Katinka removed her hand quickly, and shuddered.

"Tomorrow, in my office, you'll have the files on Sashenka and Vanya as well as Mendel and Golden," promised the Marmoset. "Everything we have."

Katinka stood up but the Magician took her hand again in a clammy grip.

"Hey, girl, wait, what's the hurry? Please tell Mr. Getman we hope this is the start of a relationship. And for you as a historian. We have some espionage materials about the Cold War period that would interest the Western media and publishers. Now you know Londongrad, you flew there. We would share a commission with you if you could interest newspapers or publishers in London . . ."

"I'll tell Mr. Getman."

"A little taste of a malt whiskey much favored by the royal families of Europe? It's Glenfiddich, a famous name," suggested the Magician. "A toast to our English historical partnership?"

"I'm late," answered Katinka, longing to be away from these disgusting hucksters, the successors of the Chekists who had arrested Sashenka and Vanya.

She fled outside. Spring in Moscow seethed with the tang of new life, and the ponds were surrounded by cherry blossom and new growth. She bought an ice cream and sat admiring the daffodils growing under the trees and the majestic swans on the pond with their grey-feathered cygnets.

At the pay phone, she called Satinov.

Mariko answered. "My father is ill. He fell. He also has respiratory problems."

"But I've got a lot to tell him. I've found Snowy, and Lala Lewis who told me what a hero he'd been to help those children—"

"You've talked enough to him already. No more calls."

And Mariko slammed down the phone.

16

Sitting of Military Tribunal, office of the Narkom L. P. Beria, at Special Object 110 [Sukhanovka Prison, Beria's special jail in the former St. Catherine's Nunnery at Vidnoe, outskirts of Moscow] *3:00 a.m. 21 January 1940*

Chairman of the Military Tribunal V. S. Ulrikh: Accused Palitysn, have you read the indictment? You understand the charges?

Palitsyn: Yes, I, Vanya Palitsyn, understand the charges.

Ulrikh: Do you object to any of the judges?

Palitsyn: No.

Ulrikh: Do you admit your guilt?

Palitsyn: Yes.

Ulrikh: Did you not meet with Mendel Barmakid and your wife Sashenka Zeitlin to plot the assassination of Comrade Stalin and the Politburo?

Palitsyn: My wife was never involved in this conspiracy.

Ulrikh: Come now, Accused Palitsyn, we have before us your full signed confession that states how you and said accused Sashenka Zeitlin . . .

Palitsyn: If the Party wants . . .

Ulrikh: The Party demands the truth. Stop playing games with us now. Speak up.

Palitsyn: Long live the Party. I have been a dedicated and devoted Bolshevik since the age of sixteen. I have never betrayed the Party. I have served Comrade Stalin and the Party with absolute fervor all my adult life. So has my wife, Sashenka. However, if the Party demands it . . .

Ulrikh: The Party demands: do you confess your guilt to all charges?

Palitysn: I do.

Ulrikh: Do you wish to add anything else, Accused Palitsyn?

Palitsyn: I remain in my heart devoted to the Communist Party and Comrade Stalin personally: I have committed grave sins and crimes. If I face the Supreme Measure of Punishment, I shall gladly die a Bolshevik with the name Stalin reverently on my lips. Long live the Party! Long live Stalin!

Ulrikh: Then let the judges retire.

3:22 a.m. The judges return.

Ulrikh: In the name of the Union of Soviet Socialist Republics, the Military Tribunal of the Supreme Court has examined the case and established that Ivan Palitsyn was a member of an anti-Soviet Trotskyite group, connected to Okhrana double agents and White Guardists, and controlled by the Japanese and French secret services, linked to his wife Alexandra "Sashenka" Zeitlin-Palitsyn (known in Party circles as Comrade Snowfox), Mendel Barmakid (known in Party circles as Comrade Furnace) and the writer Beniamin Golden. Having found Accused Palitsyn guilty of all said offenses under Article 58, the Tribunal sentences him to the Highest Measure of Punishment, to be shot. The verdict is final and to be effected without delay . . .

Katinka was sitting at the T-shaped desk in the Marmoset's office at the Lubianka, reading the transcript of Vanya's trial and the originals of his confessions. The Marmoset buffed his nails and read his Manchester United fanzine—but Katinka, her flesh creeping, could hear only the brutal verdict of the judge. Vanya Palitsyn was no longer a historical character to her. He was Roza's father—and somehow she was going to have to tell her that he'd died so terribly. She was just searching through the papers for a certificate of execution when the door opened and the archives rat, Kuzma, hobbled into the room, pushing his cart with its cats frolicking together on the lower tray.

"Collecting files, Colonel," murmured Kuzma in his white coat, placing some *papki* on his cart and sorting them into piles.

Katinka returned to Palitsyn's interrogations: he confessed to the crimes specified by Captain Sagan, whose confessions were also stowed in his file. But here was something odd: the confessions, signed by "Vanya Palitsyn" on the top right-hand corner of each page, were filthy, as if they had been splashed in a muddy winter puddle. Had the interrogator spilled his coffee? Only while she was turning the pages did she realize that this muddy spray was surely the spatter of blood. She raised the paper to her face, sniffed it and thought that she could divine the telltale copperiness . . . Katinka felt disgust for the Marmoset, and for this evil place.

"Excuse me, Colonel," said Katinka, her head full of Roza's family and their sufferings. "There's no death certificate in Palitsyn's file. What happened to it?"

"That's all there is," said the colonel.

"Was Vanya Palitsyn executed?"

"If it's in the file, yes; if it's not, no."

"I saw Mouche Zeitlin yesterday. She said that the KGB sentenced Sashenka to 'ten years without rights of correspondence.' What did that mean?"

"It means she couldn't receive or send letters or packages."

"So she could be alive?"

"Sure."

"But these files are empty. There's so much missing!"

The Marmoset shrugged and his nonchalance infuriated her.

"I thought we had a deal." Katinka was aware she was almost shouting. They both glanced at Kuzma, who was edging slowly toward the door in his stiff, cadaverous gait.

"I'm not an alchemist," said the Marmoset testily.

Now she understood what Maxy had told her: archives start out as sheets of crushed tree pulp but they come to life, they assume the grit of existence, they sing of life and death. Sometimes they are all that is left of families, and then they metamorphose. The stamps, signatures and instructions on scuffed, stained scraps of curling yellow paper can convey something approaching life, even sometimes love.

The Marmoset came round the table and pulled a chit from the back of the file: *Send files of Palitsyn case to Central Committee.*

"What does that mean?" she asked him.

"It means it's not in this file. It's in another one, and it's not here. And that is not my problem."

Just then Kuzma unleashed a jet of gob into his KGB spittoon.

"Comrade Kuzma, how good to see you," she said, jumping up. The fat marmalade cat sat on the cart licking the scrawny kitten. "How are Utesov and Tseferman, our jazz cats?"

This time, Kuzma opened a toothless mouth and emitted a high-pitched yelp of pleasure. "Ha!"

"I brought them something. I hope they like it," Katinka said, taking a bottle of milk and a tin of cat food out of her handbag.

Kuzma seized both these objects as if he were in a hurry, snorting loudly and muttering to himself. He produced a brown saucer from his cart and poured out milk for the cats, who immediately started to lap it up with pink tongues. When he spat enthusiastically in a high green arc, Katinka realized that the gobbing was the weathervane of his mood.

The Marmoset sneered at her and shook his head, but Katinka ignored him, smiled at Kuzma instead, and then returned to the next file as the cats purred in the background.

Investigation File June 1939
Case 161375
Mendel Barmakid (Comrade Furnace)

Sashenka's uncle; Roza's great-uncle; comrade of Lenin and Stalin, the so-called Conscience of the Party—but the file contained just one piece of paper.

To Narkom L. P. Beria, Commissar-General, State Security, first degree
From: Deputy Narkom B. Kobylov, Commissar-General, State Security, second degree
12 October 1939
Accused Mendel Barmakid died today 3:00 a.m. NKVD Dr. Medvedev examined prisoner and certified death by cardiac arrest. Medical report attached.

So Mendel died of natural causes. At least she had discovered the fate of one of the family.

"Put the papers down," ordered the Marmoset.

"But I haven't gotten to Sashenka's file!"

"Two more minutes."

"We paid for these files," she whispered vehemently at him.

"I don't know what you mean," he replied. "Two minutes."

"You've wasted my time. You broke your word!"

"One minute fifty seconds."

Katinka could barely stand this filthy place where those dear to her employer had suffered grievous sorrow. She wanted to weep, but not under the eyes of the Marmoset. She turned to Sashenka's file, which contained a single sheet of paper that "read *Please find enclosed the confession of Accused Zeitlin-Palitsyn (167 pages)*. But it was not in there. Just a note: *Send files of Zeitlin-Palitsyn case to Central Committee.*

She cursed herself for her rudeness to the Marmoset. "Sashenka's confession is missing: please may I have it?"

"You insult me and through me the Soviet Union and the Competent Organs!" He pointed at the white bust of Felix Dzerzhinsky. "You insult Iron Felix!"

"Please! I apologize!"

"I'll report all this to my superior, General Fursenko, but it is unlikely to be permitted."

"In that case," said Katinka, emboldened by the courage of those who had been in far greater peril than she, "I doubt very much Mr. Getman will be interested in helping you sell your spy secrets to the newspapers abroad."

The Marmoset stared at her, sucked in his cheeks, then crossly got up and opened the door. "Fuck off, you little bitch! Your sort have had their day! You blame everything on us, but America's done more damage to Russia in a few years than Stalin did in decades! And your oligarch can go fuck his mother. You're finished in here—get out!"

Katinka stood up, gathered her notebook and handbag and, trying to maintain some dignity, walked out slowly right past Kuzma, who stood outside collating some files on his cart. She was crying: she had spoiled everything with her own foolish temper.

Now she would never discover what happened to Sashenka, never find Carlo. She felt faint. It was hopeless.

17

"You again?" said Mariko sourly. "What did I tell you? Don't call."

"But Mariko, please! Just listen one second," beseeched Katinka, the desperation audible in her voice. "I'm calling from the public phone outside the Lubianka! I've been to see Lala in Tbilisi. Just listen one second. I want to thank Marshal Satinov. I've learned how your father saved those children, Snowy and Carlo, how he risked his life. They want to thank him."

A silence. She could hear Mariko breathing.

"My father's very sick. I'll tell him. Don't call again!"

"But please . . ."

The line was dead. Groaning in frustration, she called Maxy at the Redemption office.

"There you are!" he greeted her affably. "Our sort of research isn't easy—this happens to me all the time. Don't lose heart. I've got an idea. Meet me at the feet of the poet—Pushkin Square."

Katinka waved down a Lada car, handing the driver two dollars. She reached the Pushkin statue first. It was a dazzling spring day, the sky metallic blue, the breeze biting, the sunlight raw. In the gasoline fumes and lilac scent, girls were waiting for their lovers beneath the poet, bespectacled students read their notes on the benches, guides in polyester suits lectured American tourists, limousines for German bankers and Russian wheeler-dealers drew up at the Pushkin Restaurant. *My verses will be sung throughout all Russia's vastness*, Katinka read on the monument. *My ashes will outlive and know no pale decay.* Pushkin consoled her, calmed her.

A motorbike scooted up onto the pavement. Maxy pulled off his Viking helmet, holding it by the horns, and kissed her in his overfamiliar way.

"You look flustered," he said, taking her hand. "Let's sit in the sun and you can tell me everything."

Once seated, Katinka told him about her visit to Tbilisi, her night with Lala, her discovery that Roza Getman was Sashenka's daughter—and her more recent encounter with the KGB.

"You've done so well," Maxy told her. "I'm impressed! But let me interpret some of this for you. Mouche Zeitlin says the KGB told her Sashenka was sentenced to 'ten years without rights of correspondence.' Usually that was a euphemism for execution."

Katinka caught her breath. "But what about the ex-prisoner who'd seen Sashenka in the camps in the fifties?"

"The KGB liked to trick people that way. The KGB files say Mendel died of 'cardiac arrest.' That was another euphemism. It means he died under interrogation: he was beaten to death."

"So these files have their own language?" she said.

"I'm afraid so," he said. "There was a terrible randomness in the Terror, but at the same time there were no coincidences in that world: everything was linked by invisible threads. We just need to find them. *Send files of Palitsyn case to Central Committee*," he repeated. "I know what that means. Come with me. Climb on."

Katinka joined him on the back of his bike, pulling her denim skirt down over her thighs. The engine revved raucously and Maxy weaved in and out of the unruly Moscow traffic, down Tverskaya until he took a sharp left at the statue of Prince Dolgoruky, founder of Moscow, and went down a steep hill. The wind blew in Katinka's hair and she closed her eyes, allowing the rich spring air to refresh her.

They stopped alongside a Brezhnevite concrete box with a shabby glass front, a dark frieze of Marx, Engels and Lenin over the revolving door.

Maxy scissored off the bike in his leathers and tugged off his helmet, pushing back his hair. She thought him more seventies heavy-metal singer than historian. He strode ahead into a marble hall and Katinka followed him, almost running. In the grey foyer, women behind tables sold Bon Jovi CDs, hats and gloves, like a flea market, but at the back, where the entrance to the elevators was guarded by two pimply teenage soldiers, stood a white Lenin bust. Maxy showed his card and they checked Katinka's passport, kept it and gave her a chit.

Maxy led her up the steps, past a canteen with its moldy cabbage-soup fug and into an elevator, which chugged to the top of the building. Before she could take in her surroundings, he was leading her into the glass-walled reading room with its circular panorama of the roofs of Moscow.

"No time to admire the view," he whispered as disapproving old Communists looked up crossly from their studies. Maxy's leathers creaked loudly in the hushed room. "I've got a little place for us here." They sat in a cul-de-sac formed by towering bookshelves. "Wait here," he said. She listened to the rasp of his biking gear with a smile. Moments later, he returned with a pile of brown *papki* files and sat very close to her. He radiated a blend of leathers, coffee, bike oil and lemon cologne.

"This place," he whispered, "is the Party archive. You see these *papki*, numbered five hundred fifty-eight? Stalin's own archive. It's still officially closed and I don't think it'll ever open." He flipped the first files toward him. "I was looking at these earlier and I noticed Satinov's name. When it said your files were sent to the Central Committee, that meant to Stalin himself. This is Stalin's miscellaneous correspondence. Go ahead, Katinka, look under *S* for Satinov."

She opened the file and found a cover note, stamped by Poskrebyshev at 9:00 p.m. on May 6, 1939:

> *To J. V. Stalin*
> *Top Secret. It has come to my notice that Ivan "Vanya" Palitsyn ordered surveillance of his wife, Party member Alexandra "Sashenka" Zeitlin-Palitsyn, without the knowledge of Narkom NKVD or Politburo.*
> *Signed: L. P. Beria, Commissar-General, State Security, first degree, Narkom NKVD*

"You see," explained Maxy, "Beria had discovered that Palitsyn was bugging his wife."

"How did he find out?"

"Probably by a tiny bureaucratic mistake. Wiretaps were always copied to Beria, who decided which to send on to Stalin. Palitsyn, foolish with jealousy, had ordered that the transcripts of his wiretap be shown only to him. Remember how he wrote *no copies*? Probably his secretary forgot this, as secretaries do—and sent it by mistake to Beria, who, by the rules of the time, had to report this abuse of government resources to Stalin himself. Beria had no malice toward the Palitsyns and he knew that, after the May Day party, Stalin took a paternal interest in Sashenka. That's why his note"—Maxy tapped the cover note—"is neutral. Stalin was often tolerant or even amused by steamy private gossip—unless he felt he had somehow been misled."

"But then he read the transcripts?"

To: Comrade Ivan Palitsyn, Commissar-General, State Security, third degree
As requested, surveillance and transcript on Alexandra "Sashenka" Zeitlin-Palitsyn, room 403, Metropole Hotel, 6 May 1939
Midday: Zeitlin-Palitsyn left office on Petrovka and walked to Metropole, took elevator to room 403. Writer Benya Golden entered the room fifteen minutes past midday, leaving separately at 3:30 p.m. Snacks and wine were delivered to the room.

Katinka turned the pages and found a place marked with a red crayon:

Golden: God, I love you. You're so lovely to me, Sashenka.

Zeitlin-Palitsyn: I can't believe I'm here.

Golden: What, darling? Didn't I please you enough last time? Until you called my name?

Zeitlin-Palitsyn: How could I forget it? I think I imagined the whole thing. I think you've made me delusional.

Golden: Come here. Unbutton me. That's paradise. Get on your hands and knees on the bed and let me unwrap the present. Oh my God, what a delicious sight. What a sweet [word deleted]. *How* [word deleted] *you are. If only your tight-assed Communist wives' committee could see you now . . .*

Katinka was peeping into an intimate pocket of time, a vanished wrinkle of private passion, in a cruel world, long ago. Her eyes were drawn to the words underlined by three harsh thick crayon marks.

Zeitlin-Palitsyn: Oh my God, Benya, I love your [word indecipherable], *I can't believe you got me to do that, I thought I might die of pleasure . . .*

"That red crayon there, the underlining, is Stalin himself," said Maxy, pulling a fat oilskinned notebook out of his stack of files. "This is Poskrebyshev's list of visitors to Stalin's office here on Trinity Square in the Kremlin—known to the cognoscenti as the Little Corner." He opened it. Poskrebyshev's tiny, immaculate handwriting listed names, dates, times. "Look up May seventh, evening."

Katinka read the page:

10:00 p.m. L. P. Beria.
Leaves 10:30 p.m.
10:30 p.m. H. A. Satinov.
Leaves 10:45 p.m.
10:40 p.m. L. P. Beria.
Leaves 10:52 p.m.

"So Satinov was there soon after Beria showed Stalin the transcripts. Why?"

"Beria comes to see the Master and gives him the transcripts. Stalin reads this hot stuff, red crayon in hand. He orders Poskrebyshev to summon Satinov, who's at Old Square, Party headquarters, up the hill. The *vertushka* telephone rings on Satinov's desk. Poskrebyshev says, 'Comrade Satinov, Comrade Stalin awaits you now. A Buick will collect you.' Stalin's already appalled by what Sashenka and Benya have done." Maxy read Stalin's note to Beria:

I misjudged this morally corrupt woman. I thought she was a decent Soviet woman. She teaches Soviet women how to be housewives. She's the wife of a top Chekist. Who knows what secrets she chatters about? She behaves like a streetwalker. Comrade Beria, perhaps we should check her out. J. St.

"You know what 'checking out' means?" asked Maxy. "It means arrest them. You see how, in a few accidental steps, this reached Stalin?"

Katinka shook her head, her heart pounding in sympathy. If it hadn't been for Stalin's visit, if it hadn't been for Sashenka's affair, if it hadn't been for Vanya's jealousy . . .

"Isn't there anything else in the file?" she asked.

Maxy sighed. "No, not in this archive. But the Russian State Archive of Special Secret Political-Administrative Documents off Mayakovsky Square is filled with Stalin's papers and somewhere in there, one day, future generations may find out what happened, if they care. But it's closed. These are all the records we can read. Oh, except for one small thing." He picked up Stalin's note again and pointed to the top right-hand corner, where, in small letters, his red crayon had written these words: *Bicho to curate.*

"What does that mean?" Katinka asked.

"I thought I knew everything about the Stalin era," said Maxy, "but for once I can't work it out."

Katinka swayed with exhaustion and sadness. "I don't think I'll ever find Sashenka or little Carlo," she whispered. "Poor Roza, how am I going to tell her?"

18

Outside the archive, the streets were already dark. Still shocked by what they'd found, Maxy and Katinka parted awkwardly like two teenagers after an unsatisfactory date. As Maxy rode away, Katinka walked slowly up the dark hill toward the glitzy neon lights of Tverskaya just beyond Prince Dolgoruky's statue. Slowing to adjust the way her bag was hanging over her shoulder, she became aware that someone was walking much too close to her.

She quickened her step but so did the shadow. She slowed to let him overtake but he slowed too. She was suddenly frightened: was it the KGB? Or a Chechen mugger? Then the figure gathered up a wad of phlegm in his mouth and launched it in a phosphorescent, light-catching arc toward the gutter.

"Kuzma!" she gasped. "What are you—"

Without a word he pulled her aside, behind the statue, where there was no one around. He was holding a big canvas bag, which he opened to reveal the marmalade jazz cat and its kitten. "Cozy!" he blurted out in his queer, unbroken voice.

"Very cozy," Katinka said, still concerned. What did he have in mind for her?

Kuzma reached into the cat bag and pulled out an old-fashioned yellow envelope, closed with red string, which he shoved into her hands, glancing around as he did so with comical vigilance—even though she knew this was no joke. He was risking his life.

"For you," he muttered.

"But what is it?"

"You read it, you see!" Peering around again, he started to move away from her up toward Tverskaya.

"Kuzma! Wait! I want to thank you properly!" Kuzma shrank from her like a vampire before holy water but she grabbed his wrist. "One question. When it says 'the Central Committee asked for the files,' where are they now? Can I see them?"

Kuzma walked back, and stood so close his unshaven muzzle pricked her ear. He pointed into the earth, into the cellars, the dungeons, the graves, and only a hiss came out of him.

"So how will I ever know what happened?"

Kuzma shrugged but then he pointed up the hill. "Better to sing well as a goldfinch than badly as a nightingale." And then he marched stiffly away, disappearing into the blurred greyness of Tverskaya's rush-hour crowds.

The envelope burned her hands. Katinka could hardly restrain herself from opening it but she tried to stay calm. She glanced around to see if she was being followed but decided that if the KGB wanted to follow her she would never know about it anyway.

She couldn't wait to reach her hotel room so she crossed the road to the sleazy foyer of the Intourist Hotel, a hideous seventies construction of glass and concrete. Its ceiling, made up of what appeared to be white polystyrene squares, was low; its floor was a faded, frayed burgundy "carpet" and the security staff at its brown, padded-vinyl desk were aggressive, lantern-jawed Soviet "bulls."

But the place seethed like a souk. One-armed bandits rumbled and whirred, and garish whores sat about on orange sofas. As one of the security thugs approached her, Katinka pointed at the whores and he shrugged: he'd collect his share later. Sitting on a foam sofa next to two booted, stockinged girls with bare, bruised white thighs, she offered them both a cigarette. Each of them grabbed one: the first put it in her handbag, the other in her stocking top.

Katinka lit up her own, inhaled and then tore open the envelope. Inside were a few trinkets and a wad of photocopied documents. The first was dated May 1953, two months after Stalin's death:

To all case officers: Palitsyn/Zeitlin Case
For security reasons, relatives enquiring about sentences of above-mentioned state criminals are to be informed that the prisoners were resentenced after a ten-year term in Gulags.
Signed: I. V. Serov, Chairman, State Security Committee (KGB)

Anger and confusion coursed through Katinka, followed by a sinking sadness. Everything she had so far learned from Mouche and the KGB archives was a callous lie. She must have paled because one of the prostitutes leaned over and asked gently: "Your test results, love? Bad news?"

"Something like that," said Katinka, her forehead prickly with sweat.

"Tough, tough, but we survive," said the prostitute, lighting up and turning back to her friend.

Katinka looked again at the typed pages.

Sitting of Military Tribunal, office of the Narkom L. P. Beria, at Special Object 110, 2:30 a.m. 22 January 1940. Trial of Accused Alexandra "Sashenka" Zeitlin-Palitsyn (Comrade Snowfox).

Chairman of the Military Tribunal of the Supreme Court Vasily Ulrikh presiding in person.

Katinka leafed to the end, looking for the sentencing—but there was that maddening note again: *Send documents on Palitsyn case to Central Committee.*

Then she started to read Sashenka's trial notes—and what she read shocked her so deeply that she stuffed the papers back in the envelope and ran out of the hotel into the street, turning right and heading down the hill toward the Kremlin, its eight red stars glowing high above her through the hazy rhapsody of a spring night.

"You've gone too far this time!" said Mariko, barely raising her voice, which made the implied threat all the more powerful.

Marshal Satinov sat in his high chair in the elegant, breezy sitting room with an oxygen mask held onto his face by elastic and a large oxygen cylinder on wheels beside him. He appeared to have shrunk in just a few days, and his blinking eyes followed Katinka's every move.

"Please, let me talk to your father for one minute," said Katinka, breathless and flushed with running. "I've so much to tell him and he himself asked me to let him know what I found . . ."

She fixed her eyes, imploringly, onto Satinov's sharp orbs with their half-closed lids. At first they showed nothing. But then they seemed to twinkle and the old man wrenched off his oxygen mask. "Oh Mariko, stop fussing." He spoke with difficulty. "Bring us tea." Mariko sighed loudly and stomped out. "How did you get in, girl?"

"Someone let me in through the street door and then I found your door ajar."

Satinov absorbed this. "Fate, that's what it is. Don't forget that's why you're here." He gave a skull-like smile.

Katinka sat down on the sofa near him and he opened his wizened hands as if to say Go on then, girl, give it to me.

"I found Snowy." He nodded appreciatively. "Lala Lewis told me everything. You were a hero. You saved the children. Snowy wants to meet you to say thank you."

He shook his head and waved his hand. "Too late," he rasped. "Have you found her brother too?"

"Not yet. I'm still trying to work out what happened to Sashenka."

"Leave them. Concentrate on Carlo! The children, the future . . ."

"Sashenka and Vanya were your best friends, weren't they?"

"Sashenka was . . . there was no one like her—and the children . . ." His blue eyes softened and for a moment Katinka thought she saw tears. She made herself go on.

"That was why Stalin summoned you to the Little Corner when he read the transcript of Benya and Sashenka. He was aware you'd known them since Petersburg and that you were Roza's godfather. He'd seen you all together at the May Day party. Did he want to find out what you knew about them?"

Satinov blinked and said nothing.

"Beria left and you arrived at ten thirty p.m.—I've seen Stalin's appointment book. But then what happened? Sashenka had had an affair. Vanya was jealous and bugged their hotel room. How did that grow into Captain Sagan's conspiracy and the destruction of an entire family?"

"I don't know," whispered Satinov.

"Why did Stalin request all the files on the case?" She glared at him. Cold bloodshot eyes looked back. "You're not going to answer that either? How can you pretend you don't know what happened?"

"Just find Carlo," Satinov wheezed. "You must be so close."

"And what did Stalin mean when he wrote *Bicho to curate*?"

There was a long pause during which Satinov breathed painfully. "Read my memoirs carefully," he said at last.

"Believe it or not, I've read every word of your interminable speeches on peaceful coexistence and your heroic role in forging the socialist Motherland and there's not a word of humanity in it." His eyes were fixed on her but she didn't stop. "You've lied to me again and again. The KGB has concealed its crimes but today I got hold of the transcript of Sashenka's trial. You were at the trial of your best friend!"

His breathing creaked.

"Take a look," she said, pulling out the first page of the trial.

"I haven't got my glasses."

"Well, let me help you then. Here, look at this. It's you, Marshal Satinov! You didn't just attend the trial," she was almost yelling at him, "you were a judge."

"Read my judgment," he gasped.

"You sat there in judgment on your best friend, the mother of your godchild. Sashenka found *you* at the trial. What did she think when she saw you? What went through her mind? I thought you were a hero. You saved Snowy and Carlo yet you presided over Sashenka's destruction! Was she sentenced to death? Or did she die in the Gulags? Tell me, tell me! You owe it to her children!"

Satinov's face tightened as his breathing constricted and his mouth gaped open.

To her shame, Katinka fought back her own tears. "How could you have done such a thing? How could you?"

"What's going on in here?" Mariko appeared in the doorway, holding a tea tray. "What is it, Papa?"

As Katinka left the room, she looked back at the old man. The oxygen mask was on his face, his lips were blue, a wiry arm was raised—and a gnarled finger pointed toward the door.

19

Judge Ulrikh: Sashenka Zeitlin-Palitsyn, you have confessed to a remarkable conspiracy to kill our heroic leaders, Comrade Stalin and the Politburo, at your own house. We have read your confession. Do you have anything more to say?

Accused Zeitlin-Palitsyn: I plotted to kill the great Stalin at my house. I rubbed arsenic and cyanide powder onto the curtain's of the room where Comrade Stalin would stand.

Judge Ulrikh: And the gramophone?

Accused Zeitlin-Palitsyn: Yes, on the gramophone too. I had heard from various comrades, including my husband Vanya, that Comrade Stalin liked to listen to music after dinner so I dusted the gramophone with cyanide dust.

Judge Satinov: Accused Zeitlin-Palitsyn, we need more details . . .

Satinov was speaking for the first time at the trial. Katinka could almost hear the voices of these flint-hearted men in the pine-paneled office in the Sukhanovka Prison, lit up in a bright electric glare in the middle of the night. NKVD guards in blue stood armed at the doors. Ulrikh, with his bullet-like bald head, sat behind the desk with Satinov and the other judge, all in their Stalinka tunics and gleaming boots.

As soon as she had left that disastrous meeting with Satinov, Katinka had called Maxy, repeating what had been said word for word, trying to disguise her tears. But Maxy was encouraging. Satinov had told her to read his judgment, so she must read it right away. Satinov had told her to read his memoirs—and that must mean something too. Maxy proposed that they meet at midday the next day at the closed Archive for Special Secret Political-Administrative Documents, through the archway off Mayakovsky Square.

Now it was the middle of the night and Katinka was reading the trial in her seedy room at the Moskva Hotel. She poured herself a shot of vodka—for courage and to overcome her exhaustion. Through her little window, the red stars of the Kremlin glowed.

Judge Satinov: How did you procure this cyanide? Tell the Tribunal!

Katinka imagined Sashenka standing at the end of the T-shaped table, pale, thin, battered but still beautiful. But what must she have thought as she was tried for her life and found Hercules Satinov on the Tribunal right there in front of her? She must have struggled to show no emotion, not even a flicker of recognition—everyone would be watching for her reaction and his. But imagine her surprise, her shock—and her overriding concern: are the children safe? Or does Satinov's presence mean that the children . . .

Accused Zeitlin-Palitsyn: I will, Comrade Judge. Vanya procured it from the the NKVD Laboratory.

Judge Satinov: How did you know which records to poison?

Accused Zeitlin-Palitsyn: I knew Comrade Stalin enjoys Georgian folk music, the songs from the movies Volga, Volga *and* Jolly Fellows, *and the arias of Glinka and Tchaikovsky. So I poisoned those.*

Judge Satinov: You were serving the Japanese Emperor, the Polish landowners and the British lords in conspiracy with Trotsky?

Katinka's skin crawled as she pictured what was going through Sashenka's mind: Snowy and Carlo—where are you?

Accused Zeitlin-Palitsyn: Yes, Trotsky ordered the assassination in diabolical compact with the Japanese Emperor and the British lords.

Judge Satinov: And the network of the White Guard, Captain Sagan, who controlled you on Trotsky's behalf, forcing you to use the methods he had taught you as a young girl?

Accused Zeitlin-Palitsyn: You mean the sexual depravity? Yes, and I used that to recruit further agents such as the writer Benya Golden.

Judge Satinov: Did the writer Golden become an agent?

Accused Zeitlin-Palitsyn: I tried to recruit him using the wiles taught me by Captain Sagan but—as I must tell the truth before the Party—Golden was a dilettante non-Party philistine who lacked vigilance but he never joined the conspiracy. He regarded it as "play-acting."

Judge Ulrikh: You're amending your confession?

Accused Zeitlin-Palitsyn: I have to tell the truth before Comrade Stalin and the Party. I am myself guilty; my husband and Captain Sagan are guilty but Golden was a child incapable of conspiracy.

Katinka could not help but smile at this. Now she knew that Sashenka had truly loved Benya Golden too. Wasn't this insult to Golden more romantic than any love song?

Judge Satinov: Comrade Judges, I'm almost overcome with disgust at the evil and depravity of this serpent woman, this black widow spider. Are we ready to consider the case?

Katinka fought back tears as she read this tragic-comic exchange. Did Satinov mean this? Did Sashenka believe he meant it? Sashenka must have looked at her friend, sending him message after message: are the children settled? Are they safe? Or have you betrayed us? A mother's questions. Katinka lit a cigarette and read on.

Accused Zeitlin-Palitsyn: I must declare before the court that my greatest regret and shame are the crimes I've committed before the Party and that the future . . . posterity . . . will remember me as a scoundrel.

Posterity? Was this a message to Satinov?

Judge Ulrikh (presiding): All right, are we Comrade Judges ready? Any comment?

Judge Lansky (second judge): What wickedness. No other comment.

Judge Ulrikh: Comrade Satinov?

Judge Satinov (third judge): Accused Zeitlin-Palitsyn confesses to shocking crimes in a lifetime of deception and mask wearing. I must ask the court to forgive me for saying that, due to the vigilance of the NKVD investigation, we the Soviet people are grateful that our brilliant Leader of the Peoples, Comrade Stalin, is safe, that his loyal comrades Molotov, Voroshilov, Mikoyan, Andreyev and other Politburo members are now safe finally from spies, traitors and Trotskyites, safe in their offices and homes from this poisoning viper in their midst. They are now safe, quite safe. There is only one possible punishment, the way we treat mad, rabid dogs, the justice of the people . . . Thank you, Comrade Ulrikh.

Katinka could scarcely breathe. She read it again, and then again, and it was unmistakable: the sign. Satinov said 'safe,' and then repeated it four times in all. Two 'safe's for Snowy, two 'safe's for Carlo. So Satinov had not betrayed Sashenka. Instead he was really saying, "Dear friend, die easy if you can, *the children are safe! I repeat, the children are safe!*"

What relief for Sashenka. Yet the judgment was missing: did she survive after all? There it was, just the same note—*Papers sent to Central Committee.*

Dawn was coming up over Moscow, as Katinka's head fell forward onto the transcripts that still rested on her knee.

Judge Ulrikh: Thank you, Comrade Satinov, let us retire to make our judgment.

Judges retire.

20

An upstart sun in an eggshell-blue sky threw golden beams onto Mayakovsky's statue. Katinka walked up Tverskaya, first passing the statue of Prince Dolgoruky on one side and then Pushkin on the other, toward the new archive. She had woken up too early and with a crick in her neck when Maxy had phoned, then gone back to sleep. But she still ached as if she had been pummeled and only a bracing double espresso at the Coffee Bean café on Tverskaya—good coffee was one of the benefits of democracy, she thought—had restored some of her spirits.

Carrying a bulky package under her arm, she passed Mayakovsky Metro and took a left through one of those red granite archways that help give Moscow its somber and hostile grandeur. She found herself on a tiny road that seemed to be a cul-de-sac, but just when she could go no farther it turned sharply once and then again, becoming narrower. Katinka relished this unlikely, meandering lane in the midst of the unforgiving metropolis, as if she were discovering a jumbled village behind the granite walls and ramparts of those roaring boulevards. After the second twist, she came upon an ocher wall with a white top and then a black steel gate, which was open and led to some steps. Maxy's bike was parked next to a plaque engraved with Lenin's domed profile.

"You look tired—did you get any sleep? You procured what I suggested?" he asked.

Katinka nodded at her package. "It was the most expensive stuff I've ever bought and I had to ask Pasha Getman for permission."

"Three hundred dollars is nothing to him. Did you tell him what it was?"

"I thought it better not to."

"Well, it's our only hope. This woman will do *anything* for that." Then Maxy took her hand. "I fear you're becoming even more obsessed than me about the secret lives of fifty years ago. Are you ready?"

"Yes, but how are you getting us in? I thought you said—"

"Don't worry, I've organized it all. Now remember," he continued, straight-faced, "I booked you an appointment to apply to make an application to apply to peruse the list of documents held in this archive, and I can now inform you that our application to make an application will of course be refused. Go on in, Katinka. Good luck."

"I feel uneasy about this. Will it work or will I get arrested?"

"One or the other." He laughed. "Just think, two weeks ago you'd never have tried such a stunt. But be confident. Look as if you know where you're going and you're entitled to get what you want. I'll see you later."

She watched him kick-start the bike and saw the horned helmet disappear into the hidden lanes before she turned to enter the high Gothic slab with pillars and balconies embellished by heroes carved in stone and bronze.

At the wooden desk, the two teenaged Interior Ministry soldiers half dozed in their battered chairs but sat up at the sight of Katinka. The pimplier of the two conscripts slid the signing-in book along the desk, examined her passport with a sneer intended to project the power invested in him by the Russian state, checked a collage of yellow chits on his desk and found one bearing her name, wrote out another chit on a further badly printed scrap and then with the hint of a virile smirk handed back the paper, keeping the passport, and gestured grandly toward the elevators in the white marble hall behind him. "Application for archives, fourth floor."

She scarcely dared look back but sensed a presence. A skinny young man with a bald head, yellow vinyl shoes, and a grey parka was hanging up his coat in the cloakroom and watching her intently. A strange crew, these archive rats, Katinka thought, as she hurried on and entered the elevator. As its doors were about to close, a hand held them back and the archive rat came in, nodding at her nervously but saying nothing. He was pulling on his archivist's stained yellow coat, like a laboratory assistant, his red-rimmed eyes magnified and eager through his smeared spectacles.

The elevator was small and they stood so awkwardly close that the archive rat kept trying to apologize but never quite managed it, as each of his attempts at conversation ended in him starting to hum. Katinka flattened herself against the wall, horribly close to the pasty dome of his head with its sparse colorless hairs, livid blotches and beads of sweat. She pressed the bell for the fifth floor but he pressed the fourth and when the quivering elevator jolted to a halt, the doors opened and he got out, holding them open.

"Your floor." He wasn't asking, he was telling her. "Applications."

But Katinka shook her head twice. The rat looked surprised and remained standing there quizzically as the doors closed. Katinka cringed, knowing she'd been found out because, as Maxy had explained, "outside applicants are not permitted to visit the fifth floor."

The elevator opened on a landing with misted glass doors, some shabby plastic palms and a grand portrait frame—with no picture inside it. *Directorate of the Study of Dialectical Materialism and Leninist Economic-Political Historical Questions of the Soviet Union* read the plaque, to which someone had taped a note: *The Russian State Archive of Special Secret Political-Administrative Documents.*

"It would be best if you didn't meet anyone up there," Maxy had told her—so she expected the archive rat to jump out at her with the pimpled teenaged guards at any moment.

The long parquet corridors with lines of closed pine doors were hushed. The passages were much too hot—the winter heating was still on. Katinka checked the engraved plaques that announced a name and title on each door. She turned right and then right again until she heard the blare of opera—Glinka's famous aria from *A Life for the Tsar*. When she turned again, the music got louder and louder as she approached the last door.

Agrippina Constantinovna Begbulatov, Director of Manuscripts read the plaque. Quite a name. Katinka listened at the door: the music was reaching a climax. Should she have made an appointment? No, Maxy had said that was too dangerous.

She knocked. No answer. She knocked again. Nothing. Katinka cursed obstructive dinosaurs like Satinov, the maddeningly rigid bureaucrats, the frustrations of this project, and just opened the door.

A very large, white-skinned woman of advanced years lay sleeping on a divan in her underwear, her eyes covered by a mask that read *American Airways.*

The room was hot, the music rippled out of a modern CD player, and the perfumes within were heady. Katinka had only a moment to register two fans whirring, piles of yellowed manuscripts and two mountainous thighs flowing over lacy stocking tops before the woman was pulling off her mask and coming toward her.

"How dare you barge in here! Who are you? Have you no manners? Are you some sort of cultureless philistine?" The whale-sized woman looked Katinka up and down as if she had never seen a young girl in denim and boots in the sacred archive. "Who gave you permission to burst in on me?"

"Umm, no one." Katinka was lost momentarily.

"Then please leave and never return!" cried the woman, whose capacious milky bosoms strained even her rigidly structured brassiere.

"No, no." Katinka was struggling now, blushing and stammering. "I was just asked to deliver something to you. It's here . . . for you." She raised the package.

The woman angrily yanked off a mauve hairnet. "I'm not expecting anything," she said, peering craftily at the package. Katinka had little left to lose. She tried not to look at the garter belt, the generous flesh-colored underpants or any of the other eye-catching parts of the vision before her. "It's a gift from . . ." She checked up and down the corridor, to suggest that the lady might not like her colleagues to witness the delivery of the package, "well, I'd prefer to tell you in private."

The woman frowned, apparently remembering where she was and what she was wearing. "One minute!" She shoved Katinka out of the door and closed it. The music stopped. The door reopened.

"I'm Agrippina Begbulatov," declared the woman, offering a firm, sweaty hand. "I like to take a nap in the middle of the day. Please, sit!"

Katinka sat on the red divan, on which she could instantly feel the heat radiating from where the director of manuscripts' generous body had recently rested. Agrippina wore rouge and scarlet lipstick, a blue Soviet-style dress with lace over the décolletage and a pyramid of spangles on both hips. Katinka recognized the towering dyed-auburn coiffure of a Soviet grande dame of the Brezhnev era.

"You know I'm in charge of collecting all the memoirs of Party members so that they can be cataloged and filed in this special archive?" said Agrippina, sitting in a soft chair.

"Agrippina Constantinovna, thank you for receiving me," said Katinka.

"My pleasure," said Agrippina, coldly gracious, haughtily patient.

Katinka realized she had one second to explain herself—or ultimately face the Organs. When she started to speak, she hadn't yet decided which lie to tell (indeed she had never told a lie, not a serious one, ever) and she knew that every lie would carry a high risk of exposure because all these top Communists knew one another, had been to school together, then to the Institute for Foreign Languages, after which they married each other and lived close to one another in their dachas and bred the next generation of Golden Youth. But already Katinka could hear her own voice sounding different, a lying voice.

"Comrade Agrippina Constantinova," she started, "I bring you a gift from . . . Mariko Satinov. You know her, of course?"

Katinka clenched her teeth, trying to conceal her internal torment.

"Mariko?" queried Agrippina, head on one side.

"Yes."

"I know Comrade Hercules Satinov," said Agrippina reverently. "Not well of course, but I met him once at a concert at the Conservatoire and in the course of my work here, naturally."

"Naturally," agreed Katinka. "But you don't know Mariko?"

Agrippina shook her head. "But she's sent me a gift?"

"Yes, yes, by way of introducing me to you. She knows you, comrade, by name because of your dedicated and important work with her father, Comrade Marshal Satinov."

Agrippina's nostrils flared nobly as she puffed up her breast and seemed to swell with pride. "Comrade Satinov mentioned me?"

"Oh yes. I'm a friend of the family and he most certainly did mention you when he was telling me about how you helped him write his memoirs. He said he couldn't have done the job without you."

"Well, legendary Comrades Gromyko and Mikoyan, with whom I was fortunate enough to work on their books, said that their memoirs would not have been accomplished without my editorial skills."

"That does not surprise me in the least," said Katinka, finding that a lie, when it works, is an exhilarating thing, and soon leads to other lies. "Indeed, Comrade Satinov told me, 'Young comrade, visit Agrippina Constantinovna, that master of editors, that keeper of the holy flame, and she'll show you how we worked on the memoir, she'll show you the drafts . . .'"

"You are a Communist, comrade . . . ?"

"Katinka Vinsky. Yes, I was a Young Pioneer, then Komsomol and now I'm a historian writing a paper for Comrade Satinov about his role in the storming of Berlin."

"Ah. There are so few young comrades left, how refreshing to meet one," said Agrippina. She paused, and stopped smiling. "But why hasn't Comrade Satinov called me? He knows he should make an appointment . . ."

"He is very ill," said Katinka. "Lung cancer."

"I heard. But I should ring his daughter, this Mariko, and check . . ." She moved toward the phones on the T-shaped desk.

"Wait, Agrippina Constantinova," said Katinka, a little frantically, "Mariko's nursing him today . . . at the Kremlevka Hospital. That's why I just came without an appointment. Comrade Satinov, in a lucid moment, told Mariko to give you a certain gift—and you would know it was from him." She patted her package.

"It's for me?"

"Oh yes."

"From Mariko Satinov and the marshal?" Her beetle eyes fixed on the gift.

Agrippina wiggled her bottom closer to the edge of her seat so that she was closer to the package. Katinka rested her hand on it protectively. "Do you have Marshal Satinov's full memoirs here, the manuscript?" Katinka was following Maxy's instructions.

"Yes, young girl, I do, in this pile." A blue-ringed hand pointed at the heaps of yellowing manuscripts that covered every inch of the room. "You understand that our famous comrades dictated their memoirs to their assistants or to me personally and then it was my task to edit the book for the Party, according to the guidance of the Central Committee, leaving out any materials that might distract the public. Not all the episodes in Marshal Satinov's memoirs, as with all the memoirs of our leaders, were included in the final version."

"Marshal Satinov is most keen for me to glance at those sections . . . so I can appreciate your editorial work. Before he became too ill in the last day or so, he told Mariko to give you this present as another mark of his gratitude." Katinka took the package in her hands. "Do you have the manuscript?"

"I really must ring the marshal's house or speak to the Archive Director about this . . ."

"If you wish," said Katinka, "but then I would have to give the gift to someone else."

That decided the matter. Agrippina fell to her swollen, dimpled knees on the carpet and, bending over the heaps of paper, so that Katinka could again see the scaffolding of her garter belt, she began talking to herself softly, naming each manuscript. Finally, in triumph, she held up Satinov's memoir. Breathing heavily and pink in the face, she sat back on the chair and focused her eyes on the package.

Katinka waited, expecting Agrippina to hand over the document now resting so comfortably on her lap, but nothing happened. Agrippina looked at her, plucked red eyebrows raised, and Katinka looked back. The atmosphere in the room changed as the air changes when it is about to rain.

"Oh yes, Agrippina Constantinovna, I almost forgot," said Katinka at last. "A gift from the Satinovs," and she handed over the weighty package.

Agrippina, beaming, grabbed the bag and drew out an enormous three-hundred-dollar bottle of Chanel No. 5.

"My favorite!" exclaimed Agrippina, hugging the bottle. "How did the marshal remember?"

"May I look at the manuscript?" asked Katinka.

"Only in this room," answered Agrippina. "There are a few fragments that weren't published. No one has ever read them except me."

Katinka felt a sense of foreboding as she took the wad of pages.

"Put your feet up on the divan," said Agrippina. "Enjoy the cold air of the fans, and the music of Glinka. You may take notes."

Katinka glanced through the pages quickly. Much of it was familiar from Satinov's turgid book—"How we conquered the Virgin Lands," "Building homes for Soviet workers," "Creating the Motor Tractor Stations," "An interesting conversation with Comrade Gagarin on our conquest of space" and so on . . . Another waste of time, thought Katinka, but then, as Agrippina anointed her wrists and neck and even behind her ears with Madame Chanel's priceless nectar, she found something that made her heart pound.

21

A conversation with J. V. Stalin, January 1940
By Hercules Satinov

One night about 2:00 a.m., I was at my desk in Old Square when the phone rang.

"It's Poskrebyshev. Comrade Stalin wants to see you at the dacha. There's a car waiting for you downstairs."

Stalin favored me. We had made an alliance with Nazi Germany but we knew the war would come soon. The Party had ordered me to supervise the creation of new tanks and artillery for the Red Army. I had been invited to the dacha twice already to discuss my work. So I wasn't afraid, though when you went to see Stalin you never quite knew where it would end.

The car had chains on its wheels to avoid skidding on the ice—it was minus twenty degrees, a truly freezing winter. We sped up the Mozhaisk Highway and turned off into a drive through a forest of oaks, pines, firs, maples and birches. The occasional guard could be seen against the snows.

Two security gates let us through. Lastly a green steel gate opened and there was Stalin's real home, the Kuntsevo dacha, a plain two-story house, recently painted khaki in case war came.

A guard in NKVD blue met us at the door and showed me inside. I left my coat on the coatrack. Stalin's office was on the left, heaped with books and journals, but then out of the library on the right, which was filled with bookcases, came Stalin himself in a grey tunic and boots.

"Evening, *bicho*," he said quietly, grinning. He always called me *bicho*—it means "boy" in Georgian. "Come in and have a drink and some food. Have you eaten?"

Of course I had eaten already but in those days we all worked according to Stalin's nocturnal habits.

"Comrade Beria's here and the others are coming." He led the way into a big room with a huge dining-room table, heavy chairs and divans, the ceiling and walls paneled in Karelian pine, with posters by Russian artists. At one end of the table there was a buffet, a Georgian feast, with plates for us to help ourselves.

Lavrenti Beria was already standing at the table, holding a glass of wine. He greeted me in Georgian. With Stalin, you see, we were three Georgians in icy Russia!

Stalin, pouring me some wine and taking some himself, sat down at the table. I sat between the two of them.

"So," said Stalin, lighting up a Herzegovina Flor cigarette, "what happened with the Sashenka case?"

The mention of her name always had an emotional effect on me, which I hoped was invisible.

"She seemed such a decent Soviet woman," said Stalin. "I remember seeing her in Lenin's office in Petrograd . . ." He shook his head sadly. "In our world, people can wear masks for decades."

I looked at Beria.

"She confessed everything," said Beria.

"The trial went smoothly," I added.

"You knew her well, didn't you, boy?" said Stalin to me.

I nodded.

"Did they all disarm and show remorse?" asked Stalin, dropping his cigarette into the bowl of his pipe and making puffs of smoke. "At the end?"

"Vanya Palitsyn disarmed," said Beria, laughing hoarsely. "He took it well, shouting out, 'Long live Comrade Stalin!' at the last moment."

Stalin sucked on his pipe, golden eyes half closed.

"But Mendel, what an old fool!" Beria continued. "He refused to disarm."

"He was always such a stickler for rules," said Stalin rather fondly.

"I did as you asked with Mendel," said Beria.

Stalin and Beria exchanged a quick conspiratorial smile—I knew they enjoyed their intrigues. I once heard Beria talking about arranging a fatal car crash for a comrade who was too well known to arrest and execute.

"Boy, are you interested in hearing about Mendel?" Stalin asked me.

"Yes," I said, though in truth I dreaded it.

"Tell him, Lavrenti," ordered Stalin.

"I told Mendel, 'Confess your crimes and Comrade Stalin will guarantee your life,'" explained Beria, "and you know what Mendel did? He shouted, 'Never! I'm innocent and will be an honest Bolshevik until I die!' He spat at me and then in Kobylov's face . . ."

"That was a mistake," mused Stalin.

"Kobylov went crazy and gave him a real beating, and that was that."

"What pride! What foolish pride!" Stalin looked at me. "But you curated the case, boy?"

"Yes, Comrade Stalin. I curated as you asked." I could not help but give Beria a heavy look. Stalin was so sensitive, he divined it immediately.

"Well?" he asked.

"Nothing special," said Beria, and he kicked my shin hard under the table. But however dangerous Beria may have been, it was never a good idea to hide anything from Stalin.

"There was an irregularity, Comrade Stalin, in one of the executions," I said finally, feeling unwell.

"An irregularity?" repeated Stalin coldly.

Beria gave me another kick in the leg but it was too late.

"The NKVD has professional and devoted cadres but this was a rare example of philistine infantilism," I said, starting to sweat.

"Did you know about this, Comrade Beria?"

"I heard about it, Comrade Stalin, and am investigating."

"I thought you'd cleansed the Organs of this sort of shit? The guilty must be punished." He turned to us both and scrutinized us carefully. "Right. Comrades Beria and Satinov, form a commission of Comrades Shkiryatov, Malenkov, Merkulov. I want a report fast."

Just then we heard the purr of cars driving up to the house, doors slamming. Stalin stood up and went to greet members of the Politburo, who had arrived for dinner.

Beria and I were left alone.

"You motherfucker," said Beria, jabbing me in the side, "why the fuck did you have to mention that to him?" But then Molotov, Voroshilov and the other leaders joined us in the dining room.

When we were helping ourselves to dinner, Stalin appeared next to me, standing very close.

"That pretty girl Sashenka," he murmured. "What terrible decisions we have to make."

22

"Have you finished, dear?" asked Agrippina. As the Parisian perfume thickened the air, Katinka absorbed Satinov's revelation. Maxy was right; she was becoming obsessed with these strangers—people who had nothing to do with her, yet whose stories consumed her. She had longed to find out what had happened to them, but the excised pages from Satinov's memoir had raised even more questions. Saddest of all, she was now sure that Sashenka was dead. She would have to ring Roza and tell her both her parents had been killed by Stalin's thugs. Sashenka's husband had been shot crying "Long live Comrade Stalin" and her uncle Mendel had not died of a heart attack but been bludgeoned to death.

But how had Sashenka died? What had been the "irregularity?" Had she been gang-raped by the guards, tortured to death, starved? Only one person could tell her: she had to rush to Satinov. However angry he had been with her last night, she *had* to see him before he died.

"Thank you," she managed to say to Agrippina.

"Please give my regards to the comrade marshal and his daughter and thank them for remembering me with this gift."

"Yes, of course." Katinka was already on her way to the elevator.

Fighting back tears, she waited a few minutes but it didn't come, and suddenly she realized she was not alone. The archive rat who had ridden up with her to the fourth floor was standing beside her, leaning on his cart of files and humming. Finally he cleared his throat.

"This elevator's broken. You must use our elevator."

Katinka noticed that he said "must"—but she was so upset she did not care. He hummed as they walked round the rectangular building, his yellow shoes squeaking, until they reached a dirtier, rustier elevator with sawdust on its floor. It soon grunted and heaved on its way.

What would she tell Roza? A wave of despair overcame her. Satinov wouldn't see her again; Mariko would throw her out. And now she would never find Carlo.

At last the elevator jerked to a halt but they weren't in the foyer; they were underground somewhere. The archive rat held open the door.

"Please," he said.

"But this is the wrong floor," she objected.

The archive rat looked up and down an underground passageway.

"I've got some documents to show you."

"I'm sorry," Katinka said, suddenly scared and vigilant, "I don't know you. I've got to—" She pressed the button for the first floor but the man held the door.

"I'm Apostollon Shcheglov," he said, as if expecting her to know the name, which meant "goldfinch."

"I'm late. I must rush," she insisted, pressing the button again and again.

"Better to sing well as a goldfinch than badly as a nightingale," he said, quoting the Krylov fable.

Katinka stopped and stared at him.

Shcheglov's smile was adorned by two gold teeth.

"Do you remember who said that to you?" he asked. "Let me give you a clue: Utesov and Tseferman."

Of course, it was Kuzma's weird good-bye.

"We archivists all know one another. We're a secret order. Come on," he said, showing her a well-lit corridor of solid concrete. "This is one of the safest places in the world, Katinka, if I may call you that. This is where our nation's history is protected."

Still feeling nervous, Katinka allowed herself to be led. They came to a white steel door like the entrance to a submarine or a bomb shelter. Shcheglov turned a large chrome wheel, opened three different locks and then tapped a code into an electronic pad. The door shifted sideways and then slid open: it was about two feet thick. "This can withstand a full nuclear assault. If the Americans attacked us with all their H-bombs, you and I, the President in the Kremlin and the generals at headquarters would be the only people left alive in Moscow."

Another reinforced door had to be opened like the first. Katinka glanced behind her. She felt horribly vulnerable—suppose Kuzma had been caught giving her the documents and the KGB had forced him to lure her here?

Still humming, Shcheglov entered a small office to one side, always holding a tune at the back of his throat. His desk was tidy, stacked with files, but the expansive table in front of it was covered in a colored relief map, showing valleys, rivers and houses, peopled by tin soldiers, cannons, banners and horses, all exquisitely painted.

"I made and decorated every one of them myself. Would you like me to show you? Are you in a hurry?"

Katinka had never been in such a hurry. Satinov was dying, taking Sashenka's secret with him, and she had to get to him fast. But suppose this archive rat had the documents she needed? She knew that top secret and closed files were stored down here and he must have asked her to follow him for a reason. She decided to humor him.

"I'd love to see more of your toy soldiers," she said.

"Not toys. This is a historical re-enactment," he insisted, "precise in every detail, even down to the ammunition in the cannons and the shakos of the Dragoons. You're a historian, can you guess the battle?"

Katinka circled the table as Shcheglov bounced on his yellow plastic toes with pleasure.

She noted the Napoleonic Grande Armée on one side and the Russian Guards Regiments on the other. "It's 1812 of course," she said slowly. "That must be the Raevsky Redoubt, Barclay de Tolly's forces here, Prince Bagration here facing French Marshals Murat and Ney. Napoleon himself with the Guard here. It's the Battle of Borodino!" she said triumphantly.

"Hurrah!" he cried. "Now let me show you where we keep our documents." He opened a further steel door into a subterranean hall stacked with metal cabinets holding thousands upon thousands of numbered files. "Many of these will still be closed long after we're dead. This is my life's work and I wouldn't show you anything that I felt undermined the security of the Motherland. But your research is just a footnote, albeit a very interesting footnote. Please sit at my desk and I'll show you your materials."

"Why are you helping me?" she asked.

"Only as a favor to a respected comrade archivist—and uncle. Yes, Kuzma's my uncle. We archivists are all related: my father works at the State Archive and my grandfather before him."

"An imperial dynasty of archivists," said Katinka.

"Between ourselves, that's exactly how I see it!" Shcheglov beamed, gold teeth flashing in the electric light. "You're not to copy anything even into a notebook. Remember, girl, none of this is ever to be published. Agreed?"

Katinka nodded and sat at his desk. He took a shallow pile of beige files off a shelf, opened a file, licked his finger and turned some pages.

"Scene one. A list of one hundred and twenty-three names—each with a number—signed by Stalin and a quorum of the Politburo on nine January 1940."

Katinka's heart raced. A deathlist. Shcheglov hummed as he ran his finger down the list.

82. Palitsyn, I. N.
83. Zeitlin-Palitsyn, A. S. (Comrade Snowfox)
84. Barmakid, Mendel

She noted the list was addressed to Stalin and the Politburo and signed in a tiny, neat green ink by *L. P. Beria, Narkom NKVD.*

Shcheglov's finger traveled to the scrawls around the typed names:

Agreed. Molotov
Crush these traitors like snakes. I vote for the Vishka! Kaganovich
Shoot these whores and scoundrels like dogs. Voroshilov

And most decisively:

Shoot them all.
J. St.

"So they were sentenced," she said, "but were they all . . . ?"

"Scene two." Shcheglov slid the document across the desk with a flourish, turned back to the shelf, hunted around for a few moments and then presented a scuffed memorandum, bearing in its careless scrawl and clumsy blotting the grinding boredom, stained desks, greasy fingers and the rough routine of prisons.

To Comrade Commandant of Special Object 110, Golechev
21 January 1940
Transfer to Major V. S. Blokhin, Head of Command Operations, the below-mentioned prisoners condemned to be shot . . .

The 123 names on the list were typed below. Sashenka and Vanya were near the top. A bunch of more than a hundred blotched, crumpled chits—pro-forma memoranda with the names and dates filled in—was held together by a thick red string pushed through a hole in the sheaf.

Her hands shaking, Katinka found Vanya Palitsyn's chit.

On the orders of Comrade Kobylov, Deputy Narkom NKVD, the undersigned on 21 January 1940 at 4:41 a.m. carried out the sentence of shooting on . . . and here the semiliterate scribble of a half-drunk executioner added the name *Palitsyn, Ivan.* The man who carried out the sentence was *V. S. Blokhin.* Katinka had heard of him from Maxy: he usually wore a butcher's leather apron and cap to shield his beloved NKVD uniform from the spatter of blood.

Katinka felt herself in the presence of evil and nothingness. She was not crying, she was too overwhelmed for that. Instead she felt dizzy and faint.

The other chits were the same. She could only think that every scrap, so sloppily filled in, was the end of a life and a family. She could barely bring herself to look at Sashenka's—but then she started to turn the pages too fast, almost tearing them.

"I can't find her," she said, her voice shaking.

Shcheglov looked at his watch. "We haven't got long before my colleague returns. Now we go back over six months to how the case began. Take a look at this. Scene three."

He placed a yellowing piece of paper before her, headed in black type—**OFFICE OF J. V. STALIN**. Its entire surface was covered in squiggles and shading in thick green and red crayon, doodles of wolves and apparently random words. But Stalin's secretary had annotated the exact date and time: *7 May 1939. Sent to archives 11:42 p.m.* That was the evening when Beria had shown Stalin the transcript of Sashenka and Benya in bed together at the Metropole.

Katinka looked into the bottle-thick, greasy lenses of Shcheglov's spectacles, which reflected her own anxious eyes, then down at the papers before her. Slowly, she started to piece together the drama of the night that had doomed Sashenka and her whole family. She knew how Stalin had read the bugging transcript and hated it, calling Sashenka *morally corrupt . . . like a streetwalker.* She got her notebook out of her bag and glanced back at the order of Stalin's visitors that night:

10:00 p.m. L. P. Beria.
Leaves 10:30 p.m.
10:30 p.m. H. A. Satinov.
Leaves 10:45 p.m.
10:40 p.m. L. P. Beria.
Leaves 10:52 p.m.

By the time Beria left Stalin's office at 10:30 p.m., Satinov was waiting in the anteroom. Stalin called in Satinov and asked him about Sashenka's affair.

Katinka perused the new page of Stalin's squiggles and, with a rising horror, she started to understand.

Questions for Comrade Satinov: Sashenka in St. Petersburg was in the middle of the page, surrounded by circles, squares and a finely drawn fox's face, shaded in red and entitled *Comrade Snowfox.* Satinov must have answered these questions coolly because Stalin scrawled down his answer: *Old friends, devoted Bolsheviks.*

Then Stalin called in Beria again and they intensified their cross-examination of Satinov. The next words were scarcely legible.

"I can't quite read this," she said.

The archivist followed the words with his finger and read out:

Snowfox in St. Petersburg reliable/unreliable?
L. P. Beria: Molotov and Mendel in St. Petersburg?

Katinka realized that these were all questions to Satinov. She started to imagine his struggle for survival during those five minutes. What could he say? He must have been pale, sweating, his mind spinning. He had a sweet wife and a new baby, but he was a devoted Communist and an ambitious man. His answers during those five minutes would either save his life and make his career, or destroy his own life and that of his wife and baby.

When Stalin asked about Sashenka's "reliability" in Petersburg, a name must have come to Satinov's mind: Captain Sagan, whom he knew of only from his dealings with Mendel in late 1916.

Did Stalin already know about Sashenka's mission to turn Sagan, and that it had been ordered by the Petersburg Committee? If he talked about it now, and no one knew of it, it could taint Sashenka, although this was unlikely since Sagan had been dead for twenty-two years.

But what if Molotov or Mendel, the only others apart from Sashenka who knew about the Sagan operation, had already discussed it with Stalin? Satinov would then be accused of hiding it from the Party, from Stalin himself. That was unthinkable. That would mean death.

Katinka stared down at the crayoned hieroglyphics that revealed this feverish game of Russian roulette that would still decree the destinies of people fifty years later.

So what did Satinov do? Did he panic and say more than he meant? Or did he calculate and act in cold blood?

"We'll probably never know." She found she was talking aloud.

"But we do know he said *this* . . . ," replied Shcheglov, his finger showing her the next words written by Stalin on this crowded piece of paper: *Hercules S: Cpt Sagan. Petersburg. SAGAN*

Katinka went cold. So Satinov *had* told Stalin and Beria about Sashenka and Captain Sagan of the Okhrana. She felt pity for Satinov, and then anger, and then pity again. He might have answered differently if he had known that Captain Sagan was alive—and in one of Beria's camps, his name meticulously filed in the NKVD roster of prisoners. Within hours, Sagan was on his way to Moscow and Kobylov was beating him into testifying against Sashenka.

"If Satinov had brazened it out," she whispered, "they might all have survived."

"Or he might have faced the Vishka too," Shcheglov pointed out.

"Have you seen enough?" He started to gather up the papers and put them away in his orderly files where they would rest, perhaps forever.

"So Satinov doomed his best friends," Katinka mused, "but then risked everything to save their children. Does that redeem him?"

Shcheglov gestured toward the elevator, in a hurry to get her out of his office, but she gripped his arms. "Hang on, there's one thing missing. Stalin created a commission to investigate Sashenka's execution. Where is its report?"

"There was a number for the file," said Shcheglov, guiding her toward the elevator. "But the file's not here. Sorry, but only God knows everything." He pressed the button to call the elevator.

"Thank you for showing me this," she said, kissing him as she left. "You've been very kind. I can't tell you what this means to me."

"And you care too much," he said, squeezing her hands.

As she stepped into the elevator, she reviewed the combination of the extract from Satinov's memoirs and Stalin's enigmatic note, *Bicho to curate*, on the papers Maxy had shown her in the Party archive.

Bicho—boy in Georgian—was Stalin's nickname for Satinov. "Curate" was Stalin's word for what he wanted Satinov to do: supervise the destruction of a family he loved.

"Oh God," she gasped, finally understanding it all. "Satinov saw her die. What did they do to her?"

23

Rushing out of the archive and onto Mayakovsky Square, Katinka waved down a Lada. It sped her down the hill toward the Granovsky. Fizzing with urgency, she rang five bells simultaneously, the door buzzed and she raced upstairs to the Satinov apartment. The door was again open but when she entered, Mariko was standing in the hall beneath the crystal chandelier.

"Mariko, I know what you think but please—I've got to tell him what I've discovered. He's helped me every step of the way without me realizing. I know he'll want to talk to me now."

Katinka stopped and caught her breath. Mariko did not throw her out. She didn't say anything at all and Katinka, who had never really looked at her before, noticed that Mariko did not seem angry. Her dark, pointed face was desperately tired.

"Come in," she said quietly. "You can see him." She walked down the hallway, passing the sitting room. Katinka followed, peering eagerly ahead. "Go on in."

Satinov lay in bed, propped up on pillows with his eyes closed. His face, his hair, his lips seemed the color of ashes. A nurse was by the bed, adjusting the oxygen tank and the plastic mask, but when she saw them she nodded briskly and left the room.

Katinka, who had so much to ask, was suddenly uncertain what to do. Satinov's breathing was ragged; sometimes his chest rose jerkily, at other times he did not breathe for some seconds. He was sweating with effort and fear. Katinka knew she should feel pity for this dying man but instead she felt only fury and frustration. How could he escape her like this? How could he be so cruel as to leave Roza without ever telling anyone what happened to her mother?

Katinka glanced at Mariko, who gestured at the low chair by the bed. "You can talk to him," Mariko said. "For a minute or two. He asked where you were. He was thinking about you and your research. That's why I let you in."

"Can he hear me?"

"I think so. He speaks sometimes, his lips move. He's talked about my mother a bit but it's hard to understand. The doctors say . . . We're not sure." Mariko leaned back against the doorpost, stretched her back and rubbed her face.

Katinka stood up, leaned over the bed, then looked back at Mariko. "Go ahead," she said.

Katinka took Satinov's hand in hers. "It's Katinka. Your researcher. I say 'your' researcher because you've held all the cards all along and you've sent me this way and that . . . If you can hear me, let me know somehow. You can squeeze my hand or even just blink." She waited but he took another desperate breath, his entire body shivered, and he settled down again. "I know you loved Sashenka and Vanya, I know you did a terrible thing and I know how you saved their children. But what happened to Sashenka? What did you see? Please tell me how she died."

There was no reaction. Katinka realized that this old man was a study in ambiguities. He had helped and encouraged her but also tricked and obstructed her, just as he had doomed Sashenka and saved her children. She grieved for him yet at the same time she'd never felt more enraged.

He was quiet for a few minutes but then his breathing became more of a struggle, his hands clawing the bedspread as his body twisted to get oxygen. The nurse returned and gave him oxygen and an injection, and he grew calmer again.

"I'll get my brothers in a minute," said Mariko. "They're sleeping down the corridor. We've been up all night."

Katinka stood up and walked to the door.

"I'm so sorry," she said. "Thank you for letting me in. I wish now I'd brought Roza to see him . . . I had so much to ask him." She looked back at the bed, hoping for him to call her back. "I'll let myself out."

Just then they heard his voice. Katinka spun round and the two of them returned to the bedside. Satinov's lips were moving a little.

"What's he saying?" asked Katinka.

Mariko took his hands and kissed his forehead. "Papa, it's Mariko, right here with you, darling Papa."

He moved his lips again, but they could hear nothing. After a while his lips stopped moving and, as his family filed into the room, Katinka slipped away.

Outside, Maxy waited, smoking as he leaned on his bike. Katinka walked out into his arms, smelling the leather of his jacket and the smoke of his cigarette. She was very glad he was there.

"He's dying? A terrible thing to see. But you've done all you can . . ."

"It's over," she said, "and I'm exhausted. I'll phone Roza, collate my notes and put her in contact with anyone she wants to meet."

"What will you do now?"

"I'm going home. I want to see my friends, and there's a boy who wants to take me on vacation. Perhaps it's best that we never know how Sashenka died. My papa was right. I should never have taken this job. I'm going back to Catherine the Great."

"But you're so good at this," said Maxy. "Katinka, please come and work with me at the foundation. We could achieve so much together."

She shook her head and collected herself. "No thanks. There's no fruit, no harvest in this sort of history; all these fields are sown with salt. It may be old history but the poison is fresh and the unhappiness lives on. No, the turning over of old graves isn't for me. It's too painful. Good-bye, Maxy, and thanks for everything."

She wiped her eyes and started to walk away.

"Katinka!" Maxy called after her.

She half turned.

"Katinka, can I call you sometime?"

24

But Katinka had reckoned without the persuasive force of Pasha Getman.

"You can't just give up and walk away from us," he'd roared at her when she'd phoned to say she'd done all she could. Then he'd said in a quieter voice, "What about my mother? She's so fond of you. We need you to do one final thing for us. Think of it as a personal favor to Roza."

And so it was that three days later, taking Pasha's private plane,

Katinka and Roza had flown down to Tbilisi (which was, as Pasha reminded Katinka, almost on her way home). Some of Pasha's bodyguards had driven them straight to the picturesque café in the old vine-entangled mansion.

"Lala," said Katinka to the old lady in the small room upstairs. "I've brought someone to meet you."

Lala Lewis, holding her usual glass of Georgian wine, sat up in bed and focused on the doorway.

"Is it her? Is it Sashenka?" she asked.

"No, Lala, but it is almost Sashenka. This is Roza Getman, Sashenka's daughter, whom you knew as Snowy."

"Ohh," Lala sighed and held out her hands. "Come closer. I'm very old. Come sit on my bed. Let me look at you. Let me see into your eyes."

"Hello, Lala," said Roza, her voice trembling, "it's been more than fifty years since you cared for us."

Katinka watched as Roza, dressed neatly in a white blouse, blue cardigan and cream skirt, her grey hair still coiffed in the style of her youth, walked forward slowly, looking around her at the trinkets of a vanished life. She seemed to hesitate for a moment at the sight of the old nanny's outstretched hands and then, smiling, as if Lala were somehow familiar to her, she sat on the bed.

Lala took Roza's hands, not only squeezing them with all her might but shaking them too. Neither woman said a word, but from where she was standing Katinka could see Roza's shoulders shaking, and the tears streaming down Lala's cheeks. Feeling like an intruder suddenly, she walked to the window and looked out. The sounds and smells of Tbilisi—the singing of someone in the street and the aromas of *tkemali*, *lavashi* bread, ground coffee and apple blossom—rose around her.

This is the last scene of the drama, Katinka told herself. She'd done what Pasha asked. She'd brought these two women together, exposing herself in the process to more pain than she'd thought possible. Now she would go home, back to Papa and Mama—and to Andrei.

Lala stroked Roza's face. "Dear child, I dreamed of seeing your mother again. I must tell you all about her because there was no one like her. Look, there's her picture as a schoolgirl at the Smolny. See? I used to collect her in the baron's landaulet, or motorcar I should say nowadays. Samuil, the baron, was your grandfather and you never met him though he knew all about you. And not a day passed when I didn't think of you and your brother Carlo. As a girl you were so like your mother—she was blond as an angel when she was young—and you have the violet eyes of your grandmother, Ariadna. Oh darling child, think of me, a girl from England. I've lived long enough to see the Tsar fall and the barbarians come to power and fall too and now to see you here—I can't quite believe it."

"I'm hardly a child," Roza laughed, "I'm sixty."

"Methuselah's young to me!" Lala answered. "Do you remember the days we spent together before . . ."

Roza nodded. "I think so . . . Yes, I remember seeing you in a canteen in a station. You had Carlo's favorite cookies. I remember walking hand in hand with you and then . . ."

"I struggled in those times to keep my head above water," Lala continued. "I had lost my darling charge, Sashenka, and your grandfather. And then I was granted a few days of such happiness with you and Carlo. When I had settled you with your new parents, I considered killing myself. Only the thought that someone dear to me would return kept me alive. And do you know, the most unlikely person of all did come back."

"Lala," interrupted Katinka, trying not to interfere yet still burning with curiosity, "only Stalin could have saved Samuil's life. Did you ever learn why?"

Lala nodded. "After the monster died, everyone here sobbed and mourned. There were even demonstrations in his honor. But I was delighted. Samuil was very ill then so I said, 'Now you can tell me why you were released.' He said he didn't know exactly but in 1907 he had given shelter—and a hundred rubles—to a pockmarked Georgian revolutionary. He let him stay in the doorman's cottage of his house here in Tbilisi when the police were searching for him. Later he realized it was Stalin, and Stalin never forgot a slight or a favor." Lala looked back at Roza, whose hands she still held. Sometimes she raised Roza's hands to her lips and kissed them. "I'll die happy now," she said.

"You're my only connection to my mother," said Roza. "You know, I almost hated my parents all through my childhood. They'd abandoned me and I never knew why. I couldn't imagine what I had done wrong for them to reject me. Yet I thought of them all the time. Sometimes I dreamed they were dead; often I looked at the Bear in the sky because Papa had told me that he would always be there. Only when I was older did I realize that perhaps something bad had happened to them and they had had no choice but to leave me. But all through my life I've never been able to cry about them."

Roza turned to Katinka. "You've done so well, my dear. Thank you from the bottom of my heart—thank you. You've changed my life. But I know you're keen to get home and Pasha's plane's waiting at the airport to fly you to Vladikavkaz. Please go whenever you want to."

Katinka kissed Roza and Lala and walked to the door—then stopped.

"I can't go quite yet," she said, turning back. "May I stay and listen? I'm afraid I've become more involved than I should have."

Roza jumped up and hugged her. "Of course, I'm so pleased you feel like that. I've become very fond of you." She sat on the bed again. "Lala, thanks to Katinka, I know about you and my parents. But please, tell me about Carlo."

Lala took a sip of her wine and closed her eyes. "He was the sweetest child, built just like a little bear with adorable brown eyes, and he was such a child of love, so affectionate. He used to stroke my face with his hands and kiss me on the nose. The day I had to let him go was one of the cruelest of my life. We were at the Beria Orphanage—can you imagine a children's home named after that creature? The day before, Snowy, I had seen you go away with the Liberharts and I could tell they were intelligentsia, Jewish professors, but you fought and kicked and screamed, and I cried for hours. I'd have kept you myself if I'd had the chance. But Satinov said, 'Your husband won't come back; they'll come for you any day—and what of the children then? No, we must settle them so they have stable, loving families.' The next day, two peasants from the north Caucasus turned up. They were collective-farm workers, Russians with some Cossack blood, but so primitive they actually came into Tbilisi on a tractor and cart, having delivered vegetables from their collective to the marketplace. I could tell they were uneducated and tough—they had hay in their hair. But I couldn't question anything. We were so lucky that Satinov had arranged the whole thing. But Carlo was so sensitive. He had to have his Kremlin cookies because he had low blood sugar and felt faint. He had to be stroked to sleep at night, no fewer than eleven strokes—as Carolina the nanny had shown me. When they took him, I sank to the floor so distraught that I may have fainted. I don't remember much of what happened afterward but a doctor came. I was inconsolable . . ."

Katinka felt a sudden shiver of excitement. *Satinov had arranged the whole thing.* Of course, it all came back to her. What had he said at their second meeting? *Your name is Vinsky? How did you get this job? Yes, Academician Beliakov was right to choose you out of his hundreds of students.* She remembered how annoyed she'd been, how she'd felt he was playing with her. But he hadn't been. He'd been telling her something. How naïve she'd been, she thought. The spark of revelation fluttered, then blazed inside her. The Getmans' advertisement for a researcher had appeared in the faculty newsletter, but *she* had been given the job even though she hadn't even applied. Academician Beliakov had approached her in the library and told her, "The job's for you. No other applicants necessary."

"How did you choose me as your researcher?" Katinka asked Roza. "Did you interview other applicants?"

"No," she said. "We first sent a letter to Marshal Satinov. He was the only name I had. The only link. He refused to help us and said there was no connection to him. He insisted we needed a historian and put us in contact with Academician Beliakov, who placed the advert."

"What did Beliakov tell you?"

"There were lots of applicants but you were the best—we didn't need to see anyone else."

Katinka got up, aware that Roza and Lala were looking at her strangely. Her heart was pounding. Only Satinov knew the names of the adoptive families, she thought. Did this mean that he knew something about her too? If so, when he received Roza's letter, all he had to do was call his friend Academician Beliakov: "When some millionaires want to hire a student for some family research, give them the Vinsky girl." She had been searching for Carlo in the archives, when all the time he'd been much, much closer.

"I have to go," she told Roza, already at the door and running down the steps. "I have to talk to my father."

25

"We longed for a child of our own," Baba told the family as they sat in the shabby living room of their blue-shuttered cottage.

Katinka looked around the familiar room in the house where she had grown up. Every face was anguished and it was her doing. Her sturdy grandmother, Baba, in her floral housecoat and with a red kerchief on her head, sat in the middle on the frayed, sunken chair, her wide face a picture of anxiety. Katinka had never seen her so distraught. Her peppery, splenetic grandfather, Bedbug, paced the room, spitting curses at her. But it was her beloved father who caused her the greatest pain.

Dr. Vinsky had driven straight from his office, still in his white coat, to meet her at the airport. When he saw his precious daughter, he had hugged and kissed her.

"I'm so pleased you're home," he said. "The light of my life. Is everything all right? Are you OK, darling?"

She looked into his thoughtful and serious face, so matinee-idol handsome with that dimple in his chin, and realized that she was a time bomb about to shatter his family. "What is it?" he said.

Then and there, she told him the whole story.

He said nothing for a while then lit up a cigarette. Katinka waited nervously but he did not argue with her. He just went on smoking and pondering.

"Papochka, tell me, should I have kept silent? Shall we forget it?"

"No," he said. "If it's true, I want to find my sister, if I have one. I want to know who my real parents were. But beyond that, I think it will change little for me. I know who I am. My parents have loved me all my life and they'll always be my parents and I'll always be the boy they loved. But it could break their hearts—and that would break mine in turn. Let me talk to them . . ."

The rest of the drive home was silent. As they drove into the village of Beznadezhnaya, Katinka should have been full of the joy of homecoming. But now the village itself seemed different; the cottage had changed; it was as if everything had been shaken up and put together differently in a thousand little ways.

Without Katinka's mother, the family might have broken apart on her father's anguished silence and the obstinate secrecy of the grandparents. But as soon as Katinka explained everything to her, Tatiana—often so vague and featherbrained—set to work calming her husband and reassuring Bedbug and Baba.

At first, her grandparents claimed to know nothing. They said it was all a mistake and Katinka wondered if she had imagined everything. Perhaps she had become overinvolved in Sashenka's story? Perhaps she was so obsessed she was losing her mind?

"This is a dagger through my heart," Baba had told her son. "A lie, a libel!" She sat down defiantly. "What a thing to say!"

Bedbug was raging. "Haven't we loved you all your life? Haven't we been good parents? And this is how you thank us—by claiming we're nothing to you!" He turned on Katinka. "Why toss these lies in our faces? Shame on you, Katinka! Is this some trick, some joke of those rich Jews in Moscow?"

Katinka was racked with pain and doubt. She looked at her father. She had never seen his face so tormented.

Then Katinka's mother intervened. "Dear parents," she said, "you've been like parents to me and I know Valentin loves you more than you can know." She turned to her husband. "Darling, tell them how you feel. Tell them now."

"Papa, Mama," he said, kneeling at the feet of the old peasant woman and taking her hands. "You're my parents. You'll always be my beloved Mamochka and Papochka. If I was adopted, it'll change nothing for me. You've loved me all my life. I know nothing but your loving kindness. I know who I am, and I will always be the little boy you've loved as long as I can remember. If you chose not to tell me before, I understand. In those days, people didn't talk about such things. But if there is anything you'd like to tell me now, we'll all listen and love you just the same afterward."

His speech touched Katinka deeply, and she looked into Baba's face and saw it soften by degrees. The old peasants exchanged glances, then her grandmother shrugged. "I want to tell the story," she said to her husband.

"All lies," said Bedbug but he was quieter now.

Some secrets are denied for so long, thought Katinka, that they no longer seem real.

Then Bedbug waved his gnarled fingers at his wife. "Tell it if you must." He sat on the sofa and lit a cigarette.

"Go on, Mama," said Dr. Vinsky, lighting up too. He got up and poured some *cha-cha* into a tiny glass and gave it to her. "I want to hear your story—whatever it is."

Baba took a deep breath, downed the *cha-cha* and, looking round the room, opened her hands. "Me and Bedbug had been married for eight years—and no children. Nothing. It was a curse to be childless. Even though I was a true Communist, I visited the priests for a blessing; I saw the quack in the next village. Still nothing. Bedbug wouldn't discuss it . . . Then one day, I heard in the collective-farm office that a bigshot official from Moscow was coming on a tour to inspect our new tractor stations. He was talking to everyone informally and he wanted to talk to us. It was Comrade Satinov."

"Did you already know him?" asked Katinka.

"Yes," said Baba. "In 1931, the campaign to collectivize the villages and destroy the richer peasants, the kulaks, came to our region. All the kulaks were being deported; many were shot here in the villages; there were grain searches and famine. It was a time of dread. Bedbug was denounced as a kulak. We were on the list to be arrested. All the others on that list were shot. Comrade Satinov was in charge, and I don't know why but for some reason he intervened and had our names taken off the list. We owed him our lives. Eight years later, in 1939, he again blessed us. He asked us to take in a three-year-old boy. 'Love him as a treasured gift,' he said. 'Take this secret to your grave. Bring him up as if he were your own.' One day we got the call from the Beria Orphanage and we went into Tbilisi and collected . . . a little boy with brown eyes and a dimple in his chin. The most beautiful little boy in the world."

"You were our son, our own," said Bedbug.

"We loved you from the moment we saw you," added Baba.

"Did you ever contact Satinov?" asked Katinka.

"Only once." Bedbug turned to address his son. "You wanted to be a doctor. It was hard to get into the best medical schools and none of my family had ever been past grade school. So I called Comrade Satinov—and he got you into Leningrad University."

"When you were little," continued Baba, "you remembered something. You cried about your mother, and your father, and your nanny, a dacha and a journey. You had a toy rabbit that you loved so much that we raised our own rabbits in the hutch in the garden and you fed them, gave them names, loved them like we loved you. I held you at night and gradually you forgot the past and loved us. And we adored you so much in return, we could never tell you . . . And that's God's truth. If we've done wrong, tell us."

When her father kissed his parents, Katinka could not watch. She stepped outside onto the veranda to admire the budding plenty of spring, the lush honeysuckle, the trilling, diving swallows, the rushing of frothy streams and far away the snow-peaked mountains. But she could see and hear nothing—just her father's loving face and the howling of her grandmother, who cried in the uninhibited way that peasants have always cried.

26

The body of Hercules Satinov lay in a casket of glazed oak and scarlet satin in the sitting room of the Granovsky apartment. Standing on an easel behind the coffin was a portrait of Satinov that Katinka hadn't seen before: it depicted him as a dashing commissar in the civil war, in his early twenties. He was on horseback in a leather coat, Mauser pistol in his hand and a rifle slung across his back, leading a line of Red Cossacks in a charge across snowy wastes. Katinka thought that this Red Cavalry commander was probably no older than she was now.

Two days earlier, Mariko had called Katinka at home to say that her father had died the night before and to invite Sashenka's children to pay their respects.

Roza was already in Moscow so Pasha sent his plane for Katinka and her father. Roza was almost girlish in her excitement: "I'm going to meet Carlo again," she told Katinka on the phone. "I can't believe it. I don't know what I'm going to say to him, I don't know what to wear. Is your father as excited as I am?"

As she lay in bed that night, Katinka imagined the reunion of brother and sister, how happy it would have made Sashenka and Vanya and how it would play out: who would run into whose arms? Who would cry and who would laugh? Her diffident father would hold back a little while Roza would hug him passionately . . . She had made it happen; she was responsible for this meeting, and she wanted it to go according to plan.

At that moment when the black of night turns into the blue of dawn, Katinka sat up in bed, pulled on her dressing gown and hurried into the sitting room. She knew she would find her father there on the sofa, smoking in the half light. He put out his hand to take hers. "You haven't packed," she said.

"I'm not coming," he answered. "This is my home. I have all the family I need . . ."

She sat beside him. "But don't you want to meet your sister? Satinov so wanted you to meet. We can't put everything back together, but if you don't come you're letting the people who killed your mother and father win." Her father said nothing for a while. "Please, Papochka!"

He shook his head slowly. "I think they've toyed with us enough."

The plane ride to Moscow seemed desolate to Katinka, who sat forlorn and disappointed amid the resplendent luxury of Pasha's converted Boeing. She couldn't help feeling furious with her father for letting her down, yet she also respected his quiet determination. She kept thinking about the tragedy of her grandparents' lives and each time she did so she saw it differently: it was the black work of men who believed they had the right to play with the lives of others and they were still toying with hers too.

Roza was waiting on the tarmac at the private airport at Vnukovo. Pasha stood beside her with two bodyguards while behind him, parked in a fan of gleaming steel, stood the customary oligarch's cavalcade of black Bentley and two Land Cruisers filled with guards, engines purring, ready to convey them into Moscow.

When she saw Katinka's downcast face, Roza put out her arms to her. "Don't worry, Katinka. I'm disappointed too, but I think I understand. I left it all much too late." Then she squeezed Katinka's hand. "The most important thing is that I've found out who I am—and I've found a niece I never knew I had. I've got you, darling Katinka."

They stood there for a moment as if they were alone in the world—until Pasha kissed his mother gently on the top of the head.

"Let's go home," he said, walking her to the car. "It'll take time, Mama."

As he closed Roza's door, he whispered to Katinka: "It's understandable. It's not your fault. Don't you see? They're strangers. Your father didn't want to find his past. It found him."

•••

Now Katinka and Roza, her newly discovered aunt, whom she was coming to love, stood arm in arm waiting their turn in the short line that led across the sitting room at Satinov's home. Even without her brother, Roza had insisted on coming to see the man who had changed her life so decisively, once damningly, once selflessly and now, belatedly, in an attempt at redemption.

The other mourners seemed to belong, Katinka thought, in a bizarre seventies time warp. She watched as bloated women in bosom-squeezing suits and sporting giant nut-red hairdos passed by with their men, sausagey apparatchiks with oiled comb-overs on bald pates and brown suits with medals. But there were younger army officers too and some children, probably Satinov's grandchildren. Their parents kept trying to hush their giggles and games at such a solemn ritual.

At the front of the line, Katinka held Roza's hand as they stepped up onto the slightly raised plinth and looked down into the coffin. She couldn't help but look at Satinov's face with fondness, despite the games he had played with her. Death—and the attentions of a meticulous embalmer and hairdresser—had restored to him the graceful virility and serene grandeur of a Soviet hero of the older generation. Four rows of medals glinted on his chest; the starred and gilded shoulder boards of a marshal of the Soviet Union glistened; the grey hair reared up stiffly in razor-cut spikes.

"I remember playing with him long ago," said Roza, looking at him. "And he *was* the man in the car who watched me going to school in Odessa from his limousine." She leaned into the coffin and kissed Satinov's forehead, but stepping off the plinth she tottered and Katinka caught her. "I'm fine," Roza said. "It's all so much to absorb."

Katinka helped her to a chair, from where Roza watched the children running up the long corridor and sliding on their knees along the gleaming parquet floor. Katinka went to the kitchen to get Roza a glass of water. Mariko and a couple of relatives, obviously Georgians, perhaps her brothers, were drinking tea and nibbling on Georgian snacks.

"Oh, Katinka," said Mariko, "I'm pleased you came. Would you like some *chai* or a glass of wine?" Mariko looked weary in her black suit but Katinka was sure she had grown younger and prettier in the last few days. "Tomorrow he's going to lie in state in the Red Army Hall," she said proudly.

"Thanks to your father, I found Sashenka's children," explained Katinka, "and—you'll never guess—thanks to him, I learned that Sashenka was my grandmother. Imagine that!"

Mariko brought Roza into the kitchen. Mariko's relatives left them alone and she poured *chai* and offered them food.

"Do you know," said Roza as she sipped her tea, "I remember sliding on the floor of this apartment."

"Your apartment was in this building too, wasn't it?" asked Katinka.

"Not just in this building," said Roza sharply. "This was our home, this very apartment, and I remember when the men in shiny boots came here: a pile of photographs, papers in a heap on the floor over there, and us being hugged by a pretty woman in tears."

Katinka glanced at Mariko, who said nothing for a moment: she and Roza were close in age but they had led very different, almost mirrored lives.

"I was born in 1939," said Mariko, taking a sip of red wine. "I think we were granted this apartment at that time too. It was impossible to refuse a gift from the Party—it was a test of loyalty . . ."—she swallowed hard and looked away—"but I never dreamed it came to us like that. I don't know what to say."

Roza reached out and put her hand on Mariko's. "It is so wonderful to meet you. If things hadn't happened the way they did, we might have grown up together."

"I wish we had. It must be so hard for you to come here . . . It's hard to learn some things, and it was hard for my father."

"He helped me," Katinka told her, "but there were some things he didn't want me to discover."

"He so wanted you to find Sashenka's children again," said Mariko, "but he'd devoted his life to the Soviet Union and the Party. He needed to help you without undermining his beliefs. And he never wanted anyone to know the terrible thing he had done. My father saw much tragedy in his life but, you know, I think Sashenka was always in the back of his mind, in his dreams. She and all her family. He must have seen them every day in this apartment."

"But we still don't know what happened to her," said Katinka with a touch of bitterness. "The file was missing. Only your father knew, and he's taken the secret to his grave."

There was nothing else to say. Mariko stood up, collecting the plates and the cups, piling them in the sink.

"I'm sorry for your loss," said Roza.

Mariko dried her hands on a towel. "And I'm s—" but she stopped herself sharply. "Thank you for coming," she said at last.

A few minutes later, Katinka and Roza walked down the stone steps to the street where Pasha's Bentley waited. A chauffeur opened the door. History is so messy, so unsatisfactory, Katinka thought, remembering her father's sorrowful words earlier that morning. She too hated the way history toyed with people.

"Katinka!" She looked up. "Katinka!" Mariko was calling to her from the first-floor landing.

The front door was still open and Katinka turned and ran back up the steps.

"Take this." Mariko thrust a yellow envelope into Katinka's hands. "My father made me promise to destroy it. But I want you to have it. Go on, Katinka, it's your story as well as ours. Yours and Roza's."

27

"I need your help, Maxy, one last time," Katinka told him on the telephone once she and Roza were back at the Getman mansion.

"It's lovely to hear your voice," answered Maxy. "I missed you. And I've got something to show you, out in the countryside. What better place to talk and think. Can I pick you up?"

Half an hour later, Katinka heard the welcome roar of his motorbike. Feeling excited and suddenly pleased to see him, she ran outside, and soon they were racing along roads newly covered with sleek black asphalt, paid for by the oligarchs and ministers who owned dachas in that region, no longer ramshackle wooden villas but gigantic chalets and mock-Tudor palaces, guarded by watchtowers and high walls. After a while Maxy turned the bike off the road and onto a rougher lane into the forest.

The sunlight shone through the leaves of birch and pine and linden. Katinka enjoyed the bumpiness of the ride and the clarity of the air after all the hours she had spent recently on planes and in dusty archives. Finally they stopped in a clearing near an old-fashioned wooden villa. Katinka pulled off her helmet and found herself among raspberry canes and blackberry bushes.

"What a beautiful place," she said, shaking back her hair.

"I've brought some Borodinsky bread and cheese to nibble while we talk, and some juice."

"I never thought you'd be so domesticated," she said. "I'm impressed."

Maxy looked embarrassed but pleased. He put the food on the grass and sat down. "Well? Who's first?"

"You!" they both said at the same time—and then they laughed.

"No," Maxy said, "I want to hear your news first, and how I can help you. But I just wondered . . . what was it like being home?"

"Fine," she answered. She sat down on the grass, enjoying the way the dappled beams made puzzle shapes on Maxy's face. The sun heated the pine resin so that it sweetened the air.

He broke up the black bread, cut a slice of cheese and offered her both.

"How's your boyfriend down there?"

"Oh, I see what you meant. About being home."

"No, no, I didn't mean it like that. I was just . . ."

"Curious? He's the same as he was before, but I'm not sure how long I'll stay down there. Meeting Roza and Pasha, researching Sashenka"—she was surprised at how nervously he seemed to be listening to her words—"has changed things a bit, changed me in fact. So I'm thinking of staying in Moscow this summer. I might get on with my research or, if you're kind to me, I might even help you out a bit at the foundation . . ."

"That's great!" Maxy smiled so sunnily at her that Katinka wanted to laugh. But she discovered that his pleasure delighted her, though she resolved not to show it. He was too pleased with himself as it was.

"Anyway," he said, changing tone, returning to business, "what did Satinov's daughter give you?"

Katinka pulled the envelope out of her jacket, undid the string at the top and drew out an old file from the archives. "I've only glanced at it. It's the missing file."

Top Secret.
To: J. V. Stalin; L. P. Beria
Report of the Commission of Inquiry on behalf of Central Committee—Comrades Merkulov, Malenkov, Shkiryatov—on the official misconduct concerning the Highest Degree of Punishment of Object 83 at Special Object 110 on 21 January 1940. Report filed 12 March 1940.

Katinka noticed the doodlings—circles, rhomboids and crescents in green crayon—around the heading, and gasped: "It's Stalin's own copy."

"Right," said Maxy.

"How did Satinov get it?"

"That's easy. After Stalin's death in fifty-three, each leader wanted to save his own skin so they all rifled through the archives to remove any especially incriminating documents. Usually they burned them. But Satinov kept this." He studied the document carefully, absent-mindedly putting a cigarette in his mouth, striking a match but forgetting to light it.

"Now let's interpret this. The Highest Degree of Punishment is execution with a single bullet to the back of the neck. The Special Object One Hundred Ten is Beria's special prison, Sukhanovka, the former St. Catherine's Nunnery at Vidnoe, where Sashenka and Vanya were tried and executed. It was so secret that prisoners there were known by numbers, not by their names, so Object Eighty-three is—"

"Sashenka," interrupted Katinka. "It was her number on the death list." She leaned over and started to read. "First they interviewed Golechev, the prison commandant . . ."

Commission: Comrade Commandant Golechev, you were responsible for the completion of the Highest Degree of Punishment on sentenced prisoners on 21 January 1940. The Highest Degree was to be witnessed on behalf of the Central Committee by Comrade Hercules Satinov. Why did you begin early and in such a disorderly and un-Bolshevik way?

Golechev: The Highest Degrees were carried out in the professional manner expected of an NKVD officer.

Commission: I warn you, Comrade Golechev, this is a serious offense. Your conduct helped our enemies. Were you working for the enemy? You may well face the Highest Degree yourself.

Golechev : I confess before the Central Committee to serious and foolish mistakes. It was my birthday. We started drinking early, at lunchtime, and drinking helps when there's a Vishka to conduct. Cognac, champagne, wine, vodka. At midnight it was time to bring the prisoners down, but Comrade Satinov was late and we couldn't start without him.

Commission: Comrade Satinov, why were you, the witness, so late?

Satinov: I was taken ill, seriously ill, but I reported my illness to the commandant and arrived at Sukhanovka as soon as I could.

Commission: Comrade Satinov, you knew some of the convicted prisoners, especially Sashenka Zeitlin-Palitsyn. Were you suffering from a neurasthenic crisis caused by bourgeois sentimentality?

Satinov: No, on my word as a Communist. I simply had food poisoning. In our times of struggle and war, Enemies of the People must be liquidated.

"You get the picture?" asked Maxy. "The NKVD guards are wildly drunk; Sashenka, Vanya and more than a hundred others are awaiting execution; and Satinov is so upset that he is too sick to attend. So what happens?"

Golechev: As we drank, our talk turned to the depravity of our female Enemies, most particularly Prisoner Zeitlin-Palitsyn—the famous Sashenka. We'd heard about this traitor's repellent, snake-like depravity, how she used her devious female wiles to seduce and entrap other traitors, and since Comrade Satinov was not yet present, we, under the influence of alcohol and our disgust for her betrayal, decided to begin with her. We brought her up to my dining room and . . .

In green pen, beside this statement, Stalin had written one word: *Hooligans.*

"Now we hear from Blokhin," said Maxy.

Commission: Comrade Major Blokhin, you were designated to conduct the Highest Measure of the 123 prisoners on this list, yet you complained about the commandant's conduct.

"Blokhin was Stalin's top executioner," Maxy explained. "In the case of the Polish prisoners at Katyn, he personally executed about eleven thousand men in a series of nights."

Blokhin: At midnight, I arrived ready to begin my duties as Chief of the Command Operations Section in the Highest Degree of this list of 123, but I wish to report to the Central Committee that I found the commandant and his officers drunk in the presence of Prisoner

Zeitlin-Palitsyn, who was being treated in a highly unprofessional way, against the noble Chekist morality. She was already partially disrobed. I protested strongly. I offered to carry out the sentence myself at once but I was sent away. I tried to call Comrade Satinov. When he arrived I reported everything to him. These drunken and bungling amateurs made a mockery of my Chekist professionalism and skill in this special and sensitive work. They were taking bets and shouting. At approximately thirty-three minutes after midnight, they forced Prisoner Zeitlin-Palitsyn outside into the courtyard near the officers' garages, which is lit up very brightly by searchlights. The temperature was approximately minus 40 degrees.

Golechev: When she was outside, we performed the Highest Degree, the sentence of the Military Collegium against Prisoner Zeitlin-Palitsyn, but in our drunkenness and because of the unprofessional lateness of Comrade Satinov . . . we did so in an unacceptable, frivolous and depraved manner. Yes, I admit we were curious about her as a seductive agent of the Japanese Emperor and British lords, and as a woman.

Katinka felt cold. "Oh my God," she whispered. "Did they rape her?"

"No. If they had done, it would say so here," said Maxy. "But they were certainly excited by her beauty, her reputation as a seductress. They'd heard of the transcript of Sashenka and Benya."

Satinov: I arrived at 3:06 a.m. and noticed something strange in the courtyard near where my driver parked my car. I admit before the Central Committee that my lateness was partly the cause of this misconduct. Commandant Golechev was drunk and tried to conceal what he had done. I summoned Major Blokhin and reviewed the List of Prisoners to Face the Highest Measure. I noted the absence of Prisoner Zeitlin-Palitsyn. I ordered Commandant Golechev to take me to her. Afterward, I ordered Commandant Golechev and Major Blokhin to begin at once. The prisoners were brought down to the cell designed for this purpose and I observed the Vishka of 122 prisoners as the witness of the Central Committee. Major Blokhin put on a butcher's apron and conducted himself very competently. As a devoted Communist, I delighted in the liquidation of these Enemies, traitors, scoundrels and bastards.

Golechev: We committed a crime against the highest morals of the Communist Party but I'm devoted heart and soul to the Party and Comrade Stalin. I expect pitiless punishment for this but I throw myself upon the mercy of the Central Committee. At around 3:00 a.m., Comrade Satinov finally arrived and he behaved in an unprofessional manner, exposing his bourgeois sentimentality . . .

Stalin's red crayon encircled this accusation and scrawled the words *Satinov sympathy???*

"So what happened? What did Satinov see?" asked Katinka, concentrating absolutely—no question had ever seemed so vital.

Satinov: She was completely . . . exposed. Commandant Golechev displayed depraved infantilism and corrupt philistinism, as I reported in person and on paper to the Instantzia. I confess that, while questioning Golechev, I struck him twice and he fell to the ground. This was due to my outrage as a good Communist, not any bourgeois sentimentality toward the Enemy.

Maxy whistled. "So whatever happened to Sashenka, it made Satinov, an iron man of that pitiless generation, lose control. How extraordinary—to have cracked up like that in front of those secret policemen could have signed his own death warrant then and there."

"But what did he see?" Katinka realized she was actually shouting.

"Hang on . . ." Maxy went on reading. "Here." He pointed at the bottom of the document. In the midst of a maze of green shading and squiggles, Stalin had written a word.

Hose.

"Hose? Have I misread it?"

Maxy shook his head. "I don't think so . . ." He hesitated.

"But what does it mean?"

"I heard of a similar case at Vladimir Prison in 1937. I think they tied Sashenka to a post and turned the hose on her. She was naked. It was an unusually cold night. They took bets on how long it would take . . . the water to freeze. Gradually the ice encased her. Like a glass statue."

28

Neither of them spoke for a long time. The finches serenaded them in the woods, bees danced around the cherry blossoms and the lilacs peeked their white and purple heads through the silvery birches.

As Katinka wept for the grandmother she'd never known, she thought of what Sashenka must have endured during that long, terrifying night in the cold winter of 1940. After a while, Maxy put his arms around her.

"What are we doing here?" she asked finally, slipping out of his arms.

"I did a little more research and found the burial records of Sashenka, Vanya, even Uncle Mendel. After execution, they were cremated and the ashes were buried in the grounds of an NKVD dacha in the birch woods just outside Moscow. Afterward, following NKVD orders on mass graves, raspberry canes and blackberry bushes were planted on the site. Look, there's a plaque on the tree there." He pointed.

Here lie buried the remains
of the innocent tortured and executed victims
of the political repressions.
May they never be forgotten!

"She's here, isn't she?" said Katinka, standing close to him. He put his arms around her again, and this time she didn't object.

"Not just her," he said. "They're all here, together."

Evening was falling—that rosy, grainy dusk when it seems as if Moscow is lit from below, not above—as Maxy dropped Katinka back at the Getman mansion. She stood on the steps and waved as he drove off.

When the guards admitted her the house was unusually hushed, but she found Roza in the kitchen.

"You need some *chai* and honeycakes," said Roza, giving her a look. Katinka realized that her skin must be raw, and her eyes red. "Sit down."

Katinka watched as Roza made the tea, adding honey and two teaspoons of brandy to each cup. Her aunt didn't miss much, she thought.

"Here," said Roza, "drink this. We both need it. Don't worry about your father. I was rushing him too much. You know, I can still see that sturdy little boy with his beloved rabbit at our dacha. I've thought of him like that all my life and I've been aching to find him again—but of course, I don't know him anymore. Will you tell me what to do?"

"Yes, yes, of course," said Katinka, still reeling from what she had learned with Maxy, her mind stalked by visions of Sashenka's death. She suddenly longed to share what she knew, to tell Roza everything, to work out exactly how death had come to Sashenka, how it had happened, and how she had looked—what Satinov had seen. "I've got something else to show you," she said, drawing out a wad of photocopied papers from her backpack.

"Wait," answered Roza. "Before I look at that, I want to ask you—I know my father was shot but you said there was something unusual . . . How did my mother die?"

"I was just about to come to that," said Katinka but something made her keep the papers close to her.

She took a breath, eager to go on, but as she did so she saw Sashenka in the snow, her skin white in the electric glare of the searchlights . . . and Satinov, horrified, standing before Sashenka just minutes later. If he had really broken, if he hadn't supervised the other 122 executions with Stalinist toughness immediately afterward, then he too would have been tortured until he revealed how he had rescued Sashenka's children . . .

Katinka sensed Roza's gentle but penetrating gaze on her, and she shook herself—there were some secrets she should keep.

She looked into Roza's intelligent, violet eyes and saw that she was tensed, ready to absorb this blow too. Instead she took her hands. "Like the others. She died just like the others."

Roza held her stare and then smiled. "I thought so. That's good to know. But what were you going to show me?"

Katinka deftly put the investigation into Sashenka's death at the back of her papers so that another document was on top. "I've got a few things I was given by Kuzma the archive rat, including this, your mother's confession. I hadn't read it in full because she gave them two hundred pages of crazy confessions of secret meetings with enemy agents and her plot to kill Stalin by spraying cyanide onto the gramophone at the dacha—all to give Satinov time to settle you and Carlo with your families. But there's one bit that sounds strange. May I read it to you?"

Accused Zeitlin-Palitsyn: In 1933, as a reward from the Party for our work, Vanya and I were allowed to seek treatment for my neurasthenia in London. We visited a well-known clinic in Harley Street called the Cushion House, where, under cover of medical treatment, we met agents of the British secret service and Trotsky himself, who asked us to arrange the assassination of Comrade Stalin.

Interrogator Mogilchuk: At the Cushion House?

Accused Zeitlin-Palitsyn: Yes.

"This 'Cushion House' is an odd name, even in English," explained Katinka. "I checked it. There's never been a Cushion House anywhere in London, ever. Does it ring a bell?"

Roza started to laugh. "Come with me." She took Katinka's hand and led her upstairs to her tidy bedroom. "Do you see?" she asked.

"What?" asked Katinka.

"Look!" She pointed at her bed. "Here!" Roza picked up a ragged old cushion, the material so threadbare and motheaten it was almost transparent, so bleached by time it was nearly white. "This was Cushion, *moya Podoushka*, the companion of my childhood and the only thing I could take with me to my new existence."

She hugged it like a baby.

"You see how she remembered me?" said Roza. "My mother was telling me that she loved me, wasn't she? She was sending me a message. So that if I ever found out who I really was, I'd know that she always loved me."

The air in the room was suddenly taut and Roza turned her back on Katinka and looked out of the window.

"Is there anything else in there that seems strange?" she asked, hopefully, and Katinka understood that she wanted something to offer her brother.

"Yes, now I see what she was doing, there is something. You said my father loved rabbits. Well, in the confession, Sashenka says she and Vanya hid some of the cyanide in the rabbit hutch—of all places—at the dacha. So I think she left something for him too . . ."

"I'd like to tell him that myself," said Roza, "but I don't want to do anything to upset him. I thought I might wait a bit and then call him and perhaps go down to see him. What do you think?"

"Of course, but don't leave it too long," smiled Katinka, "will you?"

29

It had been an extraordinary day, Katinka thought as she came downstairs. But it was not quite over yet.

As she crossed the spacious hall toward the kitchen, she heard a convoy of cars sweeping into the drive. Pasha was back. There was the sound of doors slamming then Pasha's loud voice, his clumsy, shambling footsteps and an unfamiliar but husky chattering that stopped abruptly.

"Oh my God, it's her!" the voice said.

Katinka turned, and found herself face to face with a slim old man with a long, sensitive face and a battered blue worker's cap. He was obviously in his eighties at least but there was a jerky energy about him, and he was still dapper in a crumpled brown suit that was too baggy for his slight figure. She liked him immediately.

"Is it you, Sashenka?" said the man, looking at her intensely. "Is it you? God, am I dreaming? You're so very like her—down to her grey eyes, her mouth, even the way she stands. Is this a trick?"

"No, it's not," said Pasha, standing right behind him. "Katinka, you weren't the only one doing some research. I found someone too."

Katinka let her backpack drop onto the floor and stepped back. "Who are you?" she asked shakily. "Who the hell are you?"

The old man wiped his face with a big linen handkerchief. "Who's asking the questions here? Me or this slip of a girl?" Katinka noticed his eyes were a dazzling blue. "My name's Benya Golden. Who are you?" He took her hand and kissed it. "Tell me, for God's sake."

"Benya Golden?" exclaimed Katinka. "But I thought you were . . ."

"Well . . . ," Benya shrugged, "so did everyone else. Can I sit down? I'd like a cognac, please?" He looked round at the exquisitely restored mansion, the Old Master paintings, the fat sofas. "This place looks as if your bar will have everything. Get me a Courvoisier before I drop. It's been a long journey. Look—my hands are trembling."

They moved into the sitting room, where Pasha lit a cigar and poured them all brandies.

"So you've heard of me?" Benya said after a while.

"Of course, I've even read your *Spanish Stories*," answered Katinka.

"I didn't know I had such young fans. I didn't know I had any fans." He was silent. "You know, you really are the image of a woman called Sashenka whom I loved with all my heart a long time ago. Hasn't anyone told you that?"

Katinka shook her head but she remembered Sashenka's face in that prison photograph and how she'd felt. "She was my grandmother," she said. "I've been finding out what happened to her."

"Have you been in those vile archives?"

"Oh yes."

"And have you found how they tortured us and broke us?"

Katinka nodded. "Everything."

"And so can you tell me why it all happened, to us I mean, to me and Sashenka?"

"There was no why," Katinka said slowly. "Just a chain of events. I've discovered so much . . . But tell me, how did you survive?"

"Uh, there's not much to tell. Stalin's thugs beat me and I told them everything they wanted. But at the trial, I said I'd been lying because I'd been tortured. I knew they'd shoot me and I couldn't face the bullet knowing I'd betrayed Sashenka. But they gave me ten years in Kolyma instead. I was released in the war—and I had quite a war—but then I was rearrested afterward, and released again in the fifties. I was a husk of a man, but I met a woman in the camps, a nurse, an angel, and she put me back together again. She got me a job as editor of a journal in Birobizhan, the Jewish region, near the Chinese border, and that's the godforsaken place where we've been living ever since."

"Do you still write?"

"They'd beaten all that out of me." He brushed that aside with a gesture. "I am happy just to breathe. Do you have any food in this palace? I'm always hungry."

"Of course," said Pasha. "We can make anything you like. Just name it!"

"I'll have a steak, dear prince, and all the trimmings, and a bottle of red wine," said Benya. "Do you have any French wine? Or is that pushing this dream too far? I once loved French Bordeaux . . . I drank it in Paris, you know—do you have it? Well then, will you all join me?" He went quiet again, and Katinka could see that his eyes had filled with tears.

Finally he took her hand and kissed it a second time. "Meeting you is like a last summer for me. Not a day passes when I don't remember your grandmother. We were the world's greatest lovers, yet we were together for just eleven days." He sighed deeply. "I gave her a flower for every day . . ."

Katinka's heart gave a little skip. She reached into her backpack and pulled out the little envelope of materials from Sashenka's file that Kuzma had given her. "Does *this* mean anything to you?" She handed him a much-creased old envelope addressed to "B. Golden" at the Soviet Writers' Union, in a feminine hand.

He took it from her, opened it, fingers shaking, and pulled out a pressed mimosa so flimsy that it almost came apart in his hands.

"She sent it to you," Katinka told him, "but it arrived too late, and you'd been arrested. The Writers' Union gave it to the NKVD and they filed it."

Benya muttered something, shaking his head in disbelief. Then he raised the flower to his face, sniffed its old petals, kissed it and when he could finally speak, he sat up straight and proud, beaming at her through flooded eyes.

Suddenly he threw off his peaked cap and, with a dashing and triumphant smile, spun it across the room. "Even after fifty years," he said, "I know what this means."

30

It was a lazy *sommerki* in Moscow over a week later. A sleepy, orange-headed sun had lost the swagger of the day and struggled to remain in the sky. The light spread a tender pink veil over the cool waters while the shadows beneath the trees were dyed a dark blue. There was so much blossom on the warm breeze, it almost snowed gossamer as Katinka walked with Maxy around the Patriarchy Ponds. Katinka felt dizzy and joyful to be away from her family and the past. Here only the present mattered as she strolled around this sanctuary in the middle of the clamoring city.

She had not seen Maxy since that day out in the woods and she had things to tell him that only he would understand and that only they could share. Though they weren't touching, she felt that they moved in sync, as if their limbs were linked with invisible threads.

"I'm so glad I'm living now," she was saying to him, "because I don't think I would have been as brave as Sashenka and Vanya if I'd lived then."

"I think you might have been braver," answered Maxy as, like one, they headed toward the outdoor café beside the water.

"Well, thank God that in our times we don't need to be that brave," she said. "We're free in Russia. For the first time in history. We can do what we want, say whatever we want. No one's watching us anymore—that's all over now."

"But for how long?" asked Maxy so seriously that Katinka thought he was being absurdly gloomy. The joy of being alive and young suddenly took hold of her—and she spun around and kissed him, quite recklessly.

ACKNOWLEDGMENTS

This is the story of the women and children of a fictional family across several generations and I hope it will be enjoyed as that: an intimate novel about a family. But it was inspired by the many stories, letters and cases that I found in archives and heard in interviews over ten years of researching Russian history. My own ancestors escaped from the Tsarist Empire in the early years of the last century and sparked my lifelong interest in Russia.

There are some historical characters in the book—Rasputin and Stalin being among the most obvious—and their portrayals are as accurate as I could make them. But as I wrote this book, Sashenka and her family began to seem more real than their factual contemporaries.

Historians generally write about extraordinary people who've shaped world events. But in this novel I wanted to write about how an ordinary family coped with the triumphs and tragedies of twentieth-century Russian history. I was fascinated by the courage and endurance of the many thousands of women who lost their husbands and children and I wondered: how did they survive? And how would any of us have behaved in such terrible times?

Above all, this is a book about love and family—but I also wanted to make these strange and tragic times in Russian history interesting for readers who perhaps wouldn't read history books. The details of high society in St. Petersburg, its shops, restaurants and clubs, prisons and dives, its tycoons and secret policemen, the Smolny school and the Okhrana offices, and many of its outrageous characters such as Prince Andronnikov are mainly factual. In the Soviet period, Stalin, Beria, Rodos and Kobylov are historical, as are the details of the prisons, their guards, and the customs of the labyrinthine Soviet bureacracy. The language and details of the documents in part three are real too, although some of the archives have been invented. The village of Beznadezhnaya is imaginary, though typical of many places I've known in the north Caucasus.

The story of Sashenka and her family is inspired by many true stories, including those of the Jewish wives of Stalin's henchmen, the arrests of writers such as Isaac Babel, and the case of Zhenya, the wife of Nikolai Yezhov, the NKVD boss who destroyed all those who loved her. (This also appears in my history *Stalin: The Court of the Red Tsar.*)

I owe a huge debt to my sources, whose work I have used liberally: for part one (St. Petersburg, 1916), I used Vladimir Nabokov's famous and exquisite memoir, *Speak Memory*; a brilliant privately published memoir of a wealthy Jewish family, *The Silver Samovar* by Alexander Poliakoff, whom I knew as a boy; *The Five* by Vladimir Jabotinsky; Ilya Ehrenburg's multivolumed memoirs; as well as novels such as *The Moskat Family* and *The Manor* by Isaac Bashevis Singer.

On the history, politics, art and society, I used a superb book, *Passage Through Armageddon* by W. Bruce Lincoln. On the details of the Tsarist secret police, see *Russian Hide-and-Seek: The Tsarist Secret Police in St. Petersburg, 1906–14* by Iain Lauchlan and *The Foe Within* by William C. Fuller, Jr. But I found most of this material during the research for my latest history book, *Young Stalin.*

On the Stalin period in part two, most of the material comes from my own research into the Soviet élite for my history, *Stalin: The Court of the Red Tsar,* but I owe much to brilliant material in *The KGB's Literary Archive* by Vitaly Shentalinsky. I also used the novella *The House on the Embankment* by Yury Trifonov and the novels in the Arbat trilogy by Anatoli Rybakov.

Recent history books such as *Stalinism as a Way of Life* by Lewis Siegelbaum and Andrei Sokolov, *Thank You Comrade Stalin* by Jeffrey Brooks and *Rulers and Victims* by Geoffrey Hosking were invaluable sources. The outstanding and unforgettable book *The Whisperers* by Orlando Figes is especially enlightening because it reveals how Sashenka's story was, in many ways, commonplace. I recommend it to anyone who is intrigued by my story and wants to know what really happened to private lives and families in Russia. Even in the 1990s—

even now—Russian families are discovering their extraordinary pasts and being reunited with vanished relations.

Experts will recognize that Mendel's letter complaining of his treatment in prison is closely based on the tragic letter written by the theatrical director V. Meyerhold.

As for my sources for part three, the age of the oligarchs, and of course the mysteries and delights of archival research in Russia, all I can say is that I spent a lot of time as a journalist and then a historian in both Moscow and the Caucasus during the 1990s. Most of the material in his section has been drawn from my own experiences.

Thanks to Galina Babkova for investigating what it was like to study at the Smolny; to Galina Oleksiuk, who taught me Russian, and has corrected and checked the manuscript for Russian context; to Nestan Charkviani for giving me Georgian color; to Marc and Rachel Polonsky for having me to stay at their apartment in the Granovsky Building; and to Dominic Lieven for his encouragement.

Thanks to everyone at my publishers, Transworld, and in particular to Bill Scott-Kerr, Deborah Adams for her copy-editing skills and Claire Ward and Anne Kragelund for the cover image. I have been most blessed by the brilliant, expert, sensitive and meticulous work of my editor, Selina Walker.

My parents, Stephen and April Sebag-Montefiore, edited and improved the book. My wife Santa, an accomplished novelist as well as a loving best friend, gave me golden advice on character and plot. And the exuberant charm of my beloved children—daughter Lily and son Sasha—constantly encouraged and inspired me.

Simon Montefiore

A NOTE ON NAMES AND LANGUAGE

Places in Russia tend to change their names with the tides of history. St. Petersburg was founded by Peter the Great in 1703 and was known as such until 1914, when Nicholas II changed its Germanic sound to Petrograd, "Peter's city." In 1924, the Bolsheviks renamed it Leningrad. In 1991 it became St. Petersburg once again. Tiflis is now known as Tbilisi, the capital of independent Georgia.

The rulers of Russia were called Tsars, though in 1721 Peter the Great declared himself Emperor and thenceforth the Romanovs were known as both.

Russians use three names in a formal context: a first name, a patronymic (meaning son/daughter of) and a surname. Thus Sashenka's formal name is Alexandra Samuilovna Zeitlin and Vanya's is Ivan Nikolaievich Palitsyn. But Russians (and Georgians) usually also use diminutives as nicknames: Sashenka is the diminutive of Alexandra and Vanya is the diminutive of Ivan, etc.

In the Pale of Settlement, the Jews spoke Yiddish as their vernacular, prayed in Hebrew and petitioned in Russian. The Georgian language is totally different from Russian and has its own alphabet and literature.

CAST OF CHARACTERS

The names of historical figures are marked with an asterisk.

The Family: the Zeitlins
Sashenka (Alexandra Samuilovna) Zeitlin, schoolgirl at the Smolny Institute
Baron Samuil Moiseievich Zeitlin, St. Petersburg banker and Sashenka's father
Baroness Ariadna (Finkel Abramovna) Zeitlin, née Barmakid, Sashenka's mother
Gideon Moiseievich Zeitlin, Samuil's brother, journalist/novelist
Vera Zeitlin, his wife, and their two daughters,
Vika (Viktoria) Zeitlin and
Mouche (Sophia) Zeitlin, actress

The Family: the Barmakids
Abram Barmakid, Rabbi of Turbin, Ariadna and Mendel's father
Miriam Barmakid, Ariadna and Mendel's mother
Avigdor Abramovich "Arthur" Barmakid, Ariadna and Mendel's brother who left for England
Mendel Abramovich Barmakid, Ariadna and Avigdor's brother, Bolshevik leader
Natasha, a Yakut, Mendel's wife and Bolshevik comrade
Lena (Vladlena), only daughter of Mendel and Natasha

CAST OF CHARACTERS

The Zeitlin Household

Lala, Audrey Lewis, Sashenka's English governess
Pantameilion, chauffeur
Leonid, butler
Delphine, the French cook
Luda and Nyuna, parlormaids
Shifra, Samuil's old governess

St. Petersburg, 1916

Peter de Sagan, Captain of Gendarmes, officer of the Okhrana, penniless Baltic nobleman
Rasputin,* Grigory the "Elder," peasant healer and the Empress's "friend"
Anya Vyrubova,* Empress's close friend and Rasputin supporter
Julia "Lili" von Dehn,* Empress's close friend and Rasputin supporter
Prince Mikhail Andronnikov,* well-connected influence-peddler
Countess Missy Loris, Ariadna's American friend, married to Count Loris, St. Petersburg aristocrat
Boris Sturmer,* Premier of Tsarist Russia, 1916
D. F. Trepov,* penultimate Premier of Tsarist Russia, 1916
Prince Dmitri Golitsyn,* last Premier of Tsarist Russia, 1916–17
Alexander Protopopov,* syphilitic politician and the last Tsarist Minister of the Interior
Ivan Manuilov-Manesevich,* spy, con man, journalist and fixer for Premier Sturmer
Max Flek, Baron Zeitlin's lawyer
Dr. Mathias Gemp, fashionable doctor

The Bolsheviks and Others, 1939

Vladimir Illich Lenin,* Bolshevik leader
Grigory Zinoviev,* Bolshevik leader
Josef Vissarionovich Stalin,* né Djugashvili, nickname "Koba," a Georgian Bolshevik, later General Secretary of Communist Party, Premier and Soviet dictator

Vyechaslav Molotov,* né Scriabin, nicknamed "Vecha," Bolshevik, later Soviet Premier and Foreign Minister
Alexander Shlyapnikov,* worker and midranking Bolshevik in charge of Party during February Revolution of 1917
Hercules (Erakle Alexandrovich) Satinov, young Georgian Bolshevik
Tamara, Satinov's young wife
Mariko, Satinov's daughter
Ivan "Vanya" Palitsyn, worker, Bolshevik activist
Nikolai and Marfa Palitsyn, Vanya's parents
Razum, Vanya's driver
Nikolai Yezhov,* "the Bloody Dwarf," secret police chief (People's Commissar of Internal Affairs—NKVD), 1936–8
Lavrenti Pavlovich Beria,* a Georgian, Stalin's secret police chief (People's Commissar of Internal Affairs—NKVD), 1938 onward
Bogdan Kobylov,* Georgian secret policeman, Beria's chief henchman, "The Bull"
Pavel Mogilchuk, NKVD investigator, Serious Cases Section, State Security, and author of detective stories
Boris Rodos,* NKVD investigator, Serious Cases Section, State Security
Vasily Blokhin,* NKVD executioner, Major, State Security
Count Alexei Tolstoy,* writer
Ilya Ehrenburg,* writer
Isaac Babel,* writer
Klavdia Klimov, deputy editor of *Soviet Wife and Proletarian Housekeeping*
Misha Kalman, features editor, *Soviet Wife and Proletarian Housekeeping*
Leonid Golechev, NKVD commandant of Special Object 110, Sukhanovka Prison
Benjamin (known as "Benya") Golden, writer

The Vinsky Family of the North Caucasus
Dr. Valentin Vinsky, a Russian doctor in the village of Beznadezhnaya
Tatiana Vinsky, his wife
Katinka (Ekaterina Valentinovna), their daughter
Bedbug, Sergei Vinsky, Valentin's father, a peasant
Baba, Irina Vinsky, Valentin's mother, a peasant

The Getman Family of Odessa
Roza Getman, née Liberhart, widow from Odessa
Pasha (Pavel) Getman, Roza's son, a billionaire oligarch
Professor Enoch Liberhart, Roza Getman's father, Professor of Musicology at the Odessa Conservatoire
Dr. Perla Liberhart, Roza Getman's mother, teacher of literature at Odessa University

Moscow, 1990s
Maxy Shubin, historian of Stalin's Terror
Colonel Lentin, Russian secret policeman, KGB/FSB, the Marmoset
Colonel Trofimsky, Russian secret policeman, KGB/FSB, the Magician
Kuzma, archivist in KGB/FSB archives
Agrippina Begbulatov, archive official
Apostollon Shcheglov, archivist